# PATRICIA HIGHSMITH

*Selected Novels and Short Stories*

ALSO BY PATRICIA HIGHSMITH

*Strangers on a Train*

*The Price of Salt* (as Claire Morgan)

*The Blunderer*

*The Talented Mr. Ripley*

*Deep Water*

*Miranda the Panda Is on the Veranda* (with Doris Sanders)

*A Game for the Living*

*This Sweet Sickness*

*The Cry of the Owl*

*The Two Faces of January*

*The Glass Cell*

*A Suspension of Mercy*

*Plotting and Writing Suspense Fiction*

*Those Who Walk Away*

*The Tremor of Forgery*

*Ripley Under Ground*

*The Snail-Watcher and Other Stories*

*A Dog's Ransom*

*Ripley's Game*

*Little Tales of Misogyny*

*The Animal-Lover's Book of Beastly Murder*

*Edith's Diary*

*Slowly, Slowly in the Wind*

*The Boy Who Followed Ripley*

*The Black House*

*People Who Knock on the Door*

*Mermaids on the Golf Course*

*Found in the Street*

*Tales of Natural and Unnatural Catastrophes*

*Ripley Under Water*

*Small g: A Summer Idyll*

*The Selected Stories of Patricia Highsmith*

*Nothing That Meets the Eye: The Uncollected Stories*

# PATRICIA HIGHSMITH

*Selected Novels and Short Stories*

Edited with an Introduction by Joan Schenkar

W. W. NORTON & COMPANY
NEW YORK • LONDON

Printed in the United States of America
First Edition

For information about permission to reproduce selections from this book, write to Permissions, W. W. Norton & Company, Inc., 500 Fifth Avenue, New York, NY 10110

For information about special discounts for bulk purchases, please contact W. W. Norton Special Sales at specialsales@wwnorton.com or 800-233-4830

Manufacturing by RR Donnelley, Harrisonburg, VA
Book design by Joe Lops
Production manager: Anna Oler

Library of Congress Cataloging-in-Publication Data

Highsmith, Patricia, 1921–1995.
[Selections. 2011]
Patricia Highsmith : selected novels and short stories /
Patricia Highsmith : edited with an introduction by Joan Schenkar. – 1st ed.
p. cm.
ISBN 978-0-393-08013-1 (hardcover)
I. Title.
PS3558.I366A6 2011
813'.54—dc22 2010034589

W. W. Norton & Company, Inc.
500 Fifth Avenue, New York, N.Y. 10110
www.wwnorton.com

W. W. Norton & Company Ltd.
Castle House, 75/76 Wells Street, London W1T 3QT

1 2 3 4 5 6 7 8 9 0

# CONTENTS

# HIGHSMITH COUNTRY: AN INTRODUCTION

## BY JOAN SCHENKAR

Let's face it.

Patricia Highsmith—who spent half her life outside the United States and never wrote a novel without a crime in it—is as American as rattlesnake venom.

Rooted in Texas and Alabama, raised in Greenwich Village, Highsmith invested her considerable creative capital in the back alleys of the American Dream: a shadow world of homicidal alter egos, subverted successes, and narratives of such shimmering negativity that they are like nothing else in their immediate literary landscapes.

The secrets of her style are a coroner's eye for detail, a hyperconsciousness of the way human abnormalities can be enumerated, and the high optical refractions she was able to scan into her mostly plain prose. She liked lists, charts, maps, forgeries, and everything doubled. She believed, like any good American, in rigorous self-improvement, and murder was always on her mind. She lived for her many tumultuous love affairs—they inspired her work—but she couldn't live *with* them. She preferred writing to anything else in the world.

*Patricia Highsmith: Selected Novels and Short Stories* is a bridge to the deep disruptive shocks awaiting you in the world of Patricia Highsmith. The "news" Highsmith brought back from the ends of her nerves is never more apparent than in *Strangers on a Train* (1950) and *The Price of Salt* (1952)—the two novels she wrote from opposing sides of her psychological divide—and in the baker's dozen of short stories (selected from the six Norton short story collections) that accompany them here. ("Good short stories," she wrote, "are made from the writer's emotions alone.") Like tissue cultures excised from the skin of her imagination, these works all bare the imprint of her unruly instincts and unholy feelings.

Born in 1921 in her grandmother's boarding house in Fort Worth, Texas, on Edgar Allan Poe's birthday, Highsmith began her first short story in 1935—she was fourteen—with this sentence: "He prepared to go to sleep, removed his shoes and set them parallel, toe outward, beside his bed." Her need for order was urgent. At sixteen, she wrote her second short story, "Crime Begins," because she was tempted to steal a book from her high school library. In place of the theft, she put the story; a story about a girl who steals a book from a library. "Every artist," she wrote, "is in business for his health." Fiction was for what she *wished* would happen.

Her restless, roiling, note-taking travels across the United States and Mexico—first as a precocious teenager in the late 1930s and then as a blazingly ambitious young author in the 1940s and '50s—released her from her cramped, exotic family circumstances and gave her a cartographer's feel for the homeland she longed to leave. The publications of her first two completed novels, the dazzling double tour de force of *Strangers on a Train* (1950) and *The Price of Salt* (1952), confirmed what she had been quietly plotting for years: the slow, insidious pull of her powers on the gravitational field of modern fiction.

An outsider artist of graveled gifts, savage talents, and obsessional interests, Patricia Highsmith understood early on that she would never see the world as others do. "I am married to my mother," she wrote at nineteen, "I will never wed another." At twenty-one, her attentions were focused: "Obsessions are the only things that matter. Perversion interests me most and is my guiding darkness." In the acid bath of her detail-saturated prose, she developed her own image of an alternate earth: Highsmith Country, a territory so psychologically threatening that even her most faithful readers hope never to meet themselves in its pages.

In Highsmith Country, good intentions corrupt naturally and automatically, guilt often afflicts the innocent and not the culpable, hunter and prey reverse roles at a moment's notice, and life is a suffocating trap from which even her most accomplished escape artists cannot find a graceful exit. Highsmith furnished her houses of fiction with the large and small irritants of her daily life: if she had carpenter ants in her attic and tax bills on her back, then her iconic "hero-criminal" Tom Ripley had them too. And the deep psychological divisions her protagonists suffer as they slip into crime and finely graduated degrees of madness came from a relentless examination of her own wayward tastes: "I can't think of anything more apt to set the imagination stirring, drifting, creating, than the idea—the fact—that anyone you walk past on the pavement anywhere may be a sadist, a compulsive thief, or even a murderer."

Moving from country to country, drink to drink, and woman to woman in Europe (the worse her relationships went, the better she wrote was the general rule), she aged and iced inside her cone of watchful darkness, became a literary bestseller on the Continent, and continued to curate her private museum of American maladies. It proved to be a rich resource for the bleakly original novels and crankishly perceptive short stories that poured out of her long, strange self-exile. She kept her passionate quarrel with America hot and bright and learned the expatriate's bitter lesson—you can take the girl out of Texas, but you can't take Texas (or Greenwich Village) out of the girl—the hard way. The hard way was how Pat Highsmith learned everything.

The atmospheres and geographies that found their way into her work are legion: the state of Texas; the Alabama Confederacy; Astoria, Queens; the crooked streets of Greenwich Village (so appropriate for criminal activity, she thought—and tended to murder her fictional characters at Village addresses where she'd made love in life); an early passion for Dostoyevsky, Proust, Gide, Wilde, woodworking, and anything abnormal; her secret career as a scriptwriter of superhero comic books in 1940s Manhattan; the landscape of Mexico; half a lifetime of self-exile in Western Europe; the love of dozens of interesting women and a few good men; an achingly resentful bond with her flamboyant artist-mother (the original of all the noir bitches in her work); the divorce of her birth parents nine days before she was born.

The broken marital contract allowed Pat to say, with relish, that she was an out-of-wedlock child but still "legitimate." It was the first of the many contradictions that ruled her deeply destructive, intensely creative life.

Her slow, literary crawl over the surface of things produced hundreds of raspingly acute portraits of quietly transgressive acts—and six or seven of the most unsettling novels of the last half of the twentieth century. *Strangers on a Train* (1950), *The Price of Salt* (1952), *The Blunderer* (1954), *The Talented Mr. Ripley* (1955), *Deep Water* (1957), *This Sweet Sickness* (1960), and *The Cry of the Owl* (1962) are my own favorites. Highsmith herself would have added *The Tremor of Forgery* (1969) and *Edith's Diary* (1977) to the list—and then changed her mind the following week.

In her best-known work, *The Talented Mr. Ripley,* Pat developed a wonderfully unashamed alter-ego relationship with her protagonist, the charming, deadly, murderer/forger/identity-impersonator Tom Ripley: "I often had the feeling Ripley was writing it and I was merely typing." Ripley's confusion of love with murder and his passion for "the best" in life were Pat's own feelings—and she gave Ripley an unlikely godfather when she took the central premise of Henry James's novel *The Ambassadors,* turned it upside down (the only way she could imagine it), and smuggled it into *The Talented Mr. Ripley.* "What I predicted I would once do, I am doing already[;] showing the unequivocal triumph of evil over good, and rejoicing in it. I shall make my readers rejoice in it, too."

The toxic brilliance of her trail—thirty volumes of novels and short story collections—goes on glowing.

Did anyone work harder than the talented Miss Highsmith? Her little train of daily accomplishments—freighted with book themes, articles, short story beginnings, observations, and five to eight neatly typed pages of fiction—chugged steadily between the twin terminals of her self-regard and her depressions, and kept her very busy filling up its cars. And *still* she was afraid of not doing enough.

Along with her many published works, she left 250 unpublished manuscripts of varying length, as well as 38 writer's notebooks (or *cahiers,* as she rather grandly called them) and 18 diaries in five languages—four of which she didn't actually speak. She drew, she sketched, she made sculptures. She handcrafted furniture out of wood and carved out little statues. She pasted up her own Christmas and birthday cards and decorated the covers of all fourteen of her fat press books with cutouts and designs of her own devising.

Thousands of personal letters (in her peculiarly impersonal style) rolled from the platen of her favorite 1956 coffee-colored Olympia Deluxe portable typewriter—the machine on which she committed most of her fictional murders and unpicked the psychologies of her perpetrators. The labeling on its *E* key was entirely worn away. The Olympia got the same unsparing treatment she gave to herself.

By the time she died alone in a hospital in Locarno, Switzerland, in 1995 (always ambivalent, she expired of two competing diseases), Pat Highsmith—a literary star in Europe for decades—no longer had a publisher in her native land. It is only in the first years of this century that her entire oeuvre has begun to be reprinted in the United States.

• • •

*Strangers on a Train* was an astonishing debut novel for the twenty-nine-year-old writer. The celebrated "germ" of the book, strangers who agree to exchange murders and "get away with it," was the inspired result of a winter's walk with her mother and stepfather—the two people on earth most likely to provoke her to thoughts of homicide. This time, she transformed her little double-indemnifying nugget into what would become the essential Highsmith situation: two men bound together by the stalkerlike fixation of one upon the other, a fixation that always involves a murderous, implicitly homoerotic fantasy.

Guy Haines is an architectural genius whose moody purity, fear of failure, and perfect relationship with his girlfriend Anne (the first of the thinly drawn, fictional blonde beauties Pat would approach with a bouquet in one hand and a headsman's ax in the other) invite corruption. Charles Bruno is the psychopathic, subliterate mastermind who is "the unseen part" of Guy, and he "waits in ambush" for him. In their tranced and mutual psychological seduction, these Terrible Twins vacate their characters at the drop of a threat, exchange traits as easily as they trade hats, and like "God and the Devil" mingle their identities and misdirect their pursuer. The bulk of their narrative is conveyed in a writing voice cloaked (but not necessarily concealed) by another (but not exactly opposite) gender. From the age of twelve, Pat said, she knew she was "a boy in a girl's body."

Like much of Highsmith's work to come, *Strangers on a Train* splays across genres,[1] interrogates genders, provides as thorough an anatomy of

1 The publishing of *Strangers on a Train* in the United States as a "suspense novel" ensured the book's notice but moved Highsmith into a lifetime of mostly uncongenial partnership with the "suspense" and "crime" genres. If Pat Highsmith is anything at all, she's a *punishment* novelist, not a crime novelist.

guilt as can be found in contemporary literature, and attacks its readers right where they live. It is a masterpiece of modern fiction.

*The Price of Salt,* a love story written in the richly figured language of pursuit, betrayal, and murder, was the bookend to the intensely creative period of Highsmith's late twenties. The novel takes some of the props and elements of *Strangers on a Train* and subdues them to the subject of requited lesbian love—the "crime" Pat mostly left out of her other fictions. It was a new idea for midcentury American literature.

But requited love in Highsmith Country is not like other loves in Novel Land; redolent of Grimms' fairy tales and *Lolita* (three years *before* Nabokov published his chef d'oeuvre), *The Price of Salt* glows with a luminous halo of incest and a little light pedophilia. Its lovemaking metaphors are weaponized, and its sexual consummations are spied upon, recorded on tape, and offered up as legal threats. Pat said—who can doubt her?—that the book came right up out of her bones.

Therese Belivet, a lovely, talented, jail bait–aged set designer, with high ambitions and an unsatisfactory boyfriend, takes the same "Christmas rush" job in a grand Manhattan department store that Pat herself took in 1948, when the inspiration for *The Price of Salt* appeared in the form of an alluring blonde in expensive furs who sauntered up to Pat's toy counter and ordered a doll for her daughter.

Their two-minute encounter was so erotic for the young writer (who had her usual response to sexual appeal: she fantasized about strangling the woman) that she rushed home in a high fever to write out the entire plot of *The Price of Salt* in two hours. She called her thirty-something character Carol Aird, made her as attractively steely as her teenage lover Therese, gave her a gun to put in her glove box, and (grudgingly) granted her and her lover a fairy-tale future together.

Pat signed *The Price of Salt* with a pseudonym, Claire Morgan, took to disparaging it in later life, and never published anything like it again. The book sold hundreds of thousands of copies—and made its author uneasy all her life.

• • •

The thirteen short stories in this volume were composed between 1939 and 1973.[2] They are to *Strangers on a Train* and *The Price of Salt* what pilot fish are to giant sharks: sharing in some of the nutrients and temerities of the larger works but smaller in scope, rougher in style, and more erratic in behavior.

Eight of the stories explore the little disturbances of women. Among their characters and situations are: a mother and daughter who seem to cooperate with a prospective pedophile; a cavewoman whose violent death makes romantic and artistic history; a matron whose jealousy of another mother afflicts her infant son; a career girl humiliated by the disparagements of her married sister; two elderly roommates and their unquiet cruelties; a press representative permanently upset by her only act of creation; a dying stranger patiently watching her mean-spirited nurse; a female pigeon with marital problems.

The five stories focused on men include: a heterosexual Mexican prototype for Ripley; a collector of forgeries whose own body parts are prosthetic; a toxic social group that engineers the suicide of its least desirable member; a vaguely homosexual poet who robs and murders his vaguely homosexual patron; an expressionist serial killer whose cartoon crimes are inspired by celebrity waxworks.

Withal, Patricia Highsmith's writing is as recognizable as its resonances are indelible. Anyone who has read even one of her best novels with close attention takes out citizenship papers in the country she created—and is provided with a passport that can never be revoked. In all her long fictions and in her most accomplished short works, there is always something wounding, something disorienting, something deeply damaging to the reader. Few authors have been so willing to bite the hand that buys them.

• • •

In the many years I spent thinking about Pat Highsmith for *The Talented Miss Highsmith: The Secret Life and Serious Art of Patricia Highsmith* (2009)—and she is *very* interesting to think about—no image haunted me more than

2 The stories, selected from Highsmith's lesser-known short works, are not printed chronologically.

that of the artist who had buried herself alive, literally and figuratively, in her writing. And so, aside from a first and much-needed introduction to the pleasures and terrors of Highsmith's work, the selections in *Patricia Highsmith: Selected Novels and Short Stories* offer you an experience as intimate, as delicate, and as revealing as anything imaginative prose can provide: a portrait of the artist herself—America's most surreptitiously autobiographical author—concealed in plain sight in her fictions.

Her imagination—greatly exhilarated by transgression—is a dangerous instrument.

And now you've been warned.

Welcome to Highsmith Country.

# STRANGERS ON A TRAIN

# one

The train tore along with an angry, irregular rhythm. It was having to stop at smaller and more frequent stations, where it would wait impatiently for a moment, then attack the prairie again. But progress was imperceptible. The prairie only undulated, like a vast, pink-tan blanket being casually shaken. The faster the train went, the more buoyant and taunting the undulations.

Guy took his eyes from the window and hitched himself back against the seat.

Miriam would delay the divorce at best, he thought. She might not even want a divorce, only money. Would there really ever be a divorce from her?

Hate had begun to paralyze his thinking, he realized, to make little blind alleys of the roads that logic had pointed out to him in New York. He could sense Miriam ahead of him, not much farther now, pink and tan-freckled, and radiating a kind of unhealthful heat, like the prairie out the window. Sullen and cruel.

Automatically, he reached for a cigarette, remembered for the tenth time that he couldn't smoke in the Pullman car, then took one anyway. He tapped it twice on the face of his wristwatch, read the time, 5:12, as if it meant anything today, and fitted the cigarette into the corner of his mouth before he brought the cupped match up. The cigarette replaced the match inside his hand, and he smoked in slow, steady pulls. Again and again his brown eyes dropped to the stubborn, fascinating ground out the window. A tab of his soft shirt collar began to ride up. In the reflection the dusk had started to create in the window's glass, the peak of white collar along his jaw suggested a style of the last century, like his black hair that grew high and loose on top and lay close in back. The rise of hair and the slope of his long nose gave him a look of intense purpose and somehow of forward motion, though from the front, his heavy, horizontal brows and mouth imposed a stillness and reserve. He wore flannel trousers that needed pressing, a dark jacket that slacked over his slight body and showed faintly purple where the light struck it, and a tomato-colored woolen tie, carelessly knotted.

He did not think Miriam would be having a child unless she wanted it. Which should mean the lover intended to marry her. But why had she sent for him? She didn't need him to get a divorce. And why did he go over the same dull ground he had four days ago when he had gotten her letter? The five or six lines in Miriam's round handwriting had said only that she was going to have a child and wanted to see him. That she was pregnant guaranteed the divorce, he reasoned, so why was he nervous? A suspicion that he might, in some unreachable depth of himself, be jealous because she was going to bear another man's child and had once aborted his own tormented him above all. No, it was nothing but shame that nettled him, he told himself, shame that he had once loved such a person as Miriam. He mashed his cigarette on the heater's grilled cover. The stub rolled out at his feet, and he kicked it back under the heater.

There was so much to look forward to now. His divorce, the work in Florida—it was practically certain the board would pass on his drawings, and he would learn this week—and Anne. He and Anne could begin to plan now. For over a year he had been waiting, fretting, for something—*this*—to happen so he would be free. He felt a pleasant explosion of happiness inside him, and relaxed in the corner of the plush seat. For the last three years, really, he had been waiting for this to happen. He could have bought a divorce, of course, but he hadn't ever amassed that much spare money. Starting a career as an architect, without benefit of a job with a firm, had not been easy and still wasn't. Miriam had never asked for an income, but she plagued him in other ways, by talking of him in Metcalf as if they were still on the best of terms, as if he were up in New York only to establish himself and eventually send for her. Occasionally she wrote him for money, small but irritating amounts which he let her have because it would be so easy for her, so natural to her, to start a campaign in Metcalf against him, and his mother was in Metcalf.

A tall blond young man in a rust-brown suit dropped into the empty seat opposite Guy and, smiling with a vague friendliness, slid over into the corner. Guy glanced at his pallid, undersized face. There was a huge pimple in the exact center of his forehead. Guy looked out the window again.

The young man opposite him seemed to debate whether to start a conversation or take a nap. His elbow kept sliding along the window sill, and whenever the stubby lashes came open, the gray bloodshot eyes were looking at him and the soft smile came back. He might have been slightly drunk.

Guy opened his book, but his mind wandered after half a page. He looked up as the row of white fluorescent lights flickered on down the ceiling of the car, let his eyes wander to the unlighted cigar that still gyrated conversationally in a bony hand behind one of the seat backs, and to the monogram that trembled on a thin gold chain across the tie of the young man opposite him. The monogram was CAB, and the tie was of green silk, hand-painted with offensively orange-colored palm trees. The long rust-brown body was sprawled vulnerably now, the head thrown back so that the big pimple or boil on the forehead might have been a topmost point that had erupted. It was an interesting face, though Guy did not know why. It looked neither young nor old, neither intelligent nor entirely stupid. Between the narrow bulging forehead and the lantern jaw, it scooped degenerately, deep where the mouth lay in a fine line, deepest in the blue hollows that held the small scallops of the lids. The skin was smooth as a girl's, even waxenly clear, as if all its impurities had been drained to feed the pimple's outburst.

For a few moments, Guy read again. The words made sense to him and began to lift his anxiety. But what good will Plato do you with Miriam, an inner voice asked him. It had asked him that in New York, but he had brought the book anyway, an old text from a high school philosophy course, an indulgence to compensate him, perhaps, for having to make the trip to Miriam. He looked out the window and, seeing his own image, straightened his curling collar. Anne was always doing that for him. Suddenly he felt helpless without her. He shifted his position, accidentally touched the outstretched foot of the young man asleep, and watched fascinatedly as the lashes twitched and came open. The bloodshot eyes might have been focused on him all the while through the lids.

"Sorry," Guy murmured.

"'S all right," the other said. He sat up and shook his head sharply. "Where are we?"

"Getting into Texas."

The blond young man brought a gold flask from his inside pocket, opened it, and extended it amiably.

"No, thanks," Guy said. The woman across the aisle, Guy noticed, who had not looked up from her knitting since St. Louis, glanced over just as the flask upended with a metallic splash.

"Where you bound?" The smile was a thin wet crescent now.

"Metcalf," Guy said.

"Oh. Nice town, Metcalf. Down on business?" He blinked his sore-looking eyes politely.

"Yes."

"What business?"

Guy looked up reluctantly from his book. "Architect."

"Oh," with wistful interest. "Build houses and things?"

"Yes."

"I don't think I've introduced myself." He half stood up. "Bruno. Charles Anthony Bruno."

Guy shook his hand briefly. "Guy Haines."

"Glad to meet you. You live in New York?" The hoarse baritone voice sounded false, as if he were talking to wake himself up.

"Yes."

"I live in Long Island. Going to Santa Fe for a little vacation. Ever been to Santa Fe?"

Guy shook his head.

"Great town to relax in." He smiled, showing poor teeth. "Mostly Indian architecture there, I guess."

A conductor stopped in the aisle, thumbing through tickets. "That your seat?" he asked Bruno.

Bruno leaned possessively into his corner. "Drawing room next car."

"Number Three?"

"I guess. Yeah."

The conductor went on.

"Those guys!" Bruno murmured. He leaned forward and gazed out the window amusedly.

Guy went back to his book, but the other's obtrusive boredom, a feeling he was about to say something in another instant, kept him from concentrating. Guy contemplated going to the diner, but for some reason sat on. The train was slowing again. When Bruno looked as if he were going to speak, Guy got up, retreated into the next car, and leapt the steps to the crunchy ground before the train had quite stopped.

The more organic air, weighted with nightfall, struck him like a smothering pillow. There was a smell of dusty, sun-warm gravel, of oil and hot metal. He was hungry and lingered near the diner, pacing in slow strides with his hands in his pockets, breathing the air deeply, though he disliked it. A constellation of red and green and white lights hummed southward in the sky. Yesterday, Anne might have come this route, he thought, on her way to Mexico. He might have been with her. She had wanted him to come with her as far as Metcalf. He might have asked her to stay over a day and meet his mother, if it had not been for Miriam. Or even regardless of Miriam, if he had been another sort of person, if he could be simply unconcerned. He had told Anne about Miriam, about almost all of it, but he could not bear the thought of their meeting. He had wanted to travel alone on the train in order to think. And what had he thought so far? What good had thinking or logic ever been where Miriam was concerned?

The conductor's voice shouted a warning, but Guy paced till the last moment, then swung himself aboard the car behind the diner.

The waiter had just taken his order when the blond young man appeared in the doorway of the car, swaying, looking a little truculent with a short cigarette in his mouth. Guy had put him quite out of mind and now his tall rust-brown figure was like a vaguely unpleasant memory. Guy saw him smile as he sighted him.

"Thought you might have missed the train," Bruno said cheerfully, pulling out a chair.

"If you don't mind, Mr. Bruno, I'd like some privacy for a while. I have some things to think over."

Bruno stabbed out the cigarette that was burning his fingers and looked at him blankly. He was drunker than before. His face seemed smeared and fuzzy at the edges. "We could have privacy in my place. We could have dinner there. How about it?"

"Thanks, I'd rather stay here."

"Oh, but I insist. Waiter!" Bruno clapped his hands. "Would you have this gentleman's order sent to Drawing Room Three and bring me a steak medium rare with French fries and apple pie? And two Scotch and sodas fast as you can, huh?" He looked at Guy and smiled, the soft wistful smile. "Okay?"

Guy debated, then got up and came with him. What did it matter after all? And wasn't he utterly sick of himself?

There was no need of the Scotches except to provide glasses and ice. The four yellow-labeled bottles of Scotch lined up on an alligator suitcase were the one neat unit of the little room. Suitcases and wardrobe trunks blocked passage everywhere except for a small labyrinthine area in the center of the floor, and on top of them were strewn sports clothes and equipment, tennis rackets, a bag of golf clubs, a couple of cameras, a wicker basket of fruit and wine bedded in fuchsia paper. A splay of current magazines, comic books and novels covered the seat by the window. There was also a box of candy with a red ribbon across the lid.

"Looks kind of athletic, I guess," Bruno said, suddenly apologetic.

"It's fine." Guy smiled slowly. The room amused him and gave him a welcome sense of seclusion. With the smile his dark brows relaxed, transforming his whole expression. His eyes looked outward now. He stepped lithely in the alleys between suitcases, examining things like a curious cat.

"Brand-new. Never felt a ball," Bruno informed him, holding out a tennis racket for him to feel. "My mother makes me take all this stuff, hoping it'll keep me out of bars. Good to hock if I run out, anyway. I like to drink when I travel. It enhances things, don't you think?" The highballs arrived, and Bruno strengthened them from one of his bottles. "Sit down. Take off your coat."

But neither of them sat down or removed his coat. There was an awkward several minutes when they had nothing to say to each other. Guy took a swallow of the highball that seemed to be all Scotch, and looked down at the littered floor. Bruno had odd feet, Guy noticed, or maybe it was the shoes. Small, light tan shoes with a long plain toecap shaped like Bruno's lantern chin. Somehow old-fashioned-looking feet. And Bruno was not so slender as he had thought. His long legs were heavy and his body rounded.

"I hope you weren't annoyed," Bruno said cautiously,"when I came in the diner."

"Oh, no."

"I felt lonely. You know."

Guy said something about its being lonely traveling in a drawing room alone, then nearly tripped on something: the strap of a Rolleiflex camera. There was a new white scratch deep down the side of its leather case. He was conscious of Bruno's shy stare. He was going to be bored, of course. Why had he come? A pang of conscience made him want to return to the diner. Then the waiter arrived with a pewter-covered tray, and snapped up a table. The smell of charcoal-broiled meat cheered him. Bruno insisted so desperately on paying the check that Guy gave it up. Bruno had a big mushroom-covered steak. Guy had hamburger.

"What're you building in Metcalf?"

"Nothing," Guy said. "My mother lives there."

"Oh," Bruno said interestedly. "Visiting her? Is that where you're from?"

"Yes. Born there."

"You don't look much like a Texan." Bruno shot ketchup all over his steak and French fries, then delicately picked up the parsley and held it poised. "How long since you been home?"

"About two years."

"Your father there, too?"

"My father's dead."

"Oh. Get along with your mother okay?"

Guy said he did. The taste of Scotch, though Guy didn't much care for it, was pleasant because it reminded him of Anne. She drank Scotch, when she drank. It was like her, golden, full of light, made with careful art. "Where do you live in Long Island?"

"Great Neck."

Anne lived much farther out on Long Island.

"In a house I call the Doghouse," Bruno went on. "There's dogwood all around it and everybody in it's in some kind of doghouse, down to the chauffeur." He laughed suddenly with real pleasure, and bent again over his food.

Looking at him now, guy saw only the top of his narrow thin-haired head and the protruding pimple. He had not been conscious of the pimple since he had seen him asleep, but now that he noticed it again, it seemed a monstrous, shocking thing and he saw it alone. "Why?"Guy asked.

"Account of my father. Bastard. I get on okay with my mother, too. My mother's coming out to Santa Fe in a couple days."

"That's nice."

"It is," Bruno said as if contradicting him. "We have a lot of fun together—sitting around, playing golf. We even go to parties together." He laughed, half ashamed, half proud, and suddenly uncertain and young. "You think that's funny?"

"No," said Guy.

"I just wish I had my own dough. See, my income was supposed to start this year, only my father won't let me have it. He's deflecting it into his own exchequer. You might not think so, but I haven't got any more money now than I had when I was in school with everything paid for. I have to ask for a hundred dollars now and then from my mother." He smiled, pluckily.

"I wish you had let me pay the check."

"A-aw, no!" Bruno protested. "I just mean it's a hell of a thing, isn't it, when your own father robs you. It isn't even his money, it's my mother's family's money." He waited for Guy to comment.

"Hasn't your mother any say about it?"

"My father got his name put on it when I was a kid!" Bruno shouted hoarsely.

"Oh." Guy wondered how many people Bruno had met, bought dinners for, and told the same story about his father. "Why did he do that?"

Bruno brought his hands up in a hopeless shrug, then hid them fast in his pockets. "I said he was a bastard, didn't I? He robs everyone he can. Now he says he won't give it to me because I won't work, but that's a lie. He thinks my mother and I have too good a time as it is. He's always scheming up ways to cut in."

Guy could see him and his mother, a youngish Long Island society woman who used too much mascara and occasionally, like her son, enjoyed tough company. "Where'd you go to college?"

"Harvard. Busted out sophomore year. Drinking and gambling." He shrugged with a writhing movement of his narrow shoulders. "Not like you, huh? Okay, I'm a bum, so what?" He poured more Scotch for both of them.

"Who said you were?"

"My father says so. He should've had a nice quiet son like you, then everybody would've been happy."

"What makes you think I'm nice and quiet?"

"I mean you're serious and you choose a profession. Like architecture. Me, I don't feel like working. I don't have to work, see? I'm not a writer or a painter or a musician. Is there any reason a person should work if they don't have to? I'll get my ulcers the easy way. My father has ulcers. Hah! He still has hopes I'll enter his hardware business. I tell him his business, all business, is legalized throat-cutting, like marriage is legalized fornication. Am I right?"

Guy looked at him wryly and sprinkled salt on the French fried potato on his fork. He was eating slowly, enjoying his meal, even vaguely enjoying Bruno, as he might have enjoyed an entertainment on a distant stage. Actually, he was thinking of Anne. Sometimes the faint continuous dream he had of her seemed more real than the outside world that penetrated only in sharp fragments, occasional images, like the scratch on the Rolleiflex case, the long cigarette Bruno had plunged into his pat of butter, the shattered glass of the photograph of the father Bruno had thrown out in the hall in the story he was telling now. It had just occurred to Guy he might have time to see Anne in Mexico, between seeing Miriam and going to Florida. If he got through with Miriam quickly, he could fly to Mexico and fly to Palm Beach. It hadn't occurred to him before because he couldn't afford it. But if the Palm Beach contract came through, he could.

"Can you imagine anything more insulting? Locking the garage where my own car is?" Bruno's voice had cracked and was stuck at a shrieking pitch.

"Why?" Guy asked.

"Just because he knew I needed it bad that night! My friends picked me up finally, so what does he get out of it?"

Guy didn't know what to say. "He keeps the keys?"

"He took *my keys*! Took them out of my room! That's why he was scared of me. He left the house that night, he was so scared." Bruno was turned in his chair, breathing hard, chewing a fingernail. Some wisps of hair, darkened brown with sweat, bobbed like antennae over his forehead. "My mother wasn't home, or it never could have happened, of course."

"Of course," Guy echoed involuntarily. Their whole conversation had been leading to this story, he supposed, that he had heard only half of. Back of the bloodshot eyes that had opened on him in the Pullman car, back of the wistful smile, another story of hatred and injustice. "So you threw his picture out in the hall?" Guy asked meaninglessly.

"I threw it out of my mother's room," Bruno said, emphasizing the last three words. "My father put it in my mother's room. She doesn't like the Captain any better than I do. The Captain!— *I* don't call him anything, brother!"

"But what's he got against you?"

"Against me and my mother, too! He's different from us or any other *human*! He doesn't like anybody. He doesn't like anything but money. He cut enough throats to make a lot of money, that's all. Sure he's smart! Okay! But his conscience is sure eating him now! That's why he wants me to go into his business, so I'll cut throats and feel as lousy as he does!" Bruno's stiff hand closed, then his mouth, then his eyes.

Guy thought he was about to cry, when the puffy lids lifted and the smile staggered back.

"Boring, huh? I was just explaining why I left town so soon, ahead of my mother. You don't know what a cheerful guy I am really! Honest!"

"Can't you leave home if you want to?"

Bruno didn't seem to understand his question at first, then he answered calmly,"Sure, only I like to be with my mother."

And his mother stayed because of the money, Guy supposed. "Cigarette?"

Bruno took one, smiling. "You know, the night he left the house was the first time in maybe ten years he'd gone out. I wonder where the hell he even went. I was sore enough that night to kill him and he knew it. Ever feel like murdering somebody?"

"No."

"I do. I'm sure sometimes I could kill my father." He looked down at his plate with a bemused smile. "You know what my father does for a hobby? Guess."

Guy didn't want to guess. He felt suddenly bored and wanted to be alone.

"He collects cookie cutters!" Bruno exploded with a snickering laugh. "Cookie cutters, honest! He's got all kinds— Pennsylvania Dutch, Bavarian, English, French, a lot of Hungarian, all around the room. Animal-cracker cookie cutters framed over his desk—you know, the things kids eat in boxes? He wrote the president of the company and they sent him a whole set. The machine age!" Bruno laughed and ducked his head.

Guy stared at him. Bruno himself was funnier than what he said. "Does he ever use them?"

"Huh?"

"Does he ever make cookies?"

Bruno whooped. With a wriggle, he removed his jacket and flung it at a suitcase. For a moment he seemed too excited to say anything, then remarked with sudden quiet,"My mother's always telling him to go back to his cookie cutters."A film of sweat covered his smooth face like thin oil. He thrust his smile solicitously half across the table. "Enjoy your dinner?"

"Very much," Guy said heartily.

"Ever hear of the Bruno Transforming Company of Long Island? Makes AC-DC gadgets?"

"I don't think so."

"Well, why should you? Makes plenty of dough though. You interested in making money?"

"Not awfully."

"Mind if I ask how old you are?"

"Twenty-nine."

"Yeah? I would've said older. How old you think I look?"

Guy studied him politely. "Maybe twenty-four or five," he answered, intending to flatter him, for he looked younger.

"Yeah, I am. Twenty-five. You mean I do look twenty-five with this—this *thing* right in the center of my head?" Bruno caught his underlip between his teeth. A glint of wariness came in his eyes, and suddenly he cupped his hand over his forehead in intense and bitter shame. He sprang up and went to the mirror. "I meant to put something over it."

Guy said something reassuring, but Bruno kept looking at himself this way and that in the mirror, in an agony of self-torture. "It *couldn't* be a pimple," he said nasally. "It's a boil. It's everything I *hate* boiling up in me. It's a plague of Job!"

"Oh, now!" Guy laughed.

"It started coming Monday night after that fight. It's getting worse. I bet it leaves a scar."

"No, it won't."

"Yes, it will. A fine thing to get to Santa Fe with!"He was sitting in his chair now with his fists clenched and one heavy leg trailing, in a pose of brooding tragedy.

Guy went over and opened one of the books on the seat by the window. It was a detective novel. They were all detective novels. When he tried to read a few lines, the print swam and he closed the book. He must have drunk a lot, he thought. He didn't really care, tonight.

"In Santa Fe,"Bruno said,"I want everything there is. Wine, women, and song. Hah!"

"What do you want?"

"Something." Bruno's mouth turned down in an ugly grimace of unconcern. "Everything. I got a theory a person ought to do everything it's possible to do before he dies, and maybe die trying to do something that's really impossible."

Something in Guy responded with a leap, then cautiously drew back. He asked softly,"Like what?"

"Like a trip to the moon in a rocket. Setting a speed record in a car—blindfolded. I did that once. Didn't set a record, but I went up to a hundred sixty."

"Blindfolded?"

"And I did a robbery." Bruno stared at Guy rigidly. "Good one. Out of an apartment."

An incredulous smile started on Guy's lips, though actually he believed Bruno. Bruno could be violent. He could be insane, too. Despair, Guy thought, not insanity. The desperate boredom of the wealthy, that he often spoke of to Anne. It tended to destroy rather than create. And it could lead to crime as easily as privation.

"Not to get anything," Bruno went on. "I didn't want what I took. I especially took what I didn't want."

"What did you take?"

Bruno shrugged. "Cigarette lighter. Table model. And a statue off the mantel. Colored glass. And something else."Another shrug. "You're the only one knows about it. I don't talk much. Guess you think I do." He smiled.

Guy drew on his cigarette. "How'd you go about it?"

"Watched an apartment house in Astoria till I got the time right, then just walked in the window. Down the fire escape. Sort of easy. One of the things I cross off my list, thinking thank God."

"Why 'thank God'?"

Bruno grinned shyly. "I don't know why I said that." He refilled his glass, then Guy's.

Guy looked at the stiff, shaky hands that had stolen, at the nails bitten below the quick. The hands played clumsily with a match cover and dropped it, like a baby's hands, onto the ash-sprinkled steak. How boring it was really, Guy thought, crime. How motiveless often. A certain type turned to crime. And who would know from Bruno's hands, or his room, or his ugly wistful face that he had stolen? Guy dropped into his chair again.

"Tell me about you," Bruno invited pleasantly.

"Nothing to tell." Guy took a pipe from his jacket pocket, banged it on his heel, looked down at the ashes on the carpet, and then forgot them. The tingling of the alcohol sank deeper into his flesh. He thought, if the Palm Beach contract came through, the two weeks before work began would pass quickly. A divorce needn't take long. The pattern of the low white buildings on the green lawn in his finished drawing swam familiarly in his mind, in detail, without his trying to evoke them. He felt subtly flattered, immensely secure suddenly, and blessed.

"What kind of houses you build?" Bruno asked.

"Oh—what's known as modern. I've done a couple of stores and a small office building." Guy smiled, feeling none of the reticence, the faint vexation he generally did when people asked him about his work.

"You married?"

"No. Well, I am, yes. Separated."

"Oh. Why?"

"Incompatible," Guy replied.

"How long you been separated?"

"Three years."

"You don't want a divorce?"

Guy hesitated, frowning.

"Is she in Texas, too?"

"Yes."

"Going to see her?"

"I'll see her. We're going to arrange the divorce now." His teeth set. Why had he said it?

Bruno sneered. "What kind of girls you find to marry down there?"

"Very pretty," Guy replied. "Some of them."

"Mostly dumb though, huh?"

"They can be." He smiled to himself. Miriam was the kind of Southern girl Bruno probably meant.

"What kind of girl's your wife?"

"Rather pretty,"Guy said cautiously. "Red hair. A little plump."

"What's her name?"

"Miriam. Miriam Joyce."

"Hm-m. Smart or dumb?"

"She's not an intellectual. I didn't want to marry an intellectual."

"And you loved her like hell, huh?"

Why? Did he show it? Bruno's eyes were fixed on him, missing nothing, unblinking, as if their exhaustion had passed the point where sleep is imperative. Guy had a feeling those gray eyes had been searching him for hours and hours. "Why do you say that?"

"You're a nice guy. You take everything serious. You take women the hard way, too, don't you?"

"What's the hard way?" he retorted. But he felt a rush of affection for Bruno because Bruno had said what he thought about him. Most people, Guy knew, didn't say what they thought about him.

Bruno made little scallops in the air with his hands, and sighed.

"What's the hard way?" Guy repeated.

"All out, with a lot of high hopes. Then you get kicked in the teeth, right?"

"Not entirely." A throb of self-pity piqued him, however, and he got up, taking his drink with him. There was no place to move in the room. The swaying of the train made it difficult even to stand upright.

And Bruno kept staring at him, one old-fashioned foot dangling at the end of the crossed leg, flicking his finger again and again on the cigarette he held over his plate. The unfinished pink and black steak was slowly being covered by the rain of ashes. Bruno looked less friendly, Guy suspected, since he had told him he was married. And more curious.

"What happened with your wife? She start sleeping around?"

That irritated him, too, Bruno's accuracy. "No. That's all past anyway."

"But you're still married to her. Couldn't you get a divorce before now?"

Guy felt instantaneous shame. "I haven't been much concerned about a divorce."

"What's happened now?"

"She just decided she wanted one. I think she's going to have a child."

"Oh. Fine time to decide, huh? She's been sleeping around for three years and finally landed somebody?"

Just what had happened, of course, and probably it had taken the baby to do it. How did Bruno know? Guy felt that Bruno was superimposing upon Miriam the knowledge and hatred of someone else he knew. Guy turned to the window. The window gave him nothing but his own image. He could feel his heartbeats shaking his body, deeper than the train's vibrations. Perhaps, he thought, his heart was beating because he had never told anyone so much about Miriam. He had never told Anne as much as Bruno knew already. Except that Miriam had once been different—sweet, loyal, lonely, terribly in need of him and of freedom from her family. He would see Miriam tomorrow, be able to touch her by putting out his hand. He could not bear the thought of touching her oversoft flesh that once he had loved. Failure overwhelmed him suddenly.

"What happened with your marriage?" Bruno's voice asked gently, right behind him. "I'm really very interested, as a friend. How old was she?"

"Eighteen."

"She start sleeping around right away?"

Guy turned reflexively, as if to shoulder Miriam's guilt. "That's not the only thing women do, you know."

"But she did, didn't she?"

Guy looked away, annoyed and fascinated at the same time. "Yes." How ugly the little word sounded, hissing in his ears!

"I know that Southern redhead type," Bruno said, poking at his apple pie.

Guy was conscious again of an acute and absolutely useless shame. Useless, because nothing Miriam had done or said would embarrass or surprise Bruno. Bruno seemed incapable of surprise, only of a whetting of interest.

Bruno looked down at his plate with coy amusement. His eyes widened, bright as they could be with the bloodshot and the blue circles. "Marriage," he sighed.

The word "marriage" lingered in Guy's ears, too. It was a solemn word to him. It had the primordial solemnity of *holy, love, sin.* It was Miriam's round terra cotta-colored mouth saying,"Why should I put myself out for *you*?" and it was Anne's eyes as she pushed her hair back and looked up at him on the lawn of her house where she planted crocuses. It was Miriam turning from the tall thin window in the room in Chicago, lifting her freckled, shield-shaped face directly up to his as she always did before she told a lie, and Steve's long dark head, insolently smiling. Memories began to crowd in, and he wanted to put his hands up and push them back. The room in Chicago where it had all happened . . . He could smell the room, Miriam's perfume, and the heat from painted radiators. He stood passively, for the first time in years not thrusting Miriam's face back to a pink blur. What would it do to him if he let it all flood him again, now? Arm him against her or undermine him?

"I mean it,"Bruno's voice said distantly. "What happened? You don't mind telling me, do you? I'm interested."

Steve happened. Guy picked up his drink. He saw the afternoon in Chicago, framed by the doorway of the room, the image gray and black now like a photograph. The afternoon he had found them in the apartment, like no other afternoon, with its own color, taste, and sound, its own world, like a horrible little work of art. Like a date in history fixed in time. Or wasn't it just the opposite, that it traveled with him always? For here it was now, as clear as it had ever been. And, worst of all, he was aware of an impulse to tell Bruno everything, the stranger on the train who would listen, commiserate, and forget. The idea of telling Bruno began to comfort him. Bruno was not the ordinary stranger on the train by any means. He was cruel and corrupt enough himself to appreciate a story like that of his first love. And Steve was only the surprise ending that made the rest fall into place. Steve wasn't the first betrayal. It was only his twenty-six-year-old pride that had exploded in his face that afternoon. He had told the story to himself a thousand times, a classic story, dramatic for all his stupidity. His stupidity only lent it humor.

"I expected too much of her,"Guy said casually,"without any right to. She happened to like attention. She'll probably flirt all her life, no matter whom she's with."

"I know, the eternal high school type." Bruno waved his hand. "Can't even pretend to belong to one guy, ever."

Guy looked at him. Miriam had, of course, once.

Abruptly he abandoned his idea of telling Bruno, ashamed that he had nearly begun. Bruno seemed unconcerned now, in fact, whether he told it or not. Slumped, Bruno was drawing with a match in the gravy of his plate. The downturned half of his mouth, in profile, was sunken between nose and chin like the mouth of an old man. The mouth seemed to say, whatever the story, it was really beneath his contempt to listen.

"Women like that draw men,"Bruno mumbled,"like garbage draws flies."

## *two*

The shock of Bruno's words detached him from himself. "You must have had some unpleasant experiences yourself," he remarked. But Bruno troubled by women was hard to imagine.

"Oh, my father had one like that. Redhead, too. Named Carlotta."

He looked up, and the hatred for his father penetrated his fuzziness like a barb. "Fine, isn't it? It's men like my father keep 'em in business."

Carlotta. Guy felt he understood now why Bruno loathed Miriam. It seemed the key to Bruno's whole personality, to the hatred of his father and to his retarded adolescence.

"There's two kinds of guys!" Bruno announced in a roaring voice, and stopped.

Guy caught a glimpse of himself in a narrow panel mirror on the wall. His eyes looked frightened, he thought, his mouth grim, and deliberately he relaxed. A golf club nudged him in the back. He ran his fingertips over its cool varnished surface. The inlaid metal in the dark wood recalled the binnacle on Anne's sailboat.

"And essentially one kind of women!" Bruno went on. "Two-timers. At one end it's two-timing and the other end it's a whore! Take your choice!"

"What about women like your mother?"

"I never seen another woman like my mother," Bruno declared. "I never seen a woman take so much. She's good-looking, too, lots of men friends, but she doesn't fool around with them."

Silence.

Guy tapped another cigarette on his watch and saw it was 10:30. He must go in a moment.

"How'd you find out about your wife?" Bruno peered up at him.

Guy took his time with his cigarette.

"How many'd she have?"

"Quite a few. Before I found out." And just as he assured himself it made no difference at all now to admit it, a sensation as of a tiny whirlpool inside him began to confuse him. Tiny, but realer than the memories somehow, because he had uttered it. Pride? Hatred? Or merely impatience with himself, because all that he kept feeling now was so useless? He turned the conversation from himself. "Tell me what else you want to do before you die."

"Die? Who said anything about dying? I got a few crackproof rackets doped out. Could start one some day in Chicago or New York, or I might just sell my ideas. And I got a lot of ideas for perfect murders." Bruno looked up again with that fixity that seemed to invite challenge.

"I hope your asking me here isn't part of one of your plans." Guy sat down.

"Jesus Christ, I *like* you, Guy! I really do!"

The wistful face pled with Guy to say he liked him, too. The loneliness in those tiny, tortured eyes! Guy looked down embarrassedly at his hands. "Do all your ideas run to crime?"

"Certainly not! Just things I want to do, like—I want to give a guy a thousand dollars some day. A beggar. When I get my own dough, that's one of the first things I'm gonna do. But didn't you ever feel you wanted to steal something? Or kill somebody? You must have. Everybody feels those things. Don't you think some people get quite a kick out of killing people in wars?"

"No," Guy said.

Bruno hesitated. "Oh, they'd never admit it, of course, they're afraid! But you've had people in your life you'd have liked out of the way, haven't you?"

"No." Steve, he remembered suddenly. Once he had even thought of murdering him.

Bruno cocked his head. "Sure you have. I see it. Why don't you admit it?"

"I may have had fleeting ideas, but I'd never have done anything about them. I'm not that kind of person."

"That's exactly where you're wrong! Any kind of person can murder. Purely circumstances and not a thing to do with temperament! People get so far—and it takes just the least little thing to push them over the brink. Anybody. Even your grandmother. I know!"

"I don't happen to agree," Guy said tersely.

"I tell you I came near murdering my father a thousand times! Who'd you ever feel like murdering? The guys with your wife?"

"One of them," Guy murmured.

"How near did you come?"

"Not near at all. I merely thought of it." He remembered the sleepless nights, hundreds of them, and the despair of peace unless he avenged himself. Could something have pushed him over the line then? He heard Bruno's voice mumbling,"You were a hell of a lot nearer than you think, that's all I can say." Guy gazed at him puzzledly. His figure had the sickly, nocturnal look of a croupier's, hunched on shirtsleeved forearms over the table, thin head hanging. "You read too many detective stories," Guy said, and having heard himself, did not know where the words had come from.

"They're good. They show all kinds of people can murder."

"I've always thought that's exactly why they're bad."

"Wrong again!" Bruno said indignantly. "Do you know what percentage of murders get put in the papers?"

"I don't know and I don't care."

"One twelfth. One twelfth! Just imagine! Who do you think the other eleven twelfths are? A lot of little people that don't matter. All the people the cops know they'll never catch." He started to pour more Scotch, found the bottle empty, and dragged himself up. A gold penknife flashed out of his trousers pocket on a gold chain fine as a string. It pleased Guy aesthetically, as a beautiful piece of jewelry might have. And he found himself thinking, as he watched Bruno slash round the top of a Scotch bottle, that Bruno might murder one day with the little penknife, that he would probably go quite free, simply because he wouldn't much care whether he were caught or not.

Bruno turned, grinning, with the new bottle of Scotch. "Come to Santa Fe with me, huh? Relax for a couple days."

"Thanks, I can't."

"I got plenty of dough. Be my guest, huh?" He spilled Scotch on the table.

"Thanks," Guy said. From his clothes, he supposed, Bruno thought he hadn't much money. They were his favorite trousers, these gray flannels. He was going to wear them in Metcalf and in Palm Beach, too, if it wasn't too hot. Leaning back, he put his hands in his pockets and felt a hole at the bottom of the right one.

"Why not?"Bruno handed him his drink. "I like you a lot, Guy."

"Why?"

"Because you're a good guy. Decent, I mean. I meet a lot of guys—no pun—but not many like you. I admire you," he blurted, and sank his lip into his glass.

"I like you, too," said Guy.

"Come with me, huh? I got nothing to do for two or three days till my mother comes. We could have a swell time."

"Pick up somebody else."

"Cheeses, Guy, what d'you think I do, go around picking up traveling companions? I like you, so I ask you to come with me. One day even. I'll cut right over from Metcalf and not even go to El Paso. I'm supposed to see the Canyon."

"Thanks, I've got a job as soon as I finish in Metcalf."

"Oh." The wistful, admiring smile again. "Building something?"

"Yes, a country club." It still sounded strange and unlike himself, the last thing he would have thought he'd be building, two months ago. "The new Palmyra in Palm Beach."

"Yeah?"

Bruno had heard of the Palmyra Club, of course. It was the biggest in Palm Beach. He had even heard they were going to build a new one. He had been to the old one a couple of times.

"You designed it?" He looked down at Guy like a hero-worshiping little boy. "Can you draw me a picture of it?"

Guy drew a quick sketch of the buildings in the back of Bruno's address book and signed his name, as Bruno wanted. He explained the wall that would drop to make the lower floor one great ballroom extending onto the terrace, the louver windows he hoped to get permission for that would eliminate air-conditioning. He grew happy as he talked, and tears of excitement came in his eyes, though he kept his voice low. How could he talk so intimately to Bruno, he wondered, reveal the very best of himself? Who was less likely to understand than Bruno?

"Sounds terrific," Bruno said. "You mean, you just tell them how it's gonna look?"

"No. One has to please quite a lot of people." Guy put his head back suddenly and laughed.

"You're gonna be famous, huh? Maybe you're famous now."

There would be photographs in the news magazines, perhaps something in the newsreels. They hadn't passed on his sketches yet, he reminded himself, but he was so sure they would. Myers, the architect he shared an office with in New York, was sure. Anne was positive. And so was Mr. Brillhart. The biggest commission of his life. "I might be famous after this. It's the kind of thing they publicize."

Bruno began to tell him a long story about his life in college, how he would have become a photographer if something hadn't happened at a certain time with his father. Guy didn't listen. He sipped his drink absently, and thought of the commissions that would come after Palm Beach. Soon, perhaps, an office building in New York. He had an idea for an office building in New York, and he longed to see it come into being. Guy Daniel Haines. *A name*. No longer the irksome, never quite banished awareness that he had less money than Anne.

"Wouldn't it, Guy?" Bruno repeated.

"What?"

Bruno took a deep breath. "If your wife made a stink now about the divorce. Say she fought about it while you were in Palm Beach and made them fire you, wouldn't that be motive enough for murder?"

"Of Miriam?"

"Sure."

"No," Guy said. But the question disturbed him. He was afraid Miriam had heard of the Palmyra job through his mother, that she might try to interfere for the sheer pleasure of hurting him.

"When she was two-timing you, didn't you feel like murdering her?"

"No. Can't you get off the subject?" For an instant, Guy saw both halves of his life, his marriage and his career, side by side as he felt he had never seen them before. His brain swam sickeningly, trying to understand how he could be so stupid and helpless in one and so capable in the other. He glanced at Bruno, who still stared at him, and, feeling slightly befuddled, set his glass on the table and pushed it fingers' length away.

"You must have wanted to once," Bruno said with gentle, drunken persistence.

"No." Guy wanted to get out and take a walk, but the train kept on and on in a straight line, like something that would never stop. Suppose Miriam did lose him the commission. He was going to live there several months, and he would be expected to keep on a social par with the directors. Bruno understood such things very well. He passed his hand across his moist forehead. The difficulty was, of course, that he wouldn't know what was in Miriam's mind until he saw her. He was tired, and when he was tired, Miriam could invade him like an army. It had happened so often in the two years it had taken him to turn loose of his love for her. It was happening now. He felt sick of Bruno. Bruno was smiling.

"Shall I tell you one of my ideas for murdering my father?"

"No," Guy said. He put his hand over the glass Bruno was about to refill.

"Which do you want, the busted light socket in the bathroom or the carbon monoxide garage?"

"Do it and stop talking about it!"

"I'll do it, don't think I won't! Know what else I'll do some day? Commit suicide if I happen to feel like committing suicide, and fix it so it looks like my worst enemy murdered me."

Guy looked at him in disgust. Bruno seemed to be growing indefinite at the edges, as if by some process of deliquescence. He seemed only a voice and a spirit now, the spirit of evil. All he despised, Guy thought, Bruno represented. All the things he would not want to be, Bruno was, or would become.

"Want me to dope out a perfect murder of your wife for you? You might want to use it sometime." Bruno squirmed with self-consciousness under Guy's scrutiny.

Guy stood up. "I want to take a walk."

Bruno slammed his palms together. "Hey! Cheeses, what an idea! We murder for each other, see? I kill your wife and you kill my father! We meet on the train, see, and nobody knows we know each other! Perfect alibis! Catch?"

The wall before his eyes pulsed rhythmically, as if it were about to spring apart. *Murder*. The word sickened him, terrified him. He wanted to break away from Bruno, get out of the room, but a nightmarish heaviness held him. He tried to steady himself by straightening out the wall, by understanding what Bruno was saying, because he could feel there was logic in it somewhere, like a problem or a puzzle to be solved.

Bruno's tobacco-stained hands jumped and trembled on his knees. "Airtight alibis!"he shrieked. "It's the idea of my life! Don't you get it? I could do it sometime when you're out of town and you could do it when I was out of town."

Guy understood. No one could ever, possibly, find out.

"It would give me a great pleasure to stop a career like Miriam's and to further a career like yours." Bruno giggled. "Don't you agree she ought to be stopped before she ruins a lot of other people? Sit down, Guy!"

She hasn't ruined me, Guy wanted to remind him, but Bruno gave him no time.

"I mean, just supposing the setup was that. Could you do it? You could tell me all about where she lived, you know, and I could do the same for you, as good as if you lived there. We could leave fingerprints all over the place and only drive the dicks batty!" He snickered. "Months apart, of course, and strictly no communication. Christ, it's a cinch!" He stood up and nearly toppled, getting his drink. Then he was saying, right in Guy's face, with suffocating confidence:"You could do it, huh, Guy? Wouldn't be any hitches, I swear. I'd fix everything, I swear, Guy."

Guy thrust him away, harder than he had intended. Bruno rose resiliently from the window seat. Guy glanced about for air, but the walls presented an unbroken surface. The room had become a little hell. What was he doing here? How and when had he drunk so much?

"I'm positive you *could*!" Bruno frowned.

Shut up with your damned theories, Guy wanted to shout back, but instead his voice came like a whisper:"I'm sick of this."

He saw Bruno's narrow face twist then in a queer way—in a smirk of surprise, a look that was eerily omniscient and hideous. Bruno shrugged affably.

"Okay. I still say it's a good idea and we got the absolutely perfect setup right here. It's the idea I'll use. With somebody else, of course. Where you going?"

Guy had at last thought of the door. He went out and opened another door onto the platform where the cooler air smashed him like a reprimand and the train's voice rose to an upbraiding blare. He added his own curses of himself to the wind and the train, and longed to be sick.

"Guy?"

Turning, he saw Bruno slithering past the heavy door.

"Guy, I'm sorry."

"That's all right," Guy said at once, because Bruno's face shocked him. It was doglike in its self-abasement.

"Thanks, Guy." Bruno bent his head, and at that instant the pound-pound-pound of the wheels began to die away, and Guy had to catch his balance.

He felt enormously grateful, because the train was stopping. He slapped Bruno's shoulder. "Let's get off and get some air!"

They stepped out into a world of silence and total blackness.

"The hell's the idea?"Bruno shouted. "No lights!"

Guy looked up. There was no moon either. The chill made his body rigid and alert. He heard the homely slap of a wooden door somewhere. A spark grew into a lantern ahead of them, and a man ran with it toward the rear of the train where a boxcar door unrolled a square of light. Guy walked slowly toward the light, and Bruno followed him.

Far away on the flat black prairie a locomotive wailed, on and on, and then again, farther away. It was a sound he remembered from childhood, beautiful, pure, lonely. Like a wild horse shaking a white mane. In a burst of companionship, Guy linked his arm through Bruno's.

"I don't wanna *walk*!" Bruno yelled, wrenching away and stopping. The fresh air was wilting him like a fish.

The train was starting. Guy pushed Bruno's big loose body aboard.

"Nightcap?" Bruno said disspiritedly at his door, looking tired enough to drop.

"Thanks, I couldn't."

Green curtains muffled their whispers.

"Don't forget to call me in the morning. I'll leave the door unlocked. If I don't answer, come on in, huh?"

Guy lurched against the walls of green curtains as he made his way to his berth.

Habit made him think of his book as he lay down. He had left it in Bruno's room. His Plato. He didn't like the idea of its spending the night in Bruno's room, or of Bruno's touching it and opening it.

## *three*

He had called Miriam immediately, and she had arranged to meet him at the high school that lay between their houses.

Now he stood in a corner of the asphalt gamefield, waiting. She would be late, of course. Why had she chosen the high school, he wondered. Because it was her own ground? He had loved her when he had used to wait for her here.

Overhead, the sky was a clear strong blue. The sun poured down moltenly, not yellow but colorless, like something grown white with its own heat. Beyond the trees, he saw the top of a slim reddish building he did not know, that had gone up since he had been in Metcalf two years ago. He turned away. There was no human being in sight, as if the heat had caused everyone to abandon the school building and even the homes of the neighborhood. He looked at the broad gray steps that spilled from the dark arch of the school doors. He could still remember the inky, faintly sweaty smell on the fuzzy edges of Miriam's algebra book. He could still see the MIRIAM penciled on the edge of its pages, and the drawing of the girl with the Spencerian marcel wave on the flyleaf, when he opened the book to do her problems for her. Why had he thought Miriam any different from all the others?

He walked through the wide gate between the crisscross wire fence and looked up College Avenue again. Then he saw her, under the yellow-green trees that bordered the sidewalk. His heart began to beat harder, but he blinked his eyes with deliberate casualness. She walked at her usual rather stolid pace, taking her time. Now her head came into view, haloed by a broad, light-colored hat. Shadow and sun speckled her figure chaotically. She gave him a relaxed wave, and Guy pulled a hand out of his pocket, returned it, and went back into the gamefield, suddenly tense and shy as a boy. She knows about the Palm Beach job, he thought, that strange girl under the trees. His mother had told him, half an hour ago, that she had mentioned it to Miriam when Miriam last telephoned.

"Hello, Guy." Miriam smiled and quickly closed her broad orangey-pink lips. Because of the space between her front teeth, Guy remembered.

"How are you, Miriam?" Involuntarily he glanced at her figure, plump but not pregnant looking, and it flashed through his mind she might have lied. She wore a brightly flowered skirt and a white short-sleeved blouse. Her big white pocketbook was of woven patent leather.

She sat down primly on the one stone bench that was in the shade, and asked him dull questions about his trip. Her face had grown fuller where it had always been full, on the lower cheeks, so that her chin looked more pointed. There were little wrinkles under her eyes now, Guy noticed. She had lived a long time, for twenty-two.

"In January," she answered him in a flat voice. "In January the child's due."

It was two months advanced then. "I suppose you want to marry him."

She turned her head slightly and looked down. On her short cheek, the sunlight picked out the largest freckles, and Guy saw a certain pattern he remembered and had not thought of since a time when he had been married to her. How sure he had once been that he possessed her, possessed her every frailest thought! Suddenly it seemed that all love was only a tantalizing, a horrible next-best to knowing. He knew not the smallest part of the new world in Miriam's mind now. Was it possible that the same thing could happen with Anne?

"Don't you, Miriam?" he prompted.

"Not *right* now. See, there're complications."

"Like what?"

"Well, we might not be able to marry as soon as we'd like to."

"Oh." *We*. He knew what he would look like, tall and dark, with a long face, like Steve. The type Miriam had always been attracted to. The only type she would have a child by. And she did want this child, he could tell. Something had happened, that had nothing to do with the man, perhaps, that made her want a child. He could see it in the prim, stiff way she sat on the bench, in that self-abandoned trance he had always seen or imagined in pregnant women's faces. "That needn't delay the divorce though, I suppose."

"Well, I didn't think so—until a couple of days ago. I thought Owen would be free to marry this month."

"Oh. He's married now?"

"Yeah, he's married," she said with a little sigh, almost smiling.

Guy looked down in vague embarrassment and paced a slow step or two on the asphalt. He had known the man would be married. He had expected he would have no intention of marrying her unless he were forced to. "Where is he? Here?"

"He's in Houston," she replied. "Don't you want to sit down?"

"No."

"You never did like to sit down."

He was silent.

"Still have your ring?"

"Yes." His class ring from Chicago, that Miriam had always admired because it meant he was a college man. She was staring at the ring with a self-conscious smile. He put his hands in his pockets. "As long as I'm here, I'd like it settled. Can we do it this week?"

"I want to go away, Guy."

"For the divorce?"

Her stubby hands opened in a limp ambiguous gesture, and he thought suddenly of Bruno's hands. He had forgotten Bruno completely, getting off the train this morning. And his book.

"I'm sort of tired of staying here," she said.

"We can get the divorce in Dallas if you like." Her friends here knew, he thought, that was all.

"I want to wait, Guy. Would you mind? Just a while?"

"I should think you'd mind. Does he intend to marry you or not?"

"He could marry me in September. He'd be free then, but—"

"But what?" In her silence, in the childlike lick of her tongue on her upper lip, he saw the trap she was in. She wanted this child so much, she would sacrifice herself in Metcalf by waiting until four months before it was born to marry its father. In spite of himself, he felt a certain pity for her.

"I want to go away, Guy. With you."

There was a real effort at sincerity in her face, so much that he almost forgot what she was asking, and why. "What is it you want, Miriam? Money to go away somewhere?"

The dreaminess in her gray-green eyes was dispersing like a mist. "Your mother said you were going to Palm Beach."

"I might be going there. To work." He thought of the Palmyra with a twinge of peril. It was slipping away already.

"Take me with you, Guy? It's the last thing I'll ask you. If I could stay with you till December and then get the divorce—"

"Oh," he said quietly, but something throbbed in his chest, like the breaking of his heart. She disgusted him suddenly, she and all the people around her whom she knew and attracted. Another man's child. Go away with her, be her husband until she gave birth to another man's child. In Palm Beach!

"If you don't take me, I'll come anyway."

"Miriam, I could get that divorce now. I don't have to wait to see the child. The law doesn't." His voice shook.

"You wouldn't do that to me," Miriam replied with that combination of threat and pleading that had played on both his anger and his love when he loved her, and baffled him.

He felt it baffling him now. And she was right. He wouldn't divorce her now. But it was not because he still loved her, not because she was still his wife and was therefore due his protection, but because he pitied her and because he remembered he had once loved her. He realized now he had pitied her even in New York, even when she wrote him for money. "I won't take the job if you come out there. There'd be no use in taking it," he said evenly, but it was gone already, he told himself, so why discuss it?

"I don't think you'd give up a job like that," she challenged.

He turned away from her twisted smile of triumph. That was where she was wrong, he thought, but he was silent. He took two steps on the gritty asphalt and turned again, with his head high. Be calm, he told himself. What could anger accomplish? Miriam had used to hate him when he reacted like this, because she loved loud arguments. She would love one even this morning, he thought. She had hated him when he reacted like this, until she had learned that in the long run it hurt him more to react like this. He knew he played into her hands now, yet he felt he could react in no other way.

"I haven't even got the job yet, you know. I'll simply send them a telegram saying I don't want it." Beyond the treetops, he noticed again the new reddish building he had seen before Miriam came.

"And then what?"

"A lot of things. But you won't know about them."

"Running away?" she taunted. "Cheapest way out."

He walked again, and turned. There was Anne. With Anne, he could endure this, endure anything. And in fact, he felt strangely resigned. Because he was with Miriam now, the symbol of the failure of his youth? He bit the tip of his tongue. There was inside him, like a flaw in a jewel, not visible on the surface, a fear and anticipation of failure that he had never been able to mend. At times, failure was a possibility that fascinated him, as at times, in high school and college, when he had allowed himself to fail examinations he might have passed; as when he married Miriam, he thought, against the will of both their families and all their friends. Hadn't he known it couldn't succeed? And now he had given up his biggest commission, without a murmur. He would go to Mexico and have a few days with Anne. It would take all his money, but why not? Could he possibly go back to New York and work without having seen Anne first?

"Is there anything else?" he asked.

"I've said it," she told him, out of her spaced front teeth.

# four

He walked home slowly, approaching Ambrose Street, where he lived, through Travis Street, which was shaded and still. There was a small fruit shop now on the corner of Travis and Delancey Streets, sitting right on somebody's front lawn like a children's play store. Out of the great Washatorium building that marred the west end of Ambrose Street, girls and women in white uniforms were pouring, chattering, on their way to an early lunch. He was glad he did not meet anyone on the street he had to speak to. He felt slow and quiet and resigned, and even rather happy. Strange how remote—perhaps how foreign—Miriam seemed five minutes after talking with her, how unimportant, really, everything seemed. Now he felt ashamed of his anxiety on the train.

"Not bad, Mama," he said with a smile when he came home.

His mother had greeted him with an anxious lift of her eyebrows. "I'm glad to hear that." She pulled a rocker around and sat down to listen. She was a small woman with light brown hair, with a pretty, rather fine straight-nosed profile still, and a physical energy that seemed to twinkle off in sparks now in the silver of her hair. And she was almost always cheerful. It was this fact chiefly that made Guy feel that he and she were quite different, that had estranged him from her somewhat since the time he had suffered from Miriam. Guy liked to nurse his griefs, discover all he could about them, while his mother counseled him to forget. "What did she say? You certainly weren't gone very long. I thought you might have had lunch with her."

"No, Mama." He sighed and sank down on the brocade sofa. "Everything's all right, but I'll probably not take the Palmyra job."

"Oh, Guy. Why not? Is she—? Is it true she's going to have a child?"

His mother was disappointed, Guy thought, but so mildly disappointed, for what the job really meant. He was glad she didn't know what the job really meant. "It's true," he said, and let his head go back until he felt the cool of the sofa's wooden frame against the back of his neck. He thought of the gulf that separated his life from his mother's. He had told her very little of his life with Miriam. And his mother, who had known a comfortable, happy upbringing in Mississippi, who kept herself busy now with her big house and her garden and her pleasant, loyal friends in Metcalf—what could she understand of a total malice like Miriam's? Or, for instance, what could she understand of the precarious life he was willing to lead in New York for the sake of a simple idea or two about his work?

"Now what's Palm Beach got to do with Miriam?" she asked finally.

"Miriam wants to come with me there. Protection for a time. And I couldn't bear it." Guy clenched his hand. He had a sudden vision of Miriam in Palm Beach, Miriam meeting Clarence Brillhart, the manager of the Palmyra Club. Yet it was not the vision of Brillhart's shock beneath his calm, unvarying courtesy, Guy knew, but simply his own revulsion that made it impossible. It was just that he couldn't bear having Miriam anywhere near him when he worked on a project like this one. "I couldn't bear it," he repeated.

"Oh," was all she said, but her silence now was one of understanding. If she made any comment, Guy thought, it was bound to remind him of her old disapproval of their marriage. And she wouldn't remind him at this time. "You couldn't bear it," she added, "for as long as it would take."

"I couldn't bear it." He got up and took her soft face in his hands. "Mama, I don't care a bit," he said, kissing her forehead. "I really don't care a row of beans."

"I don't believe you do care. Why don't you?"

He crossed the room to the upright piano. "Because I'm going to Mexico to see Anne."

"Oh, are you?" she smiled, and the gaiety of this first morning with him won out. "Aren't you the gadabout!"

"Want to come to Mexico?" He smiled over his shoulder. He began to play a saraband that he had learned as a child.

"Mexico!" his mother said in mock horror. "Wild horses wouldn't get me to Mexico. Maybe you can bring Anne to see me on your way back."

"Maybe."

She went over and laid her hands shyly on his shoulders. "Sometimes, Guy, I feel you're happy again. At the funniest times."

# *five*

What has happened? Write *immediately*. Or better, telephone collect. We're here at the Ritz for another two weeks. Missed you so on the trip, seems a shame we couldn't have flown down together, but I understand. I wish you well every moment of the day, darling. This must be over soon and we'll get it over. Whatever happens, tell me and let's face it. I often feel you *don't*. Face things, I mean.

You're so close, it's absurd you can't come down for a day or so. I hope you'll be in the mood. I hope there'll be time. Would love to have *you* here, and you know the family would. Darling, I do love the drawings and I'm so terribly proud of you I can even stand the idea of your being away in the months ahead because you'll be building them. Dad most impressed, too. We talk about you all the time.

All my love, and all that goes with it. Be happy, darling.

A.

Guy wrote a telegram to Clarence Brillhart, the manager of the Palmyra Club: "Owing to circumstances, impossible for me to take commission. My deepest regrets and thanks for your championing and constant encouragement. Letter following."

Suddenly he thought of the sketches they would use in lieu of his—the imitation Frank Lloyd Wright of William Harkness Associates. Worse yet, he thought as he dictated the telegram over the phone, the board would probably ask Harkness to copy some of his ideas. And Harkness would, of course.

He telegraphed Anne that he would fly down Monday and that he was free for several days. And because there was Anne, he did not bother to wonder how many months it would be, how many years, perhaps, before another job as big as the Palmyra would come within his reach.

## *six*

That evening, Charles Anthony Bruno was lying on his back in an El Paso hotel room, trying to balance a gold fountain pen across his rather delicate, dished-in nose. He was too restless to go to bed, not energetic enough to go down to one of the bars in the neighborhood and look things over. He had looked things over all afternoon, and he did not think much of them in El Paso. He did not think much of the Grand Canyon either. He thought more of the idea that had come to him night before last on the train. A pity Guy hadn't awakened him that morning. Not that Guy was the kind of fellow to plan a murder with, but he liked him, as a person. Guy was somebody worth knowing. Besides, Guy had left his book, and he could have given it back.

The ceiling fan made a *wuz-wuz-wuz* sound because one of its four blades was missing. If the fourth had been there, he would have been just a little cooler, he thought. One of the taps in the john leaked, the clamp on the reading light over the bed was broken so it hung down, and there were fingerprints all over the closet door. And the best hotel in town, they told him! Why was there always something wrong, maybe only one thing, with every hotel room he had ever been in? Some day he was going to find the perfect hotel room and buy it, even if it was in South Africa.

He sat up on the edge of the bed and reached for the telephone. "Gimme long-distance."He looked blankly at a smudge of red dirt his shoe had put on the white counterpane. "Great Neck 166J . . . Great Neck, yeah." He waited. "Long Island . . . In *New York*, lunk, ever hear of it?"

In less than a minute, he had his mother.

"Yeah, I'm here. You still leaving Sunday? You better. . . . Well, I took that muleback trip. Just about pooped me, too. . . . Yeah, I seen the canyon. . . . Okay, but the colors are kind of corny. . . . Anyhow, how's things with you?"

He began to laugh. He pushed off his shoes and rolled back on the bed with the telephone, laughing. She was telling him about coming home to find the Captain entertaining two of her friends—two men she had met the night before—who had dropped in, thought the Captain was her father, and proceeded to say all the wrong things.

## *seven*

Propped on his elbow in bed, Guy stared at the letter addressed to him in pencil. "Guess I'll have only one more time to wake you for another good long while," his mother said.

Guy picked up the letter from Palm Beach, "Maybe not so long, Mama."

"What time does your plane leave tomorrow?"

"One-twenty."

She leaned over and superfluously tucked in the foot of his bed. "I don't suppose you'll have time to run over and see Ethel?"

"Oh, certainly I will, Mama." Ethel Peterson was one of his mother's oldest friends. She had given Guy his first piano lessons.

The letter from Palm Beach was from Mr. Brillhart. He had been given the commission. Mr. Brillhart had also persuaded the board about the louver windows.

"I've got some good strong coffee this morning," his mother said from the threshold. "Like breakfast in bed?"

Guy smiled at her. "Would I!"

He reread Mr. Brillhart's letter carefully, put it back in its envelope, and slowly tore it up. Then he opened the other letter. It was one page, scrawled in pencil. The signature with the heavy flourish below it made him smile again: Charles A. Bruno.

Dear Guy:

This is your train friend, remember? You left your book in my room that night & I found a Texas address in it which I trust is still right. Am mailing book to you. Read some in it myself, didn't know there was so much conversation in Plato.

A great pleasure dining with you that night & hope I may list you among my friends. It would be fine to see you in Santa Fe & if you possibly change your mind, address is: Hotel La Fonda, Santa Fe, New Mex. for next two weeks at least.

I keep thinking about that idea we had for a couple of murders. It could be done, I am sure. I cannot express to you my supremest confidence in the idea! Though I know subject does not interest you.

What's what with your wife as that was very interesting? Please write me soon. Outside of losing wallit in El Paso (stolen right off a bar in front of me) nothing has happened of note. Didn't like El Paso, with apologies to you.

Hoping to hear from you soon,

Your friend,

Charles A. Bruno

P.S. Very sorry for sleeping late and missing you that a.m.

C.A.B.

The letter pleased him somehow. It was pleasant to think of Bruno's freedom.

"Grits!" he said happily to his mother. "Never get grits with my fried eggs up North!"

He put on a favorite old robe that was too hot for the weather, and sat back in bed with the *Metcalf Star* and the teetery-legged bed tray that held his breakfast.

Afterward, he showered and dressed as if there were something he had to do that day, but there wasn't. He had visited the Cartwrights yesterday. He might have seen Peter Wriggs, his boyhood friend, but Peter had a job in New Orleans now. What was Miriam doing, he wondered. Perhaps manicuring her nails on her back porch, or playing checkers with some little girl neighbor who adored her, who wanted to be just like her. Miriam was never one to brood when a plan went askew. Guy lighted a cigarette.

A soft, intermittent *chink* came from downstairs, where his mother or Ursline the cook was cleaning the silver and dropping it piece by piece onto a heap.

Why hadn't he left for Mexico today? The next idle twenty-four hours were going to be miserable, he knew. Tonight, his uncle again, and probably some friends of his mother's dropping over. They all wanted to see him. Since his last visit, the *Metcalf Star* had printed a column about him and his work, mentioning his scholarships, the Prix de Rome that he hadn't been able to use because of the war, the store he had designed in Pittsburgh, and the little annex infirmary of the hospital in Chicago. It read so impressively in a newspaper. It had almost made him feel important, he remembered, the lonely day in New York when the clipping had arrived in his mother's letter.

A sudden impulse to write Bruno made him sit down at his work table, but, with his pen in his hand, he realized he had nothing to say. He could see Bruno in his rust-brown suit, camera strap over his shoulder, plodding up some dry hill in Santa Fe, grinning with his bad teeth at something, lifting his camera unsteadily and clicking. Bruno with a thousand easy dollars in his pocket, sitting in a bar, waiting for his mother. What did he have to say to Bruno? He recapped his fountain pen and tossed it back on the table.

"Mama?" he called. He ran downstairs. "How about a movie this afternoon?"

His mother said she had already been to movies twice that week. "You know you don't like movies," she chided him.

"Mama, I really want to go!" he smiled, and insisted.

## eight

The telephone rang that night at about eleven. His mother answered it, then came in and called him from the living room where he sat with his uncle and his uncle's wife and his two cousins, Ritchie and Ty.

"It's long-distance," his mother said.

Guy nodded. It would be Brillhart, of course, asking for further explanations. Guy had answered his letter that day.

"Hello, Guy," The voice said. "Charley."

"Charley who?"

"Charley Bruno."

"Oh!—How are you? Thanks for the book."

"I dint send it yet but I will," Bruno said with the drunken cheer Guy remembered from the train. "Coming out to Santa Fe?"

"I'm afraid I can't."

"What about Palm Beach? Can I visit you there in a couple weeks? I'd like to see how it looks."

"Sorry, that's all off."

"Off? Why?"

"Complications. I've changed my mind."

"Account of your wife?"

"N-no." Guy felt vaguely irritated.

"She wants you to stay with her?"

"Yes. Sort of."

"Miriam wants to come out to Palm Beach?"

Guy was surprised he remembered her name.

"You haven't got your divorce, huh?"

"Getting it," Guy said tersely.

"*Yes, I'm paying for this call!*" Bruno shouted to someone. "Cheeses!" disgustedly. "Listen, Guy, you gave up that job account of her?"

"Not exactly. It doesn't matter. It's finished."

"You have to wait till the child's born for a divorce?"

Guy said nothing.

"The other guy's not going to marry her, huh?"

"Oh, yes, he is—"

"Yeah?" Bruno interrupted cynically.

"I can't talk any longer. We've got guests here tonight. I wish you a pleasant trip, Charley."

"When can we talk? Tomorrow?"

"I won't be here tomorrow."

"Oh." Bruno sounded lost now, and Guy hoped he was. Then the voice again, with sullen intimacy, "Listen, Guy, if you want anything done, you know, all you have to do is give a sign."

Guy frowned. A question took form in his mind, and immediately he knew the answer. He remembered Bruno's idea for a murder.

"What do you want, Guy?"

"Nothing. I'm very content. Understand?" But it was drunken bravado on Bruno's part, he thought. Why should he react seriously?

"Guy, I mean it," the voice slurred, drunker than before.

"Good-by, Charley," Guy said. He waited for Bruno to hang up.

"Doesn't sound like everything's fine," Bruno challenged.

"I don't see that it's any of your business."

"Guy!" in a tearful whine.

Guy started to speak, but the line clicked and went dead. He had an impulse to ask the operator to trace the call. Then he thought, drunken bravado. And boredom. It annoyed him that Bruno had his address. Guy ran his hand hard across his hair, and went back into the living room.

## *nine*

All of what he had just told her of Miriam, Guy thought, did not matter so much as the fact he and Anne were together on the gravel path. He took her hand as they walked, and gazed around him at the scene in which every object was foreign—a broad level avenue bordered with giant trees like the Champs-Elysées, military statues on pedestals, and beyond, buildings he did not know. The Paseo de la Reforma. Anne walked beside him with her head still lowered, nearly matching his slow paces. Their shoulders brushed, and he glanced at her to see if she were about to speak, to say he was right in what he had decided, but her lips were still thoughtful. Her pale yellow hair, held by a silver bar at the back of her neck, made lazy movements in the wind behind her. It was the second summer he had seen her when the sun had only begun to tan her face, so her skin about equaled in pigment the color of her hair. Soon her face would be darker than her hair, but Guy liked her best the way she was now, like something made of white gold.

She turned to him with the faintest smile of self-consciousness on her lips because he had been staring at her. "You couldn't have borne it, Guy?"

"No. Don't ask me why. I couldn't." He saw that her smile stayed, tinged with perplexity, perhaps annoyance.

"It's such a big thing to give up."

It vexed him now. He felt done with it. "I simply loathe her," he said quietly.

"But you shouldn't loathe anything."

He made a nervous gesture. "I loathe her because I've told you all this while we're walking here!"

"Guy, really!"

"She's everything that should be loathed," he went on, staring in front of him. "Sometimes I think I hate everything in the world. No decency, no conscience. She's what people mean when they say America never grows up, America rewards the corrupt. She's the type who goes to the bad movies, acts in them, reads the love-story magazines, lives in a bungalow, and whips her husband into earning more money this year so they can buy on the installment plan next year, breaks up her neighbor's marriage—"

"Stop it, Guy! You talk so like a child!" She drew away from him.

"And the fact I once loved her," Guy added, "loved all of it, makes me ill."

They stopped, looking at each other. He had had to say it, here and now, the ugliest thing he could say. He wanted to suffer also from Anne's disapproval, perhaps from her turning away and leaving him to finish the walk by himself. She had left him on one or two other occasions, when he had been unreasonable.

Anne said, in that distant, expressionless tone that terrified him, because he felt she might abandon him and never come back, "Sometimes I can believe you're still in love with her."

He smiled, and she softened. "I'm sorry," he said.

"Oh, Guy!" She put out her hand again, like a gesture of beseeching, and he took it. "If you'd only grow up!"

"I read somewhere people don't grow emotionally."

"I don't care what you read. They do. I'll prove it to you if it's the last thing I do."

He felt secure suddenly. "What else can I think about now?" he asked perversely, lowering his voice.

"That you were never closer to being free of her than now, Guy. What do you suppose you should think about?"

He lifted his head higher. There was a big pink sign on the top of a building: TOME XX, and all at once he was curious to know what it meant and wanted to ask Anne. He wanted to ask her why everything was so much easier and simpler when he was with her, but pride kept him from asking now, and the question would have been rhetorical anyway, unanswerable by Anne in words, because the answer was simply Anne. It had been so since the day he met her, in the dingy basement of the Art Institute in New York, the rainy day he had slogged in and addressed the only living thing he saw, the Chinese red raincoat and hood. The red raincoat and hood had turned and said: "You get to 9A from the first floor. You didn't have to come all the way down here." And then her quick, amused laugh that mysteriously, immediately, lifted his rage. He had learned to smile by quarter inches, frightened of her, a little contemptuous of her new dark green convertible. "A car just makes more sense," Anne said, "when you live in Long Island." The days when he was contemptuous of everything and courses taken here and there were no more than tests to make sure he knew all the instructor had to say, or to see how fast he could learn it and leave. "How do you suppose anybody gets in if not through pull? They can still throw you out if they don't like you." He had seen it her way finally, the right way, and gone to the exclusive Deems Architectural Academy in Brooklyn for a year, through her father's knowing a man on the board of directors.

"I know you have it in you, Guy," Anne said suddenly at the end of a silence, "the capacity to be terribly happy."

Guy nodded quickly, though Anne was not looking at him. He felt somehow ashamed. Anne had the capacity to be happy. She was happy now, she had been happy before she met him, and it was only he, his problems, that ever seemed to daunt her happiness for an instant. He would be happy, too, when he lived with Anne. He had told her so, but he could not bear to tell her again now.

"What's that?" he asked.

A big round house of glass had come into view under the trees of Chapultepec Park.

"The botanical gardens," Anne said.

There was no one inside the building, not even a caretaker. The air smelled of warm, fresh earth. They walked around, reading unpronounceable names of plants that might have come from another planet. Anne had a favorite plant. She had watched it grow for three years, she said, visiting it on successive summers with her father.

"Only I can't ever remember these names," she said.

"Why should you remember?"

They had lunch at Sanborn's with Anne's mother, then walked around in the store until it was time for Mrs. Faulkner's afternoon nap. Mrs. Faulkner was a thin, nervously energetic woman, tall as Anne, and for her age as attractive. Guy had come to be devoted to her, because she was devoted to him. At first, in his mind, he had built up the greatest handicaps for himself from Anne's wealthy parents, but not one of them had come true, and gradually he had shed them. That evening, the four of them went to a concert at the Bellas Artes, then had a late supper at the Lady Baltimore Restaurant across the street from the Ritz.

The Faulkners were sorry he wouldn't be able to stay the summer with them in Acapulco. Anne's father, an importer, intended to build a warehouse on the docks there.

"We can't expect to interest him in a warehouse if he's building a whole country club," Mrs. Faulkner said.

Guy said nothing. He couldn't look at Anne. He had asked her not to tell her parents about Palm Beach until after he left. Where would he go next week? He might go to Chicago and study for a couple of months. He had stored away his possessions in New York, and his landlady awaited his word as to whether to rent his apartment or not. If he went to Chicago, he might see the great Saarinen in Evanston and Tim O'Flaherty, a young architect who had had no recognition yet, but whom Guy believed in. There might be a job or two in Chicago. But New York was too dismal a prospect without Anne.

Mrs. Faulkner laid her hand on his forearm and laughed. "He wouldn't smile if he got all New York to build over, would you, Guy?"

He hadn't been listening. He wanted Anne to take a walk with him later, but she insisted on his coming up to their suite at the Ritz to see the silk dressing gown she had bought for her cousin Teddy, before she sent it off. And then, of course, it was too late for a walk.

He was staying at the Hotel Montecarlo, about ten blocks from the Hotel Ritz, a great shabby building that looked like the former residence of a military general. One entered it through a wide carriage drive, paved in black and white tile like a bathroom floor. This gave into a huge dark lobby, also tile floored. There was a grotto-like barroom and a restaurant that was always empty. Stained marble stairs wound around the patio, and going up them behind the bellhop yesterday, Guy had seen, through open doorways and windows, a Japanese couple playing cards, a woman kneeling at prayer, people writing letters at tables or merely standing with a strange air of captivity. A masculine gloom and an untraceable promise of the supernatural oppressed the whole place, and Guy had liked it instantly, though the Faulkners, including Anne, chaffed him about his choice.

His cheap little room in a back corner was crammed with pink and brown painted furniture, had a bed like a fallen cake, and a bath down the hall. Somewhere down in the patio, water dripped continuously, and the sporadic flush of toilets sounded torrential.

When he got back from the Ritz, Guy deposited his wristwatch, a present from Anne, on the pink bed table, and his billfold and keys on the scratched brown bureau, as he might have done at home. He felt very content as he got into bed with his Mexican newspapers and a book on English architecture that he had found at the Alameda bookstore that afternoon. After a second plunge at the Spanish, he leaned his head back against the pillow and gazed at the offensive room, listened to the little ratlike sounds of human activity from all parts of the building. What was it that he liked, he wondered. To immerse himself in ugly, uncomfortable, undignified living so that he gained new power to fight it in his work? Or was it a sense of hiding from Miriam? He would be harder to find here than at the Ritz.

Anne telephoned him the next morning to say that a telegram had come for him. "I just happened to hear them paging you," she said. "They were about to give it up."

"Would you read it to me, Anne?"

Anne read: "'Miriam suffered miscarriage yesterday. Upset and asking to see you. Can you come home? Mama.'—Oh, Guy!"

He felt sick of it, all of it. "She did it herself," he murmured.

"You don't know, Guy."

"I know."

"Don't you think you'd better see her?"

His fingers tightened on the telephone. "I'll get the Palmyra back anyway," he said. "When was the telegram sent?"

"The ninth. Tuesday, at 4 p.m."

He sent a telegram off to Mr. Brillhart, asking if he might be reconsidered for the job. Of course he would be, he thought, but how asinine it made him. Because of Miriam. He wrote to Miriam:

> This changes both our plans, of course. Regardless of yours, I mean to get the divorce now. I shall be in Texas in a few days. I hope you will be well by then, but if not, I can manage whatever is necessary alone.
>
> Again my wishes for your quick recovery.
>
> Guy
>
> Shall be at this address until Sunday.

He sent it airmail special delivery.

Then he called up Anne. He wanted to take her to the best restaurant in the city that night. He wanted the most exotic cocktails in the Ritz Bar to start with, all of them.

"You really feel happy?" Anne asked, laughing, as if she couldn't quite believe him.

"Happy and—strange. *Muy extranjero.*"

"Why?"

"Because I didn't think it was fated. I didn't think it was part of my destiny. The Palmyra, I mean."

"I did."

"Oh, you did!"

"Why do you think I was so mad at you yesterday?"

He really did not expect an answer from Miriam, but Friday morning when he and Anne were in Xochimilco, he felt prompted to call his hotel to see if a message had come. There was a telegram waiting. And after saying he would pick it up in a few minutes, he couldn't wait, once he was back in Mexico City, and telephoned the hotel again from a drugstore in the Socalo. The Montecarlo clerk read it to him: "'Have to talk with you first. Please come soon. Love, Miriam.'"

"She'll make a bit of a fuss," Guy said after he repeated it to Anne. "I'm sure the other man doesn't want to marry her. He's got a wife now."

"Oh."

He glanced at her as they walked, wanting to say something to her about her patience with him, with Miriam, with all of it. "Let's forget it," he smiled, and began to walk faster.

"Do you want to go back now?"

"Certainly not! Maybe Monday or Tuesday. I want these few days with you. I'm not due in Florida for another week. That's if they keep to the first schedule."

"Miriam won't follow you now, will she?"

"This time next week," Guy said, "she won't have a single claim on me."

## *ten*

At her dressing table in Hotel La Fonda, Santa Fe, Elsie Bruno sat removing the night's dry skin cream from her face with a cleansing tissue. Now and then, with wide, absent blue eyes, she leaned closer to the mirror to examine the little mesh of wrinkles below her lids and the laugh lines that curved from the base of her nose. Though her chin was somewhat recessive, the lower part of her face projected, thrusting her full lips forward in a manner quite different from Bruno's face. Santa Fe, she thought, was the only place she could see the laugh lines in the mirror when she sat all the way back at her dressing table.

"This light around here—might as well be an X-ray," she remarked to her son.

Bruno, slumped in his pajamas in a rawhide chair, cast a puffy eye over at the window. He was too tired to go and pull the shade down. "You look good, Mom," he croaked. He lowered his pursed lips to the glass of water that rested on his hairless chest, and frowned thoughtfully.

Like an enormous walnut in feeble, jittery squirrel hands, an idea, bigger and closer than any idea he had ever known, had been revolving in his mind for several days. When his mother left town, he intended to crack open the idea and start thinking in earnest. His idea was to go and get Miriam. The time was ripe, and the time was now. Guy needed it now. In a few days, a week even, it might be too late for the Palm Beach thing, and he wouldn't.

Her face had grown fatter in these few days in Santa Fe, Elsie thought. She could tell by the plumpness of her cheeks compared to the small taut triangle of her nose. She hid the laugh lines with a smile at herself, tilted her curly blond head, and blinked her eyes.

"Charley, should I pick up that silver belt this morning?" she asked, as casually as if she spoke to herself. The belt was two hundred and fifty something, but Sam would send another thousand on to California. It was such a good-looking belt, like nothing in New York. What else was Santa Fe good for but silver?

"What else is he good for?" Bruno murmured.

Elsie picked up her shower cap and turned to him with her quick broad smile that had no variations. "Darling," coaxingly.

"Umm-m?"

"You won't do anything you shouldn't while I'm gone?"

"No, Ma."

She left the shower cap perched on the crown of her head, looked at a long narrow red nail, then reached for a sandpaper stick. Of course, Fred Wiley would be only too happy to buy the silver belt for her—he'd probably turn up at the station with something atrocious and twice as expensive anyway—but she didn't want Fred on her neck in California. With the least encouragement, he would come to California with her. Better that he only swore eternal love at the station, wept a little, and went straight home to his wife.

"I must say last night was funny though,"Elsie went on. "Fred saw it first." She laughed, and the sandpaper stick flew in a blur.

Bruno said coolly, "I had nothing to do with it."

"All right, darling, you had nothing to do with it!"

Bruno's mouth twisted. His mother had awakened him at 4 in the morning, in hysterics, to tell him there was a dead bull in the Plaza. A bull sitting on a bench with a hat and coat on, reading a newspaper. Typical of Wilson's collegiate pranks. Wilson would be talking about it today, Bruno knew, elaborating on it till he thought of something dumber to do. Last night in La Placita, the hotel bar, he had planned a murder—while Wilson dressed a dead bull. Even in Wilson's tall stories about his war service, he had never claimed to have killed anybody, not even a Jap. Bruno closed his eyes, thinking contentedly of last night. Around ten o'clock, Fred Wiley and a lot of other baldheads had trooped into La Placita half crocked, like a musical comedy stagline, to take his mother to a party. He'd been invited, too, but he had told his mother he had a date with Wilson, because he needed time to think. And last night he had decided yes. He had been thinking really since Saturday when he talked to Guy, and here it was Saturday again, and it was tomorrow or never, when his mother left for California. He was sick of the question, could he do it. How long had the question been with him? Longer than he could remember. He *felt* like he could do it. Something kept telling him that the time, the circumstances, the cause would never be better. A pure murder, without personal motives! He didn't consider the possibility of Guy's murdering his father a motive, because he didn't count on it. Maybe Guy could be persuaded, maybe not. The point was, now was the time to act, because the setup was so perfect. He'd called Guy's house again last night to make sure he still wasn't back from Mexico. Guy had been in Mexico since Sunday, his mother said.

A sensation like a thumb pressing at the base of his throat made him tear at his collar, but his pajama jacket was open all the way down the front. Bruno began to button it dreamily.

"You won't change your mind and come with me?" His mother asked, getting up. "If you did, I'd go up to Reno. Helen's there now and so's George Kennedy."

"Only one reason I'd like to see you in Reno, Mom."

"Charley—" She tipped her head to one side and back again. "Have patience? If it weren't for Sam, we wouldn't be here, would we?"

"Sure, we would."

She sighed. "You won't change your mind?"

"I'm having fun here," he said through a groan.

She looked at her nails again. "All I've heard is how bored you are."

"That's with Wilson. I'm not gonna see him again."

"You're not going to run back to New York?"

"What'd I do in New York?"

"Grannie'd be so disappointed if you fell down again this year."

"When did I ever fall down?" Bruno jested weakly, and suddenly felt sick enough to die, too sick even to throw up. He knew the feeling, it lasted only a minute, but God, he thought, let there not be time for breakfast before the train, don't let her say the word breakfast. He stiffened, not moving a muscle, barely breathing between his parted lips. With one eye shut, he watched her move toward him in her pale blue silk wrapper, a hand on her hip, looking as shrewd as she could which wasn't shrewd at all, because her eyes were so round. And she was smiling besides.

"What've you and Wilson got up your sleeves?"

"That punk?"

She sat down on the arm of his chair. "Just because he steals your thunder," she said, shaking him slightly by the shoulder. "Don't do anything too awful, darling, because I haven't got the money just now to throw around cleaning up after you."

"Stick him for some more. Get me a thousand, too."

"Darling." She laid the cool backs of her fingers against his forehead. "I'll miss you."

"I'll be there day after tomorrow probably."

"Let's have fun in California."

"Sure."

"Why're you so serious this morning!"

"I'm not, Ma."

She tweaked the thin dangling hair over his forehead, and went on into the bathroom.

Bruno jumped up and shouted against the roar of her running bath,"Ma, I got money to pay my bill here!"

"What, angel?"

He went closer and repeated it, then sank back in the chair, exhausted with the effort. He did not want his mother to know about the long-distance calls to Metcalf. If she didn't, everything was working out fine. His mother hadn't minded very much his not staying on, hadn't really minded enough. Was she meeting this jerk Fred on the train or something? Bruno dragged himself up, feeling a slow animosity rising in him against Fred Wiley. He wanted to tell his mother he was staying on in Santa Fe for the biggest experience of his life. She wouldn't be running the water in there now, paying no attention to him, if she knew a fraction of what it meant. He wanted to say, Ma, life's going to be a lot better for both of us soon, because this is the beginning of getting rid of the Captain. Whether Guy came through with his part of the deal or not, if he was successful with Miriam, he would have proved a point. A perfect murder. Some day, another person he didn't know yet would turn up and some kind of a deal could be made. Bruno bent his chin down to his chest in sudden anguish. How could he tell his mother? Murder and his mother didn't go together. "How gruesome!" she would say. He looked at the bathroom door with a hurt, distant expression. It had dawned on him that he couldn't tell anyone, ever. Except Guy. He sat down again.

"Sleepyhead!"

He blinked when she clapped her hands. Then he smiled. Dully, with a wistful realization that much would happen before he saw them again, he watched his mother's legs flex as she tightened her stockings. The slim lines of her legs always gave him a lift, made him proud. His mother had the best-looking legs he had ever seen on anyone, no matter what age. Ziegfeld had picked her, and hadn't Ziegfeld known his stuff? But she had married right back into the kind of life she had run away from. He was going to liberate her soon, and she didn't know it.

"Don't forget to mail *that*," his mother said.

Bruno winced as the two rattlesnakes' heads tipped over toward him. It was a tie rack they had bought for the Captain, made of interlocking cowhorns and topped by two stuffed baby rattlers sticking their tongues out at each other over a mirror. The Captain hated tie racks, hated snakes, dogs, cats, birds—What didn't he hate? He would hate the corny tie rack, and that was why he had talked his mother into getting it for him. Bruno smiled affectionately at the tie rack. It hadn't been hard to talk his mother into getting it.

# *eleven*

He stumbled on a goddamned cobblestone, then drew himself up pridefully and tried to straighten his shirt in his trousers. Good thing he had passed out in an alley and not on a street, or the cops might have picked him up and he'd have missed the train. He stopped and fumbled for his wallet, fumbled more wildly than he had earlier to see if the wallet was there. His hands shook so, he could hardly read the 10:20 a.m. on the railroad ticket. It was now 8:10 according to several clocks. If this was Sunday. Of course it was Sunday, all the Indians were in clean shirts. He kept an eye out for Wilson, though he hadn't seen him all day yesterday and it wasn't likely he would be out now. He didn't want Wilson to know he was leaving town.

The Plaza spread suddenly before him, full of chickens and kids and the usual old men eating piñones for breakfast. He stood still and counted the pillars of the Governor's palace to see if he could count seventeen, and he could. It was getting so the pillars weren't a good gauge anymore. On top of a bad hangover, he ached now from sleeping on the goddamned cobblestones. Why'd he drunk so much, he wondered, almost tearfully. But he had been all alone, and he always drank more alone. Or was that true? And who cared anyway? He remembered one brilliant and powerful thought that had come to him last night watching a televised shuffleboard game: *the way to see the world was to see it drunk.* Everything was created to be seen drunk. Certainly this wasn't the way to see the world, with his head splitting every time he turned his eyes. Last night he'd wanted to celebrate his last night in Santa Fe.

Today he'd be in Metcalf, and he'd have to be sharp. But had he ever known a hangover a few drinks couldn't fix? A hangover might even help, he thought: he had a habit of doing things slowly and cautiously with a hangover. Still, he hadn't planned anything, even yet. He could plan on the train.

"Any mail?" he asked mechanically at the desk, but there wasn't any.

He bathed solemnly and ordered hot tea and a raw egg sent up to make a prairie oyster, then went to the closet and stood a long while, wondering vaguely what to wear. He decided on the red-brown suit in honor of Guy. It was rather inconspicuous, too, he noticed when he had it on, and it pleased him that he might have chosen it unconsciously for this reason also. He gulped the prairie oyster and it stayed down, flexed his arms—but suddenly the room's Indian décor, the loony tin lamps, and the strips hanging down the walls were unbearable, and he began to shake all over again in his haste to get his things and leave. What things? He didn't need anything really. Just the paper on which he had written everything he knew about Miriam. He got it from the back pocket of his suitcase and stuck it into the inside pocket of his jacket. The gesture made him feel like a businessman. He put a white handkerchief into his breast pocket, then left the room and locked the door. He figured he could be back tomorrow night, sooner if he could possibly do it tonight and catch a sleeper back.

Tonight!

He could hardly believe it as he walked toward the bus station, where one caught the bus for Lamy, the railroad terminal. He had thought he would be so happy and excited—or maybe quiet and grim—and he wasn't at all. He frowned suddenly, and his pallid, shadowy-eyed face looked much younger. Was something going to take the fun out of it after all? What would take it out? But something always had taken the fun out of everything he had ever counted on. This time he wouldn't let it. He made himself smile. Maybe it was the hangover that had made him doubt. He went into a bar and bought a fifth from a barman he knew, filled his flask, and asked for an empty pint bottle to put the rest in. The barman looked, but he didn't have one.

At Lamy Bruno went on to the station, carrying nothing but the half empty bottle in a paper bag, not even a weapon. He hadn't planned yet, he kept reminding himself, but a lot of planning didn't always mean a murder was a success. Witness the—

"Hey, Charley! Where you going?"

It was Wilson, with a gang of people. Bruno forced himself to walk toward them, wagging his head boredly. They must have just got off a train, he thought. They looked tired and seedy.

"Where you been for two days?" Bruno asked Wilson.

"Las Vegas. Didn't know I was there until I was there, or I'd have asked you, Meet Joe Hanover. I told you about Joe."

"H'lo, Joe."

"What're you so mopey about?" Wilson asked with a friendly shove.

"Oh, Charley's hung over!" shrieked one of the girls, her voice like a bicycle bell right in his ear.

"Charley Hangover, meet Joe Hanover!" Joe Hanover said, convulsed.

"Haw haw." Bruno tugged his arm away gently from a girl with a lei around her neck. "Hell, I gotta catch this train." His train was waiting.

"Where *you* going?" Wilson asked, frowning so his black eyebrows met.

"I hadda see someone in Tulsa," Bruno mumbled, aware he mixed his tenses, thinking he must get away *now*. Frustration made him want to weep, lash out at Wilson's dirty red shirt with his fists.

Wilson made a movement as if he would wipe Bruno away like a chalk streak on a blackboard. "Tulsa!"

Slowly, with a try at a grin, Bruno made a similar gesture and turned away. He walked on, expecting them to come after him, but they didn't. At the train, he looked back and saw the group moving like a rolling thing out of the sunlight into the darkness below the station roof. He frowned at them, feeling something conspiratorial in their closeness. Did they suspect something? Were they whispering about him? He boarded the train casually, and it began to move before he found his seat.

When he awakened from his nap, the world seemed quite changed. The train was speeding silkily through cool bluish mountainland. Dark green valleys were full of shadows. The sky was gray. The air-conditioned car and the cool look of things outside was as refreshing as an icepack. And he was hungry. In the diner he had a delicious lunch of lamb chops, French fries and salad, and fresh peach pie washed down with two Scotch and sodas, and strolled back to his seat feeling like a million dollars.

A sense of purpose, strange and sweet to him, carried him along in an irresistible current. Merely in gazing out the window, he felt a new coordination of mind and eye. He began to realize what he intended to do. He was on his way to do a murder which not only would fulfill a desire of years, but would benefit a friend. It made Bruno very happy to do things for his friends. And his victim deserved her fate. Think of all the other good guys he would save from ever knowing her! The realization of his importance dazzled his mind, and for a long moment he felt completely and happily drunk. His energies that had been dissipated, spread like a flooded river over land as flat and boring as the Llano Estacado he was crossing now, seemed gathered in a vortex whose point strove toward Metcalf like the aggressive thrust of the train. He sat on the edge of his seat and wished Guy were opposite him again. But Guy would try to stop him, he knew; Guy wouldn't understand how much he wanted to do it or how easy it was. But for Christ's sake, he ought to understand how useful! Bruno ground his smooth, hard rubberlike fist into his palm, wishing the train would go faster. All over his body, little muscles twitched and quivered.

He took out the paper about Miriam, laid it on the empty seat opposite him, and studied it earnestly. *Miriam Joyce Haines, about twenty-two*, said his handwriting in precise, inked characters, for this was his third copy. *Rather pretty. Red hair. A little plump, not very tall. Pregnant so you could tell probably since a month. Noisy, social type. Probably flashy dressed. Maybe short curly hair, maybe a long permanent*. It wasn't very much, but it was the best he could do. A good thing she had red hair at least. Could he really do it tonight, he wondered. That depended on whether he could find her right away. He might have to go through the whole list of Joyces and Haineses. He thought she'd be living with her family probably. Once he saw her, he was sure he would recognize her. The little bitch! He hated her already. He thought of the instant he would see her and recognize her, and his feet gave an expectant jump on the floor. People came and went in the aisle, but Bruno did not look up from the paper.

*She's going to have a child*, Guy's voice said. The little floozy! Women who slept around made him furious, made him ill, like the mistresses his father used to have, that had turned all his school holidays into nightmares because he had not known if his mother knew and was only pretending to be happy, or if she did not know at all. He recreated every word he could of his and Guy's conversation on the train. It brought Guy close to him. Guy, he considered, was the most worthy fellow he had ever met. He had earned the Palm Beach job, and he deserved to keep it. Bruno wished he could be the one to tell Guy he still had it.

When Bruno finally replaced the paper in his pocket and sat back with one leg comfortably crossed, his hands folded on his knee, anyone seeing him would have judged him a young man of responsibility and character, probably with a promising future. He did not look in the pink of health, to be sure, but he did reflect poise and an inner happiness seen in few faces, and in Bruno's never before. His life up to now had been pathless, and seeking had known no direction, finding had revealed no meaning. There had been crises—he loved crises and created them sometimes among his acquaintances and between his father and mother—but he had always stepped out of them in time to avoid participation. This, and because he occasionally found it impossible to show sympathy even when it was his mother who was hurt by his father, had led his mother to think that a part of him was cruel, while his father and many other people believed him heartless. Yet an imagined coolness in a stranger, a friend he telephoned in a lonely dusk who was unable or unwilling to spend the evening with him, could plunge him into sulking, brooding melancholy. But only his mother knew this. He stepped out of crises because he found pleasure in depriving himself of excitement, too. So long had he been frustrated in his hunger for a meaning of his life, and in his amorphous desire to perform an act that would give it meaning, that he had come to prefer frustration, like some habitually unrequited lovers. The sweetness of fulfillment of anything he had felt he would never know. A quest with direction and hope he had always felt, from the start, too discouraged to attempt. Yet there had always been the energy to live one more day. Death held no terror at all, however. Death was only one more adventure untried. If it came on some perilous business, so much the better. Nearest, he thought, was the time he had driven a racing car blindfolded on a straight road with the gas pedal on the floor. He never heard his friend's gunshot that meant stop, because he was lying unconscious in a ditch with a broken hip. At times he was so bored he contemplated the dramatic finality of suicide. It had never occurred to him that facing death unafraid might be brave, that his attitude was as resigned as that of the swamis of India, that to commit suicide required a particular kind of despondent nerve. Bruno had that kind of nerve always. He was actually a little ashamed of ever considering suicide, because it was so obvious and dull.

Now, on the train to Metcalf, he had direction. He had not felt so alive, so real and like other people since he had gone to Canada as a child with his mother and father—also on a train, he remembered. He had believed Quebec full of castles that he would be allowed to explore, but there had not been one castle, not even time to look for any, because his paternal grandmother had been dying, which was the only reason they had come anyway, and since then he had never placed full confidence in the purpose of any journey. But he did in this one.

In Metcalf, he went immediately to a telephone book and checked on the Haineses. He was barely conscious of Guy's address as he frowned down the list. No Miriam Haines, and he hadn't expected any. There were seven Joyces. Bruno scribbled a list of them on a piece of paper. Three were at the same address, 1235 Magnolia Street, and one of them there was Mrs. M. J. Joyce. Bruno's pointed tongue curled speculatively over his upper lip. Certainly a good bet. Maybe her mother's name was Miriam, too. He should be able to tell a lot from the neighborhood. He didn't think Miriam would live in a fancy neighborhood. He hurried toward a yellow taxi parked at the curb.

## *twelve*

It was almost nine o'clock. The long dusk was sliding steeply into night, and the residential blocks of small flimsy-looking wooden houses were mostly dark, except for a glow here and there on a front porch where people sat in swings and on front steps.

"Lemme out here, this is okay," Bruno said to the driver. Magnolia Street and College Avenue, and this was the one-thousand block. He began walking.

A little girl stood on the sidewalk, staring at him.

"Hyah," Bruno said, like a nervous command for her to get out of the way.

"H'lo," said the little girl.

Bruno glanced at the people on the lighted porch, a plump man fanning himself, a couple of women in the swing. Either he was tighter than he thought or luck was going to be with him, because he certainly had a hunch about 1235. He couldn't have dreamt up a neighborhood more likely for Miriam to live in. If he was wrong, he'd just try the rest. He had the list in his pocket. The fan on the porch reminded him it was hot, apart from his own feverlike temperature that had been annoying him since late afternoon. He stopped and lighted a cigarette, pleased that his hands did not shake at all. The half bottle since lunch had fixed his hangover and put him in a slow mellow mood. Crickets chirruped everywhere around him. It was so quiet, he could hear a car shift gears two blocks away. Some young fellows came around a corner, and Bruno's heart jumped, thinking one might be Guy, but none of them was.

"You ol' jassack!" one said.

"Hell, I tol' her I ain't foolin' with no man don't give his brother an even break. . . ."

Bruno looked after them haughtily. It sounded like another language. They didn't talk like Guy at all.

On some houses, Bruno couldn't find a number. Suppose he couldn't find 1235? But when he came to it, 1235 was very legible in tin numerals over the front porch. The sight of the house brought a slow pleasant thrill. Guy must have hopped up those steps very often, he thought, and it was this fact alone that really set it apart from the other houses. It was a small house like all the others on the block, only its yellow-tan clapboards were more in need of paint. It had a driveway at the side, a scraggly lawn, and an old Chevvy sedan sitting at the curb. A light showed at a downstairs window and one in a back corner window upstairs that Bruno thought might be Miriam's room. But why didn't he *know*? Maybe Guy really hadn't told him enough!

Nervously, Bruno crossed the street and went back a little the way he had come. He stopped and turned and stared at the house, biting his lip. There was no one in sight, and no porch lighted except one down at the corner. He could not decide if the faint sound of a radio came from Miriam's house or the one next to it. The house next to it had two lighted windows downstairs. He might be able to walk up the driveway and take a look at the back of 1235.

Bruno's eyes slid alertly to the next-door front porch as the light came on. A man and woman came out, the woman sat down in the swing, and the man went down the walk. Bruno backed into the niche of a projecting garage front.

"Pistachio if they haven't got peach, Don," Bruno heard the woman call.

"I'll take vanilla," Bruno murmured, and drank some out of his flask.

He stared quizzically at the yellow-tan house, put a foot up behind him to lean on, and felt something hard against his thigh: the knife he had bought in the station at Big Springs, a hunting knife with a six-inch blade in a sheath. He did not want to use a knife if he could avoid it. Knives sickened him in a funny way. And a gun made noise. How would he do it? Seeing her would suggest a way. Or would it? He had thought seeing the house would suggest something, and he still felt like this was the house, but it didn't suggest anything. Could that mean this wasn't the house? Suppose he got chased off for snooping before he even found out. Guy hadn't told him enough, he really hadn't! Quickly he took another drink. He mustn't start to worry, that would spoil everything! His knee buckled. He wiped his sweaty hands on his thighs and wet his lips with a shaky tongue. He pulled the paper with the Joyce addresses out of his breast pocket and slanted it toward the street light. He still couldn't see to read. Should he leave and try another address, maybe come back here?

He would wait fifteen minutes, maybe half an hour.

A preference for attacking her out of doors had taken root in his mind on the train, so all his ideas began from a simple physical approach to her. This street was almost dark enough, for instance, very dark there under the trees. He preferred to use his bare hands, or to hit her over the head with something. He did not realize how excited he was until he felt his body start now with his thoughts of jumping to right or left, as it might be, when he attacked her. Now and then it crossed his mind how happy Guy would be when it was done. Miriam had become an object, small and hard.

He heard a man's voice, and a laugh, he was sure from the lighted upstairs room in 1235, then a girl's smiling voice: "Stop that?—Please? Plee-ee-ease?" Maybe Miriam's voice. Babyish and stringy, but somehow strong like a strong string, too.

The light blinked out and Bruno's eyes stayed at the dark window. Then the porch light flashed on and two men and a girl—*Miriam*—came out. Bruno held his breath and set his feet on the ground. He could see the red in her hair. The bigger fellow was redheaded, too—maybe her brother. Bruno's eyes caught a hundred details at once, the chunky compactness of her figure, the flat shoes, the easy way she swung around to look up at one of the men.

"Think we ought to call her, Dick?" she asked in that thin voice. "It's kinda late."

A corner of the shade in the front window lifted. "Honey? Don't be out too long!"

"No, Mom."

They were going to take the car at the curb.

Bruno faded toward the corner, looking for a taxi. Fat chance in this dead burg! He ran. He hadn't run in months, and he felt fit as an athlete.

"Taxi!" He didn't even see a taxi, then he did and dove for it.

He made the driver circle and come into Magnolia Street in the direction the Chevvy had been pointed. The Chevvy was gone. Darkness had closed in tight. Far away he saw a red taillight blinking under trees.

"Keep going!"

When the taillight stopped for a red and the taxi closed some of the distance, Bruno saw it was the Chevvy and sank back with relief.

"Where do you want to go?" asked the driver.

"Keep going!" Then as the Chevvy swung into a big avenue, "Turn right." He sat up on the edge of his seat. Glancing at a curb, he saw "Crockett Boulevard" and smiled. He had heard of Crockett Boulevard in Metcalf, the widest longest street.

"Who're the people's names you want to go to?" the driver asked. "Maybe I know 'em."

"Just a minute, just a minute," Bruno said, unconsciously assuming another personality, pretending to search through the papers he had dragged from his inside pocket, among them the paper about Miriam. He snickered suddenly, feeling very amused, very safe. Now he was pretending to be the dopey guy from out of town, who had even misplaced the address of where he wanted to go. He bent his head so the driver could not see him laughing, and reached automatically for his flask.

"Need a light?"

"Nope, nope, thank you." He took a hot swallow. Then the Chevvy backed into the avenue, and Bruno told the driver to keep going.

"Where?"

"Get going and shut up!" Bruno shouted, his voice falsetto with anxiety.

The driver shook his head and made a click with his tongue. Bruno fumed, but they had the Chevvy in sight. Bruno thought they would never stop driving and that Crockett Boulevard must cross the whole state of Texas. Twice Bruno lost and found the Chevvy. They passed roadstands and drive-in movies, then darkness put up a wall on either side. Bruno began to worry. He couldn't tail them out of town or down a country road. Then a big arch of lights appeared over the road. WELCOME TO LAKE METCALF'S KINGDOM OF FUN, it said, and the Chevvy drove under it and into a parking lot. There were all kinds of lights ahead in the woods and the jingle of merry-go-round music. An amusement park! Bruno was delighted.

"Four bucks," said the driver sourly, and Bruno poked a five through the front window.

He hung back until Miriam and the two fellows and a new girl they had picked up had gone through the turnstile, then he followed them. He stretched his eyes wide for a good look at Miriam under the lights. She was cute in a plump college-girl sort of way, but definitely second-rate, Bruno judged. The red socks with the red sandals infuriated him. How could Guy have married such a thing? Then his feet scraped and he stood still: she wasn't pregnant! His eyes narrowed in intense perplexity. Why hadn't he noticed from the first? But maybe it wouldn't show yet. He bit his underlip hard. Considering how plump she was, her waist looked even flatter than it ought to. Maybe a sister of Miriam's. Or she had had an abortion or something. Or a miscarriage. Miss Carriage! How *do* you do? Swing it, sister! She had fat little hips under a tight gray skirt. He moved on as they did, following evenly, as if magnetized. Had Guy lied about her being pregnant? But Guy wouldn't lie. Bruno's mind swam in contradictions. He stared at Miriam with his head cocked. Then something made a connection in his mind before he was aware of looking for it: if something had happened to the child, then all the more reason why he should erase her, because Guy wouldn't be able to get his divorce. She could be walking around now if she had had an abortion, for instance.

She stood in front of a sideshow where a gypsy woman was dropping things into a big fishbowl. The other girl started laughing, leaning all over the redheaded fellow.

"Miriam!"

Bruno leapt off his feet.

"Oooh, yes!" Miriam went across to the frozen custard stand.

They all bought frozen custards. Bruno waited boredly, smiling, looking up at the ferris wheel's arc of lights and the tiny people swinging in benches up there in the black sky. Far off through the trees, he saw lights twinkling on water. It was quite a park. He wanted to ride the ferris wheel. He felt wonderful. He was taking it easy, not getting excited. The merry-go-round played "Casey would waltz with the strawberry blonde . . ." Grinning, he turned to Miriam's red hair, and their eyes met, but hers moved on and he was sure she hadn't noticed him, but he mustn't do that again. A rush of anxiety made him snicker. Miriam didn't look at all smart, he decided, which amused him, too. He could see why Guy would loathe her. He loathed her, too, with all his guts! Maybe she was lying to Guy about having a baby. And Guy was so honest himself, he believed her. Bitch!

When they moved on with their frozen custards, he released the swallowtailed bird he had been fingering in the balloon seller's box, then wheeled around and bought one, a bright yellow one. It made him feel like a kid again, whipping the stick around, listening to the tail's *squee-wee-wee*!

A little boy walking by with his parents stretched his hand toward it, and Bruno had an impulse to give it to him, but he didn't.

Miriam and her friends entered a big lighted section where the bottom of the ferris wheel was and a lot of concessions and sideshows. The roller coaster made a *tat-tat-tat-tat-tat* like a machine gun over their heads. There was a clang and a roar as someone sent the red arrow all the way to the top with a sledge hammer. He wouldn't mind killing Miriam with a sledge hammer, he thought. He examined Miriam and each of the three to see if any seemed aware of him, but he was sure they weren't. If he didn't do it tonight, he mustn't let any of them notice him. Yet somehow he was sure he would do it tonight. Something would happen that he could. This was his night. The cooler night air bathed him, like some liquid that he frolicked in. He waved the bird in wide circles. He liked Texas, Guy's state! Everybody looked happy and full of energy. He let Miriam's group blend into a crowd while he took a gulp from his flask. Then he loped after them.

They were looking at the ferris wheel, and he hoped they would decide to ride it. They really did things big in Texas, Bruno thought, looking up admiringly at the wheel. He had never seen a ferris wheel big as this. It had a five-pointed star in blue lights inside it.

"Ralph, how 'bout it?" Miriam squealed, poking the last of the frozen custard cone into her mouth with her hand against her face.

"Aw, 's ain't no fun. H'bout the merry-go-round?"

And they all went. The merry-go-round was like a lighted city in the dark woods, a forest of nickel-plated poles crammed with zebras, horses, giraffes, bulls, and camels all plunging down or upward, some with necks arched out over the platform, frozen in leaps and gallops as if they waited desperately for riders. Bruno stood still, unable to take his dazzled eyes from it even to watch Miriam, tingling to the music that promised movement at any instant. He felt he was about to experience again some ancient, delicious childhood moment that the steam calliope's sour hollowness, the stitching hurdy-gurdy accompaniment, and the drum-and-cymbal crash brought almost to the margin of his grasp.

People were choosing mounts. And Miriam and her friends were eating again, Miriam diving into a popcorn bag Dick held for her. The pigs! Bruno was hungry, too. He bought a frankfurter, and when he looked again, they were boarding the merry-go-round. He scrambled for coins and ran. He got the horse he had wanted, a royal blue one with an upreared head and an open mouth, and as luck would have it, Miriam and her friends kept weaving back through the poles toward him, and Miriam and Dick took the giraffe and the horse right in front of him. Luck was with him tonight! Tonight he should be gambling!

*Just like the strain—te-te-dum—*
*Of a haunting refrain—te-te-dum—*
*She'll start upon—BOOM! a marathon—BOOM!*

Bruno loved the song and so did his mother. The music made him suck in his belly and sit his horse like a ramrod. He swung his feet gaily in the stirrups. Something swatted him in the back of the head, he turned belligerently, but it was only some fellows roughhousing with one another.

They started off slowly and militantly to "The Washington Post March." Up, up, up he went and down, down, down went Miriam on her giraffe. The world beyond the merry-go-round vanished in a light-streaked blur. Bruno held the reins in one hand as he had been taught to do in his polo lessons, and ate the frankfurter with the other.

"Yeeee-hooo!" yelled the redheaded fellow.

"Yeeee-hooo!"Bruno yelled back. "I'm a Texan!"

"Katie?" Miriam leaned forward on the giraffe's neck, and her gray skirt got round and tight. "See that fellow over there in the check shirt?"

Bruno looked. He saw the fellow in the checked shirt. He looked a little like Guy, Bruno thought, and thinking of this, he missed what Miriam said about him. Under the bright lights, he saw that Miriam was covered with freckles. She looked increasingly loathesome, so he began not to want to put his hands on her soft sticky-warm flesh. Well, he still had the knife. A clean instrument.

"A clean instrument!" Bruno shouted jubilantly, for no one could possibly hear him. His was the outside horse, and next to him was a boxed double seat thing made out of swans, which was empty. He spat into it. He flung away the rest of the frankfurter and wiped the mustard off his fingers on the horse's mane.

"Casey would waltz with the strawberry blonde, while the band—played—aaaawn!" Miriam's date sang out with vehemence.

They all joined in and Bruno with them. The whole merry-go-round was singing. If they only had drinks! Everybody should be having a drink!

"His brain was so loaded, it nearly exploded," sang Bruno at the cracking top of his lungs,"the poor girl would shake with alaa-arm!"

"Hi, Casey!" Miriam cooed to Dick, opening her mouth to catch the popcorn he was trying to throw into it.

"Yak-yak!" Bruno shouted.

Miriam looked ugly and stupid with her mouth open, as if she were being strangled and had turned pink and bloated. He could not bear to look at her, and still grinning, turned his eyes away. The merry-go-round was slowing. He hoped they would stay for another ride, but they got off, linked arms, and began to walk toward the twinkling lights on the water.

Bruno paused under the trees for another little nip from the nearly empty flask.

They were taking a rowboat. The prospect of a cool row was delightful to Bruno. He engaged a boat, too. The lake looked big and black, except for the lightless twinkles, full of drifting boats with couples necking in them. Bruno got close enough to Miriam's boat to see that the redheaded fellow was doing the rowing, and that Miriam and Dick were squeezing each other and giggling in the back seat. Bruno bent for three deep strokes that carried him past their boat, then let his oars trail.

"Want to go to the island or loaf around?" the redheaded fellow asked.

Petulantly, Bruno slumped sideways on the seat, waiting for them to make up their minds. In the nooks along the shore, as if from little dark rooms, he heard murmurs, soft radios, laughter. He tipped his flask and drained it. What would happen if he shouted "Guy!"? What would Guy think if he could see him now? Maybe Guy and Miriam had been out on dates on this lake, maybe in the same rowboat he sat in now. His hands and the lower part of his legs tingled cozily with the liquor. If he had Miriam here in the boat with him, he would hold her head under the water with pleasure. Here in the dark. Pitch dark and no moon. The water made quick licking sounds against his boat. Bruno writhed in sudden impatience. There was the sucking sound of a kiss from Miriam's boat, and Bruno gave it back to them with a pleasurable groan thrown in. *Smack, smack!* They must have heard him, because there was a burst of laughter.

He waited until they had paddled past, then followed leisurely. A black mass drew closer, pricked here and there with the spark of a match. The island. It looked like a neckers' paradise. Maybe Miriam would be at it again tonight, Bruno thought, giggling.

When Miriam's boat landed, he rowed a few yards to one side and climbed ashore, and set his boat's nose up on a little log so it would be easy to recognize from the others. The sense of purpose filled him once more, stronger and more imminent than on the train. In Metcalf hardly two hours, and here he was on an island with her! He pressed the knife against him through his trousers. If he could just get her alone and clap his hand over her mouth—or would she be able to bite? He squirmed with disgust at the thought of her wet mouth on his hand.

Slowly he followed their slow steps, up rough ground where the trees were close.

"We cain't sit here, the ground's wet," whined the girl called Katie.

"Sit on mah coat if y'wanta," a fellow said.

Christ, Bruno thought, those dumb Southern accents!

"When I'm walkin' with m'honey down honeymoon lane . . . ," somebody sang, off in the bushes.

Night murmurs. Bugs. Crickets. And a mosquito at his ear. Bruno boxed his ear and the ear rang maddeningly, drowning out the voices.

". . . shove off."

"Why cain't we find a place?" Miriam yapped.

"Ain't no place an' watch whatcha step in!"

"Watcha step-ins, gals!" laughed the redheaded fellow.

What the hell *were* they going to do? He was bored! The music of the merry-go-round sounded tired and very distant, only the *tings* coming through. Then they turned around right in his face, so he had to move off to one side as if he were going somewhere. He got tangled in some thorny underbrush and occupied himself getting free of it while they passed him. Then he followed, downward. He thought he could smell Miriam's perfume, if it wasn't the other girl's, a sweetness like a steamy bathroom that repelled him.

". . . And now," said a radio, "coming in very cautiously . . . Leon . . . *Leon* lands a hard right to the Babe's face *andlistentothecrowd*!" A roar.

Bruno saw a fellow and a girl wallowing down there in the bushes as if they were fighting, too.

Miriam stood on slightly higher ground, not three yards away from him now, and the others slid down the bank toward the water. Bruno inched closer. The lights on the water silhouetted her head and shoulders. Never had he been so close!

"Hey!" Bruno whispered, and saw her turn. "Say, isn't your name Miriam?"

She faced him, but he knew she could barely see him. "Yeah. Who're you?"

He came a step nearer. "Haven't I met you somewhere before?" he asked cynically, smelling the perfume again. She was a warm ugly black spot. He sprang with such concentrated aim, the wrists of his spread hands touched.

"Say, what d'you—?"

His hands captured her throat on the last word, stifling its abortive uplift of surprise. He shook her. His body seemed to harden like rock, and he heard his teeth crack. She made a grating sound in her throat, but he had her too tight for a scream. With a leg behind her, he wrenched her backward, and they fell to the ground together with no sound but of a brush of leaves. He sunk his fingers deeper, enduring the distasteful pressure of her body under his so her writhing would not get them both up. Her throat felt hotter and fatter. Stop, stop, stop! He willed it! And the head stopped turning. He was sure he had held her long enough, but he did not lessen his grip. Glancing behind him, he saw nothing coming. When he relaxed his fingers, it felt as if he had made deep dents in her throat as in a piece of dough. Then she made a sound like an ordinary cough that terrified him like the rising dead, and he fell on her again, hitched himself onto his knees to do it, pressing her with a force he thought would break his thumbs. All the power in him he poured out through his hands. And if it was not enough? He heard himself whimper. She was still and limp now.

"Miriam?" called the girl's voice.

Bruno sprang up and stumbled straight away toward the center of the island, then turned left to bring him out near his boat. He found himself scrubbing something off his hands with his pocket handkerchief. Miriam's spit. He threw the handkerchief down and swept it up again, because it was monogrammed. He was thinking! He felt great! It was done!

"Mi-ri-am!" with lazy impatience.

But what if he hadn't finished her, if she were sitting up and talking now? The thought shot him forward and he almost toppled down the bank. A firm breeze met him at the water's edge. He didn't see his boat.

He started to take any boat, changed his mind, then a couple of yards farther to the left found it, perched on the little log.

"Hey, she's fainted!"

Bruno shoved off, quickly, but not hurrying.

"Help, somebody!" said the girl's half gasp, half scream.

"Gawd!—Huh-*help*!"

The panic in the voice panicked Bruno. He rowed for several choppy strokes, then abruptly stopped and let the boat glide over the dark water. What was he getting scared about, for Christ's sake? Not a sign of anyone chasing him.

"Hey!"

"F'God's sake, she's *dead*! Call somebody!"

A girl's scream was a long arc in silence, and somehow the scream made it final. A beautiful scream, Bruno thought with a queer, serene admiration. He approached the dock easily, behind another boat. Slowly, as slowly as he had ever done anything, he paid the boatkeeper.

"On the island!" said another shocking, excited voice from a boat. "Girl's dead, they said!"

"Dead?"

"Somebody call the cops!"

Feet ran on the wooden dock behind him.

Bruno idled toward the gates of the park. Thank God he was so tight or hung over or something he could move so slowly! But a fluttering, unfightable terror rose in him as he passed through the turnstile. Then it ebbed quickly. No one was even looking at him. To steady himself, he concentrated on wanting a drink. There was a place up the road with red lights that looked like a bar, and he went straight toward it.

"Cutty," he said to the barman.

"Where you from, son?"

Bruno looked at him. The two men on the right were looking at him, too. "I want a Scotch."

"Can't get no hard liquor round here, man."

"What is this, part of the park?" His voice cracked like the scream.

"Can't get no hard liquor in the state of Texas."

"Gimme some of that!" Bruno pointed to the bottle of rye the men had on the counter.

"Here. Anybody wants a drink that bad." One of the men poured some rye in a glass and pushed it over.

It was rough as Texas going down, but sweet when it got there. Bruno offered to pay him, but the man refused.

Police sirens sounded, coming closer.

A man came in the door.

"What happened? Accident?" somebody asked him.

"I didn't see anything," the man said unconcernedly.

*My brother!* Bruno thought, looking the man over, but it didn't seem the thing to do to go over and talk to him.

He felt fine. The man kept insisting he have another drink, and Bruno had three fast. He noticed a streak on his hand as he lifted the glass, got out his handkerchief, and calmly wiped between his thumb and forefinger. It was a smear of Miriam's orangey lipstick. He could hardly see it in the bar's light. He thanked the man with the rye, and strolled out into the darkness, walking along the right side of the road, looking for a taxi. He had no desire to look back at the lighted park. He wasn't even thinking about it, he told himself. A streetcar passed, and he ran for it. He enjoyed its bright interior, and read all the placards. A wriggly little boy sat across the aisle, and Bruno began chatting with him. The thought of calling Guy and seeing him kept crossing his mind, but of course Guy wasn't here. He wanted some kind of celebration. He might call Guy's mother again, for the hell of it, but on second thought, it didn't seem wise. It was the one lousy note in the evening, the fact he couldn't see Guy, or even talk or write to him for a long while. Guy would be in for some questioning, of course. But he was free! It was done, done, done! In a burst of well-being, he ruffled the little boy's hair.

The little boy was taken aback for a moment, then in response to Bruno's friendly grin, he smiled, too.

At the Atchison, Topeka and Santa Fe Railroad terminal, he got an upper berth on a sleeper leaving at 1:30 a.m., which gave him an hour and a half to kill. Everything was perfect and he felt terribly happy. In a drugstore near the station, he bought a pint of Scotch to refill his flask. He thought of going by Guy's house to see what it looked like, debated it carefully, and decided he could. He was just heading for a man standing by the door, to ask directions—he knew he shouldn't go there in a taxi—when he realized he wanted a woman. He wanted a woman more than ever before in his life, and that he did pleased him prodigiously. He hadn't wanted one since he got to Santa Fe, though twice Wilson had gotten him into it. He veered away right in the man's face, thinking one of the taxi drivers outside would be better to ask. He had the shakes, he wanted a woman so badly! A different kind of shakes from liquor shakes.

"Ah don' know," said the blank, freckle-faced driver leaning against his fender.

"What d'you mean, you don't know?"

"Don' know, that's all."

Bruno left him in disgust.

Another driver down the sidewalk was more obliging. He wrote Bruno an address and a couple of names on the back of a company card, though it was so close by, he didn't even have to drive him there.

## *thirteen*

Guy leaned against the wall by his bed in the Montecarlo, watching Anne turn the pages of the family album he had brought from Metcalf. These had been wonderful days, his last two with Anne. Tomorrow he left for Metcalf. And then Florida. Mr. Brillhart's telegram had come three days ago, saying the commission was still his. There was a stretch of six months' work ahead, and in December the commencement of their own house. He had the money to build it now. And the money for the divorce.

"You know," he said quietly,"if I didn't have Palm Beach, if I had to go back to New York tomorrow and work, I could, and take anything." But almost as he said it, he realized that Palm Beach had given him his courage, his momentum, his will, or whatever he chose to call it, that without Palm Beach these days with Anne would give him only a sense of guilt.

"But you don't have to,"Anne said finally. She bent lower over the album.

He smiled. He knew she had hardly been listening to him. And, in fact, what he had said didn't matter, as Anne knew. He leaned over the album with her, identifying the people that she asked about, watching amusedly as she examined the double page of his pictures that his mother had collected, from babyhood to about twenty. He was smiling in every one of them, a shock of black hair setting off a sturdier, more careless-looking face than he had now.

"Do I look happy enough there?" he asked.

She winked at him. "And very handsome. Any of Miriam?" She let the remaining pages slip past her thumbnail.

"No," Guy said.

"I'm awfully glad you brought this."

"My mother would have my neck if she knew it was in Mexico." He put the album back in his suitcase so he wouldn't possibly leave it behind. "It's the most humane way of meeting families."

"Guy, did I put you through much?"

He smiled at her plaintive tone. "No! I never minded a bit!" He sat down on the bed and pulled her back with him. He had met all of Anne's relatives, by twos and threes, by dozens at the Faulkners' Sunday suppers and parties. It was a family joke how many Faulkners and Weddells and Morrisons there were, all living in New York State or in Long Island. Somehow he liked the fact she had so many relatives. The Christmas he had spent at the Faulkners' house last year had been the happiest of his life. He kissed both her cheeks, then her mouth. When he put his head down, he saw Anne's drawings on the Montecarlo stationery on the counterpane, and idly began to push them into a neat stack. They were ideas for designs that had come to her after their visit to the Museo Nacionale this afternoon. Their lines were black and definite, like his own rough sketches. "I'm thinking about the house, Anne."

"You want it big."

He smiled. "Yes."

"Let's have it big." She relaxed in his arms. They both sighed, like one person, and she laughed a little as he wrapped her closer.

It was the first time she had agreed to the size of the house. The house was to be Y-shaped, and the question had been whether to dispense with the front arm of it. But the idea sang in Guy's head only with both arms.

It would cost much, much more than twenty thousand, but Palm Beach would bring a flock of private commissions, Guy expected, that would be fast, well-paid jobs. Anne had said her father would like nothing better than to make them a wedding present of the front wing, but to Guy that seemed as unthinkable as removing it. He could see the house shining white and sharp against the brown bureau across the room. It projected from a certain white rock he had seen near a town called Alton in lower Connecticut. The house was long, low, and flat-roofed, as if alchemy had created it from the rock itself, like a crystal.

"I might call it 'The Crystal,'" Guy said.

Anne stared up reflectively at the ceiling. "I'm not so fond of naming houses—houses' names. Maybe I don't like 'Crystal.'"

Guy felt subtly hurt. "It's a lot better than 'Alton.' Of all the insipid names! That's New England for you. Take Texas now—"

"All right, you take Texas and I'll take New England." Anne smiled, stopping Guy in his tracks, because in reality she liked Texas and Guy liked New England.

Guy looked at the telephone, with a funny premonition it was going to ring. He felt rather giddy in his head, as if he had taken some mildly euphoric drug. It was the altitude, Anne said, that made people feel that way in Mexico City. "I feel as if I could call up Miriam tonight and talk to her and everything would be all right," Guy said slowly, "as if I could say just the right thing."

"There's the telephone," Anne said, perfectly serious.

Seconds passed, and he heard Anne sigh.

"What time is it?" she asked, sitting up. "I told Mother I'd be back by twelve."

"Eleven-seven."

"Aren't you sort of hungry?"

They ordered something from the restaurant downstairs. Their ham and eggs were an unrecognizable dish of vermilion color, but quite good, they decided.

"I'm glad you got to Mexico," Anne said. "It's been like something I knew so well and you didn't, something I wanted you to know. Only Mexico City isn't like the rest." She went on, eating slowly, "It has a nostalgia like Paris or Vienna and you want to come back no matter what's happened to you here."

Guy frowned. He had been to Paris and Vienna with Robert Treacher, a Canadian engineer, one summer when neither of them had any money. It hadn't been the Paris and Vienna Anne had known. He looked down at the buttered sweet roll she had given him. At times he wanted passionately to know the flavor of every experience Anne had ever known, what had happened to her in every hour of her childhood. "What do you mean, no matter what's happened to me here?"

"I mean whether you've been sick. Or robbed." She looked up at him and smiled. But the lamp's light that made a glow through her smoke-blue eyes, a crescent glow on their darker rims, lent a mysterious sadness to her face. "I suppose it's contrasts that make it attractive. Like people with incredible contrasts."

Guy stared at her, his finger crooked in the handle of his coffee cup. Somehow her mood, or perhaps what she said, made him feel inferior. "I'm sorry I don't have any incredible contrasts."

"Oh-ho-ho!" Then she burst out in a laugh, her familiar gay laugh that delighted him even when she laughed at him, even when she had no intention of explaining herself.

He sprang up. "How about some cake. I'm going to produce a cake like a jinni. A wonderful cake!" He got the cookie tin out of the corner of his suitcase. He had not thought of the cake until that moment, the cake his mother had baked him with the blackberry jam he had praised at his breakfasts.

Anne telephoned the bar downstairs and ordered a very special liqueur that she knew of. The liqueur was a rich purple like the purple cake, in stemmed glasses hardly bigger around than a finger. The waiter had just gone, they were just lifting the glasses, when the telephone rang, in nervous, iterant rings.

"Probably Mother," Anne said.

Guy answered it. He heard a voice talking distantly to an operator. Then the voice came louder, anxious and shrill, his mother's voice:

"Hello?"

"Hello, Mama."

"Guy, something's happened."

"What's the matter?"

"It's Miriam."

"What about her?" Guy pressed the receiver hard against his ear. He turned to Anne, and saw her face change as she looked at him.

"She's been killed, Guy. Last night—" She broke off.

"What, Mama?"

"It happened last night." She spoke in the shrill, measured tones that Guy had heard only once or twice before in his life. "Guy, she was murdered."

"Murdered!"

"Guy, *what?*" Anne asked, getting up.

"Last night at the lake. They don't know anything."

"You're—"

"Can you come home, Guy?"

"Yes, Mama.—How?" he asked stupidly, wringing the telephone as if he could wring information from its two old-fashioned parts. "How?"

"Strangled." The one word, then silence.

"Did you—?" he began. "Is—?"

"Guy, what is it?" Anne held to his arm.

"I'll be home as fast as I can, Mama. Tonight. Don't worry. I'll see you very soon." He hung up slowly and turned to Anne. "It's Miriam. Miriam's been killed."

Anne whispered, "Murdered—did you say?"

Guy nodded, but it suddenly struck him there might be a mistake. If it were just a report—

"When?"

But it was last night. "Last night, she said."

"Do they know who?"

"No. I've got to go tonight."

"My God."

He looked at Anne, standing motionless in front of him. "I've got to go tonight," he said again, dazedly. Then he turned and went to the telephone to call for a plane reservation, but it was Anne who got the reservation for him, talking rapidly in Spanish.

He began to pack. It seemed to take hours getting his few possessions into his suitcase. He stared at the brown bureau, wondering if he had already looked through it to see if everything were out of its drawers. Now, where he had seen the vision of the white house, a laughing face appeared, first the crescent mouth, then the face—Bruno's face. The tongue curved lewdly over the upper lip, and then the silent, convulsed laughter came again, shaking the stringy hair over the forehead. Guy frowned at Anne.

"What's the matter, Guy?"

"Nothing," he said. How *did* he look now?

# *fourteen*

Supposing Bruno had done it? He couldn't have, of course, but just supposing he had? Had they caught him? Had Bruno told them the murder was a plan of theirs? Guy could easily imagine Bruno hysterical, saying anything. There was no predicting what a neurotic child like Bruno would say. Guy searched his hazy memory of their conversation on the train and tried to recall if in jest or anger or drunkenness he had said anything that might have been taken as a consent to Bruno's insane idea. He hadn't. Against this negative answer, he weighed Bruno's letter that he remembered word for word: *that idea we had for a couple of murders. It could be done, I am sure. I cannot express to you my supremest confidence*—

From the plane window, Guy looked down into total blackness. Why wasn't he more anxious than he was? Up the dim cylinder of the plane's body, a match glowed at someone's cigarette. The scent of Mexican tobacco was faint, bitter, and sickening. He looked at his watch: 4:25.

Toward dawn he fell asleep, yielding to the shaking roar of the motors that seemed bent on tearing the plane apart, tearing his mind apart, and scattering the pieces in the sky. He awakened to a gray overcast morning, and a new thought: Miriam's lover had killed her. It was so obvious, so likely. He had killed her in a quarrel. One read such cases so often in the newspapers, the victims so often women like Miriam. There was a front-page story about a girl's murder in the tabloid *El Grafico* he had bought at the airport—he hadn't been able to find an American paper, though he had almost missed the plane looking for one—and a picture of her grinning Mexican lover holding the knife with which he had killed her, and Guy started to read it, becoming bored in the second paragraph.

A plainclothesman met him at the Metcalf airport and asked if he would mind answering a few questions. They got into a taxi together.

"Have they found the murderer?" Guy asked him.

"No."

The plainclothesman looked tired, as if he had been up all night, like the rest of the reporters and clerks and police in the old North Side courthouse. Guy glanced around the big wooden room, looking for Bruno before he was aware of doing so. When he lighted a cigarette, the man next to him asked him what kind it was, and accepted the one Guy offered him. They were Anne's Belmonts that he had pocketed when he was packing.

"Guy Daniel Haines, 717 Ambrose Street, Metcalf. . . . When did you leave Metcalf? . . . And when did you get to Mexico City?"

Chairs scraped. A noiseless typewriter started bumping after them.

Another plainclothesman with a badge, with his jacket open and a swagbelly protruding, strolled closer. "Why did you go to Mexico?"

"To visit some friends."

"Who?"

"The Faulkners. Alex Faulkner of New York."

"Why didn't you tell your mother where you were going?"

"I did tell her."

"She didn't know where you were staying in Mexico City," the plainclothesman informed him blandly, and referred to his notes. "You sent your wife a letter Sunday asking for a divorce. What did she reply?"

"That she wanted to talk with me."

"But you didn't care to talk with her anymore, did you?" asked a clear tenor voice.

Guy looked at the young police officer, and said nothing.

"Was her child to be yours?"

He started to answer, but was interrupted.

"Why did you come to Texas last week to see your wife?"

"Didn't you want a divorce pretty badly, Mr. Haines?"

"Are you in love with Anne Faulkner?"

Laughter.

"You know your wife had a lover, Mr. Haines. Were you jealous?"

"You were depending on that child for your divorce, weren't you?"

"That's all!" someone said.

A photograph was thrust in front of him, and the image spun with his anger before it straightened to a long dark head, handsome and stupid brown eyes, a cleft, manly chin—a face that might have been a movie actor's, and no one had to tell him this was Miriam's lover, because this was the kind of face she had liked three years ago.

"No," Guy said.

"Haven't you and he had some talks together?"

"That's all!"

A bitter smile pulled at the corner of his mouth, yet he felt he might have cried, too, like a child. He hailed a taxi in front of the courthouse. On the ride home, he read the double column on the front page of the *Metcalf Star*:

QUEST CONTINUES FOR GIRL'S SLAYER

June 12—The quest continues for the slayer of Mrs. Miriam Joyce Haines of this city, victim of strangulation by an unknown assailant on Metcalf Island Sunday night.

Two fingerprint experts arrive today who will endeavor to establish classifications of fingerprints taken from several oars and rowboats of the Lake Metcalf rowboat docks. But police and detectives fear that obtainable fingerprints are hazy. Authorities yesterday afternoon expressed the opinion that the crime might have been the act of a maniac. Apart from dubious fingerprints and several heelprints around the scene of the attack, police officials have not yet uncovered any vital clue.

Most important testimony at the inquest, it is believed, will come from Owen Markman, 30, longshoreman of Houston, and a close friend of the murdered woman.

Interment of Mrs. Haines' body will take place today at Remington Cemetery. The cortege departs from Howell Funeral Home on College Avenue at 2:00 p.m. this afternoon.

Guy lighted a cigarette from the end of another. His hands were still shaking, but he felt vaguely better. He hadn't thought of the possibility of a maniac. A maniac reduced it to a kind of horrible accident.

His mother sat in her rocker in the living room with a handkerchief pressed to her temple, waiting for him, though she did not get up when he came in. Guy embraced her and kissed her cheek, relieved to see she hadn't been crying.

"I spent yesterday with Mrs. Joyce," she said, "but I just can't go to the funeral."

"There isn't any need to, Mama." He glanced at his watch and saw it was already past 2. For an instant, he felt that Miriam might have been buried alive, that she might awaken and scream in protest. He turned, and passed his hand across his forehead.

"Mrs. Joyce," his mother said softly, "asked me if you might know something."

Guy faced her again. Mrs. Joyce resented him, he knew. He hated her now for what she might have said to his mother. "Don't see them again, Mama. You don't have to, do you?"

"No."

"And thank you for going over."

Upstairs on his bureau, he found three letters and a small square package with a Santa Fe store label. The package contained a narrow belt of braided lizard skin with a silver buckle formed like an H. A note enclosed said:

> Lost your Plato book on way to post office. I hope this will help make up.
>
> Charley

Guy picked up the penciled envelope from the Santa Fe hotel. There was only a small card inside. On the card's back was printed:

NICE TOWN METCALF

Turning the card, he read mechanically:

24 HOUR

DONOVAN TAXI SERVICE

RAIN OR SHINE

CALL 2-3333

SAFE FAST COURTEOUS

Something had been erased beneath the message on the back. Guy held the card to the light and made out one word: Ginnie. It was a Metcalf taxi company's card, but it had been mailed from Santa Fe. It doesn't mean anything, doesn't prove anything, he thought. But he crushed the card and the envelope and the package wrappings into his wastebasket. He loathed Bruno, he realized. He opened the box in the wastebasket and put the belt in, too. It was a handsome belt, but he happened also to loathe lizard and snake skin.

Anne telephoned him that night from Mexico City. She wanted to know everything that had happened, and he told her what he knew.

"They don't have any suspicion who did it?" she asked.

"They don't seem to."

"You don't sound well, Guy. Did you get any rest?"

"Not yet." He couldn't tell her now about Bruno. His mother had said that a man had called twice, wanting to talk to him, and Guy had no doubt who it was. But he knew he could not tell Anne about Bruno until he was sure. He could not begin.

"We've just sent those affidavits, darling. You know, about your being here with us?"

He had wired her for them after talking to one of the police detectives. "Everything'll be all right after the inquest," he said.

But it troubled him the rest of the night that he had not told Anne about Bruno. It was not the horror that he wished to spare her. He felt it was some sense of personal guilt that he himself could not bear.

There was a report going about that Owen Markman had not wanted to marry Miriam after the loss of the child, and that she had started a breach-of-promise action against him. Miriam really had lost the child accidentally, Guy's mother said. Mrs. Joyce had told her that Miriam had tripped on a black silk nightgown that she particularly liked, that Owen had given her, and had fallen downstairs in her house. Guy believed the story implicitly. A compassion and remorse he had never before felt for Miriam had entered his heart. Now she seemed pitiably ill-fated and entirely innocent.

# *fifteen*

"Not more than seven yards and not less than five," the grave, self-assured young man in the chair replied. "No, I did not see anyone."

"I think about fifteen feet," said the wide-eyed girl, Katherine Smith, who looked as frightened as if it had just happened. "Maybe a little more," she added softly.

"About thirty feet. I was the first one down at the boat," said Ralph Joyce, Miriam's brother. His red hair was like Miriam's, and he had the same gray-green eyes, but his heavy square jaw took away the resemblance. "I wouldn't say she had any enemy. Not enough to do something like this."

"I didn't hear one thing," Katherine Smith said earnestly, shaking her head.

Ralph Joyce said he hadn't heard anything, and Richard Schuyler's positive statement ended it:

"There weren't any sounds."

The facts repeated and repeated lost their horror and even their drama for Guy. They were like dull blows of a hammer, nailing the story in his mind forever. The nearness of the three others was the unbelievable. Only a maniac would have dared come so near, Guy thought, that was certain.

"Were you the father of the child Mrs. Haines lost?"

"Yes." Owen Markman slouched forward over his locked fingers. A glum, hangdog manner spoilt the dashing good looks Guy had seen in the photograph. He wore gray buckskin shoes, as if he had just come from his job in Houston. Miriam would not have been proud of him today, Guy thought.

"Do you know anyone who might have wanted Mrs. Haines to die?"

"Yes." Markman pointed at Guy. "Him."

People turned to look at him. Guy sat tensely, frowning straight at Markman, for the first time really suspecting Markman.

"Why?"

Owen Markman hesitated a long while, mumbled something, then brought out one word: "Jealousy."

Markman could not give a single credible reason for jealousy, but after that accusations of jealousy came from all sides. Even Katherine Smith said,"I guess so."

Guy's lawyer chuckled. He had the affidavits from the Faulkners in his hand. Guy hated the chuckle. He had always hated legal procedure. It was like a vicious game in which the objective seemed not to disclose the truth but to enable one lawyer to tilt at another, and unseat him on a technicality.

"You gave up an important commission—" the coroner began.

"I did not give it up," Guy said. "I wrote them before I had the commission, saying I didn't want it."

"You telegraphed. Because you didn't want your wife to follow you there. But when you learned in Mexico that your wife had lost her child, you sent another telegram to Palm Beach that you wished to be considered for the commission. Why?"

"Because I didn't believe she'd follow me there then. I suspected she'd want to delay the divorce indefinitely. But I intended to see her—this week to discuss the divorce." Guy wiped the perspiration from his forehead, and saw his lawyer purse his lips ruefully. His lawyer hadn't wanted him to mention the divorce in connection with his change of mind about the commission. Guy didn't care. It was the truth, and they could make of it what they wished.

"In your opinion was her husband capable of arranging for such a murder, Mrs. Joyce?"

"Yes," said Mrs. Joyce with the faintest quiver, her head high. The shrewd dark red lashes were almost closed, as Guy had so often seen them, so that one never knew where her eyes rested. "He wanted his divorce."

There was an objection that Mrs. Joyce had said a few moments before that her daughter wanted the divorce and Guy Haines did not because he still loved her. "If both wanted a divorce, and it has been proven Mr. Haines did, why wasn't there a divorce?"

The court was amused. The fingerprint experts could not come to agreement on their classifications. A hardware dealer, into whose store Miriam had come the day before her death, got tangled up as to whether her companion had been male or female, and more laughter camouflaged the fact he had been instructed to say a man. Guy's lawyer harangued on geographical fact, the inconsistencies of the Joyce family, the affidavits in his hand, but Guy was sure that his own straightforwardness alone had absolved him from any suspicion.

The coroner suggested in his summation that the murder would seem to have been committed by a maniac unknown to the victim and the other parties. A verdict was brought in of "person or persons unknown," and the case was turned over to the police.

A telegram arrived the next day, just as Guy was leaving his mother's house:

ALL GOOD WISHES FROM THE GOLDEN WEST

UNSIGNED

"From the Faulkners," he said quickly to his mother.

She smiled. "Tell Anne to take good care of my boy."

She pulled him down gently by his ear and kissed his cheek.

Bruno's telegram was still wadded in his hand when he got to the airport. He tore it into tiny bits and dropped them into a wire trashbasket at the edge of the field. Every one of the pieces blew through the wire and went dancing out across the asphalt, gay as confetti in the windy sunlight.

## *sixteen*

Guy struggled to find a definite answer about Bruno—had he or hadn't he?—and then gave it up. There was too much incredible in the possibility that Bruno had done it. What weight did the Metcalf taxi company's card have? It would be like Bruno to find such a card in Santa Fe and mail it on to him. If it were not the act of a maniac, as the coroner and everyone else believed, wasn't it far more likely that Owen Markman had arranged it?

He closed his mind to Metcalf, to Miriam, and to Bruno, and concentrated on the work for Palm Beach which, he saw from the first day, would demand all that he had in diplomacy, technical knowledge, and sheer physical strength. Except for Anne, he closed his mind to all his past that, for all his idealistic aims and the fighting for them, and the small success he had known, seemed miserable and grubbing compared to the magnificent main building of the country club. And the more he immersed himself in the new effort, the more he felt recreated also in a different and more perfect form.

Photographers from newspapers and news magazines took pictures of the main building, the swimming pool, the bathhouses, and the terracing in the early stages of construction. Members of the club were also photographed inspecting the grounds, and Guy knew that below their pictures would be printed the amount of money each had donated to the cause of princely recreation. Sometimes he wondered if part of his enthusiasm might be due to a consciousness of the money behind the project, to the lavishness of space and materials he had to work with, to the flattery of the wealthy people who continually invited him to their homes. Guy never accepted their invitations. He knew he might be losing himself the small commissions he would need next winter, but he also knew he could never force himself to the social responsibilities that most architects assumed as a matter of course. Evenings when he did not want to be alone, he caught a bus to Clarence Brillhart's house a few miles away, and they had dinner together, listened to phonograph records, and talked. Clarence Brillhart, the Palmyra Club manager, was a retired broker, a tall, white-haired old gentleman whom Guy often thought he would have liked as a father. Guy admired most of all his air of leisure, as imperturbable on the bustling, hectic construction grounds as in his own home. Guy hoped he might be like him in his own old age. But he felt he moved too fast, had always moved too fast. There was inevitably, he felt, a lack of dignity in moving fast.

Most evenings Guy read, wrote long letters to Anne, or merely went to bed, for he was always up by five and often worked all day with a blowtorch or mortar and trowel. He knew almost all the workmen by name. He liked to judge the temperament of each man, and to know how it contributed or did not contribute to the spirit of his buildings. "It is like directing a symphony," he wrote to Anne. In the dusks, when he sat smoking his pipe in a thicket of the golf course, gazing down on the four white buildings, he felt that the Palmyra project was going to be perfect. He knew it when he saw the first horizontals laid across the spaced marble uprights of the main building. The Pittsburgh store had been marred at the last moment by the client's change of mind about the window area. The hospital annex in Chicago had been ruined, Guy thought, by the cornice that was of darker stone than he had intended. But Brillhart permitted no interference, the Palmyra was going to be as perfect as his original conception, and Guy had never created anything before that he felt would be perfect.

In August, he went North to see Anne. She was working in the design department of a textile company in Manhattan. In the fall, she planned to go into partnership in a shop with another woman designer she had met. Neither of them mentioned Miriam until the fourth and last day of Guy's visit. They were standing by the brook behind Anne's house, in their last few minutes together before Anne drove him to the airport.

"Do you think it was Markman, Guy?" Anne asked him suddenly. And when Guy nodded: "It's terrible—but I'm almost sure."

Then one evening when he returned from Brillhart's house to the furnished room where he lived, a letter from Bruno awaited him with one from Anne. The letter was from Los Angeles, forwarded by his mother from Metcalf. It congratulated him on his work in Palm Beach, wished him success, and begged for just a word from him. The P.S. said:

> Hope you are not annoyed at this letter. Have written many letters and not mailed them. Phoned your mother for your address, but she wouldn't give it to me. Guy, honestly there is nothing to worry about or I wouldn't have written. Don't you know I'd be the first one to be careful? Write soon. I may go to Haiti soon. Again your friend and admirer. C.A.B.

A slow ache fell through him to his feet. He could not bear to be alone in his room. He went out to a bar, and almost before he knew what he was doing, had two ryes and then a third. In the mirror behind the bar, he saw himself glance at his sunburnt face, and it struck him that his eyes looked dishonest and furtive. *Bruno had done it.* It came thundering down with a weight that left no possibility of doubt any longer, like a cataclysm that only a madman's unreason could have kept suspended all this while. He glanced about in the little bar as if he expected the walls to topple down on him. *Bruno had done it.* There was no mistaking Bruno's personal pride in his, Guy's, freedom now. Or the P.S. Or possibly even the trip to Haiti. But what did Bruno *mean?* Guy scowled at the face in the mirror and dropped his eyes, looked down at his hands, the front of his tweed jacket, his flannel trousers, and it flashed through his mind he had put these clothes on this morning as a certain person and that he would take them off tonight as another person, the person he would be from now on. He *knew* now. This was an instant—He could not say just what was happening, but he felt his entire life would be different, must be different, from now on.

If he knew Bruno had done it, why didn't he turn him in? What did he feel about Bruno besides hatred and disgust? Was he afraid? Guy didn't clearly know.

He resisted an impulse to telephone Anne until it was too late, and finally, at three in the morning, could resist no longer. Lying on his bed in the darkness, he talked to her very calmly, about commonplace matters, and once he even laughed. Even Anne did not notice anything wrong, he thought when he had hung up. He felt somehow slighted, and vaguely alarmed.

His mother wrote that the man who had called while he was in Mexico, and said his name was Phil, had called again to ask how he might reach him. She was worried that it might have something to do with Miriam, and wondered if she should tell the police.

Guy wrote back to her: "I found out who the annoying telephoner was. Phil Johnson, a fellow I knew in Chicago."

## *seventeen*

"Charley, what're all these clippings?"

"Friend of mine, Ma!" Bruno shouted through the bathroom door. He turned the water on harder, leaned on the basin, and concentrated on the bright nickel-plated drainstop. After a moment, he reached for the Scotch bottle he kept under towels in the clothes hamper. He felt less shaky with the glass of Scotch and water in his hand, and spent a few seconds inspecting the silver braid on the sleeve of his new smoking jacket. He liked the jacket so much, he wore it as a bathrobe also. In the mirror, the oval lapels framed the portrait of a young man of leisure, of reckless and mysterious adventure, a young man of humor and depth, power and gentleness (witness the glass held delicately between thumb and forefinger with the air of an imperial toast)—a young man with two lives. He drank to himself.

"Charley?"

"Minute, Mom!"

He cast a wild eye about the bathroom. There was no window. Lately it happened about twice a week. Half an hour or so after he got up, he felt as if someone were kneeling on his chest and stifling him. He closed his eyes and dragged air in and out of his lungs as fast as he could. Then the liquor took. It bedded his leaping nerves like a hand passing down his body. He straightened and opened the door.

"Shaving," he said.

His mother was in tennis shorts and a halter, bending over his unmade bed where the clippings were strewn. "Who was she?"

"Wife of a fellow I met on the train coming down from New York. Guy Haines." Bruno smiled. He liked to say Guy's name. "Interesting, isn't it? They haven't caught the murderer yet."

"Probably a maniac," she sighed.

Bruno's face sobered. "Oh, I doubt it. Circumstances are too complicated."

Elsie stood up and slid her thumb inside her belt. The bulge just below her belt disappeared, and for a moment she looked as Bruno had seen her all her life until this last year, trim as a twenty-year-old down to her thin ankles. "Your friend Guy's got a nice face."

"Nicest fellow you ever saw. It's a shame he's dragged in on it. He told me on the train he hadn't seen his wife in a couple of years. Guy's no more a murderer than I am!" Bruno smiled at his inadvertent joke, and to cover it added,"His wife was a roundheels anyway—"

"Darling." She took him by the braid-edged lapels. "Won't you watch your language a little for the duration? I know Grannie's horrified sometimes."

"Grannie wouldn't know what a roundheels means," Bruno said hoarsely.

Elsie threw her head back and shrieked.

"Ma, you're getting too much sun. I don't like your face that dark."

"I don't like yours that pale."

Bruno frowned. The leathery look of his mother's forehead offended him painfully. He kissed her suddenly on the cheek.

"Promise me you'll sit in the sun a half hour today anyway. People come thousands of miles to get to California, and here you sit in the house!"

Bruno frowned down his nose. "Ma, you're not interested in my friend!"

"I am interested in your friend. You haven't told me much about him."

Bruno smiled shyly. No, he had been very good. He had let the clippings lie out in his room only today for the first time, because he was sure now both he and Guy were safe. If he talked a quarter of an hour about Guy now, his mother would probably forget, too. If it were even necessary that she forget. "Did you read all that?" He nodded toward the bed.

"No, not all that. How many drinks this morning?"

"One."

"I smell two."

"All right, Mom, I had two."

"Darling, won't you watch the morning drinks? Morning drinks are the end. I've seen alcoholic after alcoholic—"

"Alcoholic is a nasty word." Bruno resumed his slow circuit of the room. "I feel better since I drink a little more, Ma. You said yourself I'm more cheerful and my appetite's better. Scotch is a very pure drink. Some people it agrees with."

"You drank too much last night, and Grannie knows it. Don't think she doesn't notice, you know."

"About last night don't ask me." Bruno grinned and waved his hand.

"Sammie's coming over this morning. Why don't you get dressed and come down and keep score for us?"

"Sammie gives me ulcers."

She walked to the door as gaily as if she had not heard. "Promise me you'll get some sun today anyway."

He nodded and moistened his dry lips. He did not return her smile as she closed the door, because he felt as if a black lid had fallen on him suddenly, as if he had to escape something before it was too late. He had to see *Guy* before it was too late! He had to get rid of his father before it was too late! He had things to do! He did not want to be here, in his grandmother's house furnished just like his own house in Louis Quinze, eternal Louis Quinze! But he did not know where else he wanted to be. He was not happy if he were long away from his mother, was he? He bit his underlip and frowned, though his small gray eyes were quite blank. Why did she say he didn't need a drink in the mornings? He needed it more than any other drink of the day. He flexed his shoulders in a slow rotary movement. Why should he feel low? The clippings on the bed were about him. Week after week went by and the dumb police got nothing on him, nothing except the heelprints, and he had thrown his shoes away long ago! The party last week with Wilson in the San Francisco hotel was nothing to what he would do now if he had Guy to celebrate with. A perfect murder! How many people could do a perfect murder on an island with a couple of hundred other people around?

He was not like the dopes in the newspapers who killed "to see what it felt like," and never had a bloody thing to report except sometimes a sick-making, "It wasn't as good as I expected." If he were interviewed, he would say,"It was terrific! There's nothing in the world like it!" ("Would you ever do it again, Mr. Bruno?") "Well, I might," reflectively, with caution, as an arctic explorer when asked if he will winter up north again next year might reply uncommittingly to a reporter. ("Can you tell us a little bit about your sensations?") He would tip the microphone toward him, look up, and muse, while the world awaited his first word. How had it felt? Well, there's only *it*, see, and nothing to compare it with. She was a rotten woman anyway, you understand. It was like killing a hot little rat, only she was a girl so it made it a murder. The very warmth of her had been disgusting, and he remembered thinking that before he took his fingers away, the heat would really have stopped coming, that after he left her, she would grow chill and hideous, like she really was.("Hideous, mr. Bruno?") Yes, hideous. ("Do you think a corpse is hideous?") Bruno frowned. No, he did not really think he thought a corpse was hideous. If the victim was evil, like Miriam, people ought to be pretty glad to see the corpse, oughtn't they? ("Power, Mr. Bruno?") Oh, yes, he had felt terrific power! That was it. He had taken away a life. Now, nobody knew what life was, everybody defended it, the most priceless possession, but he had taken one away. That night there had been the danger, the ache of his hands, the fear in case she made a sound, but the instant when he felt that life had left her, everything else had fallen away, and only the mysterious *fact* of the thing he did remained, the mystery and the miracle of stopping life. People talked about the mystery of birth, of beginning life, but how explainable that was! Out of two live germ cells! What about the mystery of stopping life? Why should life stop because he held a girl's throat too tightly? What was life anyway? What did Miriam feel after he took his hands away? Where was she? No, he didn't believe in a life after death. She was stopped, and that was just the miracle. Oh, he could say a great deal at his interview with the press! ("What significance did it have for you that your victim was female?") Where had that question come from? Bruno hesitated, then recovered his poise. Well, the fact she was a female had given him greater enjoyment. No, he did not therefore conclude that his pleasure had partaken of the sexual. No, he did not hate women either. Rather not! Hate is akin to love, you know. Who said that? He didn't believe it for a minute. No, all he would say was that he wouldn't have enjoyed it quite so much, he thought, if he had killed a man. Unless it was his father.

The telephone . . .

Bruno had been staring at it. Every telephone suggested Guy. He could reach Guy now with two well-placed calls, but a call might annoy Guy. Guy might still be nervous. He would wait for Guy to write. A letter should come any day now, because Guy must have gotten his letter the end of last week. The one thing Bruno needed to make his happiness complete was to hear Guy's voice, to have a word from him saying he was happy. The bond between Guy and him now was closer than brotherhood. How many brothers liked their brothers as much as he liked Guy?

Bruno threw a leg out the window and stood up on the wrought iron balcony. The morning sunshine did feel rather good. The lawn was broad and smooth as a golf course all the way to the ocean. Then he saw Sammie Franklin, dressed in white tennis clothes with his rackets under his arm, grinning his way toward his mother. Sammie was big and flabby, like a softened-up boxer. He reminded Bruno of another Hollywood stooge who had hung around his mother when they were here three years ago, Alexander Phipps. Why did he even remember their phony names? He heard Sammie's chuckle as he extended his hand to his mother, and an old antagonism fluttered up in Bruno and lay still again. *Merde.* Disdainfully he took his eyes from Sammie's broad flannel backsides, and examined the view from left to right. A couple of pelicans flew loggily over a hedge and plopped down on the grass. Far out on the pale water he saw a sailboat. Three years ago he had begged his grandmother to get a sailboat, and now that she had one, he never felt like using it.

The tennis balls *wokked* around the tan stucco corner of the house. Chimes sounded from downstairs, and Bruno went back into his room, so he would not know what time it was. He liked to see a clock by accident as late as possible in the day, and find it was later than he had thought. If there was no letter from Guy in the noon mail, he thought, he might catch a train to San Francisco. On the other hand, his last memory of San Francisco was not pleasant. Wilson had brought a couple of Italian fellows up to the hotel, and Bruno had bought all the dinners and several bottles of rye. They had called Chicago on his telephone. The hotel had chalked up two calls to Metcalf, and he couldn't remember the second at all. And the last day, he had been twenty dollars short on the bill. He didn't have a checking account, so the hotel, the best hotel in town, had held his suitcase until his mother wired the money. No, he wouldn't go back to San Francisco.

"Charley?" called the high, sweet voice of his grandmother.

He saw the curved handle of the door start to move, made an involuntary lunge for the clippings on his bed, then circled back to the bathroom instead. He shook tooth powder into his mouth. His grandmother could smell liquor like a dry sourdough in the Klondike.

"Aren't you ready to have some breakfast with me?" his grandmother asked.

He came out combing his hair. "Gee, you're all dressed up!" She turned her small unsteady figure around for him like a fashion model, and Bruno smiled. He liked the black lace dress with the pink satin showing through it. "Looks like one of those balconies out there."

"Thank you, Charley. I'm going into town the latter part of the morning. I thought you might like to come with me."

"Could be. Yeah, I'd like that, Grannie," he said good-naturedly.

"So it's *you've* been clipping my *Times*! I thought it was one of the servants. You must be getting up awfully early these mornings."

"Yep," Bruno said agreeably.

"When I was young, we used to get poems out of newspapers for our scrapbooks. We made scrapbooks out of everything under the sun. What're you going to do with these?"

"Oh, just keep 'em."

"Don't you make scrapbooks?"

"Nope." She was looking at him, and Bruno wanted her to look at the clippings.

"Oh, you're just a *ba-aby*!" She pinched his cheek. "Hardly a bit of fuzz on your chin yet! I don't know why your mother's worried about you—"

"She's not worried."

"—when you just need time to grow up. Come on down to breakfast with me. Yes, pajamas and all."

Bruno gave her his arm on the stairs.

"I've got the least bit of shopping to do," said his grandmother as she poured his coffee, "and then I thought we'd do something nice. Maybe a good movie—with a murder in it—or maybe the amusement park. I haven't been to an amusement park in *a-ages*!"

Bruno's eyes opened as wide as they could.

"Which would you like? Well, we can look over the movies when we get there."

"I'd like the amusement park, Grannie."

Bruno enjoyed the day, helping her in and out of the car, piloting her around the amusement park, though there was not much after all his grandmother could do or eat. But they rode the ferris wheel together. Bruno told his grandmother about the big ferris wheel in Metcalf, but she did not ask him when he had been there.

Sammie Franklin was still at the house when they came home, staying for dinner. Bruno's eyebrows drew together at the first sight of him. He knew his grandmother cared as little for Sammie as he did, and Bruno felt suddenly a great tenderness for her, because she accepted Sammie so uncomplainingly, accepted any mongrel his mother brought on the place. What had he and his mother been doing all day? They had been to a movie, they said, one of Sammie's movies. And there was a letter for him upstairs in his room.

Bruno ran upstairs. The letter was from Florida. He tore it open with his hands shaking like ten hangovers. He had never wanted a letter so badly, not even at camp, when he had waited for letters from his mother.

Sept. 6

Dear Charles,

I do not understand your message to me, or for that matter your great interest in me. I know you very slightly, but enough to assure me that we have nothing in common on which to base a friendship. May I ask you please not to telephone my mother again or communicate with me?

Thank you for trying to return the book to me. Its loss is of no importance.

Guy Haines

Bruno brought it up closer and read it again, his eyes lingering incredulously on a word here and there. His pointed tongue stretched over his upper lip, then disappeared suddenly. He felt shorn. It was a feeling like grief, or like a death. Worse! He glanced about his room, hating the furniture, hating his possessions. Then the pain centered in his chest, and reflexively he began to cry.

After dinner, Sammie Franklin and he got into an argument about vermouths. Sammie said the drier the vermouth, the more one had to put into a martini, though he admitted he was not a martini drinker. Bruno said he was not a martini drinker either, but he knew better than that. The argument went on even after his grandmother said good night and left them. They were on the upstairs terrace in the dark, his mother in the glider and he and Sammie standing by the parapet. Bruno ran down to the bar for the ingredients to prove his point. They both made martinis and tasted them, and though it was clear Bruno was right, Sammie kept holding out, and chuckling as if he didn't quite mean what he said either, which Bruno found insufferable.

"Go to New York and learn something!" Bruno shouted. His mother had just left the terrace.

"How do you know what you're saying anyway?" Sammie retorted. The moonlight made his fat grinning face blue-green and yellow, like gorgonzola cheese. "You're pickled all day. You—"

Bruno caught Sammie by the shirtfront and bent him backward over the parapet. Sammie's feet rattled on the tiles. His shirt split. When he wriggled sideways to safety, the blue had left his face and it was a shadowless yellow-white.

"Th-the hell's the matter with you?" he bellowed. "You'd a shoved me over, wouldn't you?"

"No, I wouldn't!" Bruno shrieked, louder than Sammie. Suddenly he couldn't breathe, like in the mornings. He took his stiff, sweaty hands down from his face. He had done a murder, hadn't he? Why should he do another? But he had seen Sammie squirming on the points of the iron fence right below, and he had wanted him there. He heard Sammie stirring a highball fast. Bruno stumbled over the threshold of the French window into the house.

"And *stay* out!" Sammie shouted after him.

The shaking passion in Sammie's voice sent a throb of fear through him. Bruno said nothing as he passed his mother in the hall. Going downstairs, he clung to the banister with both hands, cursing the ringing, aching, unmanageable mess in his head, cursing the martinis he had drunk with Sammie. He staggered into the living room.

"Charley, what did you do to Sammie?" His mother had followed him in.

"Ah, whad I do to Sammie!" Bruno shoved his hand toward her blurred figure and sat down on the sofa with a bounce.

"Charley—come back and apologize." The white blur of her evening dress came closer, one brown arm extended toward him.

"Are you sleeping with that guy? *Are you sleeping with that guy?*" He knew he had only to lie back on the sofa and he would pass out like a light, so he lay back, and never felt her arm at all.

# eighteen

In the month after Guy returned to New York, his restlessness, his dissatisfaction with himself, with his work, with Anne, had focused gradually on Bruno. It was Bruno who made him hate to look at pictures of the Palmyra now, Bruno who was the real cause of his anxiety that he had blamed on the dearth of commissions since he had come back from Palm Beach. Bruno who had made him argue so senselessly with Anne the other evening about not getting a better office, not buying new furniture and a rug for this one. Bruno who had made him tell Anne he did not consider himself a success, that the Palmyra meant nothing. Bruno who had made Anne turn quietly away from him that evening and walk out the door, who had made him wait until he heard the elevator door close, before he ran down the eight flights of stairs and begged her to forgive him.

And who knew? Perhaps it was Bruno who kept him from getting jobs now. The creation of a building was a spiritual act. So long as he harbored his knowledge of Bruno's guilt, he corrupted himself in a sense. Such a thing could be perceived in him, he felt. Consciously, he had made up his mind to let the police trap Bruno. But as the weeks went by and they didn't, he was plagued by a feeling that he should act himself. What stopped him was both an aversion to accusing a man of murder and a senseless but lingering doubt that Bruno might not be guilty. That Bruno had committed the crime struck him at times as so fantastic, all his previous conviction was momentarily wiped out. At times, he felt he would have doubted even if Bruno had sent him a written confession. And yet, he had to admit to himself that he was *sure* Bruno had done it. The weeks that went by without the police picking up any strong trail seemed to confirm it. As Bruno had said, how could they with no motivation? His letter to Bruno in September had silenced him all the fall, but just before he left Florida, a sober note from Bruno had said he would be back in New York in December and he hoped to be able to have a talk with him. Guy was determined to have nothing to do with him.

Still he fretted, about everything and about nothing, but chiefly about his work. Anne told him to be patient. Anne reminded him that he had already proven himself in Florida. In greater measure than ever before, she offered him the tenderness and reassurance he needed so, yet he found that in his lowest, most stubborn moments he could not always accept it.

One morning in mid-December, the telephone rang as Guy sat idly studying his drawings of the Connecticut house.

"Hello, Guy. This is Charley."

Guy recognized the voice, felt his muscles tensing for a fight.

But Myers was within earshot across the room.

"How are you?" Bruno asked with smiling warmth. "Merry Christmas."

Slowly Guy put the telephone back in its cradle.

He glanced over at Myers, the architect with whom he shared the big one-room office. Myers was still bent over his drawing board. Under the edge of the green windowshade, the bobbing pigeons still pecked at the grain he and Myers had sprinkled on the sill a few moments ago.

The telephone rang again.

"I'd like to see you, Guy," Bruno said.

Guy stood up. "Sorry. I don't care to see you."

"What's the matter?" Bruno forced a little laugh. "Are you nervous, Guy?"

"I just don't care to see you."

"Oh. Okay," said Bruno, hoarse with hurt.

Guy waited, determined not to retreat first, and finally Bruno hung up.

Guy's throat was dry, and he went to the drinking fountain in the corner of the room. Behind the fountain, sunlight lay in a precise diagonal across the big aerial photograph of the four nearly finished Palmyra buildings. He turned his back to it. He'd been asked to make a speech at his old school in Chicago, Anne would remind him. He was to write an article for a leading architectural magazine. But so far as commissions went, the Palmyra Club might have been a public declaration that he was to be boycotted. And why not? Didn't he owe the Palmyra to Bruno? Or at any rate to a murderer?

On a snowy evening a few days later, as he and Anne came down the brownstone steps of his West Fifty-third Street apartment house, Guy saw a tall bareheaded figure standing on the sidewalk gazing up at them. A tingle of alarm traveled to his shoulders, and involuntarily his hand tightened on Anne's arm.

"Hello," Bruno said, his voice soft with melancholy. His face was barely visible in the dusk.

"Hello," Guy replied, as if to a stranger, and walked on.

"Guy!"

Guy and Anne turned at the same time. Bruno came toward them, hands in the pockets of his overcoat.

"What is it?" Guy asked.

"Just wanted to say hello. Ask how you are." Bruno stared at Anne with a kind of perplexed, smiling resentment.

"I'm fine," Guy said quietly. He turned away, drawing Anne with him.

"Who is he?"Anne whispered.

Guy itched to look back. He knew Bruno would be standing where they had left him, knew he would be looking after them, weeping perhaps. "He's a fellow who came around looking for work last week."

"You can't do anything for him?"

"No. He's an alcoholic."

Deliberately Guy began to talk about their house, because he knew there was nothing else he could talk about now and possibly sound normal. He had bought the land, and the foundations were being laid. After New Year's, he was going up to Alton and stay for several days. During the movie, he speculated as to how he could shake Bruno off, terrify him so that he would be afraid to contact him.

What did Bruno want with him? Guy sat with his fists clenched at the movie. The *next* time, he would threaten Bruno with police investigation. And he would carry it through, too. What vast harm was there in suggesting a man be investigated?

But what did Bruno want with him?

# nineteen

Bruno had not wanted to go to Haiti, but it offered escape. New York or Florida or anywhere in the American continent was torture so long as Guy was there, too, and would not see him. To blot out his pain and depression, he had drunk a great deal at home in Great Neck, and to occupy himself had measured the house and the grounds in paces, measured his father's room with tailor's tape, moving doggedly, stooping, measuring and remeasuring, like a tireless automaton that wavered only slightly off its track now and then, betraying the fact it was drunk and not deranged. Thus he spent ten days after seeing Guy, waiting for his mother and her friend Alice Leffingwell to get ready to go to Haiti.

There were moments when he felt his whole being in some as yet inscrutable stage of metamorphosis. There was the deed he had done, which in his hours alone in the house, in his room, he felt sat upon his head like a crown, but a crown that no one else could see. Very easily and quickly, he could break down in tears. There was the time he had wanted a caviar sandwich for lunch, because he deserved the finest, big black caviar, and when there had been only red in the house, had told Herbert to go out and get some black. He had eaten a quarter of the toasted sandwich, sipping a Scotch and water with it, then had almost fallen asleep staring at the triangle of toasted bread that finally had begun to lift at one corner. He had stared at it until it was no longer a sandwich, the glass with his drink no longer a glass, and only the golden liquid in it part of himself, and he had gulped it all. The empty glass and the curling toast had been live things that mocked him and challenged his right to use them. A butcher's truck had departed down the driveway just then and Bruno had frowned after it, because everything had suddenly come alive and was fleeing to escape him—the truck, the sandwich, and the glass, the trees that couldn't run away but were disdainful, like the house that imprisoned him. He had hit both his fists against the wall simultaneously, then seized the sandwich and broken its insolent triangular mouth and burnt it, piece by piece, in the empty fireplace, the caviar popping like little people, dying, each one a life.

Alice Leffingwell, his mother and he, and a crew of four including two Puerto Ricans left for Haiti in mid-January on the steam yacht, *Fairy Prince*, which Alice had spent all fall and winter wresting from her former husband. The trip was a celebration of her third divorce, and she had invited Bruno and his mother months before. Bruno's delight in the voyage inspired him to a pretense of indifference and boredom during the first days. No one noticed. Alice and his mother spent whole afternoons and evenings chattering together in the cabin, and in the mornings they slept. To justify his happiness to himself at such a dull prospect as being cooped up on a ship for a month with an old bag like Alice, Bruno convinced himself he had been under quite a strain watching out the police didn't get on his trail, and that he needed leisure to dope out the details of how his father could be got rid of. He also reasoned that the more time elapsed, the more likely Guy would be to change his attitude.

On shipboard, he detailed two or three key plans for the murder of his father, of which any other plans laid on the estate would be mere variations. He was very proud of his plans—one with gun in his father's bedroom, one with knife and two choices of escape, and one with either gun or knife or strangulation in the garage where his father put his car every evening at 6:30. The disadvantage of the last plan was lack of darkness, but it had compensations in comparative simplicity. He could all but hear in his ears the efficient *click-click* of his plans' operations. Yet whenever he finished a careful drawing, he felt obliged to tear it up for safety. He was eternally making drawings and tearing them up. The sea from Bar Harbor to the southernmost of the Virgin Islands was strewn with the subdivided seeds of his ideas when the *Fairy Prince* rounded Cape Maisi bound for Port-au-Prince.

"A princely harbor for my *Prince*!" cried Alice, relaxing her mind in a lull of conversation with his mother.

Around the corner from them, in the shade, Bruno fumbled up the paper he had been drawing on and lifted his head. In the left quarter of the horizon, land was visible in a gray fuzzy line. Haiti. Seeing it made it seem more distant and foreign than when he had not seen it. He was going farther and farther away from Guy. He pulled himself from the deck chair and went over to the port rail. They would spend days in Haiti before they moved on, and then they would move farther south. Bruno stood perfectly still, feeling frustration corrode him internally as the tropical sun did externally now, on the pale backs of his legs. Abruptly, he ripped the plan to pieces and released them by opening his hands over the side. The wind perversely carried the pieces forward.

As important as the plans, of course, was to find someone for the job. He would do it himself, he thought, if not for the fact Gerard, his father's private detective, would nail him no matter how carefully he planned it. Besides, he wanted to put his no-motivation scheme to the test again. Matt Levine or Carlos—the trouble was he knew them. And it was dangerous to try to negotiate without knowing if the person would agree. Bruno had seen Matt several times, and hadn't been able to mention it.

Something happened in Port-au-Prince that Bruno would never forget. He fell off the gangplank coming back aboard ship the second afternoon.

The steamy heat had stupefied him and rum had made it worse, made him hotter. He was on his way from Hotel La Citadelle to the ship to get his mother's evening shoes, when he stopped in a bar near the waterfront for a Scotch with ice. One of the Puerto Ricans of the crew, whom Bruno had disliked since the first moment he saw him, was in the bar and blind drunk, roaring around as if he owned the town, the *Fairy Prince*, and the rest of Latin America. He called Bruno a "wite bum-m"and a lot of other things Bruno could not understand but which made everybody laugh. Bruno left the bar with dignity, too tired and disgusted to fight, with a quiet determination to report it to Alice and get the Puerto Rican fired and blacklisted. A block away from the ship, the Puerto Rican caught up with him and kept on talking. Then, crossing the gangplank, Bruno lurched against the handrope and fell off into the filthy water. He couldn't say the Puerto Rican had pushed him, because he hadn't. The Puerto Rican and another sailor, also laughing, fished him out and dragged him in to his bed. Bruno crawled off the bed and got his bottle of rum. He drank some straight, then flopped on the bed and fell asleep in his wet underwear.

Later, his mother and Alice came in and shook him awake.

"What happened?" they kept asking, giggling so they could hardly talk. "What happened, Charley?"

Their figures were fuzzy but their laughs were sharp. He recoiled from Alice's fingers on his shoulder. He couldn't talk, but he knew what he wanted to say. What were they doing in his room if they didn't have a message from Guy?

"What? What guy?" asked his mother.

"G'way!" he shouted, and he meant both of them.

"Oh, he's out," said his mother deploringly, as if he were a hospital case nearly dead. "Poor boy. Poor, poor boy."

Bruno jerked his head this way and that to avoid the cool washcloth. He hated them both and he hated Guy! He had killed for him, dodged police for him, kept quiet when he asked him to, fallen in the stinking water for him, and Guy didn't even want to see him! Guy spent his time with a girl! Guy wasn't scared or unhappy, just didn't have time for him! Three times he had seen her around Guy's house in New York! If he had her here, he would kill her just like he had killed Miriam!

"Charley, Charley, hush!"

Guy would get married again and never have time for him. See what sympathy he'd get now when this girl played him for a sucker! He'd been seeing her in Mexico, not just visiting friends. No wonder he'd wanted Miriam out of the way! And he hadn't even mentioned Anne Faulkner on the train! Guy had used him. Maybe Guy would kill his father whether he liked it or not. Anybody can do a murder. Guy hadn't believed it, Bruno remembered.

# *twenty*

"Have a drink with me," Bruno said. He had appeared out of nowhere, in the middle of the sidewalk.

"I don't care to see you. I'm not asking questions. I don't care to see you."

"I don't care if you ask questions," Bruno said with a weak smile. His eyes were wary. "Come across the street. Ten minutes."

Guy glanced around him. Here he is, Guy thought. Call the police. Jump him, throw him down to the sidewalk. But Guy only stood rigidly. He saw that Bruno's hands were rammed in his pockets, as if he might have a gun.

"Ten minutes," Bruno said, luring him with the tentative smile.

Guy hadn't heard a word from Bruno in weeks. He tried to summon back the anger of that last evening in the snow, of his decision to turn Bruno over to the police. This was the critical moment. Guy came with him. They walked into a bar on Sixth Avenue and took a back booth.

Bruno's smile grew wider. "What're you scared about, Guy?"

"Not a thing."

"Are you happy?"

Guy sat stiffly on the edge of his seat. He was sitting opposite a murderer, he thought. Those hands had crushed Miriam's throat.

"Listen, Guy, why didn't you tell me about Anne?"

"What about Anne?"

"I'd have liked to know about her, that's all. On the train, I mean."

"This is our last meeting, Bruno."

"Why? I just want to be friends, Guy."

"I'm going to turn you over to the police."

"Why didn't you do that in Metcalf?" Bruno asked with the lowest pink gleam in his eyes, as only he could have asked it, impersonally, sadly, yet with triumph. Oddly, Guy felt his inner voice had asked him the question in the same way.

"Because I wasn't sure enough."

"What do I have to do, make a written statement?"

"I can still turn you over for investigation."

"No, you can't. They've got more on you than on me." Bruno shrugged.

"What're you talking about?"

"What do you think they'd get on me? Nothing."

"I could tell them!" He was suddenly furious.

"If I wanted to say you paid me for it," Bruno frowned self-righteously, "the pieces would fit like hell!"

"I don't care about pieces."

"Maybe you don't, but the law does."

"What pieces?"

"That letter you wrote Miriam," Bruno said slowly, "the cover-up of that job canceling. The whole convenient trip to Mexico."

"You're insane!"

"Face it, Guy! You're not making any sense!" Bruno's voice rose hysterically over the jukebox that had started up near them. He pushed his hand flat across the table toward Guy, then closed it in a fist. "I like you, Guy, I swear. We shouldn't be talking like this!"

Guy did not move. The edge of the bench cut against the back of his legs. "I don't want to be liked by you."

"Guy, if you say anything to the police, you'll only land us both in prison. Don't you see?"

Guy had thought of it, even before now. If Bruno clung to his lies, there could be a long trial, a case that might never be decided unless Bruno broke down, and Bruno wouldn't break down. Guy could see it in the monomaniacal intensity with which Bruno stared at him now. Ignore him, Guy thought. Keep away. Let the police catch him. He's insane enough to kill you if you make a move.

"You didn't turn me in in Metcalf because you like me, Guy. You like me in a way."

"I don't like you in the least."

"But you're not going to turn me in, are you?"

"No," Guy said between his teeth. Bruno's calm amazed him. Bruno was not afraid of him at all. "Don't order me another drink. I'm leaving."

"Wait a minute." Bruno got money from his wallet and gave it to the waiter.

Guy sat on, held by a sense of inconclusiveness.

"Good-looking suit." Bruno smiled, nodding toward Guy's chest.

His new gray flannel chalk-stripe suit. Bought with the Palmyra money, Guy thought, like his new shoes and the new alligator brief case beside him on the seat.

"Where do you have to go?"

"Downtown." He was to meet a prospective client's representative at the Fifth Avenue Hotel at 7. Guy stared at Bruno's hard, wistful eyes, feeling sure Bruno thought he was on his way to meet Anne now. "What's your game, Bruno?"

"You know," Bruno said quietly. "What we talked about on the train. The exchange of victims. You're going to kill my father."

Guy made a sound of contempt. He had known it before Bruno said it, had suspected it since Miriam's death. He stared into Bruno's fixed, still wistful eyes, fascinated by their cool insanity. Once as a child he had stared at a mongoloid idiot on a streetcar, he remembered, like this, with a shameless curiosity that nothing could shake. Curiosity and fear.

"I told you I could arrange every detail." Bruno smiled at the corner of his mouth, amusedly, apolegetically. "It'd be very simple."

He hates me, Guy thought suddenly. He'd love to kill me, too.

"You know what I'll do if you don't." Bruno made a gesture of snapping his fingers, but his hand on the table was carelessly limp. "I'll just put the police onto you."

Ignore him, Guy thought, ignore him! "You don't frighten me in the least. It'd be the easiest thing in the world to prove you insane."

"I'm no more insane than you are!"

It was Bruno who ended the interview a moment later. He had a 7 o'clock appointment with his mother, he said.

The next encounter, so much shorter, Guy felt he lost, too, though at the time he thought he had won. Bruno tried to intercept him one Friday afternoon as he was leaving his office on the way to Long Island to see Anne. Guy simply brushed past him and climbed into a taxi. Yet a feeling of having physically run away shamed him, began to undermine a certain dignity that had up to then been intact. He wished he had said something to Bruno. He wished he had faced him for an instant.

## *twenty-one*

In the next days, there was hardly an evening when Bruno was not standing on the sidewalk across the street from his office building. Or if not there, standing across the street from where he lived, as if Bruno knew the evenings he would come straight home. There was never a word now, never a sign, only the tall figure with the hands in the pockets of the long, rather military overcoat that fit him closely, like a stovepipe. There was only the eyes following him, Guy knew, though he did not look back until he was out of sight. For two weeks. Then the first letter came.

It was two sheets of paper: the first a map of Bruno's house and the grounds and roads around it and the course Guy would take, neatly drawn with dotted and ruled ink lines, and the second a typed, closely written letter lucidly setting forth the plan for the murder of Bruno's father. Guy tore it up, then immediately regretted it. He should have kept it as evidence against Bruno. He kept the pieces.

But there was no need to have kept them. He received such a letter every two or three days. They were all mailed from Great Neck, as if Bruno stayed out there now—he had not seen Bruno since the letters began—writing perhaps on his father's typewriter the letters that must have taken him two or three hours to prepare. The letters were sometimes drunken. It showed in the typing mistakes and in the emotional bursts of the last paragraphs. If he were sober, the last paragraph was affectionate and reassuring as to the ease of the murder. If he were drunk, the paragraph was either a gush of brotherly love or a threat to haunt Guy all his life, ruin his career and his "love affair," and a reminder that Bruno had the upper hand. All the necessary information might have been gotten from any one of the letters, as if Bruno anticipated he might tear most of them up unopened. But despite his determination to tear up the next, Guy would open it when it came, curious as to the variations in the last paragraph. Of Bruno's three plans, the one with a gun, using the back entrance of the house, came most often, though each letter invited him to take his choice.

The letters affected him in a perverse way. After the shock of the first, the next few bothered him hardly at all. Then as the tenth, twelfth, fifteenth appeared in his mailbox, he felt they hammered at his consciousness on his nerves in a manner that he could not analyze. Alone in his room he would spend quarter hours trying to isolate his injury and repair it. His anxiety was unreasonable, he told himself, unless he thought Bruno would turn on him and try to murder him. And he didn't really. Bruno had never threatened that. But reasoning could not alleviate the anxiety, or make it less exhausting.

The twenty-first letter mentioned Anne. "You wouldn't like Anne to know your part in Miriam's murder, would you? What girl would marry a murderer? Certainly not Anne. The time is getting short. The first two weeks in March is my deadline. Until then it would be easy."

Then the gun came. It was handed him by his landlady, a big package in brown paper. Guy gave a short laugh when the black gun toppled out. It was a big Luger, shiny and new-looking except for a chip off the crosshatched handle.

Some impulse made Guy take his own little revolver from the back of his top drawer, made him heft his own beautiful pearl-handled gun over his bed where the Luger lay. He smiled at his action, then brought the Texas gun up closer to his eyes and studied it. He had seen it in a glutted pawnshop window on lower Main Street in Metcalf when he was about fifteen, and had bought it with money from his paper route, not because it was a gun but because it was beautiful. Its compactness, the economy of its short barrel had delighted him. The more he had learned of mechanical design, the more pleased he had been with his gun. He had kept it in various top drawers for fifteen years. He opened the chamber and removed the bullets, three of them, and turned the cylinder around with six pulls of the trigger, admiring the deep pitched clicks of its perfect machinery. Then he slipped the bullets back, put the gun into its lavender-colored flannel bag, and replaced it in his drawer.

How should he get rid of the Luger? Drop it over an embankment into the river? Into some ashcan? Throw it out with his trash? Everything he thought of seemed either suspect or melodramatic. He decided to slip it under his socks and underwear in a bottom drawer until something better occurred to him. He thought suddenly of Samuel Bruno, for the first time as a person. The presence of the Luger brought the man and his potential death into juxtaposition in his mind. Here in his room was the complete picture of the man and his life, according to Bruno, the plan for his murder—a letter had been waiting in his box that morning, too, and lay on his bed now unopened—and the gun with which he was supposed to kill him. Guy got one of Bruno's recent letters from among a few in the bottom drawer.

> Samuel Bruno [Bruno seldom referred to him as "my father"] is the finest example of the worst that America produces. He comes of low-class peasants in Hungary, little better than animals. He picked a wife of good family, with his usual greed, once he could afford her. All this time my mother quietly bore his unfaithfulness, having some concept of the sacredness of marriage contract. Now in his old age he tries to act pius before it is too late, but it is too late. I wish I could kill him myself but I have explained to you due to Gerard, his private detective, it is impossible. If you ever had anything to do with him, he would be your personal enemy, too. He is the kind of man who thinks all your

ideas about architecture as beauty and about adiquate houses for everyone are idiotic & doesn't care what kind of factory he has as long as the roof doesn't leak and ruin his machinery. It may interest you to know his employees are on strike now. See *N.Y. Times* last Thurs. p. 31 bottom left. They are striking for a living wage. Samuel Bruno does not hesitate to rob his own son . . .

Who would believe such a story if he told it? Who would accept such fantasy? The letter, the map, the gun— They seemed like props of a play, objects arranged to give a verisimilitude to a story that wasn't real and never could be real. Guy burnt the letter. He burnt all the letters he had, then hurried to get ready for Long Island.

He and Anne were going to spend the day driving, walking in the woods, and tomorrow drive up to Alton. The house would be finished by the end of March, which would give them a leisurely two months before the wedding to furnish it. Guy smiled as he gazed out the train window. Anne had never said she wanted a June wedding; it was simply drifting that way. She had never said she wanted a formal wedding, only, "Let's not have anything too slapdash." Then when he had told her he wouldn't mind a formal wedding if she wouldn't, she had let out a long "Oh-h!" and grabbed him and kissed him. No, he didn't want another three-minute wedding with a stranger for a witness. He began sketching on the back of an envelope the twenty-story office building he had learned last week he had a good chance of being commissioned for, that he had been saving as a surprise for Anne. He felt the future had suddenly become the present. He had everything he wanted. Running down the platform steps, he saw Anne's leopard coat in the little crowd by the station door. Always he would remember the times she waited for him here, he thought, the shy dance of impatience she did when she caught sight of him, the way she smiled and half turned round, as if she wouldn't have waited half a minute longer.

"Anne!" He put his arm around her and kissed her cheek.

"You didn't wear a hat."

He smiled because it was exactly what he had expected her to say. "Well, neither did you."

"I'm in the car. And it's snowing."She took his hand and they ran across the crisp ash lane toward the cars. "I've got a surprise!"

"So have I. What's yours?"

"Sold five designs yesterday on my own."

Guy shook his head. "I can't beat that. I've just got one office building. Maybe."

She smiled and her eyebrows went up. "Maybe? Yes!"

"Yes, yes, yes!" he said, and kissed her again.

That evening, standing on the little wooden bridge over the stream back of Anne's house, Guy started to say, "Do you know what Bruno sent me today? A gun." Then, not that he had come close to saying it, but the remoteness of Bruno and his connection with him from his and Anne's life shocked him with a terrible realization. He wanted no secrets from Anne, and here was one bigger than all he had told her. Bruno, the name that haunted him, would mean nothing to Anne.

"What is it, Guy?"

She knew there was something, he thought. She always knew. "Nothing."

He followed her as she turned and walked toward the house. The night had blackened the earth, made the snowy ground hardly distinguishable from woods and sky. And Guy felt it again—the sense of hostility in the clump of woods east of the house. Before him, the kitchen door spilled a warm yellow light some way onto the lawn. Guy turned again, letting his eyes rest on the blackness where the woods began. The feeling he had when he gazed there was discomforting and relieving at once, like biting on an ailing tooth.

"I'll walk around again," he said.

Anne went in, and he turned back. He wanted to see if the sensation were stronger or weaker when Anne was not with him. He tried to feel rather than see. It was still there, faint and evasive, where the darkness deepened at the baseline of the woods. Nothing of course. What chance combination of shadow and sound and his own thoughts had created it?

He slipped his hands into his overcoat pockets and moved stubbornly closer.

The dull snap of a twig plummeted his consciousness to earth, focused it at a certain point. He sprinted toward it. A crackling of bushes now, and a moving black figure in the blackness. Guy released all his muscles in a long dive, caught it, and recognized the hoarse intake of breath as Bruno's. Bruno plunged in his arms like a great powerful fish underwater, twisted and hit him an agonizing blow on the cheekbone. Clasping each other, they both fell, fighting to free arms, fighting as if they both fought death. Bruno's fingers scratched frenziedly at his throat, though Guy kept his arms straight. Bruno's breath hissed in and out between his drawn-back lips. Guy hit the mouth again with his right fist that felt broken, that would no longer close.

"Guy!" Bruno burst out indignantly.

Guy caught him by the front of his collar. Suddenly they both stopped fighting.

"You knew it was me!" Bruno said in a fury. "Dirty bastard!"

"What're you doing here?" Guy pulled him to his feet.

The bleeding mouth spread wider, as if he were going to cry. "Lemme go!"

Guy shoved him. He fell like a sack to the ground and tottered up again.

"Okay, kill me if you want to! You can say it's self-defense!" Bruno whined.

Guy glanced toward the house. They had struggled a long way into the woods. "I don't want to kill you. I'll kill you next time I find you here."

Bruno laughed, the single victorious clap.

Guy advanced menacingly. He did not want to touch Bruno again. Yet a moment before, he had fought with "Kill, kill!" in his mind. Guy knew there was nothing he could do to stop Bruno's smile, not even kill him. "Clear out."

"You ready to do that job in two weeks?"

"Ready to turn you over to the police."

"Ready to turn yourself over?" Bruno jeered shrilly. "Ready to tell Anne all about it, huh? Ready to spend the next twenty years in jail? Sure, I'm ready!" He brought his palms together gently. His eyes seemed to glow with a red light. His swaying figure was like that of an evil spirit's that might have stepped from the twisted black tree behind him.

"Get someone else for your dirty work," Guy muttered.

"Look who's talking! I want you and I've got you! Okay!" A laugh. "I'll start. I'll tell your girl friend all about it. I'll write her tonight." He lurched away, tripped heavily, and staggered on, a loose and shapeless thing. He turned and shouted, "Unless I hear from *you* in a day or so."

Guy told Anne he had fought with a prowler in the woods. He suffered only a reddened eye from the battle, but he saw no way to stay on at the house, not go to Alton tomorrow, except by feigning injury. He had been hit in the stomach, he said. He didn't feel well. Mr. and Mrs. Faulkner were alarmed, and insisted to the policeman who came to look over the grounds that they have a police guard for the next few nights. But a guard was not enough. If Bruno came back, Guy wanted to be there himself. Anne suggested that he stay on Monday, so he would have someone to look after him in case he were sick. Guy did stay on.

Nothing had ever shamed him so much, he thought, as the two days in the Faulkner house. He was ashamed that he felt the need to stay, ashamed that on Monday morning he went into Anne's room and looked on the writing table where the maid put her mail to see if Bruno had written. He hadn't. Anne left each morning for her shop in New York before the mail was delivered. On Monday morning, Guy looked through the four or five letters on her writing table, then hurried out like a thief, afraid the maid might see him. But he often came into her room when she was not there, he reminded himself. Sometimes when the house was filled with people, he would escape to Anne's room for a few moments. And she loved to find him there. At the threshold, he leaned his head back against the door jamb, picking out the disorder in the room—the unmade bed, the big art books that didn't fit in the bookshelves, her last designs thumbtacked to a strip of green cork down one wall, on the corner of the table a glass of bluish water that she had neglected to empty, the brown and yellow silk scarf over the chair back, that she had evidently changed her mind about. The gardenia scent of the cologne she had touched to her neck at the last moment still lingered in the air. He longed to merge his life with hers.

Guy stayed until Tuesday morning when there was no letter from Bruno either, and then went in to Manhattan. Work had piled up. A thousand things nettled him. The contract with the Shaw Realty Company for the new office building still had not been settled. He felt his life disorganized, without direction, more chaotic than when he had heard of Miriam's murder. There was no letter from Bruno that week except one that awaited him, that had arrived Monday. It was a short note saying thank God his mother was better today and he could leave the house. His mother had been dangerously ill for three weeks with pneumonia, he said, and he had stayed with her.

Thursday evening when Guy got back from a meeting of an architectural club, his landlady Mrs. McCausland said he had had three calls. The telephone rang as they stood in the hall. It was Bruno, sullen and drunk. He asked if Guy was ready to talk sense.

"I didn't think so," Bruno said. "I've written Anne." And he hung up.

Guy went upstairs and took a drink himself. He didn't believe Bruno had written or intended to write. He tried for an hour to read, called Anne to ask how she was, then restlessly went out and found a late movie.

On Saturday afternoon, he was supposed to meet Anne in Hempstead, Long Island, to see a dog show there. If Bruno had written the letter, Anne would have gotten it by Saturday morning, Guy thought. But obviously she hadn't. He could tell from her wave to him from the car where she sat waiting for him. He asked her if she had enjoyed the party last night at Teddy's. Her cousin Teddy had had a birthday.

"Wonderful party. Only no one wanted to go home. It got so late I stayed over. I haven't even changed my clothes yet." And she shot the car through the narrow gate and into the road.

Guy closed his teeth. The letter might be waiting for her at home then. All at once, he felt sure the letter *would* be waiting for her, and the impossibility of stopping it now made him weak and speechless.

He tried desperately to think of something to say as they walked along the rows of dogs.

"Have you heard anything from the Shaw people?" Anne asked him.

"No." He stared at a nervous dachshund and tried to listen as Anne said something about a dachshund that someone in her family had.

She didn't know yet, Guy thought, but if she didn't know by today, it would be only a matter of time, a matter of a few days more, perhaps, until she did know. Know what, he kept asking himself, and going over the same answer, whether for reassurance or self-torture, he did not know: that on the train last summer he had met the man who murdered his wife, that he had consented to the murder of his wife.

That was what Bruno would tell her, with certain details to make it convincing. And in a courtroom, for that matter, if Bruno distorted only slightly their conversation on the train, couldn't it amount to an agreement between murderers? The hours in Bruno's compartment, that tiny hell, came back suddenly very clearly. It was hatred that had inspired him to say as much as he had, the same petty hatred that had made him rage against Miriam in Chapultepec Park last June. Anne had been angry then, not so much at what he had said as at his hatred. Hatred, too, was a sin. Christ had preached against hatred as against adultery and murder. Hatred was the very seed of evil. In a Christian court of justice, wouldn't he be at least partially guilty of Miriam's death? Wouldn't Anne say so?

"Anne," he interrupted her. He had to prepare her, he thought. And he had to *know*. "If someone were to accuse me of having had a part in Miriam's death, what would you—? Would you—?"

She stopped and looked at him. The whole world seemed to stop moving, and he and Anne stood at its still center.

"Had a part? What do you mean, Guy?"

Someone jostled him. They were in the middle of the walk.

"Just that. Accused me, nothing more."

She seemed to search for words.

"Just accused me,"Guy kept on. "I just want to know. Accused me for no reason. It wouldn't matter, would it?" Would she still marry him, he wanted to ask, but it was such a pitiful, begging question, he could not ask it.

"Guy, why do you say that?"

"I just want to know, that's all!"

She pressed him back so they would be out of the traffic of the path. "Guy, *has* someone accused you?"

"No!"he protested. He felt awkward and vexed. "But if someone did, if someone tried to make out a strong case against me—"

She looked at him with that flash of disappointment, of surprise and mistrust that he had seen before when he said or did something out of anger, or out of a resentment, that Anne did not approve, did not understand. "Do you expect someone to?" she asked.

"I just want to know!" He was in a hurry and it seemed so simple!

"At times like this," she said quietly, "you make me feel we're complete strangers."

"I'm sorry," he murmured. He felt she had cut an invisible bond between them.

"I don't think you're sorry, or you wouldn't keep on doing this!" She looked straight at him, keeping her voice low though her eyes had filled with tears. "It's like that day in Mexico when you indulged yourself in that tirade against Miriam. I don't care— I don't like it, I'm not that kind of person! You make me feel I don't know you at all!"

Don't love you, Guy thought. It seemed she gave him up then, gave up trying to know him or to love him. Desperate, slipping, Guy stood there unable to make a move or say a word.

"Yes, since you ask me," Anne said, "I think it would make a difference if someone accused you. I'd want to ask why you expected it. Why do you?"

"I don't!"

She turned away from him, walked to the blind end of the lane, and stood with her head bent.

Guy came after her. "Anne you do know me. You know me better than anyone in the world knows me. I don't want any secrets from you. It came to my mind and I asked you!" He felt he made a confession, and with the relief that followed it, he felt suddenly sure—as sure as he had been before that Bruno had written the letter—that Bruno hadn't and wouldn't.

She brushed a tear from the corner of her eye quickly, indifferently. "Just one thing, Guy. Will you stop expecting the worst—about everything?"

"Yes," he said. "God, yes."

"Let's go back to the car."

He spent the day with Anne, and they had dinner that evening at her house. There was no letter from Bruno. Guy put the possibility from his mind, as if he had passed a crisis.

On Monday evening at about 8, Mrs. McCausland called him to the telephone. It was Anne.

"Darling—I guess I'm a little upset."

"What's the matter?" He knew what was the matter.

"I got a letter. In this morning's mail. About what you were talking about Saturday."

"What is it, anne?"

"About Miriam—typewritten. And it's not signed."

"What does it say? Read it to me."

Anne read shakily, but in her distinct speech, "'Dear Miss Faulkner, It may interest you to know that Guy Haines had more to do with his wife's murder than the law thinks at present. But the truth will out. I think you should know in case you have any plans for marrying such a dual personality. Apart from that, this writer knows that Guy Haines will not remain a free man much longer.' Signed,'A friend.'"

Guy closed his eyes. "God!"

"Guy, do you know who it could be?—Guy? Hello?"

"Yes," he said.

"Who?"

He knew from her voice she was merely frightened, that she believed in him, was afraid only for him. "I don't know, Anne."

"Is that true, Guy?" she asked anxiously. "You should know. Something should be done."

"I don't know," Guy repeated, frowning. His mind seemed tied in an inextricable knot.

"You must know. *Think*, Guy. Someone you might call an enemy?"

"What's the postmark?"

"Grand Central. It's perfectly plain paper. You can't tell a thing from that."

"Save it for me."

"Of course, guy. And I won't tell anyone. The family, I mean." A pause. "There *must* be someone, Guy. You suspected someone Saturday —didn't you?"

"I didn't."His throat closed up. "Sometimes these things happen, you know, after a trial."And he was aware of a desire to cover Bruno as carefully as if Bruno had been himself, and he guilty. "When can I see you, Anne? Can I come out tonight?"

"Well, I'm—sort of expected to go with Mother and Dad to a benefit thing. I can mail you the letter. Special delivery, you'll get it tomorrow morning."

So it came the next morning, along with another of Bruno's plans, and an affectionate but exhorting last paragraph in which he mentioned the letter to Anne and promised more.

## *twenty-two*

Guy sat up on the edge of his bed, covered his face in his hands, then deliberately brought his hands down. It was the night that took up the body of his thoughts and distorted it, he felt, the night and the darkness and the sleeplessness. Yet the night had its truth also. In the night, one approached truth merely at a certain slant, but all truth was the same. If he told Anne the story, wouldn't she consider he had been partially guilty? Marry him? How could she? What sort of beast was he that he could sit in a room where a bottom drawer held plans for a murder and the gun to do it with?

In the frail predawn light, he studied his face in the mirror. The mouth slanted downward to the left, unlike his. The full underlip was thinner with tension. He tried to hold his eyes to an absolute steadiness. They stared back above pallid semicircles, like a part of him that had hardened with accusation, as if they gazed at their torturer.

Should he dress and go out for a walk or try to sleep? His step on the carpet was light, unconsciously avoiding the spot by the armchair where the floor squeaked. *You would skip these squeaking steps just for safety*, Bruno's letters said. *My father's door is just to the right as you know. I have gone over everything and there is no room for a hitch anywhere. See on map where the butler's (Herbert's) room is. This is the closest you'll come to anyone. The hall floor squeaks there where I marked X.* . . . He flung himself on the bed. *You should not try to get rid of the Luger no matter what happens between the house and the RR station.* He knew it all by heart, knew the sound of the kitchen door and the color of the hall carpet.

If Bruno should get someone else to kill his father, he would have ample evidence in these letters to convict Bruno. He could avenge himself for what Bruno had done to him. Yet Bruno would merely counter with his lies that would convict him of planning Miriam's murder. No, it would be only a matter of time until Bruno got someone. If he could weather Bruno's threats only a while longer, it would all be over and he could sleep. If he did it, he thought, he wouldn't use the big Luger, he would use the little revolver—

Guy pulled himself up from the bed, aching, angry, and frightened by the words that had just passed through his mind. "The Shaw Building," he said to himself, as if announcing a new scene, as if he could derail himself from the night's tracks and set himself on the day's. *The Shaw Building. The ground is all grass covered to the steps in back, except for gravel you won't have to touch. . . . Skip four, skip three, step wide at the top. You can remember it, it's got a syncopated rhythm.*

*"Mr. Haines!"*

Guy started, and cut himself. He laid his razor down and went to the door.

"Hello, Guy. Are you ready yet?" asked the voice on the telephone, lewd in the early morning, ugly with the complexities of night. "Want some more?"

"You don't bother me."

Bruno laughed.

Guy hung up, trembling.

The shock lingered through the day, tremulous and traumatic. He wanted desperately to see Anne that evening, wanted desperately that instant of glimpsing her from some spot where he had promised to wait. But he wanted also to deprive himself of her. He took a long walk up Riverside Drive to tire himself, but slept badly nevertheless, and had a series of unpleasant dreams. It would be different, Guy thought, once the Shaw contract was signed, once he could go ahead on his work.

Douglas Frear of the Shaw Realty Company called the next morning as he had promised. "Mr. Haines," said his slow, hoarse voice,"we've received a most peculiar letter concerning you."

"What? What kind of a letter?"

"Concerning your wife. I didn't know—Shall I read it to you?"

"Please."

"'To Whom It May Concern: No doubt it will interest you to learn that Guy Daniel Haines, whose wife was murdered last June, had more of a role in the deed than the courts know. This is from one who knows, and who knows also that there will be a retrial soon which will show his real part in the crime.'—I trust it's a crank letter, Mr. Haines. I just thought you should know about it."

"Of course." In the corner, Myers worked over his drawing board as calmly as on any other morning of the week.

"I think I heard about—uh—the tragedy last year. There's no question of a retrial, is there?"

"Certainly not. That is, I've heard nothing about it." Guy cursed his confusion. Mr. Frear wanted only to know if he would be free to work.

"Sorry we haven't quite made up our minds on that contract, Mr. Haines."

The Shaw Realty Company waited until the following morning to tell him they weren't entirely satisfied with his drawings. In fact, they were interested in the work of another architect.

How had Bruno found out about the building, Guy wondered. But there were any number of ways. It might have been mentioned in the papers—Bruno kept himself well informed on architectural news—or Bruno might have called when he knew he was out of the office, casually gotten the information from Myers. Guy looked at Myers again, and wondered if he had ever spoken on the telephone with Bruno. The possibility had a flavor of the unearthly.

Now that the building was gone, he began to see it in terms of what it would not mean. He would not have the extra money he had counted on by summer. Nor the prestige, the prestige with the Faulkner family. It did not once occur to him—as much at the root of his anguish as any of the other reasons—that he had suffered frustration in seeing a creation come to nothing.

It would be only a matter of time until Bruno informed the next client, and the next. This was his threat to ruin his career. And his life with Anne? Guy thought of her with a flash of pain. It seemed to him that he was forgetting for long intervals that he loved her. Something was happening between them, he could not say what. He felt Bruno was destroying his courage to love. Every slightest thing deepened his anxiety, from the fact he had lost his best pair of shoes by forgetting what repair shop he had taken them to, to the house at Alton, which already seemed more than they should have taken on, which he doubted they could fill.

In the office, Myers worked on his routine, drafting agency jobs, and Guy's telephone never rang. Once Guy thought, even Bruno doesn't call because he wants it to build up and build up, so his voice will be welcome when it comes. And disgusted with himself, Guy went down in the middle of the day and drank martinis in a Madison Avenue bar. He was to have had lunch with Anne, but she had called and broken the appointment, he could not remember why. She had not sounded precisely cool, but he thought she had not given any real reason for not lunching with him. She certainly hadn't said she was going shopping for something for the house, or he would have remembered it. Or would he have? Or was she retaliating for his breaking his promise to come out to dinner with her family last Sunday? He had been too tired and too depressed to see anyone last Sunday. A quiet, unacknowledged quarrel seemed to be going on between himself and Anne. Lately, he felt too miserable to inflict himself on her, and she pretended to be too busy to see him when he asked to see her. She was busy planning for the house, and busy quarreling with him. It did not make sense. Nothing in the world made sense except to escape from Bruno. There was no way of doing that that made sense. What would happen in a court would not make sense.

He lighted a cigarette, then noticed he already had one. Hunched over the shiny black table, he smoked them both. His arms and hands with the cigarettes seemed mirrored. What was he doing here at 1:15 in the afternoon, growing swimmy on his third martini, making himself incapable of work, assuming he had any? Guy Haines who loved Anne, who had built the Palmyra? He hadn't even the courage to throw his martini glass into the corner. Quicksand. Suppose he sank completely. Suppose he did kill for Bruno. It would be so simple, as Bruno said, when the house was empty except for his father and the butler, and Guy knew the house more exactly than his home in Metcalf. He could leave clues against Bruno, too, leave the Luger in the room. This thought became a single point of concreteness. His fists closed reflexively against Bruno, then the impotence of his clenched hands before him on the table shamed him. He must not let his mind go there again. That was exactly what Bruno wanted his mind to do.

He wet his handkerchief in the glass of water and daubed his face. A shaving cut began to sting. He looked at it in the mirror beside him. It had started to bleed, a tiny red mark just to one side of the faint cleft in his chin. He wanted to throw his fist at the chin in the mirror. He jerked himself up and went to pay his bill.

But having been there once, it was easy for his mind to go there again. In the nights when he could not sleep, he enacted the murder, and it soothed him like a drug. It was not murder but an act he performed to rid himself of Bruno, the slice of a knife that cut away a malignant growth. In the night, Bruno's father was not a person but an object, as he himself was not a person but a force. To enact it, leaving the Luger in the room, to follow Bruno's progress to conviction and death, was a catharsis.

Bruno sent him an alligator billfold with gold corners and his initials G.D.H. inside. "I thought this looked like you, Guy," said the note inside. "Please don't make things tough. I am very fond of you. As ever, Bruno." Guy's arm moved to fling it into a trash-basket on the street, then he slipped it into his pocket. He hated to throw away a beautiful thing. He would think of something else to do with it.

That same morning, Guy declined an invitation to speak on a radio panel. He was in no condition to work and he knew it. Why did he even keep coming to the office? He would have been delighted to stay drunk all day, and especially all night. He watched his hand turning and turning the folded compass on his desk top. Someone had once told him that he had hands like a Capuchin monk. Tim O'Flaherty in Chicago. Once when they had sat eating spaghetti in Tim's basement apartment, talking of Le Corbusier and the verbal eloquence that seemed innate in architects, a natural concomitant of the profession, and how fortunate it was, because generally you had to talk your way. But it had all been possible then, even with Miriam draining him, merely a clean invigorating fight ahead, and somehow right with all its difficulties. He turned the compass over and over, sliding his fingers down it and turning it, until he thought the noise might be bothering Myers and stopped.

"Pull out of it, Guy," Myers said amiably.

"It isn't anything one snaps out of. One either cracks up or doesn't," Guy retorted with a dead calm in his voice, and then, unable to stop himself, "I don't want advice, Myers. Thanks."

"Listen, Guy—" Myers stood up, smiling, lanky, tranquil. But he did not come beyond the corner of his desk.

Guy got his coat from the tree by the door. "I'm sorry. Let's forget it."

"I know what's the matter. Pre-wedding nerves. I had them, too. What do you say we go down and have a drink?"

Myers' familiarity piqued a certain sense of dignity that Guy was never aware of until it was affronted. He could not bear to look at Myers' untroubled, empty face, his smug banality. "Thanks," he said,"I really don't feel like it." He closed the door softly behind him.

## *twenty-three*

Guy glanced again at the row of brownstones across the street, sure he had seen Bruno. His eyes smarted and swam, fighting the dusk. He *had* seen him, there by the black iron gate, where he was not. Guy turned and ran up his steps. He had tickets to a Verdi opera tonight. Anne was going to meet him at the theatre at 8:30. He didn't feel like seeing Anne tonight, didn't want Anne's kind of cheering, didn't want to exhaust himself pretending he felt better than he did. She was worried about his not sleeping. Not that she said much, but that little annoyed him. Above all, he didn't want to hear Verdi. Whatever had possessed him to buy tickets to Verdi? He had wanted to do something to please Anne, but at best she wouldn't like it very much, and wasn't there something insane about buying tickets for something neither of them liked?

Mrs. McCausland gave him a number he was supposed to call. He thought it looked like the number of one of Anne's aunts. He hoped Anne might be busy tonight.

"Guy, I don't see how I can make it,"Anne said. "These two people Aunt Julie wanted me to meet aren't coming until after dinner."

"All right."

"And I can't duck out on it."

"It's perfectly all right."

"I am sorry though. Do you know I haven't seen you since Saturday?"

Guy bit the end of his tongue. An actual repulsion against her clinging, her concern, even her clear, gentle voice that had before been like an embrace itself—all this seemed a revelation he no longer loved her.

"Why don't you take Mrs. McCausland tonight? I think it'd be nice if you did."

"Anne, I don't care at all."

"There haven't been any more letters, Guy?"

"No." The third time she had asked him!

"I do love you. You won't forget, will you?"

"No, Anne."

He fled upstairs to his room, hung up his coat and washed, combed his hair, and immediately there was nothing to do, and he wanted Anne. He wanted her terribly. Why had he been so mad as to think he didn't want to see her? He searched his pockets for Mrs. McCausland's note with the telephone number, then ran downstairs and looked for it on the hall floor. It had vanished—as if someone had deliberately snatched it away to thwart him. He peered through the etched glass of the front door. Bruno, he thought, Bruno had taken it.

The Faulkners would know her aunt's number. He would see her, spend the evening with her, even if it meant spending the evening with her Aunt Julie. The telephone in Long Island rang and rang and nobody answered. He tried again to think of her aunt's last name, and couldn't.

His room seemed filled with palpable, suspenseful silence. He glanced at the low bookshelves he had built around the walls, at the ivy Mrs. McCausland had given him in the wall brackets, at the empty red plush chair by the reading lamp, at his sketch in black and white over his bed entitled "Imaginary Zoo," at the monk's cloth curtains that concealed his kitchenette. Almost boredly he went and moved the curtains aside and looked behind them. He had a definite feeling someone was waiting for him in the room, though he was not in the least frightened. He picked up the newspaper and started to read.

A few moments later, he was in a bar drinking a second martini. He had to sleep, he reasoned, even if it meant drinking alone, which he despised. He walked down to Times Square, got a haircut, and on the way home bought a quart of milk and a couple of tabloids. After he wrote a letter to his mother, he thought, he would drink some milk, read the papers, and go to bed. Or there might even be Anne's telephone number on the floor when he came in. But there wasn't.

At about 2 in the morning, he got up from bed and wandered about the room, hungry and unwilling to eat. Yet one night last week, he remembered, he had opened a can of sardines and devoured them on the blade of a knife. The night was a time for bestial affinities, for drawing closer to oneself. He plucked a notebook from the bookshelf and turned through it hastily. It was his first New York notebook, when he was about twenty-two. He had sketched indiscriminately—the Chrysler Building, the Payne Whitney Psychiatric Clinic, barges on the East River, workmen leaning on electric drills that bit horizontally into rock. There was a series on the Radio City buildings, with notes on space, on the opposite page the same building with the amendations he would make, or perhaps an entirely new building of his own conception. He closed the book quickly because it was good, and he doubted if he could do as well now. The Palmyra seemed the last spurt of that generous, happy energy of his youth. The sob he had been suppressing contracted his chest with a sickening, familiar pain— familiar from the years after Miriam. He lay down on his bed in order to stop the next.

Guy awakened to Bruno's presence in the dark, though he heard nothing. After the first small start at the suddenness, he felt no surprise at all. As he had imagined, in nights before this, he was quite happy that Bruno had come. *Really* Bruno? Yes. Guy saw the end of his cigarette now, over by the bureau.

"Bruno?"

"Hi," Bruno said softly. "I got in on a pass key. You're ready now, aren't you?" Bruno sounded calm and tired.

Guy raised himself to one elbow. Of course Bruno was there. The orangey end of his cigarette was there. "Yes," Guy said, and felt the yes absorbed by the darkness, not like the other nights when the yes had been silent, not even going out from him. It undid the knot in his head so suddenly that it hurt him. It was what he had been waiting to say, what the silence in the room had been waiting to hear. And the beasts beyond the walls.

Bruno sat down on the side of the bed and gripped both his arms above the elbows. "Guy, I'll never see you again."

"No." Bruno smelled abominably of cigarettes and sweet brilliantine, of the sourness of drink, but Guy did not draw back from him. His head was still at its delicious business of untying.

"I tried to be nice to him these last couple days," Bruno said. "Not nice, just decent. He said something tonight to my mother, just before we went out—"

"I don't want to hear it!" Guy said. Time and again he had stopped Bruno because he didn't want to know what his father had said, what he looked like, anything about him.

They were both silent for several seconds, Guy because he would not explain, and Bruno because he had been silenced.

Bruno snuffled with a disgusting rattle. "We're going to Maine tomorrow, starting by noon positively. My mother and me and the chauffeur. Tomorrow night is a good night but any night except Thursday night is just the same. Any time after 11 . . ."

He kept talking, repeating what Guy knew already, and Guy did not stop him, because he knew he was going to enter the house and it would all come true.

"I broke the lock on the back door two days ago, slamming it when I was tight. They won't get it fixed, they're too busy. But if they do—" He pressed a key into Guy's hand. "And I brought you these."

"What is it?"

"Gloves. Ladies' gloves, but they'll stretch." Bruno laughed.

Guy felt the thin cotton gloves.

"You got the gun, huh? Where is it?"

"In the bottom drawer."

Guy heard him stumble against the bureau and heard the drawer pull out. The lampshade crackled, the light came on, and Bruno stood there huge and tall in a new polo coat so pale it was nearly white, in black trousers with a thin white stripe in them. A white silk muffler hung long around his neck. Guy examined him from his small brown shoes to his stringy oiled hair, as if from his physical appearance he could discover what had caused his change of feeling, or even what the feeling was. It was familiarity and something more, something brotherly. Bruno clicked the gun shut and turned to him. His face was heavier than the last time Guy had seen it, flushed and more alive than he remembered ever having seen it. His gray eyes looked bigger with his tears and rather golden. He looked at Guy as if he tried to find words, or as if he pled with Guy to find them. Then he moistened the thin parted lips, shook his head, and reached an arm out toward the lamp. The light went out.

When he was gone, it hardly seemed he was gone. There were just the two of them in the room still, and sleep.

• • •

A gray glaring light filled the room when Guy awakened. The clock said 3:25. He imagined more than remembered that he had gotten up to go to the telephone that morning, that Myers had called to ask why he had not come in, and that he had said he didn't feel well. The devil with Myers. He lay there blinking his dullness away, letting it seep into the thinking part of his brain that tonight he was going to do it, and after tonight it would all be over. Then he got up and slowly went about his routine of shaving, showering, and dressing, aware that nothing he did mattered at all until the hour between 11 and midnight, the hour there was neither hurry nor delay about, that was coming just as it should. He felt he moved on certain definite tracks now, and that he could not have stopped himself or gotten off them if he had wanted to.

In the middle of his late breakfast in a coffee shop down the street, an eerie sensation came over him that the last time he had seen Anne he had told her everything that he was going to do, and that she had listened placidly, knowing she must for his sake, because he absolutely had to do what he was going to do. It seemed so natural and inevitable, he felt everyone in the world must know it, the man sitting beside him unconcernedly eating, Mrs. McCausland, sweeping her hall as he went out, who had given him an especially maternal smile and asked if he was feeling well. March 12 FRIDAY, said the day-by-day calendar on the coffee-shop wall. Guy stared at it a moment, then finished his meal.

He wanted to keep moving. He decided by the time he walked up Madison Avenue, then Fifth to the end of Central Park, down Central Park West to Pennsylvania Station, it would be time to catch the train to Great Neck. He began to think of his course of action for tonight, but it bored him like something in school he had already studied too much, and he stopped. The brass barometers in a Madison Avenue window had a special appeal now, as if he were soon to have a holiday and possess them and play with them. Anne's sailboat, he thought, didn't have a barometer as handsome as any of these, or he would have noticed it. He must get one before they sailed south on their honeymoon. He thought of his love, like a rich possession. He had reached the north end of Central Park, when it occurred to him he didn't have the gun with him. Or the gloves. And it was a quarter to 8. A fine, stupid beginning! He hailed a cab and hurried the driver back to his house.

There was plenty of time after all, so much that he wandered about his room absently for a while. Should he bother to wear crepe-soled shoes? Should he wear a hat? He got the Luger out of the bottom drawer and laid it on the bureau. There was a single plan of Bruno's under the gun and he opened it, but immediately every word was so familiar, he threw it into the wastebasket. Momentum smoothed his movements again. He got the purple cotton gloves from the table by his bed. A small yellow card fluttered from them. It was a ticket to Great Neck.

He stared at the black Luger which more than before struck him as outrageously large. Idiotic of *someone* to have made a gun so big! He got his own little revolver from the top drawer. Its pearl handle gleamed with a discreet beauty. Its short slender barrel looked inquisitive, willing, strong with a reserved and gallant strength. Still, he mustn't forget he'd been going to leave the Luger in the bedroom, because it was Bruno's gun. But it didn't seem worth it now, to carry the heavy gun just for that. He really felt no enmity toward Bruno now, and that was the odd thing.

For a moment, he was utterly confused. Of course take the Luger, the Luger was in the plan! He put the Luger in his overcoat pocket. His hand moved for the gloves on the bureau top. The gloves were purple and the flannel bag of his revolver was lavender. Suddenly it seemed fitting he should take the small revolver, because of the similar colors, so he put the Luger back in the bottom drawer and dropped the little revolver into his pocket. He did not check to see if anything else should be done, because he could simply feel, having gone over Bruno's plans so often, that he had done everything. At last he got a glass of water and poured it into the ivy in the wall brackets. A cup of coffee might make him more alert, he thought. He would get one at the Great Neck station.

There was a moment on the train, when a man bumped his shoulder, when his nerves seemed to go quivering up and up to a pitch at which he thought something *must* happen, and a flurry of words rushed to his mind, almost to his tongue: *It's not really a gun in my pocket. I've never thought of it as a gun. I didn't buy it because it was a gun.* And immediately he felt easier, because he knew he was going to kill with it. He was like Bruno. Hadn't he sensed it time and time again, and like a coward never admitted it? Hadn't he known Bruno was like himself? Or why had he liked Bruno? He loved Bruno. Bruno had prepared every inch of the way for him, and everything would go well because everything always went well for Bruno. The world was geared for people like Bruno.

It was drizzling in a fine, directionless mist as he stepped off the train. Guy walked straight to the row of buses Bruno had described. The air through the open window was colder than New York's, and fresh with open country. The bus moved out of the lighted community center and into a darker road with houses along both sides. He remembered he hadn't stopped for coffee in the station. The omission threw him into a state of irritation just short of making him get off the bus and go back for it. A cup of coffee might make all the difference in the world. Yes, his life! But at the Grant Street stop, he stood up automatically, and the feeling of moving on established tracks returned to comfort him.

His step had a moist elastic sound on the dirt road. Ahead of him, a young girl ran up some steps, along a front walk, and the closing of the door behind her sounded peaceful and neighborly. There was the vacant lot with the solitary tree, and off to the left, darkness and the woods. The street lamp Bruno had put in all his maps wore an oily blue and gold halo. A car approached slowly, its headlights rolling like wild eyes with the road's bumps, and passed him.

He came upon it suddenly, and it was as if a curtain had lifted on a stage scene he knew already: the long seven-foot high wall of white plaster in the foreground, darkened here and there by a cherry tree that overhung it, and beyond, the triangle of white housetop. The Doghouse. He crossed the street. From up the road came the grit of slow steps. He waited against the darker north side of the wall until the figure came into view. It was a policeman, strolling with hands and stick behind him. Guy felt no alarm whatever, less if possible than if the man hadn't been a policeman, he thought. When the policeman had passed, Guy walked fifteen paces beside the wall, sprang up and gripped its cornice across the top, and scrambled astride it. Almost directly below him, he saw the pale form of the milk crate Bruno had said he had flung near the wall. He bent to peer through the cherry tree branches at the house. He could see two of the five big windows on the first floor, and part of the rectangle of the swimming pond projecting toward him. There was no light. He jumped down.

Now he could see the start of the six white-sided steps at the back, and the misty frill of blossomless dogwoood trees that surrounded the whole house. As he had suspected from Bruno's drawings, the house was too small for its ten double gables, obviously built because the client wanted gables and that was that. He moved along the inner side of the wall until crackling twigs frightened him. *Cut cattycornered across the lawn*, Bruno had said, and the twigs were why.

When he moved toward the house, a limb took his hat off. He rammed the hat in the front of his overcoat, and put his hand back in the pocket where the key was. When had he put the gloves on? He took a breath and moved across the lawn in a gait between running and walking, light and quick as a cat. I have done this many times before, he thought, this is only one of the times. He hesitated at the edge of the grass, glanced at the familiar garage toward which the gravel road curved, then went up the six back steps. The back door opened, heavy and smooth, and he caught the knob on the other side. But the second door with the Yale lock resisted, and a flush of something like embarrassment passed over him before he pushed harder and it yielded. He heard a clock on the kitchen table to his left. He knew it was a table, though he could see only blackness with less black forms of things, the big white stove, the servants' table and chairs left, the cabinets. He moved diagonally toward the back stairs, counting off his steps. *I would have you use the main stairway but the whole stairway creaks.* He walked slowly and stiffly, stretching his eyes, skirting the vegetable bins he did not really see. A sudden thought that he must resemble an insane somnambulist brought a start of panic.

*Twelve steps up first, skip seven. Then two little flights after the turn. . . . Skip four, skip three, step wide at the top. You can remember it, it's got a syncopated rhythm.* He skipped the fourth step in the first little flight. There was a round window just at the turn before the last flight. Guy remembered from some essay, *As a house is built so the pattern of activity of those will be who live in it. . . . Shall the child pause at the window for the view before he climbs fifteen steps to his playroom?* Ten feet ahead on his left was the butler's door. *This is the closest you'll come to anyone,* said Bruno in a crescendo as he passed the door's dark column.

The floor gave the tiniest wail of complaint, and Guy resiliently withdrew his foot, waited, and stepped around the spot. Delicately his hand closed on the knob of the hall door. As he opened it, the clock's tick on the landing of the main stairway came louder, and he realized he had been hearing it for several seconds. He heard a sigh.

A sigh on the main stairs!

A chime rang out. The knob rattled, and he squeezed it hard enough to break it, he thought. *Three. Four.* Close the door before the butler hears it! Was this why Bruno had said between 11 and midnight? Damn him! And now he didn't have the Luger! Guy closed the door with a *bump-bump.* While he sweated, feeling heat rise from his overcoat collar into his face, the clock kept on and on. And a last one.

Then he listened, and there was nothing but the deaf and blind *tick-tock* again, and he opened the door and went into the main hall. *My father's door is just to the right.* The tracks were back under him again. And surely he had been here before, in the empty hall that he could feel as he stared at Bruno's father's door, with the gray carpet, the paneled creamy walls, the marble table at the head of the stairs. The hall had a smell and even the smell was familiar. A sharp tickling sensation came at his temples. Suddenly he was sure the old man stood just the other side of the door, holding his breath just as he did, awaiting him. Guy held his own breath so long the old man must have died if he too had not breathed. Nonsense! Open the door!

He took the knob in his left hand, and his right moved automatically to the gun in his pocket. He felt like a machine, beyond danger and invulnerable. He had been here many, many times before, had killed him many times before, and this was only one of the times. He stared at the inch-wide crack in the door, sensing an infinite space opening out beyond, waiting until a feeling of vertigo passed. Suppose he couldn't *see* him when he got inside? Suppose the old man saw him first? *The night light on the front porch lights the room a little bit,* but the bed was over in the opposite corner. He opened the door wider, listened, and stepped too hastily in.

But the room was still, the bed a big vague thing in the dark corner, with a lighter strip at the head. He closed the door, *the wind might blow the door*, then faced the corner.

The gun was in his hand already, aimed at the bed that looked empty however he peered at it.

He glanced at the window over his right shoulder. It was open only about a foot, and Bruno had said it would be open *all the way*. Because of the drizzle. He frowned at the bed, and then with a terrible thrill made out the form of the head lying rather near the wall side, tipped sideways as if it regarded him with a kind of gay disdain. The face was darker than the hair which blended with the pillow. The gun was looking straight at it as he was.

One should shoot the chest. Obediently the gun looked at the chest. Guy slid his feet nearer the bed and glanced again at the window behind him. There was no sound of breathing. One would really not think he were alive. That was what he had told himself he must think, that the figure was merely a target. And that, because he did not know the target, it was like killing in war. Now?

"Ha-ha-ha-a!" from the window.

Guy trembled and the gun trembled.

The laugh had come from a distance, a girl's laugh, distant but clear and straight as a shot. Guy wet his lips. The aliveness of the laugh had swept away everything of the scene for a moment, left nothing in its place, and now slowly the vacuum was filling with his standing here about to kill. It had happened in the time of a heartbeat. Life. The young girl walking in the street. With a young man, perhaps. And the man asleep in the bed, living. *No, don't think! You do it for Anne, remember? For Anne and for yourself! It is like killing in war, like killing*—

He pulled the trigger. It made a mere click. He pulled again and it clicked. It was a trick! It was all false and didn't even exist! Not even his standing here! He pulled the trigger again.

The room tore up with a roar. His fingers tightened in terror. The roar came again, as if the crust of the world burst.

"Kagh!" said the figure on the bed. The gray face moved upward, showing the line of head and shoulders.

Guy was on the porch roof, falling. The sensation awakened him like the fall at the end of a nightmare. By a miracle an awning bar slid into one of his hands, and he fell downward again, onto hands and knees. He jumped off the porch edge, ran along the side of the house, then cut across the lawn, straight for the place where the milk crate was. He awakened to the clinging earth, to the hopelessness of his pumping arms that tried to hurry his race against the lawn. This is how it feels, how it is, he thought—*life*, like the laugh upstairs. The truth was that it is like a nightmare when one is paralyzed, against impossible odds.

"Hey!" a voice called.

The butler was after him, just as he had anticipated. He felt the butler was right behind him. The nightmare!

"Hey! Hey, there!"

Guy turned under the cherry trees and stood with his fist drawn back. The butler was not just behind him. He was a long way off, but he had seen him. The crazily running figure in white pajamas wavered like leaping smoke, then curved toward him. Guy stood, paralyzed, waiting.

"Hey!"

Guy's fist shot out for the oncoming chin, and the white wraith collapsed.

Guy jumped for the wall.

Darkness ran up higher and higher about him. He dodged a little tree, leapt what looked like a ditch, and ran on. Then suddenly he was lying face down and pain was spreading from the middle of him in all directions, rooting him to the ground. His body trembled violently, and he thought he must gather up the trembling and use it to run, that this wasn't where Bruno had said to go at all, but he could not move. *You just take the little dirt road (no lights there) eastward off Newhope south of the house and keep going across two bigger streets to Columbia Street and walk south (right)* . . . To the bus line that went to another railroad station. All very well for Bruno to write his damned instructions on paper. Damn him! He knew where he was now, in the field west of the house that never in any of the plans was to be used! He looked behind him. Which way was north now? What had happened to the street light? Maybe he wouldn't be able to find the little road in the dark. He didn't know whether the house lay behind him or to his left. A mysterious pain throbbed the length of his right forearm, so sharp he thought it should have glowed in the dark.

He felt as if he had been shattered apart with the explosion of the gun, that he could never gather the energy to move again, and that he really didn't care. He remembered his being hit in the football game in high school, when he had lain face down like this, speechless with pain. He remembered the supper, the very supper and the hot-water bottle his mother had brought to him in bed, and the touch of her hands adjusting the covers under his chin. His trembling hand was sawing itself raw on a half-buried rock. He bit his lip and kept thinking vacuously, as one thinks when only half awake on an exhausted morning, that he must get up in the next moment regardless of the agony because he wasn't safe. He was still so close to the house. And suddenly his arms and legs scrambled under him as if statics had built up a charge abruptly released, and he was running again across the field.

A strange sound made him stop—a low musical moan that seemed to come from all sides.

Police sirens, of course. And like an idiot he had thought first of an airplane! He ran on, knowing he was only running blindly and directly away from the sirens that were over his left shoulder now, and that he should veer left to find the little road. He must have run far beyond the long plaster wall. He started to cut left to cross the main road that surely lay in that direction, when he realized the sirens were coming up the road. He would either have to wait—He couldn't wait. He ran on, parallel to the cars. Then something caught his foot, and cursing, he fell again. He lay in a kind of ditch with his arms outspread, the right bent up on higher ground. Frustration maddened him to a petulant sob. His left hand felt odd. It was in water up to the wrist. It'll wet my wristwatch, he thought. But the more he intended to pull it out, the more impossible it seemed to move it. He felt two forces, one that would move the arm and another that would not, balancing themselves so perfectly his arm was not even tense. Incredibly, he felt he might have slept now. *The police will surround me*, he thought out of nowhere, and was up again, running.

Close on his right, a siren shrieked in triumph as if it had found him.

A rectangle of light sprang up in front of him, and he turned and fled it. A window. He had nearly run into a house. The whole world was awake! And he *had* to cross the road!

The police car passed thirty feet before him on the road, with a blink of headlights through bushes. Another siren moaned to his left, where the house must be, and droned away to silence. Stooping, Guy crossed the road not far behind the car and entered deeper darkness. No matter where the little road was now, he could run farther from the house in this direction. *There's sort of unlighted woods all around to the south, easy to hide in in case you have to get off the little road. . . . Do not try to get rid of the Luger no matter what happens between my house and the RR station.* His hand moved to his pocket and felt the cold of the little revolver through the holes in his gloves. He didn't remember putting the gun back in his pocket. It might have been lying on the blue carpet for all he knew! And suppose he had dropped it? A fine time to think of it!

Something had caught him and was holding him. He fought it automatically with his fists, and found it was bushes, twigs, briars, and kept fighting and hurling his body through it, because the sirens were still behind him and this was the only direction to go. He concentrated on the enemy ahead of him, and on both sides and even behind him, that caught at him with thousands of sharp tiny hands whose crackling began to drown out even the sirens. He spent his strength joyfully against them, relishing their clean, straight battle against him.

He awakened at the edge of a woods, face down on a downward sloping hill. Had he awakened, or had he fallen only a moment ago? But there was grayness in the sky in front of him, the beginning of dawn, and when he stood up, his flickering vision told him he had been unconscious. His fingers moved directly to the mass of hair and wetness that stood out from the side of his head. Maybe my head is broken, he thought in terror, and stood for a moment dully, expecting himself to drop dead.

Below, the sparse lights of a little town glowed like stars at dusk. Mechanically, Guy got out a handkerchief and wrapped it tight around the base of his thumb where a cut had oozed black-looking blood. He moved toward a tree and leaned against it. His eyes searched the town and the road below. There was not a moving thing. Was this he? Standing against the tree with the memory of the gun's explosion, the sirens, the fight against the woods? He wanted water. On the dirt road that edged the town, he saw a filling station. He made his way down toward it.

There was an old-fashioned pump beside the filling station. He held his head under it. His face stung like a mask of cuts. Slowly his mind grew clearer. He couldn't be more than two miles from Great Neck. He removed his right glove that hung by one finger and the wrist, and put it in his pocket. Where was the other? Had he left it in the woods where he tied his thumb? A rush of panic comforted him with its familiarity. He'd have to go back for it. He searched his overcoat pockets, opened his overcoat and searched his trousers pockets. His hat fell at his feet. He had forgotten about the hat, and suppose he had dropped that somewhere? Then he found the glove inside his left sleeve, no more than the seam of the top that still circled his wrist, and a tatter, and pocketed it with an abstract relief like happiness. He turned up a trousers cuff that had been torn down. He decided to walk in the direction he knew was southward, catch any bus farther southward, and ride until he came to a railroad station.

As soon as he realized his objective, pain set in. How could he walk the length of this road with these knees? Yet he kept walking, holding his head high to urge himself along. It was a time of dubious balance between night and day, still dark, though a low iridescence lay everywhere. The dark might still overcome the light, it seemed, because the dark was bigger. If the night could only hold this much until he got home and locked his door!

Then daylight made a sudden thrust at the night, and cracked the whole horizon on his left. A silver line ran around the top of a hill, and the hill became mauve and green and tan, as if it were opening its eyes. A little yellow house stood under a tree on the hill. On his right, a dark field had become high grass of green and tan, gently moving like a sea. As he looked, a bird flew out of the grass with a cry and wrote a fast, jagged, exuberant message with its sharp-pointed wings across the sky. Guy stopped and watched it until it disappeared.

## *twenty-four*

For the hundredth time, he examined his face in the bathroom mirror, patiently touched every scratch with the styptic pencil, and repowdered them. He ministered to his face and hands objectively, as if they were not a part of himself. When his eyes met the staring eyes in the mirror, they slipped away as they must have slipped away, Guy thought, that first afternoon on the train, when he had tried to avoid Bruno's eyes.

He went back and fell down on his bed. There was the rest of today, and tomorrow, Sunday. He needn't see anyone. He could go to Chicago for a couple of weeks and say he was away on a job. But it might seem suspicious if he left town the day after. *Yesterday. Last night.* Except for his scratched hands, he might have believed it one of his dreams that he had done it. Because he had not wanted to do it, he thought. It had not been his will. It had been Bruno's will, working through him. He wanted to curse Bruno, curse him aloud, but he simply had not the energy now. The curious thing was that he felt no guilt, and it seemed to him now that the fact Bruno's will had motivated him was the explanation. But what was this thing, guilt, that he had felt more after Miriam's death than now? Now he was merely tired, and unconcerned about anything. Or was this how anyone would feel after killing? He tried to sleep, and his mind retraced the moments on the Long Island bus, the two workmen who had stared at him, his pretense of sleep with the newspaper over his face. He had felt more shame with the workmen. . . .

His knees buckled on the front steps and he almost fell. He did not look to see if he were being observed. It seemed an ordinary thing he did, to go down and buy a paper. But he knew also he hadn't the strength to look to see if he were being observed, the strength even to care, and he dreaded the time when the strength would come, as a sick or wounded man dreads the next inevitable operation.

The *Journal-American* had the longest account, with a silhouette of the murderer, composed from the butler's description, of a man six feet one, weighing about one hundred and seventy to eighty pounds, wearing a dark overcoat and hat. Guy read it with mild surprise, as if it might not have been about him: he was only five nine and weighed about a hundred and forty. And he had not been wearing a hat. He skipped the part of the story that told who Samuel Bruno was, and read with greatest interest the speculation about the murderer's flight. North along Newhope Road, it said, where it was believed he lost himself in the town of Great Neck, perhaps taking the 12:18 a.m. train out. Actually, he had gone southeast. He felt suddenly relieved, safe. It was an illusion, he warned himself, safety. He stood up, for the first time as panicked as he had been when he floundered in the lot beside the house. The paper was several hours old. They could have found their mistake by now. They could be coming for him, right outside his door, by now. He waited, and there was no sound anywhere, and feeling tired again, he sat down. He forced himself to concentrate on the rest of the long column. The coolness of the murderer was stressed, and the fact it seemed to be an inside job. No fingerprints, no clue except some shoe prints, size nine and a half, and the smudge of a black shoe on the white plaster wall. His clothes, he thought, he must get rid of his clothes and immediately, but when would he find the energy to do it? It was odd they overestimated his shoe size, Guy thought, with the ground so wet. ". . . an unusually small caliber of bullet," the paper said. He must get rid of his revolver, too. He felt a little wrench of grief. He would hate that, how he would hate the instant he parted from his revolver! He pulled himself up and went to get more ice for the towel he was holding against his head.

Anne telephoned him in the late afternoon to ask him to go to a party with her Sunday night in Manhattan.

"Helen Heyburn's party. You know, I told you about it."

"Yes," Guy said, not remembering at all. His voice came evenly,"I guess I don't quite feel like a party, Anne."

For the last hour or so, he had felt numb. It made Anne's words distant, irrelevant. He listened to himself saying the right things, not even anticipating, or perhaps not even caring, that Anne might notice any difference. Anne said she might get Chris Nelson to go with her, and Guy said all right, and thought how happy Nelson would be to go with her because Nelson, who had used to see a great deal of Anne before she met Guy, was still in love with her, Guy thought.

"Why don't I bring in some delicatessen Sunday evening," Anne said, "and we'll have a snack together? I could have Chris meet me later."

"I thought I might go out Sunday, Anne. Sketching."

"Oh. I'm sorry. I had something to tell you."

"What?"

"Something I think you'll like. Well—some other time."

Guy crept up the stairs, alert for Mrs. McCausland. Anne was cool to him, he thought monotonously, Anne was cool. The next time she saw him, she would know and she would hate him. Anne was through, Anne was through. He kept chanting it until he fell asleep.

He slept until the following noon, then lay in bed the rest of the day in a torpor that made it agony even to cross the room to refill his towel with ice. He felt he would never sleep enough to get back his strength. Retracing, he thought. His body and mind retracing the long road they had traveled. Coming back to what? He lay rigid and afraid, sweating and shivering with fear. Then he had to get up to go to the bathroom. He had a slight case of diarrhea. From fear, he thought. As on a battlefield.

He dreamt in half-sleep that he crossed the lawn toward the house. The house was soft and white and unresisting as a cloud. And he stood there unwilling to shoot, determined to fight it to prove he could conquer it. The gunshot awakened him. He opened his eyes to the dawn in his room. He saw himself standing by his work table, exactly as he stood in the dream, pointing the gun at a bed in the corner, where Samuel Bruno struggled to sit up. The gun roared again. Guy screamed.

He sprang out of bed, staggering. The figure vanished. At his window was the same struggling light he had seen that dawn, the same mingling of life and death. The same light would come every dawn that he lived, would always reveal that room, and the room would grow more distinct with repetition, his horror sharper. Suppose he awakened every dawn that he lived?

The doorbell rang in the kitchenette.

The police are downstairs, he thought. This was just the time they *would* catch him, at dawn. And he didn't care, didn't care at all. He would make a complete confession. He would blurt it all out at once!

He leaned on the release button, then went to his door and listened.

Light quick steps ran up. Anne's steps. Rather the police than Anne! He turned completely around, stupidly drew his shade. He thrust his hair back with both hands and felt the knot on his head.

"Me," Anne whispered as she slipped in. "I walked over from Helen's. It's a wonderful morning!" She saw his bandage, and the elation left her face. "What happened to your hand?"

He stepped back in the shadow near his bureau. "I got into a fight."

"When? Last night? And your face, Guy!"

"Yes." He had to have her, had to keep her with him, he thought. He would perish without her. He started to put his arms around her, but she pushed him back, peering at him in the half light.

"Where, Guy? Who was it?"

"A man I don't even know," he said tonelessly, hardly realizing even that he lied, because it was so desperately necessary that he keep her with him. "In a bar. Don't turn on the light," he said quickly. "Please, Anne."

"In a bar?"

"I don't know how it happened. Suddenly."

"Someone you'd never seen before?"

"Yes."

"I don't believe you."

She spoke slowly, and Guy was all at once terrified, realizing she was a separate person from himself, a person with a different mind, different reactions.

"How can I?" she went on. "And why should I believe you about the letter, about not knowing who sent it?"

"Because it's true."

"Or the man you fought with on the lawn. Was it the same one?"

"No."

"You're keeping something from me, Guy." Then she softened, but each simple word seemed to attack him: "What is it, darling? You know I want to help you. But you've got to tell me."

"I've told you," he said, and set his teeth. Behind him, the light was changing already. If he could keep Anne now, he thought, he could survive every dawn. He looked at the straight, pale curtain of her hair, and put out his hand to touch it, but she drew back.

"I don't see how we can go on like this, Guy. We can't."

"It won't go on. It's over. I swear to you, Anne. Please believe me." The moment seemed a test, as if it were now or never again. He should take her in his arms, he thought, hold her fiercely until she stopped struggling against him. But he could not make himself move.

"How do you know?"

He hesitated. "Because it was a state of mind."

"That letter was a state of mind?"

"The letter contributed to it. I felt tied in a knot. It was my work, Anne!" He bowed his head. Nailing his sins to his work!

"You once said I made you happy," she said slowly, "or that I could in spite of anything. I don't see it anymore."

Certainly he did not make her happy, she meant to say. But if she could still love him now, how he would try to make her happy! How he would worship and serve her! "You do, Anne. I have nothing else." He bent lower with sudden sobs, shameless, wracking sobs that did not cease the long moment before Anne touched his shoulder. And though he was grateful, he felt like twisting away from the touch, too, because he felt it was only pity, only humanity that made her touch him at all.

"Shall I fix you some breakfast?"

Even in the note of exasperated patience he heard in her voice, there was a hint of forgiveness that meant total forgiveness, he knew. For fighting in a bar. Never, he thought, would she penetrate to Friday night, because it was already buried too deep for her or for any other person to go.

## *twenty-five*

"I don't give a damn what you think!" Bruno said, his foot planted in his chair. His thin blond eyebrows almost met with his frown, and rose up at the ends like the whiskers of a cat. He looked at Gerard like a golden, thin-haired tiger driven to madness.

"Didn't say I thought anything," Gerard replied with a shrug of hunched shoulders,"did I?"

"You implied."

"I did not imply." The round shoulders shook twice with his laugh. "You mistake me, Charles. I didn't mean you told anyone on purpose you were leaving. You let it drop by accident."

Bruno stared at him. Gerard had just implied that if it was an inside job, Bruno and his mother must have had something to do with it, and it certainly was an inside job. Gerard knew that he and his mother had decided only Thursday afternoon to leave Friday. The idea of getting him all the way down here in Wall Street to tell him that! Gerard didn't have anything, and he couldn't fool him by pretending that he had. It was another perfect murder.

"Mind if I shove off?" Bruno asked. Gerard was fooling around with papers on his desk as if he had something else to keep him here for.

"In a minute. Have a drink." Gerard nodded toward the bottle of bourbon on the shelf across the office.

"No, thanks."Bruno was dying for a drink, but not from Gerard.

"How's your mother?"

"You asked me that." His mother wasn't well, wasn't sleeping, and that was the main reason he wanted to get home. A hot resentment came over him again at Gerard's friend-of-the-family attitude. A friend of his father's maybe! "By the way, we're not hiring you for this, you know."

Gerard looked up with a smile on his round, faintly pink-and-purple mottled face. "I'd work on this case for nothing, Charles. That's how interesting I think it is." He lighted another of the cigars that were shaped something like his fat fingers, and Bruno noticed once more, with disgust, the gravy stains on the lapels of his fuzzy, light-brown suit and the ghastly marble-patterned tie. Every single thing about Gerard annoyed Bruno. His slow speech annoyed him. Memories of the only other times he had seen Gerard, with his father, annoyed him. Arthur Gerard didn't even look like the kind of a detective who was not supposed to look like a detective. In spite of his record, Bruno found it impossible to believe that Gerard was a top-notch detective. "Your father was a very fine man, Charles. A pity you didn't know him better."

"I knew him well," said Bruno.

Gerard's small, speckled tan eyes looked at him gravely. "I think he knew you better than you knew him. He left me several letters concerning you, your character, what he hoped to make of you."

"He didn't know me at all." Bruno reached for a cigarette. "I don't know why we're talking about this. It's beside the point and it's morbid." He sat down coolly.

"You hated your father, didn't you?"

"He hated me."

"But he didn't. That's where you didn't know him."

Bruno pushed his hand off the chair arm and it squeaked with sweat. "Are we getting anywhere or what're you keeping me here for? My mother's not feeling well and I want to get home."

"I hope she'll be feeling better soon, because I want to ask her some questions. Maybe tomorrow."

Heat rose up the sides of Bruno's neck. The next few weeks would be terrible on his mother, and Gerard would make it worse because he was an enemy of both of them. Bruno stood up and tossed his raincoat over one arm.

"Now I want you to try to think once more," Gerard wagged a finger at him as casually as if he still sat in the chair, "just where you went and whom you saw Thursday night. You left your mother and Mr. Templeton and Mr. Russo in front of the Blue Angel at 2:45 that morning. Where did you go?"

"Hamburger Hearth," Bruno sighed.

"Didn't see anyone you knew there?"

"Who should I know there, the cat?"

"Then where'd you go?" Gerard checked on his notes.

"Clarke's on Third Avenue."

"See anyone there?"

"Sure, the bartender."

"The bartender said he didn't see you," Gerard smiled.

Bruno frowned. Gerard hadn't said that a half an hour ago. "So what? The place was crowded. Maybe I didn't see the bartender either."

"All the barmen know you in there. They said you weren't in Thursday night. Furthermore, the place wasn't crowded. Thursday night? Three or 3:30?—I'm just trying to help you remember, Charles."

Bruno compressed his lips in exasperation. "Maybe I wasn't in Clarke's. I usually go over for a nightcap, but maybe I didn't. Maybe I went straight home, I don't know. What about all the people my mother and I talked to Friday morning? We called up a lot of people to say good-by."

"Oh, we're covering those. But seriously, Charles—" Gerard leaned back, crossed a stubby leg, and concentrated on puffing his cigar to life—"you wouldn't leave your mother and her friends just to get a hamburger and go straight home by yourself, would you?"

"Maybe. Maybe it sobered me up."

"Why're you so vague?" Gerard's Iowan accent made his "r" a snarl.

"So what if I'm vague? I've got a right to be vague if I was tight!"

"The point is—and of course it doesn't matter whether you were at Clarke's or some other place—*who* you ran into and told you were leaving for Maine the next day. You must think yourself it's funny your father was killed the night of the same day you left."

"I didn't see anyone. I invite you to check up on everyone I know and ask them."

"You just wandered around by yourself until after 5 in the morning."

"Who said I got home after 5?"

"Herbert. Herbert said so yesterday."

Bruno sighed. "Why didn't he remember all that Saturday?"

"Well, as I say, that's how the memory works. Gone—and then it comes. Yours'll come, too. Meanwhile, I'll be around. Yes, you can go now, Charles." Gerard made a careless gesture.

Bruno lingered a moment, trying to think of something to say, and not being able to, went out and tried to slam the door but the air pressure retarded it. He walked back through the shabby, depressing corridor of the Confidential Detective Bureau, where the typewriter that had been pecking thoughtfully throughout the interview came louder—"We," Gerard was always saying, and here they all were, grubbing away back of the doors—nodded good-by to Miss Graham, the receptionist-secretary who had expressed her sympathies to him an hour ago when he had come in. How gaily he had come in an hour ago, determined not to let Gerard rile him, and now—He could never control his temper when Gerard made cracks about him and his mother, and he might as well admit it. So what? So what did they have on him? So what clues did they have on the murderer? Wrong ones.

Guy! Bruno smiled going down in the elevator. Not once had Guy crossed his mind in Gerard's office! Not one flicker even when Gerard had hammered at him about where he went Thursday night! Guy! Guy and himself! Who else was like them? Who else was their equal? He longed for Guy to be with him now. He would clasp Guy's hand, and to hell with the rest of the world! Their feats were unparalleled! Like a sweep across the sky! Like two streaks of red fire that came and disappeared so fast, everybody stood wondering if they really had seen them. He remembered a poem he had read once that said something of what he meant. He thought he still had it in a pocket of his address case. He hurried into a bar off Wall Street, ordered a drink, and pulled the tiny paper out of the address-book pocket. It was torn out of a poetry book he had had in college.

THE LEADEN-EYED
by *Vachel Lindsay*

Let not young souls be
smothered out before
They do quaint deeds and fully
flaunt their pride.

It is the world's one crime its
babes grow dull,
Its poor are ox-like, limp and leaden-eyed.

Not that they starve, but starve
so dreamlessly,
Not that they sow, but that they
seldom reap,
Not that they serve, but have no
gods to serve,
Not that they die, but that they
die like sheep.

He and Guy were not leaden-eyed. He and Guy would not die like sheep now. He and Guy would reap. He would give Guy money, too, if he would take it.

## *twenty-six*

At about the same time the next day, Bruno was sitting in a beach chair on the terrace of his house in Great Neck, in a mood of complaisance and halcyon content quite new and pleasant to him. Gerard had been prowling around that morning, but Bruno had been very calm and courteous, had seen that he and his little stooge got some lunch, and now Gerard was gone and he felt very proud of his behavior. He must never let Gerard get him down again like yesterday, because that was the way to get rattled and make mistakes. Gerard, of course, was the dumb one. If he'd just been nicer yesterday, he might have cooperated. Cooperated? Bruno laughed out loud. What did he mean cooperated? What was he doing, kidding himself?

Overhead a bird kept singing, "Tweedledee?" and answering itself, "Tweedle*dum*!" Bruno cocked his head. His mother would know what kind of a bird it was. He gazed off at the russet-tinged lawn, the white plaster wall, the dogwoods that were beginning to bud. This afternoon, he found himself quite interested in nature. This afternoon, a check had arrived for twenty thousand for his mother. There would be a lot more when the insurance people stopped yapping and the lawyers got all the red tape cut. At lunch, he and his mother had talked about going to Capri, talked sketchily, but he knew they would go. And tonight, they were going out to dinner for the first time, at a little *intime* place that was their favorite restaurant, off the highway not far from Great Neck. No wonder he hadn't liked nature before. Now that he owned the grass and the trees, it meant something.

Casually, he turned the pages of the address book in his lap. He had found it this morning, couldn't remember if he had had it with him in Santa Fe or not, and wanted to make sure there wasn't anything about Guy in it before Gerard found it. There certainly were a lot of people he wanted to look up again, now that he had the wherewithal. An idea came to him, and he took a pencil from his pocket. Under the P's he wrote:

Tommy Pandini
232 W. 76 Street

and under the S's:

"Slitch"
Life Guard Station
Hell Gate Bridge

Give Gerard a few mysterious people to look up.

*Dan 8:15 Hotel Astor*, he found in the memos at the back of the book. He didn't even remember Dan. *Get $ from Capt. by June 1.* The next page sent a little chill down him: *Item for Guy $25.* He tore the perforated page out. That Santa Fe belt for Guy. Why had he even put it down? In some dull moment—

Gerard's big black car purred into the driveway.

Bruno forced himself to sit there and finish checking the memos. Then he slipped the address book in his pocket, and poked the torn-out page into his mouth.

Gerard strolled onto the flagstones with a cigar in his mouth and his arms hanging.

"Anything new?" Bruno asked.

"Few things." Gerard let his eyes sweep from the corner of the house diagonally across the lawn to the plaster wall, as though he reappraised the distance the murderer had run.

Bruno's jaw moved casually on the little wad of paper, as if he chewed gum. "Such as what?"he asked. Past Gerard's shoulder, he saw his little stooge sitting in the driver's seat of the car, staring at them fixedly from under a gray hatbrim. Of all the sinister-looking guys, Bruno thought.

"Such as the fact the murderer didn't cut back to town. He kept going in this general direction." Gerard gestured like a country-store proprietor pointing out a road, bringing his whole arm down. "Cut through those woods over there and must have had a pretty rough time. We found these."

Bruno got up and looked at a piece of the purple gloves and a shred of dark blue material, like Guy's overcoat. "Gosh. You sure they're off the murderer?"

"Reasonably sure. One's off an overcoat. The other—probably a glove."

"Or a muffler."

"No, there's a little seam." Gerard poked it with a fat freckled forefinger.

"Pretty fancy gloves."

"Ladies' gloves." Gerard looked up with a twinkle.

Bruno gave an amused smirk, and stopped contritely.

"I first thought he was a professional killer," Gerard said with a sigh. "He certainly knew the house. But I don't think a professional killer would have lost his head and tried to get through those woods at the point he did."

"Hm-m," said Bruno with interest.

"He knew the right road to take, too. The right road was only ten yards away."

"How do you know that?"

"Because this whole thing was carefully planned, Charles. The broken lock on the back door, the milk crate out there by the wall—"

Bruno was silent. Herbert had told Gerard that he, Bruno, broke the lock. Herbert had probably also told him he put the milk crate there.

"Purple gloves!" Gerard chuckled, as gaily as Bruno had ever heard him chuckle. "What does the color matter as long as they keep fingerprints off things, eh?"

"Yeah," Bruno said.

Gerard entered the house through the terrace door.

Bruno followed him after a moment. Gerard went back to the kitchen, and Bruno climbed the stairs. He tossed the address book on his bed, then went down the hall. The open door of his father's room gave him a funny feeling, as if he were just realizing his father were dead. It was the door's hanging open that made him feel it, he thought, like a shirttail hanging out, like a guard let down, that never would have been if the Captain were alive. Bruno frowned, then went and closed the door quickly on the carpet scuffled by detectives' feet, by Guy's feet, on the desk with the looted pigeonholes and the checkbook that lay open as if awaiting his father's signatures. He opened his mother's door carefully. She was lying on her bed with the pink satin comforter drawn up to her chin, her head turned toward the inside of the room and her eyes open, as she had lain since Saturday night.

"You didn't sleep, Mom?"

"No."

"Gerard's here again."

"I know."

"If you don't want to be disturbed, I'll tell him."

"Darling, don't be silly."

Bruno sat down on the bed and bent close to her. "I wish you could sleep, Mom." She had purple wrinkled shadows under her eyes, and she held her mouth in a way he had never seen before, that drew its corners long and thin.

"Darling, are you sure Sam never mentioned anything to you—never mentioned anyone?"

"Can you imagine him saying anything like that to me?" Bruno wandered about the room. Gerard's presence in the house irked him. It was Gerard's manner that was so obnoxious, as if he had something up his sleeve against everyone, even Herbert who he knew had idolized his father, who was saying everything against him short of plain accusation. But Herbert hadn't seen him measuring the grounds, Bruno knew, or Gerard would have let him know by now. He had wandered all over the grounds, and the house while his mother was sick, and anyone seeing him wouldn't have known when he was counting his paces or not. He wanted to sound off about Gerard now, but his mother wouldn't understand. She insisted on their continuing to hire him, because he was supposed to be the best. They were not working together, his mother and he. His mother might say something else to Gerard—like the fact they'd decided only Thursday to leave Friday—of terrible importance and not mention it to him at all!

"You know you're getting fat, Charley?" his mother said with a smile.

Bruno smiled, too, she sounded so like herself. She was putting on her shower cap at her dressing table now. "Appetite's not bad," he said. But his appetite was worse and so was his digestion. He was getting fatter anyway.

Gerard knocked just after his mother had closed the bathroom door.

"She'll be quite a long time," Bruno told him.

"Tell her I'll be in the hall, will you?"

Bruno knocked on the bathroom door and told her, then went down to his own room. He could tell by the position of the address book on his bed that Gerard had found it and looked at it. Slowly Bruno mixed himself a short highball, drank it, then went softly down the hall and heard Gerard already talking to his mother.

"—didn't seem in high or low spirits, eh?"

"He's a very moody boy, you know. I doubt if I'd have noticed," his mother said.

"Oh—people pick up psychic feelings sometimes. Don't you agree, Elsie?"

His mother did not answer.

"—too bad, because I'd like more cooperation from him."

"Do you think he's withholding anything?"

"I don't know," with his disgusting smile, and Bruno could tell from his tone that Gerard expected him to be listening, too. "Do you?"

"Of course, I don't think he is. What're you getting at, Arthur?"

She was standing up to him. She wouldn't think so much of Gerard after this, Bruno thought. He was being dumb again, a dumb Iowan.

"You want me to get at the truth, don't you, Elsie?" Gerard asked, like a radio detective. "He's hazy about what he did Thursday night after leaving you. He's got some pretty shady acquaintances. One might have been a hireling of a business enemy's of Sam's, a spy or something like that. And Charles could have mentioned that you and he were leaving the next day—"

"What're you getting at, Arthur, that Charles knows something about this?"

"Elsie, I wouldn't be surprised. Would you, really?"

"Damn him!" Bruno murmured. Damn him for saying that to his *mother*!

"I'll certainly tell you everything he tells me."

Bruno drifted toward the stairway. Her submissiveness shocked him. Suppose she began to suspect? Murder was something she wouldn't be able to take. Hadn't he realized it in Santa Fe? And if she remembered Guy, remembered that he had talked about him in Los Angeles? If Gerard found Guy in the next two weeks, he might have scratches on him from getting through those woods, or a bruise or a cut that might raise suspicion. Bruno heard Herbert's soft tread in the downstairs hall, saw him come into view with his mother's afternoon drink on a tray, and retreated up the stairs again. His heart beat as if he were in a battle, a strange manysided battle. He hurried back to his own room, took a big drink, then lay down and tried to fall asleep.

He awakened with a jerk and rolled from under Gerard's hand on his shoulder.

"By-by," Gerard said, his smile showing his tobacco-stained lower teeth. "Just leaving and thought I'd say good-by."

"Is it worth waking somebody up for?" Bruno said.

Gerard chuckled and waddled from the room before Bruno could think of some mitigating phrase he really wanted to say. He plunged back on the pillow and tried to resume his nap, but when he closed his eyes, he saw Gerard's stocky figure in the light-brown suit going down the halls, slipping wraithlike through closed doors, bending to look into drawers, to read letters, to make notes, turning to point a finger at him, tormenting his mother so it was impossible not to fight back.

# twenty-seven

"What else can you make of it? He's accusing me!" Bruno shouted across the table.

"Darling, he's not. He's attending to his business."

Bruno pushed his hair back. "Want to dance, Mom?"

"You're in no condition to dance."

He wasn't and he knew it. "Then I want another drink."

"Darling, the food's coming right away."

Her patience with it all, the purple circles under her eyes, pained him so he could not look in front of him. Bruno glanced around for a waiter. The place was so crowded tonight, it was hard to tell a waiter from any other guy. His eyes stopped on a man at a table across the dance floor who looked like Gerard. He couldn't see the man he was with, but he certainly looked like Gerard, the bald head and light brown hair, except this man wore a black jacket. Bruno closed one eye to stop the rhythmic splitting of the image.

"Charley, do sit down. The waiter's coming."

It *was* Gerard, and he was laughing now, as if the other fellow had told him he was watching them. For one suspended, furious second, Bruno wondered whether to tell his mother.

Then he sat down and said with vehemence: "Gerard's over there!"

"Is he? Where?"

"Over left of the orchestra. Under the blue lamp."

"I don't see him." His mother stretched up. "Darling, you're imagining."

"I am *not* imagining!" Bruno shouted and threw his napkin in his roast beef au jus.

"I see the one you mean, and it's not Gerard," she said patiently.

"You can't see him as good as I can! It's him and I don't feel like eating in the same room with him!"

"Charles," she sighed. "Do you want another drink? Have another drink. Here's a waiter."

"I don't even feel like drinkin'with him! Want me to prove it's him?"

"What does it matter? He's not going to bother us. He's guarding us probably."

"You admit it's him! He's spying on us and he's in a dark suit so he can follow us anywhere else we go!"

"It's not Arthur anyway," she said quietly, squeezing lemon over her broiled fish. "You're having hallucinations."

Bruno stared at her with his mouth open. "What do you mean saying things like that to me, Mom?" His voice cracked.

"Sweetie, everybody's looking at us."

"I don't care!"

"Darling, let me tell you something. You're making too much out of this." She interrupted him,"You are, because you want to. You want excitement. I've seen it before."

Bruno was absolutely speechless. His mother was turning against him. He had seen her look at the Captain the way she looked at him now.

"You've probably said something to Gerard,"she went on,"in anger, and he thinks you're behaving most peculiarly. Well, you are."

"Is that any reason for him to tail me day and night?"

"Darling, I don't think that's Gerard," she said firmly.

Bruno pushed himself up and staggered away toward the table where Gerard sat. He'd prove to her it was Gerard, and prove to Gerard he wasn't afraid of him. A couple of tables blocked him at the edge of the dance floor, but he could see it was Gerard now.

Gerard looked up at him and waved a hand familiarly, and his little stooge stared at him. And *he*, he and his mother were paying for it! Bruno opened his mouth, not knowing exactly what he wanted to say, then teetered around. He knew what he wanted to do, call up Guy. Right here and now. Right in the same room with Gerard. He struggled across the dance floor toward the telephone booth by the bar. The slow, crazily revolving figures pressed him back like a sea wave, baffling him. The wave floated toward him again, buoyant but insuperable, sweeping him yet farther back, and a similar moment at a party in his house when he was a little boy, when he tried to get through the dancing couples to his mother across the living room, came back to him.

Bruno woke up early in the morning, in bed, and lay perfectly still, retracing the last moments he could remember. He knew he had passed out. Had he called Guy before he passed out? If he had, could Gerard trace it? He surely hadn't talked to Guy or he'd remember it, but maybe he'd called his house. He got up to go ask his mother if he had passed out in the telephone booth. Then the shakes came on and he went into the bathroom. The Scotch and water splashed up in his face when he lifted the glass. He braced himself against the bathroom door. It was getting him at both ends now, the shakes, early and late, waking him earlier and earlier, and he had to take more and more at night to get to sleep.

And in between was Gerard.

## *twenty-eight*

Momentarily, and faintly, as one re-experiences a remembered sensation, Guy felt secure and self-sufficient as he sat down at his work table where he had his hospital books and notes carefully arranged.

In the last month, he had washed and repainted all his bookshelves, had his carpet and curtains cleaned, and had scrubbed his kitchenette until its porcelain and aluminum gleamed. All guilt, he had thought as he poured the pans of dirty water down the sink, but since he could sleep no more than two or three hours a night, and then only after physical exercise, he reasoned that cleaning one's house was a more profitable manner of tiring oneself than walking the streets of the city.

He looked at the unopened newspaper on his bed, then got up and glanced through all its pages. But the papers had stopped mentioning the murder six weeks ago. He had taken care of every clue—the purple gloves cut up and flushed down the toilet, the overcoat (a good overcoat, and he had thought of giving it to a beggar, but who would be so base as to give even a beggar a murderer's overcoat?) and the trousers torn in pieces and disposed of gradually in the garbage. And the Luger dropped off the Manhattan Bridge. And his shoes off another. The only thing he had not disposed of was the little revolver.

He went to his bureau to look at it. Its hardness under his fingertips soothed him. The one clue he had not disposed of, and all the clue they needed if they found him. He knew exactly why he kept the revolver: it was *his*, a part of himself, the third hand that had done the murder. It was himself at fifteen when he had bought it, himself when he had loved Miriam and had kept it in their room in Chicago, looking at it now and then in his most contented, most inward moments. The best of himself, with its mechanical, absolute logic. Like him, he thought now, in its power to kill.

If Bruno dared to contact him again, he would kill him, too. Guy was sure that he could. Bruno would know it, too. Bruno had always been able to read him. The silence from Bruno now brought more relief than the silence from the police. In fact, he was not anxious at all lest the police find him, had never been. The anxiety had always been within himself, a battle of himself against himself, so torturous he might have welcomed the law's intervention. Society's law was lax compared to the law of conscience. He might go to the law and confess, but confession seemed a minor point, a mere gesture, even an easy way out, an avoidance of truth. If the law executed him, it would be a mere gesture.

"I have no great respect for the law," he remembered he had said to Peter Wriggs in Metcalf two years ago. Why should he have respect for a statute that called him and Miriam man and wife? "I have no great respect for the church," he had said sophomorishly to Peter at fifteen. Then, of course, he had meant the Metcalf Baptists. At seventeen, he had discovered God by himself. He had discovered God through his own awakening talents, and through a sense of unity of all the arts, and then of nature, finally of science—of all the creating and ordering forces in the world. He believed he could not have done his work without a belief in God. And where had his belief been when he murdered? He had forsaken God, not God him. It seemed to him that no human being had ever borne, or had needed to bear, so much guilt as he, and that he could not have borne it and lived unless his spirit was dead already, and what existed of himself now only a husk.

Awkwardly, he turned and faced his work table. A gasp hissed between his teeth, and nervously, impatiently, he passed his hand hard across his mouth. And yet, he felt, there was *something* still to come, still to be grasped, some severer punishment, some bitterer realization.

"I don't suffer enough!" burst from him suddenly in a whisper. But why had he whispered? Was he ashamed? "I don't suffer enough," he said in a normal voice, glancing about him as if he expected some ear to hear him. And he would have shouted it, if he had not felt some element of pleading in it, and considered himself unworthy of pleading for anything, from anyone.

His new books, for instance, the beautiful new books he had bought today—he could still think about them, love them. Yet he felt he had left them there long ago on his work table, like his own youth. He must go immediately and work, he thought. He had been commissioned to plan a hospital. He frowned at the little stack of notes he had already taken, spotlighted under his gooseneck lamp. Somehow it did not seem real that he had been commissioned. He would awaken soon and find that all these weeks had been a fantasy, a wishful dream. A hospital. Wasn't a hospital more fitting than even a prison? He frowned puzzledly, knowing his mind had strayed wildly, that two weeks ago when he had begun the hospital interior he had not thought once of death, that the positive requisites of health and healing alone had occupied him. He hadn't told Anne about the hospital, he remembered suddenly, that was why it seemed unreal. She was his glass of reality, not his work. But on the other hand, why hadn't he told her?

He must go immediately and work, but he could feel in his legs now that frenzied energy that came every evening, that sent him out in the streets finally in a vain effort to spend it. The energy frightened him because he could find no task that would absorb it, and because he felt at times that the task might be his suicide. Yet very deep inside him, and very much against his own will, his roots still clung to life, and he sensed that suicide was a coward's escape, a ruthless act against those who loved him.

He thought of his mother, and felt he could never let her embrace him again. He remembered her telling him that all men were equally good, because all men had souls and the soul was entirely good. Evil, she said, always came from externals. And so he had believed even months after Miriam, when he had wanted to murder her lover Steve. So he had believed even on the train, reading his Plato. In himself, the second horse of the charioteer had always been obedient as the first. But love and hate, he thought now, good and evil, lived side by side in the human heart, and not merely in differing proportions in one man and the next, but all good and all evil. One had merely to look for a little of either to find it all, one had merely to scratch the surface. All things had opposites close by, every decision a reason against it, every animal an animal that destroys it, the male the female, the positive the negative. The splitting of the atom was the only true destruction, the breaking of the universal law of oneness. Nothing could be without its opposite that was bound up with it. Could space exist in a building without objects that stopped it? Could energy exist without matter, or matter without energy? Matter and energy, the inert and the active, once considered opposites, were now known to be one.

And Bruno, he and Bruno. Each was what the other had not chosen to be, the cast-off self, what he thought he hated but perhaps in reality loved.

For a moment, he felt as if he might be mad. He thought, madness and genius often overlapped, too. But what mediocre lives most people lived! In middle waters, like most fish!

No, there was that duality permeating nature down to the tiny proton and electron within the tiniest atom. Science was now at work trying to split the electron, and perhaps it couldn't because perhaps only an idea was behind it: the one and only truth, that the opposite is always present. Who knew whether an electron was matter or energy? Perhaps God and the Devil danced hand in hand around every single electron!

He threw his cigarette at the wastebasket and missed.

When he put out the stub in the basket, he saw a crumpled page on which he had written last night one of his guilt-crazed confessions. It dragged him up sickeningly to a present that assaulted him from all sides—Bruno, Anne, this room, this night, the conference with the Department of Hospitals tomorrow.

Toward midnight, when he felt drowsy, he left his work table and lay down carefully on his bed, not daring to undress lest he awaken himself again.

He dreamed that he woke up in the night to the sound of the slow, watchful breathing that he heard every night in his room as he tried to fall asleep. It came from outside his window now. Someone was climbing the house. A tall figure in a great cape like a bat's wings sprang suddenly into the room.

"I'm here," said the figure matter-of-factly.

Guy jumped from his bed to fight him. "Who are you?" He saw it was Bruno.

Bruno resisted him rather than fought back. If Guy used his utmost strength, he could just pin Bruno's shoulders to the floor, and always in the recurrent dream, Guy had to use his utmost strength. Guy held Bruno to the floor with his knees and strangled him, but Bruno kept grinning up at him as if he felt nothing.

"You," Bruno answered finally.

Guy awakened heavy-headed and perspiring. He sat up higher, vigilantly guarding his empty room. There were slimily wet sounds in the room now, as of a snake crawling through the cement court below, slapping its moist coils against the walls. Then suddenly he recognized the sound as that of rain, a gentle, silvery summer rain, and sank back again on his pillow. He began to cry softly. He thought of the rain, rushing at a slant to the earth. It seemed to say:Where are the spring plants to water? Where is the new life that depends on me? *Where is the green vine, Anne, as we saw love in our youth?* he had written last night on the crumpled paper. The rain would find the new life awaiting it, depending on it. What fell in his court was only its excess. *Where is the green vine, Anne . . .*

He lay with his eyes open until the dawn eased its fingertips onto the sill, like the stranger who had sprung in. Like Bruno. Then he got up and turned on his lights, drew the shades, and went back to his work.

## *twenty-nine*

Guy slammed his foot on the brake pedal, but the car leapt, screaming, toward the child. There was a tinny clatter of the bicycle falling. Guy got out and ran around the car, banged his knee excruciatingly on the front bumper, and dragged the child up by his shoulders.

"I'm okay," the little boy said.

"Is he all right, Guy?" Anne ran up, white as the child.

"I think so." Guy gripped the bicycle's front wheel with his knees and straightened the handlebars, feeling the child's curious eyes on his own violently trembling hands.

"Thanks," said the boy.

Guy watched him mount the bicycle and pedal off as if he watched a miracle. He looked at Anne and said quietly, with a shuddering sigh,"I can't drive anymore today."

"All right," she replied, as quietly as he, but there was a suspicion in her eyes, Guy knew, as she turned to go around to the driver's seat.

Guy apologized to the Faulkners as he got back into the car, and they murmured something about such things happening to every driver now and then. But Guy felt their real silence behind him, a silence of shock and horror. He had seen the boy coming down the side road. The boy had stopped for him, but Guy had swerved the car toward him as if he had intended to hit him. Had he? Tremulously, he lighted a cigarette. Nothing but bad coordination, he told himself, he had seen it a hundred times in the past two weeks—collisions with revolving doors, his inability even to hold a pen against a ruler, and so often the feeling he wasn't *here*, doing what he was doing. Grimly he re-established what he was doing now, driving in Anne's car up to Alton to see the new house. The house was done. Anne and her mother had put the drapes up last week. It was Sunday, nearly noon. Anne had told him she had gotten a nice letter from his mother yesterday, and that his mother had sent her three crocheted aprons and a lot of homemade preserves to start their kitchen shelves. Could he remember all that? All he seemed to remember was the sketch of the Bronx hospital in his pocket, that he hadn't told Anne about yet. He wished he could go away somewhere and do nothing but work, see no one, not even Anne. He stole a glance at her, at her coolly lifted face with the faint arch in the bridge of the nose. Her thin strong hands swung the wheel expertly into a curve and out. Suddenly he was sure she loved her car more than she loved him.

"If anybody's hungry, speak up now," Anne said. "This little store's the last place for miles."

But no one was hungry.

"I expect to be asked for dinner at least once a year, Anne," her father said. "Maybe a brace of ducks or some quail. I hear there's some good hunting around here. Any good with a gun, Guy?"

Anne turned the car into the road that led to the house.

"Fair, sir," Guy said finally, stammering twice. His heart was flogging him to run, he could still it only by running, he was sure.

"Guy!" Anne smiled at him. Stopping the car, she whispered to him,"Have a nip when you get in the house. There's a bottle of brandy in the kitchen." She touched his wrist, and Guy jerked his hand back, involuntarily.

He must, he thought, have a brandy or something. But he knew also that he would not take anything.

Mrs. Faulkner walked beside him across the new lawn. "It's simply beautiful, Guy. I hope you're proud of it."

Guy nodded. It was finished, he didn't have to imagine it anymore as he had in the brown bureau of the hotel room in Mexico. Anne had wanted Mexican tiles in the kitchen. So many things she wore from time to time were Mexican. A belt, a handbag, huarachas. The long embroidered skirt that showed now below her tweed coat was Mexican. He felt he must have chosen the Hotel Montecarlo so that dismal pink-and-brown room and Bruno's face in the brown bureau would haunt him the rest of his life.

It was only a month until their marriage now. Four more Friday nights, and Anne would sit in the big square green chair by the fireplace, her voice would call to him from the Mexican kitchen, they would work together in the studio upstairs. What right had he to imprison her with himself? He stood staring at their bedroom, vaguely aware that it seemed cluttered, because Anne had said she wanted their bedroom "not modern."

"Don't forget to thank Mother for the furniture, will you?" she whispered to him. "Mother gave it to us, you know."

The cherry bedroom set, of course. He remembered her telling him that morning at breakfast, remembered his bandaged hand, and Anne in the black dress she had worn to Helen's party. But when he should have said something about the furniture, he didn't, and then it seemed too late. They must know something is the matter, he felt. Everyone in the world must know. He was only somehow being reprieved, being saved for some weight to fall upon him and annihilate him.

"Thinking about a new job, Guy?" Mr. Faulkner asked, offering him a cigarette.

Guy had not seen his figure there when he stepped onto the side porch. With a sense of justifying himself, he pulled the folded paper from his pocket and showed it to him, explained it to him. Mr. Faulkner's bushy, gray and brown eyebrows came down thoughtfully. But he's not listening to me at all, Guy thought. He's bending closer only to see my guilt that is like a circle of darkness about me.

"Funny Anne didn't say anything to me about it," Mr. Faulkner said.

"I'm saving it."

"Oh," Mr. Faulkner chuckled. "A wedding present?"

Later, the Faulkners took the car and went back for sandwiches from the little store. Guy was tired of the house. He wanted Anne to walk with him up the rock hill.

"In a minute," she said. "Come here." She stood in front of the tall stone fireplace. She put her hands on his shoulders and looked into his face, a little apprehensive, but still glowing with her pride in their new house. "Those are getting deeper, you know," she told him, drawing her fingertip down the hollow in his cheek. "I'm going to make you eat."

"Maybe need a little sleep," he murmured. He had told her that lately his work demanded long hours. He had told her, of all things, that he was doing some agency jobs, hack jobs, as Myers did, in order to earn some money.

"Darling, we're—we're well off. What on earth's troubling you?"

And she had asked him half a dozen times if it was the wedding, if he wanted not to marry her. If she asked him again, he might say yes, but he knew she would not ask it now, in front of their fireplace. "Nothing's troubling me," he said quickly.

"Then will you please not work so hard?" she begged him, then spontaneously, out of her own joy and anticipation, hugged him to her.

Automatically—as if it were nothing at all, he thought—he kissed her, because he knew she expected him to. She will notice, he thought, she always notices the slightest difference in a kiss, and it had been so long since he had kissed her. When she said nothing, it seemed to him only that the change in him was simply too enormous to mention.

## *thirty*

Guy crossed the kitchen and turned at the back door. "Awfully thoughtless of me to invite myself on the cook's night out."

"What's thoughtless about it? You'll just fare as we do on Thursday nights, that's all." Mrs. Faulkner brought him a piece of the celery she was washing at the sink. "But Hazel's going to be disappointed she wasn't here to make the shortcake herself. You'll have to do with Anne's tonight."

Guy went out. The afternoon was still bright with sun, though the picket fence cast long oblique bars of shadow over the crocus and iris beds. He could just see Annie's tied-back hair and the pale green of her sweater beyond a crest in the rolling sea of lawn. Many times he had gathered mint and watercress there with Anne, from the stream that flowed out of the woods where he had fought Bruno. Bruno is past, he reminded himself, gone, vanished. Whatever method Gerard had used, he had made Bruno afraid to contact him.

He watched Mr. Faulkner's neat black car enter the driveway and roll slowly into the open garage. What was he doing here, he asked himself suddenly, where he deceived everyone, even the colored cook who liked to make shortcake for him because, once perhaps, he had praised her dessert? He moved into the shelter of the pear tree, where neither Anne nor her father would easily see him. If he should step out of Anne's life, he thought, what difference would it make to her? She had not given up all her old friends, hers and Teddy's set, the eligible young men, the handsome young men who played at polo and, rather harmlessly, at the night clubs before they entered their father's business and married one of the beautiful young girls who decorated their country clubs. Anne was different, of course, or she wouldn't have been attracted to him in the first place. She was not one of the beautiful young girls who worked at a career for a couple of years just to say they had done it, before they married one of the eligible young men. But wouldn't she have been just the same, herself, without him? She had often told him he was her inspiration, he and his own ambition, but she had had the same talent, the same drive the day he met her, and wouldn't she have gone on? And wouldn't another man, like himself but worthy of her, have found her? He began to walk toward her.

"I'm almost done," she called to him. "Why didn't you come sooner?"

"I hurried," he said awkwardly.

"You've been leaning against the house ten minutes."

A sprig of watercress was floating away on the stream, and he sprang to rescue it. He felt like a possum, scooping it up. "I think I'll take a job soon, Anne."

She looked up, astoundedly. “A job? You mean with a firm?”

It was a phrase to be used about other architects,“a job with a firm.” He nodded, not looking at her. “I feel like it. Something steady with a good salary.”

“Steady?” She laughed a little. “With a year’s work ahead of you at the hospital?”

“I won’t need to be in the drafting room all the time.”

She stood up. “Is it because of money? Because you’re not taking the hospital money?”

He turned away from her and took a big step up the moist bank. “Not exactly,”he said through his teeth. “Maybe partly.”He had decided weeks ago to give his fee back to the Department of Hospitals after he paid his staff.

“But you said it wouldn’t matter, Guy. We both agreed we—you could afford it.”

The world seemed silent all at once, listening. He watched her push a strand of her hair back and leave a smudge of wet earth on her forehead. “It won’t be for long. Maybe six months, maybe a lot less.”

“But why at all?”

“I feel like it!”

“Why do you feel like it? Why do you want to be a martyr, Guy?”

He said nothing.

The setting sun dropped free of the trees and poured onto them suddenly. Guy frowned deeper, shading his eye with the brow that bore the white scar from the woods—the scar that would always show, he thought. He kicked at a stone in the ground, without being able to dislodge it. Let her think the job was still part of his depression after the Palmyra. Let her think anything.

“Guy, I’m sorry,” she said.

Guy looked at her. “Sorry?”

She came closer to him. “Sorry. I think I know what it is.”

He still kept his hands in his pockets. “What do you mean?”

She waited a long while. “I thought all this, all your uneasiness after the Palmyra—even without your knowing it, I mean—goes back to Miriam.”

He twisted away abruptly. “No. No, that’s not it at all!” He said it so honestly, yet it sounded so like a lie! He thrust his fingers in his hair and shoved it back.

"Listen, Guy," Anne said softly and clearly, "maybe you don't want the wedding as much as you think you do. If you think that's part of it, say it, because I can take that a lot easier than this job idea. If you want to wait—still—or if you want to break it off entirely, I can bear it."

Her mind was made up, and had been for a long while. He could feel it at the very center of her calmness. He could give her up at this moment. The pain of that would cancel out the pain of guilt.

"Hey, there, Anne!" her father called from the back door. "Coming in soon? I need that mint!"

"Minute, Dad!"she shouted back. "What do you say, Guy?"

His tongue pressed the top of his mouth. He thought, she is the sun in my dark forest. But he couldn't say it. He could only say,"I can't say—"

"Well—I want you now more than ever, because you need me now more than ever." She pressed the mint and watercress into his hand. "Do you want to take this to Dad? And have a drink with him. I have to change my clothes." She turned and went off toward the house, not fast, but much too fast for Guy to try to follow her.

Guy drank several of the mint juleps. Anne's father made them the old-fashioned way, letting the sugar and bourbon and mint stand in a dozen glasses all day, getting colder and more frosted, and he liked to ask Guy if he had ever tasted better ones anywhere. Guy could feel the precise degree to which his tension lessened, but it was impossible for him to become drunk. He had tried a few times and made himself sick, without becoming drunk.

There was a moment after dusk, on the terrace with Anne, when he imagined he might not have known her any better than he had the first evening he visited her, when he suddenly felt a tremendous, joyous longing to make her love him. Then he remembered the house in Alton awaiting them after the wedding Sunday, and all the happiness he had known already with Anne rushed back to him. He wanted to protect her, to achieve some impossible goal, which would please her. It seemed the most positive, the happiest ambition he had ever known. There was a way out, then, if he could feel like this. It was only a part of himself he had to cope with, not his whole self, not Bruno, or his work. He had merely to crush the other part of himself, and live in the self he was now.

# thirty-one

But there were too many points at which the other self could invade the self he wanted to preserve, and there were too many forms of invasion: certain words, sounds, lights, actions his hands or feet performed, and if he did nothing at all, heard and saw nothing, the shouting of some triumphant inner voice that shocked him and cowed him. The wedding so elaborately prepared for, so festive, so pure with white lace and linen, so happily awaited by everyone, seemed the worst act of treachery he could commit, and the closer it drew, the more frantically and vainly he debated canceling it. Up to the last hour, he wanted simply to flee.

Robert Treacher, the friend of his Chicago days, telephoned his good wishes and asked if he might come to the wedding. Guy put him off with some feeble excuse. It was the Faulkners' affair, he felt, their friends, their family church, and the presence of a friend would put a hole in his armor. He had invited only Myers, who didn't matter—since the hospital commission, he no longer shared an office with him—Tim O'Flaherty, who couldn't come, and two or three architects from the Deems Academy, who knew his work better than they knew him. But half an hour after Treacher's call from Montreal, Guy telephoned back and asked Bob if he would be his best man.

Guy realized he had not even thought of Treacher in nearly a year, had not answered his last letter. He had not thought of Peter Wriggs, or Vic De Poyster and Gunther Hall. He had used to call on Vic and his wife in their Bleecker Street apartment, had once taken Anne there. Vic was a painter, and had sent him an invitation to his exhibit last winter, Guy remembered. He hadn't even answered. Vaguely now, he remembered that Tim had been in New York and had called him to have lunch during the period when Bruno had been haunting him by telephone, and that he had refused. The Theologica Germanica, Guy recalled, said that the ancient Germans had judged an accused man innocent or guilty by the number of friends who came forth to vouch for his character. How many would vouch for him now? He had never given a great deal of time to his friends, because they were not the kind of people who expected it, but now he felt his friends were shunning him in turn, as if they sensed without seeing him that he had become unworthy of friendship.

The Sunday morning of the wedding, walking in slow circles around Bob Treacher in the vestry of the church, Guy clung to his memory of the hospital drawings as to a single last shred of hope, the single proof that he still existed. He had done an excellent job. Bob Treacher, his friend, had praised him. He had proven to himself that he could still create.

Bob had given up trying to make conversation with him. He sat with his arms folded, with a pleasant but rather absent expression on his chubby face. Bob thought he was simply nervous. Bob didn't know how he felt, Guy knew, because however much he thought it showed, it didn't. And that was the hell, that one's life could so easily be total hypocrisy. This was the essence, his wedding and his friend, Bob Treacher, who no longer knew him. And the little stone vestry with the high grilled window, like a prison cell. And the murmur of voices outside, like the self-righteous murmurings of a mob impatient to storm the prison and wreak justice.

"You didn't by any chance bring a bottle."

Bob jumped up. "I certainly did. It's weighing me down and I completely forgot it." He set the bottle on the table and waited for Guy to take it. Bob was about forty-five, a man of modest but sanguine temperament, with an indelible stamp of contented bachelorhood and of complete absorption and authority in his profession. "After you,"he prompted Guy. "I want to drink a private toast to Anne. She's very beautiful, Guy." He added softly, with a smile,"As beautiful as a white bridge."

Guy stood looking at the opened pint bottle. The hubbub out the window seemed to poke fun at him now, at him and Anne. The bottle on the table was part of it, the jaded, half-humorous concomitant of the traditional wedding. He had drunk whisky at his wedding with Miriam. Guy hurled the bottle into the corner. Its solid crack and spatter ended the hooting horns, the voices, the silly tremolo of the organ only for a second, and they began to seep back again.

"Sorry, Bob. I'm very sorry."

Bob had not taken his eyes from him. "I don't blame you a bit," he smiled.

"But I blame myself!"

"Listen, old man—"

Guy could see that Bob did not know whether to laugh or be serious.

"Wait," Treacher said. "I'll get us some more."

The door opened just as Bob reached for it, and Peter Wriggs' thin figure slipped in. Guy introduced him to Treacher. Peter had come all the way up from New Orleans to be at his wedding. He wouldn't have come to his wedding with Miriam, Guy thought. Peter had hated Miriam. There was gray at Peter's temples now, though his lean face still grinned like a sixteen-year-old's. Guy returned his quick embrace, feeling that he moved automatically now, on rails as he had the Friday night.

"It's time, Guy," Bob said, opening the door.

Guy walked beside him. It was twelve steps to the altar. The accusing faces, Guy thought. They were silent with horror, as the Faulkners had been in the back of the car. When were they going to interfere and stop it all? How much longer was everyone going to wait?

"Guy!" somebody whispered.

Six, Guy counted, seven.

"Guy!" faint and direct, from among the faces, and Guy glanced left, followed the gaze of two women who looked over their shoulders, and saw Bruno's face and no other.

Guy looked straight again. Was it Bruno or a vision? The face had been smiling eagerly, the gray eyes sharp as pins. Ten, eleven, he counted. *Twelve steps up, skip seven. . . . You can remember it, it's got a syncopated rhythm.* His scalp tingled. Wasn't that a proof it was a vision and not Bruno? He prayed, Lord, don't let me faint. Better you fainted than married, the inner voice shouted back.

He was standing beside Anne, and Bruno was here with them, not an event, not a moment, but a condition, something that had always been and always would be. Bruno, himself, Anne. And the moving on the tracks. And the lifetime of moving on the tracks until death do us part, for that was the punishment. What more punishment was he looking for?

Faces bobbed and smiled all around him, and Guy felt himself aping them like an idiot. It was the Sail and Racquet Club. There was a buffet breakfast, and everyone had a champagne glass, even himself. And Bruno was not here. There was really no one here but wrinkled, harmless, perfumed old women in hats. Then Mrs. Faulkner put an arm around his neck and kissed his cheek, and over her shoulder he saw Bruno thrusting himself through the door with the same smile, the same pinlike eyes that had already found him. Bruno came straight toward him and stopped, rocking on his feet.

"My best—best wishes, Guy. You didn't mind if I looked in, did you? It's a happy occasion!"

"Get out. Get out of here fast."

Bruno's smile faded hesitantly. "I just got back from Capri," he said in the same hoarse voice. He wore a new dark royal-blue gabardine suit with lapels broad as an evening suit's lapels. "How've you been, Guy?"

An aunt of Anne's babbled a perfumed message into Guy's ear, and he murmured something back. Turning, Guy started to move off.

"I just wanted to wish you well," Bruno declared. "There it is."

"Get out,"Guy said. "The door's behind you."But he mustn't say any more, he thought. He would lose control.

"Call a truce, Guy. I want to meet the bride."

Guy let himself be drawn away by two middle-aged women, one on either arm. Though he did not see him, he knew that Bruno had retreated, with a hurt, impatient smile, to the buffet table.

"Bearing up, Guy?" Mr. Faulkner took his half-empty glass from his hand. "Let's get something better at the bar."

Guy had half a glassful of Scotch. He talked without knowing what he was saying. He was sure he had said, Stop it all, tell everyone to go. But he hadn't, or Mr. Faulkner wouldn't be roaring with laughter. Or would he?

Bruno watched from down the table as they cut the cake, watched Anne mostly, Guy noticed. Bruno's mouth was a thin, insanely smiling line, his eyes glinted like the diamond pin on his dark blue tie, and in his face Guy saw that same combination of wistfulness, awe, determination, and humor that he had seen the first moment he met him.

Bruno came up to Anne. "I think I met you somewhere before. Are you any relation to Teddy Faulkner?"

Guy watched their hands meet. He had thought he wouldn't be able to bear it, but he was bearing it, without making a move.

"He's my cousin," Anne said with her easy smile, the same smile she had given someone a moment before.

Bruno nodded. "I played golf with him a couple of times."

Guy felt a hand on his shoulder.

"Got a minute, Guy? I'd—" It was Peter Wriggs.

"I haven't." Guy started after Bruno and Anne. He closed his fingers around Anne's left hand.

Bruno sauntered on the other side of her, very erect, very much at ease, bearing his untouched piece of wedding cake on a plate in front of him. "I'm an old friend of Guy's. An old acquaintance." Bruno winked at him behind Anne's head.

"Really? Where'd you two know each other?"

"In school. Old school friends." Bruno grinned. "You know, you're the most beautiful bride I've seen in years, Mrs. Haines. I'm certainly glad to have met you," he said, not with finality but an emphatic conviction that made Anne smile again.

"Very glad to have met you," she replied.

"I hope I'll be seeing you both. Where're you going to live?"

"In Connecticut," Anne said.

"Nice state, Connecticut," Bruno said with another wink at Guy, and left them with a graceful bow.

"He's a friend of Teddy's?" Guy asked Anne. "Did Teddy invite him?"

"Don't look so worried, darling!" Anne laughed at him. "We'll leave soon."

"Where is Teddy?" But what was the use finding Teddy, what was the sense in making an issue of it, he asked himself at the same time.

"I saw him two minutes ago up at the head of the table," Anne told him. "There's Chris. I've got to say hello to him."

Guy turned, looking for Bruno, and saw him helping himself to shirred eggs, talking gaily to two young men who smiled at him as if under the spell of a devil.

The ironic thing, Guy thought bitterly in the car a few moments later, the ironic thing was that Anne had never had time to know him. When they first met, he had been melancholic. Now his efforts, because he so rarely made efforts, had come to seem real. There had been, perhaps, those few days in Mexico City when he had been himself.

"Did the man in the blue suit go to Deems?" Anne asked.

They were driving out to Montauk Point. One of Anne's relatives had lent them her cottage for their three-day honeymoon. The honeymoon was only three days, because he had pledged to start work at Horton, Horton and Keese, Architects, in less than a month, and he would have to work on the double to get the detailed drawings for the hospital under way before he began. "No, the Institute. For a while." But why did he fall in with Bruno's lie?

"Interesting face he has," Anne said, straightening her dress about her ankles before she put her feet on the jump seat.

"Interesting?" Guy asked.

"I don't mean attractive. Just intense."

Guy set his teeth. Intense? Couldn't she see he was insane? Morbidly insane? Couldn't everyone see it?

# *thirty-two*

The receptionist at Horton, Horton and Keese, Architects, handed him a message that Charles Bruno had called and left his number. It was the Great Neck number.

"Thank you," Guy said, and went on across the lobby.

Suppose the firm kept records of telephone messages. They didn't, but suppose they did. Suppose Bruno dropped in one day. But Horton, Horton and Keese were so rotten themselves, Bruno wouldn't make much of a contrast. And wasn't that exactly why he was here, steeping himself in it, under some illusion that revulsion was atonement and that he would begin to feel better here?

Guy went into the big skylighted, leather-upholstered lounge, and lighted a cigarette. Mainwaring and Williams, two of the firm's first-string architects, sat in big leather armchairs, reading company reports.

Guy felt their eyes on him as he stared out the window. They were always watching him, because he was supposed to be something special, a genius, the junior Horton had assured everybody, so what was he doing here? He might be broker than everybody thought, of course, and he had just gotten married, but quite apart from that and from the Bronx hospital, he was obviously nervous, had lost his grip. The best lost their grip sometimes, they would say to themselves, so why should they scruple about taking a comfortable job? Guy gazed down onto the dirty jumble of Manhattan roofs and streets that looked like a floor model of how a city should not be built. When he turned around, Mainwaring dropped his eyes like a schoolboy.

He spent the morning dawdling over a job that he had been on for several days. Take your time, they told him. All he had to do was give the client what he wanted and sign his name to it. Now, this job was a department store for an opulent little community in Westchester, and the client wanted something like an old mansion, in keeping with the town, only sort of modern, too, see? And he had asked especially for Guy Daniel Haines. By adjusting his brain to the level of the trick, the cartoon, Guy could have tossed it off, but the fact it was really going to be a department store kept intruding certain functional demands. He erased and sharpened pencils all morning, and figured it would take him four or five more days, well into next week, until he got anything down as even a rough idea to show the client.

"Charley Bruno's coming tonight, too," Anne called that evening from the kitchen.

"What?" Guy came around the partition.

"Isn't that his name? The young man we saw at the wedding."

Anne was cutting chives on a wooden board.

"You invited him?"

"He seems to have heard about it, so he called up and sort of invited himself," Anne replied so casually that a wild suspicion she might be testing him sent a faint chill up his spine. "Hazel—not milk, angel, there's plenty of cream in the refrigerator."

Guy watched Hazel set the cream container down by the bowl of crumbled gorgonzola cheese.

"Do you mind his coming, Guy?" Anne asked him.

"Not at all, but he's no friend of mine, you know." He moved awkwardly toward the cabinets and got out the shoe-polish box. How could he stop him? There had to be a way, yet even as he racked his brain, he knew that the way would elude him.

"You do mind,"Anne said, with a smile.

"I think he's sort of a bounder, that's all."

"It's bad luck to turn anyone away from a housewarming. Don't you know that?"

Bruno was pink-eyed when he arrived. Everyone else had made some comment about the new house, but Bruno stepped down into the brick-red and forest-green living room as if he had been here a hundred times before. Or as if he lived here, Guy thought as he introduced Bruno around the room. Bruno focused a grinning, excited attention on Guy and Anne, hardly acknowledging the greetings of the others—two or three looked as if they knew him, Guy thought—except for that of a Mrs. Chester Boltinoff of Muncey Park, Long Island, whose hand Bruno shook in both his as if he had found an ally. And Guy watched with horror as Mrs. Boltinoff looked up at Bruno with a wide, friendly smile.

"How's every little thing?" Bruno asked Guy after he had gotten himself a drink.

"Fine. Very fine." Guy was determined to be calm, even if he had to anaesthetize himself. He had already had two or three straight shots in the kitchen. But he found himself walking away, retreating, toward the perpendicular spiral stairway in the corner of the living room. Just for a moment, he thought, just to get his bearings. He ran upstairs and into the bedroom, laid his cold hand against his forehead, and brought it slowly down his face.

"Pardon me, I'm still exploring," said a voice from the other side of the room. "It's such a terrific house, Guy, I had to retreat to the nineteenth century for a while."

Helen Heyburn, Anne's friend from her Bermuda schooldays, was standing by the bureau. Where the little revolver was, Guy thought.

"Make yourself at home. I just came up for a handkerchief. How's your drink holding up?" Guy slid out the right top drawer where lay both the gun he didn't want and the handkerchief he didn't need.

"Well—better than I am."

Helen was in another "manic" period, Guy supposed. She was a commercial artist, a good one, Anne thought, but she worked only when her quarterly allowance gave out and she slipped into a depressive period. And she didn't like him, he felt, since the Sunday evening when he hadn't gone with Anne to her party. She was suspicious of him. What was she doing now in their bedroom, pretending to feel her drinks more than she did?

"Are you always so serious, Guy? You know what I said to Anne when she told me she was going to marry you?"

"You told her she was insane."

"I said, 'But he's so serious. Very attractive and maybe a genius, but he's so serious, how can you stand it?'" She lifted her squarish, pretty blond face. "You don't even defend yourself. I'll bet you're too serious to kiss me, aren't you?"

He forced himself toward her, and kissed her.

"That's no kiss."

"But I deliberately wasn't being serious."

He went out. She would tell Anne, he thought, she would tell her that she had found him in the bedroom looking pained at 10 o'clock. She might look into the drawer and find the gun, too. But he didn't believe any of it. Helen was silly, and he hadn't the slightest idea why Anne liked her, but she wasn't a troublemaker. And she wasn't a snooper any more than Anne was. My God, hadn't he left the revolver there in the drawer next to Anne's all the time they had been living here? He was no more afraid Anne would investigate his half of the bureau than he was that she would open his mail.

Bruno and Anne were on the right-angled sofa by the fireplace when he came down. The glass Bruno wobbled casually on the sofa back had made dark green splotches on the cloth.

"He's telling me all about the new Capri, Guy." Anne looked up at him. "I've always wanted us to go there."

"The thing to do is to take a whole house," Bruno went on, ignoring Guy, "take a castle, the bigger the better. My mother and I lived in a castle so big we never walked to the other end of it until one night I couldn't find the right door. There was a whole Italian family having dinner at the other end of the veranda, and the same night they all come over, about twelve of them, and ask if they can work for us for nothing, just if we let them stay there. So of course we did."

"And you never learned any Italian?"

"No need to!" Bruno shrugged, his voice hoarse again, exactly as Guy always heard it in his mind.

Guy busied himself with a cigarette, feeling Bruno's avid, shyly flirtatious gaze at Anne boring into his back, deeper than the numbing tingle of the alcohol. No doubt Bruno had already complimented the dress she was wearing, his favorite dress of gray taffeta with the tiny blue pattern like peacocks' eyes. Bruno always noticed women's clothes.

"Guy and I," Bruno's voice said distinctly behind him as if he had turned his head,"Guy and I once talked about traveling."

Guy jabbed his cigarette into an ashtray, put out every spark, then went toward the sofa. "How about seeing our game room upstairs?" he said to Bruno.

"Sure." Bruno got up. "What kind of games you play?"

Guy pushed him into a small room lined with red, and closed the door behind them. "How far are you going?"

"Guy! You're tight!"

"What's the idea of telling everyone we're old friends?"

"Didn't tell everyone. I told Anne."

"What's the idea of telling her or anyone? What's the idea of coming here?"

"Quiet, Guy! Sh—sh—sh-h-h!" Bruno swung his drink casually in one hand.

"The police are still watching your friends, aren't they?"

"Not enough to worry me."

"Get out. Get out now." His voice shook with his effort to control it. And why should he control himself? The revolver with the one bullet was just across the hall.

Bruno looked at him boredly and sighed. The breath against his upper lip was like the breathing Guy heard in his room at night.

Guy staggered slightly, and the stagger enraged him.

"I think Anne's beautiful," Bruno remarked pleasantly.

"If I see you talking with her again, I'll kill you."

Bruno's smile went slack, then came back even broader. "Is that a threat, Guy?"

"That's a promise."

Half an hour later, Bruno passed out back of the sofa where he and Anne had been sitting. He looked extremely long on the floor, and his head tiny on the big hearthstone. Three men picked him up, then didn't know what to do with him.

"Take him—I suppose to the guest room," Anne said.

"That's a good omen, Anne," Helen laughed. "Somebody's supposed to stay overnight at every housewarming, you know. First guest!"

Christopher Nelson came over to Guy. "Where'd you dig him up? He used to pass out so often at the Great Neck Club, he can't get in anymore."

Guy had checked with Teddy after the wedding. Teddy hadn't invited Bruno, didn't know anything about him, except that he didn't like him.

Guy climbed the steps to the studio, and closed the door. On his work table lay the unfinished sketch of the cockeyed department store that conscience had made him take home to complete this weekend. The familiar lines, blurred now with drinking, almost made him sick. He took a blank sheet of paper and began to draw the building they wanted. He knew exactly what they wanted. He hoped he could finish before he became sick, and after he finished be as sick as a dog. But he wasn't sick when he finished. He only sat back in his chair, and finally went and opened a window.

## *thirty-three*

The department store was accepted and highly praised, first by the Hortons and then by the client, Mr. Howard Wyndham of New Rochelle, who came into the office early Monday afternoon to see the drawing. Guy rewarded himself by spending the rest of the day smoking in his office and thumbing through a morocco-bound copy of *Religio Medici* he had just bought at Brentano's to give Anne on her birthday. What assignment would they give him next, he wondered. He skipped through the book, remembering the passages he and Peter had used to like . . . *the man without a navel yet lives in me* . . . What atrocity would he be asked to do next? He had already fulfilled an assignment. Hadn't he done enough? Another thing like the department store would be unbearable. It wasn't self-pity, only *life*. He was still alive, if he wanted to blame himself for that. He got up from the drawing table, went to his typewriter, and began his letter of resignation.

Anne insisted they go out and celebrate that evening. She was so glad, so overflowing with gladness, Guy felt his own spirits lifting a little, uncertainly, as a kite tries to lift itself from the ground on a still day. He watched her quick, slender fingers draw her hair tight back at the sides and close the bar pin over it in back.

"And, Guy, can't we make the cruise now?" she asked as they came down into the living room.

Anne still had her heart set on the cruise down the coast in the *India*, the honeymoon trip they had put off. Guy had intended to give all his time to the drafting rooms that were doing his hospital drawings, but he couldn't refuse Anne now.

"How soon do you think we can leave? Five days? A week?"

"Maybe five days."

"Oh, I just remember," she sighed. "I've got to stay till the twenty-third. There's a man coming in from California who's interested in all our cotton stuff."

"And isn't there a fashion show the end of this month?"

"Oh, Lillian can take care of that." She smiled. "How wonderful of you to remember!"

He waited while she pulled the hood of her leopard coat up about her head, amused at the thought of her driving a hard bargain with the man from California next week. She wouldn't leave that to Lillian. Anne was the business half of the shop. He saw the long-stemmed orange flowers on the coffee table for the first time. "Where'd these come from?" he asked.

"Charley Bruno. With a note apologizing for passing out Friday night." She laughed. "I think it's rather sweet."

Guy stared at them. "What kind are they?"

"African daisies." She held the front door open for him, and they went on out to the car.

She was flattered by the flowers, Guy thought. But her opinion of Bruno, he also knew, had gone down since the night of the party. Guy thought again of how bound up they were now, he and Bruno, by the score of people at the party. The police might investigate him any day. They *would* investigate him, he warned himself. And why wasn't he more concerned? What state of mind was he in that he could no longer say even what state it was? Resignation? Suicide? Or simply a torpor of stupidity?

During the next idle days he was compelled to spend at Horton, Horton and Keese to launch the drawings of the department store interior, he even asked himself whether he could be mentally deranged, if some subtle madness had not taken possession of him. He remembered the week or so after the Friday night, when his safety, his existence, had seemed to hang in a delicate balance that a failure of nerve might upset in a second. Now he felt none of that. Yet he still dreamt of Bruno invading his room. If he woke at dawn, he could still see himself standing in the room with the gun. He still felt that he must, and very soon, find some atonement for what he had done, some atonement for which no service or sacrifice he could yet envisage sufficed. He felt rather like two people, one of whom could create and feel in harmony with God when he created, and the other who could murder. "Any kind of person can murder," Bruno had said on the train. The man who had explained the cantilever principle to Bobbie Cartwright two years ago in Metcalf? No, nor the man who had designed the hospital, or even the department store, or debated half an hour with himself over the color he would paint a metal chair on the back lawn last week, but the man who had glanced into the mirror just last night and had seen for one instant the murderer, like a secret brother.

And how could he sit at his desk thinking of murder, when in less than ten days he would be with Anne on a white ship? Why had he been given Anne, or the power to love her? And had he agreed so readily to the cruise only because he wanted to be free of Bruno for three weeks? Bruno, if he wanted to, could take Anne from him. He had always admitted that to himself, always tried to face it. But he realized that since he had seen them together, since the day of the wedding, the possibility had become a specific terror.

He got up and put on his hat to go out to lunch. He heard the switchboard buzz as he crossed the lobby. Then the girl called to him.

"Take it from here if you like, Mr. Haines."

Guy picked up the telephone, knowing it was Bruno, knowing he would agree to Bruno's seeing him sometime today. Bruno asked him to have lunch, and Guy promised to meet him at Mario's Villa d'Este in ten minutes.

There were pink and white patterned drapes in the restaurant's window. Guy had a feeling that Bruno had laid a trap, that detectives would be behind the pink and white curtain, but not Bruno. And he didn't care, he felt, didn't care at all.

Bruno spotted him from the bar and slid off his stool with a grin. Guy walking around with his head in the air again, he thought, walking right by him. Bruno laid his hand on Guy's shoulder.

"Hi, Guy. I've got a table the end of this row."

Bruno was wearing his old rust-brown suit. Guy thought of the first time he had followed the long legs, down the swaying train to the compartment, but the memory brought no remorse now. He felt, in fact, well-disposed toward Bruno, as he sometimes did by night, but never until now by day. He did not even resent Bruno's evident gratification that he had come to lunch with him.

Bruno ordered the cocktails and the lunch. He ordered broiled liver for himself, because of his new diet, he said, and eggs Benedict for Guy, because he knew Guy liked them. Guy was inspecting the table nearest them. He felt a puzzled suspicion of the four smartly dressed, fortyish women, all of whom were smiling with their eyes almost closed, all of whom lifted cocktail glasses. Beyond them, a well-fed, European-looking man hurled a smile across the table at his invisible companion. Waiters scurried zealously. Could it all be a show created and enacted by madmen, he and Bruno the main characters, and the maddest of all? For every movement he saw, every word he heard, seemed wrapped in the heroic gloom of predestination.

"Like 'em?" Bruno was saying. "I got 'em at Clyde's this morning. Best selection in town. For summer anyway."

Guy looked down at the four tie boxes Bruno had opened in their laps. There were knitted, silk and linen ties, and a pale lavender bowtie of heavy linen. There was a shantung silk tie of aqua, like a dress of Anne's.

Bruno was disappointed. Guy didn't seem to like them. "Too loud? They're summer ties."

"They're nice," Guy said.

"This is my favorite. I never saw anything like this." Bruno held up the white knitted tie with the thin red stripe down the center. "Started to get one for myself, but I wanted you to have it. Just you, I mean. They're for you, Guy."

"Thanks." Guy felt an unpleasant twitch in his upper lip. He might have been Bruno's lover, he thought suddenly, to whom Bruno had brought a present, a peace offering.

"Here's to the trip," Bruno said, lifting his glass.

Bruno had spoken to Anne this morning on the telephone, and Anne had mentioned the cruise, he said. Bruno kept telling him, wistfully, how wonderful he thought Anne was.

"She's so pure-looking. You certainly don't see a—a *kind*-looking girl like that very often. You must be awfully happy, Guy." He hoped Guy might say something, a phrase or a word, that would somehow explain just why he was happy. But Guy didn't say anything, and Bruno felt rebuffed, felt the choking lump traveling from his chest up to his throat. What could Guy take offense at about that? Bruno wanted very much to put his hand over Guy's fist, that rested lightly on the edge of the table, just for a moment as a brother might, but he restrained himself. "Did she like you right away or did you have to know her a long time? Guy?"

Guy heard him repeat the question. It seemed ages old. "How can you ask me about time? It's a fact." He glanced at Bruno's narrow, plumpening face, at the cowlick that still gave his forehead a tentative expression, but Bruno's eyes were vastly more confident than when he had seen them first, and less sensitive. Because he had his money now, Guy thought.

"Yeah. I know what you mean." But Bruno didn't, quite. Guy was happy with Anne even though the murder still haunted him. Guy would be happy with her even if he were broke. Bruno winced now for even having thought once that he might offer Guy money. He could hear the way Guy would say, "No," with that look of drawing back in his eyes, of being miles away from him in a second. Bruno knew he would never have the things Guy had no matter how much money he had or what he did with it. Having his mother to himself was no guarantee of happiness, he had found out. Bruno made himself smile. "You think Anne likes me all right?"

"All right."

"What does she like to do outside of designing? Does she like to cook? Things like that?" Bruno watched Guy pick up his martini and drain it in three swallows. "You know. I just like to know the kind of things you do together. Like take walks or work crossword puzzles."

"We do things like that."

"What do you do in the evenings?"

"Anne sometimes works in the evenings." His mind slid easily, as it never had before with Bruno, to the upstairs studio where he and Anne often worked in the evenings, Anne talking to him from time to time, or holding something up for him to comment on, as if her work were effortless. When she dabbled her paintbrush fast in a glass of water, the sound was like laughter.

"I saw her picture in *Harper's Bazaar* a couple months ago with some other designers. She's pretty good, isn't she?"

"Very good."

"I—" Bruno laid his forearms one above the other on the table. "I sure am glad you're happy with her."

Of course he was. Guy felt his shoulders relax, and his breathing grow easier. Yet at this moment, it was hard to believe she was his. She was like a goddess who descended to pluck him from battles that would certainly have killed him, like the goddesses in mythology who saved the heroes, yet introduced an element at the end of the stories that had always struck him, when he read them as a child, as extraneous and unfair. In the nights when he could not sleep, when he stole out of the house and walked up the rock hill in pajamas and overcoat, in the unchallenging, indifferent summer nights, he did not permit himself to think of Anne. "*Dea ex machina,*" Guy murmured.

"What?"

Why was he sitting here with Bruno, eating at the same table with him? He wanted to fight Bruno and he wanted to weep. But all at once he felt his curses dissolve in a flood of pity. Bruno did not know how to love, and that was all he needed. Bruno was too lost, too blind to love or to inspire love. It seemed all at once tragic.

"You've never even been in love, Bruno?" Guy watched a restive, unfamiliar expression come into Bruno's eyes.

Bruno signaled for another drink. "No, not really in love, I guess." He moistened his lips. Not only hadn't he ever fallen in love, but he didn't care too much about sleeping with women. He had never been able to stop thinking it was a silly business, that he was standing off somewhere and watching himself. Once, one terrible time, he had started giggling. Bruno squirmed. That was the most painful difference he felt separating him and Guy, that Guy could forget himself in women, had practically killed himself for Miriam.

Guy looked at Bruno, and Bruno lowered his eyes. Bruno was waiting, as if for him to tell him how to fall in love. "Do you know the greatest wisdom in the world, Bruno?"

"I know a lot of wisdoms," Bruno smirked. "Which one do you mean?"

"That everything has its opposite close beside it."

"Opposites attract?"

"That's too simple. I mean—you give me ties. But it also occurred to me you might have the police waiting for me here."

"F' Christ's sake, Guy, you're my *friend*!" Bruno said quickly, suddenly frantic. "I like you!"

I like you, I don't hate you, Guy thought. But Bruno wouldn't say that, because he did hate him. Just as he would never say to Bruno, I like you, but instead, I hate you, because he did like him. Guy set his jaw, and rubbed his fingers back and forth across his forehead. He could foresee a balance of positive and negative will that would paralyze every action before he began it. Such as that, for instance, that kept him sitting here. He jumped up, and the new drinks splashed on the cloth.

Bruno stared at him in terrified surprise. "Guy, what's the matter?" Bruno followed him. "Guy, wait! You don't think I'd do a thing like that, do you? I wouldn't in a million years!"

"Don't touch me!"

"*Guy!*" Bruno was almost crying. Why did people do these things to him? *Why?* He shouted on the sidewalk: "Not in a million years! Not for a million dollars! Trust me, Guy!"

Guy pushed his hand into Bruno's chest and closed the taxi door. Bruno would not in a million years betray him, he knew. But if everything were as ambiguous as he believed, how could he really be sure?

## *thirty-four*

"What's your connection with Mrs. Guy Haines?"

Bruno had expected it. Gerard had his latest charge accounts, and this was the flowers he had sent Anne. "Friend. Friend of her husband."

"Oh. Friend?"

"Acquaintance." Bruno shrugged, knowing Gerard would think he was trying to brag because Guy was famous.

"Known him long?"

"Not long." From his horizontal slump in his easy chair, Bruno reached for his lighter.

"How'd you happen to send flowers?"

"Feeling good, I guess. I was going to a party there that night."

"Do you know him that well?"

Bruno shrugged again. "Ordinary party. He was one of the architects we thought of when we were talking about building a house." That had just popped out, and it was rather good, Bruno thought.

"Matt Levine. Let's get back to him."

Bruno sighed. Skipping Guy, maybe because he was out of town, maybe just skipping him. Now Matt Levine—they didn't come any shadier, and without realizing it might be useful, he had seen a lot of Matt before the murder. "What about him?"

"How is it you saw him the twenty-fourth, twenty-eighth, and thirtieth of April, the second, fifth, sixth, seventh of March, and two days before the murder?"

"Did I?" he smiled. Gerard had had only three dates the last time.

Matt didn't like him either. Matt had probably said the worst. "He was interested in buying my car."

"And you were interested in selling it? Why, because you thought you'd get a new one soon?"

"Wanted to sell it to get a little car," Bruno said obliviously. "The one in the garage now. Crosley."

Gerard smiled. "How long have you known Mark Lev?"

"Since he was Mark Levitski," Bruno retorted. "Go back a little farther and you'll find he killed his own father in Russia." Bruno glared at Gerard. The "own" sounded funny, he shouldn't have said it, but Gerard trying to be smart with the aliases!

"Matt doesn't care for you either. What's the matter, couldn't you two come to terms?"

"About the car?"

"Charles," Gerard said patiently.

"I'm not saying anything." Bruno looked at his bitten nails, and thought again how well Matt matched Herbert's description of the murderer.

"You haven't seen Ernie Schroeder much lately."

Bruno opened his mouth boredly to answer.

# *thirty-five*

Barefoot, in white duck trousers, Guy sat cross-legged on the *India*'s forward deck. Long Island had just come in sight, but he did not want to look at it yet. The gently rolling movement of the ship rocked him pleasantly and familiarly, like something he had always known. The day he had last seen Bruno, in the restaurant, seemed a day of madness. Surely he had been going insane. Surely Anne must have seen it.

He flexed his arm and pinched up the thin brown skin that covered its muscles. He was brown as Egon, the half-Portuguese ship's boy they had hired from the Long Island dock at the start of the cruise. Only the little scar in his right eyebrow remained white.

The three weeks at sea had given him a peace and resignation he had never known before, and that a month ago he would have declared foreign to him. He had come to feel that his atonement, whatever it might be, was a part of his destiny, and like the rest of his destiny would find him without his seeking. He had always trusted his sense of destiny. As a boy with Peter, he had known that he would not merely dream, as he had somehow known, too, that Peter would do nothing but dream, that he would create famous buildings, that his name would take its proper place in architecture, and finally—it had always seemed to him the crowning achievement—that he would build a bridge. It would be a white bridge with a span like an angel's wing, he had thought as a boy, like the curving white bridge of Robert Maillart in his architecture books. It was a kind of arrogance, perhaps, to believe so in one's destiny. But, on the other hand, who could be more genuinely humble than one who felt compelled to obey the laws of his own fate? The murder that had seemed an outrageous departure, a sin against himself, he believed now might have been a part of his destiny, too. It was impossible to think otherwise. And if it were so, he would be given a way to make his atonement, and given the strength to make it. And if death by law overtook him first, he would be given the strength to meet that also, and strength besides sufficient for Anne to meet it. In a strange way, he felt humbler than the smallest minnow of the sea, and stronger than the greatest mountain on earth. But he was not arrogant. His arrogance had been a defense, reaching its height at the time of the break with Miriam. And hadn't he known even then, obsessed by her, wretchedly poor, that he would find another woman whom he could love and who would love him always? And what better proof did he need that all this was so than that he and Anne had never been closer, their lives never more like one harmonious life, than during these three weeks at sea?

He turned himself with a movement of his feet, so he could see her as she leaned against the mainmast. There was a faint smile on her lips as she gazed down at him, a half-repressed, prideful smile like that of a mother, Guy thought, who had brought her child safely through an illness, and smiling back at her, Guy marveled that he could put such trust in her infallibility and rightness and that she could still be merely a human being. Most of all, he marveled that she could be his. Then he looked down at his locked hands and thought of the work he would begin tomorrow on the hospital, of all the work to come, and the events of his destiny that lay ahead.

Bruno telephoned a few evenings later. He was in the neighborhood, he said, and wanted to come by. He sounded very sober, and a little dejected.

Guy told him no. He told him calmly and firmly that neither he nor Anne wanted to see him again, but even as he spoke, he felt the sands of his patience running out fast, and the sanity of the past weeks crumbling under the madness of their conversing at all.

Bruno knew that Gerard had not spoken to Guy yet. He did not think Gerard would question Guy more than a few minutes. But Guy sounded so cold, Bruno could not bring himself to tell him now that Gerard had gotten his name, that he might be interviewed, or that he intended to see Guy strictly secretly from now on—no more parties or even lunches—if Guy would only let him.

"Okay," Bruno said mutedly, and hung up.

Then the telephone rang again. Frowning, Guy put out the cigarette he had just lighted relievedly, and answered it.

"Hello. This is Arthur Gerard of the Confidential Detective Bureau. . . ." Gerard asked if he could come over.

Guy turned around, glancing warily over the living room, trying to reason away a feeling that Gerard had just heard his and Bruno's conversation over tapped wires, that Gerard had just captured Bruno. He went upstairs to tell Anne.

"A private detective?" Anne asked, surprised. "What's it about?"

Guy hesitated an instant. There were so many, many places where he might hesitate too long! Damn Bruno! Damn him for dogging him! "I don't know."

Gerard arrived promptly. He fairly bowed over Anne's hand, and after apologizing for intruding on their evening, made polite conversation about the house and the strip of garden in front. Guy stared at him in some astonishment. Gerard looked dull, tired, and vaguely untidy. Perhaps Bruno wasn't entirely wrong about him. Even his absent air, heightened by his slow speech, did not suggest the absent-mindedness of a brilliant detective. Then as Gerard settled himself with a cigar and a highball, Guy caught the shrewdness in the light hazel eyes and the energy in the chunky hands. Guy felt uneasy then. Gerard looked unpredictable.

"You're a friend of Charles Bruno, Mr. Haines?"

"Yes. I know him."

"His father was murdered last March as you probably know, and the murderer has not been found."

"I didn't know that!" Anne said.

Gerard's eyes moved slowly from her back to Guy.

"I didn't know either," said Guy.

"You don't know him that well?"

"I know him very slightly."

"When and where did you meet?"

"At—" Guy glanced at Anne—"the Parker Art Institute, I think around last December." Guy felt he had walked into a trap. He had repeated Bruno's flippant reply at the wedding, simply because Anne had heard Bruno say it, and Anne had probably forgotten. Gerard regarded him, Guy thought, as if he didn't believe a word of it. Why hadn't Bruno warned him about Gerard? Why hadn't they *settled* on the story Bruno had once proposed about their having met at the rail of a certain midtown bar?

"And when did you see him again?" Gerard asked finally.

"Well—not until my wedding in June." He felt himself assuming the puzzled expression of a man who does not yet know his inquisitor's object. Fortunately, he thought, fortunately, he had already assured Anne that Bruno's assertion they were old friends was only Bruno's style of humor. "We didn't invite him," Guy added.

"He just came?" Gerard looked as if he understood. "But you did invite him to the party you gave in July?" He glanced at Anne also.

"He called up," Anne told him, "and asked if he could come, so—I said yes."

Gerard then asked if Bruno knew about the party through any friends of his who were coming, and Guy said possibly, and gave the name of the blond woman who had smiled so horrifically at Bruno that evening. Guy had no other names to give. He had never seen Bruno with anyone.

Gerard leaned back. "Do you like him?" he smiled.

"Well enough," Anne replied finally, politely.

"All right," Guy said, because Gerard was waiting. "He seems a bit pushing." The right side of his face was in shadow. Guy wondered if Gerard were scanning his face now for scars.

"A hero-worshiper. Power-worshiper, in a sense." Gerard smiled, but the smile no longer looked genuine, or perhaps it never had. "Sorry to bother you with these questions, Mr. Haines."

Five minutes later, he was gone.

"What does it mean?" Anne asked. "Does he suspect Charles Bruno?"

Guy bolted the door, then came back. "He probably suspects one of his acquaintances. He might think Charles knows something, because he hated his father so. Or so Charles told me."

"Do you think Charles might know?"

"There's no telling. Is there?" Guy took a cigarette.

"Good lord." Anne stood looking at the corner of the sofa, as if she still saw Bruno where he had sat the night of the party. She whispered, "Amazing what goes on in people's lives!"

## thirty-six

"Listen," Guy said tensely into the receiver. "Listen, Bruno!" Bruno was drunker than Guy had ever heard him, but he was determined to penetrate to the muddled brain. Then he thought suddenly that Gerard might be with him, and his voice grew even softer, cowardly with caution. He found out Bruno was in a telephone booth, alone. "Did you tell Gerard we met at the Art Institute?"

Bruno said he had. It came through the drunken mumblings that he had. Bruno wanted to come over. Guy couldn't make it register that Gerard had already come to question him. Guy banged the telephone down, and tore open his collar. Bruno calling him now! Gerard had externalized his danger. Guy felt it was more imperative to break completely with Bruno even than to arrange a story with him that would tally. What annoyed him most was that he couldn't tell from Bruno's driveling what had happened to him, or even what kind of mood he was in.

Guy was upstairs in the studio with Anne when the door chime rang. He opened the door only slightly, but Bruno bumped it wide, stumbled across the living room, and collapsed on the sofa. Guy stopped short in front of him, speechless first with anger, then disgust. Bruno's fat, flushed neck bulged over his collar. He seemed more bloated than drunk, as if an edema of death had inflated his entire body, filling even the deep eye sockets so the red-gray eyes were thrust unnaturally forward. Bruno stared up at him. Guy went to the telephone to call a taxi.

"Guy, who is it?" Anne whispered down the stairway.

"Charles Bruno. He's drunk."

"Not drunk!" Bruno protested suddenly.

Anne came halfway down the stairs, and saw him. "Shouldn't we just put him upstairs?"

"I don't want him here." Guy was looking in the telephone book, trying to find a taxi company's number.

"Yess-s!" Bruno hissed, like a deflating tire.

Guy turned. Bruno was staring at him out of one eye, the eye the only living point in the sprawled, corpselike body. He was muttering something, rhythmically.

"What's he saying?" Anne stood closer to Guy.

Guy went to Bruno and caught him by the shirtfront. The muttered, imbecilic chant infuriated him, Bruno drooled onto his hand as he tried to pull him upright. "Get up and get out!" Then he heard it:

"I'll *tell* her, I'll *tell* her—I'll *tell* her, I'll *tell* her," Bruno chanted, and the wild red eye stared up. "Don't send me away, I'll *tell* her—I'll—"

Guy released him in abhorrence.

"What's the matter, Guy? What's he saying?"

"I'll put him upstairs," Guy said.

Guy tried with all his strength to get Bruno over his shoulder, but the flaccid, dead weight defeated him. Finally, Guy stretched him out across the sofa. He went to the front window. There was no car outside. Bruno might have dropped out of the sky. Bruno slept noiselessly, and Guy sat up watching him, smoking.

Bruno awakened about 3 in the morning, and had a couple of drinks to steady himself. After a few moments, except for the bloatedness, he looked almost normal. He was very happy at finding himself in Guy's house, and had no recollection of arriving. "I had another round with Gerard," he smiled. "Three days. Been seeing the papers?"

"No."

"You're a fine one, don't even look at the papers!" Bruno said softly. "Gerard's hot on a bum scent. This crook friend of mine, Matt Levine. He doesn't have an alibi for that night. Herbert thinks it could be him. I been talking with all three of them for three days. Matt might get it."

"Might die for it?"

Bruno hesitated, still smiling. "Not die, just take the rap. He's got two or three killings on him now. The cops're glad to have him." Bruno shuddered, and drank the rest in his glass.

Guy wanted to pick up the big ashtray in front of him and smash Bruno's bloated head, burn out the tension he felt would grow and grow until he did kill Bruno, or himself. He caught Bruno's shoulders hard in both hands. "Will you get out? I swear this is the last time!"

"No," Bruno said quietly, without any movement of resistance, and Guy saw the old indifference to pain, to death, that he had seen when he had fought him in the woods.

Guy put his hands over his own face, and felt its contortion against his palms. "If this Matt gets blamed,"he whispered,"I'll tell them the whole story."

"Oh, he won't. They won't have enough. It's a joke, son!" Bruno grinned. "Matt's the right character with the wrong evidence. You're the wrong character with the right evidence. You're an important guy, f' Christ's sake!"He pulled something out of his pocket and handed it to Guy. "I found this last week. Very nice, Guy."

Guy looked at the photograph of "The Pittsburgh Store," funereally backgrounded by black. It was a booklet from the Modern Museum. He read: "Guy Daniel Haines, hardly thirty, follows the Wright tradition. He has achieved a distinctive, uncompromising style noted for a rigorous simplicity without starkness, for the grace he calls 'singingness' . . ." Guy closed it nervously, disgusted by the last word that was an invention of the Museum's.

Bruno repocketed the booklet. "You're one of the tops. If you kept your nerve up, they could turn you inside out and never suspect."

Guy looked down at him. "That's still no reason for you to see me. Why do you do it?" But he knew. Because his life with Anne fascinated Bruno. Because he himself derived something from seeing Bruno, some torture that perversely eased.

Bruno watched him as if he knew everything that passed through his mind. "I like you, Guy, but remember—they've got a lot more against you than against me. I could wiggle out if you turned me in, but you couldn't. There's the fact Herbert might remember you. And Anne might remember you were acting funny around that time. And the scratches and the scar. And all the little clues they'd shove in front of you, like the revolver, and glove pieces—" Bruno recited them slowly and fondly, like old memories. "With me against you, you'd crack up, I bet."

## *thirty-seven*

Guy knew as soon as Anne called to him that she had seen the dent. He had meant to get it fixed, and had forgotten. He said first that he didn't know how it got there, then that he did. He had taken the boat out last week, he said, and it had bumped a buoy.

"Don't be terribly sorry," she mocked him,"it isn't worth it." She took his hand as she stood up. "Egon said you had the boat out one afternoon. Is that why you didn't say anything about it?"

"I suppose."

"Did you take it out by yourself?"Anne smiled a little, because he wasn't a good-enough sailor to take the boat out by himself.

Bruno had called up and insisted they go out for a sail. Gerard had come to a new deadend with Matt Levine, deadends everywhere, and Bruno had insisted that they celebrate. "I took it out with Charles Bruno one afternoon," he said. And he had brought the revolver with him that day, too.

"It's all right, Guy. Only why'd you see him again? I thought you disliked him so."

"A whim," he murmured. "It was the two days I was doing that work at home." It wasn't all right, Guy knew. Anne kept the *India*'s brass and white-painted wood gleaming and spotless, like something of chryselephantine. And Bruno! She mistrusted Bruno now.

"Guy, he's not the man we saw that night in front of your apartment, is he? The one who spoke to us in the snow?"

"Yes. He's the same one." Guy's fingers, supporting the weight of the revolver in his pocket, tightened helplessly.

"What's his interest in you?" Anne followed him casually down the deck. "He isn't interested in architecture particularly. I talked with him the night of the party."

"He's got no interest in me. Just doesn't know what to do with himself." When he got rid of the revolver, he thought, he could talk.

"You met him at school?"

"Yes. He was wandering around a corridor." How easy it was to lie when one *had* to lie! But it was wrapping tendrils around his feet, his body, his brain. He would say the wrong thing one day. He was doomed to lose Anne. Perhaps he had already lost her, at this moment when he lighted a cigarette and she stood leaning against the mainmast, watching him. The revolver seemed to weight him to the spot, and determinedly he turned and walked toward the prow. Behind him, he heard Anne's step onto the deck, and her soft tread in her tennis shoes, going back toward the cockpit.

It was a sullen day, promising rain. The *India* rocked slowly on the choppy surface, and seemed no farther from the gray shore than it had been an hour ago. Guy leaned on the bowsprit and looked down at his white-clad legs, the blue gilt-buttoned jacket he had taken from the *India*'s locker, that perhaps had belonged to Anne's father. He might have been a sailor instead of an architect, he thought. He had been wild to go to sea at fourteen. What had stopped him? How different his life might have been without—what? Without Miriam, of course. He straightened impatiently and pulled the revolver from the pocket of the jacket.

He held the gun in both hands over the water, his elbow on the bowsprit. How intelligent a jewel, he thought, and how innocent it looked now. Himself— He let it drop. The gun turned once head-over, in perfect balance, with its familiar look of willingness, and disappeared.

"What was that?"

Guy turned and saw her standing on the deck near the cabin. He measured the ten or twelve feet between them. He could think of nothing, absolutely nothing to say to her.

# thirty-eight

Bruno hesitated about the drink. The bathroom walls had that look of breaking up in little pieces, as if the walls might not really have been there, or he might not really have been here.

"Ma!" But the frightened bleat shamed him, and he drank his drink.

He tiptoed into his mother's room and awakened her with a press of the button by her bed, which signaled to Herbert in the kitchen that she was ready for her breakfast.

"Oh-h," she yawned, then smiled. "And how are you?" She patted his arm, slid up from the covers, and went into the bathroom to wash.

Bruno sat quietly on her bed until she came out and got back under the cover again.

"We're supposed to see that trip man this afternoon. What's his name, Saunders? You'd better feel like going in with me."

Bruno nodded. It was about their trip to Europe, that they might make into a round-the-world trip. It didn't have any charm this morning. He might like to go around the world with Guy. Bruno stood up, wondering whether to go get another drink.

"How're you feeling?"

His mother always asked him at the wrong times. "Okay," he said, sitting down again.

There was a knock on the door, and Herbert came in. "Good morning, madam. Good morning, sir," Herbert said without looking at either of them.

With his chin in his hand, Bruno frowned down at Herbert's silent, polished, turned-out shoes. Herbert's insolence lately was intolerable! Gerard had made him think he was the key to the whole case, if they just produced the right man. Everyone said how brave he was to have chased the murderer. And his father had left him twenty thousand in his will. Herbert *might* take a vacation!

"Does madam know if there'll be six or seven for dinner?"

As Herbert spoke, Bruno looked up at his pink, pointed chin and thought, Guy whammed him there and knocked him right out.

"Oh, dear, I haven't called yet, Herbert, but I think seven."

"Very good, madam."

Rutledge Overbeck II, Bruno thought. He had known his mother would end up having him, though she pretended to be doubtful because he would make an odd number. Rutledge Overbeck was madly in love with his mother, or pretending to be. Bruno wanted to tell his mother Herbert hadn't sent his clothes to be pressed in six weeks, but he felt too sickish to begin.

"You know, I'm dying to see Australia," she said through a bite of toast. She had propped a map up against her coffee pot.

A tingling, naked sensation spread over his buttocks. He stood up. "Ma, I don't feel so hot."

She frowned at him concernedly, which frightened him more, because he realized there was nothing in the world she could do to help him. "What's the matter, darling? What do you want?"

He hurried from the room, feeling he might have to be sick. The bathroom went black. He staggered out, and let the still corked Scotch bottle topple onto his bed.

"What, Charley? What is it?"

"I wanna lie down." He flopped down, but that wasn't it. He motioned his mother away so he could get up, but when he sat up he wanted to lie down again, so he stood up. "Feel like I'm dying!"

"Lie down, darling. How about some—some hot tea?"

Bruno tore off his smoking jacket, then his pajama top. He was suffocating. He had to pant to breathe. He *did* feel like he was dying!

She hurried to him with a wet towel. "What is it, your stomach?"

"Everything." He kicked off his slippers. He went to the window to open it, but it was already open. He turned, sweating. "Ma, maybe I'm dying. You think I'm dying?"

"I'll get you a drink!"

"No, get the doctor!" he shrieked. "Get me a drink, too!" Feebly he pulled his pajama string and let the pants drop. What was it? Not just the shakes. He was too weak to shake. Even his hands were weak and tingly. He held up his hands. The fingers were curved inward. He couldn't open them. "Ma, somp'n's the matter with my hands! Look, Ma, what is it, what is it?"

"Drink this!"

He heard the bottle chatter on the rim of the glass. He couldn't wait for it. He trotted into the hall, stooped with terror, staring at his limp, curling hands. It was the two middle fingers on each hand. They were curving in, almost touching the palm.

"Darling, put your robe on!" she whispered.

"*Get the doctor!*" A robe! She talked about a robe! What did it matter if he was stark naked? "Ma, but don't let 'em take me away!" He plucked at her as she stood at the telephone. "Lock all the doors! You know what they do?"He spoke fast and confidentially, because the numbness was working up and he knew what was the matter now. He was a case! He was going to be like this all his life! "Know what they do, Ma, they put you in a straitjacket without a drop and it'll kill me!"

"Dr. Packer? This is Mrs. Bruno. Could you recommend a doctor in the neighborhood?"

Bruno screamed. How would a doctor get out here in the Connecticut sticks? "Massom—" He gasped. He couldn't talk, couldn't move his tongue. It had gone into his vocal cords! "Aaaaagh!" He wriggled from under the smoking jacket his mother was trying to throw over him. Let Herbert stand there gaping at him if he wanted to!

"Charles!"

He gestured toward his mouth with his crazy hands. He trotted to the closet mirror. His face was white, flat around the mouth as if someone had hit him with a board, his lips drawn horribly back from his teeth. And his hands! He wouldn't be able to hold a glass anymore, or light a cigarette. He wouldn't be able to drive a car. He wouldn't even be able to go to the john by himself!

"*Drink* this!"

Yes, liquor, liquor. He tried to catch it all in his stiff lips. It burnt his face and ran down his chest. He motioned for more. He tried to remind her to lock the doors. Oh, Christ, if it went away, he would be grateful all his life! He let Herbert and his mother push him onto the bed.

"Tehmeh!" he choked. He twisted his mother's dressing gown and nearly pulled her down on top of him. But at least he could hold to something now. "Dome tehmeh way!" he said with his breath, and she assured him she wouldn't. She told him she would lock all the doors.

*Gerard,* he thought. Gerard was still working against him, and he would keep on and on and on. Not only Gerard but a whole army of people, checking and snooping and visiting people, hammering typewriters, running out and running back with more pieces, pieces from Santa Fe now, and one day Gerard might put them together right. One day Gerard might come in and find him like this morning, and ask him and he would tell everything. He had killed someone. They killed *you* for killing someone. Maybe he couldn't cope. He stared up at the light fixture in the center of the ceiling. It reminded him of the round chromium drainstop in the basin at his grandmother's house in Los Angeles. Why did he think of that?

The cruel jab of the hypodermic needle shocked him to sharper consciousness.

The young, jumpy-looking doctor was talking to his mother in a corner of the darkened room. But he felt better. They wouldn't take him away now. It was okay now. He had just been panicky. Cautiously, just under the top of the sheet, he watched his fingers flex. "Guy," he whispered. His tongue was still thick, but he could talk. Then he saw the doctor go out.

"Ma, I don't want to go to Europe!" he said in a monotone as his mother came over.

"All right, darling, we won't go." She sat down gently on the side of the bed, and he felt immediately better.

"The doctor didn't say I couldn't go, did he?" As if he wouldn't go if he wanted to! What was he afraid of? Not even of another attack like this! He touched the puffed shoulder of his mother's dressing gown, but he thought of Rutledge Overbeck at dinner tonight, and let his hand drop. He was sure his mother was having an affair with him. She went to see him too much at his studio in Silver Springs, and she stayed too long. He didn't want to admit it, but why shouldn't he when it was under his nose? It was the first affair, and his father was dead so why shouldn't she, but why did she have to pick such a jerk? Her eyes looked darker now, in the shaded room. She hadn't improved since the days after his father's death. She was going to be like this, Bruno realized now, stay like this, never be young again the way he liked her. "Don't look so sad, Mom."

"Darling, will you promise me you'll cut down? The doctor said this is the beginning of the end. This morning was a warning, don't you see? Nature's warning." She moistened her lips, and the sudden softness of the rouged, lined underlip so close to him was more than Bruno could bear.

He closed his eyes tight shut. If he promised, he would be lying. "Hell, I didn't get the D.T.'s, did I? I never had 'em."

"But this is worse. I talked with the doctor. It's destroying your nerve tissue, he said, and it can kill you. Doesn't that mean anything to you?"

"Yes, Ma."

"Promise me?" She watched his eyelids flutter shut again, and heard him sigh. The tragedy was not this morning, she thought, but years ago when he had taken his first drink by himself. The tragedy was not even the first drink, because the first drink was not the first resort but the last. There'd had to be first the failure of everything else—of her and Sam, of his friends, of his hope, of his interests, really. And hard as she tried, she could never discover why or where it might have begun, because Charley had always been given everything, and both she and Sam had done their best to encourage him in everything and anything he had ever shown interest in. If she could only discover the place in the past where it might have begun— She got up, needing a drink herself.

Bruno opened his eyes tentatively. He felt deliciously heavy with sleep. He saw himself halfway across the room, as if he watched himself on a screen. He was in his red-brown suit. It was the island in Metcalf. He saw his younger, slimmer body arc toward Miriam and fling her to the earth, those few short moments separate from time before and time after. He felt he had made special movements, thought special brilliant thoughts in those moments, and that such an interval would never come again. Like Guy had talked about himself, the other day on the boat, when he built the Palmyra. Bruno was glad those special moments for both of them had come so near the same time. Sometimes he thought he could die without regrets, because what else could he ever do that would measure up to the night in Metcalf? What else wouldn't be an anticlimax? Sometimes, like now, he felt his energy might be winding down, and something, maybe his curiosity, dying down. But he didn't mind, because he felt so wise now somehow, and really so content. Only yesterday he had wanted to go around the world. And why? To say he had been? To say to whom? Last month he had written to William Beebe, volunteering to go down in the new super-bathysphere that they were testing first without a man inside.

Why? Everything was silly compared to the night in Metcalf. Every person he knew was silly compared to Guy. Silliest of all to think he'd wanted to see a lot of European women! Maybe the Captain's whores had soured him, so what? Lots of people thought sex was overrated. No love lasts forever, the psychologists said. But he really shouldn't say that about Guy and Anne. He had a feeling theirs might last, but just why he didn't know. It wasn't only that Guy was so wrapped up in her he was blind to all the rest. It wasn't just that Guy had enough money now. It was something invisible that he hadn't even thought of yet. Sometimes he felt he was right on the brink of thinking of it. No, he didn't want the answer for himself. Purely in the spirit of scientific inquiry.

He turned on his side, smiling, clicking and unclicking the top of his gold Dunhill lighter. That trip man wouldn't see them today or any other day. Home was a hell of a lot more comfortable than Europe. And Guy was here.

# *thirty-nine*

Gerard was chasing him through a forest, waving all the clues at him—the glove scraps, the shred of overcoat, even the revolver, because Gerard already had Guy. Guy was tied up back in the forest, and his right hand was bleeding fast. If he couldn't circle around and get to him, Guy would bleed to death. Gerard giggled as he ran, as if it were a good joke, a good trick they'd played, but he'd guessed it after all. In a minute, Gerard would touch him with those ugly hands!

"Guy!" But his voice sounded feeble. And Gerard was almost touching him. That was the game, when Gerard *touched* him!

With all his power, Bruno struggled to sit up. The nightmare slid from his brain like heavy slabs of rock.

Gerard! There he was!

"What's the matter? Bad dream?"

The pink-purply hands touched him, and Bruno whirled himself off the bed onto the floor.

"Woke you just in time, eh?" Gerard laughed.

Bruno set his teeth hard enough to break them. He bolted to the bathroom and took a drink with the door wide open. In the mirror, his face looked like a battlefield in hell.

"Sorry to intrude, but I found something new," Gerard said in the tense, high-pitched voice that meant he had scored a little victory. "About your friend Guy Haines. The one you were just dreaming about, weren't you?"

The glass cracked in Bruno's hand, and meticulously he gathered up the pieces from the basin and put them in the jagged bottom of the glass. He staggered boredly back to his bed.

"When did you meet him, Charles? Not last December." Gerard leaned against the chest of drawers, lighting a cigar. "Did you meet him about a year and a half ago? Did you go with him on the train down to Santa Fe?" Gerard waited. He pulled something from under his arm and tossed it on the bed. "Remember that?"

It was Guy's Plato book from Santa Fe, still wrapped and with its address half rubbed off. "Sure, I remember it."Bruno pushed it away. "I lost it going to the post office."

"Hotel La Fonda had it right on the shelf. How'd you happen to borrow a book of Plato?"

"I found it on the train." Bruno looked up. "It had Guy's address in it, so I meant to mail it. Found it in the dining car, matter of fact." He looked straight at Gerard, who was watching him with his sharp, steady little eyes that didn't always have anything behind them.

"When did you meet him, Charley?" Gerard asked again, with the patient air of one questioning a child he knows is lying.

"In December."

"You know about his wife's murder, of course."

"Sure, I read about it. Then I read about him building the Palmyra Club."

"And you thought, how interesting, because you had found a book six months before that belonged to him."

Bruno hesitated. "Yeah."

Gerard grunted, and looked down with a little smile of disgust.

Bruno felt odd, uncomfortable. When had he seen it before, a smile like that after a grunt? Once when he had lied to his father about something, very obviously lied and clung to it, and his father's grunt, the disbelief in the smile, had shamed him. Bruno realized that his eyes pled with Gerard to forgive him, so he deliberately looked off at the window.

"And you made all those calls to Metcalf not even knowing Guy Haines." Gerard picked up the book.

"What calls?"

"Several calls."

"Maybe one when I was tight."

"Several. About what?"

"About the damned book!" If Gerard knew him so well, he should know that was exactly the kind of thing he would do. "Maybe I called when I heard his wife got murdered."

Gerard shook his head. "You called before she was murdered."

"So what? Maybe I did."

"So what? I'll have to ask Mr. Haines. Considering your interest in murder, it's remarkable you didn't call him after the murder, isn't it?"

"I'm sick of murder!" Bruno shouted.

"Oh, I believe it, Charley, I believe it!" Gerard sauntered out, and down the hall toward his mother's room.

Bruno showered and dressed with slow care. Gerard had been much, much more excited about Matt Levine, he remembered. As far as he knew, he had made only two calls to Metcalf from Hotel La Fonda, where Gerard must have picked up the bills. He could say Guy's mother was mistaken about the others, that it hadn't been he.

"What'd Gerard want?" Bruno asked his mother.

"Nothing much. Wanted to know if I knew a friend of yours. Guy Haines." She was brushing her hair with upward strokes, so it stood out wildly around the calm, tired face. "He's an architect, isn't he?"

"Uh-huh. I don't know him very well." He strolled along the floor behind her. She had forgotten the clippings in Los Angeles, just as he had thought she would. Thank Christ, he hadn't reminded her he knew Guy when all the Palmyra pictures came out! The back of his mind must have known he was going to get Guy to do it.

"Gerard was talking about your calling him last summer. What was all that?"

"Oh, Mom, I get so damn sick of Gerard's dumb steers!"

# forty

A few moments later that morning, Guy stepped out of the director's office at Hanson and Knapp Drafters, happier than he had felt in weeks. The firm was copying the last of the hospital drawings, the most complex Guy had ever supervised, the last okays had come through on the building materials, and he had gotten a telegram early that morning from Bob Treacher that made Guy rejoice for his old friend. Bob had been appointed to an advisory committee of engineers for the new Alberta Dam in Canada, a job he had been looking forward to for the last five years.

Here and there at one of the long tables that fanned out on either side of him, a draftsman looked up and watched him as he walked toward the outer door. Guy nodded a greeting to a smiling foreman. He detected the smallest glow of self-esteem. Or maybe it was nothing but his new suit, he thought, only the third suit in his life he had ever had made for him. Anne had chosen the gray-blue glen plaid material. Anne had chosen the tomato-colored woolen tie this morning to go with it, an old tie but one that he liked. He tightened its knot in the mirror between the elevators. There was a wild gray hair sticking up from one black, heavy eyebrow. The brows went up a little in surprise. He smoothed the hair down. It was the first gray hair he had ever noticed on himself.

A draftsman opened the office door. "Mr. Haines? Lucky I caught you. There's a telephone call."

Guy went back, hoping it wouldn't be long, because he was to meet Anne for lunch in ten minutes. He took the call in an empty office off the drafting room.

"Hello, Guy? Listen, Gerard found that Plato book. . . . Yeah, in Santa Fe. Now, listen, it doesn't change anything. . . ."

Five minutes had passed before Guy was back at the elevators. He had always known the Plato might be found. Not a chance, Bruno had said. Bruno could be wrong. Bruno could be caught, therefore. Guy scowled as if it were incredible, the idea Bruno could be caught. And somehow it had been incredible, until now.

Momentarily, as he came out into the sunlight, he was conscious again of the new suit, and he clenched his fist in frustrated anger with himself. "I found the book on the train, see?" Bruno had said. "If I called you in Metcalf, it was on account of the book. But I didn't meet you until December . . ." The voice more clipped and anxious than Guy had ever heard it before, so alert, so harried, it hardly seemed Bruno's voice. Guy went over the fabrication Bruno had just given him as if it were something that didn't belong to him, as if it were a swatch of material he indifferently considered for a suit, he thought. No, there were no holes in it, but it wouldn't necessarily wear. Not if someone remembered seeing them on the train. The waiter, for instance, who had served them in Bruno's compartment.

He tried to slow his breathing, tried to slow his pace. He looked up at the small disc of the winter sun. His black brows with the gray hair, with the white scar, his brows that were growing shaggier lately, Anne said, broke the glare into particles and protected him. If one looks directly into the sun for fifteen seconds, one can burn through the cornea, he remembered from somewhere. Anne protected him, too. His work protected him. *The new suit, the stupid new suit.* He felt suddenly inadequate and dull-witted, helpless. Death had insinuated itself into his brain. It enwrapped him. He had breathed its air so long, perhaps, he had grown quite used to it. Well, then, he was not afraid. He squared his shoulders superfluously.

Anne had not arrived when he got to the restaurant. Then he remembered she had said she was going to pick up the snapshots they had made Sunday at the house. Guy pulled Bob Treacher's telegram from his pocket and read it again and again:

> JUST APPOINTED TO ALBERTA COMMITTEE. HAVE RECOMMENDED YOU. THIS IS A BRIDGE, GUY. GET FREE SOON AS POSSIBLE. ACCEPTANCE GUARANTEED. LETTER COMING.
>
> BOB

Acceptance guaranteed. Regardless of how he engineered his life, his ability to engineer a bridge was beyond question. Guy sipped his martini thoughtfully, holding the surface perfectly steady.

# *forty-one*

"I've wandered into another case," Gerard murmured pleasantly, gazing at the typewritten report on his desk. He had not looked at Bruno since the young man had come in. "Murder of Guy Haines' first wife. Never been solved."

"Yeah, I know."

"I thought you'd know quite a lot about it. Now tell me everything you know." Gerard settled himself.

Bruno could tell he had gone all the way into it since Monday when he had the Plato book. "Nothing," Bruno said. "Nobody knows. Do they?"

"What do you think? You must have talked a great deal with Guy about it."

"Not particularly. Not at all. Why?"

"Because murder interests you so much."

"What do you mean, murder interests me so much?"

"Oh, come, Charles, if I didn't know from you, I'd know that much from your father!" Gerard said in a rare burst of impatience.

Bruno started to reach for a cigarette and stopped. "I talked with him about it,"he said quietly, respectfully. "He doesn't know anything. He didn't even know his wife very well then."

"Who do you think did it? Did you ever think Mr. Haines might have arranged it? Were you interested maybe in how he'd done it and gotten away with it?"At his ease again, gerard leaned back with his hands behind his head, as if they were talking about the good weather that day.

"Of course I don't think he arranged it," Bruno replied. "You don't seem to realize the caliber of the person you're talking about."

"The only caliber ever worth considering is the gun's, Charles."Gerard picked up his telephone. "As you'd be the first to tell me probably.—Have Mr. Haines come in, will you?"

Bruno jumped a little, and Gerard saw it. Gerard watched him in silence as they listened to Guy's footsteps coming closer in the hall. He had expected Gerard would do this, Bruno told himself. So what, so what, so what?

Guy looked nervous, Bruno thought, but his usual air of being nervous and in a hurry covered it. He spoke to Gerard, and nodded to Bruno.

Gerard offered him his remaining chair, a straight one. "My whole purpose in asking you to come down here, Mr. Haines, is to ask you a very simple question. What does Charles talk with you about most of the time?"Gerard offered Guy a cigarette from a pack that must have been years old, Bruno thought, and Guy took it.

Bruno saw Guy's eyebrows draw together with the look of irritation that was exactly appropriate. "He's talked to me now and then about the Palmyra Club," Guy replied.

"And what else?"

Guy looked at Bruno. Bruno was nibbling, so casually the action seemed nonchalant, at a fingernail of the hand that propped his cheek. "Can't really say," Guy answered.

"Talked to you about your wife's murder?"

"Yes."

"How does he talk to you about the murder?" Gerard asked kindly. "I mean your wife's murder."

Guy felt his face flush. He glanced again at Bruno, as anybody might, he thought, as anybody might in the presence of a discussed party who is being ignored. "He often asked me if I knew who might have done it."

"And do you?"

"No."

"Do you like Charles?" Gerard's fat fingers trembled slightly, incongruously. They began playing with a match cover on his desk blotter.

Guy thought of Bruno's fingers on the train, playing with the match cover, dropping it onto the steak. "Yes, I like him," Guy answered puzzledly.

"Hasn't he annoyed you? Hasn't he thrust himself on you many times?"

"I don't think so," Guy said.

"Were you annoyed when he came to your wedding?"

"No."

"Did Charles ever tell you that he hated his father?"

"Yes, he did."

"Did he ever tell you he'd like to kill him?"

"No," he replied in the same matter-of-fact tone.

Gerard got the brown paper-wrapped book from a drawer in his desk. "Here's the book Charles meant to mail you. Sorry I can't let you have it just now, because I may need it. How did Charles happen to have your book?"

"He told me he found it on the train." Guy studied Gerard's sleepy, enigmatic smile. He had seen a trace of it the night Gerard called at the house, but not like this. This smile was calculated to inspire dislike. This smile was a professional weapon. What it must be, Guy thought, facing that smile day after day. Involuntarily, he looked over at Bruno.

"And you didn't see each other on the train?" Gerard looked from Guy to Bruno.

"No," said Guy.

"I spoke with the waiter who served you two dinner in Charles' compartment."

Guy kept his eyes on Gerard. This naked shame, he thought, was more annihilating than guilt. This was annihilation he was feeling, even as he sat upright, looking straight at Gerard.

"So what?" Bruno said shrilly.

"So I'm interested in why you two take such elaborate trouble," Gerard wagged his head amusedly, "to say you met months later." He waited, letting the passing seconds eat at them. "You won't tell me the answer. Well, the answer is obvious. That is, one answer, as a speculation."

All three of them were thinking of the answer, Guy thought. It was visible in the air now, linking him and Bruno, Bruno and Gerard, Gerard and himself. The answer Bruno had declared beyond thought, the eternally missing ingredient.

"Will you tell me, Charles, you who read so many detective stories?"

"I don't know what you're getting at."

"Within a few days, your wife was killed, Mr. Haines. Within a few months, Charles' father. My obvious and first speculation is that you both knew those murders were going to happen—"

"Oh, crap!" Bruno said.

"—and discussed them. Pure speculation, of course. That's assuming you met on the train. Where did you meet?" Gerard smiled. "Mr. Haines?"

"Yes," Guy said, "we met on the train."

"And why've you been so afraid of admitting it?" Gerard jabbed one of his freckled fingers at him, and again Guy felt in Gerard's prosaicness his power to terrify.

"I don't know," Guy said.

"Wasn't it because Charles told you he would like to have his father killed? And you were uneasy then, Mr. Haines, because you knew?"

Was that Gerard's trump? Guy said slowly, "Charles said nothing about killing his father."

Gerard's eyes slid over in time to catch Bruno's tight smirk of satisfaction. "Pure speculation, of course," Gerard said.

Guy and Bruno left the building together. Gerard had dismissed them together, and they walked together down the long block toward the little park where the subways were, and the taxicabs. Bruno looked back at the tall narrow building they had left.

"All right, he still hasn't anything," Bruno said. "Any way you look at it, he hasn't anything."

Bruno was sullen, but calm. Suddenly Guy realized how cool Bruno had been under Gerard's attack. Guy was continually imagining Bruno hysterical under pressure. He glanced quickly at Bruno's tall hunched figure beside him, feeling that wild, reckless comradeship of the day in the restaurant. But he had nothing to say. Surely, he thought, Bruno must know that Gerard wasn't going to tell them everything he had discovered.

"You know, the funny thing," Bruno continued, "Gerard's not looking for us, he's looking for other people."

## *forty-two*

Gerard poked a finger between the bars and waggled it at the little bird that fluttered in terror against the opposite side of the cage. Gerard whistled a single soft note.

From the center of the room, Anne watched him uneasily. She didn't like his having just told her Guy had been lying, then his strolling off to frighten the canary. She hadn't liked Gerard for the last quarter hour, and because she had thought she did like him on his first visit, her misjudgment annoyed her.

"What's his name?" Gerard asked.

"Sweetie," Anne replied. She ducked her head a little, embarrassedly, and swung half around. Her new alligator pumps made her feel very tall and graceful, and she had thought, when she bought them that afternoon, that Guy would like them, that they would coax a smile from him as they sat having a cocktail before dinner. But Gerard's arrival had spoilt that.

"Do you have any idea why your husband didn't want to say he met Charles June before last?"

The month Miriam was murdered, Anne thought again. June before last meant nothing else to her. "It was a difficult month for him," she said. "It was the month his wife died. He might have forgotten almost anything that happened that month." She frowned, feeling Gerard was making too much of his little discovery, that it couldn't matter so very much, since Guy hadn't even seen Charles in the six months afterwards.

"Not in this case," Gerard said casually, reseating himself. "No, I think Charles talked with your husband on the train about his father, told him he wanted him dead, maybe even told him how he intended to go about—"

"I can't imagine Guy listening to that," Anne interrupted him.

"I don't know," Gerard went on blandly, "I don't know, but I strongly suspect Charles knew about his father's murder and that he may have confided to your husband that night on the train. Charles is that kind of a young man. And I think the kind of man your husband is would have kept quiet about it, tried to avoid Charles from then on. Don't you?"

It would explain a great deal, Anne thought. But it would also make Guy a kind of accomplice. Gerard seemed to want to make Guy an accomplice. "I'm sure my husband wouldn't have tolerated Charles even to this extent," she said firmly, "if Charles had told him anything like that."

"A very good point. However—" Gerard stopped vaguely, as if lost in his own slow thoughts.

Anne did not like to look at the top of his bald freckled head, so she stared at the tile cigarette box on the coffee table, and finally took a cigarette.

"Do you think your husband has any suspicion who murdered his wife, Mrs. Haines?"

Anne blew her smoke out defiantly. "I certainly do not."

"You see, if that night on the train, Charles went into the subject of murder, he went into it thoroughly. And if your husband did have some reason to think his wife's life was in danger, and if he mentioned it to Charles—why then they have a sort of mutual secret, a mutual peril even. It's only a speculation," he hurried to add,"but investigators always have to speculate."

"I know my husband couldn't have said anything about his wife's being in danger. I was with him in Mexico City when the news came, and with him days before in New York."

"How about March of this year?" Gerard asked in the same even tone. He reached for his empty highball glass, and submitted to Anne's taking it to refill.

Anne stood at the bar with her back to Gerard, remembering March, the month Charles' father was killed, remembering Guy's nervousness then. Had that fight been in February or March? And *hadn't* he fought with Charles Bruno?

"Do you think your husband could have been seeing Charles now and then around the month of March without your knowing about it?"

Of course, she thought, that might explain it: that Guy had known Charles intended to kill his father, and had tried to stop him, had fought with him, in a bar. "He could have, I suppose," she said uncertainly. "I don't know."

"How did your husband seem around the month of March, if you can remember, Mrs. Haines?"

"He was nervous. I think I know the things he was nervous about."

"What things?"

"His work—" Somehow she couldn't grant him a word more than that about Guy. Everything she said, she felt Gerard would incorporate in the misty picture he was composing, in which he was trying to see Guy. She waited, and Gerard waited, as if he vied with her not to break the silence first.

Finally, he tapped out his cigar and said, "If anything does occur to you about that time in regard to Charles, will you be sure and tell me? Call me any time during the day or night. There'll be somebody there to take messages." He wrote another name on his business card, and handed it to Anne.

Anne turned from the door and went directly to the coffee table to remove his glass. Through the front window, she saw him sitting in his car with his head bent forward, like a man asleep, while, she supposed, he made his notes. Then with a little stab, she thought of his writing that Guy might have seen Charles in March without her knowing about it. Why had she said it? She did know about it. Guy said he hadn't seen Charles, between December and the wedding.

When Guy came in about an hour later, Anne was in the kitchen, tending the casserole that was nearly done in the oven. She saw Guy put his head up, sniffing the air.

"Shrimp casserole," Anne told him. "I guess I should open a vent."

"Was Gerard here?"

"Yes. You knew he was coming?"

"Cigars," he said laconically. Gerard had told her about the meeting on the train, of course. "What did he want this time?"he asked.

"He wanted to know more about Charles Bruno." Anne glanced at him quickly from the front window. "If you'd said anything to me about suspecting him of anything. And he wanted to know about March."

"About March?" He stepped onto the raised portion of the floor where Anne stood.

He stopped in front of her, and Anne saw the pupils of his eyes contract suddenly. She could see a few of the hair-fine scars over his cheekbone from that night in March, or February. "Wanted to know if you suspected Charles was going to have his father killed that month."But Guy only stared at her with his mouth in a familiar straight line, without alarm, and without guilt. She stepped aside, and went down into the living room. "It's terrible, isn't it," she said,"murder?"

Guy tapped a fresh cigarette on his watch face. It tortured him to hear her say "murder." He wished he could erase every memory of Bruno from her brain.

"You didn't know, did you, Guy—in March?"

"No, Anne. What did you tell Gerard?"

"Do you believe Charles had his father killed?"

"I don't know. I think it's possible. But it doesn't concern us." And he did not realize for seconds that it was even a lie.

"That's right. It doesn't concern us." She looked at him again. "Gerard also said you met Charles June before last on the train."

"Yes, I did."

"Well—what does it matter?"

"I don't know."

"Was it because of something Charles said on the train? Is that why you dislike him?"

Guy shoved his hands deeper in his jacket pockets. He wanted a brandy suddenly. He knew he showed what he felt, that he could not hide it from Anne now. "Listen, Anne," he said quickly. "Bruno told me on the train he wished his father were dead. He didn't mention any plans, he didn't mention any names. I didn't like the way he said it, and after that I didn't like him. I refuse to tell Gerard all that, because I don't know if Bruno had his father killed or not. That's for the police to find out. Innocent men have been hanged because people reported their saying something like that."

But whether she believed him or not, he thought, he was finished. It seemed the basest lie he had ever told, the basest thing he had ever done—the transferring of his guilt to another man. Even Bruno wouldn't have lied like this, wouldn't have lied against him like this. He felt himself totally false, totally a lie. He flung his cigarette into the fireplace and put his hands over his face.

"Guy, I do believe you're doing what you should," Anne's voice said gently.

His face was a lie, his level eyes, the firm mouth, the sensitive hands. He whipped his hands down and put them in his pockets. "I could use a brandy."

"Wasn't it Charles you fought with in March?" she asked as she stood at the bar.

There was no reason not to lie about this also, but he could not. "No, Anne." He knew from the quick sidelong glance she gave him that she didn't believe him. She probably thought he had fought with Bruno to stop him. She was probably proud of him! Must there always be this protection, that he didn't even want? Must everything always be so easy for him? But Anne would not be satisfied with this. She would come back to it and back to it until he told her, he knew.

That evening, Guy lighted the first fire of the year, the first fire in their new house. Anne lay on the long hearthstone with her head on a sofa pillow. The thin nostalgic chill of autumn was in the air, filling Guy with melancholy and a restless energy. The energy was not buoyant as autumnal energy had been in his youth, but underlaid with frenzy and despair, as if his life were winding down and this might be his last spurt. What better proof did he need that his life was winding down than that he had no dread of what lay ahead? Couldn't Gerard guess it now, knowing that he and Bruno had met on the train? Wouldn't it dawn on him one day, one night, one instant as his fat fingers lifted a cigar to his mouth? What were they waiting for, Gerard and the police? He had sometimes the feeling that Gerard wanted to gather every tiniest contributing fact, every gram of evidence against them both, then let it fall suddenly upon them and demolish them. But however they demolished him, Guy thought, they would not demolish his buildings. And he felt again the strange and lonely isolation of his spirit from his flesh, even from his mind.

But suppose his secret with Bruno were never found out? There were still those moments of mingled horror at what he had done, and of absolute despondency, when he felt that secret bore a charmed inviolability. Perhaps, he thought, that was why he was not afraid of Gerard or the police, because he still believed in its inviolability. If no one had guessed it so far, after all their carelessness, after all Bruno's hints, wasn't there something making it impregnable?

Anne had fallen asleep. He stared at the smooth curve of her forehead, paled to silver by the fire's light. Then he lowered his lips to her forehead and kissed her, so gently she would not awaken. The ache inside him translated itself into words: "I forgive you."

He wanted Anne to say it, no one but Anne.

In his mind, the side of the scale that bore his guilt was hopelessly weighted, beyond the scale's measure, yet into the other side he continually threw the equally hopeless featherweight of self-defense. He had committed the crime in self-defense, he reasoned. But he vacillated in completely believing this. If he believed in the full complement of evil in himself, he had to believe also in a natural compulsion to express it. He found himself wondering, therefore, from time to time, if he might have enjoyed his crime in some way, derived some primal satisfaction from it—how else could one really explain in mankind the continued toleration of wars, the perennial enthusiasm for wars when they came, if not for some primal pleasure in killing?—and because the capacity to wonder came so often, he accepted it as true that he had.

# *forty-three*

District attorney Phil Howland, immaculate and gaunt, as sharp of outline as Gerard was fuzzy, smiled tolerantly through his cigarette smoke. "Why don't you let the kid alone? It was an angle at first, I grant you. We combed through his friends, too. There's nothing, Gerard. And you can't arrest a man on his personality."

Gerard recrossed his legs and allowed himself a complaisant smile. This was his hour. His satisfaction was heightened by the fact he had sat here smiling in the same way during other less momentous interviews.

Howland pushed a typewritten sheet with his fingertips to the edge of the desk. "Twelve new names here, if you're interested. Friends of the late Mr. Samuel furnished us by the insurance companies," Howland said in his calm, bored voice, and Gerard knew he pretended especial boredom now, because as District Attorney he had so many hundreds of men at his disposal, could throw so much finer nets so much farther.

"You can tear them up," Gerard said.

Howland hid his surprise with a smile, but he couldn't hide the sudden curiosity in his dark, wide eyes. "I suppose you've already got your man. Charles Bruno, of course."

"Of course," Gerard chuckled. "Only I've got him for another murder."

"Only one? You always said he was good for four or five."

"I never said," Gerard denied quietly. He was smoothing out a number of papers, folded in thirds like letters, on his knees.

"Who?"

"Curious? Don't you know?" Gerard smiled with his cigar between his teeth. He pulled a straight chair closer to him, and proceeded to cover its seat with his papers. He never used Howland's desk, however many papers he had, and Howland knew now not to bother offering it. Howland disliked him, personally as well as professionally, Gerard knew. Howland accused him of not being cooperative with the police. The police had never been in the least cooperative with him, but with all their hindrance, Gerard in the last decade had solved an impressive number of cases the police hadn't even been warm on.

Howland got up and strolled slowly toward Gerard on his long thin legs, then hung back, leaning against the front of his desk. "But does all this shed any light on the *case*?"

"The trouble with the police force is that it has a single-track mind," Gerard announced. "This case, like many others, took a double-track mind. Simply couldn't have been solved without a double-track mind."

"Who and when?" Howland sighed.

"Ever hear of Guy Haines?"

"Certainly. We questioned him last week."

"His wife. June eleventh of last year in Metcalf, Texas.

Strangulation, remember? The police never solved it."

"Charles Bruno?" Howland frowned.

"Did you know that Charles Bruno and Guy Haines were on the same train going South on June first? Ten days before the murder of Haines' wife. Now, what do you deduce from that?"

"You mean they knew each other before last June?"

"No, I mean they met each other on that train. Can you put the rest together? I'm giving you the missing link."

The District Attorney smiled faintly. "You're saying Charles Bruno killed Guy Haines' wife?"

"I certainly am." Gerard looked up from his papers, finished. "The next question is, what's my proof? There it is. All you want." He gestured toward the papers that overlapped in a long row, like cards in a game of solitaire. "Read from the bottom up."

While Howland read, Gerard drew a cup of water from the tank in the corner and lighted another cigar from the one he had been smoking. The last statement, from Charles' taxi driver in Metcalf, had come in this morning. He hadn't even had a drink on it yet, but he was going to have three or four as soon as he left Howland, in the lounge car of an Iowa-bound train.

The papers were signed statements from Hotel La Fonda bellhops, from one Edward Wilson who had seen Charles leaving the Santa Fe station on an eastbound train the day of Miriam Haines' murder, from the Metcalf taxi driver who had driven Charles to the Kingdom of Fun Amusement Park at Lake Metcalf, from the barman in the roadhouse where Charles had tried to get hard liquor, plus telephone bills of long-distance calls to Metcalf.

"But no doubt you know that already," Gerard remarked.

"Most of it, yes," Howland answered calmly, still reading.

"You knew he made a twenty-four-hour trip to Metcalf that day, too, did you?" Gerard asked, but he was really in too good spirits for sarcasm. "That taxi driver was certainly hard to find. Had to trace him all the way up to Seattle, but once we found him, it didn't take any jostling for him to remember. People don't forget a young man like Charles Bruno."

"So you're saying Charles Bruno is so fond of murder," Howland remarked amusedly,"that he murders the wife of a man he meets on a train the week before? A woman he's never even seen? Or had he seen her?"

Gerard chuckled again. "Of course he hadn't. My Charles had a plan." The "my" slipped out, but Gerard didn't care. "Can't you see it? Plain as the nose on your face? And this is only half."

"Sit down, Gerard, you'll work yourself into a heart attack."

"You can't see it. Because you didn't know and don't know Charles' personality. You weren't interested in the fact he spends most of his time planning perfect crimes of various sorts."

"All right, what's the rest of your theory?"

"That Guy Haines killed Samuel Bruno."

"Ow!" Howland groaned.

Gerard smiled back at the first grin Howland had given him since he, Gerard, had made a mistake in a certain case years ago. "I haven't finished checking on Guy Haines yet," Gerard said with deliberate ingenuousness, puffing away at the cigar. "I want to take it easy, and that's the only reason I'm here, to get you to take it easy with me. I didn't know but what you'd grab Charles, you see, with all your information against him."

Howland smoothed his black mustache. "Everything you say confirms my belief you should have retired about fifteen years ago."

"Oh, I've solved a few cases in the last fifteen years."

"A man like Guy Haines?" Howland laughed again.

"Against a fellow like Charles? Mind you, I don't say Guy Haines did it of his own free will. He was made to do it for Charles' unsolicited favor of freeing him of his wife. Charles hates women," he remarked in a parenthesis. "That was Charles' plan. Exchange. No clues, you see. No motives. Oh, I can just hear him! But even Charles is human. He was too interested in Guy Haines to leave him alone afterward. And Guy Haines was too frightened to do anything about it. Yes—" Gerard jerked his head for emphasis, and his jowls shook—"Haines was coerced. How terribly probably no one will ever know."

Howland's smile went away momentarily at Gerard's earnestness. The story had the barest possibility, but still a possibility. "Hmm-m."

"Unless he tells us," Gerard added.

"And how do you propose to make him tell us?"

"Oh, he may yet confess. It's wearing him down. But otherwise, confront him with the facts. Which my men are busy gathering. One thing, Howland—" Gerard jabbed a finger at his papers on the chair seat. "When you and your—your army of oxes go out checking these statements, don't question Guy Haines' mother. I don't want Haines forewarned."

"Oh. Cat-and-mouse technique for Mr. Haines," Howland smiled. He turned to make a telephone call about an inconsequential matter, and Gerard waited, resenting that he had to turn his information over to Howland, that he had to leave the Charles–Guy Haines spectacle. "Well—" Howland let his breath out in a long sigh—"what do you want me to do, work over your little boy with this stuff? Think he'll break down and tell all about his brilliant plan with Guy Haines, architect?"

"No, I don't want him worked over. I like clean jobs. I want a few days more or maybe weeks to finish checking on Haines, then I'll confront them both. I'm giving you this on Charles, because from now on I'm out of the case personally, so far as they're to know. I'm going to Iowa for a vacation, I really am, and I'm going to let Charles know it." Gerard's face lighted with a big smile.

"It's going to be hard to hold the boys back," Howland said regretfully, "especially for all the time it'll take you to get evidence against Guy Haines."

"Incidentally—" Gerard picked up his hat and shook it at Howland. "You couldn't crack Charles with all that, but I could crack Guy Haines with what I've got this minute."

"Oh, you mean *we* couldn't crack Guy Haines?"

Gerard looked at him with elaborate contempt. "But you're not interested in cracking him, are you? You don't think he's the man."

"Take that vacation, Gerard!"

Methodically, Gerard gathered his papers and started to pocket them.

"I thought you were going to leave those."

"Oh, if you think you'll need them." Gerard presented the papers courteously, and turned toward the door.

"Mind telling me what you've got that'll crack Guy Haines?"

Gerard made a disdainful sound in his throat. "The man is tortured with guilt," he said, and went out.

## *forty-four*

"You know, in the whole world," Bruno said, and tears started in his eyes so he had to look down at the long hearthstone under his feet, "I wouldn't want to be anywhere else but here tonight, Anne." He leaned his elbow jauntily on the high mantel.

"Very nice of you to say," Anne smiled, and set the plate of melted cheese and anchovy canapés on the sawbuck table. "Have one of these while they're hot."

Bruno took one, though he knew he wouldn't be able to get it down. The table looked beautiful, set for two with gray linen and big gray plates. Gerard was off on a vacation. They had beaten him, Guy and he, and the lid was off his brains! He might have tried to kiss Anne, he thought, if she didn't belong to Guy. Bruno stood taller and adjusted his cuffs. He took great pride in being a perfect gentleman with Anne. "So Guy thinks he's going to like it up there?" Bruno asked. Guy was in Canada now, working on the big Alberta dam. "I'm glad all this dumb questioning is over, so he won't have to worry about it when he's working. You can imagine how I feel. Like celebrating!" He laughed, mainly at his understatement.

Anne stared at his tall restless figure by the mantel, and wondered if Guy, despite his hatred, felt the same fascination she did. She still didn't know, though, whether Charles Bruno would have been capable of arranging his father's murder, and she had spent the whole day with him in order to make up her mind. He slid away from certain questions with joking answers, he was serious and careful about answering others. He hated Miriam as if he had known her. It rather surprised Anne that Guy had told him so much about Miriam.

"Why didn't you want to tell anyone you'd met Guy on the train?" Anne asked.

"I didn't mind. I just made the mistake of kidding around about it first, said we'd met in school. Then all those questions came up, and Gerard started making a lot out of it. I guess because it looked bad, frankly. Miriam killed so soon after, you know. I think it was quite nice of Guy at the inquest on Miriam not to drag in anybody he'd just met by accident." He laughed, a single loud clap, and dropped into the armchair. "Not that I'm a suspicious character, by any means!"

"But that didn't have anything to do with the questioning about your father's death."

"Of course not. But Gerard doesn't pay any attention to logic. He should have been an inventor!"

Anne frowned. She couldn't believe that Guy would have fallen in with Charles' story simply because telling the truth would have looked bad, or even because Charles had told him on the train that he hated his father. She must ask Guy again. There was a great deal she had to ask him. About Charles' hostility to Miriam, for instance, though he had never seen her. Anne went into the kitchen.

Bruno strolled to the front window with his drink, and watched a plane alternating its red and green lights in the black sky. It looked like a person exercising, he thought, touching fingertips to shoulders and stretching arms out again. He wished Guy might be on that plane, coming home. He looked at the dusky pink face of his new wristwatch, thinking again, before he read the time on its tall gold numerals, that Guy would probably like a watch like this, because of its modern design.

In just three hours more, he would have been with Anne twenty-four hours, a whole day. He had driven by last evening instead of telephoning, and it had gotten so late, Anne had invited him to spend the night. He had slept up in the guest room where they had put him the night of the party, and Anne had brought him some hot bouillon before he went to sleep. Anne was terribly sweet to him, and he really loved her! He spun around on his heel, and saw her coming in from the kitchen with their plates.

"Guy's very fond of you, you know," Anne said during the dinner.

Bruno looked at her, having already forgotten what they had been talking about. "There's *nothing* I wouldn't do for him! I feel a tremendous tie with him, like a brother. I guess because everything started happening to him just after we met each other on the train." And though he had started out to be gay, even funny, the seriousness of his real feeling for Guy got the better of him. He fingered the rack of Guy's pipes near him on an end table. His heart was pounding. The stuffed potato was beautiful, but he didn't dare eat another mouthful. Nor the red wine. He had an impulse to try to spend the night again. Couldn't he manage to stay again tonight, if he didn't feel well? On the other hand, the new house was closer than Anne thought. Saturday he was giving a big party. "You're sure Guy'll be back this weekend?" he asked.

"So he said." Anne ate her green salad thoughtfully. "I don't know whether he'll feel like a party, though. When he's been working, he usually doesn't like anything more distracting than a sail."

"I'd like a sail. If you wouldn't mind company."

"Come along." Then she remembered, Charles had already been out on the *India*, had invited himself with Guy, had dented the gunwail, and suddenly she felt puzzled, tricked, as if something had prevented her remembering until now. And she found herself thinking, Charles could probably do anything, atrocious things, and fool everyone with the same ingratiating naïveté, the same shy smile. Except Gerard. Yes, he could have arranged his father's murder. Gerard wouldn't be speculating in that direction if it weren't possible. She might be sitting opposite a murderer. She felt a little pluck of terror as she got up, a bit too abruptly as if she were fleeing, and removed the dinner plates. And his grim, merciless pleasure in talking of his loathing for Miriam. He would have enjoyed killing her, Anne thought. A fragile suspicion that he might have killed her crossed her mind like a dry leaf blown by the wind.

"So you went on to Santa Fe after you met Guy?" she almost stammered, from the kitchen.

"Uh-huh." Bruno was deep in the big green armchair again.

Anne dropped a demitasse spoon and it made an outrageous clatter on the tiles. The odd thing, she thought, was that it didn't seem to matter what one said to Charles or asked him. Nothing would shock him. But instead of making it simpler to talk to him, this was the very quality that she felt rattling her and throwing her off.

"Have you ever been to Metcalf?" she heard her own voice call around the partition.

"No,"Bruno replied. "No, I always wanted to. Have you?"

Bruno sipped his coffee at the mantel. Anne was on the sofa, her head tipped back so the curve of her throat above the tiny ruffled collar of her dress was the lightest thing about her. *Anne is like light to me*, Bruno remembered Guy once saying. If he could strangle Anne, too, then Guy and he could really be together. Bruno frowned at himself, then laughed and shifted on his feet.

"What's funny?"

"Just thinking," he smiled. "I was thinking of what Guy always says, about the doubleness of everything. You know, the positive and negative, side by side. Every decision has a reason against it." He noticed suddenly he was breathing hard.

"You mean two sides to everything?"

"Oh, no, that's too simple!" Women were really so crude sometimes! "People, feelings, everything! Double! Two people in each person. There's also a person exactly the opposite of you, like the unseen part of you, somewhere in the world, and he waits in ambush." It thrilled him to say Guy's words, though he hadn't liked hearing them, he remembered, because Guy had said the two people were mortal enemies, too, and Guy had meant him and himself.

Anne brought her head up slowly from the sofa back. It sounded so like Guy, yet he had never said it to her. Anne thought of the unsigned letter last spring. Charles must have written it. Guy must have meant Charles when he talked of ambush. There was no one else beside Charles to whom Guy reacted so violently. Surely it was Charles who alternated hatred with devotion.

"It's not all good and evil either, but that's how it shows itself best, in action," Bruno went on cheerfully. "By the way, I mustn't forget to tell Guy about giving the thousand dollars to a beggar. I always said when I had my own money, I'd give a thousand to a beggar. Well, I did, but you think he thanked me? It took me twenty minutes to prove to him the money was real! I had to take a hundred in a bank and break if for him! Then he acted as if he thought I was crazy!" Bruno looked down and shook his head. He had counted on its being a memorable experience, and then to have the bastard look practically *sore* at him the next time he saw him—still begging on the same street corner, too—because he hadn't brought him *another* thousand! "As I was saying anyway—"

"About good and evil," Anne said. She loathed him. She knew all that Guy felt now about him. But she didn't yet know why Guy tolerated him.

"Oh. Well, these things come out in actions. But for instance, murderers. Punishing them in the law courts won't make them any better, Guy says. Every man is his own law court and punishes himself enough. In fact, every man is just about everything to Guy!" He laughed. He was so tight, he could hardly see her face now, but he wanted to tell her everything that he and Guy had ever talked about, right up to the last little secret that he couldn't tell her.

"People without consciences don't punish themselves, do they?" Anne asked.

Bruno looked at the ceiling. "That's true. Some people are too dumb to have consciences, other people too evil. Generally the dumb ones get caught. But take the two murderers of Guy's wife and my father." Bruno tried to look serious. "Both of them must have been pretty brilliant people, don't you think?"

"So they have consciences and don't deserve to get caught?"

"Oh, I don't say that. Of course not! But don't think they aren't suffering a little. In their fashion!" He laughed again, because he was really too tight to know just where he was going. "They weren't just madmen, like they said the murderer of Guy's wife was. Shows how little the authorities know about real criminology. A crime like that took planning." Out of the blue, he remembered he hadn't planned that one at all, but he certainly had planned his father's, which illustrated his point well enough. "What's the matter?"

Anne laid her cold fingers against her forehead. "Nothing."

Bruno fixed her a highball at the bar Guy had built into the side of the fireplace. Bruno wanted a bar just like it for his own house.

"Where did Guy get those scratches on his face last March?"

"What scratches?" Bruno turned to her. Guy had told him she didn't know about the scratches.

"More than scratches. Cuts. And a bruise on his head."

"I didn't see them."

"He fought with you, didn't he?" Charles stared at her with a strange pinkish glint in his eyes. She was not deceitful enough to smile now. She was sure. She felt Charles was about to rush across the room and strike her, but she kept her eyes fixed on his. If she told Gerard, she thought, the fight would be proof of Charles' knowledge of the murder. Then she saw Charles' smile waver back.

"No!" he laughed. He sat down. "Where did he say he got the scratches? I didn't see him anyway in March. I was out of town then." He stood up. He suddenly didn't feel well in the stomach, and it wasn't the questions, it was his stomach. Suppose he was in for another attack now. Or tomorrow morning. He mustn't pass out, mustn't let Anne see *that* in the morning! "I'd better go soon," he murmured.

"What's the matter? You're not feeling well? You're a little pale."

She wasn't sympathetic. He could tell by her voice. What woman ever was, except his mother? "Thank you very much, Anne, for—for all day."

She handed him his coat, and he stumbled out the door, gritting his teeth as he started the long walk toward his car at the curb.

The house was dark when Guy came home a few hours later. He prowled the living room, saw the cigarette stub ground on the hearth, the pipe rack askew on the end table, the depression in a small pillow on the sofa. There was a peculiar disorder that couldn't have been created by Anne and Teddy, or by Chris, or by Helen Heyburn. Hadn't he known?

He ran up to the guest room. Bruno wasn't there, but he saw a tortured roll of newspaper on the bed table and a dime and two pennies domestically beside it. At the window, the dawn was coming in like that dawn. He turned his back on the window, and his held breath came out like a sob. What did Anne mean by doing this to him? Now of all times when it was intolerable—when half of himself was in Canada and the other half here, caught in the tightening grip of Bruno, Bruno with the police off his trail. The police had given him a little insulation! But he had overreached now. There was no enduring much longer.

He went into the bedroom and knelt beside Anne and kissed her awake, frightenedly, harshly, until he felt her arms close around him. He buried his face in the soft muss of the sheets over her breast. It seemed there was a rocking, roaring storm all around him, all around both of them, and that Anne was the only point of stillness, at its center, and the rhythm of her breathing the only sign of a normal pulse in a sane world. He got his clothes off with his eyes shut.

"I've missed you," were the first words Anne said.

Guy stood near the foot of the bed with his hands in the pockets of his robe, clenched. The tension was still in him, and all the storm seemed gathered in his own core now. "I'll be here three days. Have you missed me?"

Anne slid up a few inches in the bed. "Why do you look at me like that?"

Guy did not answer.

"I've seen him only once, Guy."

"Why did you see him at all?"

"Because—" Her cheeks flushed as pink as the spot on her shoulder, Guy noticed. His beard had scratched her shoulder. He had never spoken to her like this before. And the fact she was going to answer him reasonably seemed only to give more reason to his anger. "Because he came by—"

"He always comes by. He always telephones."

"Why?"

"He slept here!" Guy burst out, then he saw Anne's recoil in the subtle lift of her head, the flicker of her lashes.

"Yes. Night before last," her steady voice challenged him. "He came by late, and I asked him to stay over."

It had crossed his mind in Canada that Bruno might make advances to Anne, simply because she belonged to him, and that Anne might encourage him, simply because she wanted to know what he had not told her. Not that Bruno would go very far, but the touch of his hand on

Anne's, the thought of Anne permitting it, and the reason for which she would permit it, tormented him. "And he was here last evening?"

"Why does it bother you so?"

"Because he's dangerous. He's half insane."

"I don't think that's the reason he bothers you," Anne said in the same slow steady voice. "I don't know why you defend him, Guy. I don't know why you don't admit he's the one who wrote that letter to me and the one who almost drove you insane in March."

Guy stiffened with guilty defensiveness. Defense of Bruno, he thought, always defense of Bruno! Bruno hadn't admitted sending the letter to Anne, he knew. It was just that Anne, like Gerard, with different facts, was putting pieces together. Gerard had quit, but Anne would never quit. Anne worked with the intangible pieces, and the intangible pieces were the ones that would make the picture. But she didn't have the picture yet. It would take time, a little more time, and a little more time to torture him! He turned to the window with a tired leaden movement, too dead even to cover his face or bow his head. He did not care to ask Anne what she and Bruno had talked of yesterday. Somehow he could *feel* exactly what they had said, exactly how much more Anne had learned. There was some allotted period of time, he felt suddenly, in this agony of postponement. It had gone on beyond all logical expectation, as life sometimes did against a fatal disease, that was all.

"Tell me, Guy,"Anne said quietly, not pleading with him now, her voice merely like the tolling of a bell that marked another length of time. "Tell me, will you?"

"I shall tell you," he replied, still looking at the window, but hearing himself say it now, believing himself, such a lightness filled him, he was sure Anne must see it in the half of his face, in his whole being, and his first thought was to share it with her, though for a moment he could not take his eyes from the sunlight on the window sill. *Lightness*, he thought, both a lifting of darkness and of weight, weightlessness. He would tell Anne.

"Guy, come here." She held up her arms for him, and he sat beside her, slipped his arms around her, and held her tight against him. "There's going to be a baby," she said. "Let's be happy. Will you be happy, Guy?"

He looked at her, feeling suddenly like laughing for happiness, for surprise, for her shyness. "A baby!" he whispered.

"What'll we do these days you're here?"

"When, Anne?'

"On—not for ages. I guess in May. What'll we do tomorrow?"

"We'll definitely go out on the boat. If it's not too rough." And the foolish, conspiratorial note in his voice made him laugh out loud now.

"Oh, Guy!"

"Crying?"

"It's so good to hear you laugh!"

# *forty-five*

Bruno telephoned Saturday morning to congratulate Guy on his appointment to the Alberta Committee, and to ask if he and Anne would come to his party that evening. Bruno's desperate, elated voice exhorted him to celebrate. "Talking over my own private wires, Guy. Gerard's gone back to Iowa. Come on, I want you to see my new house." Then, "Let me talk to Anne."

"Anne's out right now."

Guy knew the investigations were over. The police had notified him and so had Gerard, with thanks.

Guy went back into the living room where he and Bob Treacher were finishing their late breakfast. Bob had flown down to New York a day ahead of him, and Guy had invited him for the weekend. They were talking of Alberta and the men they worked with on the Committee, of the terrain, the trout fishing, and of whatever came into their heads. Guy laughed at a joke Bob told in French-Canadian dialect. It was a fresh, sunny November morning, and when Anne got back from her marketing, they were going to take the car to Long Island and go for a sail. Guy felt a boyish, holiday delight in having Bob with him. Bob symbolized Canada and the work there, the project in which Guy felt he had entered another vaster chamber of himself where Bruno could not follow. And the secret of the coming child gave him a sense of impartial benevolence, of magical advantage.

Just as Anne came in the door, the telephone rang again. Guy stood up, but Anne answered it. Vaguely, he thought, Bruno always knows exactly when to call. Then he listened, incredulously, to the conversation drifting toward the sail that afternoon.

"Come along then," Anne said. "Oh, I suppose some beer would be nice if you must bring something."

Guy saw Bob staring at him quizzically.

"What's up?" Bob asked.

"Nothing." Guy sat down again.

"That was Charles. You don't mind too much if he comes, do you, Guy?" Anne walked briskly across the room with her bag of groceries. "He said Thursday he'd like to come sailing if we went, and I practically invited him."

"I don't mind," Guy said, still looking at her. She was in a gay, euphoric mood this morning, in which it would have been difficult to imagine her refusing anybody anything, but there was more than that, Guy knew, in her inviting Bruno. She wanted to see them together again. She couldn't wait, even today. Guy felt a rise of resentment, and said quickly to himself, she doesn't realize, she can't realize, and it's all your own fault anyway for the hopeless muddle you've made. So he put the resentment down, refused even to admit the odium Bruno would inspire that afternoon. He determined to keep himself under the same control all day.

"You could do worse than watch your nerves a bit, old man," Bob told him. He lifted his coffee cup and drained it, contentedly. "Well, at least you're not the coffee fiend you used to be. What was it, ten cups a day?"

"Something like that." No, he had cut out coffee entirely, trying to sleep, and now he hated it.

They stopped for Helen Heyburn in Manhattan, then crossed the Triboro Bridge to Long Island. The winter sunlight had a frozen clarity at the shore, lay thin on the pale beach, and sparkled nervously on the choppy water. The *India* was like an iceberg at anchor, Guy thought, remembering when its whiteness had been the essence of summer. Automatically, as he rounded the corner of the parking lot, his eye fell on Bruno's long, bright blue convertible. The merry-go-round horse Bruno had ridden on, Guy remembered Bruno saying, had been royal blue, and that was why he had bought the car. He saw Bruno standing under the shed of the dockhouse, saw everything of him except his head, the long black overcoat and the small shoes, the arms with the hands in the pockets, the familiar anxiety of his waiting figure.

Bruno picked up the sack of beer and strolled toward the car with a shy smile, but even at a distance, Guy could see the pent elation, ready to explode. He wore a royal-blue muffler, the same color as his car. "Hello. Hello, Guy. Thought I'd try and see you while I could." He glanced at Anne for help.

"Nice to see you!" Anne said. "This is Mr. Treacher. Mr. Bruno."

Bruno greeted him. "You couldn't possibly make it to the party tonight, Guy? It's quite a big party. All of you?" His hopeful smile included Helen and Bob.

Helen said she was busy or she would love to. Glancing at her as he locked the car, Guy saw her leaning on Bruno's arm, changing into her moccasins. Bruno handed Anne the sack of beer with an air of departure.

Helen's blond eyebrows fluted troubledly. "You're coming with us, aren't you?"

"Not exactly dressed," Bruno protested feebly.

"Oh, there's lots of slickers on board," Anne said.

They had to take a rowboat from the dock. Guy and Bruno argued politely but stubbornly about who should row, until Helen suggested they both row. Guy pulled in long deep strokes, and Bruno, beside him on the center thwart, matched him carefully. Guy could feel Bruno's erratic excitement mounting as they drew near the *India.* Bruno's hat blew off twice, and at last he stood up and spun it spectacularly into the sea.

"I hate hats anyway!" he said with a glance at Guy.

Bruno refused to put on a slicker, though the spray dashed now and then over the cockpit. It was too gusty to raise sail. The *India* entered the Sound under engine power, with Bob steering.

"Here's to Guy!" Bruno shouted, but with the odd hitch of repression and inarticulateness Guy had noticed since he first spoke that morning. "Congratulations, salutations!" He brought the beautiful, fruit-ornamented silver flask down suddenly and presented it to Anne. He was like some clumsy, powerful machine that could not catch its proper timebeat to start. "Napoleon brandy. Five-star."

Anne declined, but Helen, who was already feeling the cold, drank some, and so did Bob. Under the tarpaulin, Guy held Anne's mittened hand and tried not to think about anything, not about Bruno, not about Alberta, not about the sea. He could not bear to look at Helen, who was encouraging Bruno, nor at Bob's polite, vaguely embarrassed smile as he faced front at the wheel.

"Anybody know 'Foggy, Foggy Dew'?" Bruno asked, brushing spray fussily off a sleeve. His pull from the silver flask had pushed him over the line into drunkenness.

Bruno was nonplussed because no one wanted any more of his specially selected liquor, and because no one wanted to sing. It also crushed him that Helen said "Foggy, Foggy Dew" was depressing. He loved "Foggy, Foggy Dew." He wanted to sing or shout or do *something*. When else would they all be together again like this? He and Guy. Anne. Helen. And Guy's friend. He twisted up in his corner seat and looked all around him, at the thin line of horizon that appeared and disappeared behind the swells of sea, at the diminishing land behind them. He tried to look at the pennant at the top of the mast, but the mast's swaying made him dizzy.

"Some day Guy and I are going to circle the world like an isinglass ball, and tie it up in a ribbon!" he announced, but no one paid any attention.

Helen was talking with Anne, making a gesture like a ball with her hands, and Guy was explaining something about the motor to Bob. Bruno noticed as Guy bent over that the creases in his forehead looked deeper, his eyes as sad as ever.

"Don't you realize anything!" Bruno shook Guy's arm. "You have to be so serious *today*?"

Helen started to say something about Guy's always being serious, and Bruno roared her down, because she didn't know a damned thing about the way Guy was serious or why. Bruno returned Anne's smile gratefully, and produced the flask again.

But still Anne did not want any, and neither did Guy.

"I brought it specially for you, Guy. I thought you'd like it," Bruno said, hurt.

"Have some, Guy," Anne said.

Guy took it and drank a little.

"To Guy! Genius, friend, and partner!" Bruno said and drank after him. "Guy *is* a genius. Do you all realize that?" He looked around at them, suddenly wanting to call them all a bunch of numbskulls.

"Certainly," said Bob agreeably.

"As you're an old friend of Guy's," Bruno raised his flask, "I salute you also!"

"Thank you. A very old friend. One of the oldest."

"How old?" Bruno challenged.

Bob glanced at Guy and smiled. "Ten years or so."

Bruno frowned. "I've known Guy all his life," he said softly, menacingly. "Ask him."

Guy felt Anne wriggle her hand from his tight hold. He saw Bob chuckling, not knowing what to make of it. Sweat made his forehead cold. Every shred of calm had left him, as it always did. Why did he always think he could endure Bruno, given one more chance?

"Go on and tell him I'm your closest friend, Guy."

"Yes," Guy said. He was conscious of Anne's small tense smile and of her silence. Didn't she know everything now? Wasn't she merely waiting for him and Bruno to put it into words in the next seconds? And suddenly it was like the moment in the coffee shop, the afternoon of the Friday night, when he felt he had already told Anne everything that he was going to do. He was going to tell her, he remembered. But the fact he hadn't quite yet told her, that Bruno was once more dancing around him, seemed the last good measure of excoriation for his delay.

"Sure I'm mad!" Bruno shouted to Helen, who was inching away from him on the seat. "Mad enough to take on the whole world and whip it! Any man doesn't think I whipped it, I'll settle with him privately!" He laughed, and the laugh, he saw, only bewildered the blurred, stupid faces around him, tricked them into laughing with him. "Monkeys!" he threw at them cheerfully.

"Who is he?" Bob whispered to Guy.

"Guy and I are supermen!" Bruno said.

"You're a superman drinker," Helen remarked.

"That's not true!" Bruno struggled onto one knee.

"Charles, calm *down*!" Anne told him, but she smiled, too, and Bruno only grinned back.

"I defy what she said about my drinking!"

"What's he talking about?" Helen demanded. "Have you two made a killing on the stock market?"

"Stock market, cr—!" Bruno stopped, thinking of his father. "Yee-hoo-oo! I'm a Texan! Ever ride the merry-go-round in Metcalf, Guy?"

Guy's feet jerked under him, but he did not get up and he did not look at Bruno.

"Awright, I'll sit down," Bruno said to him. "But you disappoint me. You disappoint me horribly!" Bruno shook his empty flask, then lobbed it overboard.

"He's crying," Helen said.

Bruno stood up and stepped out of the cockpit onto the deck. He wanted to take a long walk away from all of them, even away from Guy.

"Where's he going?" Anne asked.

"Let him go," Guy murmured, trying to light a cigarette.

Then there was a splash, and Guy knew Bruno had fallen overboard. Guy was out of the cockpit before any of them spoke.

Guy ran to the stern, trying to get his overcoat off. He felt his arms pinned behind him and, turning, hit Bob in the face with his fist and flung himself off the deck. Then the voices and the rolling stopped, and there was a moment of agonizing stillness before his body began to rise through the water. He shed the overcoat in slow motion, as if the water that was so cold it was merely a pain had frozen him already. He leapt high, and saw Bruno's head incredibly far away, like a mossy, half-submerged rock.

"You can't reach him!" Bob's voice blared, cut off by a burst of water against his ear.

"Guy!" Bruno called from the sea, a wail of dying.

Guy cursed. He could reach him. At the tenth stroke, he leapt up again. "Bruno!" But he couldn't see him now.

"There, Guy!" Anne pointed from the stern of the *India*.

Guy couldn't see him, but he threshed toward the memory of his head, and went down at the place, groping with his arms wide, the farthest tips of his fingers searching. The water slowed him. As if he moved in a nightmare, he thought. As on the lawn. He came up under a wave and took a gasp of water. The *India* was in a different place, and turning. Why didn't they direct him? They didn't care, those others!

"Bruno!"

Perhaps behind one of the wallowing mountains. He threshed on, then realized he was directionless. A wave bashed the side of his head. He cursed the gigantic, ugly body of the sea. Where was his friend, his brother?

He went down again, deep as he could, spreading his ridiculous length as wide as he could. But now there seemed nothing but a silent gray vacuum filling all space, in which he was only a tiny point of consciousness. The swift, unbearable loneliness pressed him closer, threatening to swallow his own life. He stretched his eyes desperately. The grayness became a brown, ridged floor.

"Did you find him?" he blurted, raising himself up. "What time is it?"

"Lie still, Guy," Bob's voice said.

"He went down, Guy," Anne said. "We saw him."

Guy closed his eyes and wept.

He was aware that, one by one, they all went out of the bunkroom and left him, even Anne.

## *forty-six*

Carefully, so as not to awaken Anne, Guy got out of bed and went downstairs to the living room. He drew the drapes together and turned on the light, though he knew there was no shutting out the dawn that slithered now under the Venetian blinds, between the green drapes, like a silvery-mauve and amorphous fish. He had lain upstairs in the darkness awaiting it, knowing it would come for him finally over the foot of the bed, fearing more than ever the grip of the mechanism it set in motion, because he knew now that Bruno had borne half his guilt. If it had been almost unbearable before, how would he bear it now alone? He knew that he couldn't.

He envied Bruno for having died so suddenly, so quietly, so violently, and so young. And so easily, as Bruno had always done everything. A tremor passed through him. He sat rigidly in the armchair, his body under the thin pajamas as hard and tense as in the first dawns. Then on the spasmic snap that always broke his tension, he got up and went upstairs to the studio before he actually knew what he intended to do. He looked at the big sleek-surfaced sheets of drawing paper on his work table, four or five lying as he had left them after sketching something for Bob. Then he sat down and began to write from the upper left-hand corner across, slowly at first, then more and more rapidly. He wrote of Miriam and of the train, the telephone calls, of Bruno in Metcalf, of the letters, the gun, and his dissolution, and of the Friday night. As if Bruno were still alive, he wrote every detail he knew that might contribute to an understanding of him. His writing blackened three of the big sheets. He folded the sheets, put them into an oversized envelope, and sealed it. For a long while he stared at the envelope, savoring its partial relief, wondering at its separateness now from himself. Many times before he had written passionate, scribbled admissions but, knowing no one would ever see them, they had never really left him. This was for Anne. Anne would touch this envelope. Her hands would hold the sheets of paper, and her eyes would read every word.

Guy put his palms up to his own hot, aching eyes. The hours of writing had tired him almost to a point of sleepiness. His thoughts drifted, resting on nothing, and the people he had been writing about—Bruno, Miriam, Owen Markman, Samuel Bruno, Arthur Gerard, Mrs. McCausland, Anne—the people and the names danced around the edge of his mind. *Miriam.* Oddly, she was more a person to him now than ever before. He had tried to describe her to Anne, tried to evaluate her. It had forced him to evaluate her to himself. She was not worth a great deal as a person, he thought, by Anne's standards or by anyone's. But she had been a human being. Neither had Samuel Bruno been worth a great deal—a grim, greedy maker of money, hated by his son, unloved by his wife. Who had really loved him? Who had really been hurt by either Miriam's death or Samuel Bruno's? If there were someone who had been hurt—Miriam's family, perhaps? Guy remembered her brother on the witness stand at the inquest, the small eyes that had held nothing but malicious, brutal hatred, not grief. And her mother, vindictive, as vicious of spirit as ever, not caring where the blame fell as long as it fell on someone, unbroken, unsoftened by grief. Was there any purpose, even if he wanted to, in going to see them and giving them a target for their hatred? Would it make them feel any better? Or him? He couldn't see that it would. If anyone had really loved Miriam— Owen Markman.

Guy took his hands down from his eyes. The name had swum into his mind mechanically. He hadn't thought of Owen at all until he wrote the letter. Owen had been a dim figure in the background. Guy had held him of less value than Miriam. But Owen must have loved her. He had been going to marry her. She had been carrying his child. Suppose Owen had staked all his happiness on Miriam. Suppose he had known the grief in the months afterward that Guy himself had known when Miriam died to him in Chicago. Guy tried to recall every detail of Owen Markman at the inquest. He remembered his hangdog manner, his calm, straightforward answers until his accusation of jealousy. Impossible to tell what really might have been going on in his head.

"Owen," Guy said.

Slowly, he stood up. An idea was taking form in his mind even as he tried to weigh his memories of the long, dark face and tall, slouching figure that was Owen Markman. He would go and see Markman and talk with him, tell him everything. If he owed it to anyone, he owed it to Markman. Let Markman kill him if he would, call the police in, anything. But he would have told him, honestly, and face to face. Suddenly it was an urgent necessity. Of course. It was the only step and the next step. After that, after his personal debt, he would shoulder whatever the law put upon him. He would be ready then. He could catch a train today, after the questions they were supposed to answer about Bruno. The police had told him to be at the station with Anne this morning. He could even catch a plane this afternoon, if he was lucky. Where was it? Houston. If Owen was still there. He mustn't let Anne go with him to the airport. She must think he was going to Canada as he had planned. He didn't want Anne to know yet. The appointment with Owen was more urgent. It seemed to transform him. Or perhaps it was like the shedding of an old and worn-out coat. He felt naked now, but not afraid any longer.

# *forty-seven*

Guy sat on a jumpseat in the aisle of a plane bound for Houston. He felt miserable and nervous, as out of place and wrong, somehow, as the little lump of the seat itself that clogged the aisle and spoilt the symmetry of the plane's interior. Wrong, unnecessary, and yet he was convinced that what he was doing was necessary. The difficulties he had hurdled in getting this far had put him in a mood of stubborn determination.

Gerard had been at the police station to hear the questioning on Bruno's death. He had flown over from Iowa, he said. It was too bad, Charles' end, but Charles had never been cautious about anything. It was too bad it had had to happen on Guy's boat. Guy had been able to answer the questions without any emotion whatever. It had seemed so insignificant, the details of the disappearance of his body. Guy had been more disturbed by Gerard's presence. He didn't want Gerard to follow him down to Texas. To be doubly safe, he had not even canceled his ticket on the plane to Canada, which had left earlier in the afternoon. Then he had waited nearly four hours at the airport for this plane. But he was safe. Gerard had said he was going back to Iowa by train this afternoon.

Nevertheless, Guy took another look around him at the passengers, a slower and more careful look than he had dared take the first time. There was not one who seemed the least interested in him.

The thick letter in his inside pocket crackled as he bent over the papers in his lap. The papers were sectional reports of the Alberta work, which Bob had given him. Guy couldn't have read a magazine, he didn't want to look out the window, but he knew he could memorize, mechanically and efficiently, the items in the reports that had to be memorized. He found a page from an English architectural magazine torn out and stuck between the mimeographed sheets. Bob had circled a paragraph in red pencil:

> Guy Daniel Haines is the most significant architect yet to emerge from the American South. With his first independent

work at the age of twenty-seven, a simple, two-story building which has become famous as "The Pittsburgh Store," Haines set forth principles of grace and function to which he has steadfastly held, and through which his art has grown to its present stature. If we seek to define Haines' peculiar genius, we must depend chiefly upon that elusive and aery term, "grace," which until Haines has never distinguished modern architecture. It is Haines' achievement to have made classic in our age his own concept of grace. His main building of the widely known Palmyra group in Palm Beach, Florida, has been called "The American Parthenon" . . .

An asterisked paragraph at the bottom of the page said:

Since the writing of this article, Mr. Haines has been appointed a member of the Advisory Committee of the Alberta Dam project in Canada. Bridges have always interested him, he says. He estimates that this work will occupy him happily for the next three years.

"Happily," he said. How had they happened to use such a word?

A clock was striking 9 as Guy's taxi crossed the main street of Houston. Guy had found Owen Markman's name in a telephone book at the airport, had checked his bags and gotten into a taxi. It won't be so simple, he thought. You can't just arrive at 9 in the evening and find him at home, and alone, and willing to sit in a chair and listen to a stranger. He won't be home, or he won't be living there anymore, or he won't even be in Houston anymore. It might take days.

"Pull up at this hotel," Guy said.

Guy got out and reserved a room. The trivial, provident gesture made him feel better.

Owen Markman was not living at the address in Cleburne Street. It was a small apartment building. The people in the hall downstairs, among them the superintendent, looked at him very suspiciously and gave him as little information as possible. No one knew where Owen Markman was.

"You're not the police, are you?" asked the superintendent finally.

Despite himself, he smiled. “No.”

Guy was on his way out when a man stopped him on the steps and, with the same air of cautious reluctance, told him that he might be able to find Markman at a certain café in the center of town.

Finally, Guy found him in a drugstore, sitting at the counter with two women whom he did not introduce. Owen Markman simply slid off his stool and stood up straight, his brown eyes a little wide. His long face looked heavier and less handsome than Guy remembered it. He slid his big hands warily into the slash pockets of his short leather jacket.

“You remember me,” Guy said.

“Reckon I do.”

“Would you mind if I had a talk with you? Just for a little while.” Guy looked around him. The best thing was to invite him to his hotel room, he supposed. “I’ve got a room here at the Rice Hotel.”

Markman looked Guy slowly up and down once more, and after a long silence said,“All right.”

Passing the cashier’s desk, Guy saw the shelves of liquor bottles. It might be hospitable to offer Markman a drink. “Do you like Scotch?”

Markman loosened up a bit as Guy bought it. “Coke’s fine, but it tastes better with a little something in it.”

Guy bought some bottles of Coca-Cola, too.

They rode to the hotel in silence, rode up in the elevator and entered the room in silence. How would he begin, Guy wondered. There were a dozen beginnings. Guy discarded them all.

Owen sat down in the armchair, and divided his time between eying Guy with insouciant suspicion, and savoring the long glass of Scotch and Coca-Cola.

Guy began stammeringly,“What—”

“What?” asked Owen.

“What would you do if you knew who murdered Miriam?”

Markman’s foot thudded down to the floor, and he sat up. His frowning brows made a black, intense line above his eyes. “Did you?”

“No, but I know the man who did.”

“Who?”

What was he feeling as he sat there frowning, Guy wondered. Hatred? Resentment? Anger? “I know, and so will the police very soon.”Guy hesitated. "It was a man from New York whose name was Charles Bruno. He died yesterday. He was drowned."

Owen sat back a little. He took a sip of his drink. "How do you know? Confessed?"

"I know. I've known for some time. That's why I've felt it was my fault. For not betraying him." He moistened his lips. It was difficult every syllable of the way. And why did he uncover himself so cautiously, inch by inch? Where were all his fantasies, the imagined pleasure and relief of blurting it all out? "That's why I blame myself. I—" Owen's shrug stopped him. He watched Owen finish his glass, then automatically, Guy went and mixed another for him. "That's why I blame myself," he repeated. "I have to tell you the circumstances. It was very complex. You see, I met Charles Bruno on a train, coming down to Metcalf. The train in June, just before she was killed. I was coming down to get my divorce." He swallowed. There it was, the words he had never said to anyone before, said of his own will, and it felt so ordinary now, so ignominious even. He had a huskiness in his throat he could not get rid of. Guy studied Owen's long, dark attentive face. There was less of a frown now. Owen's leg was crossed again, and Guy remembered suddenly the gray buckskin work shoes Owen had worn at the inquest. These were plain brown shoes with elastic sidepieces. "And—"

"Yeah," Owen prompted.

"I told him Miriam's name. I told him I hated her. Bruno had an idea for a murder. A double murder."

"Jesus!" Owen whispered.

The "Jesus" reminded him of Bruno, and Guy had a horrible, an utterly horrible thought all at once, that he might ensnare Owen in the same trap that Bruno had used for him, that Owen in turn would capture another stranger who would capture another, and so on in infinite progression of the trapped and the hunted. Guy shuddered and clenched his hands. "My mistake was in speaking to him. My mistake was in telling a stranger my private business."

"He told you he was going to kill her?"

"No, of course not. It was an idea he had. He was insane. He was a psychopath. I told him to shut up and to go to hell. I got rid of him!" He was back in the compartment. He was leaving it to go onto the platform. He heard the bang of the train's heavy door. Got rid of him, he had thought!

"You didn't tell him to do it."

"No. He didn't say he was going to do it."

"Why don't you have a straight shot? Why don't you sit down?" Owen's slow, rasping voice made the room steady again. His voice was like an ugly rock, solidly lodged in dry ground.

He didn't want to sit down, and he didn't want to drink. He had drunk Scotch like this in Bruno's compartment. This was the end and he didn't want it to be like the beginning. He touched the glass of Scotch and water that he had fixed for himself only for politeness' sake. When he turned around, Owen was pouring more liquor into his glass, continued to pour it, as if to show Guy that he hadn't been trying to do it behind his back.

"Well,"Owen drawled,"if the fellow was a nut like you say— That was the court's opinion finally, too, wasn't it, that it must have been a madman?"

"Yes."

"I mean, sure I can understand how you felt afterwards, but if it was just a conversation like you say, I don't see where you should blame yourself so awful much."

Guy was staring at him incredulously. Didn't it matter to Owen more than this? Maybe he didn't entirely understand. "But you see—"

"When did you find out about it?" Owen's brown eyes looked slurry.

"About three months after it happened. But you see, if not for me, Miriam would be alive now." Guy watched Owen lower his lips to the glass again. He could taste the sickening mess of Coca-Cola and Scotch sliding into Owen's wide mouth. What was Owen going to do? Leap up suddenly and fling the glass down, throttle him as Bruno had throttled Miriam? He couldn't imagine that Owen would continue to sit there, but the seconds went by and Owen did not move. "You see, I had to tell you,"Guy persisted. "I considered you the one person I might have hurt, the one person who suffered. Her child had been yours. You were going to marry her. You loved her. It was you—"

"Hell, I didn't love her." Owen looked at Guy with no change whatever in his face.

Guy stared back at him. Didn't love her, didn't love her, Guy thought. His mind staggered back, trying to realign all the past equations that no longer balanced. "Didn't love her?" he said.

"No. Well, not the way you seem to think. I certainly didn't want her to die—and understand, I'd have done anything to prevent it, but I was glad enough not to have to marry her. Getting married was her idea. That's why she had the child. That's not a man's fault, I wouldn't say. Would you?" Owen was looking at him with a tipsy earnestness, waiting, his wide mouth the same firm, irregular line it had been on the witness stand, waiting for Guy to say something, to pass judgment on his conduct with Miriam.

Guy turned away with a vaguely impatient gesture. He couldn't make the equations balance. He couldn't make any sense to it, except an ironic sense. There was no reason for his being here now, except for an ironic reason. There was no reason for his sweating, painful self-torture in a hotel room for the benefit of a stranger who didn't care, except for an ironic reason.

"Do you think so?" Owen kept on, reaching for the bottle on the table beside him.

Guy couldn't have made himself say a word. A hot, inarticulate anger was rising inside him. He slid his tie down and opened his shirt collar, and glanced at the open windows for an air-conditioning apparatus.

Owen shrugged. He looked quite comfortable in his open-collared shirt and unzipped leather jacket. Guy had an absolutely unreasonable desire to ram something down Owen's throat, to beat him and crush him, above all to blast him out of his complacent comfort in the chair.

"Listen," Guy began quietly,"I am a—"

But Owen had begun to speak at the same instant, and he went on, droningly, not looking at Guy who stood in the middle of the floor with his mouth still open. ". . . the second time. Got married two months after my divorce, and there was trouble right away. Whether Miriam would of been any different, I don't know, but I'd say she'd of been worse. Louisa up and left two months ago after damn near setting the house on fire, a big apartment house." He droned on, and poured more Scotch into his glass from the bottle at his elbow, and Guy felt a disrespect, a definite affront, directed against himself, in the way Owen helped himself. Guy remembered his own behavior at the inquest, undistinguished behavior, to say the least, for the husband of the victim. Why should Owen have respect for him? "The awful thing is, the man gets the worst of it, because the women do more talking. Take Louisa, she can go back to that apartment house and they'll give her a welcome, but let me so much—"

"Listen!" Guy said, unable to stand it any longer. "I—I killed someone, too! I'm a murderer, too!"

Owen's feet came down to the floor again, he sat up again, he even looked from Guy to the window and back again, as if he contemplated having to escape or having to defend himself, but the befuddled surprise and alarm on his face was so feeble, so halfhearted, that it seemed a mockery itself, seemed to mock Guy's seriousness. Owen started to set his glass on the table and then didn't. "How's that?" he asked.

"Listen!" Guy shouted again. "Listen, I'm a dead man. I'm as good as dead right now, because I'm going to give myself up. Immediately! Because I killed a man, do you understand? Don't look so unconcerned, and don't lean back in that chair again!"

"Why shouldn't I lean back in this chair?" Owen had both hands on his glass now, which he had just refilled with Coca-Cola and Scotch.

"Doesn't it mean anything to you that I am a murderer, and took a man's life, something no human being has a right to do?"

Owen might have nodded, or he might not have. At any rate, he drank again, slowly.

Guy stared at him. The words, unutterable tangles of thousands and thousands of words, seemed to congest even his blood, to cause waves of heat to sweep up his arms from his clenched hands. The words were curses against Owen, sentences and paragraphs of the confession he had written that morning, that were growing jumbled now because the drunken idiot in the armchair didn't want to hear them. The drunken idiot was determined to look indifferent. He didn't look like a murderer, he supposed, in his clean white shirtsleeves and his silk tie and his dark blue trousers, and maybe even his strained face didn't look like a murderer's to anybody else. "That's the mistake," Guy said aloud, "that nobody knows what a murderer looks like. A murderer looks like anybody!" He laid the back of his fist against his forehead and took it down again, because he had known the last words were coming, and had been unable to stop them. It was exactly like Bruno.

Abruptly Guy went and got himself a drink, a straight three-finger shot, and drank it off.

"Glad to see I've got a drinking companion," Owen mumbled. Guy sat down on the neat, green-covered bed opposite Owen. Quite suddenly, he had felt tired. "It doesn't mean anything,"he began again,"it doesn't mean anything to you, does it?"

"You're not the first man I seen that killed another man. Or woman."He chuckled. "Seems to me there's more women that go free."

"I'm not going free. I'm not free. I did this in cold blood. I had no reason. Don't you see that might be worse? I did it for—" He wanted to say he did it because there had been that measure of perversity within him sufficient to do it, that he had done it because of the worm in the wood, but he knew it would make no sense to Owen, because Owen was a practical man. Owen was so practical, he would not bother to hit him, or flee from him, or call the police, because it was more comfortable to sit in the chair.

Owen waggled his head as if he really did consider Guy's point. His lids were half dropped over his eyes. He twisted and reached for something in his hip pocket, a bag of tobacco. He got cigarette papers from the breast pocket of his shirt.

Guy watched his operations for what seemed like hours. "Here," Guy said, offering him his own cigarettes.

Owen looked at them dubiously. "What kind are they?"

"Canadian. They're quite good. Try one."

"Thanks, I—" Owen drew the bag closed with his teeth— "prefer my own brand." He spent at least three minutes rolling the cigarette.

"This was just as if I pulled a gun on someone in a public park and shot him," Guy went on, determined to go on, though it was as if he talked to an inanimate thing like a dictaphone in the chair, with the difference that his words didn't seem to be penetrating in any way. Mightn't it dawn on Owen that he could pull a gun on him now in this hotel room? Guy said,"I was driven to it. That's what I'll tell the police, but that won't make any difference, because the point is, I did it. You see, I have to tell you Bruno's idea."At least Owen was looking at him now, but his face, far from being rapt, seemed actually to wear an expression of pleasant, polite, drunken attention. Guy refused to let it stop him. "Bruno's idea was that we should kill for each other, that he should kill Miriam and I should kill his father. Then he came to Texas and killed Miriam, behind my back. Without my knowledge or consent, do you see?" His choice of words was abominable, but at least Owen was listening. At least the words were coming out. "I didn't know about it, and I didn't even suspect—not really. Until months later. And then he began to haunt me. He began to tell me he would pin the blame for Miriam's death on me, unless I went through with the rest of his damned plan, do you see? Which was to kill his father. The whole idea rested on the fact that there was no reason for the murders. No personal motives. So we couldn't be traced, individually. Provided we didn't see each other. But that's another point. The point is, I did kill him. I was broken down. Bruno broke me down with letters and blackmail and sleeplessness. He drove me insane, too. And listen, I believe any man can be broken down. I could break you down. Given the same circumstances, I could break you down and make you kill someone. It might take different methods from the ones Bruno used on me, but it could be done. What else do you think keeps the totalitarian states going? Or do you ever stop to wonder about things like that, Owen? Anyway, that's what I'll tell the police, but it won't matter, because they'll say I shouldn't have broken down.

"It won't matter, because they'll say I was weak. But I don't care now, do you see? I can face anyone now, do you see?" He bent to look into Owen's face, but Owen seemed scarcely to see him. Owen's head was sagged sideways, resting in his hand. Guy stood up straight. He couldn't make Owen see, he could feel that Owen wasn't understanding the main point at all, but that didn't matter either. "I'll accept it, whatever they want to do to me. I'll say the same thing to the police tomorrow."

"Can you prove it?" Owen asked.

"Prove what? What is there to prove about my killing a man?"

The bottle slipped out of Owen's fingers and fell onto the floor, but there was so little in it now that almost nothing spilled. "You're an architect, aren't you?"Owen asked. "I remember now." He righted the bottle clumsily, leaving it on the floor.

"What does it matter?"

"I was wondering."

"Wondering what?" Guy asked impatiently.

"Because you sound a little touched—if you want my honest opinion. Ain't saying you do." And behind Owen's fogged expression now was a simple wariness lest Guy might walk over and hit him for his remark. When he saw that Guy didn't move, he sat back in his chair again, and slumped lower than before.

Guy groped for a concrete idea to present to Owen. He didn't want his audience to slip away, indifferent as it was. "Listen, how do you feel about the men you know who've killed somebody? How do you treat them? How do you act with them? Do you pass the time of day with them the same as you'd do with anybody else?"

Under Guy's intense scrutiny, Owen did seem to try to think. Finally he said with a smile, blinking his eyes relaxedly, "Live and let live."

Anger seized him again. For an instant, it was like a hot vise, holding his body and brain. There were no words for what he felt. Or there were too many words to begin. The word formed itself and spat itself from between his teeth: "*Idiot!*"

Owen stirred slightly in his chair, but his unruffledness prevailed. He seemed undecided whether to smile or to frown. "What business is it of mine?" he asked firmly.

"What business? Because you—you are a part of society!"

"Well, then it's society's business," Owen replied with a lazy wave of his hand. He was looking at the Scotch bottle, in which only half an inch remained.

What business, Guy thought. Was that his real attitude, or was he drunk? It must be Owen's attitude. There was no reason for him to lie now. Then he remembered it had been his own attitude when he had suspected Bruno, before Bruno had begun to dog him. Was that most people's attitude? If so, who was society?

Guy turned his back on Owen. He knew well enough who society was. But the society he had been thinking about in regard to himself, he realized, was the law, was inexorable rules. Society was people like Owen, people like himself, people like—Brillhart, for instance, in Palm Beach. Would Brillhart have reported him? No. He couldn't imagine Brillhart reporting him. Everyone would leave it for someone else, who would leave it for someone else, and no one would do it. Did he care about rules? Wasn't it a rule that had kept him tied to Miriam? Wasn't it a person who was murdered, and therefore people who mattered? If people from Owen to Brillhart didn't care sufficiently to betray him, should he care any further? Why did he think this morning that he had wanted to give himself up to the police? What masochism was it? He wouldn't give himself up. What, concretely, did he have on his conscience now? What human being would inform on him?

"Except a stool-pigeon," Guy said. "I suppose a stool-pigeon would inform."

"That's right," Owen agreed. "A dirty, stinking stool-pigeon." He gave a loud, relieving laugh.

Guy was staring into space, frowning. He was trying to find solid ground that would carry him to something he had just seen as if by a flash, far ahead of him. The law was not society, it began. Society was people like himself and Owen and Brillhart, who hadn't the right to take the life of another member of society. And yet the law did. "And yet the law is supposed to be the will of society at least. It isn't even that. Or maybe it is collectively," he added, aware that as always he was doubling back before he came to a point, making things as complex as possible in trying to make them certain.

"Hmm-m?" Owen murmured. His head was back against the chair, his black hair tousled over his forehead, and his eyes almost closed.

"No, people collectively might lynch a murderer, but that's exactly what the law is supposed to guard against."

"Never hold with lynchings," Owen said. "'S not true! Gives the whole South a bad name—unnec'sarily."

"My point is, that if society hasn't the right to take another person's life, then the law hasn't either. I mean, considering that the law is a mass of regulations that have been handed down and that nobody can interfere with, no human being can touch. But it's human beings the law deals with, after all. I'm talking about people like you and me. My case in particular. At the moment, i'm only talking about my case. But that's only logic. Do you know something, Owen? Logic doesn't always work out, so far as people go. It's all very well when you're building a building, because the material behaves then, but—" His argument went up in smoke. There was a wall that prevented him from saying another word, simply because he couldn't think any further. He had spoken loudly and distinctly, but he knew Owen hadn't been hearing, even if he was trying to listen. And yet Owen *had* been indifferent, five minutes ago, to the question of his guilt. "What about a jury, I wonder," Guy said.

"What jury?"

"Whether a jury is twelve human beings or a body of laws. It's an interesting point. I suppose it's always an interesting point." He poured the rest of the bottle into his glass and drank it. "But I don't suppose it's interesting to you, is it, Owen? What is interesting to you?"

Owen was silent and motionless.

"Nothing is interesting to you, is it?" Guy looked at Owen's big scuffed brown shoes extended limply on the carpet, the toes tipped inward toward each other, because they rested on their heels. Suddenly, their flaccid, shameless, massive stupidity seemed the essence of all human stupidity. It translated itself instantly into his old antagonism against the passive stupidity of those who stood in the way of the progress of his work, and before he knew how or why, he had kicked, viciously, the side of Owen's shoe. And still, Owen did not move. His work, Guy thought. Yes, there was his work to get back to. Think later, think it all out right later, but he had work to do.

He looked at his watch. Ten past 12. He didn't want to sleep here. He wondered if there was a plane tonight. There must be something out. Or a train.

He shook Owen. "Owen, wake up. Owen!"

Owen mumbled a question.

"I think you'll sleep better at home."

Owen sat up and said clearly,"That I doubt."

Guy picked up his topcoat from the bed. He looked around, but he hadn't left anything because he hadn't brought anything. It might be better to telephone the airport now, he thought.

"Where's the john?" Owen stood up. "I don't feel so good."

Guy couldn't find the telephone. There was a wire by the bed table, though. He traced the wire under the bed. The telephone was off the hook, on the floor, and he knew immediately it hadn't fallen, because both parts were dragged up near the foot of the bed, the hand piece eerily focused on the armchair where Owen had been sitting. Guy pulled the telephone slowly toward him.

"Hey, ain't there a john anywheres?" Owen was opening a closet door.

"It must be down the hall." His voice was like a shudder. He was holding the telephone in a position for speaking, and now he brought it closer to his ear. He heard the intelligent silence of a live wire. "Hello?" he said.

"Hello, Mr. Haines." The voice was rich, courteous, and just the least brusque.

Guy's hand tried unavailingly to crush the telephone, and then he surrendered without a word. It was like a fortress falling, like a great building falling apart in his mind, but it crumbled like powder and fell silently.

"There wasn't time for a dictaphone. But I heard most of it from just outside your door. May I come in?"

Gerard must have had his scouts at the airport in New York, Guy thought, must have followed in a chartered plane. It was possible. And here it was. And he had been stupid enough to sign the register in his own name. "Come in," Guy echoed. He put the telephone on the hook and stood up, rigidly, watching the door. His heart was pounding as it never had before, so fast and hard, he thought surely it must be a prelude to his dropping dead. Run, he thought. Leap, attack as soon as he comes in. This is your very last chance. But he didn't move. He was vaguely aware of Owen being sick in the basin in the corner behind him. Then there was a rap at the door, and he went toward it, thinking, wouldn't it have to be like this after all, by surprise, with someone, a stranger who didn't understand anything, throwing up in a basin in a corner of the room, without his thoughts ordered, and worse, having already uttered half of them in a muddle. Guy opened the door.

"Hello," Gerard said, and he came in with his hat on and his arms hanging, just as he had always looked.

"Who is it?" Owen asked.

"Friend of Mr. Haines," Gerard said easily, and glancing at Guy with his round face as serious as before, he gave him a wink. "I suppose you want to go to New York tonight, don't you?"

Guy was staring at Gerard's familiar face, at the big mole on his cheek, at the bright, living eye that had winked at him, undoubtedly had winked at him. Gerard was the law, too. Gerard was on his side, so far as any man could be, because Gerard knew Bruno. Guy knew it now, as if he had known it the whole time, yet it had never even occurred to him before. He knew, too, that he had to face Gerard. That was part of it all, and always had been. It was inevitable and ordained, like the turning of the earth, and there was no sophistry by which he could free himself from it.

"Eh?" Gerard said.

Guy tried to speak, and said something entirely different from what he had intended. "Take me."

# EARLY STORIES

# A MIGHTY NICE MAN

The child Charlotte sat on the narrow curbstone, her cheek against one knee, drawing idly in the dust with a stick. She sniffed at the flesh of her leg, smelt the dust and the sweat on it. Then she sighed and threw away the stick.

"Em'lie," she said.

Emilie, age nine, was standing behind her, with her back against the sun-warm wooden post, her toes braced on the edge of the sidewalk.

"Huh?" Emilie breathed.

"Play like I've got a store. Play like I've got a grocer store an' you've gotta buy stuff. . . . Huh, Em'lie?"

Emilie was so bored and sleepy she did not reply. Her gray sullen eyes looked out across the road and the whole scene was yellow to her, the dirt of the road, the squatting house just beyond, the dry fields: yellow pulsing heat and silence.

"Em'lie! You crazy? . . . Answer me!" Charlotte turned around on the curb and glowered at her.

"Wha'?" said Emilie, and pushed herself away from the post.

"I've gotta store an' you must buy stuff." She reached for the tiny red truck that was their common property and began filling it with pebbles. "An' then I must deliver it. You gotta go home first an' then you must telephone." She clutched the truck in one dirty hand as she scowled at Emilie.

They heard footsteps in the grit of the road. Charlotte forgot her game and they both looked up the slope. Emilie brushed the mottled blond hair out of her eyes and squinted. Her left eye was cast, and she twisted up that side of her face whenever she looked at anything.

"I betcha it's a boarder from Mrs. Osterman's," Charlotte said. "I betcha he's from New York, too."

He turned onto the sidewalk that began half a block from Charlotte's house. Emilie could see him now, a short figure in unpressed white trousers. He saw them, too, and began whistling a tune.

"Hello," he said, taking in both of them.

"H'lo," they replied in unison.

He stopped a minute, looked about him. "Gonna be here when I get back?" He spoke quietly, smiling. "I'll bring you some candy."

Charlotte and Emilie surveyed him silently.

"I like . . . I like *any* kind of candy," Charlotte told him.

He laughed, winked at them and walked on down the sidewalk. Once he turned and waved, but only Charlotte saw that. They were both motionless a long time, watching.

"Reckon he'll come back, Em'lie?"

"Huh?"

"Reckon he'll come back this way?"

"Huh?"

"I sed . . . reckon he'll come *back*?"

But Emilie moved off without a word toward her house and Charlotte sat on the curb, resting her face against one knee as she traced in the dust. Soon the screen door to Emilie's house screeched, closed with a double slap, and Emilie's bare heels thudded across the porch.

"Huh," said Emilie, and handed Charlotte a small pale peach. Charlotte took it silently, bit into the fruit with darkish baby teeth.

"Betcha that man's got a car."

"Huh?"

"I sed"—she took a deep breath—"I betcha that man's got a *ca-ar.*"

"Wha' man?"

"That *ma-an* . . . what just passed."

Emilie licked her peach-stained fingers. "He ain't comin' back." She sighed, looked across the hot road to the blurry yellowish fields. The bugs in the grass, in the trees, were singing rhythmically. Two clicks and a long buzz. Down the road where it met the street that led into town they heard Mr. Wynecoop's station wagon. They knew it from all the other cars in the neighborhood. Charlotte and Emilie sat on the edge of the curb and looked.

As he passed, Mr. Wynecoop waved a stiff-fingered hand at them, and they chanted, "H'lo, ol' man Wynecoop."

The car pulled up the hill, reached the top, sighed as it hit level ground. Charlotte kept watching for the man in white. She stood up once and looked toward town, but the view was mostly shut out by the trees along the sidewalk.

Emilie smirked and grunted contemptuously.

Charlotte held the empty truck in one hand and stared down the walk. "*You* cou'nt see him if he *was* comin'." Suddenly she drew in her breath. "He's comin', all right," she whispered, and ran stooping over to Emilie by the curb. She began stabbing in the dust, her heart beating fast.

Then Emilie heard his footsteps and twisted around and peered into the yellowness. He was whistling again. The blur of white came closer.

"He's got candy!" Charlotte said.

The man took his cigarette out of his mouth and threw it down.

"Hello," he said quietly, then glanced at the houses and back at the two little girls on the curb. He handed the bag to Charlotte. Two licorice sticks stuck out of the top, and she was disappointed to see that it was all penny candy, unwrapped caramels and sugar hearts that sell five for a cent. Once an old man from Mrs. Osterman's had brought her five-cent candy bars.

Slowly she put one end of a licorice stick into her mouth. The man shuffled uneasily, leaned against a tree and lighted another cigarette. "You didn't tell me your name," he said finally.

She told him, and he said his name was Robbie.

"I've got a car. . . . Want to go riding sometime?" He kept shifting and taking his hands in and out of his pockets. "I bet you like riding, Charlotte."

"I sure do," she said, and a dark stream of licorice juice ran down her chin.

The man leaning against the tree sprang toward her, drew a wadded handkerchief out of his hip pocket. He put one hand back of her head and wiped her face hard. "You're . . . pretty messy." Then he stood up again and put the handkerchief back. Emilie was watching him steadily, curiously. He felt the hostility in her twisted mouth.

He drew viciously on his cigarette. "How'd you like to go riding this evening?" he whispered. "After dinner."

"I'd like that," Charlotte said.

Then he went off quietly, looking back at them, smiling and friendly.

Charlotte was proud of herself. She leaned back on her hands and the thin muscles in her thighs showed under the dirt-streaked skin.

"He didn't ask *you* to go."

Emilie sighed. "He ain't comin'. You wait an' see."

So Charlotte waited. She finished the candy alone, picked at her noon meal, and brooded happily in the shade of the house, humming to herself. Then she lay in the patched-up hammock on her front porch and looked at the pictures in a frayed funny paper book. The afternoon was hot and long and silent.

After supper Charlotte went out to the road and stood by the tree. Her mother had given her a sponge bath, and she had a cotton dress on instead of the thin romper suit she wore all day. She had told her mother nothing about the man from Mrs. Osterman's. The fast-setting sun sent hot horizontal rays into her face. She was sure he would come. She tried to picture the car, like the ones she had seen in the movies. That was the kind of car *he* would have. And she would step into the big front seat and they would drive away with hardly a sound. They would drive fast.

But after a while she got tired and came in to the front porch. The wood was hot to her bare feet. She leaned on one side of the hammock, pushed herself into it. Still she listened and there was no sound of a car. Then the screen door to Emilie's house shrieked, stopped and shrieked again. Emilie appeared, unwashed and tousled, eating the remains of a slice of bread and butter. She came deliberately onto Charlotte's porch, stood chewing reflectively as she stared at her in the hammock. Charlotte disdained to look at her.

"Oh . . . *he* ain't comin'," she said, and turned around and walked to the steps. She heard something down the walk. "That your mother comin'? *She* don't know, I betcha."

Charlotte bounced out of the hammock. "Listen, Em'lie . . ." She frowned furiously. "If you . . . if you say to her . . ." She clenched her fists at her sides and Emilie gazed at her solemnly.

"Huh!"

But Charlotte had won.

There was no more sun, but it was still light. Charlotte's mother came back from the store. None of them said a word. The woman went into the house and Charlotte could hear her drawing water for the baby. Finally Emilie went hop-skipping across the front yard, into her house.

Charlotte lay in the hammock and listened for him. Someone was walking, whistling. She ran down to the sidewalk and saw him coming. He was dressed in white again with his jacket unbuttoned. He stopped when he saw her, smiled and beckoned. And she glanced once at her house, then ran up the warm pavement to where he stood.

"Where's your car?"

He looked about him, grinned and jerked his head. "Up the road. . . . We don't want nobody to know. You didn't tell nobody, did you?"

"No."

They walked together. She could hardly keep up with him, so he took her hand. The fields opened up on either side after the pavement stopped. Charlotte strained up to see the car, and then the road turned suddenly and they came upon it parked by the roadside. It was big, but not so bright as those in the movies. He opened the door and lifted her in, her feet dangling over the edge of the seat. Then he came in from the other side.

"All set?"

"Uh-huh." Charlotte was looking at the car inside.

"Like it?" he asked, and wiped his nose on the back of his hand.

They didn't drive off immediately. Charlotte was examining the gaudily colored dashboard, its clock with green numbers and silver hands. The other circles she did not understand, but they were all beautiful, colored and shining. The man caught her hand suddenly and she felt his fingers warm and moist, felt her mouth twist up as though she were about to cry. Then she wished that she had not come, wished that she were back on the front porch with Emilie. But he was smiling, laughing, even, as he started the car.

"You like to go fast?"

Charlotte tried to answer, but her lips were stiff. He squeezed her hand again.

"I like a lot of speed."

Then through the engine's noise she heard someone calling her name. The man heard it, too, and released her hand. But the car was moving on toward her house.

"Charlotte! Charlo-otte!"

"That's my mother," Charlotte said quietly.

Charlotte noticed that he frowned and that his hands tightened on the steering wheel. She felt the cool breeze in her face and she wanted to go on riding, but they were not going fast and she wanted to go fast. As they came near the house, she pressed herself against the seat, hoping her mother would not see her.

The woman stood with one foot on the curb, her apron hanging almost to the ground. She waved at them and he slowed the car. She came nearer, hiding her hands under her apron.

"Charlotte." She grinned, but she looked at the man almost flirtatiously. "Em'lie said you were out ridin'. I just wanted to make sure where you was . . . an' I need you to help with the baby now." She pushed some strands of hair behind her ear.

The man at the wheel smiled broadly and said, "How d'you do?"

Charlotte's mother nodded to him. "I allus have Charlotte help me with the baby 'bout this time after supper. . . . It's awful nice o' you to take her out ridin', mister, but she didn't say nothin' to me about it." She laughed nervously.

"Sure, I know," he said. He stretched one arm across and opened the door gallantly. "Maybe tomorrow, then. I'll be around for a few days."

The woman looked in awe at the shiny dials and knobs, the upholstered seats. "Why . . . I'd like you to take her ridin' . . . most anytime."

Then Charlotte and her mother walked hand in hand down the sidewalk. Once the woman cast a timid glance back at the car. "He's a mighty nice man for a city fellah, Charlotte. Where'd you meet up with him? . . . An' say, ain't that a pretty car?"

Charlotte watched the ground pass below her bare feet. Her free hand brushed along the coarse grass that grew high.

"Maybe he'll be around tomorrow," her mother said.

One blade of grass Charlotte caught convulsively and the edges jerked through her fingers. As she looked at her thumb, two thin red lines came out of the flesh.

# THE STILL POINT OF THE TURNING WORLD

There is a small park, hardly more than a square, far over on the West Side in the lower Twenties, that is almost always deserted. A low iron fence runs around it, setting it off from a used car lot, a big redstone public dispensary of some sort, and the plain gray backs of shabby apartment buildings that share the same block with it. Three or four benches stand in pleasant places along the two curving cement paths that one may enter by, and that meet in the center at a cement drinking fountain forever bubbling an inch or so of cool water.

From quite a distance up or down the avenue the little park shines like an emerald isle, a bright and inviting surprise in a sea of drab grayness. Mrs. Robertson noticed it one day from a corner of the Castle Terrace Apartments three blocks away, where she lived. She took her small son Philip to play there that afternoon. It was a splendid place for him, because the low iron fence kept him within bounds even when her back was turned, and it was quiet and sunny, unlittered and untrodden. For a city park it was unusually pretty, too, as if the gardeners had been inspired by a special and personal pride when they made it. The fine close-cropped grass extended into the very corners of the four vaguely triangular lawns. If the grass was not to be walked on, there was no one about to tell her so. Of course, the neighborhood was an abruptly sordid contrast with nearby Castle Terrace, but so was the neighborhood in every direction around Castle Terrace. Its square block of apartments stood like a feudal castle in the center of vassal land in which even the dingiest shops and restaurants bore sycophantic names like the King George, the Crown Tavern, the Belvedere Bar and Grill, as if to curry patronage from the manor. The only people Mrs. Robertson saw near the park, however, were the busy truck drivers who came and went around a diner a block away, and an occasional old man in a pinned-together overcoat who shuffled by too drunk or too tired even to glance at the park. Mrs. Robertson read her book until she grew tired of it, then picked up some knitting she had brought, and after a while just sat and daydreamed in the tranquillity. She debated the item she always left until last in her dinner, the vegetable she would buy in a frozen package on the way home.

She had just decided on mixed carrots and peas when a young woman with a child about the age of Philip came into the park and sat down on one of the benches. The little boy was dark-haired and had a blue and white beach ball which interested Philip.

The dark-haired little boy climbed over the scalloped wire fence into the lawn where Philip played. "Hello," he said.

"Hello," said Philip.

In a minute they were playing together, Philip with the beach ball and the dark-haired little boy with Philip's tricycle. Mrs. Robertson did not like Philip's playing with just any child, but this had happened so quickly there was nothing to be done about it. She intended to leave in about fifteen minutes anyway. Idly, she studied the other woman, surmising immediately that she was rather poor and that she lived in one of the shabby apartment buildings close by. She had very light blond hair that did not quite look bleached, though, and she was rather pretty. She sat with her hands in the pockets of her black polo coat, her knees close together, almost as if she were cold, and she paid little attention to her child, Mrs. Robertson thought, if it was hers. She stared straight before her with a faint smile on her lips, as if she were miles away in thought.

Soon Mrs. Robertson got up and went to get Philip. He and the dark-haired child had become such good friends, Philip cried a little when she loosened his hands from the beach ball and drew him and his tricycle toward the path. Mrs. Robertson and the blond woman exchanged a smile of understanding, but they did not speak to each other. Mrs. Robertson was not given to speaking to strangers, and the other woman seemed still lost in her trance.

The next afternoon, the blond young woman was in the park when

Mrs. Robertson arrived, on the same bench, in the same attitude in the black polo coat.

"Dickie!" Philip shrieked when he saw the little boy, and his baby voice cracked with joy.

It gave Mrs. Robertson a tweak of surprise, somehow of unease, that Philip knew the other little boy's name. She watched Philip run totteringly along the path to meet Dickie, who stood with a wide smile, holding his beach ball toward Philip in two outstretched arms. Philip's rush of greeting knocked the other little boy down, and they both scrambled after the rolling ball. Mrs. Robertson knew suddenly in that instant they were together, bound up as one being in play, what had made her uneasy: she was not sure the other little boy was clean. He might even have things in his hair. Mrs. Robertson had lived until recently in a suburb of Philadelphia, but she had heard about the unsanitary conditions of New York's tenement apartments. The dark-haired little boy *looked* washed enough in his pink-and-white striped play overalls, but one never knew what kind of disease a child who lived in a tenement might carry, and Philip would not have the resistance of a child brought up in such an environment. She would have to watch to see he did not put things in his mouth.

Mrs. Robertson gave the blond woman a nod and a smile as she sat down on the bench where she had been the day before. The other woman responded with a nod that Mrs. Robertson could just detect, and her eyes resumed their vacant gaze, quite above the figures of the two little boys playing on the grass. Her expression was so completely oblivious, it aroused Mrs. Robertson's curiosity. Her smile suggested that she saw into some pleasant and fascinating spectacle in a definite place in space. She was quite young, she decided, probably about twenty-one or -two. What was she thinking of? she wondered. And what would her little boy have to do to make her pay him any notice?

On the bench across the path, nearer the fountain than Mrs. Robertson, the blond young woman was awaiting her lover. She was thinking what a beautiful sunny, quiet day it was, and wishing, almost, that these meetings in the little park in April afternoons were all that he and she would know, could know, or would want to know. She was thinking that a mood came upon her every afternoon as she and Dickie left the house, as she descended the brownstone steps, feeling the warmth of the spring sunlight and its calm clarity upon her before she could take her eyes from Dickie's feet to look around her. The street where she lived was especially free of traffic, and at two or three in the afternoons almost as tranquil as the park itself. It presented two smooth parallel walls of brownstone, and even the gray-blue band of street between them was sharp and clear. Here and there a window was dotted by a white bottle of milk on the sill, or a pair of arms at rest on a flattened pillow. Above the arms, resigned and mildly curious eyes gazed down, athirst for any movement on the street, and there was so little: a woman in a housedress airing a nondescript white dog along the curb, a solitary child bouncing a ball beside a stoop post, maybe a boy with a rattly laundry cart, a passing cat. Everyone except the aged and a few women were off at work. Like her husband, Charles, who drove a bus on Broadway, who was gone by eight in the morning and generally did not return until after five. To her, the street seemed empty even of people, because she did not think the woman with her white dog or the arms on the two or three windowsills were alive in the way she knew she was alive. She did not believe they were aware in the same way of the serenity of the street, an odd kind of serenity that clamored to be noticed, or even of its dazzling cleanliness at that hour of the afternoon in the month of April. The woman with the dog did not feel the same as she, coming down her own steps onto the sidewalk, did not sense that the afternoon there belonged to women, to the wives who were alone now with the chores they were complete mistresses of, whose schedule they could rearrange with the flexibility of a woman's day, to an hour earlier if they chose, an hour later, or perhaps not until tomorrow—a woman's world, the street and its two or three reedy trees in iron cages, their thin heads green once more, the street and its unutterable peace. She did not, however, consider herself an ordinary housewife. And there was not the stillness of the street or of the park inside her on the afternoons when he was to come to meet her, though her perception of its stillness and the park's were dependent upon him. On the afternoons she was to see him, she saw beyond the street and the park. She would look eastward where the street disappeared in a huddled jagged mass of buildings, and imagine noise and seething people. She would look west and something in her would leap at the sight of the pier on the river, at a ship's high short mast rising in a cross like a strong and mystic promise above the sooty front of the dock building, above the squared top where the pier's number was written. From this very pier, so close to where she slept every night, she might leave for any corner of the earth, she supposed. And she would wonder if she and Lance would ever really make voyages to foreign places. If she asked him, of course, he would answer such a firm, "Certainly we will. Why not?" she would believe and not wonder any longer. Did the woman with the dog ever lift her eyes to look at the pier? Or the woman who had come to the park again today, with the washed and combed little blond boy, who must live in Castle Terrace, did she ever get chills at the sight and smell and sound of the river? But she had probably been all over the world already, been to Europe so many times she knew how each thing would look, what was going to happen next. She would not care to look at the pier.

The blond young woman looked at her now, sitting reading her book, glancing once in a while to see if her little boy was safe. What could happen to anyone in this park? The sweater she wore over her dress was beautiful in the sunlight, the color of a stick of grape ice held to light. Cashmere. She was young, too, she thought, but her manner was so formal she seemed older. She had not talked with her, she supposed, because she considered her an inferior, but she did not care at all. She was not in a mood for talking. She was not in a mood for reading, either. She could have sat all day happily, dreaming on the bench and gazing into space with the green of the park beneath her eyes and reflecting up into them. She was waiting for Lance. And in this park, wasn't she able to sit like this even on the days when he could not come? After the hours here, she could smile, very quietly, as if it amused her, when Charles came in very drunk and cheerful late at night, having drunk up all his pay. Strangely, she did not even blame him, if she had spent the afternoon in the park. His job had ruined his nerves—the pushing crowds, the making change, stopping and starting, the schedules to be met, the dodging of darting pedestrians that made him start up in his sleep at night—so he drank to deaden his nerves. He drank to find the stillness that she found in the park. Once, months ago, before she had met Lance, she had brought Charles to the park and he had not liked it, because he could not sit still anymore anywhere. Now the park belonged to her and

Lance. After the hours in the park, she could not blame Charles or herself for what had happened. They simply had stopped loving each other, first Charles, then herself. It might have been the lack of quiet that had exhausted them, from the very first when they lived in the ground-floor apartment on the East Side, that had left Charles not enough energy to love her any longer. If he could be bathed in stillness, drink it and hear it, see it and breathe it, sleep for hours in it, she could imagine his forehead smooth again, his eyes opening to look at her again as if he loved her. But she did not even want this now, it was too late. She had found Lance and she loved him. And Lance would love her no matter where he or she were, together or apart, in silence or noise, movement or stillness. Lance had something within him that Charles had not and never had. She knew now. She was not eighteen any longer, as she had been when she married Charles.

"Philip!"

Philip stood up and looked guiltily at his mother, who was waiting for him to say, "Yes, Mama," which he did, with the accent on the last syllable.

"Don't get mud on your playsuit, darling! Be careful, now."

"Yes, Mama." And he turned back and squatted down by his friend and finished pouring the Dixie cup of water from the fountain into the little pit they had dug in the smooth grass. Dickie had found the discarded cup at the end of the path, and Philip had automatically kept it out of sight when he spoke to his mother. They did not know what they were going to do with the little pit that kept drinking the water, but they were happy and they found something to say to each other every second, so that both talked at once almost all the time. Neither of them in his life had ever found anyone he liked so much as the other.

Mrs. Robertson looked up immediately when the man came into the park, so few people ever came into the park. He was bareheaded, in a dark suit, and he stopped and stood for a moment on the cement walk, looking at the woman on the bench. Mrs. Robertson's first reaction was the least sensation of alarm: there was something sinister in his intensity, in his half-smiling observation of the blond woman, in his hands rammed into the pockets of his jacket almost as if he were cold—and as she recognized this single similarity between them, she recognized also that they knew each other, though neither made a sign of greeting. Now he walked with a kind of rigid caution in his shortened step toward the woman and sat down easily beside her, not taking his hands from his pockets or his eyes from her face. And the woman's expression of bemused content that Mrs. Robertson had remarked both yesterday and today did not alter even in the least. The man's lips moved, the woman looked at him and smiled, and Mrs. Robertson again felt subtly disturbed by what she beheld. It was vaguely disturbing that a man had come in and sat down on a bench at all. That he was a stranger making advances had flitted into her mind and out, because of the aura of intimacy that wrapped them both. Both looked before them now, leaned very slightly toward each other, though between them was one of the iron arms that divided the bench into four or five seats, and then the man reached over and took the young woman's hand gently from her pocket, drawing it by the wrist beneath the iron bar until he held it in his own hand, resting it on his crossed leg. And suddenly Mrs. Robertson knew: they were lovers. Of course! Why had it taken her so long to guess? Now she began to watch fascinatedly, covertly. For a few moments she was captured by the obvious and attractive happiness in both of them, by the pride in the lift of their heads as they gazed, he, too, now in the sightless, half-smiling way she had seen first in the woman, straight ahead of them as if at something far beyond the park's iron fence. They were certainly unlike husband and wife, she thought, with a strange rise of excitement, yet neither did they behave quite as intensely as she thought lovers should behave, though she reminded herself she had probably never seen a pair of clandestine lovers, only read about them. And these were certainly clandestine lovers. She saw it all: a husband (with dark hair) who worked during the day and came home at six o'clock, all unsuspecting that his wife had spent the afternoon with another man. Mrs. Robertson felt a pang of compassion for the deceived husband. Yes, the blond woman was clearly rather cheap—her high-heeled pumps, her hair lightened with peroxide probably. Would she take the lover home with her? Mrs. Robertson hoped she would not have to witness that. And in the next moment, she admitted to herself she *would* like to see just that, see them go away together. She turned a page she hadn't read, conscious of the sound of her thin gold bracelet touching her watch. She looked over her reading glasses again. The man was talking, but so low she could hear not even a murmur. His head was back, resting on the back of the bench, and the woman watched his face, more alert now than Mrs. Robertson had yet seen her, though still with her soft unconscious-looking smile. The man spread his fingers and took firmer grip on her hand, and Mrs. Robertson felt a small wave of pleasure break over her. What did he talk to her about? she wondered. Or could she possibly be wrong about the whole thing? Was the woman not the child's mother, only a paid sitter, or a nursemaid? But both the woman and the child did not look well enough dressed for such a relationship to be likely. And as if to asseverate her opinion, the child suddenly came running across the path, she watched the woman gather him in her arms, take a handkerchief from her bag, and wipe his nose with a twist, and she caught a quality, in both of them, beyond a shadow of doubt now, that was like a statement that they were mother and child. The man had brought his other hand from his pocket with a handkerchief, too, and having put the handkerchief back, he held now, as if he had just discovered it, a small blue automobile on his palm. The woman said something, and the little boy threw his arms about the man's neck, kissed his cheek, and darted away, so quickly Mrs. Robertson could hardly believe she had seen it. Yet she had seen it, of course, and there had been in that, too, an unmistakable look of its having been done before. She stared at the two unabashedly as they leaned forward together, smilingly watching the children.

Philip! He was playing with the automobile, too. The little boy was sharing it with him. Mrs. Robertson stood up involuntarily, then sat down again. She did not like his playing with the toy, felt somehow that the automobile was not quite right, not quite clean, either, like the little boy. Again she looked at the two on the bench—she could look at them openly for all they appeared aware of her—and again they were leaning back comfortably, more comfortably than seemed possible on the hard bench, and their arms were interlocked, their hands clasped more closely under the iron bar between them. The man talked, and the woman now and again said something in response. It was unusual that he should be so fond of the child. Or was he only pretending? What were they talking about? How they must hate the bench arm between them! And she felt a taut, righteous satisfaction that the iron bar was between them. What would the park be like without the iron arms? Men sleeping along the benches. Couples . . .

"He's half you, isn't he?" Lance was saying.

"One day we'll have a child that's all us."

Then they said nothing for a while. A bird sang a few annunciatory notes in a nearby tree—there were only three or four trees in the whole park—then swooped past so that both saw it. Not far away, on the river, a boat sounded its steam toot, not deep enough to be a big liner, not high enough to be a tug: a middle-sized vessel whose toot still said proudly, however, that it could go everywhere on earth and furthermore had been there.

"We'll make a lot of trips," he remarked.

"I want to go to Scotland," the girl said, even more quietly, but her tone was as if she had bought a ticket from someone.

"Scotland must be terrific. We'll definitely go to Scotland . . . the Hebrides."

"Hebrides?"

"'As we in dreams behold the Hebrides.'"

"What are they? Mountains?"

"Mountains and islands. Mountains." He said the words so slowly, so roundly, it was as if he built the islands and the mountains right there.

"Don't say 'dreams,'" the girl chided. "Or is that another poem?"

"It's a poem. But poems are true."

"Sometimes, I guess."

He did not argue. They were silent a longer while.

"Then will you build me a house—after we've finished traveling?"

"I will build you not one house but three . . . four," he said distinctly. "One for every season of the year. A white house for spring, a red house for winter. For autumn, a brown house—"

"I don't like brown."

"For autumn, a *tan* house."

"Lance, are you watching the time?" she barely whispered, like an aside.

"Yes, I am watching the time. The clock in the steeple says five of four."

The clock in the steeple of the little church was only half a block down the avenue, but she had told him she would never look at it while he was with her in the park. The clock in the steeple was always six minutes slow. At 4:09, therefore, he would have to leave in order to report back at his job in a big bookstore in Nassau Street, far downtown. Tomorrow he would not be able to come, nor the next day. He delivered only on Tuesdays and Fridays, an unpopular duty he had asked for so he might manage, perhaps, half an hour or forty-five minutes with her. It was the only time he could see her. As long as she was married to Charles, she would never let him see her in the evening. He put his other hand over hers and smiled at her with sudden tenderness. Somehow, in her mind, his meeting her in the park partook of the accidental, he knew. The one time he had seen her in the evening was the evening they had met, over by the park in Gramercy Square, a park they could not enter because it was locked. In the darkness he had seen her standing before the tall spears of the fence, and with a sense sharpened by his own solitude and loneliness, he had known that whoever and whatever she was, there was something of himself in her, so he had said good evening. They had both been to the same movie in Twenty-third Street that evening, each alone. The one evening they had seen each other, yet in his mind he liked to call himself her lover. What did she call him? She would not call him that, he thought. He lifted his head higher, lolled it back on the edge of the bench back, and one would have thought he had not a care in the world, that he would stay relaxed there the rest of the afternoon.

"This park is the still point of the turning world," he said, and his low voice was steadied with reverence.

"I feel that, too. Yes. And the street where I live. And these days."

"These days." But suddenly he felt guilty for his idleness, even for these half hours with her, because there was so much he had to do. Not guilty so much because he spent the time with her, but that he allowed himself and her to dream so foolishly. Or were the dreams foolish? One could never really tell. He felt guilty because the little park was so good for dreaming, too good, he knew, too quiet and too like an imaginary heaven. And he began to examine caressingly, as he did every afternoon he sat here, the delicate convexity of the little lawns, the sharp delineation of the scalloped fences against their bright green fields. His eyes moved casually over Dickie and the other little boy playing with the new automobile. Dickie was always a part of the park, the cherub of its heaven. Today he looked happier than usual because he had the other little boy to play with. He looked at the woman over on the bench, who was again glancing at them, and he smiled a little at her, but she looked down at once at her knitting.

The knitting had got into a small snarl, and Mrs. Robertson was plucking at it anxiously. There was a sensation of clash and disorder within her, as of a distant battle, for which she blamed the knitting. She was dimly aware of an impulse to take Philip and leave the park, correct the knitting at home, as well as a desire to remain because Philip was having such a good time and because the park—perhaps, she admitted, the sight of the two on the other bench—gave her a pleasure akin to an enchantment. The two forces were not at all clear in her mind, but the sense of struggle was as she plucked at the knitting, and while the crystals of herself suffered disorganization, she sat perfectly still except for her fingers, which worked skillfully to rescue the hitherto flawless mitten for Philip. And when the snarl was smoothed out and her course resumed, when the mysterious armies fell silent within her, the outcome of the struggle was veiled, too, leaving her only a subtle sense of irritation, of impatience and somehow of disappointment. *I shall not come here again,* she thought suddenly, and in that decision alone, which seemed to come out of nowhere, she felt substantiality. She would, however, stay just a few minutes more. There was nothing she need run from.

The sunlight stirred all at once like a living thing, climbed over the scalloped fence and fell lightly, soundlessly, half across the walk. Now it lay over the feet of Lance and the girl beside him. A long point of it strove diagonally across the path toward the woman on the bench. He saw her look at it even as he did, but she did not glance up again.

"The still point of the world," the girl whispered.

"The turning world." And again he felt the guilt: the world turned all around them, here on this green island of asylum, machines turned, clocks turned, but he and she were motionless and there was so much to be done and to be fought for.

"Yes, the turning world is nicer. I can feel it—but I can never say it like you. I felt it this afternoon, leaving the house—" But she would not be able to describe it, she knew. "And now."

"Only I didn't say it. That's Eliot. There's another part of it, '. . . at the still point, there the dance is.'" He stopped, knowing suddenly that beside one's beloved is no fixity, though the stillness surpass all other stillnesses and all other kinds of peace, knowing suddenly as if it had been an eternal truth he had just stumbled over and discovered first, that beside one's beloved the beauty of a daydream is never thin, never motionless and flat like a picture as it is in solitude, because beside her there is movement forward and electrical energy in the air and a roundness, a wholeness to things real or imagined. He turned toward her, and he saw her glance prudently at the woman on the bench. But he had not intended to kiss her now.

Bells tinkled. Distant sheep bells on rolling green hills half hidden in mist, he thought: the Hebrides.

"There's the ice-cream man," she said.

The ice-cream wagon came into the path at the downtown end of the park, pushed by a slender young man in white trousers, shirt, and cap.

"Mother," Dickie said, climbing over the path fence, "can I have some ice cream?"

Lance reached into his pocket.

Mrs. Robertson watched the man give the coin to the little boy, who skipped with it to the ice-cream man. Philip stood where he was, watching, knowing he would not be allowed ice cream so soon before his suppertime.

"Can he have one, too?" The man had stood up and was smiling at her, reaching into his pocket again.

"Oh, thank you very much," Mrs. Robertson replied. "It's a bit too near his suppertime."

Her heart was beating faster, she noticed. It had excited her, in a way neither pleasant nor unpleasant, the exchange of conversation with him. His manner, even his face, she decided, were nicer than she had thought, than his unpressed suit had led her to believe. The dark-haired little boy clambered back over the fence in the act of taking his first bite of the ice-cream stick, then ran straight to Philip. She stood up, impelled to stop Philip before he could put the ice cream into his mouth.

"Philip, I don't think—"

She was too late. Philip had the whole top of the ice cream in his mouth, and the other little boy was holding it for him. She did not mean to snatch Philip away, but her tension made it a snatch, and the ice cream suddenly held by no one fell to the grass between the two children.

"Oh!" said Mrs. Robertson, with genuine regret. "I'm terribly sorry!"

After the first stunned moment, the dark-haired little boy stooped to pick it up. But the ice cream fell off the stick, hopelessly broken now, too far gone even for a three-year-old to rescue. Its chocolate crust cracked again even as he watched, as if it were determined to lose itself in the thick smooth grass. He stood up and looked at her, and wiped his hands shyly behind him.

"Where'd the ice-cream man go?" Mrs. Robertson looked around for him, but he was out of sight. She heard his bell up the avenue.

"Lose your ice cream, Dickie?" called the man sympathetically.

"Oh, that's okay," said the little boy, half to him, half to her. He was not angry, but he did not smile, either.

"It's my fault, I'm afraid," Mrs. Robertson said. Then, feeling suddenly ridiculous, she took Philip's arm in one hand and his tricycle handlebar in the other and urged them toward the scalloped fence.

"You have to go now, Philip?" asked the dark-haired little boy.

"Yes," sighed Philip, with resignation. But at the fence he looked back sadly past the arm his mother lifted straight up, as if he had just realized he was actually going.

"See you tomorrow, Philip," said the other little boy, a precocity of phrase that surprised Mrs. Robertson.

He would not see him tomorrow. She did not want Philip to play with him again. She could not say why precisely, but she did not want it. She had been foolish not to take him away as soon as she realized what sort of person his mother was. There was something, somehow she knew it, impure about the little boy no matter how well he might be scrubbed, because his mother was impure. Yet she found herself going past the woman and the man on the bench, though it was the long way out of the park for her, found herself glancing once more at them, quite involuntarily and much to her own annoyance, a furtive sidewise glance that did not even feel like her own. But the man and the woman seemed lost in themselves again, holding hands. She was relieved they hadn't seen her.

When she reached the end of the path, she knew she had left the man and the woman, the little boy and the park forever.

The blond girl had seen the glance, seen in it for all its fleetness the ancient and imperishable look that one woman gives another she knows is well loved, a look made up of desire, admiration, wistfulness, of envy and vicarious pleasure, unveiled for an instant and then veiled again. Seeing it, she had pressed Lance's hand more tightly in quick reflexive pride. Had Lance seen it, too? But probably only a woman would have seen. She would have liked to tell him, but the words for it would be far more difficult to find even than the words about her inner peace as she came down the brownstone steps every afternoon, so instead she said:

"I don't think she likes me. She was here yesterday, too."

Lance only smiled and tucked her arm closer. He had seven minutes more. He drew her arm close until he could feel it all along his side, not feeling any longer the iron arm cutting tense muscles through his jacket sleeve. "Now there's no one," he said.

There was no one. The long point of the wedge of sunlight had reached the bench the woman had been sitting on, had captured one of the curved metal legs. The bird dipped again, crossing their vision, asserting its absolute freedom and security within the tiny park. Now there was no human being along the avenue, not even a blind and impersonal truck hurrying past beyond the boundary of the low iron fence. Yes, there was a nun coming down the steps of the church half a block away, black-clad and in black bonnet, an erect and archaic figure, black skirts rippling with her pace like the carved robes of a ship's figurehead. They turned to each other and their lips met above their clasped hands and entwined arms, above the iron arm, and the kiss became the center of the stillness. The kiss became the narrowed center of the still point of the turning world, so that even the park was turning in comparison to the still peace at their lips.

Then, because there were only three minutes until he had to go, he began to talk casually, but seriously and quickly, of their plans, his work, their money, as if to fortify himself in these last moments before they parted for two days and nights. In three more months they would have enough money to open the next campaign in their struggle, her divorce. It was impossible to talk to her husband now about a divorce so long as she had to live with him. Only three more months. Twenty-four more meetings like this afternoon, he reckoned for the first time, and knew he could not prevent himself from counting them off from now on. Twenty-four . . .

Mrs. Robertson did not go the next day to the little park down the avenue. She took Philip to a court in the center of Castle Terrace where there was a big sandbox and many small children for him to play with.

Philip stood where his mother had turned him loose and looked up at the building that rose like a great tan hollowed-out mountain around him, and asked, “Aren’t we going to the park later?”

“Aren’t we going to the park later, Mama?” he asked again, when his mother had settled herself in a comfortable metal chair. “I want to see Dickie.”

“No, darling, we’re not going to the park today.” She tried to make her voice gentle and casual, too, and it was difficult. And perhaps she had failed, she thought as she watched Philip pedal off very slowly on his tricycle, with an air of seeing nothing around him.

There were many other young mothers in the play court, and Mrs. Robertson was soon occupied in conversation. She felt right, here in the court of her own apartment building. Why had she tried to be different and find a nicer place? The park was pretty and Philip would miss it, of course, for a few days, but she did not regret her decision not to go back. Here there was sun, too, things for Philip to play on, and an abundance of children for him to make friends with, children she could be sure were clean and being well brought up. And other women, like herself, with whom she could exchange ideas.

“I want Dickie,” said Philip, coming up slowly on his tricycle. He had cruised the playground and found it unsatisfactory.

“Darling, there’s some little boys over by the sandbox. Don’t you want to go play with them?” She turned back to the women she had been talking with, lest she seem as concerned as she felt to Philip.

“I want Dickie!” said Philip two minutes later. Now he had got off his tricycle and stood away from it, as if he would never mount it again unless it was to go see his friend. He had tears in his eyes. He looked at his mother with resentment, and with determined, uncomprehending accusation.

This was the moment to be firm, Mrs. Robertson knew, to ignore it or to say something that would satisfy or silence forever. She hesitated, at a loss.

"Who's Dickie?" asked one of the women.

"He's a little boy he met down the street," Mrs. Robertson answered.

As if piqued at their mention of his friend, Philip about-faced and wandered off with his head up, and thus his mother was spared making the answer she could not find.

Philip asked for Dickie the next afternoon, and the next and the next. But the fifth afternoon he did not ask.

# WHERE THE DOOR IS ALWAYS OPEN AND THE WELCOME MAT IS OUT

Riding home on the Third Avenue bus, sitting anxiously on the very edge of the seat she had captured, Mildred made rapid calculations for the hundredth time that day.

Her sister Edith was arriving from Cleveland at 6:10 at Penn Station. It was already 5:22, later than she had anticipated, because some letters Mr. Sweeney wanted sent out at the last minute had delayed her at the office. She would have only about twenty-two minutes at home to straighten anything that might have gotten unstraightened since last night's cleaning, lay the table and organize their delicatessen supper, and fix her face a bit before she left for Penn Station. It was lucky she'd done the marketing in her lunch hour. All the last half of the afternoon, though, she had watched the dark spot on the grocery bag grow bigger—the dill pickles leaking—and she'd been too busy at the office to drag all the things out and rearrange them. Now, with her firm, square hand over the wet place, she felt better.

The bus swayed to a stop, and she twisted and ducked her head to see a street marker. Only Thirty-sixth Street.

Dill pickles, pumpernickel bread, rollmops (maybe it was the rollmops leaking, not the pickles), liverwurst, salami, celery and garlic for the potato salad, coffee ring for dessert, and oranges for breakfast tomorrow. She'd found some gladiolas in her lunch hour, too, and their blossoms still looked as fresh as when she'd bought them. It seemed like everything, but she knew better than to think there wouldn't be something at the last minute she'd forgotten.

Edith's telegram last evening had taken her completely by surprise, but Mildred had just pitched in and cleaned everything, spent all last evening and early this morning at it, washing windows, cleaning out closets, as well as the usual dusting and sweeping and scouring. Her sister Edith was such a neat housekeeper herself, Mildred knew she would have to have things in apple pie order, if her sister was to take a good report back to their Cleveland relations. Well, at least none of the folks in Cleveland could say she'd lost her hospitality because she'd become a New Yorker. "The welcome mat is always out," Mildred had written many a time to friends and members of the family who showed any signs of coming to New York. Her guests were treated to a home-cooked meal—though she did depend on the delicatessen quite a bit, she supposed—and to every comfort she could offer for as long as they cared to stay. Edith probably wouldn't stay more than two or three days, though. She was just passing through on her way to Ithaca to visit her son Arthur and his wife.

She got off at Twenty-sixth Street. Five twenty-seven, said a clock in a hardware store window. She certainly would have to rush. Well, wasn't she always rushing? A lot Edith, with nothing but a household to manage, knew of a life as busy as hers!

Mildred's apartment house was a six-story red brick building on Third Avenue over a delicatessen. The delicatessen's crowded window prompted her to go over everything again. The coleslaw! And milk, of course. How could she have forgotten?

There were two women ahead of her, their shopping bags full of empty bottles, and they chatted with Mr. Weintraub and had their items charged in the notebook he kept hanging by the cash register. Mildred shifted and trembled inwardly with impatience and frustration, regretted that neighborliness had such a price these days, but her tense smile was a pleasant one.

"Coleslaw and milk," repeated Mr. Weintraub. "Anything else?"

"No, that's all, thank you," Mildred said quickly, not wanting to delay the woman who had come in after her.

Some children playing tag on the sidewalk deliberately dragged an ash can into her path, but Mildred ignored them and fumbled for her keys. Necessity had taught her the trick of pushing the key with a thumb as she turned the knob with the same hand, a method she used even on those rare occasions when both arms were not full. She saw mail in her box, but she could get it later. No, it might be something from Edith.

It was a beauty parlor advertisement and a postcard about a new dry-cleaning process for rugs.

"Plumber's upstairs, Miss Stratton," said the superintendent, who was on his way down.

"Oh? What's happened?"

"Nothing much. Woman above had her bowl run over, and the plumber thinks the trouble might be in your place."

"But I haven't—" It was quicker to suffer accusation, however, so she plodded up the stairs.

The door of her apartment was ajar. She went into a narrow room whose two close-set windows looked out on the avenue. Crossing her room, she felt a lift of pride at the unaccustomed orderliness of everything. On the coffee table lay the single careless touch: a program of the performance of *Hansel and Gretel* she had attended last Christmas in Brooklyn. She'd found it in cleaning the bookcase, and had put it out for Edith to see.

But the sight of the bathroom made her gasp. There were black smudges on everything, even on the frame of the mirror over the basin. What *didn't* plumbers and superintendents manage to touch, and weren't their hands always black!

"All fixed, ma'am. Here's what the trouble was." The plumber held up something barely recognizable as a toothbrush, and smiled. "Remember it?"

"No, I don't," she said, letting her parcels slide onto a kitchen chair. It wasn't *her* toothbrush, she was sure of that, but the less talk about it, the sooner he would leave.

While she waited to get at the bathroom, she spread her best tablecloth on the gateleg table in the kitchen, pulled the window shade down so the people in the kitchen three feet away across the air chute couldn't see in, then dashed the morning coffee grounds into the garbage pail and stuck the dirty coffeepot into the sink. Keeping one foot on the pedal of the garbage pail, she pivoted in a half dozen directions, reached even the bag of groceries on the chair and began to unload it.

The closing of the door told her the plumber was gone, and crushing the last paper bag into the garbage—she generally saved them for old Sam the greengrocer, but there was no time now—she went into the bathroom and erased every black fingerprint with rag and scouring powder, and mopped up the floor as she backed her way out. In the minute she allowed for the floor to dry, she pushed off her medium-heeled oxfords at the closet door and stepped into identical newer oxfords. But their laces were tied from a hasty removal, too. She stooped down, and felt a dart over her bent knee. A run. She mustn't forget to change the stocking before she left for the station. Or had she another good stocking? Buying stockings was one of the errands she had intended to do today in her lunch hour.

Twenty-one minutes of six, she saw as she trotted into the bathroom. Eleven minutes before she ought to leave the house.

Even after the brisk scrubbing with a washrag, her squarish face looked as colorless as her short jacket of black and gray tweed. Her hair, of which the gray had recently gotten an edge over the brown, was naturally wavy, and now the more wiry gray hairs stood out from her head, making her look entirely gray, unfortunately, and giving her an air of harassed untidiness no matter what she did to correct it. But her eyes made up for the dullness of the rest of her face, she thought. Her round but rather small gray eyes still looked honest and kind, though sometimes there was a bewildered, almost frightened expression in them that shocked her. She saw it now. It was because she was hurrying so, she supposed. She must remember to look calm with Edith. Edith was so calm.

She daubed a spot of rouge on one cheek and was spreading it outward with timid strokes when the peal of the doorbell made her jump.

"Miss," said a frail voice in the semidarkness of the hall, "take a ten-cent chance on the St. Ant'ny School lottery Saturday May twenny-second?"

"No. No, child, I haven't time," Mildred said, closing the door. She hated to be harsh with the little tykes, but at seventeen minutes of six . . .

As a matter of fact, the alarm clock shouldn't be out on the coffee table, she thought, it looked too much as if she slept on the living room couch, which of course she did. She put the clock in a bureau drawer.

For a moment, she stood in the center of the room with her mind a complete blank. What should she do next? Why was her heart beating so fast? One would think she'd been running, or at least that she was terribly excited about something, and she wasn't really.

Maybe a bit of whiskey would help. Her father had always said a little nip was good when a person was under a strain, and she was under a slight strain, she supposed. After all, she hadn't seen Edith in nearly two years, not since she'd been to Cleveland on her vacation two summers ago.

Mr. Sweeney had given her the whiskey last Christmas, and she hadn't touched it since she made the eggnog Christmas Day for old Mrs. Chevlov upstairs. The bottle was still almost full. Cautiously, she poured an inch into a small glass that had once contained cheese, then added another half inch, and drank it off at a gulp to save time. The drink landed with a warm explosion inside her.

"Dear old Edith!" she said aloud, and smiled with anticipation.

The doorbell rang.

Those children again, she thought, they always tried twice. Absently, she plucked a piece of thread from the carpet, and rolled it between her thumb and forefinger, wondering if she should answer the door or not. Then the bell came again, with a rap besides, and she plunged toward it. It might be the plumber about something else.

"Miss, take a ten-cent chance on the St. Ant'ny—"

"No," Mildred said with a shudder. "No, thank you, children." But she found a coin in the pocket of her jacket and thrust it at them.

Then she dashed into the kitchen and set out plates, cups and saucers, and paper napkins in buffet style. It looked nice to have everything out, and would save considerable time later. She put the big mixing bowl for the potato salad on the left, and lined up beside it the smaller mixing bowl for the dressing, the salad oil, the vinegar, mustard, paprika, salt and pepper, the jar of stuffed olives—a little moldy, best wash them off—in a militarily straight row. The sugar bowl was low, she noticed, and lumpy, too. And only three minutes left! She hacked at the lumps in the bowl with a teaspoon, but not all of them would dislodge, so finally she gave it up and just added more sugar. Some of it spilled on the floor. She seized broom and dustpan and went after it. Her heart was pounding again. What on earth ailed her?

Thoughtfully, she took down the whiskey and poured another inch or two into the glass. Soothing sensations crept from her stomach in all directions, made their way even into her hands and feet. She swept up the sugar with renewed fortitude and patience, and whisked the remaining grains under the sink so they wouldn't crackle underfoot.

The kitchen curtains caught her eye for the first time in months, but she resolutely refused to worry about their streaks of black grit. A person was allowed *one* fault in a household, she thought.

As she pulled on her coat, it occurred to her she hadn't boiled the eggs for the salad, and she'd meant to do it the first thing when she came home. She put three eggs into a saucepan of water and turned the gas on high. At least she could start them in the few moments she'd be here, and turn them off as she went out the door.

Now. Had she keys? Money? Her hat. She snatched up her hat—a once-stiff pillbox of Persian lamb, much the same color as her hair—and pressed it on with the flat of her hand. Nice to have the kind of hats one didn't have to worry about being straight or crooked, she thought, but she allowed herself one glance in the hall mirror as she passed by, and it was enough to reveal one rouged cheek and one plain one. She hurried back into the bathroom, where the light was best.

It was six minutes to six when she flew downstairs.

She'd better take a taxi to the station after all. She regretted the extravagance, though she felt herself yielding to a gaiety and abandonment that had been plucking at her ever since she thought of taking a nip of whiskey. She didn't really care about eighty-five cents, a dollar with tip. A dollar was just a little more than one-hundredth of her weekly salary. Or a little more than one-thousandth? No, than one-hundredth, of course.

Crossing the lobby of Penn Station toward the information center, she felt the run in her stocking travel upward and was afraid to look. She'd forgotten to change it, but she wouldn't, really wouldn't have had time to look for a good stocking, even if she'd remembered. She could tell Edith she'd gotten the run hurrying to meet her. In fact, she thought brilliantly, Edith didn't have to know she'd been home at all, which would make her house and herself, after some apologies, look very nice indeed.

"Downstairs for incoming train information," the clerk told her.

Mildred trotted downstairs, and was referred to a blackboard, where she learned that the Cleveland Flyer would be twenty minutes late. Suddenly something collapsed in her, and she felt terribly tired. She started for a nearby bench, but she knew she was too restless to sit still. She wandered back upstairs. Her nervous system was not adjusted to waiting. She could wait in the office for Mr. Sweeney to finish a long telephone conversation and get back to whatever work they were doing together, but she could not wait on her own time—for an elevator, for a clerk in a department store, or on a line in the post office—without growing anxious and jumpy. Maybe another touch of whiskey would be a good idea, she thought, a leisurely one she could sip while she composed herself.

A big, softly lighted, pink and beige bar came into view almost immediately. And there were several women inside, she was relieved to see. Feeling strange and somehow very special, Mildred went in through the revolving door. Every table was in use, so she stood shyly behind two men at the bar, over whose shoulders she could see the barman now and then.

"Whiskey," she said, when the barman seemed to be looking at her.

"What kind?"

"Oh, it doesn't matter," she said cheerfully.

Everybody in the place seemed to be having such a good time, it was fun just to watch them. She never gave such places a thought, yet they were going full blast all over New York every evening, she supposed. It occurred to her she was probably a more sophisticated person than she realized.

She wondered if Edith still wore her hair in those stiff marcel waves. The last time she had seen Edith, she had looked like one of those dummies with wigs they have in beauty parlor windows. That wasn't a nice thing to think about one's sister, but Edith really had looked like them. For the first time now, Mildred realized that Edith was actually coming, that she would see her within minutes. She could hear Edith's slow voice as clearly as if she stood beside her, saying, "Well, that's fate, Millie," as she often did, and as she probably would say about her daughter Phyllis's marriage. Phyllis's husband was only nineteen and without a job, and, according to a letter Cousin John in Toledo had written her a few weeks ago, without ambition, either. "Well, that's fate," Edith would say by way of passing it off. "Parents can't boss their children anymore, once the children think they're grown." Mildred's heart went out to her sister.

The square-numeraled clock on the wall said only 6:17. Just about an hour ago, she had been on the bus going home. The crowded bus seemed suddenly dismal and hideous. It was as if another person had been riding on it an hour ago, not herself, not this person who sipped whiskey in a bar where dance music played, this person who awaited a train from Cleveland.

One of the men offered her a high red stool, but she was so short, she decided just to lean against it. Then all at once it was 6:28. She paid her check, clutched her handbag, and dashed off.

Now, really now, her sister was pulling into the station. She giggled excitedly. A bell went *whang-whang-whang!* A metal gate folded back. People rushed up the slope, people rushed down, among them herself. And there was Edith, walking toward her!

"Edith!"

"Millie!"

They fell upon each other. My own flesh and blood, Mildred thought, patting Edith's back and feeling a little weepy. There was confusion for a few minutes while Edith found her suitcase, Mildred asked questions about the family, and they looked for a cab. With a flash of pain, Mildred remembered the eggs on the stove at home. They would be burning now, aflame probably, the gas was so high. How did burning eggs smell? In the taxi, Mildred braced Edith's suitcase against the jump seat with her foot and tried to listen to everything Edith was telling her, but she couldn't keep track of anything for thinking of the eggs.

"How is Arthur?" Mildred asked, one eye out the window to see if the driver was going right.

"Just as well as can be. He has a new baby."

Mildred hoped every child in the neighborhood wasn't cluttering the front steps. Sometimes they played cards right in the doorway. "Oh, a new baby! Oh, has he?"

"Yes, another little girl," said Edith. "Just last week. I was saving it to tell you."

"So now you're twice a grandmother! I'll have to send Arthur and Helen something right away."

Edith protested she shouldn't.

Mildred paid the driver, then struggled out with the suitcase, waving Edith's assistance aside, and not waiting for the driver to help, because drivers usually didn't. She realized too late that she might have added another dime to the tip, and hoped Edith hadn't noticed. Pinching each other's fingers under the suitcase handle, the sisters climbed the three flights. Mildred felt a rough corner of the suitcase tearing at her good stocking.

"Are you hungry?" she asked cheerily as she felt for her keys, trying not to sound out of breath. She sniffed for burning eggs.

"I had a snack on the train about five o'clock," Edith replied, "so I'm bearing up, as they say."

"Well, here it is, such as it is!" Mildred smiled fearfully as she swung the door open for Edith, braced for any kind of odor.

"It's just lovely," Edith said, even before the light was turned on.

Mildred had flown past her into the kitchen. The eggs were turned off, resting quietly in their water. She stared at them incredulously for a second or two. "It's just the one room and a bit of a kitchen this time," Mildred remarked as she returned to her sister, for Edith, standing in the middle of the room, seemed to be expecting her to show her the rest. "But it's much more convenient to the office than the Bronx apartment was. I know you'll want to wash up, Edie, so just have your coat off and I'll show you where everything is."

But Edith did not want to wash up.

"As Father used to say, 'I propose we have a wee nip in honor of the occasion!'" Mildred said a bit wildly, her voice rising over the roar of a passing truck on Third Avenue. She thought Edith looked at her in a funny way, so she added, "Not that I've become a drinking woman, by any means! I did have one while I was waiting for you in the station, though. Could you tell?"

"No. You mean you went in a bar by yourself and had a drink?"

"Why, yes," Mildred replied, wishing now that she hadn't mentioned it. "Women often go into bars in New York, you know. It's not like Cleveland." Mildred turned a little unsteadily and went into the kitchen. She did want another bit of a drink, just to continue feeling as calm as she did now, for it certainly was helping to calm her. She took a quick nip, then fixed a tray with the bottle and glasses and ice. "Well, down the hatch!" Mildred said as she set the tray down on the coffee table.

Edith had refused the maroon-covered easy chair Mildred had offered her, and now she sat tensely on the couch and sipped her whiskey as if it were poison. She gazed off now and then at the windows—the curtains,

Mildred admitted, were not so clean as Cleveland curtains, but at least she had brushed them down last night—and at the brown bureau that was her least attractive piece of furniture. Why didn't Edith look over at the kitchen table where everything was lined up as neatly as a color photograph in a magazine?

"The gladiolas are beautiful, Millie," Edith said, looking at the gladiolas Mildred had set in a blue vase atop the bureau. "I grow gladiolas in the backyard."

Mildred lighted up appreciatively at Edith's compliment. "How long am I to have the pleasure of your company, sister?"

"Oh, just till—" Edith broke off and looked at the windows with an expression of annoyance.

A truck or perhaps a cement mixer was rattling and clanking up the avenue. Suddenly Mildred, whose ears had adjusted long ago to the street noises, realized how it must sound to Edith, and writhed with shame. She had quite forgotten the worst feature of her apartment—the noise. The garbage trucks that started grinding around three A. M. were going to be worse.

"It's a nuisance," Mildred said carelessly, "but one gets used to it. What with the housing—" Something else was passing, backfiring like pistol shots, and Mildred realized she couldn't hear her own voice. She waited, then resumed. "What with the housing being—"

But Edith silenced her with a hopeless shake of her head.

A war of horns was going on now, probably a little traffic jam at the corner. That was the way it went, Mildred tried to convey to Edith with a smile and a shrug, all at once or nothing at all. For a few moments their ears, even Mildred's ears, were filled with the cacophony of car horns, of snarling human voices.

"Really, Millie, I don't see how you stand this noise day after day," Edith said.

Mildred shrugged involuntarily, started to say something, and said nothing after all. She felt inexplicably foolish all at once.

"What were you going to say before?" Edith prompted.

"Oh. Well, what with the housing being what it is today, New Yorkers can't be too picky where they live. I have my budget, and I didn't have any choice but this place and something on Tenth Avenue when I wanted to move from the Bronx. Took me three months to find this." She said it with a little pride that was instantly quelled by her sister's troubled regard of the windows. Well, there weren't any trucks passing now, Mildred thought a bit resentfully, and the traffic jam had evidently cleared up. What was she looking at? Self-consciously, Mildred got up and lowered the window, though she knew it would not help much to lessen the noise. She looked at her geranium. The geranium was nothing but a crooked dry stalk in its pot now, at the extreme left of the window-sill where the sun lingered longest. It must have been three weeks since she'd watered it, and now she felt overcome with remorse. Why was she always rushing so, she forgot all about doing the nice things, all the little things that gave her real pleasure? A wave of self-pity brought tears to her eyes. A lot her sister knew about all she had to contend with, the million and one things she had to think of all by herself, not only at home but at the office, too. You could tell just by looking at Edith she never had to worry or rush about anything, even to take a hard-boiled egg off the stove.

With a smile, Mildred turned to Edith, and under cover of a "Hungry yet?" ducked into the kitchen to see about the hard-boiled eggs. She balanced the three hot eggs on top of the block of ice in the icebox, so they would cool as fast as possible.

"Remember the time we took the raw eggs by mistake on the picnic, Edie?" Mildred said, laughing as she came back into the living room. It was an old family joke, and one or the other of them mentioned it almost every time they cooked hard-boiled eggs.

"Will I ever forget!" Edith shrieked, bringing her hands down gently on her knees. "I still say Billy Reed switched them on us. He's the same rascal today he always was."

"Those were happy old days, weren't they?" Mildred said vaguely, wondering if she shouldn't perhaps cook the eggs even longer. She made a start for the kitchen and changed her mind.

"Millie, do you think it's really worth it to live in New York?" Edith asked suddenly.

"Worth it? How do you mean worth it?—I suppose I earn fairly good money." She didn't mean to sound superior to her sister, but she was proud of her independence. "I'm able to save a little, too."

"I mean, it's such a hard life you lead and all, being away from the family. New York's so unfriendly, and no trees to look at or anything. I think you're more nervous than you were two years ago."

Mildred stared at her. Maybe New York had made her more nervous, quicker about things. But wasn't she as happy and healthy as Edith? "They're starting trees right here on Third Avenue. They're pretty small yet, but tomorrow you can see them.—I don't think it's such an unfriendly town," she went on defensively. "Why, just this afternoon, I heard the delicatessen man talking with a woman about— And even the plumber—" She broke off, knowing she wouldn't be able to express what she meant.

"Well, I don't know," Edith said, twiddling her hands limply in her lap. "My last trip here, I asked a policeman where the Radio City Music Hall was, and you'd have thought I was asking him to map me a way to the North Pole or something, he seemed so put out about it. Nobody's got time for anybody else—have they?" Her voice trailed off, and she looked at Mildred for an answer.

Mildred moistened her lips. Something in her struggled slowly and painfully to the surface. "I—I've always found our policemen very courteous. Maybe yours was a traffic officer or something. They're pretty busy, of course. But New York policemen are famous for their courtesy, especially to out-of-towners. Why, they even call them New York's Finest!" A tingle of civic pride swept over her. She remembered the morning she had stood in the rain at Forty-second Street and Fifth Avenue and watched the companies of policemen—*New York's Finest*—march down the avenue. And the mounted policemen! How handsome they had looked, row upon row with their horses' hoofs clattering! She had stood there not caring that she was all by herself then, or that the rain was soaking her, she felt so proud of her big city. A man with a little boy perched on his shoulder had turned around in the crowd and smiled at her, she remembered. "New York's *very* friendly," Mildred protested earnestly.

"Well, maybe, but that's not the way it seems to me." Edith slipped off a shoe and rubbed her instep against the heel of her other foot. "And sister," she continued in a more subdued tone, "I hope you're not indulging more than you should."

Mildred's eyes grew wide. "Do you mean drinking? Goodness, no! Why, at least I don't think so. I just took these in your honor, Edie. Gracious, you don't think I do this every night, do you?"

"Oh, I didn't mean I thought *that*!" Edith said, forcing a smile.

Mildred chewed her underlip and wondered whether she should think of some other excuse for herself, or let the matter drop.

"You know, Millie, I'd meant to speak to you about maybe coming back to Cleveland to live. Everybody's talking about the interesting new jobs opening up there, and you're not—well, so deep-fixed in this job that you couldn't leave, are you?"

"Of course, I could leave if I wanted to. But Mr. Sweeney depends a great deal on me. At least he says he does." She swallowed, and tried to collect all that clamored inside her for utterance. "It's not a very big job, I suppose, but it's a good one. And we've all been working together for seven years, you know," she asserted, but she knew this by itself couldn't express to Edith how the four of them—she had written Edith many a time about Louise who handled the books and the files, and Carl their salesman, and Mr. Sweeney, of course—were much more of a family than many families were. "Oh, New York's my home now, Edie."

"You've always got a home with us, Millie."

Mildred was about to say that was very sweet of her, but a truck's brakes were mounting to a piercing crescendo outside. She dropped her eyes from Edith's disappointed face.

"I've got some things I ought to put on hangers overnight," Edith said finally. "And do you mind if I wash my white gloves? They'll just about dry by morning. I'll have to leave early."

"What time?" Mildred asked, in order to be cooperative, but, aware that her worried expression might make her seem eager for Edith's departure, she smiled, which was almost worse.

"The train's at eight forty-eight," Edith replied, going to her suitcase.

"That's too bad. I'm sorry you're not staying longer, Edith." She really did feel sorry. They'd hardly have time to talk at all. And Edith probably wouldn't notice half the things she had done around the house, the neat closets, the half of the top drawer she had cleared for her in the bureau, the container of soft drinks Edith liked that she had thought of the first thing last evening.

Mildred wiped the back of her hand across her eyes, and went into the kitchen. She got the stew pan of boiled potatoes from the icebox and dumped them into the salad bowl. She separated the celery under running water, bunched it, and sliced it onto the potatoes. The old habit of rushing, of saving split seconds, caught her up in its machinery as if she no longer possessed a volition of her own, and she surrendered to it with a kind of tortured enjoyment. She hardly breathed except to gasp at intervals, and she moved faster and faster. The jar of olives flew into the bowl at one burst, followed by a shower of onion chips and a cloud of paprika that made her cough. Finally, she seized knife and fork and began to slice everything in the bowl every which way. Her muscles grew so taut, it hurt her even to move to the icebox to get the eggs. The eggs had descended three inches or more into the ice, and she could not extract them with her longest fingers. She peered at their murkily enlarged forms through the ice cake, then burst out laughing.

"Edie!" she cried. "Edie, come here and look!"

But her only reply was the flushing of the toilet. Mildre bent over in silent, paroxysmic hilarity. If her sister only knew about the toilet! The toothbrush the plumber had dragged out that hadn't even *looked* like a toothbrush!

Mildred straightened and grimly wrestled the ice cake from the box. She shook the eggs into the sink, holding the ice with hands and forearms. The eggs had bright, gooey orange centers, but they were fairly cold. She hacked them into the salad, listening the while for Edith's coming out of the bathroom. She was racing to have the supper ready when Edith came out, but what did it matter really whether she was ready or not? Why was she in such a hurry? She giggled at herself, then, with her mouth still smiling, set her teeth and stirred the dressing so fast it rose high up the sides of the mixing bowl.

"Can I help you, Millie?"

"Not a thing to do, thank you, Edie." Mildred dragged the coleslaw out of the icebox so hastily, she dropped it face down on the floor, but Edith had just turned away and didn't see.

Within moments, she was ready, the table laid, the coffee perking, the pumpernickel bread—but there wasn't any butter. She'd forgotten butter for herself yesterday, and forgotten it again today.

"There isn't any butter," Mildred said in an agony of apology as Edith took her place at the table. She thought of running down for some, but felt it would be rude to make Edith wait. "It's the same old-fashioned potato salad Mama used to make at home, though."

"It looks delicious. Don't you ever have hot meals here at home?"

"Why, most of the time. I try to eat a very balanced diet." She knew what her sister was thinking now, that she lived off delicatessen sandwiches, probably. She passed Edith the coleslaw. "Here's something very healthful, if you like." Her throat closed up. She felt ready to cry again. "I'm sorry, Edie. I suppose you'd have preferred a hot meal."

"No, this tastes very nice. Now, don't you worry," Edith said, poking at the potato salad.

At the end of the supper, Mildred realized she had not put out the dill pickles. Or the rollmops.

"Would you like to step out tonight? Take a look at the big city?" Mildred came in from the kitchen, where she had just finished cleaning up.

Edith was lying on the couch. "Well, maybe. I don't think I can nap after all, with all the traffic going. I suppose it lets up at night, though."

"There's a nice movie a few blocks uptown within walking distance," Mildred said, feeling a sink of defeat. How would she ever break it to Edith that there was some kind of noise on Third Avenue all night long?

They went to a shabby little movie house on Thirty-fourth Street, whose gay lights Edith had seen and fixed upon.

"Is this your neighborhood theater?" Edith asked.

"Oh, no. There's any number of better theaters around," Mildred answered rather shortly. Edith had chosen the place. She almost wished Edith had wanted to go up to Broadway. She'd have spent more money, but at least the theater would have been nicer, and Edith couldn't have complained. Mildred was so tired, she dozed during some of the picture.

That night, Mildred was aware that Edith got out of bed several times, to get glasses of water or to stand by the window. Mildred suggested that Edith get some cotton from the medicine cabinet to put in her ears. But Mildred slept so hard herself, even on the too-short sofa, most of her impressions might have come from a great distance.

"Are they mixing cement at this hour?" Edith asked.

"No, that's our garbage disposal, I'm afraid," Mildred said with an automatic little smile, though it was too dark for Edith to see her. She had dreaded this: the clatter of ash cans, the uninterrupted moaning of machinery chewing up cans, bottles, cartons, and anything else that was dumped into the truck's open rear. Mildred bared her set teeth and tried to estimate just how awful it sounded to her sister: the clank of bottles now, the metallic bump of an emptied ash can carelessly dropped on the sidewalk, and under it all the relentless *rrrr-rrrr-rrr-rrr*. Quite bad, she decided, and quite ugly, if one wasn't used to it. "They have their job to do," Mildred added. "I don't know what a big city like this would do without them."

"Um-m. Looks to me like they could do it in the daytime when nobody's trying to sleep," said Edith.

"What?"

Edith repeated it more loudly. "I don't see how you stand it, even with the cotton in your ears."

"I don't use cotton anymore," Mildred murmured.

Mildred did not feel too wide awake the next morning, and Edith said she hadn't slept all night and was dead tired, so neither said very much. At the core of Mildred's silence was both her ignominy at having failed as a hostess and a desire not to waste a second, for despite having gotten up early, they were a bit pressed to get off when they should. At eight o'clock sharp, the pneumatic drill burst out like a fanfare of machine guns: a big apartment house was going up directly across the street. Edith just glanced at Mildred and shook her head, but around 8:15, there was an explosion across the street that made Edith jump and drop something she had in her hands.

Mildred smiled. "They have to blast some. New York has rock foundations, you know. You'd be surprised how fast they build things, though."

Edith's suitcase was not closed for the last time until 8:27, and they arrived at the station with no time to spare.

"I hope you can manage a longer visit on your return trip, Edith," Mildred said.

"Well, Arthur did say something about going back to Cleveland with me for a while, but we'll let you know. I can't thank you enough for the lovely time, Millie."

A pressed hand, a brushed cheek, and that was all. Mildred watched the train doors close down the platform, but she had no time to watch the train pull out. What time was it? Eight forty-nine on the dot, her wristwatch said. If she hurried, she might be at the office by nine as usual. Of course, Mr. Sweeney wouldn't mind her being late on such a special morning, but for that very reason, she thought it would be nice to be prompt.

She darted to the corner of Seventh Avenue and Thirty-fourth Street and caught the crosstown bus. She could catch the Third Avenue bus uptown and be at the office on Second Avenue in no time. At the Third Avenue bus stop, an anxious frown came on her face as she estimated the speed and distance of an oncoming truck, then ran. She mustn't forget to buy stockings today during her lunch hour, she thought. And tonight, she ought to drop a note to Edith in Ithaca, telling her how she had enjoyed her stay, and inviting her again when she could make it. And a note to Arthur, of course, about the new baby. Maybe Edith and Arthur both could stay with her awhile, if they went back to Cleveland together. She'd be able to make them comfortable somehow.

# QUIET NIGHT

Hattie pulled the little chain of the reading lamp, drew the covers over her shoulders, and lay tense, listening till Alice's sniffs and coughs should subside.

"Alice," she whispered.

No response. Yes, she was sleeping already, though she insisted she never closed an eye before the clock struck eleven.

Hattie eased herself to the edge of the bed, slowly put out a white stockinged foot. She twisted around to look at Alice, of whom nothing was visible except a thin nose projecting between the ruffle of her night-cap and the sheet pulled over her mouth. She was quite still.

Hattie rose gently from the bed, her breath coming short with excitement. In the semidarkness she could see the two sets of false teeth sitting in their glasses of water on the bed table. She giggled nervously.

Like a white ghost she made her way across the room, past the Victorian upholstered settee. She stopped at the sewing table, lifted the folding top, and groped among the spools and pattern papers till she found the cold metal of the scissors. Then holding them tightly, she crossed the room again. She had left the door of the closet slightly ajar earlier in the evening, and it swung open noiselessly. Hattie reached a trembling hand into the blackness, felt the two stiff woolen coats, a few dresses. Finally she touched a fuzzy thing hanging next to the wall. She was giggling as she lifted the hanger down, and the scissors slipped out of her hand. There was a loud clatter, followed by some half-suppressed laughter. Hattie peeked round the door at Alice, motionless on the bed. Alice was rather hard of hearing.

With her white toes turned up stiffly, Hattie clumped to the easy chair by the window where a bar of moonlight slanted, and sat down with the scissors and the Angora sweater in her lap. In the moonlight her face gleamed, toothless and demoniacal. She examined the sweater in the manner of a person who plays with a piece of steak with a fork before deciding where to put his knife.

It was really a beautiful sweater. Alice had received it the week before from her niece. It was a birthday present, for Alice would never have indulged in such a luxury herself. She was happy as a child with it, and had worn it every day with her dresses.

The scissors cut purringly up the soft wool sleeves, between the wristband and the shoulder. She considered. There should be one more cut. The back, of course. But only about a foot long so it should not be immediately visible.

A few seconds later, she had put the scissors back into the table, hung the sweater in the closet, and was lying between the two feather mattresses. She heaved a tremendous sigh. She thought of the gaping sleeves, of Alice's face the next morning. The sweater was utterly beyond repair and she was immensely pleased with herself.

• • •

They were awakened at eight-thirty by the hotel maid. It was a ritual that never failed: three bony raps on the door and a bawling voice, with a hint of insolence: "Eight-thirty. You can get breakfast now." Then Hattie, who always woke first, would poke Alice's shoulder.

Mechanically they sat up on their respective sides of the bed and pulled their nightgowns over their heads, revealing clean white undergarments. They said nothing. Five years of coexistence had dwindled their conversation to rock-bottom efficiency.

This morning, however, Hattie was thinking of the sweater. She felt self-conscious, but she could think of nothing to say or do to relieve the tension. Hattie spent some fifteen minutes doing her hair. She had a braid nearly two feet long when she fixed it at night, and twice a day she would take it down for its hundred strokes. Her hair was her only vanity. Already dressed, she stood shifting uneasily, pretending to be fastening her snaps.

But Alice seemed to take an age at the wash basin, gargling with her solution of salt and tepid water. She held stubbornly to salt and water in the morning, in spite of Hattie's tempting bottle of red mouthwash sitting on the shelf.

"What are you giggling at now?" Alice turned from the basin, her face wet and smiling a little. Hattie could say nothing, looked at the teeth in the glass and snickered again.

"Here's your teeth." She reached the glass awkwardly to Alice. "I thought you were going down to breakfast without them."

"Now when did I ever go off without my teeth, Hattie?"

Alice smiled in spite of herself. It was going to be a good day, she thought. Mrs. Crumm and her sister were back from a weekend, and they could all play rummy together in the afternoon. She walked to the closet in her stocking feet, a smile playing absently about her mouth.

Hattie watched as she took down the powder blue dress, the one that went best with the beige Angora. She fastened all the little buttons in front. She took the sweater off the hanger and put one arm into the sleeve.

"Oh," she breathed painfully. Then like a hurt child her eyes squinted and her face twisted petulantly. Tears came quickly down her cheeks. "H-Hattie . . ." She turned to her and could say nothing else.

Hattie smirked, uncomfortable yet enjoying herself thoroughly. "Well I do know!" she exclaimed. "Who might have done a trick like that!" She went to the bed and sat down, doubled up with laughter.

"Hattie . . . Hattie you did this," Alice declared in unsteady tones. She clutched the sweater to her. "Hattie . . . you're just mean."

Lying across the bed, Hattie was almost hysterical. "You know I didn't now, Alice. . . . Hah-haw! . . . Why do you think I'd . . . ?" Her voice was choked off with uncontrolled laughter.

She lay there several minutes before she was calm enough to go down to breakfast. And when she left the room, Alice was sitting in the big chair by the window, sobbing, her face buried in the Angora sweater.

• • •

Alice did not come down until she was called for lunch. She chatted at the table with Mrs. Crumm and her sister and took no notice of Hattie. She sat opposite Alice, silent and restless, but she was not at all sorry for what she had done. She could have endured days of indifference on Alice's part, without feeling the slightest remorse.

It was a beautiful day. After lunch, they went with Mrs. Crumm, her sister, and the hotel hostess, Mrs. Holland, and sat in Gramercy Park.

Alice pretended to be absorbed in her book. It was a detective story by her favorite author, borrowed from the hotel's circulating library. Mrs. Crumm and her sister did most of the talking. A weekend trip was of sufficient importance to provide a topic of conversation for several afternoons, and Mrs. Crumm was able to remember every item of food she ate on visits for days running.

The monotonous tones of the voices, the warmth of the sunlight lulled Alice into half sleep. The page was blurred to her eyes.

Earlier in the day she had planned to adopt an attitude toward Hattie. She should be cold and aloof, even hostile. It was not the first time Hattie had committed such an outrage. There was the ink spilt on her lace tablecloth four months ago, and her missing morocco volume of Tennyson. She was sure Hattie had it, somewhere. And that evening, she would calmly pack her bag, write Hattie a note, short but carefully worded, and leave the hotel. She could go to another hotel in the neighborhood, let it be known through Mrs. Crumm where she was, and have the satisfaction of Hattie's coming to her and apologizing. But the fact of it was, she was not at all sure that Hattie would come to her, and this embarrassing possibility, plus a characteristic lack of enterprise prevented her taking such a dangerous course. . . . What if she had to spend the rest of her life alone? . . . It was much easier to stay where she was, to have a pleasant game of rummy in the afternoon, with ice cream and cookies, and to take out her revenge in little ways. It was also more ladylike, she consoled herself. She did not think beyond this, of the particular situations when she would say or do things calculated to hurt Hattie. The opportunities would just come of themselves.

Mrs. Holland nudged her. "We're going to get some ice cream now. Then we're going back to play some rummy."

"I was just at the most exciting part of the book." But she rose with the others and was almost cheerful as they walked to the drug store.

She won at rummy, too, and she felt pleased with herself. Hattie, watching her uneasily all day, was much relieved when Alice decreed speaking terms again.

Nevertheless, the thought of the ruined sweater rankled in Alice's mind, prodded her with a sense of injustice. Indeed, she was ashamed of herself for being able to consider it as lightly as she did. It was letting Hattie walk over her. She wished she could muster a really strong hatred.

They were in their room reading at nine o'clock. Every vestige of Hattie's shyness or pretended contrition had vanished.

"Wasn't it a nice day?" she ventured.

"H-m-m." Alice did not raise her head.

"Well," she made the inevitable remark through the inevitable yawn, "I reckon I'll be going off to bed."

And a few minutes later they were both in bed, propped up by four pillows, reading; Hattie with the newspaper and Alice with her detective story. They were silent for a while, then Hattie adjusted her pillows and lay down.

"Good night, Alice."

"Good night."

Soon Alice pulled out the light, and there was absolute silence in the room except for the soft ticking of the clock and the occasional purr of an automobile. The timepiece on the mantel whirred and then began to strike ten.

Alice lay open-eyed. All day her tears had been restrained and now, automatically, she began to cry. She wiped her nose on the top of the sheet. But they were not childish tears.

She raised herself on one elbow. The darkish braid of hair outlined Hattie's neck and shoulder against the white bedclothes. She felt very strong, strong enough to murder Hattie with her own hands. But the idea of murder passed from her mind as swiftly as it had entered. Her revenge had to be something that would last, that would hurt, something that Hattie must endure and that she, Alice, could enjoy.

Then it came to her, and she was out of bed, walking boldly to the sewing table as Hattie had done twenty-four hours before . . . and she was standing by the bed, bending over Hattie, peering at her placid, innocent face through her tears and her short-sighted eyes. Two quick strokes could cut the braid, right near the head.

But suddenly her fingers were limp, hardly strong enough to hold the scissors, much less slice through a rope of hair.

She steadied herself on the bed table . . . Hattie, dear Hattie . . . Hattie meant well. Hattie was just mischievous. She laid the scissors on the table and gave a great sob.

Hattie yawned and squinted her eyes open.

"I . . . I was just getting a drink of water," Alice said. She moved toward the basin.

Hattie yawned and grunted.

"Would you like some?"

"I don't mind if I do," Hattie murmured.

She brought her a tumbler half full, and Hattie took it without a word as a child would. Alice felt her way around the bed and climbed in. She lay there looking at the ceiling with sore tear-pink eyes, and after a moment she heard Hattie set the glass down on the table.

# IN THE PLAZA

He was born in a hut made of twigs and mud that leaned against a straw-colored hill. The road to the village went past the door, and at the age of one, he knew that the people who said "Hello" instead of "*Adiós*" were *americanos* and very rich. They gave money away for nothing, his father said. Money bought sweet rolls and candy sticks. So he had no time to play on the dirt floor with his older brother. He had no time to wonder, as his father and grandfather had wondered, sitting on the same wooden doorstep, whether the huddled hills were the backs of giant burros, as an old story told, or if the distant mountains that lay in great golden-tan curves held bubbles of air that might escape at the puncture of a pick and let the whole world down. He had time only to watch for *americanos*. He could tell them by their pale faces and their new clean clothes. When he saw one, he would rush out into the road, naked as he was, grin and say, "Ai-lo!" and hold out his palm. The coins always fell.

At four, he loitered around the smaller plaza in the village, where the buses unloaded. He learned to say, "Can I help you, lady?" and "Can I help you, sir?" and always he was given centavos, because the words meant, Could he carry the suitcases that were as big as he was and weighed a lot more? If he talked fast, he could get money from all the *turistas* before the older boys, his brother Antonio among them, could carry off their suitcases. He learned to say, "That is the best hotel," as he pointed up the road to a big white house, and if people went there, he trotted after them and collected a peso from the hotel manager. The rate at the hotel was one hundred and twenty-five pesos a day, but for the *americanos* this fortune was nothing.

When he saw an American, he did not see a person at all, but centavo pieces and red-and-green peso notes. It fascinated him to watch them buy in the silver shops. They selected things quickly, as if they were eager to get rid of their money, and there was never any back-and-forth talk about the price. The women had even more pesos than the men. Every American was a moneybag he had merely to puncture with a smile and hold his hands to. His only competition was a loose army of other small boys which roamed the village, but the competition was not serious because he, in distinction from all the rest, was cute. "Cute" was a word nearly all the Americans said when they gave him money. It meant he did not have to carry suitcases as the others did, that all he had to do was smile and hold out his palm. His last name happened to be Palma, but several years were to pass before he learned the English word "palm."

In the evening, he impressed his parents by shouting the *inglés* he had learned. "Easy on that camera!" and "Put that with the rest!"

"*Por dios, Alejandro!*" his pious mother exclaimed. She was beginning to worry about him. He was home only to sleep. Already he did not want to go to the cathedral because, he said, the Americans did not go and were much richer than the Mexicans.

He was supposed to lay the money he had earned on the table every evening, as Antonio did, but Alejandro could always conceal most of it in his pockets, because his father was not clever. He could buy all the ice-cream sodas and chocolates he wanted. He could buy factory-made shirts in the marketplace. Never did he buy anything for his parents, like Antonio. Wasn't it enough that what his father took from him enabled them to have coffee and fresh meat all the time? Without him, they would still be eating nothing but tortillas and frijoles that his father got in exchange for his wooden saddles and his mother's serapes. The cleverest Mexicans, he told his parents, were not farmers of corn or makers of wooden saddles, but guides, silver shop owners and hotel owners, people who did things for the Americans. Therefore his parents were stupid. So was Antonio, who worked like a burro carrying suitcases but did not earn half what he did just by smiling. He taunted Antonio for his stupidity, in English that Antonio could not understand, and in the older boy arose a jealousy that became hatred.

It was true that the town subsisted on money that came from the tourists. The village whored after money. Some of the natives had much money, some hardly any, but all paid the high prices for basic needs which the extravagance of the tourists had brought about. The tourists took the best houses and the best food because they had the money to pay for them, while the natives whose great-great-grandparents had been born here lived on what was left. It was ironic that this had happened to their village simply because the village happened to be so pretty. Beneath a superficial cheerfulness, hatred against the tourists ran like an underground stream that rose in the eyes of bent old men sometimes, and in the faces of small children who had not yet learned to hide it. Most American tourists moved too fast to detect it, but some Americans who had made the village their home detected it and then began to see it everywhere, even in the eyes of the stray dogs in the plaza and behind the smile of the hotel managers who spoke English perfectly. They could never escape it, except by drinking.

Alejandro learned English almost as easily as Spanish and in time the languages were side by side in his mind. He listened for new English words and earned extra centavos if he asked the Americans what a certain word meant. He learned the value of dissembling friendship, of remembering names. If he smiled, waved a hand and called, "Hello, there, Mr. So-and-So!" to a tourist he had got money from before, he would be tossed more money. By tagging after a group of tourists, babbling English, he would be invited sometimes as a kind of court jester to one of the hotel dining rooms to share a meal his parents could not imagine even after he described it.

One day when he was about seven, his offer to help a lady was accepted, and he had to carry a small bag up the longest hill to a hotel. He took his two-peso tip sullenly, and when he had walked back down the hill, he was resolved to become a *guia*, a guide. All the guides did was walk around and talk. So he went past the buses to the main plaza, where under the tall plane trees before the cathedral the guides made up their parties.

"Can I show you the town, ladies and sirs?" he asked with the same winning smile he had used at the bus stop.

He competed with boys much older than he, more capable of supporting the plump, middle-aged women who turned their ankles going down the steep cobblestones, but generally the women would say something to their men with the word "cute" in it; and he would be beckoned to. In the plaza also was his brother Antonio, who at fourteen had just graduated from porter to guide in the town's curriculum. Antonio with his indifferent English and his square, serious face. Alejandro laughed at him and took his customers from under his nose. Antonio had memorized the whole guidebook and did not know how to pronounce the words right, and besides, what American on a holiday wanted such a sad lecture? Antonio and he were real rivals now and seldom spoke to each other. It was hard to believe they were brothers, solemn Antonio and the happy-eyed little Alejandro.

Alejandro had trailed the guides often enough to know the things they pointed at and what they said, such as, "This cathedral costed ten billions of pesos," but he varied the ordinary tour. With the gestures of an experienced host, his small figure led groups of ten and twelve from Silver Shop to A Picturesque Street, to Silver Shop (the guides made commissions on the purchases), to the Cathedral, to A Beautiful View, a tour neither too short nor too long, that ended happily at one of the two high-class bars in the plaza, where a drink made with two jiggers of tequila and mentioned in every guidebook was served. Alejandro became the most popular guide of the village. His age and size were a novelty, his customers told their friends to ask for him, and there were always those tourists who came every year and had known him since he was four, who took pleasure in introducing him to their friends who were seeing the village for the first time.

He made from sixty to seventy pesos a day. The bulge of banknotes so delighted him, he got the habit of walking with one hand in his pocket to feel it, which emphasized his easy, jaunty poise. He bought brilliantine for his softly curling hair to make it shine with blue highlights. He bought trousers like the Americans wore, that sold for forty pesos in the market, kept them freshly washed and pressed and never forgot to close the zipper as many Mexican boys did, an omission he knew was remarked unfavorably by the American women. He struggled to read American magazines. He went to every American movie that came to the two picture houses in the town, and learned new words by comparing them with the Spanish written at the bottom of the screen. He cut and parted his hair after the fashion of American actors and dressed himself as nearly like them as he could.

The word "cute" he heard less often now than "good-looking." He was twelve years old. Already his face was lean and manly, with an astute expression that suggested more years than he had. His body was a lithe five feet five inches and weighed one hundred and fifteen pounds, in American measurements. Of all the young men of the village, he was the most handsome, and he noticed the effect of this on women. It was the furtive embraces of the American women as they caught at him slipping down the lanes, their hasty, shy pecks on his cheeks and lips after their second tequilas that awakened his desires. All the guides were familiar with this nervous lovemaking of the American women and laughed at it. Often they boasted to their comrades, as they pointed out this or that pretty American girl, that it had been she with whom they spent the night, half jokingly, half as if they expected to be believed.

So did Alejandro boast, though he had seduced only one girl and she was a Mexican, Concha, the prettiest *muchacha* in the village. He had been eleven and she thirteen. But this was nothing. One little peck from an American woman, no matter how old or ugly she was, counted more, because she was American. And really, Mexican girls had never attracted him. He liked American girls with blond hair, like those he saw in the movies, and sometimes getting off the buses or driving into the village in their cars. He longed to seduce one. This desire began to be stronger even than his passion for money.

His first American girl was a well-developed blue-eyed young lady of fifteen with blond hair that curled at the ends and hung partway down her back. It was the blond hair that fascinated him, the blank staring blue eyes that encouraged him. Her name was Mary Jane Howell, and she was with her mother. He took them and some other tourists around the village, then was invited to lunch at a hotel by Mrs. Howell, to whom he had been especially courteous. After lunch, Mrs. Howell wanted to go shopping, but Mary Jane said she would stay behind. Having directed Mrs. Howell to a silver shop, Alejandro returned to the hotel just as Mary Jane was stepping from behind a potted palm in the lobby with her eyes even wider, even more fixed.

He gave her his most charming smile, copied from a certain American actor, on the left side of his face with his eyes narrowed to crescents of long black lashes. "I show you that map I told you upstairs, yes? There is much breeze down here, no?"

"Yes!" she said.

He could have spoken better English, but he knew when to use an accent. He followed her into the room, and almost before he could close the door, Mary Jane had locked her arms around his neck and planted a moist warm kiss on his lips.

Hardly half an hour later, he was downstairs, walking automatically, though buoyantly, toward the plaza. His tongue leapt in his mouth to tell of his conquest, and in the next quarter hour he told it four times, in increasing detail, to as many guides and plaza loiterers as would listen. They believed him now, because he believed himself. The realization of his triumph was stronger in the plaza than it had been in Mary Jane's room. A blond American girl! Later, when Mary Jane and her mother walked about the village, they were followed by the eyes of almost the entire male population.

Thereafter came many American girls. There were a few rebuffs, but Alejandro could take success and failure with the same pleasant bow and smile—which often turned matters his way after all. He came to be known as the "bad boy" of the village, and enjoyed a worse reputation than he deserved. His walk was haughty, its tense grace suggestive of a well-cared-for tomcat, and he was always walking, roving the town. He held his narrow head high. Merely the glance of his dark eyes was half the conquest of the women he wanted.

At fifteen, he received two or three letters a week from American girls, schoolteachers, married women, beginning, "Dearest Boy," "Darling," "My Spanish Angel," ending with dirges of their boring existences in the States and a wish that the joys they had known might sometime, somewhere be relived. These letters he read conspicuously, sitting on the benches in the plaza where the plane trees dappled them with rich shadow and glaring sunspots. He put them in his hip pocket with the American stamp showing at the top, and strolled off in quest of more girls. Some of the letters he answered in careful English, most were not worth the trouble. He had found a new ambition. He wanted to marry an American woman, a wealthy one, and live like the prince he was for the rest of his life. There were many marriages between Mexican boys and American women in the village. One of their homes was the most palatial house he had ever seen. But he was still young, and it was difficult for a Mexican boy to marry an American woman before he was seventeen. He must act older, concentrate on the wealthiest and freest of the American women and charm them out of their senses.

For six months he charmed a score of American women out of their senses, but none seemed to want marriage. American women expected casual romances as part of the village's entertainment. They enjoyed the jealousy of the American men, their nervous anger or their badly pretended boredom, when they made engagements with young Mexicans. The women seemed to play a game just for the pleasure of reconciliation with their men at the end of their stay. Alejandro took his disappointments with a smile and a shrug. American women were not all so elusive. The woman for him would come.

One day, a woman like none Alejandro had seen before strolled into the plaza on the arm of a well-dressed gentleman with red hair. Was she American? Alejandro examined her from head to toe. She held herself as proudly as he did. She carried a long cigarette holder and wore high-heeled green lizard pumps in which she seemed to glide rather than walk over the cobbles that turned other women's ankles even when they wore straw sandals. She looked bored, and it seemed to be the man's idea that they see the town, though it was she who selected him as their guide. She did not look at the things he pointed to, but kept her gray-green eyes on him in a sleepy, thoughtful way that gave Alejandro an odd feeling. She was not attractive and yet she was. At any rate, and the thought gave him his bearings again, there was no doubt she had much money. Earrings of hammered gold circles hung below the lacquered upswept black hair. The pale green tweed skirt had been made for her and the gray silk blouse, too, and perhaps also the green lizard belt that matched her shoes.

She did not want to enter the cantina with the others at the end of the tour. She stopped just outside the door, looking at Alejandro, who hung there, too, as if she were the only member of his party.

"What is your name?" she asked him in a voice like a distant pipe organ and with a smile that revealed interesting teeth, one partially of gold.

"Alejandro Palma, at your service." He could not look back at her face after his bow. Never had he felt like this, and he did not know if it was shyness, attraction, or dislike.

"Alejandro," she repeated, rolling the *r* as easily as he. The gray-green eyes, half shaded by crinkly lids, blinked at him affectionately. "Well, perhaps I see you tomorrow again, Alejandro. Today I was too tired to enjoy your village."

"My pleasure." Alejandro bowed.

Her escort offered his arm with an absentminded resignation, and Alejandro watched her move off in a slinking gait that set one foot in a line with the other. Then he dispatched for fifty centavos a small boy to ascertain at what hotel she was staying, her name and that of the man. The boy reported back that she was a countess.

The next morning, she was in the plaza before nine o'clock, before Alejandro had begun to make up his first party. She wore flat iguana sandals now that made her feet look even longer and narrower. She said she wanted a drink, so they went to Cesar's Cantina, a tequila-soaked niche in the wall of one of the lanes off the plaza, since the better cantinas were not yet open. In Cesar's, the fleas were so thick one could see them hopping here and there on the red-tile floor in search of a human leg. Two dirty Mexicans slouched over the low bar.

In an open-collared white shirt and white linen trousers, Alejandro sat erectly at a little table with the Countess. He spoke English loudly and distinctly, proud to be seen by Cesar and the two Mexicans with the elegant woman who also spoke English, used a holder for her Russian cigarettes, and was in every respect beyond the iron tradition that forbade women to enter such a cantina. To her questions, Alejandro replied that he was eighteen, though he was only sixteen, and said that he had been educated at the Academia Inglesa in Mexico City.

She lifted the tiny tequila glass in her bony hand, drank it off without salt or lime, and looked at him calmly. "You are very handsome. You appear a little Spanish. Is it so?"

"My father and mother—they were pure Castilian," Alejandro said, lowering his eyes sensitively. One of Cesar's fighting cocks, combless and limping like an old man, was entering the cantina pecking at the floor.

The Countess smiled and blinked her eyes at him, and though it was a tender smile, he felt she knew he lied. "Me, I am nothing. Because I am everything. Do you understand?" She smiled again. "Like you."

He did not understand, and he did. "What about your friend?"

"Robert?" She laughed and waved a hand that drifted back to the silver cigarette case that had initials on it and a crest. "Robert told me yesterday a good-bye forever."

Again Alejandro could not look at her, could not say any of the things it was now time for him to say.

"No, do not walk back with me, Alejandro." With a bored air, she had got up. "Visit me tonight at ten if you care to. You know my name already, don't you? Countess Lomolkov—Paula."

Alejandro was there at ten. He had been unable to work all day for anxiety. In the disorderly room where her possessions obliterated the Mexican decor, the Countess made bewildering love to him, wooed and won him and covered him with heavy, tender kisses, insulted him by laughing at his lovemaking, though she made Alejandro laugh, too. She told him his language of love was more broken than his English. She made him frantic to please her. All he desired was that she let him see her again.

"Of course. Tomorrow we are going to Acapulco." She lay on her back, blowing the smoke of her Russian cigarette toward the ceiling. "Already I have telephoned reservations in an hotel."

In the morning, he packed some of his best shirts and slacks into a valise he had just bought.

"Where are you going?" asked his mother, who was putting on a pot of beans in the outdoor kitchen.

"*Quien sabe?*" he answered sourly, then began to smile as he walked down the hill. His mother would think he was merely going to Mexico City again, and this might be the last time he would see his home! He did not look back. The world spread bigger and bigger before him. The Countess filled it all.

He drove the Countess's shiny black Jaguar out of the village and turned its chromium radiator cap on the road to Acapulco. The Countess was quiet and thoughtful, and kept her eyes on the road even when she took swallows out of the long thin bottle of tequila añeja she had bought "to celebrate."

Alejandro had never felt so happy and so carefree. Though his time had always been his own, his days spent in the out-of-doors, he had always been working to earn money. Now he did not think about money. He did not want money from the Countess. He did not want to marry her unless she wished it. He thought of his marriage to anyone as a fraud, and he did not want to cheat the Countess. Just how he felt, he could not say, because he did not know the meaning of the words *respect*, *affection*, or *love*, and they did not occur to him now.

In Acapulco they stayed at the favorite hotel of the season, where their suite and meals were three hundred and fifty pesos a day. The Countess bought him a bathing suit consisting of a strip of chartreuse material splotched with vermilion flowers. With this wrapped around his narrow hips he swam at Hornos Beach in the mornings and at Coleta in the afternoons, lolled with the Countess on the sand, while she, marking with her sunglasses her place in the book she never read for gazing at him, stroked the curls back from his forehead or dribbled the white sand down the brown hairless arch of his chest. Often, after tamarind highballs on the hotel terrace, they drove to Pie de la Cuesta, a promontory fifteen kilometers away. Here they lay in hammocks strung only a few feet from the waves' edge, sipped coconuts through straws, and watched the sun drop into the water like a world on fire. They dined at all the hotels for variety, and had whole banquets sent up to their rooms. Generally, they retired early, because the Countess needed much sleep.

She told him of her childhood in Poland on her father's great estate where three hundred serfs tended vast wheat fields, of her narrow escape when Hitler came, of her life afterward in Paris and in New York. Alejandro did not believe a tenth of it, but he listened with the respect he would have demanded of a listener if he had told a comparable story of his life in Mexico. And this was what drew them together, their common habit of lying, their fellowship of falseness, their dependence on the timid man's fascination by the outrageous. Where had she got her money? She had none, she said. She lived on credit.

"When my credit will be gone, then I shall be gone also." And when Alejandro looked alarmed, "I could not live at all if I did not live in danger! Neither can you, Alejandro, even after you marry, you will see. Make a wise marriage, not a stupid one. Marry an ugly woman if you can, or if she is pretty be sure she is stupid, but they usually are. . . . You don't yet understand all, but you will."

She taught him as if she were a school of manners, morals, love, hypocrisy, and opportunism. He was her protégé, son, lover, and husband, because he would finally need to know how to be a husband, quite a different art from that of lover. She supervised the cutting of his hair, dramatizing the ripples in back and at his temples, balancing the curve of his head with an orderly clump that fell partially over his forehead. She imposed an English restraint in his dress, taught him a thousand little graces for different places and occasions, all without embarrassing him, even contriving to flatter him. And Alejandro learned with the ease and pleasure of one whose life is devoted to ease and pleasure and the pleasing of others. He burst into bloom. The Countess and the tropical sun caressed him. He caressed the whole world. Happiness! How could she make him so happy, he wondered, when a thousand times a day she criticized him, caught him in a lie, impressed some trivial matter on his mind like a schoolteacher? Yet he felt that his happiness was traced with every movement of his body like an invisible design in the air. Wasn't that why everyone gazed at him on the beaches? Even men, who always loathed him, took secret pleasure in watching him disport himself. His figure poised for a moment against the bright blue water as he sought the Countess, his flight up the beach to the older woman who was clearly not his mother and to whom he seemed so devoted began many conversations, he knew.

Two blond American women angled for him at the hotel, but Alejandro was not once tempted to be false to the Countess. He spent his evenings close by her side, usually in white linen slacks (the Countess liked him in white linen), a dark green or blue sport shirt with one of her silk handkerchiefs knotted at his throat, listening and talking to her as if she were the only woman in the world. People in the hotel could not figure them out, but how they loved to watch!

Alejandro never stopped to ask himself if he were in love with the Countess, and, probably because his emotions for sixteen years had been so false, he could not have given himself a truthful answer. He dropped postcards to his friends back in the village, telling of his extravagant, carefree life, of how voluptuous was *la condesa*, and of course of how many new conquests he had made. He wrote also to Concha, his first *amor* and now the betrothed of Antonio, and sent her a necklace of small gray seashells that he bought from a peddler for two pesos.

After six weeks, the Countess could find only the most minute faults in Alejandro. The sandpapering was over, she told him. The rest would be with emery dust. Now he learned how to make at least one incontrovertible statement on such subjects as abstract art, Negroes in America, communism in Latin America, and Wagnerian opera.

"I do not want you should anymore be a guide," the Countess said one day in the absent monotone that meant her thoughts were far ahead of her words. "You should be manager of a fine hotel in your village."

Alejandro said something evasive. He was much too busy being happy to think about working or about the future.

The Countess turned from the window in fury. "Do not be lazy! You have in you that stupid laziness of your stupid country, and if you cannot step it down we say good-bye forever this minute! . . . Yes, your country is full of stupid, lazy people! Like your parent—Yes, I know all about your parents, stupid boy! Like you would be without me! *Don't deny it!*" She shook him hard by the shoulders. "You will not grow up to be a lazy, fat bum, you will grow up to be zome—*zing!* Understand?"

Alejandro got up, bowed as she wished him to do, and murmured, "The woman I love can make the impossible possible."

"And this is not even the impossible, my sly one, you know that." The Countess smiled.

The next morning, she did not join him on the beach after her usual letter-writing period after breakfast. Alejandro went back to the hotel and was told she had checked out. Trembling, he opened the envelope the clerk handed him, conscious of the dramatic figure he made before the clerk and the two blond Americans standing nearby, of the tragedy in his young face, of the new blue banknotes he let flutter to his feet. A short letter with many interpolated terms of affection told him she had spoken with the manager of the hotel at which she had stopped in his village, and that it was all but certain he could become the receptionist there—second in importance only to the manager himself, she reminded him. The bill was paid at the Acapulco hotel for the next five days, and he was to enjoy himself and not think of her, forget her with someone else if he wanted to. "How strange I should have found in Mexico one so like myself! Bless you and thank you, my darling! But do not try to thank me except by to remember a few of the things I have told you. Never think you may see me again, never think I forget you. Your Paula. Countess Lomolkov." The last two words were underlined.

Alejandro was too lonely to stay on. Dimly, he realized he cared more for her than he had admitted, and he could not bear to face it, so he caught a bus back to the village. Once more, the world opened itself wide to him on the mountain road. He could face the world more easily than the loss of the Countess. He must turn his eyes outward, live dangerously, as she had said. Before nightfall, he had spoken to Señor Martinez, the manager of the hotel. Alejandro's bearing, his knowledge of English—even Señor Martinez did not know much English—got him the job. Señor Martinez, a shy, serious man eager for the Americanization of the hotel, had agreed with the Countess on the telephone that an English-speaking receptionist would be an advantage. Alejandro then was the likely young man she had promised to send. Alejandro's reputation would have proscribed him, but the manager's monastic habits had kept it from reaching his ears.

In the hotel, Alejandro wore either white or gray flannel with a red flower always in his buttonhole. It was his job to welcome guests, see that their rooms were satisfactory, that their breakfast orders were correctly filled before the trays left the kitchen, to invite lonely women guests out for cocktails occasionally, the bills to be paid by the hotel. He flew smoothly about the two-story patioed building, set a vase of bougainvilleas in a certain room, brought raw meat for the dog in another, replaced small light bulbs with larger ones, and gave every guest the impression that he or she was his favorite. There was never a complaint against Alejandro, and there were many tips, many commendations to Señor Martinez. When some of the *señor*'s friends remarked that Alejandro had reformed, the *señor* did not know what they meant.

Alejandro did not earn quite as much as he had as a guide, but his new position carried greater dignity, and dignity was important, the Countess had told him, to an American woman who considered marrying a Mexican. Since starting his job at the hotel, his ambition to marry a wealthy American woman had returned with new force. He was so much better equipped now. He longed to succeed.

Only the wealthiest women merited his invitations to cocktails. He made engagements with wealthy women staying at other hotels, too. All the bills were sent to Señor Martinez with notations that they were for such and such *señoras* or *señoritas* stopping at the hotel. Often he invited young ladies to the hotel to spend the evening in a room that happened to be free. This deception might have gone on indefinitely, if not for one indiscretion that would certainly have brought the severest tongue-lashing from the Countess.

Concha had married Antonio, who was now twenty-four and still not graduated from the guide class. Alejandro and Concha saw each other every Saturday night, when Antonio was busy taking tourists on a round of the bars until they closed at midnight. Antonio was now trying to teach Pancho, their fourteen-year-old cousin, how to be a guide, so he was quite occupied. Pancho tagged along with him everywhere, even on Saturday nights, and since he was as serious and stupid as Antonio, Alejandro knew he would turn out the same way as his brother—adequate as a guide, perhaps, but without a very interesting future.

Alejandro and Concha were fond of each other, but far from being in love. It was just that they enjoyed reliving the childhood *amor* they had known six years before. Concha liked to laugh, and Alejandro laughed so much more than Antonio. And it amused Alejandro to give horns to his brother.

It was Concha's birthday. Señor Martinez was in Mexico City overnight on business, and the bridal suite in the hotel happened to be free. Alejandro thought it would be fun to bring Concha there. Concha was delighted with the idea. She and Alejandro went to the hotel, telephoned down for rum and tostadas with sour cream, and pretended they were newlyweds. At eleven-thirty when they came downstairs, whom should they see behind the desk but Señor Martinez. Alejandro said, "*Buenas noches, señor,*" like a gentleman, escorted Concha home, but he knew it was the end. Señor Martinez knew that Concha was a married woman who lived in the village. Alejandro could have bribed the help, but not Señor Martinez, who would never forgive him. Alejandro was discharged that same night.

Alejandro was too optimistic to fear that Antonio would hear of the evening through Señor Martinez, but he spent over a thousand pesos bribing the staff. For a few days, Alejandro felt nervous and resentful. He was a little afraid of his brother, though when he watched him in the plaza from time to time, he could see no change in him. And when the idea occurred to him that Antonio might take action, he dismissed it as he dismissed his family—he had lived at the hotel since his return from Acapulco—because Antonio was essentially as stupid and ineffectual as his parents. Meanwhile, Alejandro had moved in with an emotionally starved American woman resident of the village, whose young Mexican husband had just abandoned her. He had often called on her before, and now she welcomed him for as long as he cared to stay.

Not long after his discharge from the hotel, on one of the afternoons he was idling about the village, too proud, still too well off to worry about earning more money so soon, he wandered into a bookshop off the plaza and saw Mrs. Kootz. Mrs. Chester Kootz came every summer to the village and stayed three or four months. Though she was a millionairess and a widow, Alejandro had never considered her because she was so ugly. She wore her hair in a gray bun that could hardly be seen under the strands that escaped it and that hung down like gray rags. Her dresses were uniformly gray, too, and so shapeless they might have been slept in. The joke was, she had been cited year after year as one of the ten wealthiest women of America, and that if she did not look it, then she must be all the wealthier for not spending money on adornment.

In a bitter mood, Alejandro flirted brazenly with Mrs. Kootz in the bookshop. Mrs. Kootz glanced at him, dragged on her cigarette, and chose a book. She had known Alejandro by sight since he had been a little centavo-beggar at the bus stop. Alejandro smiled cockily to himself and strolled out of the bookshop in the tracks of Mrs. Kootz's run-over oxfords. She started up the lane that led to the big house she always rented. But the way was so steep, Alejandro lazily turned back, slouched onto a bench in the shade of the plaza's trees, locked his fingers over his flat waist, and dozed for a while, lulled by the hum of Spanish voices around him, by the squeals of children at play.

The idea took form in the middle of a little dream: he was enjoying some delicious pleasure because he was married to Mrs. Kootz and had money. The dream fell away, but the idea remained. He would court Mrs. Kootz and try to marry her. It made him snicker now to think about it. But would the Countess laugh? Alejandro quit the shade of the plane tree as Gautama had quit his Bodhi Tree, with a purpose.

At about six that evening, Alejandro glanced up at the balcony of a bar in the plaza and saw Mrs. Kootz at a table alone, drinking one of her brandies. Alejandro went up the stairs without even raking a comb through his hair or pulling his thumbs down the sides of his collar, his habit before going into action. He walked directly to her table, and asked if he might join her.

She drew on her cigarette, squinted up at him, then gestured to the opposite chair.

Alejandro changed his tactics from those of the afternoon. Now he was the gentleman the Countess would have advised him to be. He behaved as if the sleek Countess had been sitting opposite him instead of dowdy Mrs. Kootz. He asked if she was enjoying her stay, and she replied not particularly, that she came every year because of her asthma. She spoke briefly of her ailment and with an unfeminine frankness. She was interested in buying a house in the village but couldn't because she was not a citizen or a permanent resident. This gave an opening for the remark that if she married a Mexican, she could buy it in his name, but even he felt it so pointed he could not say it.

"Do you know the Countess Lomolkov?"

Mrs. Kootz shook her head. "Who's she?"

"A lady who was here in the spring. From New York, too. We spent a month together in Acapulco."

Mrs. Kootz said nothing.

Alejandro talked pleasantly for nearly an hour, but nothing of his charm seemed to penetrate. Mrs. Kootz only drank brandy after brandy, sipping from a glass of Carta Blanca as a chaser. Then she said something about the fleas in her leather chair eating her alive and that she wanted to go. He accompanied her to her house, lending her an arm over the rough spots. He lingered at her door, waiting to be asked in to dinner.

"Good night," she said, without glancing over her shoulder.

Alejandro turned away cheerfully, remembering the hundred-peso bill she had taken out to pay the check, one of many others in her big worn alligator wallet. He had insisted on paying the check, of course. Appraisingly he looked at her dark green convertible parked in the alley, flecked with Mexican mud, but still showing its thirty-five-thousand-peso lines.

In the plaza he saw Antonio and Pancho. Antonio came toward him with one hand outstretched.

"Is from your mother," Antonio muttered in Spanish as he passed him at arm's length, as if he did not want to befoul himself with touching him. Even Pancho had barely greeted him with a nod.

Alejandro looked at what had been dropped into his hand. It was a rosary with a small silver cross he had seen before. He had not been home in over two months, and evidently his mother was concerned for his soul.

With a big bouquet of red frangipani, Alejandro called on Mrs. Kootz the next morning at eleven. A Mexican girl opened the gate, then went to see if Mrs. Kootz would admit him. Finally Mrs. Kootz herself came slowly down the flagstone walk, frowning against the sun and the smoke from her cigarette, wearing the same dress she had worn yesterday. Her forefinger was in the pages of Guizot's *History of France*.

"What's up?" she asked hoarsely.

"Good morning." He smiled, twiddling the bouquet. "I beg to see you a moment. Inside?"

She looked at him. "Come on in."

He followed her up the steps to the front hall and into a large sunny room with a tile floor and scatter rugs, with comfortable-looking corners that held books and reading lamps and Mexican leather easy chairs. Mrs. Kootz went toward one corner where a laden ashtray and an open bottle of brandy showed she had been sitting.

"Drink?" she asked, refilling her glass.

Alejandro shook his head. "These are for you." He advanced with the bouquet and bowed as he presented it.

She took the flowers as if she had not noticed them before. "Thanks," she said in a tone of surprise. "Juana?" When the girl appeared, she gave her the flowers and made gestures at a nearby vase. "Aq-wah."

The girl started to remove the tamarind pods from the vase she had indicated.

"No, not that one," Mrs. Kootz said impatiently. "Find an empty one."

The girl looked blank.

Alejandro rapped out a sentence or two in Spanish and Juana left the room promptly.

Mrs. Kootz stared after the girl, said "Damn," and tossed off the brandy. She put another cigarette in her mouth, but before Alejandro could get her a light, she had struck on her thumbnail one of the American wooden matches she always carried about her.

"Do you like Wagner?" Alejandro asked, fingering a biography of Wagner that lay on a table.

"Some. His art songs." She sat down heavily in her chair.

"He is too noisy for me," Alejandro said prissily.

Mrs. Kootz looked at him as she had looked at the flowers. "Say, what's your name?"

"Alejandro. Alejandro Palma, at your service." He bowed again, then seated himself gently on the arm of a divan. "Do you know why I came to see you, Mrs. Kootz?"

"Why?"

He stood up. An amused smile had forced itself to his lips and he lowered his head. "Because I am in love with you." He had decided the simple, direct approach was best. "I admire your mind, your . . ." But what could he say about her? The hag!

Mrs. Kootz got up, too, started to pour another brandy, then strolled out onto the side porch, the only move inspired by self-consciousness she could recall ever making.

Alejandro was beside her, insinuating his slight body into her arms. He kissed her before she could recover from her surprise to thrust him away, kissed her again.

A few yards below and in front of them, a girl named Hermalinda Herrera glanced up from her own roofless terrace, where she sat chewing gum and reading the latest issue of *Hoy*, and saw an unbelievable sight: the "bad boy" Alejandro kissing Señora Kootz *muy caliente* and the *señora* liking it, too! That afternoon, the whole village learned of it.

No one would have believed it, if Alejandro and the *señora* had not been seen together so often thereafter. Could they be thinking of getting married? Alejandro's Mexican girlfriends twitted him, and he told them frankly that he was going to marry the *señora* and for her millions of pesos. He told the guides in the plaza and his friends in Cesar's Cantina. Whether it got back to Mrs. Kootz before he clinched the marriage was no worry to him. It would sound like typical gossip, might even be good propaganda: he was having trouble convincing Mrs. Kootz that their getting married was at all possible, that someone could love her and want to make her his wife. Mrs. Kootz had somehow forgotten she was a human being, but he was teaching her to remember. But the bridge between the two languages did not seem likely to be crossed. Only the Mexicans seemed to talk, and Mrs. Kootz had no Mexican friends and only a nodding acquaintance with a few Americans.

They were married in a little chapel of the village with the traditional ceremony of two rings and thirteen pieces of silver money, symbolic of the union of their worldly estates. Antonio would not even look at Alejandro now when they met, and Concha only stole sidelong glances at him. All his Mexican friends were in awe of him, and he could make them comfortable with him only by getting them drunk.

Immediately, Señora Palma bought in the name of Alejandro Palma the house she had rented for so many years from Ysidro Barrera, a gift shop owner in the village. Interior decorators came from New York and Mexico City and argued with one another over the deployment of mountains of furniture and drapes Señora Palma had ordered, and when they at last went to work, each seemed bent on making his or her contribution as hideous as possible in order to blame the others. The house became a famous atrocity of the town, and Señora Palma allowed groups of gaping tourists to shuffle through it twice a day, conducted by guides who told them it was an example of the "luxuriant embellishment" of the Americans who had made the village their permanent home, which it was, and told them it was exquisite, which most of them believed. Señora Palma was flattered, as she had been flattered by Alejandro's attentions. She had grown less introverted, and for a while Gibbon, Toynbee, Guizot, and Prescott were forgotten in the planning of her house and the honeymoon trip she and Alejandro would make in the fall. After the house was running smoothly under the care of three maids who would be paid two hundred pesos each per month, she and Alejandro were going to drive in the green convertible to Mexico City, New Orleans, Charleston, New York, the American West, San Francisco, and home again, enjoying themselves where they found things to enjoy, spending money as they pleased. She had never known what pleasure it was to have money until Alejandro showed her how to spend it. She had never known what pleasure companionship was, or what it was to be loved. And she was proud of him: he was handsome, and his grooming inspired a kind of terror and reverence in her. Most of all, and with her self-analyzing temperament she realized it and admitted it, the novelty of him pleased her, the fact that he was a Mexican, that he was so young, that despite all the odds he had come so far with his ludicrous ambitions, his veneer of cosmopolitan gentleman. And his crumbs of information on the Negro problem, Wagnerian music, and Russian history! In another environment such determination might have made a Napoleon of him, or a Henry Ford. As a historian, she respected his intensity.

While preparations for the American tour went on, Alejandro indulged himself in sprees around the village. He bought drinks for whole cantinas, bought gifts of silver and leather for Mexican girlfriends and many new American girls. How much easier it was to get an American girl now that his tailor-made clothes proclaimed from across the plaza that he was rich! There was really no limit to the money he could spend now. He gazed with a dreamy smile at the five-figured numbers in the *señora*'s account books, at her stock reports, the Mexican bank account that was in his name as well as hers. And he owned the house, too, one of the biggest in the village. At seventeen!

The night before their departure for the honeymoon, Alejandro decided to visit Cesar's for a final tequila with his old cronies. He heard the jukebox from the cantina as he turned up the lane from the plaza. It played a gay ranchero song that he loved, and he sang with it:

*Quien dijo miedo, muchachos?*
*Si, para morir nacimo-o-os!*
*Traigo mi cuarenta y cinco*
*Con sus cuatro cargadores!*

He stood for a moment on the threshold of the cantina, smiling on everyone. Drunken shouts greeted him, many stood up and opened their arms, because even if he were not everyone's personal friend, he had money and would buy rounds of drinks. As the jukebox stopped, a mariachi in the corner began a fast rollicking song on his guitar.

Then Alejandro saw his brother Antonio sitting at one of the little tables. His was the only unfriendly face. Antonio was drunk, and Pancho was beside him, his solemn face frowning and worried. There was something so unfitting in Antonio's being here, something so frightening in Antonio's being drunk, that Alejandro hesitated to go in.

Then Pancho stood up and, with his hands in his pockets, still frowning, strolled forward, veered toward the jukebox just to the right of Alejandro, then furtively motioned for Alejandro to step back from the door. Alejandro stepped back into the alley.

"Go home!" Pancho whispered. "To the house of your parents! By way of the barranca!"

Alejandro smiled, but Pancho had turned away and was already strolling back to Antonio.

"Alejandro! Coming in?" someone yelled.

Still smiling, Alejandro waved a hand in a general good-bye, and walked back down the alley. Go home to the house of his parents, indeed, and by the back way? Not on the night before the great trip. He didn't care to get into a fight with Antonio, so he'd give up Cesar's tonight, but back to that mud hovel his parents lived in?

It happened at the foot of the steep lane that led to his big house. Two figures stepped out of the shadows only inches away from his shoulders, and simultaneously they struck at his back. The impact nearly pitched him forward on his face, and when he staggered upright again, he felt he was going to faint.

"*'Ey!*" he called, but they had already disappeared, on the run.

Then the cobblestones came up and hit him in the face. He crawled around, trying to rise, murmuring for help, for someone, anyone. Then, after a long time, two men came and with loud voices lifted him up and asked him questions.

"To the house of my parents," Alejandro said in a voice as weak as a whisper. He waved a hand in a certain direction, and he spoke in Spanish. He was dying. No doubt of it. Dying, and there would be no more honeymoon, no more pesos to spend, no more American girls. As the men bore him away, he thought of Antonio sitting at the very table in Cesar's where he and *la contesa* . . .

His mother, who undressed him in the hut, found the wounds in his back. Then she called to her husband, who had been standing outside while she did the work of undressing and washing the body. When her husband opened the door, the music of an American dance tune came louder from the hotel on the hill. She pointed to the two tiny spots of blood on either side of Alejandro's spine. He had been killed by the daggers with square, notched blades that close up the flesh when they are withdrawn, so there is almost no bleeding. In between her sobs, the American dance music came. Finally, the man went to the window and closed the shutter against it, but still the music came.

A few minutes later, they heard a hesitant knock at the door. Alejandro's mother opened the door cautiously, a candle in her hand. She saw an American woman, a very ugly American woman of about fifty years.

"What do you wish?" she asked politely.

"Is Alejandro here?" the woman asked in heavily accented Spanish.

The mother hesitated. "He is here. Who are you, if I may ask you?"

She knew how to say it. She remembered it from the day of the wedding. "I am his wife," she said.

Then Alejandro's mother slowly raised her hands, the candle dropped, and she let out a wailing, insane scream that reached all the way to the village, and echoed and reechoed across the black hills.

# THE GREAT CARDHOUSE

Lucien Montlehuc started a little when he saw the notice. He read it twice, slowly, and then, as if he finally believed it, put down his newspaper and removed his monocle. A habitual expression of amusement returned to his face, and his lids fluttered over his bright blue eyes. "Imagine Gaston Potin taken in by it!" he said to himself. "Of all people to be fooled!"

This thought made him even more gleeful. It would not be the first time that he had proven Gaston Potin wrong. This particular Giotto was a forgery, and Gaston was putting it up for sale as a genuine. Lucien meant to have it, and the sale was that very afternoon. How fortunate he had been to see the notice in time! The magnificent counterfeit might have slipped through his fingers again.

Lucien put his monocle back in the grip of his slightly protruding brow, summoned François and ordered him to pack their bags for an overnight stay in Aix-en-Provence. While he waited, he turned to *The Revelation to the Shepherds* in his book of Giotto reproductions and studied it. Again he thought how odd it was that poor Gaston Potin would not have suspected it to be a forgery. Perhaps it was the too-rigid faces of the kneeling shepherds that told him the painting was not from Giotto's hand. There was no real religious feeling there. The annunciatory angel's robe was a too-brilliant pink. The composition itself was not right, not Giotto—but it *was* magnificent, as a forgery. Lucien did not need a magnifying glass to detect a forgery. Something within him, some inner sensory apparatus, betrayed the spurious instantly and always. It never failed.

Besides, hadn't an Englishman, Sir Ronald Dunsenny, questioned the authenticity of this *Revelation* around the time of the Fruehlingen purchase? Indeed, Sir Ronald had ventured that the original had been destroyed in a fire in the middle of the eighteenth century! Evidently Gaston Potin didn't know that.

It was Lucien's passion to collect the most perfect imitations, and only the imitations, of the great artists. He did not want genuine paintings. And he prided himself that his sham masterpieces were such fine shams that any could, if presented as the original, fool the eyes of the most astute dealers and critics in the world.

Lucien had played many such tricks during the fifteen years he had been collecting forgeries. He might submit one of his forgeries as a loan from an individual who owned the original, for instance, then attend the exhibition and remark his suspicions publicly, to be proven right in the end, of course. Twice he had subjected Gaston Potin—with his great reputation as an art dealer—to such embarrassment. And once, Lucien had made Gaston uneasy about an original by presenting one of his forgeries that was so good it had taken six experts three days to decide which picture *was* the original. All in all, it had caused Gaston Potin to refer scathingly to Lucien's well-known collection and to his lamentable taste for the bogus. Lamentable to whom? Lucien wondered. And why? His pranks had cost him a few friendships, perhaps, but then he cared as little for friendship as he cared for the true Leonardos, the true Renis, the true anything: friendship and bona fide masterpieces were too natural, too easy, too boring. Not that he actually disliked people, and people liked Lucien well enough, but if friendship threatened, Lucien withdrew.

His six-million-franc Delahaye sped along the Route Napoleon from Paris toward Aix at a hundred kilometers an hour. Plane trees in full leaf, their smooth bark peeling in purplish, pink, and beige patches, flickered by at the edges of the road like picket fences. A landscape of dusky orange and green and tan, the occasional blue of a farmer's cart—a landscape as beautifully composed as a Gobelin tapestry—unfolded continuously on right and left, but Lucien had no eye for it. Nature's creations did not interest him compared to man's, and his stocky body sat deep in the seat of the car. Today there was the Fruehlingen Giotto to think about, and he looked forward to the auction with the keen, single-minded anticipation of a hunter or a lover. Merely for Lucien Montlehuc to bid for a painting meant that the painting was, or most likely was, a counterfeit, and would in this case immediately throw suspicion upon Gaston, who was sponsoring the auction. Some of the audience at Aix might think he was trying to play another trick on Gaston, of course, by bidding. So much the better when the experts confirmed the falsity after the picture was his.

• • •

"Excellent snails," Lucien remarked with satisfaction, his pink cheeks glowing after his luncheon. He and François walked quickly to the car.

"Excellent, monsieur," François replied agreeably. His good humor reflected that of his master. François was tall and lean and congenitally lazy, though he never failed to carry out an order from Lucien. He had not forgotten that he had once been earmarked for execution by the Spanish government for being in possession of a false passport. Because François had been amused and cool about the whole thing, he had won Lucien's admiration, and Lucien had managed to buy his freedom. Since then François, actually a Russian who had escaped to Czechoslovakia with a price on his head, had lived in France, safe and content to be alive and in Lucien's employ.

Lucien himself had once lived in Czechoslovakia. In 1926, most European papers had carried an account of a very young Captain Lucas Minchovik, a soldier of fortune who had been severely wounded in a skirmish on the Yugoslav border. Years ago, in Czechoslovakia, people had sometimes asked him about the 1926 report, the young captain's heroism having made the story memorable, but Lucien had always disclaimed any knowledge of it. It had been another soldier of the same name, he said. Finally, he had changed his name and come to France.

In Aix, Lucien and François stopped first at the Hôtel des Étrangers to reserve a three-room suite, then drove on to the Musée de Tapisserie beside the Cathedral Saint-Sauveur. The auction was to be held in the open court of the *musée*, and was scheduled to begin in half an hour, but things in Aix were always late. Cars of all sizes and manufacture cluttered the narrow streets around the cathedral, and the courtyard was a bedlam of hurrying workmen and chattering agents and dealers and private buyers who had not yet begun to seat themselves.

"Do you see M. Potin?" Lucien asked François, who was a good deal taller than Lucien.

"No, monsieur."

An acquaintance of Lucien's, a dealer from Strasbourg, told him that M. Potin was giving a luncheon at his villa just outside the town, and that he had not yet arrived.

Lucien decided to pay Gaston Potin a visit. He was eager to let Gaston know of his interest in the Giotto. As they drew up to Gaston's Villa Madeleine, Lucien heard the treble notes of a piano from within. Faint but bell-like, it was a Scarlatti sonata. He was shown into the hall by a servant. Through the open door of the salon, Lucien saw a slender woman seated at the piano, and a score of men and a few women standing or sitting motionless, listening to her. Lucien paused at the threshold, adjusted his monocle, and espied Gaston just behind the piano, concentrating on the music with an expression of rapt and sentimental enjoyment. Lucien's eyes swept the rest of the company. They were all here—Font-Martigue of the Dauberville Gallery in Paris, Fritz Heber of Vienna, Martin Palmer of London. Certainly the cream.

And they were all listening to the sonata—with the same absorption as Gaston. Lucien's appearance in the doorway had not even been noticed. The fast movement the woman was playing was splendid indeed. The notes sparkled from her fingers like drops of pure springwater. But to Lucien's ear, which was as infallible as his eye, an ingredient was missing—a pleasure in the performance. It was audible to Lucien that she detested Scarlatti, if not music itself. Lucien smiled. Could she really be holding the company as spellbound as it looked? But of course she was. How obtuse people were, even those who professed a knowledge of the arts! There was a perfect crash of applause from the little audience when she finished.

Lucien saw Gaston coming toward him with the pianist on his arm. Gaston smiled at Lucien as if the music had made him forget that there had ever been unpleasantnesses between them.

"Very happy and surprised to see you, Lucien!" Gaston said. "May I present the music teacher of my childhood—Mlle. Claire Duhamel of Aix."

"*Enchanté, mademoiselle*," said Lucien. He observed with satisfaction the stir of interest his entry into the salon had caused.

"She plays superbly, doesn't she?" Gaston went on. "She has just been asked to give a series of concerts in Paris, but she has refused, *n'est-ce pas*, Mlle. Claire? Aix should not be deprived of your music for so long!"

Lucien smiled politely, then said, "I learned of your sale only this morning, Gaston. Why didn't you send me an announcement?"

"Because I was sure there is nothing here that would interest you. These are all authentic pictures of my own choosing."

"But *The Revelation to the Shepherds* interests me enormously!" Lucien told him with a smile. "I don't suppose if it's here you might let me see it now."

Behind Gaston's frank surprise, there was just the least alarm. "But with the greatest pleasure, Lucien. Follow me."

Mlle. Duhamel, who had been gazing at Lucien all the while, checked him with the question, "Are you an admirer of Giotto, too, M. Montlehuc?"

Lucien looked at her. She was a typical *vieille femme*—an old maid—of a Provencal town, drab and shy, yet with an air of tenacious purpose in her own narrow, cramped way of life, a look of wiry vigor that suggested a plant growing at the edge of a wind-whipped cliff. Gentle, sad gray eyes looked out of her small face with such depression of spirit that one wanted to turn away immediately, because of an inability to help her. A less attractive person Lucien could not have imagined. "Yes, mademoiselle," he said, and hurried after Gaston.

Lucien's first sight of the picture brought that leap of excitement and recognition that only the finest forgeries gave him. From the patina, he judged the picture to be more than two hundred years old. And today it would be his.

"You see?" Gaston smiled confidently.

Lucien sighed, in mock defeat. "I see. A beautiful piece indeed. My congratulations, Gaston."

• • •

Lucien attended the auction in the subdued manner of one who watches from the outside, a bystander. He waited with impatience while an indifferent Messina and a miserable "Ignoto Veneziano" from the Fruehlingen collection were put up and sold. Apart from the false Giotto, Lucien thought mischievously, the Barons von Fruehlingen did have execrable taste!

Mlle. Duhamel, on a bench against the side wall, was again staring at him, he noticed, with what thoughts behind her quiet gray eyes, he could not guess. Lucien found something disturbing, something arrogantly omniscient in her scrutiny. For an instant, he resented her fiercely and unreasonably. Lucien removed his monocle and passed his fingertips lightly across his lids. When he looked up again, the *Revelation* was on the dais.

A man whom Lucien could not see bid a million new francs.

"A million and a half," said Lucien calmly. He was in the last row.

Heads turned to look at him. There was a murmur as the crowd recognized Lucien Montlehuc.

"Two million!" cried the same unseen bidder.

"Two million ten thousand," replied Lucien, intending to provoke laughter, as he did, by the insultingly small raise. He heard the sibilant whisper of "Lucien" among the crowd. Someone laughed, a sardonic laugh that made a corner of Lucien's mouth go up in response. Lucien knew from the rising hum that people had begun to ask one another if the Giotto were indisputably genuine.

The unseen bidder stood up. It was Font-Martigue of Paris. His bald head turned its eagle profile for a moment to glance at Lucien coldly. "Three million."

Lucien also stood up. "Three million five hundred."

"Three million seven," replied Font-Martigue, more to Lucien than to the auctioneer.

Lucien raised it to three million eight hundred and Font-Martigue to four million.

"And a hundred thousand," added Lucien.

At this rate, the figure might be driven beyond the price of a genuine Giotto, but Lucien did not care. The joke on Gaston would be worth it. And the audience was wavering already. Only Font-Martigue was bidding. Everyone knew that Gaston Potin had been wrong a few times, but Lucien never.

"Four million two hundred thousand," said Font-Martigue.

"Four million three," said Lucien.

The audience tittered. Lucien wished he could see Gaston at this moment, but he couldn't. Gaston was doubtless in the front row with his back to Lucien. A pity. It was no longer a contest of bidding. It had become a contest of faith versus nonfaith, of believer versus nonbeliever. Fifteen meters away on the dais the *Revelation* stood like a reliquary in its golden-leaf frame, a reliquary of the divine fire of art—as each of them saw it.

"Four million four," said Font-Martigue in a tone of finality.

"Four million five," Lucien promptly replied.

Font-Martigue folded his arms and sat down.

The auctioneer rapped. "Four million five hundred thousand new francs?"

Lucien smiled. Who could afford to outbid him when he wanted something?

"Four million six," said a voice on Lucien's left.

A man who looked like a young Charles de Gaulle leaned forward on his knees, focusing his attention on the auctioneer. Lucien knew the type, the de Gaulle type indeed, another believer, an idealist. He was in for five million francs at least.

Five minutes later, the auctioneer pronounced *The Revelation to the Shepherds* the property of Lucien Montlehuc for the sum of five million two hundred and fifty thousand new francs.

Lucien came forward immediately to write his check and to take possession.

"My congratulations, Lucien," Gaston Potin said. His forehead was damp with perspiration, but he managed a bewildered smile. "A genuine work of art at last. The only one in your collection, I'm sure."

"What is genuine?" Lucien asked. "Is art genuine? What is more sincere than imitation, Gaston?"

"Do you mean to say you think this painting is a forgery?"

"If it is not, I shall give it back to you. What would I want with it if it were genuine? You know, though, you should not have represented it as a genuine painting. It ran my price up."

Gaston's face was growing pink. "There are a dozen men here who could prove you wrong, Lucien."

"I invite them to prove me wrong," Lucien said courteously. "Seriously, Gaston, ask them to come to my suite at the Hôtel des Étrangers for aperitifs this afternoon. Let them bring their magnifying glasses and their history books. At six o'clock: May I expect you?"

"You *may*," said Gaston Potin.

Lucien walked out of the courtyard to his waiting car. François had already strapped the *Revelation* carefully between the seat back and the spare tire. Lucien happened to look behind him as he reached the car. He saw Mlle. Duhamel walking slowly from the doorway of the courtyard toward him, and he felt a throb in his chest, a strange premonition. Sunlight, broken into droplets by the trees, played like silent music over her moving figure, light and quick as her own fingers had played in Gaston's salon. He remembered his feeling, as he listened to her Scarlatti sonata, that she loathed playing it. And yet to play so brilliantly! That took a kind of genius, Lucien thought. He was aware suddenly of a great respect for Mlle. Duhamel, and of something else, something he could not identify, perhaps compassion. It pained him that anyone with Mlle. Duhamel's ability should take so little joy in it, that she should look so crushed, so agonizingly self-effacing.

"Do you know that I am receiving some friends at six o'clock this afternoon, Mlle. Duhamel?" Lucien said with an unwonted awkwardness as she came closer. "I should be honored if you would join us."

Mlle. Duhamel accepted with pleasure.

"Come a little early, if you will."

• • •

"Five million two hundred and fifty thousand francs for a counterfeit," Mlle. Duhamel whispered with awe. She sat on the edge of a chair in the salon of Lucien's suite, gazing at the picture Lucien had leaned against the divan.

Lucien strolled back and forth before her, smiling, smoking a Turkish cigarette. François had gone out a few moments before to fetch Cinzano and pâté and biscuits, and now they were alone. Mlle. Duhamel had been surprised, but not overly surprised, when he told her the Giotto was a forgery. Her reaction had been exactly right. And now she regarded the picture with the respect that was due it.

"One usually pays more dearly for the false than for the true, mademoiselle," Lucien said, feeling expansive in his hour of triumph. "This hair I touch, for instance," he said, patting the top of his light brown, gently waving hair, "is a toupee, the finest that Paris can make. Grown by nature, it would have cost nothing. Strictly speaking, it would have been worthless. It *is* worthless, to a man with hair of his own. But when I must buy it to hide a deficiency of nature, I must pay a hundred and fifty thousand francs for it. And it is a just price, when one thinks of the skill and labor that went into its creation." Lucien swept off his toupee and held it in his hand, lustrous side uppermost. His bald crown was a healthy pink-tan, like his face, and really detracted little from the liveliness of his appearance, which was extraordinary for his age. The bald head was a surprise, that was all.

"I had no idea you wore a toupee, M. Montlehuc."

Lucien eyed her sharply. He thought he saw amusement in her tilted head. She had one element of charm, he conceded; she had humor. "And applying this same principle to the false Giotto," Lucien continued, inspired by Mlle. Duhamel's attention, "we might say Giotto's genius was a thing of nature, too, a gift of the gods, perhaps, but certainly a faculty which cost him nothing, and in a sense cost him no effort, since he created as every artist creates, out of necessity. But consider the poor mortal who created this almost perfect imitation. Think of his travail in reproducing every stroke of the master exactly! Consider *his* effort!"

Mlle. Duhamel was absorbing every word. "Yes," she said.

"You understand then why I value the imitators so highly, or rather give them their proper value?"

"I understand," she answered.

Lucien felt perhaps she did. "And you, Mlle. Duhamel, may I say that is why I find you so valuable? You have a superb talent for deceiving. Your performance of Scarlatti this afternoon was by no means inferior to the best—technically. It was inferior in only one respect." He hesitated, wondering if he dared go on.

"Yes?" Mlle. Duhamel prompted, a little fearfully.

"You hated it, didn't you?"

She looked down at her slim, tense hands in her lap, hands that were still as smooth and flexible as a young girl's. "Yes. Yes, I hated it. I hate music. It's—" She stopped. Her eyes had grown shiny with tears, but she held her head up and the tears did not drop.

Lucien smiled nervously. He was not good at comforting people, but he wanted to comfort Mlle. Duhamel and did not know how to begin. "What a silly thing to cry about!" he burst out. "Such a talent! You play exquisitely! Why, if you could endure the boredom—and I really admire you for not being able to endure it—you might play in concerts all over the world! I daresay not a music critic in a thousand would recognize your real feelings. And what would he do if he did? Make some trifling comment that's all. But your playing would enchant millions and millions of people. Just as my forgeries could enchant millions and millions of people." He laughed and, before he realized what he did, put out his hand and pressed her thin shoulder affectionately.

She shuddered under his touch and relaxed in her chair. She seemed to shrink until she was nothing but that small, unhappy core of herself. "You are the only one who has ever known," she said. "It was my father who made me study music as a child and as a young girl, study and study until I had no time to do anything else—even to make a friend. My father was organist of the church here in Aix. He wanted me to be a concert pianist, but I knew I never could be, because I hated music too much. And finally—I was thirty-eight when my father died—it was too late to think of marriage. So I stayed on in the village, earning my living in the only way I could, by teaching music. And how ashamed I am! To pretend to love what I hate! To teach others to love what I hate—the piano!"

Her voice trailed off on "piano" like a plaintive sob itself.

"You fooled Gaston," Lucien reminded her, smiling. An excitement, a joy of life was rising in him. He could not stand still. He wanted—he did not know exactly what he wanted to do, except to convince Mlle. Duhamel that she was wrong to feel ashamed, wrong to torture herself inwardly. "Don't you see it isn't at all logical," he began, "to take seriously something you were never serious about in the first place?—Look, mademoiselle!" With a graceful movement, Lucien removed his right hand. He held the detached and perfectly natural-looking right hand in his left. His right arm ended in an empty white cuff.

Mille. Duhamel gasped.

"You never suspected that, did you?" asked Lucien, grinning like a schoolboy who has brought off a practical joke with success.

"No." Obviously, Mlle. Duhamel hadn't suspected that.

"You see, it's exactly the mate of the left, and by certain movements which have now become automatic, I can give the impression that my useless hand cooperates with the other." Lucien replaced his hand quickly.

"Why, it's like a miracle!" Mlle. Duhamel said.

"A miracle of modern plastics, that's all. And my right foot, I might add, too." Lucien pulled up his trouser leg a few inches, though there was nothing to be seen but a normal-looking black shoe and sock. "I was wounded once, literally blown apart, but should I have crept about the world like a crab, disgusting everyone, an object of horror and pity? Life is to be enjoyed, is it not? Life is to give and take pleasure, is it not? You give pleasure, Mlle. Duhamel. It remains only for you to take it!" Lucien gave a great laugh that was so truly out of his heart, that rolled so solidly from his broad chest, Mlle. Duhamel began to smile, too.

Then she laughed. At first, her laugh was no more than a feeble crack, like the opening of a door that had been closed for an incalculable length of time. But the laugh grew, seemed to reach out in all directions, like a separate being taking form, taking courage.

"And my ear!" Lucien went on with delight. "It wasn't necessary to have two ears to hear what I heard in your music, mademoiselle. An excellent match, is it not, of my left ear? But not too perfect, because ears are never exactly alike." He could not remove his grafted right ear, but he pinched it and winked at her. "And my right eye—I will spare you that, but suffice it to say that it's made of glass. People often speak of my 'magic monocle' when they mention my uncanny judgments. I wear the monocle as a joke, by way of adding an insult to an injury, as the English would say. Can you tell the difference between my eyes, Mlle. Duhamel?" Lucien bent forward and looked into her gray eyes that were beginning to glow behind the tears.

"Indeed, I cannot," she told him.

Lucien beamed with satisfaction. "Did I say my foot? My entire *leg* is of hollow plastic!" Lucien struck his thigh with a pencil he picked up from the table, and it gave a hollow report. "But does it stop me from dancing? And did anyone ever suggest that I limp? I don't limp. Shall I go on?" His affirmative clap of laughter came again.

Mlle. Duhamel looked at him, fascinated. "I've never—"

"Needles to say, my teeth!" Lucien interrupted her. "I had scarcely three whole teeth left after my injury. I was a young man then. But that doesn't matter, I saved my employer's life, and he rewarded me with a trust fund that enables me to spend my life in luxury. Anyway, my teeth are the product of an artist in deception, a Japanese whose ingenuity and powers of depiction certainly rank him with the great Leonardo. His name is Tao Mishugawa, but few on earth will ever hear of him. My teeth are full of faults, of course, like real ones. Every so often, just to deceive myself, I go to Tao and have some more fillings or an inlay put in. Tell me, mademoiselle, did you suspect?"

"I certainly did not," she assured him sincerely.

"If I could remove every artificial part of myself including the silver shin of my other leg and my plastic ribs, there wouldn't be much left of me, would there? Except the spirit. There would be *that* even more than now, I think! Does it seem strange to you that I speak of the spirit, Mlle. Duhamel?"

"Not at all. Of course it doesn't."

"I knew it wouldn't. There was no need to ask. You, too, are among the great in spirit, who respond to challenge and make nature appear niggardly. Your hours of tortured practice at the piano are not lost, mademoiselle. Not because of these words I say to you, but because you gave pleasure to a score of people this afternoon. Because you are able to give pleasure!"

Mlle, Duhamel looked down at her hands again, but now there was a flush of her own pleasure in her cheeks.

"The critics and the art dealers call me a dilettante, the idiots! That I am an artist escapes them, of course. Let it! They are the real dilettanti, the do-nothings. You understand me because you are like me, Mlle. Duhamel, but all those who sneer, who stare, who laugh at me and envy and admire me at once because I am not ashamed to confess what I love— And here they are now!"

Someone had rapped on the door.

Lucien glanced at his watch. François was having trouble finding the right kind of pâté, perhaps. Lucien did not like to answer his door himself.

Mlle. Duhamel stood up. "May I open the door for your guests?"

Lucien stared at her. She looked taller than before, and almost—he could hardly believe it—happy. The glow he had seen in her gray eyes seemed to have spread through her entire body. Lucien, too, felt a happiness he had never known before. Perhaps the kind of happiness an artist feels after creating something, he thought, an artist whose talent is given by nature.

"I should be honored," Lucien said.

• • •

Gaston had come, and with him four other dealers, one of whom carried a picture which Lucien recognized as Giotto's *Magi in Bethlehem* from a private collection. Lucien greeted them hospitably. Then more people arrived, and finally François with the refreshments. The man with the picture set it next to Lucien's against the divan, and all got out their magnifying glasses.

"I assure you, you possess an original," Gaston said cheerfully to Lucien. "Not that you didn't pay a fitting price for it." All of Gaston's confidence had returned.

Lucien gestured with his false hand at the group beside the divan. "The experts have not said so yet, have they? Let their magnifying glasses discover what I can see with my naked eyes." He strolled off toward Mlle. Duhamel and M. Palissy, who were talking in a corner of the room. How charming she looked, Lucien thought. A half hour ago, she would have been afraid to use her beautiful hands to gesture as she spoke.

Gaston intercepted Lucien before he reached Mlle. Duhamel. "You agree that this picture is genuine, Lucien?" he said, pointing to the picture the dealer had brought.

"Certainly," said Lucien, "That *Magi*—a careless piece of work, I've always thought, but certainly genuine."

"Examine the brushstrokes, Lucien. Compare them with the brushstrokes on your picture. It's so obvious, a child could see it. There is a fault in the brush that he used to paint the backgrounds of both pictures, a couple of bristles that made a scratch here and there. Evidently these pictures were painted at about the same time. It's the general opinion that they were, you know." Gaston stooped down beside the pictures. "One doesn't even need a magnifying glass to see it. But I had some photographs made and enlarged, just to be sure. Here they are, Lucien."

Lucien ignored the photographs on the divan. He could see it, with his good eye; a hair-line scratch here and there with an even finer scratch beside it, the scratches of a single brushstroke, made by the same brush. It was the same in both pictures, like a pattern, obvious enough when one looked for it, yet not obvious enough to be worthy of forging. Lucien's head grew swimmy. For an instant, he felt only a keen discomfort. He was aware that the eyes of everyone in the room were upon him as he bent over the two pictures. Most painfully of all, he was aware of Mlle. Duhamel. He felt he had failed her. He had been proven fallible.

"Now you see," said Gaston calmly, without malice, merely as if he were pointing out something that Lucien might have seen from the first.

Lucien felt as if a house of cards were tumbling down inside him, all that was himself, in fact. He could see now, looking at the picture he had believed to be false, that a misconception—a quick, initial misconception—was possible. Just as it would have been equally possible to judge the picture correctly, as he did now, and to sense that it was genuine. But he had made the misjudgment.

Lucien turned to the room. "I admit my error," he said, his tongue as dry as ashes.

He had expected laughter, but there was only a murmur, a kind of sigh in the room. He would rather they had laughed at him. No, at least there was one exchange of smiles, one nod of satisfaction from Font-Martigue that Lucien Montlehuc could be wrong. Lucien would have felt quite lost if he had not seen it. Yet no one seemed to realize the catastrophe that was taking place inside him. The great cardhouse was still falling. For the first time in his life, he felt near tears. He had a vision of himself without his artifices, without his arrogant faith in his infallibility—a piece of a man, unable even to stand upright, a miserable fragment. For a few moments, Lucien's spirit bore the full weight of reality, and almost broke beneath it.

"If you'd like to sell it back, of course, Lucien," Gaston's voice said kindly, distantly, whispering into the false ear, "I'll pay you the same price—"

"No. No, thank you, Gaston." Now he was being unreasonable to boot! What did he want with a genuine painting? Lucien stumbled toward Mlle. Duhamel. He stumbled on his artificial leg.

Mlle. Duhamel's face was as calm as if nothing had happened. "Why don't you tell them you were pretending?" she asked him, out of hearing of the others. "Why don't you pretend the whole afternoon was a great joke?"

Her face was even victorious, Lucien thought. He looked at it for a long moment, trying to draw strength from it, and failing. "But I wasn't joking," he said.

Then the guests were gone. Only he and Mlle. Duhamel remained. And the genuine Giotto. François, who had witnessed his master's defeat, standing in the background like a silent tragic chorus, had excused himself last of all and gone out.

Lucien sat down heavily on the divan.

"I shall keep the painting," Lucien said slowly, and with quiet, profound bitterness. He did not recognize his own voice, though he recognized that it was his real voice. It was the voice of the fragment of a man. "It will be the one original that will spoil the purity of my forgeries. Nothing in life is pure. Nothing is one thing and nothing more. Nothing is absolute. When I was a young man, I believed no bullet would ever touch me. And then one day I was struck by a grenade. I thought I could never misjudge a painting. And today a public misjudgment!"

"But didn't you know that nothing is absolute? Why, even my kitten knows that much!"

Lucien glanced at Mlle. Duhamel with the fiercest impatience. He had scarcely been aware of her the past few moments. Now he resented her presence as much as he had when she had spoken to him first in Gaston's salon.

She was standing by the little three-legged console table where lay her green string gloves and her big square pocketbook that was as flat as her own body. She looked at him anxiously, as if she were puzzled for a moment as to what to do. Then she came toward him, sat down beside him on the divan, and took his hand in hers. It happened to be his false hand, but she betrayed no surprise, if she felt any. She held his hand affectionately, as if it were real.

Lucien started to take his hand away, but only sighed instead. What did it matter? But then, with the touch he could not feel, he realized another misjudgment, a much older one. He had thought he could never feel close to any human being, never allow himself to be close.

But now he did feel close to Mlle. Duhamel. He felt closer to her than François, the only other person who knew of the great cardhouse that was Lucien Montlehuc. François had not suffered as Mlle. Duhamel had suffered, the idiot. It was a tenderness he felt for Mlle. Duhamel, and admiration. She lived within a cardhouse, too. Yet, if nothing was absolute, a cardhouse was not absolute, either. He might rebuild it, but it would never be perfect, and had never been perfect. How stupid he had been! He who had always prided himself that he knew the imperfections of everything, even art. Lucien looked down in wonder at his and Mlle. Duhamel's clasped hands. It had been so many years since he had had a friend.

His heart began to thump like a lover's. How pleasant it would be, Lucien thought suddenly, to have Mlle. Duhamel in his home, to have her play for him and his guests, to give her luxuries that she had never been able to afford. Lucien smiled, for the thought had only flitted across his mind like the shadow of a bird across the grass. Marriage, indeed! Hadn't he just realized that nothing was ever perfect? Why should he try to better what couldn't be bettered—the happiness he felt with Mlle. Duhamel at this instant?

"Mlle. Duhamel, would you consider being my friend?" Lucien asked, more seriously, he realized abashedly, than most men ask women to be their wives. "Would you consider friendship with a man who is sincere only at the core of his ambiguous heart and in the way he wishes to be a friend to you? A man whose very right hand is false?"

Mlle. Duhamel murmured adoringly, "I was just thinking that I held a hero's hand."

Lucien sat up a little. The words had taken him completely by surprise. "A hero's hand," he said sarcastically, but not without contentment.

# THE BABY SPOON

Claude Lamm, Professor of English Literature and Poetry, had been on the faculty of Columbia University for ten years. Short and inclined to plumpness, with a bald spot in the middle of his close-cropped black hair, he did not look like a college professor, but rather like a small businessman hiding for some reason in the clothes he thought a college professor should wear—good tweed jackets with leather patches on the elbows, unpressed gray flannels and unshined shoes of any sort. He lived in one of the great dreary apartment buildings that clump east and south of Columbia University, a gloomy, ash-colored building with a shaky elevator and an ugly miscellany of smells old and new inside it. Claude Lamm rendered his sunless, five-room apartment still more somber by cramming it with sodden-looking sofas, with books and periodicals and photographs of classic edifices and landscapes about which he professed to be sentimental but actually was not.

Seven years ago he had married Margaret Cullen, one of those humdrum, colorless individuals who look as if they might be from anywhere except New York and turn out, incredibly, to be native New Yorkers. She was fifty, eight years older than Claude, with a plain, open countenance and an air of desperate inferiority. Claude had met her through another professor who knew Margaret's father, and had married her because of certain unconscious drives in himself towards the maternal. But under Margaret's matronly exterior lay a nature that was half childish, too, and peculiarly irritating to Claude. Apart from her cooking and sewing—she did neither well—and the uninspired routine that might be called the running of the house, she had no interests. Except for an occasional exchange of letters, which she bored

Claude by reading aloud at the table, she had detached herself from her old friends.

Claude came home about five most afternoons, had some tea and planned his work and reading for the evening. At 6:15, he drank a martini without ice and read the evening paper in the living room, while Margaret prepared their early dinner. They dined on shoulder lamb chops or meat loaf, often on cheese and macaroni, which Margaret was fond of, and Margaret stirred her coffee with the silver baby spoon she had used the first evening Claude had met her, holding the spoon by the tip end of the handle in order to reach the bottom of the cup. After dinner, Claude retired to his study—a book-glutted cubicle with an old black leather couch in it, although he did not sleep here—to read and correct papers and to browse in his bookshelves for anything that piqued his aimless curiosity.

Every two weeks or so, he asked Professor Millikin, a Shakespeare scholar, or Assistant Professor George and his wife to come to dinner. Three or four times a year, the apartment was thrown open to about twelve students from his special readings classes, who came and ate Dundee cake and drank tea. Margaret would sit on a cushion on the floor, because there were never enough chairs, and of course one young man after another would offer his chair to her. "Oh, no, thank you!" Margaret would protest with a lisping coyness quite unlike her usual manner, "I'm perfectly comfortable here. Sitting on the floor makes me feel like a little girl again." She would look up at the young men as if she expected them to tell her she looked like a little girl, too, which to Claude's disgust the young men sometimes did. The little girl mood always came over Margaret in the company of men, and always made Claude sneer when he saw it. Claude sneered easily and uncontrollably, hiding it unconsciously in the act of putting his cigarette holder between his teeth, or rubbing the side of his nose with a forefinger. Claude had keen, suspicious brown eyes. No feature of his face was remarkable, but it was not a face one forgot either. It was the restlessness, the furtiveness in his face that one noticed first and remembered. At the teas, Margaret would use her baby spoon, too, which as likely as not would start a conversation. Then Claude would move out of hearing.

Claude did not like the way the young men looked at his wife—

disappointedly, a little pityingly, always solemnly. Claude was ashamed of her before them. She should have been beautiful and gay, a nymph of the soul, a fair face that would accord with the love poems of Donne and Sidney. Well, she wasn't.

Claude's marriage to Margaret might have been comparable to a marriage to his housekeeper, if not for emotional entanglements that made him passionately hate her as well as passionately need her. He hated her childishness with a vicious, personal resentment. He hated almost as much her competent, maternal ministerings to him, her taking his clothes to the cleaners, for instance; which was all he tolerated her for, he knew, and why he had her now instead of his nymph. When he had been down with flu one winter and Margaret had waited on him hand and foot, he had sneered often at her retreating back, hating her, really hating her obsequious devotion to him. Claude had despised his mother and she, too, between periods of neglect and erratic ill-temper, had been capable of smothering affection and attention. But the nearest he came to expressing his hatred was when he announced casually, once a week or oftener:

"Winston's coming over for a while tonight."

"Oh," Margaret would reply with a tremor in her voice. "Well, I suppose he'd like some of the raisin cake later. Or maybe a sandwich of the meat loaf."

Winston loved to eat at Claude's house. Or rather, he was always hungry. Winston was a genuinely starving poet who lived in a genuine garret at the top of a brownstone house in the West Seventies. He had been a student of Claude's three years ago, a highly promising student whose brilliant, aggressive mind had so dominated his classmates that the classes had been hardly more than conversations between Claude and Winston. Claude was immensely fond of Winston and flattered by Winston's fondness for him. From the first, it had excited Claude in a strange and pleasant way to catch Winston's smile, Winston's wink even, the glint of mad humor in his eyes, in the midst of Winston's flurry of words in class. While at Columbia, Winston had published several poems in poetry magazines and literary magazines. He had written a poem called "The Booming Bittern," a mournful satire on an undergraduate's life and directionless rebellion, that Claude had thought might take the place in Winston's career that "Prufrock" had taken in Eliot's. The poem had been published in some quarterly but had attracted no important attention.

Claude had expected Winston to go far and do him credit. Winston had published only one small book of verse since leaving college. Something had happened to Winston's easy, original flow of thought. Something had happened to his self-confidence after leaving college, as if the wells of inspiration were drying up along with the sap and vitality of his twenty-four-year-old body. Winston was thin as a rail now. He had always been thin, but now he slouched, hung his head like a wronged and resentful man, and his eyes under the hard, straight brows looked anxious, hostile and unhappy. He clung to Claude with the persistence of a maltreated child clinging to the one human being who had ever given him kindness and encouragement. Winston was working now on a novel in the form of a long poem. He had submitted part of it to his publishers a year ago, and they had refused to give him an advance. But Claude liked it, and Winston's attitude was, the rest of the world be damned. Claude was keenly aware of Winston's emotional dependence upon him, and managed to hide his own dependence upon Winston in a superior, patronizing manner that he assumed with Winston. Claude's hostility to Margaret found some further release in the contempt that Winston openly showed for her intellect.

One evening, more than usually late in arriving, Winston slouched into the living room without a reply to Claude's greeting. He was a head and a half taller than Claude, even stooped, his dark brown hair untidy with wind and rain, his overcoat clutched about his splinter of a body by the hands that were rammed into his pockets. Slowly and without a glance at Margaret, Winston walked across the living room towards Claude's study.

Claude was a little annoyed. This was a mood he didn't know.

"Listen, old man, can you lend me some money?" Winston asked when they were alone in the study, then went on over Claude's surprised murmur, "You've no idea what it took for me to come here and ask you, but now it's done, anyway." He sighed heavily.

Claude had a sudden feeling it hadn't taken anything, and that the despondent mood was only playacting. "You know I've always let you have money if you needed it, Winston. Don't take it so seriously. Sit down." Claude sat down.

Winston did not move. His eyes had their usual fierceness, yet there was an impatient pleading in them, too, like the eyes of a child demanding something rightfully his own. "I mean a lot of money. Five hundred dollars. I need it to work on. Five hundred will see me through six weeks, and I can finish my book without any more interruptions."

Claude winced a little. He'd never see the money again if he lent it to Winston. Winston owed him about two hundred now. It occurred to Claude that Winston had not been so intense about anything since his university days. And it also came to him, swiftly and tragically, that Winston would never finish his book. Winston would always be stuck at the anxious, furious pitch he was now, which was contingent upon his not finishing the book.

"You've got to help me out this last time, Claude," Winston said in a begging tone.

"Let me think it over. I'll write you a note about it tomorrow. How's that, fellow?"

Claude got up and went to his desk for a cigarette. Suddenly he hated Winston for standing there begging for money. Like anybody else, Claude thought bitterly. His lip lifted as he set the cigarette holder between his teeth, and Winston saw it, he knew. Winston never missed anything. Why couldn't tonight have been like all the other evenings, Claude thought, Winston smoking his cigarettes, propping his feet on the corner of his desk, Winston laughing and making him laugh, Winston adoring him for all the jibes he threw at the teaching profession?

"You crumb," Winston's voice said steadily. "You fat, smug sonovabitch of a college professor. You stultifier and castrator of the intellect."

Claude stood where he was, half turned away from Winston. The words might have been a blunt ramrod that Winston had thrust through his skull and down to his feet. Winston had never spoken to him like that, and Claude literally did not know how to take it. Claude was not used to reacting to Winston as he reacted to other people. "I'll write you a note about it tomorrow. I'll just have to figure out how and when," he said shortly, with the dignity of a professor whose position, though not handsomely paid, commanded a certain respect.

"I'm sorry," Winston said, hanging his head.

"Winston, what's the matter with you?"

"I don't know." Winston covered his face with his hands.

Claude felt a swift sense of regret, of disappointment at Winston's weakness. He mustn't let Margaret know, he thought. "Sit down."

Winston sat down. He sipped the little glass of whiskey Claude poured from the bottle in his desk as if it were a medicine he desperately needed. Then he sprawled his scarecrow legs out in front of him and said something about a book Claude had lent him the last time he was here, a book of poetry criticism. Claude was grateful for the change of subject. Winston talked with his eyes sleepily half-shut, jerking his big head now and then for emphasis, but Claude could see the glint of interest, of affection, of some indefinable speculation about himself through the half closed lids, and could feel the focus of Winston's intense and personal interest like the life-bringing rays of a sun.

Later, they had coffee and sandwiches and cake in the living room with Margaret. Winston grew very animated and entertained them with a story of his quest for a hotel room in the town of Jalapa in Mexico, a story pulled like an unexpected toy from the hotchpotch of Winston's mind, and by Winston's words set in motion and given a life of its own. Claude felt proud of Winston. "See what I amuse myself with behind the door of my study, while you creep about in the dull prison of your own mind," Claude might have been saying aloud as he glanced at Margaret to see if she were appreciating Winston.

Claude did not write to Winston the next day. Claude felt he was in no more need of money than usual, and that Winston's crisis would pass if he and Winston didn't communicate for a while. Then on the second evening, Margaret told Claude that she had lost her baby spoon. She had looked the house over for it, she said.

"Maybe it fell behind the refrigerator," Claude suggested.

"I was hoping you'd help me move it."

A smile pulled at Claude's mouth as he seesawed the refrigerator away from the wall. He hoped she had lost the spoon. It was a silly thing to treasure at the age of fifty, sillier than her high school scrapbooks and the gilt baby shoe that had sat on her father's desk and that Margaret had so unbecomingly claimed after his death. Claude hoped she had swept the spoon into the garbage by accident and that it was out of the house forever.

"Nothing but dust," Claude said, looking down at the mess of fine, sticky gray dust on the floor and the refrigerator wires.

The refrigerator was only the beginning. Claude's cooperation inspired Margaret. That evening she turned the kitchen inside out, looked behind all the furniture in the living room, even looked in the bathroom medicine cabinet and the clothes hamper.

"It's just not in the house," she kept saying to Claude in a lost way. After another day of searching, she gave up.

Claude heard her telling the woman in the next apartment about it.

"You remember it, I suppose. I think I once showed it to you when we had coffee and cake here."

"Yes, I do remember. That's too bad," said the neighbor.

Margaret told the news-store man, too. It embarrassed Claude painfully as he stood there staring at the rows of candy bars and Margaret said hesitantly to the man she'd hardly dared to speak to before, "I did mean to pay our bill yesterday, but I've been a little distracted. I lost a very old keepsake—an old piece of silver I was very fond of. A baby spoon."

Then at the phrase "an old piece of silver," Claude realized. *Winston* had taken it. Winston might have thought it had some value, or he might have taken it out of malice. He could have palmed it that last night he was at the house. Claude smiled to himself.

Claude had known for years that Winston stole little things—a glass paperweight, an old cigarette lighter that didn't work, a photograph of Claude. Until now, Winston had chosen Claude's possessions. For sentimental reasons, Claude thought. Claude suspected that Winston had a vaguely homosexual attachment to him, and Claude had heard that homosexuals were apt to take something from someone they cared for. What then was more likely than that Winston would take an intimate possession or two from him, which he probably made a fetish of?

Three more days passed without the spoon's turning up, and without a word from Winston. Margaret wrote some letters in the evenings, and Claude knew she was saying in each and every one of them that she had lost her baby spoon and that it was unforgivably careless of her. It was like a confession of some terrible sin that she had to make to everyone. And more, she seemed to want to tell everyone, "Here I stand, bereft." She wanted to hear their words of comfort, their reassuring phrases about such things happening to everybody. Claude had seen her devouring the sympathy the delicatessen woman had offered her. And he saw her anxiety in the way she opened the letter from her sister in Staten Island. Margaret read the letter at the table, and though it didn't say anything about the baby spoon, it put Margaret in better spirits, as if her sister's not mentioning it were a guarantee of her absolution.

Leonard George and his wife Lydia came to dinner one evening, and Margaret told them about the spoon. Lydia, who was by no means stupid but very good at talking about nothing, went on and on about how disquieting the losses of keepsakes were at first, and how unimportant they seemed later. Margaret's face grew gradually less troubled until finally she was smiling. After dinner, she said on her own initiative, "Well, who wants to play some bridge?"

Margaret put on a little lipstick now when they sat down to dinner. It all happened in about ten days. The inevitable pardons she got from people after confessing the loss of her baby spoon seemed to be breaking the barriers between herself and the adult world. Claude began to think he might never see that horrible coyness again when young men came to semester teas. He really ought to thank Winston for it, he supposed. It amused him to think of grasping Winston's hand and thanking him for relieving the household of the accursed baby spoon. He would have to be careful how he did it, because Winston didn't know that he knew about his petty thieveries. But perhaps it was time Winston did. Claude still resented Winston's money-begging and that shocking moment of rudeness the last time he had visited. Yes, Winston wanted bringing into line. He would let Winston know he knew about the spoon, and he would also let him have three hundred dollars.

Winston hadn't yet called, so Claude wrote a note to him, inviting him to dinner Sunday night, and saying he was prepared to lend him three hundred dollars. "Come early so we can have a little talk first," Claude wrote.

Winston was smiling when he arrived, and he was wearing a clean white shirt. But the white collar only accented the grayness of his face, the shadows in his cheeks.

"Working hard?" Claude asked as they went into his study.

"You bet," Winston said. "I want to read you a couple of pages about the subway ride Jake takes." Jake was the main character in Winston's book.

Winston was about to begin reading, when Margaret arrived with a shaker of whiskey sours and a plate of canapés.

"By the way, Winston," Claude began when Margaret had left. "I want to thank you for a little service I think you rendered the last time you were here."

Winston looked at him. "What was that?"

"Did you see anything of a silver spoon, a little silver baby spoon?" Claude asked him with a smile.

Winston's eyes were suddenly wary. "No. No, I didn't."

Winston was guilty, and embarrassed, Claude saw. Claude laughed easily. "Didn't you take it, Winston? I'd be delighted if you did."

"Take it? No, I certainly didn't." Winston started towards the cocktail tray and stopped, frowning harder at Claude, his stooped figure rigid.

"Now look here—" Why had he begun it before Winston had had a couple of cocktails? Claude thought of Winston's hollow stomach and felt as if his words were dropping into it. "Look here, Winston, you know I'm terribly fond of you."

"What's this all about?" Winston demanded, and now his voice shook and he looked completely helpless to conceal his guilt. He half turned round and turned back again, as if guilt pinned his big shoes to the floor.

Claude tipped his head back and drank all his glass. He said with a smile, "You know I know you've taken a few things from me. It couldn't matter to me less. I'm glad you wanted to take them, in fact." He shrugged.

"What things? That's not true, Claude." Winston laid his sprawling hand over the conch shell on the bookcase. He stood upright now, and there was something even militant about his tall figure and the affronted stare he gave Claude.

"Winston, have a drink." Claude wished now that he hadn't begun it. He should have known Winston wouldn't be able to take it. Maybe he had destroyed their friendship—for nothing. Claude wondered if he should try to take it all back, pretend he had been joking. "Have a drink," he repeated.

"But you can't accuse me of being a thief!" Winston said in a horrified tone. And suddenly his body began trembling.

"No, no, you've got the whole thing wrong," Claude said. He walked slowly across the room to get a cigarette from the box on his desk.

"That's what you said, isn't it?" Winston's voice cracked.

"No, I didn't. Now let's sit down and have a drink and forget it." Claude spoke with elaborate casualness, but he knew it sounded patronizing just the same. Maybe Winston *hadn't* stolen the spoon: after all, it belonged to Margaret. Maybe Winston was reacting with guilt because he had taken other things, and he now knew that Claude realized it.

That was his last thought—that he had sounded false and patronizing, that the spoon might have disappeared by some means other than Winston—before the quick step behind him, the brief whir of something moving fast through the air, and the shattering impact at the back of his head caused his arms to fling up in a last empty, convulsive gesture.

# THE PRICE OF SALT

# PART I

## *one*

The lunch hour in the coworkers' cafeteria at Frankenberg's had reached its peak.

There was no room left at any of the long tables, and more and more people were arriving to wait back of the wooden barricades by the cash register. People who had already got their trays of food wandered about between the tables in search of a spot they could squeeze into, or a place that somebody was about to leave, but there was no place. The roar of dishes, chairs, voices, shuffling feet, and the *bra-a-ack* of the turnstiles in the bare-walled room was like the din of a single huge machine.

Therese ate nervously, with the "Welcome to Frankenberg's" booklet propped up in front of her against a sugar container. She had read the thick booklet through last week, in the first day of training class, but she had nothing else with her to read, and in the coworkers' cafeteria, she felt it necessary to concentrate on something. So she read again about vacation benefits, the three weeks' vacation given to people who had worked fifteen years at Frankenberg's, and she ate the hot plate special of the day—a grayish slice of roast beef with a ball of mashed potatoes covered with brown gravy, a heap of peas, and a tiny paper cup of horseradish. She tried to imagine what it would be like to have worked fifteen years in Frankenberg's department store, and she found she was unable to. "Twenty-five Yearers" got four weeks' vacation, the booklet said. Frankenberg's also provided a camp for summer and winter vacationers. They should have a church, too, she thought, and a hospital for the birth of babies. The store was organized so much like a prison, it frightened her now and then to realize she was a part of it.

She turned the pages quickly, and saw in big black script across two pages: "Are *You* Frankenberg Material?"

She glanced across the room at the windows and tried to think of something else. Of the beautiful black and red Norwegian sweater she had seen at Saks and might buy for Richard for Christmas, if she couldn't find a better-looking wallet than the ones she had seen for twenty dollars. Of the possibility of driving with the Kellys next Sunday up to West Point to see a hockey game. The great square window across the room looked like a painting by—who was it? Mondrian. The little square section of window in the corner open to a white sky. And no bird to fly in or out. What kind of a set would one make for a play that took place in a department store? She was back again.

But it's so different with you, Terry, Richard had said to her. You've got an absolute conviction you'll be out of it in a few weeks and the others haven't. Richard said she could be in France next summer. Would be. Richard wanted her to go with him, and there was really nothing that stood in the way of her going with him. And Richard's friend Phil McElroy had written him that he might be able to get her a job with a theater group next month. Therese had not met Phil yet, but she had very little faith that he could get her a job. She had combed New York since September, gone back and combed it a few times more, and she hadn't found anything. Who gave a job in the middle of the winter to a stage-designer apprentice just beginning to be an apprentice? It didn't seem real either that she might be in Europe with Richard next summer, sitting with him in sidewalk cafés, walking with him in Arles, finding the places Van Gogh had painted, she and Richard choosing towns to stop in for a while and paint. It seemed less real these last few days since she had been working at the store.

She knew what bothered her at the store. It was the sort of thing she wouldn't try to tell Richard. It was that the store intensified things that had always bothered her, as long as she could remember. It was the pointless actions, the meaningless chores that seemed to keep her from doing what she wanted to do, might have done—and here it was the complicated procedures with moneybags, coat checkings, and time clocks that kept people even from serving the store as efficiently as they might—the sense that everyone was incommunicado with everyone else and living on an entirely wrong plane, so that the meaning, the message, the love, or whatever it was that each life contained, never could find its expression. It reminded her of conversations at tables, on sofas, with people whose words seemed to hover over dead, unstirrable things, who never touched a string that played. And when one tried to touch a live string, looked at one with faces as masked as ever, making a remark so perfect in its banality that one could not even believe it might be subterfuge. And the loneliness, augmented by the fact one saw within the store the same faces day after day, the few faces one might have spoken to and never did, or never could. Not like the face on the passing bus that seems to speak, that is seen once and at least is gone forever.

She would wonder, standing in the time-clock queue in the basement every morning, her eyes sorting out unconsciously the regular employees from the temporary ones, just how she had happened to land here—she had answered an ad, of course, but that didn't explain fate—and what was coming next instead of a stage-designing job. Her life was a series of zigzags. At nineteen, she was anxious.

"You must learn to trust people, Therese. Remember that," Sister Alicia had often told her. And often, quite often, Therese tried to apply it.

"Sister Alicia," Therese whispered carefully, the sibilant syllables comforting her.

Therese sat up again and picked up her fork, because the cleanup boy was working in her direction.

She could see Sister Alicia's face, bony and reddish like pink stone when the sunlight was on it, and the starched blue billow of her bosom. Sister Alicia's big bony figure coming around a corner in a hall, between the white enamel tables in the refectory. Sister Alicia in a thousand places, her small blue eyes always finding her out among the other girls, seeing her differently, Therese knew, from all the other girls, yet the thin pink lips always set in the same straight line. She could see Sister Alicia handing her the knitted green gloves wrapped in tissue, not smiling, only presenting them to her directly, with hardly a word, on her eighth birthday. Sister Alicia telling her with the same straight mouth that she must pass her arithmetic. Who else had cared if she passed her arithmetic? Therese had kept the green gloves at the bottom of her tin locker at school, for years after Sister Alicia had gone away to California. The white tissue had become limp and crackleless like ancient cloth, and still she had not worn the gloves. Finally, they were too small to wear.

Someone moved the sugar container, and the propped booklet fell flat.

Therese looked at the pair of hands across from her, a woman's plump, aging hands, stirring her coffee, breaking a roll now with a trembling eagerness, daubing half the roll greedily into the brown gravy of the plate that was identical with Therese's. The hands were chapped, there was dirt in the parallel creases of the knuckles, but the right hand bore a conspicuous silver filigree ring set with a clear green stone, the left a gold wedding ring, and there were traces of red polish in the corners of the nails. Therese watched the hand carry a forkful of peas upward, and she did not have to look at the face to know what it would be like. It would be like all the fifty-year-old faces of women who worked at Frankenberg's, stricken with an everlasting exhaustion and terror, the eyes distorted behind glasses that enlarged or made smaller, the cheeks splotched with rouge that did not brighten the grayness underneath. Therese could not look.

"You're a new girl, aren't you?" The voice was shrill and clear in the din, almost a sweet voice.

"Yes," Therese said, and looked up. She remembered the face. It was the face whose exhaustion had made her see all the other faces. It was the woman Therese had seen creeping down the marble stairs from the mezzanine at about six-thirty one evening when the store was empty, sliding her hands down the broad marble banister to take some of the weight from her bunioned feet. Therese had thought: she is not ill, she is not a beggar, she simply works here.

"Are you getting along all right?"

And here was the woman smiling at her, with the same terrible creases under her eyes and around her mouth. Her eyes were actually alive now, and rather affectionate.

"Are you getting along all right?" the woman repeated, for there was a great clatter of voices and dishes all around them.

Therese moistened her lips. "Yes, thank you."

"Do you like it here?"

Therese nodded.

"Finished?" A young man in a white apron gripped the woman's plate with an imperative thumb.

The woman made a tremulous, dismissing gesture. She pulled her saucer of canned sliced peaches toward her. The peaches, like slimy little orange fishes, slithered over the edge of the spoon each time the spoon lifted, all except one which the woman would eat.

"I'm on the third floor in the sweater department. If you want to ask me anything"—the woman said with nervous uncertainty, as if she were trying to deliver a message before they would be cut off or separated—"come up and talk to me some time. My name is Mrs. Robichek, Mrs. Ruby Robichek, five forty-four."

"Thank you very much," Therese said. And suddenly the woman's ugliness disappeared, because her reddish brown eyes behind the glasses were gentle, and interested in her. Therese could feel her heart beating, as if it had come to life. She watched the woman get up from the table, and watched her short, thick figure move away until it was lost in the crowd that waited behind the barricade.

Therese did not visit Mrs. Robichek, but she looked for her every morning when the employees trickled into the building around a quarter to nine, and she looked for her in the elevators and in the cafeteria. She never saw her, but it was pleasant to have someone to look for in the store. It made all the difference in the world.

Nearly every morning when she came to work on the seventh floor, Therese would stop for a moment to watch a certain toy train. The train was on a table by itself near the elevators. It was not a big fine train like the one that ran on the floor at the back of the toy department, but there was a fury in its tiny pumping pistons that the bigger trains did not possess. Its wrath and frustration on the closed oval track held Therese spellbound.

*Awrr rr rr rrgh!* it said as it hurled itself blindly into the papier-mâché tunnel. And *Urr rr rr rrgh!* as it emerged.

The little train was always running when she stepped out of the elevator in the morning, and when she finished work in the evening. She felt it cursed the hand that threw its switch each day. In the jerk of its nose around the curves, in its wild dashes down the straight lengths of track, she could see a frenzied and futile pursuit of a tyrannical master. It drew three Pullman cars in which minuscule human figures showed flinty profiles at the windows, behind these an open boxcar of real miniature lumber, a boxcar of coal that was not real, and a caboose that snapped round the curves and clung to the fleeing train like a child to its mother's skirts. It was like something gone mad in imprisonment, something already dead that would never wear out, like the dainty, springy footed foxes in the Central Park Zoo, whose complex footwork repeated and repeated as they circled their cages.

This morning, Therese turned away quickly from the train, and went on toward the doll department, where she worked.

At five past nine, the great block-square toy department was coming to life. Green cloths were being pulled back from the long tables. Mechanical toys began to toss balls into the air and catch them, shooting galleries popped and their targets rotated. The table of barnyard animals squawked, cackled, and brayed. Behind Therese, a weary *rat-tat-tat-tat-tat* had started up, the drumbeats of the giant tin soldier who militantly faced the elevators and drummed all day. The arts and handicrafts table gave out a smell of fresh modeling clay, reminiscent of the art room at school when she was very small, and also of a kind of vault on the school grounds, rumored to be the real tomb of someone, which she had used to stick her nose into through iron bars.

Mrs. Hendrickson, section manager of the doll department, was dragging dolls from the stock shelves and seating them, splay legged, on the glass counters.

Therese said hello to Miss Martucci, who stood at the counter counting the bills and coins from her moneybag with such concentration she could give Therese only a deeper nod of her rhythmically nodding head. Therese counted twenty-eight fifty from her own moneybag, recorded it on a slip of white paper for the sales receipts envelope, and transferred the money by denominations into her drawer in the cash register.

By now, the first customers were emerging from the elevators, hesitating a moment with the bewildered, somewhat startled expressions that people always had on finding themselves in the toy department, then starting off on weaving courses.

"Do you have the dolls that wet?" a woman asked her.

"I'd like this doll, but with a yellow dress," a woman said, pushing a doll toward her, and Therese turned and got the doll she wanted out of a stock shelf.

The woman had a mouth and cheeks like her mother's, Therese noticed, slightly pocked cheeks under dark pink rouge, separated by a thin red mouth full of vertical lines.

"Are the Drinksy-Wetsy dolls all this size?"

There was no need of salesmanship. People wanted a doll, any doll, to give for Christmas. It was a matter of stooping, pulling out boxes in search of a doll with brown eyes instead of blue, calling Mrs. Hendrickson to open a showcase window with her key, which she did grudgingly if she were convinced the particular doll could not be found in stock, a matter of sidling down the aisle behind the counter to deposit a purchased doll on the mountain of boxes on the wrapping counter that was always growing, always toppling, no matter how often the stock boys came to take the packages away. Almost no children came to the counter. Santa Claus was supposed to bring the dolls, Santa Claus represented by the frantic faces and the clawing hands. Yet there must be a certain goodwill in all of them, Therese thought, even behind the cool, powdered faces of the women in mink and sable, who were generally the most arrogant, who hastily bought the biggest and most expensive dolls, the dolls with real hair and changes of clothing. There was surely love in the poor people, who waited their turn and asked quietly how much a certain doll cost, and shook their heads regretfully and turned away. Thirteen dollars and fifty cents for a doll only ten inches high.

"Take it," Therese wanted to say to them. "It really is too expensive, but I'll give it to you. Frankenberg's won't miss it."

But the women in the cheap cloth coats, the timid men huddled inside shabby mufflers would be gone, wistfully glancing at other counters as they made their way back to the elevators. If people came for a doll, they didn't want anything else. A doll was a special kind of Christmas gift, practically alive, the next thing to a baby.

There were almost never any children, but now and again one would come up, generally a little girl, very rarely a little boy, her hand held firmly by a parent. Therese would show her the dolls she thought the child might like. She would be patient, and finally a certain doll would bring that metamorphosis in the child's face, that response to make-believe that was the purpose of all of it, and usually that was the doll the child went away with.

Then one evening after work, Therese saw Mrs. Robichek in the coffee and doughnut shop across the street. Therese often stopped in the doughnut shop to get a cup of coffee before going home. Mrs. Robichek was at the back of the shop, at the end of the long curving counter, dabbling a doughnut into her mug of coffee.

Therese pushed and thrust herself toward her, through the press of girls and coffee mugs and doughnuts. Arriving at Mrs. Robichek's elbow, she gasped, "Hello," and turned to the counter, as if a cup of coffee had been her only objective.

"Hello," said Mrs. Robichek, so indifferently that Therese was crushed.

Therese did not dare look at Mrs. Robichek again. And yet their shoulders were actually pressed together! Therese was half finished with her coffee when Mrs. Robichek said dully, "I'm going to take the Independent subway. I wonder if we'll ever get out of here." Her voice was dreary, not as it had been that day in the cafeteria. Now she was like the hunched old woman Therese had seen creeping down the stairs.

"We'll get out," Therese said reassuringly.

Therese forced a path for both of them to the door. Therese was taking the Independent subway, too. She and Mrs. Robichek edged into the sluggish mob at the entrance of the subway, and were sucked gradually and inevitably down the stairs, like bits of floating waste down a drain. They found they both got off at the Lexington Avenue stop, too, though Mrs. Robichek lived on Fifty-fifth Street, just east of Third Avenue. Therese went with Mrs. Robichek into the delicatessen where she was going to buy something for her dinner. Therese might have bought something for her own dinner, but somehow she couldn't in Mrs. Robichek's presence.

"Do you have food at home?"

"No, I'm going to buy something later."

"Why don't you come and eat with me? I'm all alone. Come on." Mrs. Robichek finished with a shrug, as if that were less effort than a smile.

Therese's impulse to protest politely lasted only a moment. "Thank you. I'd like to come." Then she saw a cellophane-wrapped cake on the counter, a fruit cake like a big brown brick topped with red cherries, and she bought it to give to Mrs. Robichek.

It was a house like the one Therese lived in, only brownstone and much darker and gloomier. There were no lights at all in the halls, and when Mrs. Robichek put on the light in the third-floor hall, Therese saw that the house was not very clean. Mrs. Robichek's room was not very clean either, and the bed was unmade. Did she get up as tired as she went to bed, Therese wondered. Therese was left standing in the middle of the room while Mrs. Robichek moved on dragging feet toward the kitchenette, carrying the bag of groceries she had taken from Therese's hands. Now that she was home, Therese felt, where no one could see her, she allowed herself to look as tired as she really was.

Therese could never remember how it began. She could not remember the conversation just before and the conversation didn't matter, of course. What happened was that Mrs. Robichek edged away from her, strangely, as if she were in a trance, suddenly murmuring instead of talking, and lay down flat on her back on the unmade bed. It was because of the continued murmuring, the faint smile of apology, and the terrible, shocking ugliness of the short, heavy body with the bulging abdomen, and the apologetically tilted head still so politely looking at her, that she could not make herself listen.

"I used to have my own dress shop in Queens. Oh, a fine big one," Mrs. Robichek said, and Therese caught the note of boasting and began to listen despite herself, hating it. "You know, the dresses with the V at the waist and the little buttons running up. You know, three, five years ago—" Mrs. Robichek spread her stiff hands inarticulately across her waist. The short hands did not nearly span the front half of herself. She looked very old in the dim lamplight that made the shadows under her eyes black. "They called them Caterina dresses. You remember? I designed them. They come out of my shop in Queens. They famous, all right!"

Mrs. Robichek left the table and went to a small trunk that stood against the wall. She opened it, talking all the while, and began to drag out dresses of dark, heavy-looking material, which she let fall on the floor. Mrs. Robichek held up a garnet-red velvet dress with a white collar and tiny white buttons that came to a V down the front of the narrow bodice.

"See, I got lots of them. I made them. Other stores copied." Above the white collar of the dress, which she gripped with her chin, Mrs. Robichek's ugly head was tilted grotesquely. "You like this? I give you one. Come here. Come here, try one on."

Therese was repelled by the thought of trying one on. She wished Mrs. Robichek would lie down and rest again, but obediently Therese got up, as if she had no will of her own, and came toward her.

Mrs. Robichek pressed a black velvet dress upon Therese with trembling and importunate hands, and Therese suddenly knew how she would wait on people in the store, thrusting sweaters upon them helter-skelter, for she could not have performed the same action in any other way. For four years, Therese remembered, Mrs. Robichek had said she had worked at Frankenberg's.

"You like the green one better? Try it on." And in the instant Therese hesitated, she dropped it and picked up another, the dark red one. "I sell five of them to girls at the store, but you I give one. Left over, but they still in style. You like this one better?"

Therese liked the red better. She liked red, especially garnet red, and she loved red velvet. Mrs. Robichek pressed her toward a corner, where she could take off her clothing and lay it on an armchair. But she did not want the dress, did not want to be given it. It reminded her of being given clothing at the Home, hand-me-downs, because she was considered practically as one of the orphan girls, who made up half the school, who never got packages from outside. Therese pulled off her sweater and felt completely naked. She gripped her arms above the elbow, and her flesh there felt cold and sensationless.

"I sewed," Mrs. Robichek was saying ecstatically to herself, "how I sewed, morning to night! I managed four girls. But my eyes got bad. One blind, this one. Put the dress on." She told Therese about the operation on the eye. It was not blind, only partially blind. But it was very painful. Glaucoma. It still gave her pain. That and her back. And her feet. Bunions.

Therese realized she was relating all her troubles and her bad luck so that she, Therese, would understand why she had sunk so low as to work in a department store.

"It fits?" Mrs. Robichek asked confidently.

Therese looked in the mirror in the wardrobe door. It showed a long thin figure with a narrowish head that seemed ablaze at the outline, bright yellow fire running down to the bright red bar on either shoulder. The dress hung in straight draped folds down almost to her ankles. It was the dress of queens in fairy tales, of a red deeper than blood. She stepped back, and pulled in the looseness of the dress behind her, so it fitted her ribs and her waist, and she looked back at her own dark hazel eyes in the mirror. Herself meeting herself. This was she, not the girl in the dull plaid skirt and the beige sweater, not the girl who worked in the doll department at Frankenberg's.

"Do you like it?" Mrs. Robichek asked.

Therese studied the surprisingly tranquil mouth, whose modeling she could see distinctly, though she wore no more lipstick than she might if someone had kissed her. She wished she could kiss the person in the mirror and make her come to life, yet she stood perfectly still, like a painted portrait.

"If you like it, take it," Mrs. Robichek urged impatiently, watching from a distance, lurking against the wardrobe as saleswomen lurk while women try on coats and dresses in front of mirrors in department stores.

But it wouldn't last, Therese knew. She would move, and it would be gone. Even if she kept the dress, it would be gone, because it was a thing of a minute, this minute. She didn't want the dress. She tried to imagine the dress in her closet at home, among her other clothing, and she couldn't. She began to unbutton the buttons, to unfasten the collar.

"You like it, yes?" Mrs. Robichek asked as confidently as ever.

"Yes," Therese said firmly, admitting it.

She couldn't get the hook and eye unfastened at the back of the collar. Mrs. Robichek had to help her, and she could hardly wait. She felt as if she were being strangled. What was she doing here? How did she happen to have put on a dress like this? Suddenly Mrs. Robichek and her apartment were like a horrible dream that she had just realized she was dreaming. Mrs. Robichek was the hunchbacked keeper of the dungeon. And she had been brought here to be tantalized.

"What's the matter? A pin stick you?"

Therese's lips opened to speak, but her mind was too far away. Her mind was at a distant point, at a distant vortex that opened on the scene in the dimly lighted, terrifying room where the two of them seemed to stand in desperate combat. And at the point of the vortex where her mind was, she knew it was the hopelessness that terrified her and nothing else. It was the hopelessness of Mrs. Robichek's ailing body and her job at the store, of her stack of dresses in the trunk, of her ugliness, the hopelessness of which the end of her life was entirely composed. And the hopelessness of herself, of ever being the person she wanted to be and of doing the things that person would do. Had all her life been nothing but a dream, and was *this* real? It was the terror of this hopelessness that made her want to shed the dress and flee before it was too late, before the chains fell around her and locked.

It might already be too late. As in a nightmare, Therese stood in the room in her white slip, shivering, unable to move.

"What's the matter? You cold? It's hot."

It was hot. The radiator hissed. The room smelled of garlic and the fustiness of old age, of medicines, and of the peculiar metallic smell that was Mrs. Robichek's own. Therese wanted to collapse in the chair where her skirt and sweater lay. Perhaps if she lay on her own clothing, she thought, it wouldn't matter. But she shouldn't lie down at all. If she did, she was lost. The chains would lock, and she would be one with the hunchback.

Therese trembled violently. She was suddenly out of control. It was a chill, not merely fright or tiredness.

"Sit down," Mrs. Robichek's voice said from a distance, and with shocking unconcern and boredom, as if she were quite used to girls feeling faint in her room, and from a distance, too, her dry, rough-tipped fingers pressed against Therese's arms.

Therese struggled against the chair, knowing she was going to succumb to it, and even aware that she was attracted to it for that reason. She dropped into the chair, felt Mrs. Robichek tugging at her skirt to pull it from under her, but she couldn't make herself move. She was still at the same point of consciousness, however, still had the same freedom to think, even though the dark arms of the chair rose about her.

Mrs. Robichek was saying, "You stand up too much at the store. It's hard these Christmases. I seen four of them. You got to learn how to save yourself a little."

Creeping down the stairs clinging to the banister. Save herself by eating lunch in the cafeteria. Taking shoes off bunioned feet like the row of women perched on the radiator in the women's room, fighting for a bit of the radiator to put a newspaper on and sit for five minutes.

Therese's mind worked very clearly. It was astonishing how clearly it worked, though she knew she was simply staring into space in front of her, and that she could not have moved if she had wanted to.

"You just tired, you baby," Mrs. Robichek said, tucking a woolen blanket about her shoulders in the chair. "You need to rest, standing up all day and standing up tonight, too."

A line from Richard's Eliot came to Therese. *That is not what I meant at all. That is not it, at all.* She wanted to say it, but she could not make her lips move. Something sweet and burning was in her mouth. Mrs. Robichek was standing in front of her, spooning something from a bottle, and pushing the spoon between her lips. Therese swallowed it obediently, not caring if it were poison. She could have moved her lips now, could have gotten up from the chair, but she didn't want to move. Finally, she lay back in the chair, and let Mrs. Robichek cover her with the blanket, and she pretended to go to sleep. But all the while she watched the humpbacked figure moving about the room, putting away the things from the table, undressing for bed. She watched Mrs. Robichek remove a big laced corset and then a strap device that passed around her shoulders and partially down her back. Therese closed her eyes then in horror, pressed them tight shut, until the creaking of a spring and a long groaning sigh told her that Mrs. Robichek had gone to bed. But that was not all. Mrs. Robichek reached for the alarm clock and wound it, and, without lifting her head from the pillow, groped with the clock for the straight chair beside the bed. In the dark, Therese could barely see her arm rise and fall four times before the clock found the chair.

I shall wait fifteen minutes until she is asleep and then go, Therese thought.

And because she was tired, she tensed herself to hold back that spasm, that sudden seizure that was like falling, that came every night long before sleep, yet heralded sleep. It did not come. So after what she thought was fifteen minutes, Therese dressed herself and went silently out the door. It was easy, after all, simply to open the door and escape. It was easy, she thought, because she was not really escaping at all.

# two

"Terry, remember that fellow Phil McElroy I told you about? The one with the stock company? Well, he's in town, and he says you've got a job in a couple of weeks."

"A real job? Where?"

"A show in the Village. Phil wants to see us tonight. I'll tell you about it when I see you. I'll be over in about twenty minutes. I'm just leaving school now."

Therese ran up the three flights of stairs to her room. She was in the middle of washing up, and the soap had dried on her face. She stared down at the orange washcloth in the basin.

"A job!" she whispered to herself. The magic word.

She changed into a dress, and hung a short silver chain with a St. Christopher medallion, a birthday present from Richard, around her neck, and combed her hair with a little water so it would look neater. Then she set some loose sketches and cardboard models just inside the closet where she could reach them easily when Phil McElroy asked to see them. No, I haven't had much actual experience, she would have to say, and she felt a sink of failure. She hadn't even an apprentice's job behind her, except that two-day job in Montclair, making the cardboard model that the amateur group had finally used, if that could be called a job. She had taken two courses in scenic design in New York, and she had read a lot of books. She could hear Phil McElroy—an intense and very busy young man, probably, a little annoyed at having come to see her for nothing—saying regretfully that she wouldn't do after all. But with Richard present, Therese thought, it wouldn't be quite as crushing as if she were alone. Richard had quit or been fired from about five jobs since she had known him. Nothing bothered Richard less than losing and finding jobs. Therese remembered being fired from the Pelican Press a month ago, and she winced. They hadn't even given her notice, and the only reason she had been fired, she supposed, was that her particular research assignment had been finished. When she had gone in to speak to Mr. Nussbaum, the president, about not being given notice, he had not known, or had pretended not to know, what the term meant. "Notiz?—

Wuss?" he had said indifferently, and she had turned and fled, afraid of bursting into tears in his office. It was easy for Richard, living at home with a family to keep him cheerful. It was easier for him to save money. He had saved about two thousand in a two-year hitch in the Navy, and a thousand more in the year since. And how long would it take her to save the fifteen hundred dollars that a junior membership in the stage designers' union cost? After nearly two years in New York, she had only about five hundred dollars of it.

"Pray for me," she said to the wooden Madonna on the bookshelf. It was the one beautiful thing in her apartment, the wooden Madonna she had bought the first month she had been in New York. She wished there were a better place for it in the room than on the ugly bookshelf. The bookshelf was like a lot of fruit crates stacked up and painted red. She longed for a bookshelf of natural-colored wood, smooth to the touch and sleek with wax.

She went down to the delicatessen and bought six cans of beer and some blue cheese. Then, when she came upstairs, she remembered the original purpose of her going to the store, to buy some meat for dinner. She and Richard had planned to have dinner in tonight. That might be changed now, but she didn't like to take it on her own initiative to alter plans where Richard was concerned, and she was about to run down again for the meat when Richard's long ring sounded. She pressed the release button.

Richard came up the steps at a run, smiling. "Did Phil call?"

"No," she said.

"Good. That means he's coming."

"When?"

"In a few minutes, I guess. He probably won't stay long."

"Does it really sound like a definite job?"

"Phil says so."

"Do you know what kind of play it is?"

"I don't know anything except they need somebody for sets, and why not you?" Richard looked her over critically, smiling. "You look swell tonight. Don't be nervous, will you? It's just a little company in the Village, and you've probably got more talent than all the rest of them put together."

She took the overcoat he had dropped on a chair and hung it in the closet. Under the overcoat was a roll of charcoal paper he had brought from art school. "Did you do something good today?" she asked.

"So-so. That's something I want to work on at home," he said carelessly. "We had that redheaded model today, the one I like."

Therese wanted to see his sketch, but she knew Richard probably didn't think it good enough. Some of his first paintings were good, like the lighthouse in blues and blacks that hung over her bed, that he had done when he was in the Navy and just starting to paint. But his life drawing was not good yet, and Therese doubted that it ever would be. There was a new charcoal smudge all over one knee of his tan cotton trousers. He wore a shirt inside the red and black checked shirt, and buckskin moccasins that made his big feet look like shapeless bear paws. He was more like a lumberjack or a professional athlete of some sort, Therese thought, than anything else. She could more easily imagine him with an ax in his hand than a paintbrush. She had seen him with an ax once, cutting wood in the yard back of his house in Brooklyn. If he didn't prove to his family that he was making some progress in his painting, he would probably have to go into his father's bottled-gas business this summer, and open the branch in Long Island that his father wanted him to.

"Will you have to work this Saturday?" she asked, still afraid to talk about the job.

"Hope not. Are you free?"

She remembered now, she was not. "I'm free Friday," she said resignedly. "Saturday's a late day."

Richard smiled. "It's a conspiracy." He took her hands and drew her arms around his waist, his restless prowling of the room at an end. "Maybe Sunday? The family asked if you could come out for dinner, but we don't have to stay long. I could borrow a truck and we could drive somewhere in the afternoon."

"All right." She liked that and so did Richard, sitting up in front of the big empty gas tank, and driving anywhere, as free as if they rode a butterfly. She took her arms from around Richard. It made her feel self-conscious and foolish, as if she stood embracing the stem of a tree, to have her arms around Richard. "I did buy a steak for tonight, but they stole it at the store."

"Stole it? From where?"

"Off the shelf where we keep our handbags. The people they hire for

Christmas don't get any regular lockers." She smiled at it now, but this afternoon she had almost wept. Wolves, she had thought, a pack of wolves, stealing a bloody bag of meat just because it was food, a free meal. She had asked all the salesgirls if they had seen it, and they had all denied it. Bringing meat into the store wasn't allowed, Mrs. Hendrickson had said indignantly. But what was one to do, if all the meat stores closed at six o'clock?

Richard lay back on the studio couch. His mouth was thin and its line uneven, half of it downward slanting, giving an ambiguity to his expression, a look sometimes of humor, sometimes of bitterness, a contradiction that his rather blank and frank blue eyes did nothing to clarify. He said slowly and mockingly, "Did you go down to the lost and found? Lost, one pound of beefsteak. Answers to the name Meatball."

Therese smiled, looking over the shelves in her kitchenette. "Do you think you're joking? Mrs. Hendrickson did tell me to go down to the lost and found."

Richard gave a hooting laugh and stood up.

"There's a can of corn here and I've got lettuce for a salad. And there's bread and butter. Shall I go get some frozen pork chops?"

Richard reached a long arm over her shoulder and took the square of pumpernickel bread from the shelf. "You call that bread? It's fungus. Look at it, blue as a mandrill's behind. Why don't you eat bread once you buy it?"

"I use that to see in the dark with. But since you don't like it—" She took it from him and dropped it into the garbage bag. "That wasn't the bread I meant anyway."

"Show me the bread you meant."

The doorbell shrieked right beside the refrigerator, and she jumped for the button.

"That's them," Richard said.

There were two young men. Richard introduced them as Phil McElroy and his brother, Danny. Phil was not at all what Therese had expected. He did not look intense or serious, or even particularly intelligent. And he scarcely glanced at her when they were introduced.

Danny stood with his coat over his arm until Therese took it from him. She could not find an extra hanger for Phil's coat, and Phil took it back and tossed it onto a chair, half on the floor. It was an old dirty polo coat. Therese served the beer and cheese and crackers, listening all the while for

Phil and Richard's conversation to turn to the job. But they were talking about things that had happened since they had seen each other last in Kingston, New York. Richard had worked for two weeks last summer on some murals in a roadhouse there, where Phil had had a job as a waiter.

"Are you in the theater, too?" she asked Danny.

"No, I'm not," Danny said. He seemed shy, or perhaps bored and impatient to leave. He was older than Phil and a little more heavily built. His dark brown eyes moved thoughtfully from object to object in the room.

"They haven't got anything yet but a director and three actors," Phil said to Richard, leaning back on the couch. "A fellow I worked with in Philly once is directing. Raymond Cortes. If I recommend you, it's a cinch you'll get in," he said with a glance at Therese. "He promised me the part of the second brother in the play. It's called *Small Rain.*"

"A comedy?" Therese asked.

"Comedy. Three acts. Have you done any sets so far by yourself?"

"How many sets will it take?" Richard asked, just as she was about to answer.

"Two at the most, and they'll probably get by on one. Georgia Halloran has the lead. Did you happen to see that Sartre thing they did in the fall down there? She was in that."

"Georgia?" Richard smiled. "Whatever happened with her and Rudy?"

Disappointedly, Therese heard their conversation settling down on Georgia and Rudy and other people she didn't know. Georgia might have been one of the girls Richard had had an affair with, Therese supposed. He had once mentioned about five. She couldn't remember any of their names except Celia.

"Is this one of your sets?" Danny asked her, looking at the cardboard model that hung on the wall, and when she nodded he got up to see it.

And now Richard and Phil were talking about a man who owed Richard money from somewhere. Phil said he had seen the man last night in the San Remo bar. Phil's elongated face and his clipped hair was like an El Greco, Therese thought, yet the same features in his brother looked like an American Indian. And the way Phil talked completely destroyed the illusion of El Greco. He talked like any of the people one saw in Village bars, young people who were supposed to be writers or actors, and who usually did nothing.

"It's very attractive," Danny said, peering behind one of the little suspended figures.

"It's a model for *Petrushka*. The fair scene," she said, wondering if he would know the ballet. He might be a lawyer, she thought, or even a doctor. There were yellowish stains on his fingers, not the stains of cigarettes.

Richard said something about being hungry, and Phil said he was starving, but neither of them ate any of the cheese that was in front of them.

"We're due in half an hour, Phil," Danny repeated.

Then, a moment later, they were all standing up, putting on their coats.

"Let's eat out somewhere, Terry," Richard said. "How about the Czech place up on Second?"

"All right," she said, trying to sound agreeable. This was the end of it, she supposed, and nothing was definite. She had an impulse to ask Phil a crucial question, but she didn't.

And on the street, they began to walk downtown instead of up. Richard walked with Phil, and only glanced back once or twice at her, as if to see if she were still there. Danny held her arm at the curbs, and across the patches of dirty slippery stuff, neither snow nor ice, that were the remains of a snowfall three weeks ago.

"Are you a doctor?" she asked Danny.

"Physicist," Danny replied. "I'm taking graduate courses at NYU now." He smiled at her, but the conversation stopped there for a while.

Then he said, "That's a long way from stage designing, isn't it."

She nodded. "Quite a long way." She started to ask him if he intended to do any work pertaining to the atom bomb, but she didn't, because what would it matter if he did or didn't? "Do you know where we're going?" she asked.

He smiled broadly, showing square white teeth. "Yes. To the subway. But Phil wants a bite somewhere first."

They were walking down Third Avenue. And Richard was talking to Phil about their going to Europe next summer. Therese felt a throb of embarrassment as she walked along behind Richard, like a dangling appendage, because Phil and Danny would naturally think she was Richard's mistress. She wasn't his mistress, and Richard didn't expect her to be in Europe. It was a strange relationship, she supposed, and who would believe it? Because from what she had seen in New York, everybody slept with everybody they had dates with more than once or twice. And the two people she had gone out with before Richard—Angelo and Harry—had certainly dropped her when they discovered she didn't care for an affair with them. She had tried to have an affair with Richard three or four times in the year she had known him, though with negative results; Richard said he preferred to wait. He meant wait until she cared more for him. Richard wanted to marry her, and she was the first girl he had ever proposed to, he said. She knew he would ask her again before they left for Europe, but she didn't love him enough to marry him. And yet she would be accepting most of the money for the trip from him, she thought with a familiar sense of guilt. Then the image of Mrs. Semco, Richard's mother, came before her, smiling approval on them, on their marrying, and Therese involuntarily shook her head.

"What's the matter?" Danny asked.

"Nothing."

"Are you cold?"

"No. Not at all."

But he tucked her arm closer anyway. She was cold, and felt rather miserable in general. It was the half-dangling, half-cemented relationship with Richard, she knew. They saw more and more of each other, without actually growing closer. She still wasn't in love with him, not after ten months, and maybe she never could be, though the fact remained that she liked him better than any one person she had ever known, certainly any man. Sometimes she thought she was in love with him, waking up in the morning and looking blankly at the ceiling, remembering suddenly that she knew him, remembering suddenly his face shining with affection for her because of some gesture of affection on her part, before her sleepy emptiness had time to fill up with the realization of what time it was, what day, what she had to do, the solider substance that made up one's life. But the feeling bore no resemblance to what she had read about love. Love was supposed to be a kind of blissful insanity. Richard didn't act blissfully insane either, in fact.

"Oh, everything's called St. Germain-des-Près!" Phil shouted with a wave of his hand. "I'll give you some addresses before you go. How long do you think you'll be there?"

A truck with rattling, slapping chains turned in front of them, and

Therese couldn't hear Richard's answer. Phil went into the Riker's shop on the corner of Fifty-third Street.

"We don't have to eat here. Phil just wants to stop a minute." Richard squeezed her shoulder as they went in the door. "It's a great day, isn't it, Terry? Don't you feel it? It's your first real job!"

Richard was convinced, and Therese tried hard to realize it might be a great moment. But she couldn't recapture even the certainty she remembered when she had looked at the orange washcloth in the basin after Richard's telephone call. She leaned against the stool next to Phil's, and Richard stood beside her, still talking to him. The glaring white light on the white tile walls and the floor seemed brighter than sunlight, for here there were no shadows. She could see every shiny black hair in Phil's eyebrows, and the rough and smooth spots on the pipe Danny held in his hand, unlighted. She could see the details of Richard's hand, which hung limply out of his overcoat sleeve, and she was conscious again of their incongruity with his limber, long-boned body. They were thick, even plump-looking hands, and they moved in the same inarticulate, blind way if they picked up a saltshaker or the handle of a suitcase. Or stroked her hair, she thought. The insides of his hands were extremely soft, like a girl's, and a little moist. Worst of all, he generally forgot to clean his nails, even when he took the trouble to dress up. Therese had said something about it a couple of times to him, but she felt now that she couldn't say anything more without irritating him.

Danny was watching her. She was held by his thoughtful eyes for a moment, then she looked down. Suddenly she knew why she couldn't recapture the feeling she had had before: she simply didn't believe Phil McElroy could get her a job on his recommendation.

"Are you worried about that job?" Danny was standing beside her.

"No."

"Don't be. Phil can give you some tips." He poked his pipe stem between his lips, and seemed to be about to say something else, but he turned away.

She half listened to Phil's conversation with Richard. They were talking about boat reservations.

Danny said, "By the way, the Black Cat Theater's only a couple of blocks from Morton Street where I live. Phil's staying with me, too. Come and have lunch some time with us, will you?"

"Thanks very much. I'd like to." It probably wouldn't be, she thought, but it was nice of him to ask her.

"What do you think, Terry?" Richard asked. "Is March too soon to go to Europe? It's better to go early than wait till everything's so crowded over there."

"March sounds all right," she said.

"There's nothing to stop us, is there? I don't care if I don't finish the winter term at school."

"No, there's nothing to stop us." It was easy to say. It was easy to believe all of it, and just as easy not to believe any of it. But if it were all true, if the job were real, the play a success, and she could go to France with at least a single achievement behind her—Suddenly, Therese reached out for Richard's arm, slid her hand down it to his fingers. Richard was so surprised, he stopped in the middle of a sentence.

The next afternoon, Therese called the Watkins number that Phil had given her. A very efficient-sounding girl answered. Mr. Cortes was not there, but they had heard about her through Phil McElroy. The job was hers, and she would start work December twenty-eighth at fifty dollars a week. She could come in beforehand and show Mr. Cortes some of her work, if she wanted to, but it wasn't necessary, not if Mr. McElroy had recommended her so highly.

Therese called up Phil to thank him, but nobody answered the telephone. She wrote him a note, care of the Black Cat Theater.

## *three*

Roberta Walls, the youngest supervisor in the toy department, paused just long enough in her midmorning flurry to whisper to Therese, "If we don't sell this twenty-four ninety-five suitcase today, it'll be marked down Monday and the department'll take a two-dollar loss!" Roberta nodded at the brown pasteboard suitcase on the counter, thrust her load of gray boxes into Miss Martucci's hands, and hurried on.

Down the long aisle, Therese watched the salesgirls make way for

Roberta. Roberta flew up and down counters and from one corner of the floor to the other, from nine in the morning until six at night. Therese had heard that Roberta was trying for another promotion. She wore red harlequin glasses, and unlike the other girls always pushed the sleeves of her green smock up above her elbows. Therese saw her flit across an aisle and stop Mrs. Hendrickson with an excited message delivered with gestures. Mrs. Hendrickson nodded agreement, Roberta touched her shoulder familiarly, and Therese felt a small start of jealousy. Jealousy, though she didn't care in the least for Mrs. Hendrickson, even disliked her.

"Do you have a doll made of cloth that cries?"

Therese didn't know of such a doll in stock, but the woman was positive Frankenberg's had it, because she had seen it advertised. Therese pulled out another box, from the last spot it might possibly be, and it wasn't.

"Wotcha lookin' fuh?" Miss Santini asked her. Miss Santini had a cold.

"A doll made of cloth that cries," Therese said. Miss Santini had been especially courteous to her lately. Therese remembered the stolen meat. But now Miss Santini only lifted her eyebrows, stuck out her bright red underlip with a shrug, and went on.

"Made of cloth? With pigtails?" Miss Martucci, a lean, straggly-haired Italian girl with a long nose like a wolf's, looked at Therese. "Don't let Roberta hear you," Miss Martucci said with a glance around her. "Don't let anybody hear you, but those dolls are in the basement."

"Oh." The upstairs toy department was at war with the basement toy department. The tactics were to force the customer into buying on the seventh floor, where everything was more expensive. Therese told the woman the dolls were in the basement.

"Try and sell this today." Miss Davis said to her as she sidled past, slapping the battered imitation alligator suitcase with her red-nailed hand.

Therese nodded.

"Do you have any stiff-legged dolls? One that stands up?"

Therese looked at the middle-aged woman with the crutches that thrust her shoulders high. Her face was different from all the other faces across the counter, gentle, with a certain cognizance in the eyes, as if they actually saw what they looked at.

"That's a little bigger than I wanted," the woman said when Therese showed her a doll. "I'm sorry. Do you have a smaller one?"

"I think so." Therese went further down the aisle, and was aware that the woman followed her on her crutches, circling the press of people at the counter, so as to save Therese walking back with the doll. Suddenly Therese wanted to take infinite pains, wanted to find exactly the doll the woman was looking for. But the next doll wasn't quite right, either. The doll didn't have real hair. Therese tried in another place and found the same doll with real hair. It even cried when it bent over. It was exactly what the woman wanted. Therese laid the doll down carefully in fresh tissue in a new box.

"That's just perfect," the woman repeated. "I'm sending this to a friend in Australia who's a nurse. She graduated from nursing school with me, so I made a little uniform like ours to dress a doll in. Thank you so much. And I wish you a merry Christmas!"

"Merry Christmas to you!" Therese said, smiling. It was the first Merry Christmas she had heard from a customer.

"Have you had your relief yet, Miss Belivet?" Mrs. Hendrickson asked her, as sharply as if she reproached her.

Therese hadn't. She got her pocketbook and the novel she was reading from the shelf under the wrapping counter. The novel was Joyce's *Portrait of the Artist as a Young Man*, which Richard was anxious for her to read. How anyone could have read Gertrude Stein without reading any Joyce, Richard said, he didn't know. She felt a bit inferior when Richard talked with her about books. She had browsed all over the bookshelves at school, but the library assembled by the Order of St. Margaret had been far from catholic, she realized now, though it had included such unexpected writers as Gertrude Stein.

The hall to the employees' rest rooms was blocked by big shipping carts piled high with boxes. Therese waited to get through.

"Pixie!" one of the shipping-cart boys shouted to her.

Therese smiled a little because it was silly. Even down in the cloakroom in the basement, they yelled "Pixie!" at her morning and night.

"Pixie, waiting for me?" the raw-edged voice roared again, over the crash and bump of the stock carts.

She got through, and dodged a shipping cart that hurtled toward her with a clerk aboard.

"No smoking here!" shouted a man's voice, the very growly voice of an executive, and the girls ahead of Therese who had lighted cigarettes blew their smoke into the air and said loudly in chorus just before they reached the refuge of the women's room, "Who does he think *he* is, Mr. Frankenberg?"

"Yoo-hoo! Pixie!"

"Ah'm juss bahdin mah tahm, Pixie!"

A shipping cart skidded in front of her, and she struck her leg against its metal corner. She went on without looking down at her leg, though pain began to blossom there, like a slow explosion. She went on into the different chaos of women's voices, women's figures, and the smell of disinfectant. Blood was running to her shoe, and her stocking was torn in a jagged hole. She pushed some skin back into place and, feeling sickened, leaned against the wall and held on to a water pipe. She stayed there a few seconds, listening to the confusion of voices among the girls at the mirror. Then she wet toilet paper and daubed until the red was gone from her stocking, but the red kept coming.

"It's all right, thanks," she said to a girl who bent over her for a moment, and the girl went away.

Finally, there was nothing to do but buy a sanitary napkin from the slot machine. She used a little of the cotton from inside it, and tied it on her leg with the gauze. And then it was time to go back to the counter.

Their eyes met at the same instant, Therese glancing up from a box she was opening, and the woman just turning her head so she looked directly at Therese. She was tall and fair, her long figure graceful in the loose fur coat that she held open with a hand on her waist. Her eyes were gray, colorless, yet dominant as light or fire, and, caught by them, Therese could not look away. She heard the customer in front of her repeat a question, and Therese stood there, mute. The woman was looking at Therese, too, with a preoccupied expression, as if half her mind were on whatever it was she meant to buy here, and though there were a number of salesgirls between them, Therese felt sure the woman would come to her. Then Therese saw her walk slowly toward the counter, heard her heart stumble to catch up with the moment it had let pass, and felt her face grow hot as the woman came nearer and nearer.

"May I see one of those valises?" the woman asked, and leaned on the counter, looking down through the glass top.

The damaged valise lay only a yard away. Therese turned around and got a box from the bottom of a stack, a box that had never been opened. When she stood up, the woman was looking at her with the calm gray eyes that Therese could neither quite face nor look away from.

"That's the one I like, but I don't suppose I can have it, can I?" she said, nodding toward the brown valise in the show window behind Therese.

Her eyebrows were blonde, curving around the bend of her forehead. Her mouth was as wise as her eyes, Therese thought, and her voice was like her coat, rich and supple, and somehow full of secrets.

"Yes," Therese said.

Therese went back to the stockroom for the key. The key hung just inside the door on a nail, and no one was allowed to touch it but Mrs. Hendrickson.

Miss Davis saw her and gasped, but Therese said, "I need it," and went out.

She opened the show window, took the suitcase down and laid it on the counter.

"You're giving me the one on display?" She smiled as if she understood. She said casually, leaning both forearms on the counter, studying the contents of the valise, "They'll have a fit, won't they?"

"It doesn't matter," Therese said.

"All right. I'd like this. That's COD. And what about clothes? Do these come with it?"

There were cellophane-wrapped clothes in the lid of the suitcase, with a price tag on them. Therese said, "No, they're separate. If you want dolls' clothes—these aren't as good as the clothes in the dolls' clothing department across the aisle."

"Oh! Will this get to New Jersey before Christmas?"

"Yes, it'll arrive Monday." If it didn't, Therese thought, she would deliver it herself.

"Mrs. H. F. Aird," the woman's soft, distinct voice said, and Therese began to print it on the green COD slip.

The name, the address, the town appeared beneath the pencil point like a secret Therese would never forget, like something stamping itself in her memory forever.

"You won't make any mistakes, will you?" the woman's voice asked.

Therese noticed the woman's perfume for the first time, and instead of replying could only shake her head. She looked down at the slip to which she was laboriously adding the necessary figures, and wished with all her power to wish anything that the woman would simply continue her last words and say, "Are you really so glad to have met me? Then why can't we see each other again? Why can't we even have lunch together today?" Her voice was so casual, and she might have said it so easily. But nothing came after the "will you?"—nothing to relieve the shame of having been recognized as a new salesgirl, hired for the Christmas rush, inexperienced and liable to make mistakes. Therese slid the book toward her for her signature.

Then the woman picked up her gloves from the counter, and turned, and slowly went away, and Therese watched the distance widen and widen. Her ankles below the fur of the coat were pale and thin. She wore plain black suede shoes with high heels.

"That's a COD order?"

Therese looked into Mrs. Hendrickson's ugly meaningless face. "Yes, Mrs. Hendrickson."

"Don't you know you're supposed to give the customer the strip at the top? How do you expect them to claim the purchase when it comes? Where's the customer? Can you catch her?"

"Yes." She was only ten feet away, across the aisle at the dolls'-clothing counter. And with the green slip in her hand, she hesitated a moment, then carried it around the counter, forcing herself to advance, because she was suddenly abashed by her appearance, the old blue skirt, the cotton blouse—whoever assigned the green smocks had missed her—and the humiliating flat shoes. And the horrible bandage through which the blood was probably showing again.

"I'm supposed to give you this," she said, laying the miserable little scrap beside the hand on the edge of the counter, and turning away.

Behind the counter again, Therese faced the stock boxes, sliding them thoughtfully out and back, as if she were looking for something. Therese waited until the woman must have finished at the counter and gone away. She was conscious of the moments passing like irrevocable time, irrevocable happiness, for in these last seconds she might turn and see the face she would never see again. She was conscious, too, dimly now and with a different horror, of the old, unceasing voices of customers at the counter calling for assistance, calling to her, and of the low, humming *rrrrrr* of the little train, part of the storm that was closing in and separating her from the woman.

But when she turned finally, she looked directly into the gray eyes again. The woman was walking toward her, and as if time had turned back, she leaned gently on the counter again and gestured to a doll and asked to see it.

Therese got the doll and dropped it with a clatter on the glass counter, and the woman glanced at her.

"Sounds unbreakable," the woman said.

Therese smiled.

"Yes, I'll get this, too," she said in the quiet slow voice that made a pool of silence in the tumult around them. She gave her name and address again, and Therese took it slowly from her lips, as if she did not already know it by heart. "That really will arrive before Christmas?"

"It'll come Monday at the latest. That's two days before Christmas."

"Good. I don't mean to make you nervous."

Therese tightened the knot in the string she had put around the doll box, and the knot mysteriously came open. "No," she said. In an embarrassment so profound there was nothing left to defend, she got the knot tied under the woman's eyes.

"It's a rotten job, isn't it?"

"Yes." Therese folded the COD slips around the white string, and fastened them with a pin.

"So forgive me for complaining."

Therese glanced at her, and the sensation returned that she knew her from somewhere, that the woman was about to reveal herself, and they would both laugh then, and understand. "You're not complaining. But I know it'll get there." Therese looked across the aisle, where the woman had stood before, and saw the tiny slip of green paper still on the counter. "You really are supposed to keep that COD slip."

Her eyes changed with her smile now, brightened with a gray, colorless fire that Therese almost knew, almost could place. "I've gotten things before without them. I always lose them." She bent to sign the second COD slip.

Therese watched her go away with a step as slow as when she had come, saw her look at another counter as she passed it, and slap her black gloves across her palm twice, three times. Then she disappeared into an elevator.

And Therese turned to the next customer. She worked with an indefatigable patience, but her figures on the sales slips bore faint tails where the pencil jerked convulsively. She went to Mr. Logan's office, which seemed to take hours, but when she looked at the clock only fifteen minutes had passed, and now it was time to wash up for lunch. She stood stiffly in front of the rotating towel, drying her hands, feeling unattached to anything or anyone, isolated. Mr. Logan had asked her if she wanted to stay on after Christmas. She could have a job downstairs in the cosmetic department. Therese had said no.

In the middle of the afternoon, she went down to the first floor and bought a card in the greetings-card department. It was not a very interesting card, but at least it was simple, in plain blue and gold. She stood with the pen poised over the card, thinking of what she might have written—"You are magnificent" or even "I love you"—finally writing quickly the excruciatingly dull and impersonal: "Special salutations from Frankenberg's." She added her number, 645-A, in lieu of a signature. Then she went down to the post office in the basement, hesitated at the letter drop, losing her nerve suddenly at the sight of her hand holding the letter half in the slot. What would happen? She was going to leave the store in a few days, anyway. What would Mrs. H. F. Aird care? The blonde eyebrows would perhaps lift a little, she would look at the card a moment, then forget it. Therese dropped it.

On the way home, an idea came to her for a stage set, a house interior with more depth than breadth, with a kind of vortex down the center, from which rooms would go off on either side. She wanted to begin the cardboard model that night, but at last she only elaborated on her pencil sketch of it. She wanted to see someone—not Richard, not Jack or Alice Kelly downstairs, maybe Stella, Stella Overton, the stage designer she had met during her first weeks in New York. Therese had not seen her, she realized, since she had come to the cocktail party Therese had given before she left her other apartment. Stella was one of the people who didn't know where she lived now. Therese was on her way down to the telephone in the hall when she heard the short, quick rings of her doorbell that meant there was a call for her.

"Thank you," Therese called down to Mrs. Osborne.

It was Richard's usual call around nine o'clock. Richard wanted to know if she felt like seeing a movie tomorrow night. It was the movie at the Sutton they still hadn't seen. Therese said she wasn't doing anything, but she wanted to finish a pillow cover. Alice Kelly had said she could come down and use her sewing machine tomorrow night. And besides, she had to wash her hair.

"Wash it tonight and see me tomorrow night," Richard said.

"It's too late. I can't sleep if my head's wet."

"I'll wash it tomorrow night. We won't use the tub, just a couple of buckets."

She smiled. "I think we'd better not." She had fallen into the tub the time Richard had washed her hair. Richard had been imitating the tub drain with writhings and gluggings, and she had laughed so hard her feet slipped on the floor.

"Well, what about that art show Saturday? It's open Saturday afternoon."

"But Saturday's the day I have to work to nine. I can't get away till nine-thirty."

"Oh. Well, I'll stay around school and meet you on the corner about nine-thirty. Forty-fourth and Fifth. All right?"

"All right."

"Anything new today?"

"No. With you?"

"No. I'm going to see about boat reservations tomorrow. I'll call you tomorrow night."

Therese did not telephone Stella after all.

The next day was Friday, the last Friday before Christmas, and the busiest day Therese had known since she had been working at Frankenberg's, though everyone said tomorrow would be worse. People were pressed alarmingly hard against the glass counters. Customers she started to wait on got swept away and lost in the gluey current that filled the aisle. It was impossible to imagine any more people crowding onto the floor, but the elevators kept emptying people out.

"I don't see why they don't close the doors downstairs!" Therese remarked to Miss Martucci, when they were both stooping by a stock shelf.

"What?" Miss Martucci answered, unable to hear.

"Miss Belivet!" somebody yelled, and a whistle blew.

It was Mrs. Hendrickson. She had been using a whistle to get attention today. Therese made her way toward her, past salesgirls and through empty boxes on the floor.

"You're wanted on the telephone," Mrs. Hendrickson told her, pointing to the telephone by the wrapping table.

Therese made a helpless gesture that Mrs. Hendrickson had no time to see. It was impossible to hear anything on a telephone now. And she knew it was probably Richard being funny. He had called her once before.

"Hello?" she said.

"Hello, is this coworker six forty-five A, Therese Belivet?" the operator's voice said over clickings and buzzings. "Go ahead."

"Hello?" she repeated, and barely heard an answer. She dragged the telephone off the table and into the stockroom a few feet away. The wire did not quite reach, and she had to stoop on the floor. "Hello?"

"Hello," the voice said. "Well—I wanted to thank you for the Christmas card."

"Oh. Oh, you're—"

"This is Mrs. Aird," she said. "Are you the one who sent it? Or not?"

"Yes," Therese said, rigid with guilt suddenly, as if she had been caught in a crime. She closed her eyes and wrung the telephone, seeing the intelligent, smiling eyes again as she had seen them yesterday. "I'm very sorry if it annoyed you," Therese said mechanically, in the voice with which she spoke to customers.

The woman laughed. "This is very funny," she said casually, and Therese caught the same easy slur in her voice that she had heard yesterday, loved yesterday, and she smiled herself.

"Is it? Why?"

"You must be the girl in the toy department."

"Yes."

"It was extremely nice of you to send me the card," the woman said politely.

Then Therese understood. She had thought it was from a man, some other clerk who had waited on her. "It was very nice waiting on you," Therese said.

"Was it? Why?" She might have been mocking Therese. "Well—since it's Christmas, why don't we meet for a cup of coffee, at least? Or a drink."

Therese flinched as the door burst open and a girl came into the room, stood right in front of her. "Yes—I'd like that."

"When?" the woman asked. "I'm coming in to New York tomorrow in the morning. Why don't we make it for lunch? Do you have any time tomorrow?"

"Of course. I have an hour, from twelve to one," Therese said, staring at the girl's feet in front of her in splayed flat moccasins, the back of her heavy ankles and calves in lisle stockings, shifting like an elephant's legs.

"Shall I meet you downstairs at the Thirty-fourth Street entrance at about twelve?"

"All right. I—" Therese remembered now she went to work at one sharp tomorrow. She had the morning off. She put her arm up to ward off the avalanche of boxes the girl in front of her had pulled down from the shelf. The girl herself teetered back onto her. "Hello?" she shouted over the noise of tumbling boxes.

"I'm sow-ry," Mrs. Zabriskie said irritatedly, plowing out the door again.

"Hello?" Therese repeated.

The line was dead.

## *four*

"Hello," the woman said, smiling.

"Hello."

"What's the matter?"

"Nothing." At least the woman had recognized her, Therese thought.

"Do you have any preference as to restaurants?" the woman asked on the sidewalk.

"No. It'd be nice to find a quiet one, but there aren't any in this neighborhood."

"You haven't time for the East Side? No, you haven't, if you've only got an hour. I think I know a place a couple of blocks west on this street. Do you think you have time?"

"Yes, certainly." It was twelve-fifteen already. Therese knew she would be terribly late, and it didn't matter at all.

They did not bother to talk on the way. Now and then the crowds made them separate, and once the woman glanced at Therese, across a pushcart full of dresses, smiling. They went into a restaurant with wooden rafters and white tablecloths, that miraculously was quiet, and not half filled. They sat down in a large wooden booth, and the woman ordered an old-fashioned without sugar, and invited Therese to have one, or a sherry, and when Therese hesitated, sent the waiter away with the order.

She took off her hat and ran her fingers through her blonde hair, once on either side, and looked at Therese. "And where did you get the nice idea of sending me a Christmas card?"

"I remembered you," Therese said. She looked at the small pearl earrings, that were somehow no lighter than her hair itself, or her eyes. Therese thought her beautiful, though her face was a blur now because she could not bear to look at it directly. She got something out of her handbag, a lipstick and compact, and Therese looked at her lipstick case—golden like a jewel, and shaped like a sea chest. She wanted to look at the woman's mouth, but the gray eyes so close drove her away, flickering over her like fire.

"You haven't been working there very long, have you?"

"No. Only about two weeks."

"And you won't be much longer—probably." She offered Therese a cigarette.

Therese took one. "No. I'll have another job." She leaned toward the lighter the woman was holding for her, toward the slim hand with the oval red nails and a sprinkling of freckles on its back.

"And do you often get inspired to send postcards?"

"Postcards?"

"Christmas cards?" She smiled at herself.

"Of course not," Therese said.

"Well, here's to Christmas." She touched Therese's glass and drank. "Where do you live? In Manhattan?"

Therese told her. On Sixty-third Street. Her parents were dead, she said. She had lived in New York the past two years, and before that at a school in New Jersey. Therese did not tell her that the school was semireligious, Episcopalian. She did not mention Sister Alicia whom she adored and thought of so often, with her pale blue eyes and her ugly nose and her loving sternness. Because since yesterday morning, Sister Alicia had been thrust far away, far below the woman who sat opposite her.

"And what do you do in your spare time?" The lamp on the table made her eyes silvery, full of liquid light. Even the pearl at her earlobe looked alive, like a drop of water that a touch might destroy.

"I—" Should she tell her she usually worked on her stage models? Sketched and painted sometimes, carved things like cats' heads and tiny figures to go in her ballet sets, but that she liked best to take long walks practically anywhere, liked best simply to dream? Therese felt she did not have to tell her. She felt the woman's eyes could not look at anything without understanding completely. Therese took some more of her drink, liking it, though it was like the woman to swallow, she thought, terrifying, and strong.

The woman nodded to the waiter, and two more drinks arrived.

"I like this."

"What?" Therese asked.

"I like it that someone sent me a card, someone I didn't know. It's the way things should be at Christmas. And this year I like it especially."

"I'm glad." Therese smiled, wondering if she were serious.

"You're a very pretty girl," she said. "And very sensitive, too, aren't you?"

She might have been speaking of a doll, Therese thought, so casually had she told her she was pretty. "I think you are magnificent," Therese said with the courage of the second drink, not caring how it might sound, because she knew the woman knew anyway.

She laughed, putting her head back. It was a sound more beautiful than music. It made a little wrinkle at the corner of her eyes, and it made her purse her red lips as she drew on her cigarette. She gazed past

Therese for a moment, her elbows on the table and her chin propped up on the hand that held her cigarette. There was a long line from the waist of her fitted black suit up to the widening shoulder, and then the blond head with the fine, unruly hair held high. She was about thirty or thirty-two, Therese thought, and her daughter, for whom she had bought the valise and the doll, would be perhaps six or eight. Therese could imagine the child, blonde-haired, the face golden and happy, the body slim and well proportioned, and always playing. But the child's face, unlike the woman's with its short cheeks and rather Nordic compactness, was vague and nondescript. And the husband? Therese could not see him at all.

Therese said, "I'm sure you thought it was a man who sent you the Christmas card, didn't you?"

"I did," she said through a smile. "I thought it just might be a man in the ski department who'd sent it."

"I'm sorry."

"No, I'm delighted." She leaned back in the booth. "I doubt very much if I'd have gone to lunch with him. No, I'm delighted."

The dusky and faintly sweet smell of her perfume came to Therese again, a smell suggestive of dark green silk, that was hers alone, like the smell of a special flower. Therese leaned closer toward it, looking down at her glass. She wanted to thrust the table aside and spring into her arms, to bury her nose in the green and gold scarf that was tied close about her neck. Once the backs of their hands brushed on the table, and Therese's skin there felt separately alive now, and rather burning. Therese could not understand it, but it was so. Therese glanced at her face that was somewhat turned away, and again she knew that instant of half-recognition. And knew, too, that it was not to be believed. She had never seen the woman before. If she had, could she have forgotten? In the silence, Therese felt they both waited for the other to speak, yet the silence was not an awkward one. Their plates had arrived. They had ordered creamed spinach with an egg on top, steamy and buttery smelling.

"How is it you live alone?" the woman asked, and before Therese knew it, she had told the woman her life story.

But not in tedious detail. In six sentences, as if it all mattered less to her than a story she had read somewhere. And what did the facts matter after all, whether her mother was French or English or Hungarian, or if her father had been an Irish painter, or a Czechoslovakian lawyer, whether he had been successful or not, or whether her mother had presented her to the Order of St. Margaret as a troublesome, bawling infant, or as a troublesome, melancholy eight-year-old? Or whether she had been happy there. Because she was happy now, starting today. She had no need of parents or background.

"What could be duller than past history!" Therese said, smiling.

"Maybe futures that won't have any history."

Therese did not ponder it. It was right. She was still smiling, as if she had just learned how to smile and did not know how to stop. The woman smiled with her, amusedly, and perhaps she was laughing at her, Therese thought.

"What kind of a name is Belivet?" she asked.

"It's Czech. It's changed," Therese explained awkwardly. "Originally—"

"It's very original."

"What's your name?" Therese asked. "Your first name?"

"My name? Carol. Please don't ever call me *Carole*."

"Please don't ever call me Thereese," Therese said, pronouncing the *th*.

"How do you like it pronounced? *Therese*?"

"Yes. The way you do," she answered. Carol pronounced her name the French way, *Terez*. She was used to a dozen variations, and sometimes she herself pronounced it differently. She liked the way Carol pronounced it, and she liked her lips saying it. An indefinite longing, that she had been only vaguely conscious of at times before, became now a recognizable wish. It was so absurd, so embarrassing a desire, that Therese thrust it from her mind.

"What do you do on Sundays?" Carol asked.

"I don't always know. Nothing in particular. What do you do?"

"Nothing—lately. If you'd like to visit me sometime, you're welcome to. At least there's some country around where I live. Would you like to come out this Sunday?" The gray eyes regarded her directly now, and for the first time Therese faced them. There was a measure of humor in them, Therese saw. And what else? Curiosity, and a challenge, too.

"Yes," Therese said.

"What a strange girl you are."

"Why?"

"Flung out of space," Carol said.

# five

Richard was standing on the street corner, waiting for her, shifting from foot to foot in the cold. She wasn't cold at all tonight, she realized suddenly, even though other people on the streets were hunched in their overcoats. She took Richard's arm and squeezed it affectionately tight.

"Have you been inside?" she asked. She was ten minutes late.

"Of course not. I was waiting." He pressed his cold lips and nose into her cheek. "Did you have a rough day?"

"No."

The night was very black, in spite of the Christmas lights on some of the lampposts. She looked at Richard's face in the flare of his match. The smooth slab of his forehead overhung his narrowed eyes, strong-looking as a whale's front, she thought, strong enough to batter something in. His face was like a face sculpted in wood, planed smooth and unadorned. She saw his eyes open like unexpected spots of blue sky in the darkness.

He smiled at her. "You're in a good mood tonight. Want to walk down the block? You can't smoke in there. Like a cigarette?"

"No, thanks."

They began to walk. The gallery was just beside them, a row of lighted windows, each with a Christmas wreath, on the second floor of the big building. Tomorrow she would see Carol, Therese thought, tomorrow morning at eleven. She would see her only ten blocks from here, in a little more than twelve hours. She started to take Richard's arm again, and suddenly felt self-conscious about it. Eastward, down Forty-third Street, she saw Orion exactly spread in the center of the sky between the buildings. She had used to look at him from windows in school, from the window of her first New York apartment.

"I got our reservations today," Richard said. "The *President Taylor* sailing March seventh. I talked with the ticket fellow, and I think he can get us outside rooms, if I keep after him."

"March seventh?" She heard the start of excitement in her voice, though she did not want to go to Europe now at all.

"About ten weeks off," Richard said, taking her hand.

"Can you cancel the reservation in case I can't go?" She could as well tell him now that she didn't want to go, she thought, but he would only argue, as he had before when she hesitated.

"Of . . . of course, Terry!" And he laughed.

Richard swung her hand as they walked. As if they were lovers, Therese thought. It would be almost like love, what she felt for Carol, except that Carol was a woman. It was not quite insanity, but it was certainly blissful. A silly word, but how could she possibly be happier than she was now, and had been since Thursday?

"I wish we could share one together," Richard said.

"Share what?"

"Share a room!" Richard boomed out, laughing, and Therese noticed the two people on the sidewalk who turned to look at them. "Should we have a drink somewhere just to celebrate? We can go in the Mansfield around the corner."

"I don't feel like sitting still. Let's have it later."

They got into the show at half price on Richard's art-school passes. The gallery was a series of high-ceilinged, plush-carpeted rooms, a background of financial opulence for the commercial advertisements, the drawings, lithographs, illustrations, or whatever that hung in a crowded row on the walls. Richard pored over some of them for minutes at a time, but Therese found them a little depressing.

"Did you see this?" Richard asked, pointing to a complicated drawing of a lineman repairing a telephone wire that Therese had seen somewhere before, that tonight actually pained her to look at.

"Yes," she said. She was thinking of something else. If she stopped scrimping to save money for Europe—which had been silly anyway because she wasn't going—she could buy a new coat. There would be sales right after Christmas. The coat she had now was a kind of black polo coat, and she always felt drab in it.

Richard took her arm. "You haven't enough respect for technique, little girl."

She gave him a mocking frown, and took his arm again. She felt very close to him suddenly, as warm and happy with him as she had been the first night she met him, at the party down on Christopher Street where Frances Cotter had taken her. Richard had been a little drunk, as he had never been since with her, talking about books and politics and people more positively than she had ever heard him talk since, too. He had talked with her all evening, and she had liked him so very much that night for his enthusiasms, his ambitions, his likes and dislikes, and because it was her first real party and he had made it a success for her.

"You're not looking," Richard said.

"It's exhausting. I've had enough when you have."

Near the door, they met some people Richard knew from the League, a young man, a girl, and a young black man. Richard introduced Therese to them. She could tell they were not close friends of Richard's, but he announced to all of them, "We're going to Europe in March."

And they all looked envious.

Outside, Fifth Avenue seemed empty and waiting, like a stage set, for some dramatic action. Therese walked along quickly beside Richard, her hands in her pockets. Somewhere today she had lost her gloves. She was thinking of tomorrow, at eleven o'clock. She wondered if she would possibly still be with Carol this time tomorrow night.

"What about tomorrow?" Richard asked.

"Tomorrow?"

"You know. The family asked if you could come out this Sunday and have dinner with us."

Therese hesitated, remembering. She had visited the Semcos four or five Sunday afternoons. They had a big dinner around two o'clock, and then Mr. Semco, a short man with a bald head, would want to dance with her to polkas and Russian folk music on the phonograph.

"Say, you know Mamma wants to make you a dress?" Richard went on. "She's already got the material. She wants to measure you for it."

"A dress—that's so much work." Therese had a vision of Mrs.

Semco's embroidered blouses, white blouses with rows upon rows of stitches. Mrs. Semco was proud of her needlework. Therese did not feel she should accept such a colossal labor.

"She loves it," Richard said. "Well, what about tomorrow? Want to come out around noon?"

"I don't think I want to this Sunday. They haven't made any great plans, have they?"

"No," Richard said, disappointed. "You just want to work or something tomorrow?"

"Yes. I'd rather." She didn't want Richard to know about Carol, or even ever meet her.

"Not even take a drive somewhere?"

"I don't think so, thanks." Therese didn't like his holding her hand now. His hand was moist, which made it icy cold.

"You don't think you'll change your mind?"

Therese shook her head. "No." There were some mitigating things she might have said, excuses, but she did not want to lie about tomorrow either, any more than she had already lied. She heard Richard sigh, and they walked along in silence for a while.

"Mamma wants to make you a white dress with lace edging. She's going crazy with frustration with no girls in the family but Esther."

That was his cousin by marriage, whom Therese had seen only once or twice. "How is Esther?"

"Just the same."

Therese extricated her fingers from Richard's. She was hungry suddenly. She had spent her dinner hour writing something, a kind of letter to Carol that she hadn't mailed and didn't intend to. They caught the uptown bus at Third Avenue, then walked east to Therese's house. Therese did not want to invite Richard upstairs, but she did anyway.

"No, thanks, I'll shove on," Richard said. He put a foot on the first step. "You're in a funny mood tonight. You're miles away."

"No, I'm not," she said, feeling inarticulate and resenting it.

"You are now. I can tell. After all, don't you—"

"What?" she prompted.

"We aren't getting very far, are we?" he said, suddenly earnest. "If you don't even want to spend Sundays with me, how're we going to spend months together in Europe?"

"Well—if you want to call it all off, Richard."

"Terry, I love you." He brushed his palm over his hair, exasperatedly. "Of course, I don't want to call it all off, but—" He broke off again.

She knew what he was about to say, that she gave him practically nothing in the way of affection, but he wouldn't say it, because he knew very well that she wasn't in love with him, so why did he really expect her affection? Yet the simple fact that she wasn't in love with him made Therese feel guilty, guilty about accepting anything from him, a birthday present, or an invitation to dinner at his family's, or even his time. Therese pressed her fingertips hard on the stone banister. "All right—I know. I'm not in love with you," she said.

"That's not what I mean, Terry."

"If you ever want to call the whole thing off—I mean, stop seeing me at all, then do it." It was not the first time she had said that, either.

"Terry, you know I'd rather be with you than anyone else in the world. That's the hell of it."

"Well, if it's hell—"

"Do you love me at all, Terry? How do you love me?"

Let me count the ways, she thought. "I don't love you, but I like you. I felt tonight, a few minutes ago," she said, hammering the words out however they sounded, because they were true, "that I felt closer to you than I ever have, in fact."

Richard looked at her, a little incredulously. "Do you?" He started slowly up the steps, smiling, and stopped just below her. "Then—why not let me stay with you tonight, Terry? Just let's try, will you?"

She had known from his first step toward her that he was going to ask her that. Now she felt miserable and ashamed, sorry for herself and for him, because it was so impossible, and so embarrassing because she didn't want it. There was always that tremendous block of not even wanting to try it, which reduced it all to a kind of wretched embarrassment and nothing more, each time he asked her. She remembered the first night she had let him stay, and she writhed again inwardly. It had been anything but pleasant, and she had asked right in the middle of it, "Is this right?" How could it be right and so unpleasant, she had thought. And Richard had laughed, long and loud and with a heartiness that had made her angry. And the second time had been even worse, probably because Richard had thought all the difficulties had been gotten over. It was painful enough to make her weep, and Richard had been very apologetic and had said she made him feel like a brute. And then she had protested that he wasn't. She knew very well that he wasn't, that he was angelic compared to what Angelo Rossi would have been, for instance, if she had slept with him the night he stood here on the same steps, asking her the same question.

"Terry, darling—"

"No," Therese said, finding her voice at last. "I just can't tonight, and I can't go to Europe with you either," she finished with an abject and hopeless frankness.

Richard's lips parted in a stunned way. Therese could not bear to look at the frown above them. "Why not?"

"Because. Because I can't," she said, every word agony. "Because I don't want to sleep with you."

"Oh, Terry!" Richard laughed. "I'm sorry I asked you. Forget about it, honey, will you? And in Europe, too?"

Therese looked away, noticed Orion again, tipped at a slightly different angle, and looked back at Richard. But I can't, she thought. I've got to think about it sometime, because you think about it. It seemed to her that she spoke the words and that they were solid as blocks of wood in the air between them, even though she heard nothing. She had said the words before to him, in her room upstairs, once in Prospect Park when she was winding a kite string. But he wouldn't consider them, and what could she do now, repeat them? "Do you want to come up for a while anyway?" she asked, tortured by herself, by a shame she could not really account for.

"No," Richard said with a soft laugh that shamed her all the more for its tolerance and its understanding. "No, I'll go on. Good night, honey. I love you, Terry." And with a last look at her, he went.

## *six*

Therese stepped out into the street and looked, but the streets were empty with a Sunday morning emptiness. The wind flung itself around the tall cement corner of Frankenberg's as if it were furious at finding no human figure there to oppose. No one but her, Therese thought, and grinned suddenly at herself. She might have thought of a more pleasant place to meet than this. The wind was like ice against her teeth. Carol was a quarter of an hour late. If she didn't come, she would probably keep on waiting, all day and into the night. One figure came out of the subway's pit, a splintery thin hurrying figure of a woman in a long black coat under which her feet moved as fast as if four feet were rotating on a wheel.

Then Therese turned around and saw Carol in a car drawn up by the curb across the street. Therese walked toward her.

"Hi!" Carol called, and leaned over to open the door for her.

"Hello. I thought you weren't coming."

"Awfully sorry I'm late. Are you freezing?"

"No." Therese got in and pulled the door shut. The car was warm inside, a long dark green car with dark green leather upholstery. Carol drove slowly west.

"Shall we go out to the house? Where would you like to go?"

"It doesn't matter," Therese said. She could see freckles along the bridge of Carol's nose. Her short fair hair that made Therese think of perfume held to a light was tied back with the green and gold scarf that circled her head like a band.

"Let's go out to the house. It's pretty out there."

They drove uptown. It was like riding inside a rolling mountain that could sweep anything before it, yet was absolutely obedient to Carol.

"Do you like driving?" Carol asked without looking at her. She had a cigarette in her mouth. She drove with her hands resting lightly on the wheel, as if it were nothing to her, as if she sat relaxed in a chair somewhere, smoking. "Why're you so quiet?"

They roared into the Lincoln Tunnel. A wild, inexplicable excitement mounted in Therese as she stared through the windshield. She wished the tunnel might cave in and kill them both, that their bodies might be dragged out together. She felt Carol glancing at her from time to time.

"Have you had breakfast?"

"No, I haven't," Therese answered. She supposed she was pale. She had started to have breakfast, but she had dropped the milk bottle in the sink, and then given it all up.

"Better have some coffee. It's there in the thermos."

They were out of the tunnel. Carol stopped by the side of the road.

"There," Carol said, nodding at the thermos between them on the seat. Then Carol took the thermos herself and poured some into the cup, steaming and light brown.

Therese looked at the coffee gratefully. "Where'd it come from?"

Carol smiled. "Do you always want to know where things come from?"

The coffee was very strong and a little sweet. It sent strength through her. When the cup was half empty, Carol started the car. Therese was silent. What was there to talk about? The gold four-leaf clover with Carol's name and address on it that dangled from the key chain on the dashboard? The stand of Christmas trees they passed on the road? The bird that flew by itself across a swampy-looking field? No. Only the things she had written to Carol in the unmailed letter were to be talked about, and that was impossible.

"Do you like the country?" Carol asked as they turned into a smaller road.

They had just driven into a little town and out of it. Now on the driveway that made a great semicircular curve, they approached a white two-story house that had projecting side wings like the paws of a resting lion.

There was a metal doormat, a big shining brass mailbox, a dog barking hollowly from around the side of the house, where a white garage showed beyond some trees. The house smelled of some spice, Therese thought, mingled with a separate sweetness that was not Carol's perfume either. Behind her, the door closed with a light, firm double report. Therese turned and found Carol looking at her puzzledly, her lips parted a little as if in surprise, and Therese felt that in the next second Carol would ask, "What are you doing here?" as if she had forgotten, or had not meant to bring her here at all.

"There's no one here but the maid. And she's far away," Carol said, as if in reply to some question of Therese's.

"It's a lovely house," Therese said, and saw Carol's little smile that was tinged with impatience.

"Take off your coat." Carol took the scarf from around her head and ran her fingers through her hair. "Wouldn't you like a little breakfast? It's almost noon."

"No, thanks."

Carol looked around the living room, and the same puzzled dissatisfaction came back to her face. "Let's go upstairs. It's more comfortable."

Therese followed Carol up the wide wooden staircase, past an oil painting of a small girl with yellow hair and a square chin like Carol's, past a window where a garden with an S-shaped path, a fountain with a blue-green statue appeared for an instant and vanished. Upstairs, there was a short hall with four or five rooms around it. Carol went into a room with green carpet and walls, and took a cigarette from a box on a table. She glanced at Therese as she lighted it. Therese didn't know what to do or say, and she felt Carol expected her to do or say something, anything. Therese studied the simple room with its dark green carpet and the long green pillowed bench along one wall. There was a plain table of pale wood in the center. A game room, Therese thought, though it looked more like a study with its books and music albums and its lack of pictures.

"My favorite room," Carol said, walking out of it. "But that's my room over there."

Therese looked into the room opposite. It had flowered cotton upholstery and plain blonde woodwork like the table in the other room. There was a long plain mirror over the dressing table, and throughout a look of sunlight, though no sunlight was in the room. The bed was a double bed. And there were military brushes on the dark bureau across the room. Therese glanced in vain for a picture of him. There was a picture of Carol on the dressing table, holding up a small girl with blonde hair. And a picture of a woman with dark curly hair, smiling broadly, in a silver frame.

"You have a little girl, haven't you?" Therese asked.

Carol opened a wall panel in the hall. "Yes," she said. "Would you like a Coke?"

The hum of the refrigerator came louder now. Through all the house, there was no sound but those they made. Therese did not want the cold drink, but she took the bottle and carried it downstairs after Carol, through the kitchen and into the back garden she had seen from the window. Beyond the fountain were a lot of plants some three feet high and wrapped in burlap bags that looked like something, standing there in a group, Therese thought, but she didn't know what. Carol tightened a string that the wind had loosened. Stooped in the heavy wool skirt and the blue cardigan sweater, her figure looked solid and strong, like her face, but not like her slender ankles. Carol seemed oblivious of her for several minutes, walking about slowly, planting her moccasined feet firmly, as if in the cold flowerless garden she was at last comfortable. It was bitterly cold without a coat, but because Carol seemed oblivious of that, too, Therese tried to imitate her.

"What would you like to do?" Carol asked. "Take a walk? Play some records?"

"I'm very content," Therese told her.

She was preoccupied with something, and regretted after all inviting her out to the house, Therese felt. They walked back to the door at the end of the garden path.

"And how do you like your job?" Carol asked in the kitchen, still with her air of remoteness. She was looking into the big refrigerator. She lifted out two plates covered with wax paper. "I wouldn't mind some lunch, would you?"

Therese had intended to tell her about the job at the Black Cat Theater. That would count for something, she thought, that would be the single important thing she could tell about herself. But this was not the time. Now she replied slowly, trying to sound as detached as Carol, though she heard her shyness predominating, "I suppose it's educational. I learn how to be a thief, a liar, and a poet all at once." Therese leaned back in the straight chair so her head would be in the warm square of sunlight. She wanted to say, and how to love. She had never loved anyone before Carol, not even Sister Alicia.

Carol looked at her. "How do you become a poet?"

"By feeling things—too much, I suppose," Therese answered conscientiously.

"And how do you become a thief?" Carol licked something off her thumb and frowned. "You don't want any caramel pudding, do you?"

"No, thank you. I haven't stolen yet, but I'm sure it's easy there. There are pocketbooks all around, and one just takes something. They steal the meat you buy for dinner." Therese laughed. One could laugh at it with Carol. One could laugh at anything, with Carol.

They had sliced cold chicken, cranberry sauce, green olives, and crisp white celery. But Carol left her lunch and went into the living room. She came back carrying a glass with some whiskey in it, and added some water to it from the tap. Therese watched her. Then for a long moment, they looked at each other, Carol standing in the doorway and Therese at the table, looking over her shoulder, not eating.

Carol asked quietly, "Do you meet a lot of people across the counter this way? Don't you have to be careful whom you start talking to?"

"Oh, yes," Therese smiled.

"Or whom you go out to lunch with?" Carol's eyes sparkled. "You might run into a kidnapper." She rolled the drink around in the iceless glass, then drank it off, the thin silver bracelets on her wrist rattling against the glass. "Well—do you meet many people this way?"

"No," Therese said.

"Not many? Just three or four?"

"Like you?" Therese met her eyes steadily.

And Carol looked fixedly at her, as if she demanded another word, another phrase from Therese. But then she set the glass down on the stove top and turned away. "Do you play the piano?"

"Some."

"Come and play something." And when Therese started to refuse, she said imperatively, "Oh, I don't care how you play. Just play something."

Therese played some Scarlatti she had learned at the Home. In a chair on the other side of the room, Carol sat listening, relaxed and motionless, not even sipping the new glass of whiskey and water. Therese played the C major Sonata, which was slowish and rather simple, full of broken octaves, but it struck her as dull, then pretentious in the trill parts, and she stopped. It was suddenly too much, her hands on the keyboard that she knew Carol played, Carol watching her with her eyes half closed, Carol's whole house around her, and the music that made her abandon herself, made her defenseless. With a gasp, she dropped her hands in her lap.

"Are you tired?" Carol asked calmly.

The question seemed not of now but of always. "Yes."

Carol came up behind her and set her hands on Therese's shoulders. Therese could see her hands in her memory—flexible and strong, the delicate tendons showing as they pressed her shoulders. It seemed an age as her hands moved toward her neck and under her chin, an age of tumult so intense it blotted out the pleasure of Carol's tipping her head back and kissing her lightly at the edge of her hair. Therese did not feel the kiss at all.

"Come with me," Carol said.

She went with Carol upstairs again. Therese pulled herself up by the banister and was reminded suddenly of Mrs. Robichek.

"I think a nap wouldn't hurt you," Carol said, turning down the flowered cotton bedspread and the top blanket.

"Thanks, I'm not really—"

"Slip your shoes off," Carol said softly, but in a tone that commanded obedience.

Therese looked at the bed. She had hardly slept the night before. "I don't think I shall sleep, but if I do—"

"I'll wake you in half an hour." Carol pulled the blanket over her when she lay down. Carol sat down on the edge of the bed. "How old are you, Therese?"

Therese looked up at her, unable to bear her eyes now but bearing them nevertheless, not caring if she died that instant, if Carol strangled her, prostrate and vulnerable in her bed, the intruder. "Nineteen." How old it sounded. Older than ninety-one.

Carol's eyebrows frowned, though she smiled a little. Therese felt that she thought of something so intensely, one might have touched the thought in the air between them. Then Carol slipped her hands under her shoulders, and bent her head down to Therese's throat, and Therese felt the tension go out of Carol's body with the sigh that made her neck warm, that carried the perfume that was in Carol's hair.

"You're a child," Carol said, like a reproach. She lifted her head. "What would you like?"

Therese remembered what she had thought of in the restaurant, and she set her teeth in shame.

"What would you like?" Carol repeated.

"Nothing, thanks."

Carol got up and went to her dressing table and lighted a cigarette. Therese watched her through half-closed lids, worried by Carol's restlessness, though she loved the cigarette, loved to see her smoke.

"What would you like, a drink?"

Therese knew she meant water. She knew from the tenderness and the concern in her voice, as if she were a child sick with fever. Then Therese said it: "I think I'd like some hot milk."

The corner of Carol's mouth lifted in a smile. "Some hot milk," she mocked. Then she left the room.

And Therese lay in a limbo of anxiety and sleepiness all the long while until Carol reappeared with the milk in a straight-sided white cup with a saucer under it, holding the saucer and the cup handle, and closing the door with her foot.

"I let it boil and it's got a scum on it," Carol said, sounding annoyed. "I'm sorry."

But Therese loved it, because she knew this was exactly what Carol would always do, be thinking of something else and let the milk boil.

"Is that the way you like it? Plain like that?"

Therese nodded.

"Ugh," Carol said, and sat down on the arm of a chair and watched her.

Therese was propped on one elbow. The milk was so hot, she could barely let her lip touch it at first. The tiny sips spread inside her mouth and released a mélange of organic flavors. The milk seemed to taste of bone and blood, of warm flesh, or hair, saltless as chalk yet alive as a growing embryo. It was hot through and through to the bottom of the cup, and Therese drank it down, as people in fairy tales drink the potion that will transform, or the unsuspecting warrior the cup that will kill. Then Carol came and took the cup, and Therese was drowsily aware that Carol asked her three questions, one that had to do with happiness, one about the store, and one about the future. Therese heard herself answering. She heard her voice rise suddenly in a babble, like a spring that she had no control over, and she realized she was in tears. She was telling Carol all that she feared and disliked, of her loneliness, of Richard, and of gigantic disappointments. And of her parents. Her mother was not dead. But Therese had not seen her since she was fourteen.

Carol questioned her, and she answered, though she did not want to talk about her mother. Her mother was not that important, not even one of the disappointments. Her father was. Her father was quite different. He had died when she was six—a lawyer of Czechoslovakian descent who all his life had wanted to be a painter. He had been quite different, gentle, sympathetic, never raising his voice in anger against the woman who had nagged at him, because he had been neither a good lawyer nor a good painter. He had never been strong, he had died of pneumonia, but in Therese's mind, her mother had killed him. Carol questioned and questioned her, and Therese told of her mother's bringing her to the school in Montclair when she was eight, of her mother's infrequent visits afterward, for her mother had traveled a great deal around the country. She had been a pianist—no, not a first-rate one, how could she be, but she had always found work because she was pushing. And when Therese was about ten, her mother had remarried. Therese had visited at her mother's house in Long Island in the Christmas holidays, and they had asked her to stay with them, but not as if they wanted her to stay. And Therese had not liked the husband, Nick, because he was exactly like her mother, big and dark-haired, with a loud voice, and violent and passionate gestures. Therese was sure their marriage would be perfect. Her mother had been pregnant even then, and now there were two children. After a week with them, Therese had returned to the Home. There had been perhaps three or four visits from her mother afterward, always with some present for her, a blouse, a book, once a cosmetic kit that Therese had loathed simply because it reminded her of her mother's brittle, mascaraed eyelashes, presents handed her self-consciously by her mother, like hypocritical peace offerings. Once her mother had brought the little boy, her half brother, and then Therese had known she was an outsider. Her mother had not loved her father, had chosen to leave her at a school when she was eight, and why did she bother now even to visit her, to claim her at all? Therese would have been happier to have no parents, like half the girls in the school. Finally, Therese had told her mother she did not want her to visit again, and her mother hadn't, and the ashamed, resentful expression, the nervous sidewise glance of the brown eyes, the twitch of a smile and the silence—that was the last she remembered of her mother. Then she had become fifteen. The sisters at the school had known her mother was not writing. They had asked her mother to write, and she had, but Therese had not answered. Then when graduation came, when she was seventeen, the school had asked her mother for two hundred dollars. Therese hadn't wanted any money from her, had half believed her mother wouldn't give her any, but she had, and Therese had taken it.

"I'm sorry I took it. I never told anyone but you. Someday I want to give it back."

"Nonsense," Carol said softly. She was sitting on the arm of the chair, resting her chin in her hand, her eyes fixed on Therese, smiling. "You were still a child. When you forget about paying her back, then you'll be an adult."

Therese did not answer.

"Don't you think you'll ever want to see her again? Maybe in a few years from now?"

Therese shook her head. She smiled, but the tears still oozed out of her eyes. "I don't want to talk any more about it."

"Does Richard know all this?"

"No. Just that she's alive. Does it matter? This isn't what matters." She felt if she wept enough, it would all go out of her, the tiredness and the loneliness and the disappointment, as though it were in the tears themselves. And she was glad Carol left her alone to do it now. Carol was standing by the dressing table, her back to her. Therese lay rigid in the bed, propped up on her elbow, racked with the half-suppressed sobs.

"I'll never cry again," she said.

"Yes, you will." And a match scraped.

Therese took another cleansing tissue from the bed table and blew her nose.

"Who else is in your life besides Richard?" Carol asked.

She had fled them all. There had been Lily, and Mr. and Mrs. Anderson in the house where she had first lived in New York. Frances Cotter and Tim at the Pelican Press. Lois Vavrica, a girl who had been at the Home in Montclair, too. Now who was there? The Kellys who lived on the second floor at Mrs. Osborne's. And Richard. "When I was fired from that job last month," Therese said, "I was ashamed and I moved—" She stopped.

"Moved where?"

"I didn't tell anyone where, except Richard. I just disappeared. I suppose it was my idea of starting a new life, but mostly I was ashamed. I didn't want anyone to know where I was."

Carol smiled. "Disappeared! I like that. And how lucky you are to be able to do it. You're free. Do you realize that?"

Therese said nothing.

"No," Carol answered herself.

Beside Carol on the dressing table, a square gray clock ticked faintly, and as Therese had done a thousand times in the store, she read the time and attached a meaning to it. It was four-fifteen and a little more, and suddenly she was anxious lest she had lain there too long, lest Carol might be expecting someone to come to the house.

Then the telephone rang, sudden and long like the shriek of an hysterical woman in the hall, and they saw each other start.

Carol stood up, and slapped something twice in her palm, as she had slapped the gloves in her palm in the store. The telephone screamed again, and Therese was sure Carol was going to throw whatever it was she held in her hand, throw it across the room against the wall. But Carol only turned and laid the thing down quietly, and left the room.

Therese could hear Carol's voice in the hall. She did not want to hear what she was saying. She got up and put her skirt and her shoes on. Now she saw what Carol had held in her hand. It was a shoehorn of tan-colored wood. Anyone else would have thrown it, Therese thought. Then she knew one word for what she felt about Carol: pride. She heard Carol's voice repeating the same tones, and now, opening the door to leave, she heard the words, "I have a guest," for the third time calmly presented as a barrier. "I think it's an excellent reason. What better? . . . What's the matter with tomorrow? If you—"

Then there was no sound until Carol's first step on the stair, and Therese knew whoever had been talking to her had hung up on her. Who dared, Therese wondered.

"Shouldn't I leave?" Therese asked.

Carol looked at her in the same way she had when they first entered the house. "Not unless you want to. No. We'll take a drive later, if you want to."

She knew Carol did not want to take another drive. Therese started to straighten the bed.

"Leave the bed." Carol was watching her from the hall. "Just close the door."

"Who is it that's coming?"

Carol turned and went into the green room. "My husband," she said. "Hargess."

Then the doorbell chimed twice downstairs, and the latch clicked at the same time.

"No end prompt today," Carol murmured. "Come down, Therese."

Therese felt sick with dread suddenly, not of the man but of Carol's annoyance at his coming.

He was coming up the stairs. When he saw Therese, he slowed, and a faint surprise crossed his face, and then he looked at Carol.

"Harge, this is Miss Belivet," Carol said. "Mr. Aird."

"How do you do?" Therese said.

Harge only glanced at Therese, but his nervous blue eyes inspected her from head to toe. He was a heavily built man with a rather pink face. One eyebrow was set higher than the other, rising in an alert peak in the center, as if it might have been distorted by a scar. "How do you do?" Then to Carol, "I'm sorry to disturb you. I only wanted to get one or two things." He went past her and opened the door to a room Therese had not seen. "Things for Rindy," he added.

"Pictures on the wall?" Carol asked.

The man was silent.

Carol and Therese went downstairs. In the living room Carol sat down but Therese did not.

"Play some more, if you like," Carol said.

Therese shook her head.

"Play some," Carol said firmly.

Therese was frightened by the sudden white anger in her eyes. "I can't," Therese said, stubborn as a mule.

And Carol subsided. Carol even smiled.

They heard Harge's quick steps cross the hall and stop, then descend the stairs slowly. Therese saw his dark-clad figure and then his pinkish-blond head appear.

"I can't find that watercolor set. I thought it was in my room," he said complainingly.

"I know where it is." Carol got up and started toward the stairs.

"I suppose you want me to take her something for Christmas," Harge said.

"Thanks, I'll give the things to her." Carol went up the stairs.

They are just divorced, Therese thought, or about to be divorced.

Harge looked at Therese. He had an intense expression that curiously mingled anxiety and boredom. The flesh around his mouth was firm and heavy, rounding into the line of his mouth so that he seemed lipless. "Are you from New York?" he asked.

Therese felt the disdain and incivility in the question, like the sting of a slap in the face. "Yes, from New York," she answered.

He was on the brink of another question to her, when Carol came down the stairs. Therese had steeled herself to be alone with him for minutes. Now she shuddered as she relaxed, and she knew that he saw it.

"Thanks," Harge said as he took the box from Carol. He walked to his overcoat that Therese had noticed on the loveseat, sprawled open with its black arms spread as if it were fighting and would take possession of the house. "Good-bye," Harge said to her. He put the overcoat on as he walked to the door. "Friend of Abby's?" he murmured to Carol.

"A friend of mine," Carol answered.

"Are you going to take the presents to Rindy? When?"

"What if I gave her nothing, Harge?"

"Carol—" He stopped on the porch, and Therese barely heard him say something about making things unpleasant. Then, "I'm going over to see Cynthia now. Can I stop by on the way back? It'll be before eight."

"Harge, what's the purpose?" Carol said wearily. "Especially when you're so disagreeable."

"Because it concerns Rindy." Then his voice faded unintelligibly.

Then, an instant later, Carol came in alone and closed the door. Carol stood against the door with her hands behind her, and they heard the car outside leaving. Carol must have agreed to see him tonight, Therese thought.

"I'll go," Therese said. Carol said nothing. There was a deadness in the silence between them now, and Therese grew more uneasy. "I'd better go, hadn't I?"

"Yes. I'm sorry. I'm sorry about Harge. He's not always so rude. It was a mistake to say I had any guest here at all."

"It doesn't matter."

Carol's forehead wrinkled and she said with difficulty, "Do you mind if I put you on the train tonight, instead of driving you home?"

"No." She couldn't have borne Carol's driving her home and driving back alone tonight in the darkness.

They were silent also in the car. Therese opened the door as soon as the car stopped at the station.

"There's a train in about four minutes," Carol said.

Therese blurted suddenly, "Will I see you again?"

Carol only smiled at her, a little reproachfully, as the window between them rose up. "Au revoir," she said.

Of course, of course, she would see her again, Therese thought. An idiotic question.

The car backed fast and turned away into the darkness.

Therese longed for the store again, longed for Monday, because Carol might come in again on Monday. But it wasn't likely. Tuesday was Christmas Eve. Certainly she could telephone Carol by Tuesday, if only to wish her a merry Christmas.

But there was not a moment when she did not see Carol in her mind, and all she saw, she seemed to see through Carol. That evening, the dark flat streets of New York, the tomorrow of work, the milk bottle dropped and broken in her sink, became unimportant. She flung herself on her bed and drew a line with a pencil on a piece of paper. And another line, carefully, and another. A world was born around her, like a bright forest with a million shimmering leaves.

## *seven*

The man looked at it, holding it carelessly between thumb and forefinger. He was bald except for long strands of black hair that grew from a former brow line, plastered sweatily down over the naked scalp. His underlip was thrust out with the contempt and negation that had fixed itself on his face as soon as Therese had come to the counter and spoken her first words.

"No," he said at last.

"Can't you give me anything for it?" Therese asked.

The lip came out further. "Maybe fifty cents." And he tossed it back across the counter.

Therese's fingers crept over it possessively. "Well, what about this?" From her coat pocket she dragged up the silver chain with the St. Christopher medallion.

Again the thumb and forefinger were eloquent of scorn, turning the coin like filth. "Two fifty."

But it cost at least twenty dollars, Therese started to say, but she didn't because that was what everybody said. "Thanks." She picked up the chain and went out.

Who were all the lucky people, she wondered, who had managed to sell their old pocketknives, broken wristwatches and carpenters' planes that hung in clumps in the front window? She could not resist looking back through the window, finding the man's face again under the row of hanging hunting knives. The man was looking at her, too, smiling at her. She felt he understood every move she made. Therese hurried down the sidewalk.

In ten minutes, Therese was back. She pawned the silver medallion for two dollars and fifty cents.

She hurried westward, ran across Lexington Avenue, then Park, and turned down Madison. She clutched the little box in her pocket until its sharp edges cut her fingers. Sister Beatrice had given it to her. It was inlaid brown wood and mother-of-pearl, in a checked pattern. She didn't know what it was worth in money, but she had assumed it was rather precious. Well, now she knew it wasn't. She went into a leather goods shop.

"I'd like to see the black one in the window—the one with the strap and the gold buckles," Therese said to the salesgirl.

It was the handbag she had noticed last Saturday morning on the way to meet Carol for lunch. It had looked like Carol, just at a glance. She had thought, even if Carol didn't keep the appointment that day, if she could never see Carol again, she must buy the bag and send it to her anyway.

"I'll take it," Therese said.

"That's seventy-one eighteen with the tax," the salesgirl said. "Do you want that gift-wrapped?"

"Yes, please." Therese counted six crisp ten-dollar bills across the counter and the rest in singles. "Can I leave it here till about six-thirty tonight?"

Therese left the shop with the receipt in her billfold. It wouldn't do to risk bringing the handbag into the store. It might be stolen, even if it was Christmas Eve. Therese smiled. It was her last day of work at the store. And in four more days came the job at the Black Cat. Phil was going to bring her a copy of the play the day after Christmas.

She passed Brentano's. Its window was full of satin ribbons, leather-bound books, and pictures of knights in armor. Therese turned back and went into the store, not to buy but to look, just for a moment, to see if there was anything here more beautiful than the handbag.

An illustration in one of the counter displays caught her eye. It was a young knight on a white horse, riding through a bouquetlike forest, followed by a line of page boys, the last bearing a cushion with a gold ring on it. She took the leather-bound book in her hand. The price inside the cover was twenty-five dollars. If she simply went to the bank now and got twenty-five dollars more, she could buy it. What was twenty-five dollars? She hadn't needed to pawn the silver medallion. She knew she had pawned it only because it was from Richard, and she didn't want it any longer. She closed the book and looked at the edges of the pages that were like a concave bar of gold. But would Carol really like it, a book of love poems of the Middle Ages? She didn't know. She couldn't remember the slightest clue as to Carol's taste in books. She put the book down hurriedly and left.

Upstairs in the doll department, Miss Santini was strolling along behind the counter, offering everybody candy from a big box.

"Take two," she said to Therese. "Candy department sent 'em up."

"I don't mind if I do." Imagine, she thought, biting into a nougat, the Christmas spirit had struck the candy department. There was a strange atmosphere in the store today. It was unusually quiet, first of all. There were plenty of customers, but they didn't seem in a hurry, even though it was Christmas Eve. Therese glanced at the elevators, looking for Carol. If Carol didn't come in, and she probably wouldn't, Therese was going to telephone her at six-thirty, just to wish her a happy Christmas. Therese knew her telephone number. She had seen it on the telephone at the house.

"Miss Belivet!" Mrs. Hendrickson's voice called, and Therese jumped to attention. But Mrs. Hendrickson only waved her hand for the benefit of the Western Union messenger who laid a telegram in front of Therese.

Therese signed for it in a scribble, and tore it open. It said: "MEET YOU DOWNSTAIRS AT 5 P.M. CAROL."

Therese crushed it in her hand. She pressed it hard with her thumb into her palm, and watched the messenger boy who was really an old man walk back toward the elevators. He walked ploddingly, with a stoop that thrust his knees far ahead of him, and his puttees were loose and wobbly.

"You look happy," Mrs. Zabriskie said dismally to her as she went by.

Therese smiled. "I am." Mrs. Zabriskie had a two-months'-old baby, she had told Therese, and her husband was out of work now. Therese wondered if Mrs. Zabriskie and her husband were in love with each other, and really happy. Perhaps they were, but there was nothing in Mrs. Zabriskie's blank face and her trudging gait that would suggest it. Perhaps once Mrs. Zabriskie had been as happy as she. Perhaps it had gone away. She remembered reading—even Richard once saying—that love usually dies after two years of marriage. That was a cruel thing, a trick. She tried to imagine Carol's face, the smell of her perfume, becoming meaningless. But in the first place could she say she was in love with Carol? She had come to a question she could not answer.

At a quarter to five, Therese went to Mrs. Hendrickson and asked permission to leave a half hour early. Mrs. Hendrickson might have thought the telegram had something to do with it, but she let Therese go without even a complaining look, and that was another thing that made the day a strange one.

Carol was waiting for her in the foyer where they had met before.

"Hello!" Therese said. "I'm through."

"Through what?"

"Through with working. Here." But Carol seemed depressed, and it dampened Therese instantly. She said anyway, "I was awfully happy to get the telegram."

"I didn't know if you'd be free. Are you free tonight?"

"Of course."

And they walked on, slowly, amid the jostling crowd, Carol in her delicate-looking suede pumps that made her a couple of inches taller than Therese. It had begun to snow about an hour before, but it was stopping already. The snow was no more than a film underfoot, like thin white wool drawn across the street and sidewalk.

"We might have seen Abby tonight, but she's busy," Carol said. "Anyway, we can take a drive, if you'd like. It's good to see you. You're an angel to be free tonight. Do you know that?"

"No," Therese said, still happy in spite of herself, though Carol's mood was disquieting. Therese felt something had happened.

"Do you suppose there's a place to get a cup of coffee around here?"

"Yes. A little further east."

Therese was thinking of one of the sandwich shops between Fifth and Madison, but Carol chose a small bar with an awning in front. The waiter was reluctant at first, and said it was the cocktail hour, but when Carol started to leave, he went away and got the coffee. Therese was anxious about picking up the handbag. She didn't want to do it when Carol was with her, even though the package would be wrapped.

"Did something happen?" Therese asked.

"Something too long to explain." Carol smiled at her but the smile was tired, and a silence followed, an empty silence as if they traveled through space away from each other.

Probably Carol had had to break an engagement she had looked forward to, Therese thought. Carol would of course be busy on Christmas Eve.

"I'm not keeping you from doing anything now?" Carol asked.

Therese felt herself growing tense, helplessly. "I'm supposed to pick up a package on Madison Avenue. It's not far. I can do it now, if you'll wait for me."

"All right."

Therese stood up. "I can do it in three minutes with a taxi. But I don't think you will wait for me, will you?"

Carol smiled and reached for her hand. Indifferently, Carol squeezed her hand and dropped it. "Yes, I'll wait."

The bored tone of Carol's voice was in her ears as she sat on the edge of the taxi seat. On the way back, the traffic was so slow, she got out and ran the last block.

Carol was still there, her coffee only half finished.

"I don't want my coffee." Therese said, because Carol seemed ready to go.

"My car's downtown. Let's get a taxi down."

They went down into the business section not far from the Battery. Carol's car was brought up from an underground garage. Carol drove west to the West Side Highway.

"This is better." Carol shed her coat as she drove. "Throw it in back, will you?"

And they were silent again. Carol drove faster, changing her lane to pass cars, as if they had a destination. Therese set herself to say something, anything at all, by the time they reached the George Washington Bridge. Suddenly it occurred to her that if Carol and her husband were divorcing, Carol had been downtown to see a lawyer today. The district there was full of law offices. And something had gone wrong. Why were they divorcing? Because Harge was having an affair with the woman called Cynthia? Therese was cold. Carol had lowered the window beside her, and every time the car sped, the wind burst through and wrapped its cold arms around her.

"That's where Abby lives," Carol said, nodding across the river.

Therese did not even see any special lights. "Who's Abby?"

"Abby? My best friend." Then Carol looked at her. "Aren't you cold with this window open?"

"No."

"You must be." They stopped for a red light, and Carol rolled the window up. Carol looked at her, as if really seeing her for the first time that evening, and under her eyes that went from her face to her hands in her lap, Therese felt like a puppy Carol had bought at a roadside kennel, that Carol had just remembered was riding beside her.

"What happened, Carol? Are you getting a divorce now?"

Carol sighed. "Yes, a divorce," she said quite calmly, and started the car.

"And he has the child?"

"Just tonight."

Therese was about to ask another question, when Carol said, "Let's talk about something else."

A car went by with the radio playing Christmas carols and everyone singing.

And she and Carol were silent. They drove past Yonkers, and it seemed to Therese she had left every chance of talking further to Carol somewhere behind on the road. Carol insisted suddenly that she should eat something, because it was getting on to eight, so they stopped at a little restaurant by the roadside, a place that sold fried clam sandwiches.

They sat at the counter and ordered sandwiches and coffee, but Carol did not eat. Carol asked her questions about Richard, not in the concerned way she had Sunday afternoon, but rather as if she talked to keep Therese from asking more questions about her. They were personal questions, yet Therese answered them mechanically and impersonally. Carol's quiet voice went on and on, much quieter than the voice of the counter boy talking with someone three yards away.

"Do you sleep with him?" Carol asked.

"I did. Two or three times." Therese told her about those times, the first time and the three times afterward. She was not embarrassed, talking about it. It had never seemed so dull and unimportant before. She felt Carol could imagine every minute of those evenings. She felt Carol's objective, appraising glance over her, and she knew Carol was about to say she did not look particularly cold, or, perhaps, emotionally starved. But Carol was silent, and Therese stared uncomfortably at the list of songs on the little music box in front of her. She remembered someone telling her once she had a passionate mouth, she couldn't remember who.

"Sometimes it takes time," Carol said. "Don't you believe in giving people another chance?"

"But—why? It isn't pleasant. And I'm not in love with him."

"Don't you think you might be, if you got this worked out?"

"Is that the way people fall in love?"

Carol looked up at the deer's head on the wall behind the counter. "No," she said, smiling. "What do you like about Richard?"

"Well, he has—" But she wasn't sure if it really was sincerity. He wasn't sincere, she felt, about his ambition to be a painter. "I like his attitude—more than most men's. He does treat me like a person instead of just a girl he can go so far with or not. And I like his family—the fact that he has a family."

"Lots of people have families."

Therese tried again. "He's flexible. He changes. He's not like most men that you can label doctor or—or insurance salesman."

"I think you know him better than I knew Harge after months of marriage. At least you're not going to make the same mistake I did, to marry because it was the thing to do when you were about twenty, among the people I knew."

"You mean you weren't in love?"

"Yes, I was, very much. And so was Harge. And he was the kind of man who could wrap your life up in a week and put it in his pocket. Were you ever in love, Therese?"

She waited, until the word from nowhere, false, guilty, moved her lips. "No."

"But you'd like to be." Carol was smiling.

"Is Harge still in love with you?"

Carol looked down at her lap, impatiently, and perhaps she was shocked at her bluntness, Therese thought, but when Carol spoke her voice was the same as before. "Even I don't know. In a way, he's the same emotionally as he's always been. It's just that now I can see how he really is. He said I was the first woman he'd ever been in love with. I think it's true, but I don't think he was in love with me—in the usual sense of the word—for more than a few months. He's never been interested in anyone else, it's true. Maybe he'd be more human if he were. That I could understand and forgive."

"Does he like Rindy?"

"Dotes on her." Carol glanced at her, smiling. "If he's in love with anyone, it's Rindy."

"What kind of a name is that?'

"Nerinda. Harge named her. He wanted a son, but I think he's even more pleased with a daughter. I wanted a girl. I wanted two or three children."

"And—Harge didn't?"

"I didn't." She looked at Therese again. "Is this the right conversation for Christmas Eve?" Carol reached for a cigarette, and accepted the one Therese offered her, a Philip Morris.

"I like to know all about you," Therese said.

"I didn't want any more children, because I was afraid our marriage was going on the rocks anyway, even with Rindy. So you want to fall in love? You probably will soon, and if you do, enjoy it, it's harder later on."

"To love someone?"

"To fall in love. Or even to have the desire to make love. I think sex flows more sluggishly in all of us than we care to believe, especially men care to believe. The first adventures are usually nothing but a satisfying of curiosity, and after that one keeps repeating the same actions, trying to find—what?"

"What?" Therese asked.

"Is there a word? A friend, a companion, or maybe just a sharer. What good are words? I mean, I think people often try to find through sex things that are much easier to find in other ways."

What Carol said about curiosity, she knew was true. "What other ways?" she asked.

Carol gave her a glance. "I think that's for each person to find out. I wonder if I can get a drink here."

But the restaurant served only beer and wine, so they left. Carol did not stop anywhere for her drink as they drove back toward New York. Carol asked her if she wanted to go home or come out to her house for a while, and Therese said to Carol's house. She remembered the Kellys had asked her to drop in on the wine and fruitcake party they were having tonight, and she had promised to, but they wouldn't miss her, she thought.

"What a rotten time I give you," Carol said suddenly. "Sunday and now this. I'm not the best company this evening. What would you like to do? Would you like to go to a restaurant in Newark where they have lights and Christmas music tonight? It's not a nightclub. We could have a decent dinner there, too."

"I really don't care about going anywhere—for myself."

"You've been in that rotten store all day, and we haven't done a thing to celebrate your liberation."

"I just like to be here with you," Therese said, and hearing the explanatory tone in her voice, she smiled.

Carol shook her head, not looking at her. "Child, child, where do you wander—all by yourself?"

Then, a moment later, on the New Jersey highway, Carol said, "I know what." And she turned the car into a graveled section off the road and stopped. "Come out with me."

They were in front of a lighted stand piled high with Christmas trees. Carol told her to pick a tree, one not too big and not too small. They put the tree in the back of the car, and Therese sat in front beside Carol with her arms full of holly and fir branches. Therese pressed her face into them and inhaled the dark green sharpness of their smell, their clean spice that was like a wild forest and like all the artifices of Christmas—tree baubles, gifts, snow, Christmas music, holidays. It was being through with the store and being beside Carol now. It was the purr of the car's engine, and the needles of the fir branches that she could touch with her fingers. I am happy, I am happy, Therese thought.

"Let's do the tree now," Carol said as soon as they entered the house.

Carol turned the radio on in the living room, and fixed a drink for both of them. There were Christmas songs on the radio, bells breaking resonantly, as if they were inside a great church. Carol brought a blanket of white cotton for the snow around the tree, and Therese sprinkled it with sugar so it would glisten. Then she cut an elongated angel out of some gold ribbon and fixed it to the top of the tree, and folded tissue paper and cut a string of angels to thread along the branches.

"You're very good at that," Carol said, surveying the tree from the hearth. "It's superb. Everything but presents."

Carol's present was on the sofa beside Therese's coat. The card she had made for it was at home, however, and she didn't want to give it without the card. Therese looked at the tree. "What else do we need?"

"Nothing. Do you know what time it is?"

The radio had signed off. Therese saw the mantel clock. It was after one. "It's Christmas," she said.

"You'd better stay the night."

"All right."

"What do you have to do tomorrow?"

"Nothing."

Carol got her drink from the radio top. "Don't you have to see Richard?"

She did have to see Richard, at twelve noon. She was to spend the day at his house. But she could make some kind of excuse. "No. I said I might see him. It's not important."

"I can drive you in early."

"Are you busy tomorrow?"

Carol finished the last inch of her drink. "Yes," she said.

Therese began to clean up the mess she had made, the scraps of tissue and snippets of ribbon. She hated cleaning up after making something.

"Your friend Richard sounds like the kind of man who needs a woman around him to work for. Whether he marries her or not," Carol said. "Isn't he like that?"

Why talk of Richard now, Therese thought irritably. She felt that Carol liked Richard—which could only be her own fault—and a distant jealousy pricked her, sharp as a pin.

"Actually, I admire that more than the men who live alone or think they live alone, and end by making the stupidest blunders with women."

Therese stared at Carol's pack of cigarettes on the coffee table. She had absolutely nothing to say on the subject. She could find Carol's perfume like a fine thread in the stronger smell of evergreen, and she wanted to follow it, to put her arms around Carol.

"It has nothing to do with whether people marry, has it?"

"What?" Therese looked at her and saw her smiling a little.

"Harge is the kind of man who doesn't let a woman enter his life. And on the other hand, your friend Richard might never marry. But the pleasure Richard will get out of thinking he wants to marry." Carol looked at Therese from head to foot. "The wrong girls," she added. "Do you dance, Therese? Do you like to dance?"

Carol seemed suddenly cool and bitter, and Therese could have wept. "No," she said. She should never have told her anything about Richard, Therese thought, but now it was done.

"You're tired. Come on to bed."

Carol took her to the room that Harge had gone into on Sunday, and turned down the covers of one of the twin beds. It might have been Harge's room, Therese thought. There was certainly nothing about it that suggested a child's room. She thought of Rindy's possessions that Harge had taken from this room, and imagined Harge moving first from the bedroom he shared with Carol, then letting Rindy bring her things into this room, keeping them here, closing himself and Rindy away from Carol.

Carol laid some pajamas on the foot of the bed. "Good night, then," she said at the door. "Merry Christmas. What do you want for Christmas?"

Therese smiled suddenly. "Nothing."

That night she dreamed of birds, long, bright red birds like flamingos, zipping through a black forest and making scallopy patterns, arcs of red that curved like their cries. Then her eyes opened and she heard it really, a soft whistle curving, rising and coming down again with an extra note at the end, and behind it the real, feebler twitter of birds. The window was a bright gray. The whistling began again, just below the window, and Therese got out of bed. There was a long open-topped car in the driveway, and a woman standing in it, whistling. It was like a dream she looked out on, a scene without color, misty at the edges.

Then she heard Carol's whisper, as clearly as if all three of them were in the same room together. "Are you going to bed or getting up?"

The woman in the car with her foot on the seat said, just as softly, "Both," and Therese heard the tremor of repressed laughter in the word and liked her instantly. "Go for a ride?" the woman asked. She was looking up at Carol's window with a big smile that Therese had just begun to see.

"You nitwit," Carol whispered.

"You alone?"

"No."

"Oh-oh."

"It's all right. Do you want to come in?"

The woman got out of the car.

Therese went to the door of her room and opened it. Carol was just coming into the hall, tying the belt of her robe.

"Sorry I wakened you," Carol said. "Go back to bed."

"I don't mind. Can I come down?"

"Well, of course!" Carol smiled suddenly. "Get a robe out of the closet."

Therese got a robe, probably a robe of Harge's, she thought, and went downstairs.

"Who made the Christmas tree?" the woman was asking.

They were in the living room.

"She did." Carol turned to Therese. "This is Abby. Abby Gerhard, Therese Belivet."

"Hello," Abby said.

"How do you do." Therese had hoped it was Abby. Abby looked at her now with the same bright, rather pop-eyed expression of amusement that Therese had seen when she stood in the car.

"You made a fine tree," Abby told her.

"Will everybody stop whispering?" Carol asked.

Abby chafed her hands together and followed Carol into the kitchen. "Got any coffee, Carol?"

Therese stood by the kitchen table, watching them, feeling at ease because Abby paid no further attention to her, only took off her coat and started helping Carol with the coffee. Her waist and hips looked perfectly cylindrical, without any front or back, under her purple knitted suit. Her hands were a little clumsy, Therese noticed, and her feet had none of the grace of Carol's. She looked older than Carol, and there were two wrinkles across her forehead that cut deep when she laughed, and her strong arched eyebrows rose higher. And she and Carol kept laughing now, while they fixed coffee and squeezed orange juice, talking in short phrases about nothing, or nothing that was important enough to be followed.

Except Abby's sudden, "Well"—fishing a seed out of the last glass of orange juice and wiping her finger carelessly on her own dress—"how's old Harge?"

"The same," Carol said. Carol was looking for something in the refrigerator, and, watching, Therese failed to hear all of what Abby said next, or maybe it was another of the fragmentary sentences that Carol alone understood, but it made Carol straighten up and laugh, suddenly and hard, made her whole face change, and Therese thought with sudden envy, she could not make Carol laugh like that, but Abby could.

"I'm going to tell him that," Carol said. "I can't resist."

It was something about a Boy Scout pocket gadget for Harge.

"And tell him where it came from," Abby said, looking at Therese and smiling broadly, as if she should share in the joke, too. "Where're you from?" she asked Therese as they sat down in the table alcove at one side of the kitchen.

"She's from New York," Carol answered for her, and Therese thought Abby was going to say, why, how unusual, or something silly, but Abby said nothing at all, only looked at Therese with the same expectant smile, as if she awaited the next cue from her.

For all their fussing about breakfast, there was only orange juice and coffee and some unbuttered toast that nobody wanted. Abby lighted a cigarette before she touched anything.

"Are you old enough to smoke?" she asked Therese, offering her a red box that said Craven A's.

Carol put her spoon down. "Abby, what is this?" she asked with an air of embarrassment that Therese had never seen before.

"Thanks, I'd like one," Therese said, taking a cigarette.

Abby settled her elbows on the table. "Well, what's what?" she asked Carol.

"I suspect you're a little tight," Carol said.

"Driving for hours in the open air? I left New Rochelle at two, got home and found your message, and here I am."

She probably had all the time in the world, Therese thought, probably did nothing all day except what she felt like doing.

"Well?" Abby said.

"Well—I didn't win the first round," Carol said.

Abby drew on her cigarette, showing no surprise at all. "For how long?"

"For three months."

"Starting when?"

"Starting now. Starting last night, in fact." Carol glanced at Therese, then looked down at her coffee cup, and Therese knew Carol would not say any more with her sitting there.

"That's not set already, is it?" Abby asked.

"I'm afraid it is," Carol answered casually, with a shrug in her tone. "Just verbally, but it'll hold. What're you doing tonight? Late."

"I'm not doing anything early. Dinner's at two today."

"Call me sometime."

"Sure."

Carol kept her eyes down, looking down at the orange juice glass in her hand, and Therese saw a downward slant of sadness in her mouth now, a sadness not of wisdom but of defeat.

"I'd take a trip," Abby said. "Take a little trip away somewhere." Then Abby looked at Therese, another of the bright, irrelevant, friendly glances, as if to include her in something it was impossible she could be included in, and anyway, Therese had gone stiff with the thought that Carol might take a trip away from her.

"I'm not much in the mood," Carol said, but Therese heard the play of possibility in it nevertheless.

Abby squirmed a little and looked around her. "This place is gloomy as a coalpit in the mornings, isn't it?"

Therese smiled a little. A coalpit, with the sun beginning to yellow the windowsill, and the evergreen tree beyond it?

Carol was looking at Abby fondly, lighting one of Abby's cigarettes. How well they must know each other, Therese thought, so well that nothing either of them said or did to the other could ever surprise, ever be misunderstood.

"Was it a good party?" Carol asked.

"Mm," Abby said indifferently. "Do you know someone called Bob Haversham?"

"No."

"He was there tonight. I met him somewhere before in New York. Funnily enough, he said he was going to work for Rattner and Aird in the brokerage department."

"Really."

"I didn't tell him I knew one of the bosses."

"What time is it?" Carol asked after a moment.

Abby looked at her wristwatch, a small watch set in a pyramid of gold panels. "Seven-thirty. About. Do you care?"

"Want to sleep some more, Therese?"

"No. I'm fine."

"I'll drive you in whenever you have to go," Carol said.

But it was Abby who drove her finally, around ten o'clock, because she had nothing else to do, she said, and she would enjoy it.

Abby was another one who liked cold air, Therese thought as they picked up speed on the highway. Who rode in an open-topped car in December?

"Where'd you meet Carol?" Abby yelled at her.

Therese felt she might almost, but not quite, have told Abby the truth. "In a store," Therese yelled back.

"Oh?" Abby drove erratically, whipping the big car around curves, putting on speed where one didn't expect it. "Do you like her?"

"Of course!" What a question! Like asking her if she believed in God.

Therese pointed out her house to Abby when they turned into the street. "Do you mind doing something for me?" Therese asked. "Could you wait here a minute? I want to give you something to give to Carol."

"Sure," Abby said.

Therese ran upstairs and got the card she had made, and stuck it under the ribbon of Carol's present. She took it back down to Abby. "You're going to see her tonight, aren't you?"

Abby nodded, slowly, and Therese sensed the ghost of a challenge in Abby's curious black eyes, because she was going to see Carol and Therese wasn't, and what could Therese do about it?

"And thanks for the ride in."

Abby smiled. "Sure you don't want me to take you anywhere else?"

"No, thanks," Therese said, smiling, too, because Abby would certainly have been glad to take her even to Brooklyn Heights.

She climbed her front steps and opened her mailbox. There were two or three letters in it, Christmas cards, one from Frankenberg's. When she looked into the street again, the big cream-colored car was gone, like a thing she had imagined, like one of the birds in the dream.

# *eight*

"And now you make a wish," Richard said. Therese wished it. She wished for Carol.

Richard had his hands on her arms. They were standing under a thing that looked like a beaded crescent, or a section of a starfish, that hung from the hall ceiling. It was ugly, but the Semco family attributed almost magical powers to it, and hung it up on special occasions. Richard's grandfather had brought it from Russia.

"What did you wish?" He smiled down at her possessively. This was his house, and he had just kissed her, though the door was open and the living room filled with people.

"You're not supposed to tell," Therese said.

"You can tell in Russia."

"Well, I'm not in Russia."

The radio roared louder suddenly, voices singing a carol. Therese drank the rest of the pink eggnog in her glass.

"I want to go up to your room," she said.

Richard took her hand, and they started up the stairs.

"Ri-chard?"

The aunt with the cigarette holder was calling him from the living room door.

Richard said a word Therese didn't understand, and waved a hand at her. Even on the second floor, the house trembled with the crazy dancing below, the dancing that had nothing to do with the music. Therese heard another glass fall, and pictured the pink foamy eggnog rolling across the floor. This was tame compared to the real Russian Christmases they had used to celebrate in the first week in January, Richard said. Richard smiled at her as he closed the door of his room.

"I like my sweater," he said.

"I'm glad." Therese swept her full skirt in an arc and sat on the edge of Richard's bed. The heavy Norwegian sweater she had given Richard was on the bed behind her, lying across its tissued box. Richard had given her a skirt from an East India shop, a long skirt with green and gold bands and embroidery. It was lovely, but Therese did not know where she could ever wear it.

"How about a real shot? That stuff downstairs is sickening," Richard got his bottle of whiskey from his closet floor.

Therese shook her head. "No, thanks."

"This'd be good for you."

She shook her head again. She looked around her at the high-ceilinged, almost square room, at the wallpaper with the barely discernible pattern of pink roses, at the two peaceful windows curtained in slightly yellowed white muslin. From the door, there were two pale trails in the green carpet, one to the bureau and one to the desk in the corner. The pot of brushes and the portfolio on the floor by the desk were the only signs of Richard's painting. Just as painting took up only a corner of his brain, she felt, and she wondered how much longer he would go on with it before he dropped it for something else. And she wondered, as she had often wondered before, if Richard liked her only because she was more sympathetic with his ambitions than anyone else he happened to know now, and because he felt her criticism was a help to him. Therese got up restlessly and went to the window. She loved the room—because it stayed the same and stayed in the same place—yet today she felt an impulse to burst from it. She was a different person from the one who had stood here three weeks ago. This morning she had awakened in Carol's house. Carol was like a secret spreading through her, spreading through this house, too, like a light invisible to everyone but her.

"You're different today," Richard said, so abruptly that a thrill of peril passed down her body.

"Maybe it's the dress," she said.

She was wearing a blue taffeta dress that was God knows how old, that she hadn't put on since her first months in New York. She sat down on the bed again, and looked at Richard who stood in the middle of the floor with the little glass of straight whiskey in his hand, his clear blue eyes moving from her face to her feet in the new high-heeled black shoes, back to her face again.

"Terry." Richard took her hands, pinned her hands to the bed on either side of her. The smooth, thin lips, descended on hers, firmly, with the flick of his tongue between her lips and the aromatic smell of fresh whiskey. "Terry, you're an angel," Richard's deep voice said, and she thought of Carol saying the same thing.

She watched him pick up his little glass from the floor and set it with the bottle into the closet. She felt immensely superior to him suddenly, to all the people below stairs. She was happier than any of them. Happiness was a little like flying, she thought, like being a kite. It depended on how much one let the string out—

"Pretty?" Richard said.

Therese sat up. "It's a beauty!"

"I finished it last night. I thought if it was a good day, we'd go to the park and fly it." Richard grinned like a boy, proud of his handiwork. "Look at the back."

It was a Russian kite, rectangular and bowed like a shield, its slim frame notched and tied at the corners. On the front, Richard had painted a cathedral with whirling domes and a red sky behind it.

"Let's go fly it now," Therese said.

They carried the kite downstairs. Then everybody saw them and came into the hall, uncles, aunts, and cousins, until the hall was a din and Richard had to hold the kite in the air to protect it. The noise irritated Therese, but Richard loved it.

"Stay for the champagne, Richard!" one of the aunts shouted, one of the aunts with a fat midriff straining like a second bosom under a satin dress.

"Can't," Richard said, and added something in Russian, and Therese had a feeling she often had, seeing Richard with his family, that there must have been a mistake, that Richard might be an orphan himself, a changeling, left on the doorstep and brought up a son of this family. But there was his brother Stephen standing in the doorway, with Richard's blue eyes, though Stephen was even taller and thinner.

"What roof?" Richard's mother asked shrilly. "This roof?"

Someone had asked if they were going to fly the kite on the roof, and since the house hadn't a roof one could stand on, Richard's mother had gone off into peals of laughter. Then the dog began to bark.

"I'm going to make you that dress!" Richard's mother called to Therese, wagging her finger admonishingly. "I know your measurements!"

They had measured her with a tape in the living room, in the midst of all the singing and present opening, and a couple of the men had tried to help, too. Mrs. Semco put her arm around Therese's waist, and suddenly Therese embraced her and kissed her firmly on the cheek, her lips sinking into the soft powdered cheek, in that one second pouring out in the kiss, and in the convulsive clasp of her arm, the affection Therese really had for her, that Therese knew would hide itself again as if it did not exist, in the instant she released her.

Then she and Richard were free and alone, walking down the front sidewalk. It wouldn't be any different, if they were married, Therese thought, visiting the family on Christmas Day. Richard would fly his kites even when he was an old man, like his grandfather who had flown kites in Prospect Park until the year he died, Richard had told her.

They took the subway to the park, and walked to the treeless hill where they had come a dozen times before. Therese looked around here. There were some boys playing with a football down on the flat field at the edge of the trees, but otherwise the park looked quiet and still. There was not much wind, not really enough, Richard said, and the sky was densely white as if it carried snow.

Richard groaned, failing again. He was trying to get the kite up by running with it.

Therese, sitting on the ground with her arms around her knees, watched him put his head up and turn in all directions, as if he had lost something in the air. "Here it is!" She got up, pointing.

"Yes, but it's not steady."

Richard ran the kite into it anyway, and the kite sagged on its long string, then jerked up as if something had sprung it. It made a big arc, then began to climb in another direction.

"It's found its own wind!" Therese said.

"Yes, but it's slow."

"What a gloomy Gus! Can I hold it?"

"Wait'll I get it higher."

Richard pumped at it with long swings of his arms, but the kite stayed at the same place in the cold sluggish air. The golden domes of the cathedral wagged from side to side, as if the whole kite were shaking its head saying no, and the long limp tail followed foolishly, repeating the negation.

"Best we can do," Richard said. "It can't carry any more string."

Therese did not take her eyes from it. Then the kite steadied and stopped, like a picture of a cathedral pasted on the thick white sky. Carol wouldn't like kites probably, Therese thought. Kites wouldn't amuse her. She would glance at one, and say it was silly.

"Want to take it?"

Richard poked the string stick into her hands, and she got to her feet. She thought, Richard had worked on the kite last night when she was with Carol, which was why he hadn't called her, and didn't know she had not been home. If he had called, he would have mentioned it. Soon there would come the first lie.

Suddenly the kite broke its mooring in the sky and tugged sharply to get away. Therese let the stick turn fast in her hands, as long as she dared to under Richard's eyes, because the kite was still low. And now it rested again, stubbornly still.

"Jerk it!" Richard said. "Keep working it up."

She did. It was like playing with a long elastic band. But the string was so long and slack now, it was all she could do to stir the kite. She pulled and pulled and pulled. Then Richard came and took it, and Therese let her arms hang. Her breath came harder, and little muscles in her arms were quivering. She sat down on the ground. She hadn't won against the kite. It hadn't done what she wanted it to do.

"Maybe the string's too heavy," she said. It was a new string, soft and white and fat as a worm.

"String's very light. Look now. Now it's going!"

Now it was climbing in short, upward darts, as if it had found its own mind suddenly, and a will to escape.

"Let out more string!" she shouted.

Therese stood up. A bird flew under the kite. She stared at the rectangle that was growing smaller and smaller, jerking back and back like a ship's billowed sail going backward. She felt the kite meant something, this particular kite, at this minute.

"Richard?"

"What?"

She could see him in the corner of her eye, crouched with his hands out in front of him, as if he rode a surfboard. "How many times were you in love?" she asked.

Richard laughed, a short, hoarse laugh. "Never till you."

"Yes, you were. You told me about two times."

"If I count those, I might count twelve others, too," Richard said quickly, with the bluntness of preoccupation.

The kite was starting to take arcing steps downward.

Therese kept her voice on the same level. "Were you ever in love with a boy?"

"A boy?" Richard repeated, surprised.

"Yes."

Perhaps five seconds passed before he said, "No," in a positive and final tone.

At least he troubled to answer, Therese thought. What would you do if you were, she had an impulse to ask, but the question would hardly serve a purpose. She kept her eyes on the kite. They were both looking at the same kite, but with what different thoughts in their minds. "Did you ever hear of it?" she asked.

"Hear of it? You mean people like that? Of course." Richard was standing straight now, winding the string in with figure-of-eight movements of the stick.

Therese said carefully, because he was listening, "I don't mean people like that. I mean two people who fall in love suddenly with each other, out of the blue. Say two men or two girls."

Richard's face looked the same as it might have if they had been talking about politics. "Did I ever know any? No."

Therese waited until he was working with the kite again, trying to pump it higher. Then she remarked, "I suppose it could happen, though, to almost anyone, couldn't it?"

He went on, winding the kite. "But those things don't just happen. There's always some reason for it in the background."

"Yes," she said agreeably. Therese had thought back into the background. The nearest she could remember to being "in love" was the way she had felt about a boy she had seen a few times in the town of Montclair, when she rode in the school bus. He had curly black hair and a handsome, serious face, and he had been perhaps twelve years old, older than she then. She remembered a short time when she had thought of him every day. But that was nothing, nothing like what she felt for Carol. Was it love or wasn't it that she felt for Carol? And how absurd it was that she didn't even know. She had heard about girls falling in love, and she knew what kind of people they were and what they looked like. Neither she nor Carol looked like that. Yet the way she felt about Carol passed all the tests for love and fitted all the descriptions. "Do you think I could?" Therese asked simply, before she could debate whether she dared to ask.

"What!" Richard smiled. "Fall in love with a girl? Of course not! My God, you haven't, have you?"

"No," Therese said, in an odd, inconclusive tone, but Richard did not seem to notice the tone.

"It's going again. Look, Terry!"

The kite was wobbling straight up, faster and faster, and the stick was whirling in Richard's hands. At any rate, Therese thought, she was happier than she had ever been before. And why worry about defining everything?

"Hey!" Richard sprinted after the stick that was leaping crazily around the ground, as if it were trying to leave the earth, too. "Want to hold it?" he asked, capturing it. "Practically takes you up!"

Therese took the stick. There was not much string left, and the kite was all but invisible now. When she let her arms go all the way up, she could feel it lifting her a little, delicious and buoyant, as if the kite might really take her up if it got all its strength together.

"Let it out!" Richard shouted, waving his arms. His mouth was open, and two spots of red had come in his cheeks. "Let it out!"

"There's no more string!"

"I'm going to cut it!"

Therese couldn't believe she had heard it, but glancing over at him, she saw him reaching under his overcoat for his knife. "Don't," she said.

Richard came running over, laughing.

"Don't!" she said angrily. "Are you crazy?" Her hands were tired, but she clung all the harder to the stick.

"Let's cut it! It's more fun!" And Richard bumped into her rudely, because he was looking up.

Therese jerked the stick sideways, out of his reach, speechless with anger and amazement. There was an instant of fear, when she felt Richard might really have lost his mind, and then she staggered backward, the pull gone, the empty stick in her hand. "You're mad!" she yelled at him. "You're insane!"

"It's only a kite!" Richard laughed, craning up at the nothingness.

Therese looked in vain, even for the dangling string. "Why did you do it?" Her voice was shrill with tears. "It was such a beautiful kite!"

"It's only a kite!" Richard repeated. "I can make another kite!"

## *nine*

Therese started to get dressed, then changed her mind. She was still in her robe, reading the script of *Small Rain* that Phil had brought over earlier, and that was now spread all over the couch. Carol had said she was at Forty-eighth and Madison. She could be here in ten minutes. Therese glanced around her room, and at her face in the mirror, and decided to let it all go.

She took some ashtrays to the sink and washed them, and stacked the play script neatly on her worktable. She wondered if Carol would have her new handbag with her. Carol had called her last night from some place in New Jersey where she was with Abby, had told her she thought the bag was beautiful but much too grand a present. Therese smiled, remembering Carol's suggesting that she take it back. At least Carol liked it.

The doorbell sounded in three quick rings.

Therese looked down the stairwell, and saw Carol was carrying something. She ran down.

"It's empty. It's for you," Carol said, smiling.

It was a suitcase, wrapped. Carol slipped her fingers from under the handle and let Therese carry it. Therese put it on the couch in her room, and cut the brown paper off carefully. The suitcase was of thick light brown leather, perfectly plain.

"It's terribly good-looking!" Therese said.

"Do you like it? I don't even know if you need a suitcase."

"Of course, I like it." This was the kind of suitcase for her, this exactly and no other. Her initials were on it in small gold letters—TMB. She remembered Carol asking her her middle name on Christmas Eve.

"Work the combination and see if you like the inside."

Therese did. "I like the smell, too," she said.

"Are you busy? If you are, I'll leave."

"No. Sit down. I'm not doing anything—except reading a play."

"What play?"

"A play I have to do sets for." She realized suddenly she had never mentioned stage designing to Carol.

"Sets for?"

"Yes—I'm a stage designer." She took Carol's coat.

Carol smiled astonishedly. "Why the hell didn't you tell me?" she asked quietly. "How many other rabbits are you going to pull out of your hat?"

"It's the first real job. And it's not a Broadway play. It's going to be done in the Village. A comedy. I haven't got a union membership yet. I'll have to wait for a Broadway job for that."

Carol asked her about the union, the junior and senior memberships that cost fifteen hundred and two thousand dollars respectively. Carol asked her if she had all that money saved up.

"No—just a few hundred. But if I get a job, they'll let me pay it off in installments."

Carol was sitting on the straight chair, the chair Richard often sat in, watching her, and Therese could read in Carol's expression that she had risen suddenly in Carol's estimation, and she couldn't imagine why she hadn't mentioned before that she was a stage designer, and in fact already had a job. "Well," Carol said, "if a Broadway job comes out of this, would you consider borrowing the rest of the money from me? Just as a business loan?"

"Thanks. I—"

"I'd like to do it for you. You shouldn't be bothered paying off two thousand dollars at your age."

"Thanks. But I won't be ready for one for another couple of years."

Carol lifted her head and blew her smoke out in a thin stream. "Oh, they don't really keep track of apprenticeships, do they?'

Therese smiled. "No. Of course not. Would you like a drink? I've got a bottle of rye."

"How nice. I'd love one, Therese." Carol got up and peered at her kitchenette shelves as Therese fixed the two drinks. "Are you a good cook?"

"Yes. I'm better when I have someone to cook for. I can make good omelets. Do you like them?"

"No," Carol said flatly, and Therese laughed. "Why don't you show me some of your work?"

Therese got a portfolio down from the closet. Carol sat on the couch and looked at everything carefully, but from her comments and questions, Therese felt she considered them too bizarre to be usable, and perhaps not very good either. Carol said she liked best the *Petrushka* set on the wall.

"But it's the same thing," Therese said. "The same thing as the drawings, only in model form."

"Well, maybe it's your drawings. They're very positive, anyway. I like that about them." Carol picked up her drink from the floor and leaned back on the couch. "You see, I didn't make a mistake, did I."

"About what?"

"About you."

Therese did not know exactly what she meant. Carol was smiling at her through her cigarette smoke, and it rattled her. "Did you think you had?"

"No," Carol said. "What do you have to pay for an apartment like this?"

"Fifty a month."

Carol clicked her tongue. "Doesn't leave you much out of your salary, does it?"

Therese bent over her portfolio, tying it up. "No. But I'll be making more soon. I won't be living here forever either."

"Of course you won't. You'll travel, too, the way you do in imagination. You'll see a house in Italy you'll fall in love with. Or maybe you'll like France. Or California, or Arizona."

The girl smiled. She probably wouldn't have the money for it, when that happened. "Do people always fall in love with things they can't have?"

"Always," Carol said, smiling, too. She pushed her fingers through her hair. "I think I shall take a trip after all."

"For how long?"

"Just a month or so."

Therese set the portfolio in the closet. "How soon will you be going?"

"Right away. I suppose as soon as I can arrange everything. And there isn't much to arrange."

Therese turned around. Carol was rolling the end of her cigarette in the ashtray. It meant nothing to her, Therese thought, that they wouldn't see each other for a month. "Why don't you go somewhere with Abby?"

Carol looked up at her, and then at the ceiling. "I don't think she's free in the first place."

Therese stared at her. She had touched something, mentioning Abby. But Carol's face was unreadable now.

"You're very nice to let me see you so often," Carol said. "You know, I don't feel like seeing the people I generally see just now. One can't, really. Everything's supposed to be done in pairs."

How frail she is, Therese felt suddenly, how different from the day of the first lunch. Then Carol got up, as if she knew her thoughts, and

Therese sensed a flaunt of assurance in her lifted head, in her smile as she passed her so close their arms brushed.

"Why don't we do something tonight?" Therese asked. "You can stay here if you want to, and I'll finish reading the play. We can spend the evening together."

Carol didn't answer. She was looking at the flower box in the bookshelf. "What kind of plants are these?"

"I don't know."

"You don't know?"

They were all different, a cactus with fat leaves that hadn't grown a bit since she bought it a year ago, another plant like a miniature palm tree, and a droopy red-green thing that had to be supported by a stick. "Just plants."

Carol turned around, smiling. "Just plants," she repeated.

"What about tonight?"

"All right. But I won't stay. It's only three. I'll give you a ring around six." Carol dropped her lighter in her handbag. It was not the handbag Therese had given her. "I feel like looking at furniture this afternoon."

"Furniture? In stores?"

"In stores or at the Parke-Bernet. Furniture does me good." Carol reached for her coat on the armchair, and again Therese noticed the long line from her shoulder to the wide leather belt, continued in her leg. It was beautiful, like a chord of music or a whole ballet. She was beautiful, and why should her days be so empty now, Therese wondered, when she was made to live with people who loved her, to walk in a beautiful house, in beautiful cities, along blue seacoasts with a long horizon and a blue sky to background her.

"Bye-bye," Carol said, and in the same movement with which she put on her coat, she put her arm around Therese's waist. It was only an instant, too disconcerting with Carol's arm suddenly about her, to be relief or end or beginning, before the doorbell rang in their ears like the tearing of a brass wall. Carol smiled. "Who is it?" she asked.

Therese felt the sting of Carol's thumbnail in her wrist as she released her. "Richard probably." It could only be Richard, because she knew his long ring.

"Good. I'd like to meet him."

Therese pressed the bell, then heard Richard's firm, hopping steps on the stairs. She opened the door.

"Hello," Richard said. "I decided—"

"Richard, this is Mrs. Aird," Therese said. "Richard Semco."

"How do you do?" Carol said.

Richard nodded, with almost a bow. "How do you do," he said, his blue eyes stretched wide.

They stared at each other, Richard with a square box in his hands as if he were about to present it to her, and Carol standing, neither staying nor leaving. Richard put the box on an end table.

"I was so near, I thought I'd come up," he said, and under its note of explanation Therese heard the unconscious assertion of a right, just as she had seen behind his inquisitive stare a spontaneous mistrust of Carol. "I had to take a present to a friend of Mamma's. This is *lebkuchen.*" He nodded at the box and smiled, disarmingly. "Anybody want some now?"

Carol and Therese declined. Carol was watching Richard as he opened the box with his pocketknife. She liked his smile, Therese thought. She likes him, the gangling young man with unruly blond hair, the broad lean shoulders, and the big funny feet in moccasins.

"Please sit down," Therese said to Carol.

"No, I'm going," she answered.

"I'll give you half, Terry, then I'll be going too," he said.

Therese looked at Carol, and Carol smiled at her nervousness and sat down on a corner of the couch.

"Anyway, don't let me rush you off," Richard said, lifting the paper with the cake in it to a kitchen shelf.

"You're not. You're a painter, aren't you, Richard?"

"Yes." He popped some loose icing into his mouth, and looked at Carol, poised because he was incapable of being unpoised, Therese thought, his eyes frank because he had nothing to hide. "Are you a painter, too?"

"No," Carol said with another smile. "I'm nothing."

"The hardest thing to be."

"Is it? Are you a good painter?"

"I will be. I can be," said Richard, unperturbed. "Have you got any beer, Terry? I've got an awful thirst."

Therese went to the refrigerator and got out the two bottles that were there. Richard asked Carol if she would like some, but Carol refused. Then Richard strolled past the couch, looking at the suitcase and the wrappings, and Therese thought he was going to say something about it, but he didn't.

"I thought we might go to a movie tonight, Terry. I'd like to see that thing at the Victoria. Do you want to?"

"I can't tonight. I've got a date with Mrs. Aird."

"Oh." Richard looked at Carol.

Carol put out her cigarette and stood up. "I must be going." She smiled at Therese. "Call you back around six. If you change your mind it's not important. Good-bye, Richard."

"Good-bye," Richard said.

Carol gave her a wink as she went down the stairs. "Be a good girl," Carol said.

"Where'd the suitcase come from?" Richard asked when she came back in the room.

"It's a present."

"What's the matter, Terry?"

"Nothing's the matter."

"Did I interrupt anything important? Who is she?"

Therese picked up Carol's empty glass. There was a little lipstick at the rim. "She's a woman I met at the store."

"Did she give you that suitcase?"

"Yes."

"It's quite a present. Is she that rich?"

Therese glanced at him. Richard's aversion to the wealthy, to the bourgeois, was automatic. "Rich? You mean the mink coat? I don't know. I did her a favor. I found something she lost in the store."

"Oh?" he said. "What? You didn't say anything about it."

She washed and dried Carol's glass and set it back on the shelf. "She left her billfold on the counter and I took it to her, that's all."

"Oh. Damned nice reward." He frowned. "Terry, what is it? You're not still sore about that silly kite, are you?"

"No, of course not," she said impatiently. She wished he would go. She put her hands in her robe pockets and walked across the room, stood where Carol had stood, looking at the box of plants. "Phil brought the play over this morning. I started reading it."

"Is that what you're worried about?"

"What makes you think I'm worried?" She turned around.

"You're in another of those miles-away moods again."

"I'm not worried and I'm not miles away." She took a deep breath. "It's funny—you're so conscious of some moods and so unconscious of others."

Richard looked at her. "All right, Terry," he said with a shrug, as if he conceded it. He sat down in the straight chair and poured the rest of the beer into his glass. "What's this date you have with that woman tonight?"

Therese's lips widened in a smile as she ran the end of her lipstick over them. For a moment, she stared at the eyebrow tweezers that lay on the little shelf fixed to the inside of the closet door. Then she put the lipstick down on the shelf. "It's sort of a cocktail party, I think. Sort of a Christmas benefit thing. In some restaurant, she said."

"Hmm. Do you want to go?"

"I said I would."

Richard drank his beer, frowning a little over his glass. "What about afterward? Maybe I could hang around here and read the play while you're gone, and then we could grab a bite and go to the movie."

"Afterward, I thought I'd better finish the play. I'm supposed to start on Saturday, and I ought to have some ideas in my head."

Richard stood up. "Yep," he said casually, with a sigh.

Therese watched him idle over to the couch and stand there, looking down at the manuscript. Then he bent over, studying the title page, and the cast pages. He looked at his wristwatch, and then at her.

"Why don't I read it now?" he asked.

"Go ahead," she answered with a brusqueness that Richard either didn't hear or ignored, because he simply lay back on the couch with the manuscript in his hands and began to read. She picked up a book of matches from the shelf. No, he only recognized the "miles-away" moods, she thought, when he felt himself deprived of her by distance. And she thought suddenly of the times she had gone to bed with him, of her distance then compared to the closeness that was supposed to be, that everyone talked about. It hadn't mattered to Richard then, she supposed, because of the physical fact they were in bed together. And it crossed her mind now, seeing Richard's complete absorption in his reading, seeing the plump, stiff fingers catch a front lock of his hair between them and pull it straight down toward his nose, as she had seen him do a thousand times before, it occurred to her Richard's attitude was that his place in her life was unassailable, her tie with him permanent and beyond question, because he was the first man she had ever slept with. Therese threw the match cover at the shelf, and a bottle of something fell over.

Richard sat up, smiling a little, surprised. "'S matter, Terry?"

"Richard, I feel like being alone—the rest of the afternoon. Would you mind?"

He got up. The surprise did not leave his face. "No. Of course not." He dropped the manuscript on the couch again. "All right, Terry. It's probably better. Maybe you ought to read this now—read it alone," he said argumentatively, as if he persuaded himself. He looked at his watch again. "Maybe I'll go down and try to see Sam and Joan for a while."

She stood there, not moving, not even thinking of anything except of the few seconds of time to pass until he would be gone, while he brushed his hand once, a little clingy with its moisture, over her hair, and bent to kiss her. Then quite suddenly she remembered the Degas book she had bought days ago, the book of reproductions that Richard wanted and hadn't been able to find anywhere. She got it from the bottom drawer of the bureau. "I found this. The Degas book."

"Oh, swell. Thanks." He took it in both hands. It was still wrapped. "Where'd you find it?"

"Frankenberg's. Of all places."

"Frankenberg's." Richard smiled. "It's six bucks, isn't it?"

"Oh, that's all right."

Richard had his wallet out. "But I asked you to get it for me."

"Never mind, really."

Richard protested, but she didn't take the money. And a minute later he was gone, with a promise to call her tomorrow at five. They might do something tomorrow night, he said.

Carol called at ten past six. Did she feel like going to Chinatown, Carol asked. Therese said, of course.

"I'm having cocktails with someone in the St. Regis," Carol said. "Why don't you pick me up here? It's the little room, not the big one. And listen, we're going on to some theater thing you've asked me to. Get it?"

"Some sort of Christmas benefit cocktail party?"

Carol laughed. "Hurry up."

Therese flew.

• • •

Carol's friend WAS a man called Stanley McVeigh, a tall and very attractive man of about forty with a mustache and a boxer dog on a leash. Carol was ready to go when Therese arrived. Stanley walked out with them, put them into a taxi, and gave the driver some money through the window.

"Who's he?" Therese asked.

"An old friend. Seeing more of me now that Harge and I are separating."

Therese looked at her. Carol had a wonderful little smile in her eyes tonight. "Do you like him?"

"So-so," Carol said. "Driver, will you make that Chinatown instead of the other?"

It began to rain while they were having dinner. Carol said it always rained in Chinatown, every time she had been here. But it didn't matter much, because they ducked from one shop to another, looking at things and buying things. Therese saw some sandals with platform heels that she thought were beautiful, rather more Persian-looking than Chinese, and she wanted to buy them for Carol, but Carol said Rindy wouldn't approve. Rindy was a conservative, and didn't like her even to go without stockings in summer, and Carol conformed to her. The same store had Chinese suits of a black shiny material, with plain trousers and a high-collared jacket, and Carol bought one for Rindy. Therese bought the sandals for Carol, anyway, while Carol was arranging for Rindy's suit to be sent. She knew the right size just by looking at the sandals, and it pleased Carol after all that she bought them. Then they spent a weird hour in a Chinese theater where people in the audience were sleeping through all the clangor. And finally they went uptown for a late supper in a restaurant where a harp played. It was a glorious evening, a really magnificent evening.

# *ten*

On Tuesday, the fifth day of work, Therese sat in a little bare room with no ceiling at the back of the Black Cat Theater, waiting for Mr. Donohue, the new director, to come and look at her cardboard model. Yesterday morning, Donohue had replaced Cortes as director, had thrown out her first model, and had also thrown out Phil McElroy as the second brother in the play. Phil had walked out yesterday in a huff. It was lucky she hadn't been thrown out along with her model, Therese thought, so she had followed Mr. Donohue's instructions to the letter. The new model hadn't the movable section she had put into the first, which would have permitted the living room scene to be converted into the terrace scene for the last act. Mr. Donohue seemed to be adamant against anything unusual or even simple. By setting the whole play in the living room, a lot of the dialogue had to be changed in the last act, and some of the cleverest lines had been lost. Her new model indicated a fireplace, broad French windows giving on to a terrace, two doors, a sofa and a couple of armchairs, and a bookcase. It would look, when finished, like a room in a model house at Sloan's, lifelike down to the last ashtray.

Therese stood up, stretched herself, and reached for the corduroy jacket that was hanging on a nail on the door. The place was cold as a barn. Mr. Donohue probably wouldn't come in until afternoon, or not even today if she didn't remind him again. There was no hurry about the scenery. It might have been the least important matter in the whole production, but she had sat up until late last night, enthusiastically working on the model.

She went out to stand in the wings again. The cast was all on stage with scripts in hand. Mr. Donohue kept running the cast through the whole play, to get the flow of it, he said, but today it seemed to be only putting them to sleep. All the cast looked lazy except Tom Harding, a tall blond young man who had the male lead, and he was a little too energetic. Georgia Halloran was suffering with sinus headaches, and had to stop every hour to put drops in her nose and lie down for a few minutes. Geoffrey Andrews, a middle-aged man who played the heroine's father, grumbled constantly between his lines because he didn't like Donohue.

"No, no, no, no," said Mr. Donohue for the tenth time that morning, stopping everything and causing everybody to lower his script and turn to him with a puzzled, irritated docility. "Let's start again from page twenty-eight."

Therese watched him waving his arms to indicate the speakers, putting up a hand to silence them, following the script with his head down as if he led an orchestra. Tom Harding winked at her, and pulled his hand down his nose. After a moment, Therese went back to the room behind the partition, where she worked, where she felt a little less useless. She knew the play almost by heart now. It had a rather Sheridanesque comedy-of-errors plot—two brothers who pretend to be valet and master in order to impress an heiress with whom one of the brothers is in love. The dialogue was witty and altogether not bad, but the dreary, matter-of-fact set that Donohue had ordered for it—Therese hoped something could be done with the color they would use.

Mr. Donohue did come in just after twelve o'clock. He looked at her model, lifted it up and looked at it from below and from both sides, without any change in his nervous, harassed expression. "Yes, this is fine. I like this very much. You see how much better this is than those empty walls you had before, don't you?"

Therese took a deep breath of relief. "Yes," she said.

"A set grows out of the needs of the actors. This isn't a ballet set you're designing, Miss Belivet."

She nodded, looking at the model, too, and trying to see how it possibly was better, possibly more functional.

"The carpenter's coming in this afternoon about four. We'll get together and have a talk about this." Mr. Donohue went out.

Therese stared at the cardboard model. At least she would see it used. At least she and the carpenters would make it something real. She went to the window and looked out at the gray but luminous winter sky, at the backs of some five-story houses garlanded with fire escapes. In the foreground was a small vacant lot with a runted leafless tree in it, all twisted up like a signpost gone wild. She wished she could call Carol and invite her for lunch. But Carol was an hour and a half away by car.

"Is your name Beliver?"

Therese turned to the girl in the doorway. "Belivet. Telephone?"

"The phone by the lights."

"Thanks." Therese hurried, hoping it was Carol, knowing more likely it was Richard. Carol hadn't yet called her here.

"Hello, this is Abby."

"Abby?" Therese smiled. "How'd you know I was here?"

"You told me, remember? I'd like to see you. I'm not far away. Have you had lunch yet?"

They agreed to meet at the Palermo, a restaurant a block or two from the Black Cat.

Therese whistled a song as she walked there, happy as if she were meeting Carol. The restaurant had sawdust on the floor, and a couple of black kittens played around under the rail of the bar. Abby was sitting at a table in the back.

"Hi," Abby said as she came up. "You're looking very chipper. I almost didn't recognize you. Would you like a drink?"

Therese shook her head. "No, thanks."

"You mean, you're so happy without it?" Abby asked, and she chuckled with that secret amusement that in Abby was somehow not offensive.

Therese took the cigarette that Abby offered her. Abby knew, she thought. And perhaps she was in love with Carol, too. It put Therese on guard with her. It created a tacit rivalry that gave her a curious exhilaration, a sense of certain superiority over Abby—emotions that Therese had never known before, never dared to dream of, emotions consequently revolutionary in themselves. So their lunching together in the restaurant became nearly as important as the meeting with Carol.

"How is Carol?" Therese asked. She had not seen Carol in three days.

"She's very fine," Abby said, watching her.

The waiter came, and Abby asked him if he could recommend the mussels and the scaloppine.

"Excellent, madame!" He beamed at her as if she were a special customer.

It was Abby's manner, the glow in her face, as if today, or every day, were a special holiday for her. Therese liked that. She looked admiringly at Abby's suit of red and blue weave, her cuff links that were scrolly G's, like filigree buttons in silver. Abby asked her about her job at the Black Cat. It was tedious to Therese, but Abby seemed impressed. Abby was impressed, Therese thought, because she did nothing herself.

"I know some people in the producing end of the theater," Abby said. "I'll be glad to put in a word for you anytime."

"Thanks." Therese played with the lid of the grated cheese bowl in front of her. "Do you know anyone called Andronich? I think he's from Philadelphia."

"No," Abby said.

Mr. Donohue had told her to go and see Andronich next week in New York. He was producing a show that would open this spring in Philadelphia, and then on Broadway.

"Try the mussels." Abby was eating hers with gusto. "Carol likes these, too."

"Have you known Carol a long time?"

"Um-hm," Abby nodded, looking at her with the bright eyes that revealed nothing.

"And you know her husband, too, of course."

Abby nodded again, silently.

Therese smiled a little. Abby was out to question her, she felt, but not to disclose anything about herself or about Carol.

"How about some wine? Do you like Chianti?" Abby summoned a waiter with a snap of her fingers. "Bring us a bottle of Chianti, please. A good one. Builds up the blood," she added to Therese.

Then the main course arrived, and two waiters fussed around the table, uncorking the Chianti, pouring more water and bringing fresh butter. The radio in the corner played a tango—a little cheesebox of a radio with a broken front, but the music might have come from a string orchestra behind them, at Abby's request. No wonder Carol likes her, Therese thought. She complemented Carol's solemnity, she could remind Carol to laugh.

"Did you always live by yourself?" Abby asked.

"Yes. Since I got out of school." Therese sipped her wine. "Do you? Or do you live with your family?"

"With my family. But I've got my own half of the house."

"And do you work?" Therese ventured.

"I've had jobs. Two or three of them. Didn't Carol tell you we had a furniture shop once? We had a shop just outside of Elizabeth on the highway. We bought up antiques or plain secondhand stuff and fixed it up. I never worked so hard in my life." Abby smiled at her gaily, as if every word might be untrue. "Then my other job. I'm an entomologist. Not a very good one, but good enough to pull bugs out of Italian lemon crates and things like that. Bahama lilies are full of bugs."

"So I've heard," Therese smiled.

"I don't think you believe me."

"Yes, I do. Do you still work at that?"

"I'm on reserve. Just in time of emergency, I work. Like Easter."

Therese watched Abby's knife cutting the scaloppine into small bites before she picked any up. "Do you take trips a lot with Carol?"

"A lot? No, why?" Abby asked.

"I should think you'd be good for her. Because Carol's so serious." Therese wished she could lead the conversation to the heart of things, but just what the heart of things was, she didn't know. The wine ran slow and warm in her veins, down to her fingertips.

"Not all the time," Abby corrected, with the laughter under the surface of her voice, as it had been in the first word Therese had heard her say.

The wine in her head promised music or poetry or truth, but she was stranded on the brink. Therese could not think of a single question that would be proper to ask, because all her questions were so enormous.

"How'd you meet Carol?" Abby asked.

"Didn't Carol tell you?"

"She just said she met you at Frankenberg's when you had a job there."

"Well, that's how," Therese said, feeling a resentment in her against Abby building up, uncontrollably.

"You just started talking?" Abby asked with a smile, lighting a cigarette.

"I waited on her," Therese said, and stopped.

And Abby waited, for a precise description of that meeting, Therese knew, but she wouldn't give it to Abby or to anyone else. It belonged to her. Surely Carol hadn't told Abby, she thought, told her the silly story of the Christmas card. It wouldn't be important enough to Carol for Carol to have told her.

"Do you mind telling me who started talking first?"

Therese laughed suddenly. She reached for a cigarette and lighted it, still smiling. No, Carol hadn't told her about the Christmas card, and Abby's question struck her as terribly funny. "I did," Therese said.

"You like her a lot, don't you?" Abby asked.

Therese explored it for hostility. It was not hostile, but jealous. "Yes."

"Why do you?"

"Why do I? Why do you?"

Abby's eyes still laughed. "I've known Carol since she was four years old."

Therese said nothing.

"You're awfully young, aren't you? Are you twenty-one?"

"No. Not quite."

"You know Carol's got a lot of worries right now, don't you?"

"Yes."

"And she's lonely now," Abby added, her eyes watching.

"Do you mean that's why she sees me?" Therese asked calmly. "Do you want to tell me I shouldn't see her?"

Abby's unblinking eyes blinked twice after all. "No, not a bit. But I don't want you to get hurt. I don't want you to hurt Carol either."

"I'd never hurt Carol," Therese said. "Do you think I would?"

Abby was still watching her alertly, had never taken her eyes from her. "No, I don't think you would," Abby replied as if she had just decided it. And she smiled now as if she were especially pleased about something.

But Therese did not like the smile, and realizing her face showed her feelings, she looked down at the table. There was a glass of hot zabaglione standing on a plate in front of her.

"Would you like to come to a cocktail party this afternoon, Therese? It's uptown at about six o'clock. I don't know if there'll be any stage designers there, but one of the girls who's giving it is an actress."

Therese put her cigarette out. "Is Carol going to be there?"

"No. She won't be. But they're all easy to get along with. It's a small party."

"Thanks. I don't think I should go. I may have to work late today, too."

"Oh. I was going to give you the address anyway, but if you won't come—"

"No," Therese said.

Abby wanted to walk around the block after they came out of the restaurant. Therese agreed, though she was tired of Abby now. Abby with her cocksureness, her blunt, careless questions, made Therese feel she had gotten an advantage over her. And Abby had not let her pay the bill.

Abby said, "Carol thinks a lot of you, you know. She says you have a lot of talent."

"Does she?" Therese said, only half believing it. "She never told me." She wanted to walk faster, but Abby held their pace back.

"You must know she thinks a lot of you, if she wants you to take a trip with her."

Therese glanced and saw Abby smiling at her, guilelessly. "She didn't say anything to me about that either," Therese said quietly, though her heart had begun pumping.

"I'm sure she will. You'll go with her, won't you?"

Why should Abby know about it before she did, Therese wondered. She felt a flush of anger in her face. What was it all about? Did Abby hate her? If she did, why wasn't she consistent about it? Then in the next instant, the rise of anger fell and left her weak, left her vulnerable and defenseless. She thought, if Abby pressed her against the wall at that moment and said: Out with it. What do you want from Carol? How much of her do you want to take from me? she would have babbled it all. She would have said: I want to be with her. I love to be with her, and what has it got to do with you?

"Isn't that for Carol to talk about? Why do you ask me these things?" Therese made an effort to sound indifferent. It was hopeless.

Abby stopped walking. "I'm sorry," she said, turning to her. "I think I understand better now."

"Understand what?"

"Just—that you win."

"Win what?"

"What," Abby echoed with her head up, looking up at the corner of a building, at the sky, and Therese suddenly felt furiously impatient.

She wanted Abby to go so she could telephone Carol. Nothing mattered but the sound of Carol's voice. Nothing mattered but Carol, and why did she let herself forget for a moment?

"No wonder Carol thinks such a lot of you," Abby said, but if it was a kind remark, Therese did not accept it as such. "So long, Therese. I'll see you again no doubt." Abby held out her hand.

Therese took it. "So long," she said. She watched Abby walking toward Washington Square, her step quicker now, her curly head high.

Therese went into the drugstore at the next corner and called Carol. She got the maid and then Carol.

"What's the matter?" Carol asked. "You sound low."

"Nothing. It's dull at work."

"Are you doing anything tonight? Would you like to come out?"

Therese came out of the drugstore smiling. Carol was going to pick her up at five-thirty. Carol insisted on picking her up, because it was such a rotten trip by train.

Across the street, walking away from her, she saw Danny McElroy, striding along without a coat, carrying a naked bottle of milk in his hand.

"Danny!" she called.

Danny turned and walked toward her. "Come by for a few minutes?" he yelled.

Therese started to say no, then, as he came up to her, she took his arm. "Just for a minute. I've had a long lunch hour already."

Danny smiled down at her. "What time is it? I've been studying till I'm blind."

"After two." She felt Danny's arm tensed hard against the cold. There were goosepimples under the dark hair on his forearm. "You're mad to go out without a coat," she said.

"It clears my head." He held the iron gate for her that led to his door. "Phil's out somewhere."

The room smelled of pipe smoke, rather like hot chocolate cooking. The apartment was a semibasement, generally darkish, and the lamp made a warm pool of light on the desk that was always cluttered. Therese looked down at the opened books on his desk, the pages and pages covered with symbols that she could not understand, but that she liked to look at. Everything the symbols stood for was true and proven. The symbols were stronger and more definite than words. She felt Danny's mind swung on them, from one fact to another, as if he bore himself on strong chains, hand over hand through space. She watched him assembling a sandwich, standing at the kitchen table. His shoulders looked very broad and rounded with muscle under his white shirt, shifting a little with the motions of laying the salami and cheese slices onto the big piece of rye bread.

"I wish you'd come by more often, Therese. Wednesday's the only day I'm not home at noon. We wouldn't bother Phil, having lunch, even if he's sleeping."

"I will," Therese said. She sat down in his desk chair that was half turned around. She had come once for lunch, and once after work. She liked visiting Danny. One did not have to make small talk with him.

In the corner of the room, Phil's sofa bed was unmade, a tangle of blankets and sheets. The two times she had come in before, the bed had been unmade, or Phil had still been in it. The long bookcase pulled out at right angles to the sofa made a unit of Phil's corner of the room, and it was always in disorder, in a frustrated and nervous disorder not at all like the working disorder of Danny's desk.

Danny's beer can hissed as he opened it. He leaned against the wall with the beer and the sandwich, smiling, delighted to have her here. "Remember what you said about physics not applying to people?"

"Umm. Vaguely."

"Well, I'm not sure you're right," he said as he took a bite. "Take friendships, for instance. I can think of a lot of cases where the two people have nothing in common. I think there's a definite reason for every friendship just as there's a reason why certain atoms unite and others don't—certain missing factors in one, or certain present factors in the other—what do you think? I think friendships are the result of certain needs that can be completely hidden from both people, sometimes hidden forever."

"Maybe. I can think of a few cases, too." Richard and herself, for one. Richard got on with people, elbowed his way through the world in a way she couldn't. She had always been attracted to people with Richard's kind of self-assurance. "And what's weak about you, Danny?"

"Me?" he said, smiling. "Do you want to be my friend?"

"Yes. But you're about the strongest person I know."

"Really? Shall I enumerate my shortcomings?"

She smiled, looking at him. A young man of twenty-five who had known where he was going since he was fourteen. He had driven all his energy into one channel—just the opposite of what Richard had done.

"I have a secret and very buried need for a cook," Danny said, "and a dancing teacher, and someone to remind me to do little things like take my laundry and get haircuts."

"I can't remember to take my laundry either."

"Oh," he said sadly. "Then it's out. And I'd had some hope. I'd had a little feeling of destiny. Because, you see, what I mean about affinities is true from friendships down to even the accidental glance at someone on the street—there's always a definite reason somewhere. I think even the poets would agree with me."

She smiled. "*Even* the poets?" She thought of Carol, and then of Abby, of their conversation at lunch that had been so much more than a glance and so much less, and the sequence of emotions it had evoked in her. It depressed her. "But you have to make allowances for people's perversities, things that don't make much sense."

"Perversities? That's only a subterfuge. A word used by the poets."

"I thought it was used by the psychologists," Therese said.

"I mean, to make allowances—that's a meaningless term. Life is an exact science on its own terms, it's just a matter of finding them and defining them. What doesn't make any sense to you?"

"Nothing. I was thinking of something that doesn't matter anyway." She was suddenly angry again, as she had been on the sidewalk after the lunch.

"What?" he persisted, frowning.

"Like the lunch I just had," she said.

"With whom?"

"It doesn't matter. If it did, I'd go into it. It's just a waste, like losing something, I thought. But maybe something that didn't exist anyway." She had wanted to like Abby because Carol did.

"Except in your mind? That can still be a loss."

"Yes—but there are some people or some things people do that you can't salvage anything from finally, because nothing connects with you." It was of something else she wanted to talk about, though, not this at all.

Not Abby or Carol, but before. Something that made perfect connection and perfect sense. She loved Carol. She leaned her forehead against her hand.

Danny looked at her for a moment, then pushed himself off from the wall. He turned to the stove, and got a match from his shirt pocket, and Therese sensed that the conversation dangled, would always dangle and never be finished, whatever they went on to say. But she felt if she told Danny every word that she and Abby had exchanged, he could clear away its subterfuges with a phrase, as if he sprinkled a chemical in the air that would dry up the mist instantly. Or was there always something that logic couldn't touch? Something illogical, behind the jealousy, the suspicion, and the hostility in Abby's conversation, that was Abby all by herself?

"Everything's not as simple as a lot of combinations," Therese added.

"Some things don't react. But everything's alive." He turned around with a broad smile, as if quite another train of thought had entered his head. He was holding up the match, which was still smoking. "Like this match. And I'm not talking physics, about the indestructibility of smoke. In fact, I feel rather poetic today."

"About the match?"

"I feel as if it were growing, like a plant, not disappearing. I feel everything in the world must have the texture of a plant sometimes to a poet. Even this table, like my own flesh." He touched the table edge with his palm. "It's like a feeling I had once riding up a hill on a horse. It was in Pennsylvania. I didn't know how to ride very well then, and I remember the horse turning his head and seeing the hill, and deciding by himself to run up it, his hind legs sank before we took off, and suddenly we were going like blazes and I wasn't afraid at all. I felt completely in harmony with the horse and the land, as if we were a whole tree simply being stirred by the wind in its branches. I remember being sure that nothing would happen to me then, but some other time, yes, eventually. And it made me very happy. I thought of all the people who are afraid and hoard things, and themselves, and I thought, when everybody in the world comes to realize what I felt going up the hill, then there'll be a kind of right economy of living and of using and using up. Do you know what I mean?" Danny had clenched his fist, but his eyes were bright as if he still laughed at himself. "Did you ever wear out a sweater you particularly liked, and throw it away finally?"

She thought of the green woolen gloves of Sister Alicia, which she had neither worn nor thrown away. "Yes," she said.

"Well, that's all I mean. And the lambs who didn't realize how much wool they were losing when somebody sheared them to make the sweater, because they could grow more wool. It's very simple." He turned to the coffeepot he had reheated, which was already boiling.

"Yes." She knew. And like Richard and the kite, because he could make another kite. She thought of Abby with a sense of vacuity suddenly, as if the luncheon had been eradicated. For an instant, she felt as if her mind had overflowed a brim and was swimming emptily into space. She stood up.

Danny came toward her, put his hands on her shoulders, and though she felt it was only a gesture, a gesture instead of a word, the spell was broken. She was uneasy at his touch, and the uneasiness was a point of concreteness. "I should go back," she said. "I'm way late."

His hands came down, pinning her elbows hard against her sides, and he kissed her suddenly, held his lips hard against hers for a moment, and she felt his warm breath on her upper lip before he released her.

"You are," he said, looking at her.

"Why did you—" She stopped, because the kiss had so mingled tenderness and roughness, she didn't know how to take it.

"*Why*, Terry?" he said, turning away from her, smiling. "Did you mind?"

"No," she said.

"Would Richard mind?"

"I suppose." She buttoned her coat. "I must go," she said, moving toward the door.

Danny swung the door open for her, smiling his easy smile, as if nothing had happened. "Come back tomorrow? Come for lunch."

She shook her head. "I don't think so. I'm busy this week."

"All right, come—next Monday, maybe?"

"All right." She smiled, too, and put her hand out automatically and Danny shook it once, politely.

She ran the two blocks to the Black Cat. A little like the horse, she thought. But not enough, not enough to be perfect, and what Danny meant was perfect.

# *eleven*

"The pastimes of idle people," Carol said, stretching her legs out before her on the swing seat. "It's time Abby got herself a job again."

Therese said nothing. She hadn't told Carol all the conversation at lunch, but she didn't want to talk about Abby anymore.

"Don't you want to sit in a more comfortable chair?"

"No," Therese said. She was sitting on a leather stool near the swing seat. They had finished dinner a few moments ago, and then come up to this room that Therese had not seen before, a glass-enclosed porch off the plain green room.

"What else did Abby say that bothers you?" Carol asked, still looking straight before her, down her long legs in the navy blue slacks.

Carol seemed tired. She was worried about other things, Therese thought, more important things than this. "Nothing. Does it bother you, Carol?"

"Bother me?"

"You're different with me tonight."

Carol glanced at her. "You imagine," she said, and the pleasant vibration of her voice faded into silence again.

The page she had written last night, Therese thought, had nothing to do with this Carol, was not addressed to her. *I feel I am in love with you,* she had written, *and it should be spring. I want the sun throbbing on my head like chords of music. I think of a sun like Beethoven, a wind like Debussy, and birdcalls like Stravinsky. But the tempo is all mine.*

"I don't think Abby likes me," Therese remarked. "I don't think she wants me to see you."

"That's not true. You're imagining again."

"I don't mean she said it." Therese tried to sound as calm as Carol. "She was very nice. She invited me to a cocktail party."

"Whose party?"

"I don't know. She said uptown. She said you wouldn't be there, so I didn't particularly want to go."

"Where uptown?"

"She didn't say. Just that one of the girls giving it was an actress."

Carol set her lighter down with a click on the glass table, and Therese sensed her displeasure. "She did," Carol murmured, half to herself. "Sit over here, Therese."

Therese got up, and sat down at the very foot of the swing seat.

"You mustn't think Abby feels that way about you. I know her well enough to know she wouldn't."

"All right," Therese said.

"But Abby's incredibly clumsy sometimes in the way she talks."

Therese wanted to forget the whole thing. Carol was still so distant even when she spoke, even when she looked at her. A bar of light from the green room lay across the top of Carol's head, but she could not see Carol's face now.

Carol poked her with the back of her toe. "Hop up."

But Therese was slow to move, and Carol swung her feet over Therese's head and sat up. Then Therese heard the maid's step in the next room, and the plump, Irish-looking maid in the gray and white uniform came in bearing a coffee tray, shaking the porch floor with her quick, eager little steps that sounded so eager to please.

"The cream's in here, ma'am," she said, pointing to a pitcher that didn't match the demitasse set. Florence glanced at Therese with a friendly smile and round blank eyes. She was about fifty, with a bun at the back of her neck under the starched white band of her cap. Therese could not establish her somehow, could not determine her allegiance. Therese had heard her refer to Mr. Aird twice as if she were very devoted to him, and whether it was professional or genuine, Therese did not know.

"Will there be anything else, ma'am?" Florence asked. "Shall I put out the lights?"

"No, I like the lights. We won't need anything else, thanks. Did Mrs. Riordan call?"

"Not yet, ma'am."

"Will you tell her I'm out when she does?"

"Yes, ma'am." Florence hesitated. "I was wondering if you were finished with that new book, ma'am. The one about the Alps."

"Go in my room and get it, if you'd like it, Florence. I don't think I want to finish it."

"Thank you, ma'am. Good night, ma'am. Good night, miss."

"Good night," Carol said.

While Carol was pouring the coffee, Therese asked, "Have you decided how soon you're going away?"

"Maybe in about a week." Carol handed her the demitasse with cream in it. "Why?"

"Just that I'll miss you. Of course."

Carol was motionless for a moment, and then she reached for a cigarette, a last one, and crumpled the pack up. "I was thinking, in fact, you might like to go with me. What do you think, for three weeks or so?"

There it was, Therese thought, as casual as if she suggested their taking a walk together. "You mentioned it to Abby, didn't you?"

"Yes," Carol said. "Why?"

Why? Therese could not put into words why it hurt her that Carol had. "It just seems strange you'd tell her before you said anything to me."

"I didn't tell her. I only said I might ask you." Carol came over to her and put her hands on Therese's shoulders. "Look, there's no reason for you to feel like this about Abby—unless Abby said a lot else to you at lunch that you didn't tell me."

"No," Therese said. No, but it was the undercurrents, it was worse. She felt Carol's hands leave her shoulders.

"Abby's a very old friend of mine," Carol said. "I talk over everything with her."

"Yes," Therese said.

"Well, do you think you'd like to go?"

Carol had turned away from her, and suddenly it meant nothing, because of the way Carol asked her, as if she didn't really care one way or the other if she went. "Thanks—I don't think I can afford it just now."

"You wouldn't need much money. We'd go in the car. But if you have a job offered you right away, that's different."

As if she wouldn't turn down a job on a ballet set to go away with Carol—to go with her through country she had never seen before, over rivers and mountains, not knowing where they would be when night came. Carol knew that, and knew she would have to refuse if Carol asked her in this way. Therese felt suddenly sure that Carol taunted her, and she resented it with the bitter resentment of a betrayal. And the resentment resolved itself into a decision never to see Carol again. She glanced at Carol, who was waiting for her answer, with that defiance only half masked by an air of indifference, an expression that Therese knew would not change at all if she should give a negative answer. Therese got up and went to the box on the end table for a cigarette. There was nothing in the box but some phonograph needles and a photograph.

"What is it?" Carol asked, watching her.

Therese felt Carol had been reading all her thoughts. "It's a picture of Rindy," Therese said.

"Of Rindy? Let's see it."

Therese watched Carol's face as she looked at the picture of the little girl with the white-blonde hair and the serious face, with the taped white bandage on her knee. In the picture, Harge was standing in a rowing boat, and Rindy was stepping from a dock into his arms.

"It's not a very good picture," Carol said, but her face had changed, grown softer. "That's about three years old. Would you like a cigarette? There's some over here. Rindy's going to stay with Harge for the next three months."

Therese had supposed that from the conversation in the kitchen that morning with Abby. "Is that in New Jersey, too?"

"Yes. Harge's family lives in New Jersey. They've a big house." Carol waited. "The divorce will come through in a month, I think, and after March, I'll have Rindy the rest of the year."

"Oh. But you'll see her again before March, won't you?"

"A few times. Probably not much."

Therese looked at Carol's hand holding the photograph, beside her on the swing seat, carelessly. "Won't she miss you?"

"Yes, but she's very fond of her father, too."

"Fonder than she is of you?"

"No. Not really. But he's bought her a goat to play with now. He takes her to school on his way to work, and he picks her up at four. Neglects his business for her—and what more can you ask of a man?"

"You didn't see her Christmas, did you?" Therese said.

"No. Because of something that happened in the lawyer's office. That was the afternoon Harge's lawyer wanted to see us both, and Harge had brought Rindy, too. Rindy said she wanted to go to Harge's house for Christmas. Rindy didn't know I wasn't going to be there this year. They have a big tree that grows on the lawn and they always decorate it, so Rindy was set on it. Anyway, it made quite an impression on the lawyer, you know, the child asking to go home for Christmas with her father. And naturally I didn't want to tell Rindy then I wasn't going, or she'd have been disappointed. I couldn't have said it anyway, in front of the lawyer. Harge's machinations are enough."

Therese stood there, crushing the unlighted cigarette in her fingers. Carol's voice was calm, as it might have been if she talked to Abby, Therese thought. Carol had never said so much to her before. "But the lawyer understood?

Carol shrugged. "It's Harge's lawyer, not mine. So I agreed to the three-month arrangement now, because I don't want her to be tossed back and forth. If I'm to have her nine months and Harge three—it might as well start now."

"You won't even visit her?"

Carol waited so long to answer, Therese thought she was not going to. "Not very often. The family isn't too cordial. I talk to Rindy every day on the telephone. Sometimes she calls me."

"Why isn't the family cordial?"

"They never cared for me. They've been complaining ever since Harge met me at some deb party. They're very good at criticizing. I sometimes wonder just who would pass with them."

"What do they criticize you for?"

"For having a furniture shop, for instance. But that didn't last a year. Then for not playing bridge, or not liking to. They pick out the funny things, the most superficial things."

"They sound horrid."

"They're not horrid. One's just supposed to conform. I know what they'd like, they'd like a blank they could fill in. A person already filled in disturbs them terribly. Shall we play some music? Don't you ever like the radio?"

"Sometimes."

Carol leaned against the windowsill. "And now Rindy's got television every day. Hopalong Cassidy. How she'd love to go out west. That's the last doll I'll ever buy for her, Therese. I only got it because she said she wanted one, but she's outgrown them."

Behind Carol, an airport searchlight made a pale sweep in the night, and disappeared. Carol's voice seemed to linger in the darkness. In its richer, happier tone, Therese could hear the depths within her where she loved Rindy, deeper than she would probably ever love anyone else. "Harge doesn't make it easy for you to see her, does he?"

"You know that," Carol said.

"I don't see how he could be so much in love with you."

"It's not love. It's a compulsion. I think he wants to control me. I suppose if I were a lot wilder but never had an opinion on anything except his opinion—Can you follow all this?"

"Yes."

"I've never done anything to embarrass him socially, and that's all he cares about really. There's a certain woman at the club I wish he'd married. Her life is entirely filled with giving exquisite little dinner parties and being carried out of the best bars feet first—She's made her husband's advertising business a great success, so he smiles on her little faults. Harge wouldn't smile, but he'd have some definite reason for complaint. I think he picked me out like a rug for his living room, and he made a bad mistake. I doubt if he's capable of loving anyone, really. What he has is a kind of acquisitiveness, which isn't much separate from his ambition. It's getting to be a disease, isn't it, not being able to love?" She looked at Therese. "Maybe it's the times. If one wanted to, one could make out a case for racial suicide. Man trying to catch up with his own destructive machines."

Therese said nothing. It reminded her of a thousand conversations with Richard, Richard mingling war and big business and congressional witch hunts and finally certain people he knew into one grand enemy, whose only collective label was hate. Now Carol, too. It shook Therese in the profoundest part of her where no words were, no easy words like death or dying or killing. Those words were somehow future, and this was present. An inarticulate anxiety, a desire to *know*, know anything, for certain, had jammed itself in her throat so for a moment she felt she could hardly breathe. Do you think, do you think, it began. Do you think both of us will die violently someday, be suddenly shut off? But even that question wasn't definite enough. Perhaps it was a statement after all: I don't want to die yet without knowing you. Do you feel the same way, Carol? She could have uttered the last question, but she could not have said all that went before it.

"You're the young generation," Carol said. "And what have you got to say?" She sat down on the swing seat.

"I suppose the first thing is not to be afraid." Therese turned and saw Carol's smile. "You're smiling because you think I am afraid, I suppose."

"You're about as weak as this match." Carol held it burning for a moment after she lighted her cigarette. "But given the right conditions, you could burn a house down, couldn't you?"

"Or a city."

"But you're even afraid to take a little trip with me. You're afraid because you think you haven't got enough money."

"That's not it."

"You've got some very strange values, Therese. I asked you to go with me, because it would give me pleasure to have you. I should think it'd be good for you, too, and good for your work. But you've got to spoil it by a silly pride about money. Like that handbag you gave me. Out of all proportion. Why don't you take it back, if you need the money? I don't need the handbag. It gave you pleasure to give it to me, I suppose. It's the same thing, you see. Only I make sense and you don't." Carol walked by her and turned to her again, poised with one foot forward and her head up, the short blonde hair as unobtrusive as a statue's hair. "Well, do you think it's funny?"

Therese was smiling. "I don't care about the money," she said quietly.

"What do you mean?"

"Just that," Therese said. "I've got the money to go. I'll go."

Carol stared at her. Therese saw the sullenness leave her face, and then Carol began to smile, too, with surprise, a little incredulously.

"Well, all right," Carol said. "I'm delighted."

"I'm delighted."

"What brought this happy change about?"

Doesn't she really know, Therese thought. "You do seem to care whether I go or not," Therese said simply.

"Of course I care. I asked you, didn't I?" Carol said, still smiling, but with a twist of her toe she turned her back on Therese and walked toward the green room.

Therese watched her go, her hands in her pockets and her moccasins making light slow clicks on the floor. Therese looked at the empty doorway. Carol would have walked out exactly the same way, she thought, if she had said no, she wouldn't go. She picked up her half-finished demitasse, then set it down again.

She went out and across the hall, to the door of Carol's room. "What are you doing?"

Carol was bending over her dressing table, writing. "What am I doing?" She stood up and slipped a piece of paper into her pocket. She was smiling now, really smiling in her eyes, like the moment in the kitchen with Abby. "Something," Carol said. "Let's have some music."

"Fine." A smile spread over her face.

"Why don't you get ready for bed first? It's late, do you know that?"

"It always gets late with you."

"Is that a compliment?"

"I don't feel like going to bed tonight."

Carol crossed the hall to the green room. "You get ready. You've got circles under your eyes."

Therese undressed quickly in the room with the twin beds. The phonograph in the other room played "Embraceable You." Then the telephone rang. Therese opened the top drawer of the bureau. It was empty except for a couple of men's handkerchiefs, an old clothes brush and a key. And a few papers in the corner. Therese picked up a card covered in isinglass. It was an old driver's license belonging to Harge. Hargess Foster Aird. Age: 37. Height: 5' 8½". Weight: 168. Hair: blond. Eyes: blue. She knew all that. A 1950 Oldsmobile. Color: dark blue. Therese put it back and closed the drawer. She went to the door and listened.

"I am sorry, Tessie, but I did get stuck after all," Carol was saying regretfully, but her voice was happy. "Is it a good party? . . . Well, I'm not dressed and I'm tired."

Therese went to the bed table and got a cigarette from the box there. A Philip Morris. Carol had put them there, not the maid, Therese knew, because Carol remembered that she liked them. Naked now, Therese stood listening to the music. It was a song she didn't know.

Was Carol on the telephone again?

"Well, I don't like it," she heard Carol say, half angry, half joking, "one damn bit."

*. . . It's easy to live . . . when you're in love . . .*

"How do I know what kind of people they are? . . . Oh-ho! Is that so?"

Abby, Therese knew. She blew her smoke out and snuffled at the slightly sweet-smelling wisps of it, remembering the first cigarette she had ever smoked, a Philip Morris, on the roof of a dormitory at the home, four of them passing it around.

"Yes, we're going," Carol said emphatically. "Well, I am. Don't I sound it?"

*. . . For you . . . maybe I'm a fool but it's fun . . . People say you rule me with one . . . wave of your hand . . . Darling, it's grand . . . they just don't understand . . .*

It was a good song. Therese closed her eyes and leaned on the half-open door, listening. Behind the voice was a slow piano that rippled all over the keyboard. And a lazy trumpet.

Carol said, "That's nobody's business but mine, is it? . . . Nonsense!" and Therese smiled at her vehemence.

Therese closed the door. The phonograph had dropped another record.

"Why don't you come say hello to Abby?" Carol said.

Therese had ducked behind the bathroom door because she was naked. "Why?"

"Come along," Carol said, and Therese put on a robe and went.

"Hello," Abby said. "I hear you're going."

"Is that news to you?"

Abby sounded silly, as if she wanted to talk all night. She wished Therese a pleasant trip, and told her about the roads in the corn belt, how bad they could be in winter.

"Will you forgive me if I was rude today?" Abby said for the second time. "I like you OK, Therese."

"Cut it, cut it!" Carol called down.

"She wants to talk to you again," Therese said.

"Tell Abigail I'm in the tub."

Therese told her, and got away.

Carol had brought a bottle and two little glasses into the room.

"What's the matter with Abby?" Therese asked.

"What do you mean, what's the matter with her?" Carol poured a brown-colored liquor into the two glasses. "I think she's had a couple tonight."

"I know. But why did she want to have lunch with me?"

"Well—I guess a lot of reasons. Try some of this stuff."

"It just seems vague," Therese said.

"What does?"

"The whole lunch."

Carol gave her a glass. "Some things are always vague, darling."

It was the first time Carol had called her darling. "What things?" Therese asked. She wanted an answer, a definite answer.

Carol sighed. "A lot of things. The most important things. Taste your drink."

Therese sipped it, sweet and dark brown, like coffee, with the sting of alcohol. "Tastes good."

"You would think so."

"Why do you drink it if you don't like it?"

"Because it's different. This is to our trip, so it's got to be something different." Carol grimaced and drank the rest of her glass.

In the light of the lamp, Therese could see all the freckles on half of Carol's face. Carol's white-looking eyebrow bent like a wing around the curve of her forehead. Therese felt ecstatically happy all at once. "What's that song that was playing before, the one with just the voice and the piano?"

"Hum it."

She whistled part of it, and Carol smiled.

" 'Easy Living,' " Carol said. "That's an old one."

"I'd like to hear it again."

"I'd like you to get to bed. I'll play it again."

Carol went into the green room, and stayed there while it played. Therese stood by the door of her room, listening, smiling.

*. . . I never regret . . . the years I'm giving . . . They're easy to give, when you're in love . . . I'm happy to do whatever I do for you . . .*

That was her song. That was everything she felt about Carol. She went in the bathroom before it was over, and turned the water on in the tub, got in and let the greenish-looking water tumble about her feet.

"Hey!" Carol called. "Have you ever been to Wyoming?"

"No."

"It's time you saw America."

Therese lifted the dripping rag and pressed it against her knee. The water was so high now, her breasts looked like flat things floating on the surface. She studied them, trying to decide what they looked like besides what they were.

"Don't go to sleep in there," Carol called in a preoccupied voice, and Therese knew she was sitting on the bed, looking at a map.

"I won't."

"Well, some people do."

"Tell me more about Harge," she said as she dried herself. "What does he do?"

"A lot of things."

"I mean, what's his business?"

"Real estate investment."

"What's he like? Does he like to go to the theater? Does he like people?"

"He likes a little group of people who play golf," Carol said with finality. Then in a louder voice, "And what else? He's very very meticulous about everything. But he forgot his best razor. It's in the medicine cabinet and you can see it if you want to and you probably do. I've got to mail it to him, I suppose."

Therese opened the medicine cabinet. She saw the razor. The medicine cabinet was still full of men's things, aftershave lotions and lather brushes. "Was this his room?" she asked as she came out of the bathroom. "Which bed did he sleep in?"

Carol smiled. "Not yours."

"Can I have some more of this?" Therese asked, looking at the liqueur bottle.

"Of course."

"Can I kiss you good night?"

Carol was folding the road map, pursing her lips as if she would whistle, waiting. "No," she said.

"Why not?" Anything seemed possible tonight.

"I'll give you this instead." Carol pulled her hand out of her pocket.

It was a check. Therese read the sum, two hundred dollars, made out to her. "What's this for?"

"For the trip. I don't want you to spend the money you'll need for that union membership thing." Carol took a cigarette. "You won't need all of that, I just want you to have it."

"But I don't need it," Therese said. "Thanks. I don't care if I spend the union money."

"No backtalk," Carol interrupted her. "It gives me pleasure, remember?"

"But I won't take it." She sounded curt, so she smiled a little as she put the check down on the tabletop by the liqueur bottle. But she had thumped the check down, too. She wished she could explain it to Carol. It didn't matter at all, the money, but since it did give Carol pleasure, she hated not to take it. "I don't like the idea," Therese said. "Think of something else." She looked at Carol. Carol was watching her, was not going to argue with her, Therese was glad to see.

"To give me pleasure?" Carol asked.

Therese's smile broadened. "Yes," she said, and picked up the little glass.

"All right," Carol said. "I'll think. Good night." Carol had stopped by the door.

It was a funny way of saying good night, Therese thought, on such an important night. "Good night," Therese answered.

She turned to the table and saw the check again. But it was for Carol to tear up. She slid it under the edge of the dark blue linen table runner, out of sight.

# PART II

## *twelve*

January.

It was all things. And it was one thing, like a solid door. Its cold sealed the city in a gray capsule. January was moments, and January was a year. January rained the moments down, and froze them in her memory: the woman she saw peering anxiously by the light of a match at the names in a dark doorway, the man who scribbled a message and handed it to his friend before they parted on the sidewalk, the man who ran a block for a bus and caught it. Every human action seemed to yield a magic. January was a two-faced month, jangling like jester's bells, crackling like snow crust, pure as any beginning, grim as an old man, mysteriously familiar yet unknown, like a word one can almost but not quite define.

A young man named Red Malone and a bald-headed carpenter worked with her on the *Small Rain* set. Mr. Donohue was very pleased with it. He said he had asked a Mr. Baltin to come in and see her work. Mr. Baltin was a graduate of a Russian academy, and had designed a few sets for theaters in New York. Therese had never heard of him. She tried to get Mr. Donohue to arrange an appointment for her to see Myron Blanchard or Ivor Harkevy, but Mr. Donohue never promised anything. He couldn't, Therese supposed.

Mr. Baltin came in one afternoon, a tall, bent man in a black hat and a seedy overcoat, and looked intently at the work she showed him. She had brought only three or four models down to the theater, her very best ones. Mr. Baltin told her of a play that was to start in production in about six weeks. He would be glad to recommend her as an assistant, and Therese said that would work out very well, because she would be out of town until then, anyway. Everything was working out very well in these last days. Mr. Andronich had promised her a two-week job in Philadelphia in the middle of February, which would be just about the time she would be back from the trip with Carol. Therese wrote down the name and address of the man Mr. Baltin knew.

"He's looking for someone now, so call him the first of the week," Mr. Baltin said. "It'll just be a helper's job, but his former helper, a pupil of mine, is working with Harkevy now."

"Oh. Do you suppose you—or he could arrange for me to see Harkevy?"

"Nothing easier. All you have to do is call Harkevy's studio and ask to speak to Charles. Charles Winant. Tell him that you've spoken with me. Let's see—call him Friday. Friday afternoon around three."

"All right. Thank you." Friday was a whole week off. Harkevy was not unapproachable, Therese had heard, but he had the reputation of never making appointments, much less keeping them if he did make them, because he was very busy. But maybe Mr. Baltin knew.

"And don't forget to call Kettering," Mr. Baltin said as he left.

Therese looked again at the name he had given her: Adolph Kettering, Theatrical Investments, Inc., at a private address. "I'll call him Monday morning. Thanks a lot."

That was the day, a Saturday, when she was to meet Richard in the Palermo after work. There were eleven days left before the date she and Carol planned to leave. She saw Phil standing with Richard at the bar.

"Well, how's the old Cat?" Phil asked her, dragging up a stool for her. "Working Saturdays, too?"

"The cast didn't work. Just my department," she said.

"When's the opening?"

"The twenty-first."

"Look," Richard said. He pointed to a spot of dark green paint on her skirt.

"I know. I did that days ago."

"What would you like to drink?" Phil asked her.

"I don't know. Maybe I'll have a beer, thanks." Richard had turned his back on Phil, who stood on the other side of him, and she sensed an ill-feeling between them. "Did you do any painting today?" she asked Richard.

Richard's mouth was down at both corners. "Had to pinch hit for some driver who was sick. Ran out of gas in the middle of Long Island."

"Oh. That's rotten. Maybe you'd rather paint than go anywhere tomorrow." They had talked of going over to Hoboken tomorrow, just to walk around and eat at the Clam House. But Carol would be in town tomorrow, and had promised to call her.

"I'll paint if you'll sit for me," Richard said.

Therese hesitated uncomfortably. "I just don't feel in the mood for sitting these days."

"All right. It's not important." He smiled. "But how can I ever paint you if you'll never sit?"

"Why don't you do it out of the air?"

Phil slid his hand out and held the bottom of her glass. "Don't drink that. Have something better. I'll drink this."

"All right. I'll try a rye and water."

Phil was standing on the other side of her now. He looked cheerful, but a little dark around the eyes. For the past week, in a sullen mood, he had been writing a play. He had read a few scenes of it aloud at his New Year's party. Phil called it an extension of Kafka's "Metamorphosis." She had drawn a rough sketch for a set New Year's morning, and showed it to Phil when she came down to see him. And suddenly it occurred to her that was what was the matter with Richard.

"Terry, I wish you'd make a model we can photograph from that sketch you showed me. I'd like to have a set to go with the script." Phil pushed the rye and water toward her, and leaned on the bar close beside her.

"I might," Therese said. "Are you really going to try to get it produced?"

"Why not?" Phil's dark eyes challenged her above his smile. He snapped his fingers at the barman. "Check?"

"I'll pay," Richard said.

"No, you won't. This is mine." Phil had his old black wallet in his hand.

His play would never be produced, Therese thought, might not even be finished, because Phil's moods were capricious.

"I'll be moving along," Phil said. "Drop by soon, Terry. Cheerio, Rich."

She watched him go off and up the little front stairs, shabbier than she had ever seen him in his sandals and threadbare polo coat, yet with an attractive nonchalance about his shabbiness. Like a man walking through his house in his favorite old bathrobe, Therese thought. She waved back at him through the front window.

"I hear you took Phil sandwiches and beer New Year's Day," Richard said.

"Yes. He called up and said he had a hangover."

"Why didn't you mention it?"

"I forgot, I suppose. It wasn't important."

"Not important. If you—" Richard's stiff hand gestured slowly, hopelessly. "If you spend half the day in a guy's apartment, bringing him sandwiches and beer? Didn't it occur to you I might have wanted some sandwiches, too?"

"If you did, you had plenty of people to get them for you. We'd eaten and drunk everything in Phil's house. Remember?"

Richard nodded his long head, still smiling the downward, disgruntled smile. "And you were alone with him, just the two of you."

"Oh, Richard—" She remembered, and it was so unimportant. Danny hadn't been back from Connecticut that day. He had spent New Year's at the house of one of his professors. She had hoped Danny would come in that afternoon at Phil's, but Richard would probably never think that, never guess she liked Danny a lot better than Phil.

"If any other girl did that, I'd suspect something was brewing and I'd be right," Richard went on.

"I think you're being silly."

"I think you're being naïve." Richard was looking at her stonily, resentfully, and Therese thought, it surely couldn't be only this he was so resentful about. He resented the fact that she wasn't and never could be what he wished her to be, a girl who loved him passionately and would love to go to Europe with him. A girl like herself, with her face, her ambitions, but a girl who adored him. "You're not Phil's type, you know," he said.

"Whoever said I was? Phil?"

"That twerp, that half-baked dilettante," Richard murmured. "And he has the nerve to sound off tonight and say you don't give a damn for me."

"He hasn't any right to say that. I don't discuss you with him."

"Oh, that's a fine answer. Meaning if you had, he'd know you didn't give a damn, eh?" Richard said it quietly, but his voice shook with anger.

"What's Phil suddenly got against you?" she asked.

"That's not the point!"

"What is the point?" she said impatiently.

"Oh, Terry, let's stop it."

"You can't find any point," she said, but seeing Richard turn away from her and shift his elbows on the bar, almost as if he writhed physically under her words, she felt a sudden compassion for him. It was not now, not last week, that galled him, but the whole past and future futility of his own feelings about her.

Richard plunged his cigarette into the ashtray on the bar. "What do you want to do tonight?" he asked.

Tell him about the trip with Carol, she thought. Twice before she had meant to tell him, and put it off. "Do you want to do anything?" She emphasized the last word.

"Of course," he said depressedly. "What do you say we have dinner, then call up Sam and Joan? Maybe we can walk up and see them tonight."

"All right." She hated it. Two of the most boring people she had ever met, a shoe clerk and a secretary, happily married on West Twentieth Street, and she knew Richard meant to show her an ideal life in theirs, to remind her that they might live together the same way one day. She hated it, and any other night she might have protested, but the compassion for Richard was still in her, dragging after it an amorphous wake of guilt and a necessity to atone. Suddenly, she remembered a picnic they had had last summer, off the road near Tarrytown, remembered precisely Richard's reclining on the grass, working ever so slowly with his pocketknife at the cork in the wine bottle, while they talked of—what? But she remembered that moment of contentment, that conviction that they shared something wonderfully real and rare together that day, and she wondered now where it had gone to, on what it had been based. For now even his long flat figure standing beside her seemed to oppress her with its weight. She forced down her resentment, but it only grew heavy inside her, like a thing of substance. She looked at the chunky figures of the two Italian workmen standing at the bar, and at the two girls at the end of the bar whom she had noticed before, and now that they were leaving, she saw that they were in slacks. One had hair cut like a boy's. Therese looked away, aware that she avoided them, avoided being seen looking at them.

"Want to eat here? Are you hungry yet?" Richard asked.

"No. Let's go somewhere else."

So they went out and walked north, in the general direction of where Sam and Joan lived.

Therese rehearsed the first words until all their sense was rubbed out. "Remember Mrs. Aird, the woman you met in my house that day?"

"Sure."

"She's invited me to go on a trip with her, a trip West in a car for a couple of weeks or so. I'd like to go."

"West? California?" Richard said, surprised. "Why?"

"Why?"

"Well—do you know her as well as that?"

"I've seen her a few times."

"Oh. Well, you didn't mention it." Richard walked along with his hands swinging at his sides, looking at her. "Just the two of you?"

"Yes."

"When would you be leaving?"

"Around the eighteenth."

"Of this month?—Then you won't get to see your show."

She shook her head. "I don't think it's so much to miss."

"Then it's definite?"

"Yes."

He was silent a moment. "What kind of a person is she? She doesn't drink or anything, does she?"

"No." Therese smiled. "Does she look like she drinks?"

"No. I think she's very good-looking, in fact. It's just damned surprising, that's all."

"Why?"

"You so seldom make up your mind about anything. You'll probably change your mind again."

"I don't think so."

"Maybe I can see her again sometime with you. Why don't you arrange it?"

"She said she'd be in the city tomorrow. I don't know how much time she's got—or really whether she'll call or not."

Richard didn't continue and neither did Therese. They did not mention Carol again that evening.

Richard spent Sunday morning painting, and came to Therese's apartment around two. He was there when Carol telephoned a little later. Therese told her that Richard was with her, and Carol said, "Bring him along." Carol said she was near the Plaza, and they might meet there in the Palm Room.

Half an hour later, Therese saw Carol look up at them from a table near the center of the room, and almost like the first time, like the echo of an impact that had been tremendous, Therese was jolted by the sight of her. Carol was wearing the same black suit with the green and gold scarf that she had worn the day of the luncheon. But now Carol paid more attention to Richard than to her.

The three of them talked of nothing, and Therese, seeing the calm in Carol's gray eyes that only once turned to her, seeing a quite ordinary expression on Richard's face, felt a kind of disappointment. Richard had gone out of his way to meet her, but Therese thought it was even less from curiosity than because he had nothing else to do. She saw Richard looking at Carol's hands, the nails manicured in a bright red, saw him notice the ring with the clear green sapphire, and the wedding ring on the other hand. Richard could not say they were useless hands, idle hands, despite the longish nails. Carol's hands were strong, and they moved with an economy of motion. Her voice emerged from the flat murmur of other voices around them, talking of nothing at all with Richard, and once she laughed.

Carol looked at her. "Did you tell Richard we might go on a trip?" she asked.

"Yes. Last night."

"West?" Richard asked.

"I'd like to go up to the Northwest. It depends on the roads."

And Therese was suddenly impatient. Why did they sit here having a conference about it? Now they were talking about temperatures, and the state of Washington.

"Washington's my home state," Carol said. "Practically."

Then a few moments later, Carol asked if anyone wanted to take a walk in the park. Richard paid for their beer and coffee, pulling a bill from the tangle of bills and change that bulged a pocket of his trousers. How indifferent he was to Carol after all, Therese thought. She felt he didn't see her, as he sometimes hadn't seen figures in rock or cloud formations when she had tried to point them out to him. He was looking down at the table now, the thin, careless line of his mouth half smiling as he straightened up and shoved his hand quickly through his hair.

They walked from the entrance of the park at Fifty-ninth Street toward the zoo, and through the zoo at a strolling pace. They walked on under the first bridge over the path, where the path bent and the real park began. The air was cold and still, a little overcast, and Therese felt a motionlessness about everything, a lifeless stillness even in their slowly moving figures.

"Shall I hunt up some peanuts?" Richard asked.

Carol was stooped at the edge of the path, holding her fingers out to the squirrel. "I have something," she said softly, and the squirrel started at her voice but advanced again, seized her fingers in a nervous grip, and fixed its teeth on something, and dashed away. Carol stood up, smiling. "Had something in my pocket from this morning."

"Do you feed squirrels out where you live?" Richard asked.

"Squirrels and chipmunks," Carol replied.

What dull things they talked of, Therese thought.

Then they sat on a bench and smoked a cigarette, and Therese, watching a diminutive sun bring its orange fire down finally into the scraggly black twigs of a tree, wished the night were here already and that she were alone with Carol. They began to walk back. If Carol had to go home now, Therese thought, she would do something violent. Like jump off the Fifty-ninth Street Bridge. Or take the three Benzedrine tablets Richard had given her last week.

"Would you people like to have some tea somewhere?" Carol asked as they neared the zoo again. "How about that Russian place over by Carnegie Hall?"

"Rumpelmayer's is right here," Richard said. "Do you like Rumpelmayer's?"

Therese sighed. And Carol seemed to hesitate. But they went there. Therese had been here once with Angelo, she remembered. She did not care for the place. Its bright lights gave her a feeling of nakedness, and it was annoying not to know if one were looking at a real person or at a reflection in a mirror.

"No, none of that, thanks," Carol said, shaking her head at the great tray of pastry the waitress was holding.

But Richard chose something, chose two pastries, though Therese had declined.

"What's that for, in case I change my mind?" she asked him, and Richard winked at her. His nails were dirty again, she noticed.

Richard asked Carol what kind of car she had, and they began discussing the merits of various car makes. Therese saw Carol glance about at the tables in front of her. She doesn't like it here either, Therese thought. Therese stared at a man in the mirror that was set obliquely behind Carol. His back was to Therese, and he leaned forward, talking animatedly to a woman, jerking his spread left hand for emphasis. She looked at the thin, middle-aged woman he spoke to, and back at him, wondering if the aura of familiarity about him were real or an illusion like the mirror, until a memory fragile as a bubble swam upward in her consciousness and burst at the surface. It was Harge.

Therese glanced at Carol, but if Carol had noticed him, she thought, Carol would not know that he was in the mirror behind her. A moment later, Therese looked over her shoulder, and saw Harge in profile, much like one of the images she carried in her memory from the house—the short high nose, the full lower face, the receding twist of blond hair above the usual hairline. Carol must have seen him, only three tables away to her left.

Carol looked from Richard to Therese. "Yes," she said to her, smiling a little, and turned back to Richard and went on with her conversation. Her manner was just as before, Therese thought, not different at all. Therese looked at the woman with Harge. She was not young, not very attractive. She might have been one of his relatives.

Then Therese saw Carol mash out a long cigarette. Richard had stopped talking. They were ready to leave. Therese was looking at Harge the moment he saw Carol. After his first glimpse of her, his eyes drew almost shut as if he had to squint to believe her, and then he said something to the woman he was with and stood up and went to her.

"Carol," Harge said.

"Hello, Harge." She turned to Therese and Richard. "Would you excuse me a minute?"

Watching from the doorway where she stood with Richard, Therese tried to see it all, to see beyond the pride and aggressiveness in Harge's anxious, forward-leaning figure that was not quite so tall as the crown of Carol's hat, to see beyond Carol's acquiescent nods as he spoke, to surmise not what they talked of now but what they had said to each other five years ago, three years ago, that day of the picture in the rowing boat. Carol had loved him once, and that was hard to remember.

"Can we get free now, Terry?" Richard asked her.

Therese saw Carol nod good-bye to the woman at Harge's table, then turn away from Harge. Harge looked past Carol, to her and Richard, and without apparently recognizing her, he went back to his table.

"I'm sorry," Carol said as she rejoined them.

On the sidewalk, Therese drew Richard aside and said, "I'll say good night, Richard. Carol wants me to visit a friend of hers tonight with her."

"Oh." Richard frowned. "I had those concert tickets for tonight, you know."

Therese remembered suddenly. "Alex's. I forgot. I'm sorry."

He said gloomily, "It's not important."

It wasn't important. Richard's friend Alex was accompanying somebody in a violin concert, and had given Richard the tickets, she remembered, weeks ago.

"You'd rather see her than me, wouldn't you?" he asked.

Therese saw that Carol was looking for a taxi. Carol would leave them both in a moment. "You might have mentioned the concert this morning, Richard, reminded me, at least."

"Was that her husband?" Richard's eyes narrowed under his frown. "What is this, Terry?"

"What's what?" she said. "I don't know her husband."

Richard waited a moment, then the frown left his eyes. He smiled, as if he conceded he had been unreasonable. "Sorry. I just took it for granted I'd see you tonight." He walked toward Carol. "Good night," he said.

He looked as if he were leaving by himself, and Carol said, "Are you going downtown? Maybe I can drop you."

"I'm walking, thanks."

"I thought you two had a date," Carol said to Therese.

Therese saw that Richard was lingering, and she walked toward Carol, out of his hearing. "Not an important one. I'd rather stay with you."

A taxi had slid up beside Carol. Carol put her hand on the door handle. "Well, neither is our date so important, so why don't you go on with Richard tonight?"

Therese glanced at Richard, and saw that he had heard her.

"Bye-bye, Therese," Carol said.

"Good night," Richard called.

"Good night," Therese said, and watched Carol pull the taxi door shut after her.

"So," Richard said.

Therese turned toward him. She wouldn't go to the concert, and neither would she do anything violent, she knew, nothing more violent than walk quickly home and get to work on the set she wanted to finish by Tuesday for Harkevy. She could see the whole evening ahead, with a half-dismal, half-defiant fatality, in the second it took for Richard to walk to her. "I still don't want to go to the concert," she said.

To her surprise, Richard stepped back and said angrily, "All right, don't!" and turned away.

He walked west on Fifty-ninth Street in his loose, lopsided gait that jutted his right shoulder ahead of the other, hands swinging unrhythmically at his sides, and she might have known from the walk alone that he was angry. And he was out of sight in no time. The rejection from Kettering last Monday flashed across her mind. She stared at the darkness where Richard had disappeared. She did not feel guilty about tonight. It was something else. She envied him. She envied him his faith that there would always be a place, a home, a job, someone else for him. She envied him that attitude. She almost resented his having it.

# thirteen

Richard began it.

"Why do you like her so much?"

It was an evening on which she had broken a date with Richard on the slim chance Carol would come by. Carol hadn't, and Richard had come by instead. Now at five past eleven in the huge pink-walled cafeteria on Lexington Avenue, she had been about to begin, but Richard was ahead of her.

"I like being with her, I like talking with her. I'm fond of anybody I can talk to." The phrases of some letter she had written to Carol and never mailed drifted across her mind as if to answer Richard. *I feel I stand in a desert with my hands outstretched, and you are raining down upon me.*

"You've got a hell of a crush on her," Richard announced, explanatorily and resentfully.

Therese took a deep breath. Should she be simple and say yes, or should she try to explain it? What could he ever understand of it, even if she explained it in a million words?

"Does she know it? Of course she knows it." Richard frowned and drew on his cigarette. "Don't you think it's pretty silly? It's like a crush that schoolgirls get."

"You don't understand," she said. She felt so very sure of herself. *I will comb you like music caught in the heads of all the trees in the forest . . .*

"What's there to understand? But she understands. She shouldn't indulge you. She shouldn't play with you like this. It's not fair to you."

"Not fair to me?"

"What's she doing, amusing herself with you? And then one day she'll get tired of you and kick you out."

Kick me out, she thought. What was in or out? How did one kick out an emotion? She was angry, but she did not want to argue. She said nothing.

"You're in a daze!"

"I'm wide awake. I never felt more awake." She picked up the table knife and rubbed her thumb back and forth on the ridge at the base of the blade. "Why don't you leave me alone?"

He frowned. "Leave you alone?"

"Yes."

"You mean, about Europe, too?"

"Yes," she said.

"Listen, Terry—" Richard wriggled in his chair and leaned forward, hesitated, then took another cigarette, lighting it distastefully, throwing the match on the floor. "You're in some kind of trance! It's worse—"

"Just because I don't want to argue with you?"

"It's worse than being lovesick, because it's so completely unreasonable. Don't you understand that?"

No, she didn't understand a word.

"But you're going to get over it in about a week. I hope. My God!" He squirmed again. "To say—to say for a minute you practically want to say good-bye to me because of some silly crush!"

"I didn't say that. You said it." She looked back at him, at his rigid face that was beginning to redden in the center of the flat cheeks. "But why should I want to be with you if all you do is argue about this?"

He sat back. "Wednesday, next Saturday, you won't feel like this at all. You haven't known her three weeks yet."

She looked over toward the steam tables, where people edged slowly along, choosing this and that, drifting toward the curve in the counter where they dispersed. "We may as well say good-bye," she said, "because neither of us will ever be any different from what we are this minute."

"Therese, you're like a person gone so crazy, you think you're saner than ever!"

"Oh, let's stop it!"

Richard's hand with its row of knuckles embedded in the white, freckled flesh was clenched on the table motionless, but a picture of a hand that had hammered some ineffectual, inaudible point. "I'll tell you one thing, I think your friend knows what she's doing. I think she's committing a crime against you. I've half a mind to report her to somebody, but the trouble is you're not a child. You're just acting like one."

"Why do you make so much out of it?" she asked. "You're practically in a frenzy."

"You make enough out of it to want to say good-bye to me! What do you know about her?"

"What do *you* know about her?"

"Did she ever make any passes at you?"

"God!" Therese said. She felt like saying it a dozen times. It summed up everything, her imprisonment now, here, yet. "You don't understand." But he did, and that was why he was angry. But did he understand that she would have felt the same way if Carol had never touched her? Yes, and if Carol had never even spoken to her after that brief conversation about a doll's valise in the store. If Carol, in fact, had never spoken to her at all, for it had all happened in that instant she had seen Carol standing in the middle of the floor, watching her. Then the realization that so much had happened after that meeting made her feel incredibly lucky suddenly. It was so easy for a man and woman to find each other, to find someone who would do, but for her to have found Carol—"I think I understand you better than you understand me. You don't really want to see me again, either, because you said yourself I'm not the same person. If we keep on seeing each other, you'll only get more and more—like this."

"Terry, forget for a minute I ever said I wanted you to love me, or that I love you. It's you as a person, I mean. I like you. I'd like—"

"I wonder sometimes why you think you like me, or did like me. Because you didn't even know me."

"You don't know yourself."

"But I do—and I know you. You'll drop painting some day, and me with it. Just as you've dropped everything else you ever started, as far as I can see. The dry cleaning thing, or the used car lot—"

"That's not true," Richard said sullenly.

"But why do you think you like me? Because I paint a little, too, and we can talk about that? I'm just as impractical as a girlfriend for you as painting is as a business for you." She hesitated a minute, then said the rest of it. "You know enough about art anyway to know you'll never make a good painter. You're like a little boy playing truant as long as you can, knowing all the time what you ought to be doing and what you'll finally be doing, working for your father."

Richard's blue eyes had gone suddenly cold. The line of his mouth was straight and very short now, the thin upper lip faintly curling. "All that isn't quite the point now, is it?"

"Well—yes. It's part of your hanging on when you know it's hopeless, and when you know you'll finally let go."

"I will not!"

"Richard, there's no point—"

"You're going to change your mind, you know."

She understood that. It was like a song he kept singing to her.

• • •

A week later, Richard stood in her room with the same expression of sullen anger on his face, talking in the same tone. He had called up at the unusual hour of three in the afternoon, and insisted on seeing her for a moment. She was packing a bag to take to Carol's for the weekend. If she hadn't been packing for Carol's house, Richard might have been in quite another mood, she thought, because she had seen him three times the past week, and he had never been pleasanter, never been more considerate of her.

"You can't just give me marching orders out of your life," he said, flinging his long arms out, but there was a lonesome tone in it, as if he had already started on that road away from her. "What really makes me sore is that you act like I'm not worth anything, that I'm completely ineffectual. It isn't fair to me, Terry. I can't compete!"

No, she thought, of course he couldn't. "I don't have any quarrel with you," she said. "It's you who choose to quarrel over Carol. She hasn't taken anything away from you, because you didn't have it in the first place. But if you can't go on seeing me—" She stopped, knowing he could and probably would go on seeing her.

"What logic," he said, rubbing the heel of his hand into his eye.

Therese watched him, caught by the idea that had just come to her, that she knew suddenly was a fact. Why hadn't it occurred to her the night of the theater, days ago? She might have known it from a hundred gestures, words, looks, this past week. But she remembered the night of the theater especially—he had surprised her with tickets to something she particularly wanted to see—the way he had held her hand that night, and from his voice on the telephone, not just telling her to meet him here or there, but asking her very sweetly if she could. She hadn't liked it. It was not a manifestation of affection, but rather a means of ingratiating himself, of somehow paving the way for the sudden questions he had asked so casually that night: "What do you mean you're fond of her?

Do you want to go to bed with her?" Therese had replied, "Do you think I would tell you if I did?" while a quick succession of emotions—humiliation, resentment, loathing of him—had made her speechless, had made it almost impossible for her to keep walking beside him. And glancing at him, she had seen him looking at her with that soft, inane smile that in memory now looked cruel, and unhealthy. And its unhealthiness might have escaped her, she thought, if it weren't that Richard was so frankly trying to convince her she was unhealthy.

Therese turned and tossed into the overnight bag her toothbrush and her hairbrush, then remembered she had a toothbrush at Carol's.

"Just what do you want from her, Therese? Where's it going to go from here?"

"Why are you so interested?"

He stared at her, and for a moment beneath the anger she saw the fixed curiosity she had seen before, as if he were watching a spectacle through a keyhole. But she knew he was not so detached as that. On the contrary, she sensed that he was never so bound to her as now, never so determined not to give her up. It frightened her. She could imagine the determination transformed to hatred and to violence.

Richard sighed, and twisted the newspaper in his hands. "I'm interested in *you*. You can't just say to me, 'Find someone else.' I've never treated you the way I treated the others, never thought of you that way."

She didn't answer.

"Damn!" Richard threw the newspaper at the bookshelf, and turned his back on her.

The newspaper flicked the Madonna, and it tipped back against the wall as if astonished, fell over, and rolled off the edge. Richard made a lunge for it and caught it in both hands. He looked at Therese and smiled involuntarily.

"Thanks." Therese took it from him. She lifted it to set it back, then brought her hands down quickly and smashed the figure to the floor.

"Terry!"

The Madonna lay in three or four pieces.

"Never mind it," she said. Her heart was beating as if she were angry, or fighting.

"But—"

"To hell with it!" she said, pushing the pieces aside with her shoe.

Richard left a moment later, slamming the door.

What was it, Therese wondered, the Andronich thing or Richard? Mr. Andronich's secretary had called about an hour ago and told her that Mr. Andronich had decided to hire an assistant from Philadelphia instead of her. So that job would not be there to come back to, after the trip with Carol. Therese looked down at the broken Madonna. The wood was quite beautiful inside. It had cracked cleanly along the grain.

• • •

Carol asked her in detail that evening about her talk with Richard. It irked Therese that Carol was so concerned as to whether Richard were hurt or not.

"You're not used to thinking of other people's feelings," Carol said bluntly to her.

They were in the kitchen fixing a late dinner, because Carol had given the maid the evening off.

"What real reason have you to think he's not in love with you?" Carol asked.

"Maybe I just don't understand how he works. But it doesn't seem like love to me."

Then in the middle of dinner, in the middle of a conversation about the trip, Carol remarked suddenly, "You shouldn't have talked to Richard at all."

It was the first time Therese had told Carol any of it, any of the first conversation in the cafeteria with Richard. "Why not? Should I have lied to him?"

Carol was not eating. Now she pushed back her chair and stood up. "You're much too young to know your own mind. Or what you're talking about. Yes, in that case, lie."

Therese laid her fork down. She watched Carol get a cigarette and light it. "I had to say good-bye to him and I did. I have. I won't see him again."

Carol opened a panel in the bottom of the bookcase and took out a bottle. She poured some into an empty glass and slammed the panel shut. "Why did you do it now? Why not two months ago or two months from now? And why did you mention me?"

"I know—I think it fascinates him."

"It probably does."

"But if I simply don't see him again—" She couldn't finish it, about his not being apt to follow her, spy on her. She didn't want to say such things to Carol. And besides, there was the memory of Richard's eyes. "I think he'll give it up. He said he couldn't compete."

Carol struck her forehead with her hand. "Couldn't compete," she repeated. She came back to the table and poured some of the water from her glass into the whiskey. "How true. Finish your dinner. I may be making too much of it, I don't know."

But Therese did not move. She had done the wrong thing. And at best, even doing the right thing, she could not make Carol happy as Carol made her happy, she thought as she had thought a hundred times before. Carol was happy only at moments here and there, moments that Therese caught and kept. One had been in the evening they put away the Christmas decorations, and Carol had refolded the string of angels and put them between the pages of a book. "I'm going to keep these," she had said. "With twenty-two angels to defend me, I can't lose." Therese looked at Carol now, and though Carol was watching her, it was through that veil of preoccupation that Therese so often saw, that kept them a world apart.

"Lines," Carol said. "I can't compete. People talk of classics. These lines are classic. A hundred different people will say the same words. There are lines for the mother, lines for the daughter, for the husband and the lover. I'd rather see you dead at my feet. It's the same play repeated with different casts. What do they say makes a play a classic, Therese?"

"A classic—" Her voice sounded tight and stifled. "A classic is something with a basic human situation."

• • •

When Therese awakened, the sun was in her room. She lay for a moment, watching the watery looking sunspots rippling on the pale green ceiling, listening for any sound of activity in the house. She looked at her blouse, hanging over the edge of the bureau. Why was she so untidy in Carol's house? Carol didn't like it. The dog that lived somewhere beyond the garages was barking intermittently, halfheartedly. There had been one pleasant interval last evening, the telephone call from Rindy. Rindy back from a birthday party at nine-thirty. Could she give a birthday party on her birthday in April. Carol said of course. Carol had been different after that. She had talked about Europe, and summers in Rapallo.

Therese got up and went to the window, raised it higher and leaned on the sill, tensing herself against the cold. There were no mornings anywhere like the mornings from this window. The round bed of grass beyond the driveway had darts of sunlight in it, like scattered gold needles. There were sparks of sun in the moist hedge leaves, and the sky was a fresh solid blue. She looked at the place in the driveway where Abby had been that morning, and at the bit of white fence beyond the hedges that marked the end of the lawn. The ground looked breathing and young, even though the winter had browned the grass. There had been trees and hedges around the school in Montclair, but the green had always ended in part of a red brick wall, or a gray stone building that was part of the school—an infirmary, a woodshed, a toolhouse—and the green each spring had seemed old already, used and handed down by one generation of children to the next, as much a part of school paraphernalia as textbooks and uniforms.

She dressed in the plaid slacks she had brought from home, and one of the shirts she had left from another time, which had been laundered. It was twenty past eight. Carol liked to get up about eight-thirty, liked to be awakened by someone with a cup of coffee, though Therese had noticed she never had Florence do it.

Florence was in the kitchen when she went down, but she had only just started the coffee.

"Good morning," Therese said. "Do you mind if I fix the breakfast?" Florence hadn't minded the two other times she had come in and found Therese fixing them.

"Go ahead, miss," Florence said. "I'll just make my own fried eggs. You like doing things for Mrs. Aird yourself, don't you?" she said like a statement.

Therese was getting two eggs out of the refrigerator. "Yes," she said, smiling. She dropped one of the eggs into the water, which was just beginning to heat. Her answer sounded rather flat, but what other answer was there? When she turned around after setting the breakfast tray, she saw Florence had put the second egg in the water. Therese took it out with her fingers. "She wants only one egg," Therese said. "That's for my omelet."

"Does she? She always used to eat two."

"Well—she doesn't now," Therese said.

"Shouldn't you measure that egg anyway, miss?" Florence gave her the pleasant professional smile. "Here's the egg timer, top of the stove."

Therese shook her head. "It comes out better when I guess." She had never gone wrong yet on Carol's egg. Carol liked it a little better done than the egg timer made it. Therese looked at Florence, who was concentrating now on the two eggs she was frying in the skillet. The coffee was almost all filtered. In silence, Therese prepared the cup to take up to Carol.

Later in the morning, Therese helped Carol take in the white iron chairs and the swing seat from the lawn in back of the house. It would be simpler with Florence there, Carol said, but Carol had sent her away marketing, then had a sudden whim to get the furniture in. It was Harge's idea to leave them out all winter, she said, but she thought they looked bleak. Finally only one chair remained by the round fountain, a prim little chair of white metal with a bulging bottom and four lacy feet. Therese looked at it and wondered who had sat there.

"I wish there were more plays that happened out of doors," Therese said.

"What do you think of first when you start to make a set?" Carol asked. "What do you start from?"

"The mood of the play, I suppose. What do you mean?"

"Do you think of the kind of play it is, or of something you want to see?"

One of Mr. Donohue's remarks brushed Therese's mind with a vague unpleasantness. Carol was in an argumentative mood this morning. "I think you're determined to consider me an amateur," Therese said.

"I think you're rather subjective. That's amateurish, isn't it?"

"Not always." But she knew what Carol meant.

"You have to know a lot to be absolutely subjective, don't you? In those things you showed me, I think you're too subjective—without knowing enough."

Therese made fists of her hands in her pockets. She had so hoped Carol would like her work, unqualifiedly. It had hurt her terribly that Carol hadn't liked in the least a certain few sets she had shown her. Carol knew nothing about it, technically, yet she could demolish a set with a phrase.

"I think a look at the West would do you good. When did you say you had to be back? The middle of February?"

"Well, now I don't—I just heard yesterday."

"What do you mean? It fell through? The Philadelphia job?"

"They called me up. They want somebody from Philadelphia."

"Oh, baby. I'm sorry."

"Oh, it's just this business," Therese said. Carol's hand was on the back of her neck, Carol's thumb rubbing behind her ear as Carol might have fondled a dog.

"You weren't going to tell me."

"Yes, I was."

"When?"

"Sometime on the trip."

"Are you very disappointed?"

"No," Therese said positively.

They heated the last cup of coffee and took it out to the white chair on the lawn and shared it.

"Shall we have lunch out somewhere?" Carol asked her. "Let's go to the club. Then I ought to do some shopping in Newark. How about a jacket? Would you like a tweed jacket?"

Therese was sitting on the edge of the fountain, one hand pressed against her ear because it was aching from the cold. "I don't particularly need one," she said.

"But I'd particularly like to see you in one."

Therese was upstairs, changing her clothes, when she heard the telephone ring. She heard Florence say, "Oh, good morning, Mr. Aird. Yes, I'll call her right now," and Therese crossed the room and closed the door. Restlessly, she began to put the room in order, hung her clothes in the closet, and smoothed the bed she had already made. Then Carol knocked on the door and put her head in. "Harge is coming by in a few minutes. I don't think he'll be long."

Therese did not want to see him. "Would you like for me to take a walk?"

Carol smiled. "No. Stay up here and read a book, if you want to."

Therese got the book she had bought yesterday, the *Oxford Book of English Verse*, and tried to read it, but the words stayed separate and meaningless. She had a disquieting sense of hiding, so she went to the door and opened it.

Carol was just coming from her room, and for an instant Therese saw the same look of indecision cross her face that Therese remembered from the first moment she had entered the house. Then she said, "Come down."

Harge's car drove up as they walked into the living room. Carol went to the door, and Therese heard their greeting, Carol's only cordial, but Harge's very cheerful, and Carol came in with a long flower box in her arms.

"Harge, this is Miss Belivet. I think you met her once," Carol said.

Harge's eyes narrowed a little, then opened. "Oh, yes. How do you do?"

"How do you do?"

Florence came in, and Carol handed the flower box to her.

"Would you put these in something?" Carol said.

"Ah, here's that pipe. I thought so." Harge reached behind the ivy on the mantel, and brought forth a pipe.

"Everything is fine at home?" Carol asked as she sat down at the end of the sofa.

"Yes. Very." Harge's tense smile did not show his teeth, but his face and the quick turns of his head radiated geniality and self-satisfaction. He watched with proprietary pleasure as Florence brought in the flowers, red roses, in a vase, and set them on the coffee table in front of the sofa.

Therese wished suddenly that she had brought Carol flowers, brought them on any of a half a dozen occasions past, and she remembered the flowers Danny had brought to her one day when he simply dropped in at the theater. She looked at Harge, and his eyes glanced away from her, the peaked brow lifting still higher, the eyes darting everywhere, as if he looked for little changes in the room. But it might all be pretense, Therese thought, his air of good cheer. And if he cared enough to pretend, he must also care in some way for Carol.

"May I take one for Rindy?" Harge asked.

"Of course." Carol got up, and she would have broken a flower, but Harge stepped forward and put a little knife blade against the stem and the flower came off. "They're very beautiful. Thank you, Harge."

Harge lifted the flower to his nose. Half to Carol, half to Therese, he said, "It's a beautiful day. Are you going to take a drive?"

"Yes, we were," Carol said. "By the way, I'd like to drive over one afternoon next week. Perhaps Tuesday."

Harge thought a moment. "All right. I'll tell her."

"I'll speak to her on the phone. I meant tell your family."

Harge nodded once, in acquiescence, then looked at Therese. "Yes, I remember you. Of course. You were here about three weeks ago. Before Christmas."

"Yes. One Sunday." Therese stood up. She wanted to leave them alone. "I'll go upstairs," she said to Carol. "Good-bye, Mr. Aird."

Harge made her a little bow. "Good-bye."

As she went up the stairs, she heard Harge say, "Well, many happy returns, Carol. I'd like to say it. Do you mind?"

Carol's birthday, Therese thought. Of course, Carol wouldn't have told her.

She closed the door and looked around the room, realized she was looking for any sign that she had spent the night. There was none. She stopped at the mirror and looked at herself for a moment, frowningly. She was not so pale as she had been three weeks ago when Harge saw her; she did not feel like the drooping, frightened thing Harge had met then. From the top drawer, she got her handbag and took her lipstick out of it. Then she heard Harge knock on the door, and she closed the drawer.

"Come in."

"Excuse me. I must get something." He crossed the room quickly, went into the bathroom, and he was smiling as he came back with the razor in his hand. "You were in the restaurant with Carol last Sunday, weren't you?"

"Yes," Therese said.

"Carol said you do stage designing."

"Yes."

He glanced from her face to her hands, to the floor, and up again. "I hope you see that Carol gets out enough," he said. "You look young and spry. Make her take some walks."

Then he went briskly out the door, leaving behind him a faint shaving-soap scent. Therese tossed her lipstick onto the bed, and wiped her palms down the side of her skirt. She wondered why Harge troubled to let her know he took it for granted she spent a great deal of time with Carol.

"Therese!" Carol called suddenly. "Come down!"

Carol was sitting on the sofa. Harge had gone. She looked at Therese with a little smile. Then Florence came in and Carol said, "Florence, you can take these somewhere else. Put them in the dining room."

"Yes, ma'am."

Carol winked at Therese.

Nobody used the dining room, Therese knew. Carol preferred to eat anywhere else. "Why didn't you tell me it was your birthday?" Therese asked her.

"Oh!" Carol laughed. "It's not. It's my wedding anniversary. Get your coat and let's go."

As they backed out of the driveway, Carol said, "If there's anything I can't stand, it's a hypocrite."

"What did he say?"

"Nothing of any importance." Carol was still smiling.

"But you said he was a hypocrite."

"Par excellence."

"Pretending all this good humor?"

"Oh—just partially that."

"Did he say anything about me?"

"He said you looked like a nice girl. Is that news?" Carol shot the car down the narrow road to the village. "He said the divorce will take about six weeks longer than we'd thought, due to some more red tape. That's news. He has an idea I still might change my mind in the meantime. That's hypocrisy. I think he likes to fool himself."

Was life, were human relations like this always, Therese wondered. Never solid ground underfoot. Always like gravel, a little yielding, noisy so the whole world could hear, so one always listened, too, for the loud, harsh step of the intruder's foot.

"Carol, I never took that check, you know," Therese remarked suddenly. "I stuck it under the cloth on the table by the bed."

"What made you think of that?"

"I don't know. Do you want me to tear it up? I started to that night."

"If you insist," Carol said.

## *fourteen*

Therese looked down at the big cardboard box. "I don't want to take it." Her hands were full. "I can let Mrs. Osborne take the food out and the rest can stay here."

"Bring it," Carol said, going out the door. She carried down the last dribble of things, the books and the jackets Therese had decided at the last minute that she wanted.

Therese came back upstairs for the box. It had come an hour ago by messenger—a lot of sandwiches in wax paper, a bottle of blackberry wine, a cake, and a box containing the white dress Mrs. Semco had promised her. Richard had had nothing to do with the box, she knew, or there would have been a book or an extra note in it.

An unwanted dress still lay out on the couch, a corner of the rug was turned back, but Therese was impatient to be off. She pulled the door shut, and hurried down the steps with the box, past the Kellys' who were both away at work, past Mrs. Osborne's door. She had said good-bye to Mrs. Osborne an hour ago when she had paid the next month's rent.

Therese was just closing the car door when Mrs. Osborne called her from the front steps.

"Telephone call!" Mrs. Osborne shouted, and reluctantly Therese got out, thinking it was Richard.

It was Phil McElroy, calling her to ask about the interview with Harkevy yesterday. She had told Danny about it last night when they had had dinner together. Harkevy hadn't promised her a job, but he had said to keep in touch, and Therese felt he meant it. He had let her come to see him backstage in the theater where he was supervising the set for *Winter Town.* He had chosen three of her cardboard models and looked very carefully at them, dismissed one as a little dull, pointed out some impracticality in the second, and liked best the hall-like set Therese had started the evening she had come back from the first visit to Carol's house. He was the first person who had ever given her less conventional sets a serious consideration. She had called Carol up immediately and told her about the meeting. She told Phil about the Harkevy interview, but she didn't mention that the Andronich job had fallen through. She knew it was because she didn't want Richard to hear about it. Therese asked Phil to let her know what play Harkevy was doing sets for next, because he said he hadn't decided himself between two plays. There was more of a chance he would take her on as apprentice if he chose the English play he had talked about yesterday.

"I don't know any address to give you yet," Therese said. "I know we'll get to Chicago."

Phil said he might drop her a letter general delivery there.

"Was that Richard?" Carol asked when she came back.

"No. Phil McElroy."

"So you haven't heard from Richard?"

"I haven't for the last few days. He sent me a telegram this morning." Therese hesitated, then took it from her pocket and read it. "I HAVE NOT CHANGED. NEITHER HAVE YOU. WRITE TO ME. I LOVE YOU. RICHARD."

"I think you should call him," Carol said. "Call him from my house."

They were going to spend the night at Carol's house and leave early tomorrow morning.

"Will you put on that dress tonight?" Carol asked.

"I'll try it on. It looks like a wedding dress."

Therese put on the dress just before dinner. It hung below her calf, and the waist tied in back with long white bands that in front were stitched down and embroidered. She went down to show it to Carol. Carol was in the living room writing a letter.

"Look," Therese said, smiling.

Carol looked at her for a long moment, then came over and examined the embroidery at the waist. "That's a museum piece. You look adorable. Wear it this evening, will you?"

"It's so elaborate." She didn't want to wear it, because it made her think of Richard.

"What the hell kind of style is it, Russian?"

Therese gave a laugh. She liked the way Carol cursed, always casually, and when no one else could hear her.

"Is it?" Carol repeated.

Therese was going upstairs. "Is it what?"

"Where did you get this habit of not answering people?" Carol demanded, her voice suddenly harsh with anger.

Carol's eyes had the angry white light she had seen in them the time she refused to play the piano. And what angered her now was just as trifling. "I'm sorry, Carol. I guess I didn't hear you."

"Go ahead," Carol said, turning away. "Go on up and take it off."

It was Harge still, Therese thought. Therese hesitated a minute, then went upstairs. She untied the waist and the sleeves, glanced at herself in the mirror, then tied them all back again. If Carol wanted her to keep it on, she would.

They fixed dinner themselves, because Florence had already started her three weeks' leave. They opened some special jars of things that Carol said she had been saving, and they made stingers in the cocktail shaker just before dinner. Therese thought Carol's mood had passed, but when she started to pour a second stinger for herself, Carol said shortly, "I don't think you should have any more of that."

And Therese deferred, with a smile. And the mood went on. Nothing Therese said or did could change it, and Therese blamed the inhibiting dress for not being able to think of the right things to say. They took brandied chestnuts and coffee up to the porch after dinner, but they said even less to each other in the semidarkness, and Therese only felt sleepy and rather depressed.

The next morning, Therese found a paper bag on the back doorstep. Inside it was a toy monkey with gray and white fur. Therese showed it to Carol.

"My God," Carol said softly, and smiled. "Jacopo." She took the monkey and rubbed her forefinger against its slightly dirty white cheek. "Abby and I used to have him hanging in the back of the car," Carol said.

"Abby brought it? Last night?"

"I suppose." Carol went on to the car with the monkey and a suitcase.

Therese remembered wakening from a doze on the swing seat last night, awakening to an absolute silence, and Carol sitting there in the dark, looking straight before her. Carol must have heard Abby's car last night. Therese helped Carol arrange the suitcases and the lap rug in the back of the car.

"Why didn't she come in?" Therese asked.

"Oh, that's Abby," Carol said with a smile, with the fleeting shyness that always surprised Therese. "Why don't you go call Richard?"

Therese sighed. "I can't now, anyway. He's left the house by this time." It was eight-forty, and his school began at nine.

"Call his family then. Aren't you going to thank them for the box they sent you?"

"I was going to write them a letter."

"Call them now, and you won't have to write them a letter. It's much nicer to call anyway."

Mrs. Semco answered the telephone. Therese praised the dress and Mrs. Semco's needlework, and thanked her for all the food and the wine.

"Richard just left the house," Mrs. Semco said. "He's going to be awfully lonely. He mopes around already." But she laughed, her vigorous, high-pitched laugh that filled the kitchen where Therese knew she stood, a laugh that would ring through the house, even to Richard's empty room upstairs. "Is everything all right with you and Richard?" Mrs. Semco asked with the faintest suspicion, though Therese could tell she still smiled.

Therese said yes. And she promised she would write. Afterward, she felt better because she had called.

Carol asked her if she had closed her window upstairs, and Therese went up again, because she couldn't remember. She hadn't closed the window, and she hadn't made her bed either, but there wasn't time now. Florence could take care of the bed when she came in on Monday to lock the house up.

Carol was on the telephone when Therese came downstairs. She looked up at Therese with a smile and held the telephone toward her. Therese knew from the first tone that it was Rindy.

". . . at—uh—Mr. Byron's. It's a farm. Have you ever been there, Mother?"

"Where is it, sweetheart?" Carol said.

"At Mr. Byron's. He has horses. But not the kind you would like."

"Oh. Why not?"

"Well, these are heavy."

Therese tried to hear anything in the shrill, rather matter-of-fact voice that resembled Carol's voice, but she couldn't.

"Hello," Rindy said. "Mother?"

"I'm still here."

"I've got to say good-bye now. Daddy's ready to leave." And she coughed.

"Have you got a cough?" Carol asked.

"No."

"Then don't cough into the phone."

"I wish you would take me on the trip."

"Well, I can't because you're in school. But we'll have trips this summer."

"Can you still call me?"

"On the trip? Of course I will. Every day." Carol took the telephone and sat back with it, but she still watched Therese the minute or so more that she talked.

"She sounds so serious," Therese said.

"She was telling me all about the big day yesterday. Harge let her play hooky."

Carol had seen Rindy the day before yesterday, Therese remembered. It had evidently been a pleasant visit, from what Carol had told Therese over the telephone, but she hadn't mentioned any details about it, and Therese had not asked her anything.

Just as they were about to leave, Carol decided to make a last call to Abby. Therese wandered back into the kitchen, because the car was too cold to sit in.

"I don't know any small towns in Illinois," Carol was saying. "Why

Illinois? . . . All right, Rockford . . . I'll remember, I'll think of Roquefort . . . Of course I'll take good care of him. I wish you'd come in, nitwit . . . Well, you're mistaken, very mistaken."

Therese took a sip from Carol's half-finished coffee on the kitchen table, drank from the place where the lipstick was.

"Not a word," Carol said, drawling the phrase. "No one, so far as I know, not even Florence . . . Well, you do that, darling. Cheerio now."

Five minutes later, they were leaving Carol's town on the highway marked on the strip map in red, the highway they would use until Chicago. The sky was overcast. Therese looked around her at the country that had grown familiar now, the clump of woods off to the left that the road to New York passed, the tall flagstaff in the distance that marked the club Carol belonged to.

Therese let a crack of air in at her window. It was quite cold, and the heater felt good on her ankles. The clock on the dashboard said quarter to ten, and she thought suddenly of the people working in Frankenberg's, penned in there at a quarter to ten in the morning, this morning and tomorrow morning and the next, the hands of clocks controlling every move they made. But the hands of the clock on the dashboard meant nothing now to her and Carol. They would sleep or not sleep, drive or not drive, whenever it pleased them. She thought of Mrs. Robichek, selling sweaters this minute on the third floor, commencing another year there, her fifth year.

"Why so silent?" Carol asked. "What's the matter?"

"Nothing." She did not want to talk. Yet she felt there were thousands of words choking her throat, and perhaps only distance, thousands of miles, could straighten them out. Perhaps it was freedom itself that choked her.

Somewhere in Pennsylvania they went through a section of pale sunshine, like a leak in the sky, but around noon it began to rain. Carol cursed, but the sound of the rain was pleasant, drumming irregularly on the windshield and the roof.

"You know what I forgot?" Carol said. "A raincoat. I'll have to pick one up somewhere."

And suddenly, Therese remembered she had forgotten the book she was reading. And there was a letter to Carol in it, one sheet that stuck out both ends of the book. Damn. It had been separate from her other books, and that was why she had left it behind, on the table by the bed. She hoped Florence wouldn't decide to look at it. She tried to remember if she had written Carol's name in the letter, and she couldn't. And the check. She had forgotten to tear that up, too.

"Carol, did you get that check?"

"That check I gave you?—You said you were going to tear it up."

"I didn't. It's still under the cloth."

"Well, it's not important," Carol said.

When they stopped for gas, Therese tried to buy some stout, which Carol liked sometimes, at a grocery store next to the gas station, but they had only beer. She bought one can, because Carol didn't care for beer. Then they drove into a little road off the highway and stopped, and opened the box of sandwiches Richard's mother had put up. There was also a dill pickle, a mozzarella cheese, and a couple of hard-boiled eggs. Therese had forgotten to ask for an opener, so she couldn't open the beer, but there was coffee in the thermos. She put the beer can on the floor in the back of the car.

"Caviar. How very, very nice of them," Carol said, looking inside a sandwich. "Do you like caviar?"

"No. I wish I did."

"Why?"

Therese watched Carol take a small bite of the sandwich from which she had removed the top slice of bread, a bite where the most caviar was. "Because people always like caviar so much when they do like it," Therese said.

Carol smiled, and went on nibbling, slowly. "It's an acquired taste. Acquired tastes are always more pleasant—and hard to get rid of."

Therese poured more coffee into the cup they were sharing. She was acquiring a taste for black coffee. "How nervous I was the first time I held this cup. You brought me coffee that day. Remember?"

"I remember."

"How'd you happen to put cream in it that day?"

"I thought you'd like it. Why were you so nervous?"

Therese glanced at her. "I was so excited about you," she said, lifting the cup. Then she looked at Carol again and saw a sudden stillness, like a shock, in Carol's face. Therese had seen it two or three times before when she had said something like that to Carol about the way she felt, or paid Carol an extravagant compliment. Therese could not tell if she was pleased or displeased. She watched Carol fold the wax paper around the other half of her sandwich.

There was cake, but Carol didn't want any. It was the brown-colored spice cake that Therese had often had at Richard's house. They put everything back, into the valise that held the cartons of cigarettes and the bottle of whiskey, with a painstaking neatness that would have annoyed Therese in anyone but Carol.

"Did you say Washington was your home state?" Therese asked her.

"I was born there, and my father's there now. I wrote him I might visit him, if we get out that far."

"Does he look like you?"

"Do I look like him, yes—more than like my mother."

"It's strange to think of you with a family," Therese said.

"Why?"

"Because I just think of you as you. Sui generis."

Carol smiled, her head lifted as she drove. "All right, go ahead."

"Brothers and sisters?" Therese asked.

"One sister. I suppose you want to know all about her, too? Her name is Elaine, she has three children, and she lives in Virginia. She's older than I am, and I don't know if you'd like her. You'd think she was dull."

Yes. Therese could imagine her, like a shadow of Carol, with all Carol's features weakened and diluted.

Late in the afternoon, they stopped at a roadside restaurant which had a miniature Dutch village in the front window. Therese leaned on the rail beside it and looked at it. There was a little river that came out of a faucet at one end, which flowed in an oval stream and turned a windmill. Little figures in Dutch costume stood about the village, stood on patches of live grass. She thought of the electric train in Frankenberg's toy department, and the fury that drove it on the oval course that was about the same size as the stream.

"I never told you about the train in Frankenberg's," Therese remarked to Carol. "Did you notice it when you—"

"An electric train?" Carol interrupted her.

Therese had been smiling, but something constricted her heart suddenly. It was too complicated to go into, and the conversation stopped there.

Carol ordered some soup for both of them. They were stiff and cold from the car.

"I wonder if you'll really enjoy this trip," Carol said. "You so prefer things reflected in a glass, don't you? You have your private conception of everything. Like that windmill. It's practically as good as being in Holland to you. I wonder if you'll even like seeing real mountains and real people."

Therese felt as crushed as if Carol had accused her of lying. She felt Carol meant, too, that she had a private conception of her, and that Carol resented it. Real people? She thought suddenly of Mrs. Robichek. And she had fled her because she was hideous.

"How do you ever expect to create anything if you get all your experiences secondhand?" Carol asked her, her voice soft and even, and yet merciless.

Carol made her feel she had done nothing, was nothing at all, like a wisp of smoke. Carol had lived like a human being, had married, and had a child.

The old man from behind the counter was coming toward them. He had a limp. He stood by the table next to them and folded his arms. "Ever been to Holland?" he asked pleasantly.

Carol answered. "No, I haven't. I suppose you've been. Did you make the village in the window?"

He nodded. "Took me five years to make."

Therese looked at the man's bony fingers, the lean arms with the purple veins twisting just under the thin skin. She knew better than Carol the work that had gone into the little village, but she could not get a word out.

The man said to Carol, "Got some fine sausages and hams next door, if you like real Pennsylvania made. We raise our own hogs and they're killed and cured right here."

They went into the whitewashed box of a store beside the restaurant. There was a delicious smell of smoked ham inside it, mingled with the smell of woodsmoke and spice.

"Let's pick something we don't have to cook," Carol said, looking into the refrigerated counter. "Let's have some of this," she said to the young man in the earlapped cap.

Therese remembered standing in the delicatessen with Mrs. Robichek, her buying the thin slices of salami and liverwurst. A sign on the wall said they shipped anywhere, and she thought of sending Mrs. Robichek one of the big cloth-wrapped sausages, imagined the delight on Mrs. Robichek's face when she opened the package with her trembling hands and found a sausage. But should she after all, Therese wondered, make a gesture that was probably motivated by pity, or by guilt, or by some perversity in her? Therese frowned, floundering in a sea without direction or gravity, in which she knew only that she could mistrust her own impulses.

"Therese—"

Therese turned around, and Carol's beauty struck her like a glimpse of the Winged Victory of Samothrace. Carol asked her if she thought they should buy a whole ham.

The young man slid all the bundles across the counter, and took Carol's twenty-dollar bill. And Therese thought of Mrs. Robichek tremulously pushing her single dollar bill and a quarter across the counter that evening.

"See anything else?" Carol asked.

"I thought I might send something to somebody. A woman who works in the store. She's poor and she once asked me to dinner."

Carol picked up her change. "What woman?"

"I don't really want to send her anything." Therese wanted suddenly to leave.

Carol frowned at her through her cigarette smoke. "Do it."

"I don't want to. Let's go, Carol." It was like the nightmare again, when she couldn't get away from her.

"Send it," Carol said. "Close the door and send her something."

Therese closed the door and chose one of the six-dollar sausages, and wrote on a gift card: "This comes from Pennsylvania. I hope it'll last a few Sunday mornings. With love from Therese Belivet."

Later, in the car, Carol asked her about Mrs. Robichek, and Therese answered as she always did, succinctly, and with the involuntary and absolute honesty that always depressed her afterward. Mrs. Robichek and the world she lived in was so different from that of Carol, she might have been describing another species of animal life, some ugly beast that lived on another planet. Carol made no comment on the story, only questioned and questioned her as she drove. She made no comment when there was nothing more to ask, but the taut, thoughtful expression with which she had listened stayed on her face even when they began to talk of other things. Therese gripped her thumbs inside her hands. Why did she let Mrs. Robichek haunt her? And now she had spread it into Carol and could never take it back.

"Please don't mention her again, will you, Carol? Promise me."

## *fifteen*

Carol walked barefoot with little short steps to the shower room in the corner, groaning at the cold. She had red polish on her toenails, and her blue pajamas were too big for her.

"It's your fault for opening the window so high," Therese said.

Carol pulled the curtain across, and Therese heard the shower come on with a rush. "Ah, divinely hot!" Carol said. "Better than last night."

It was a luxurious tourist cabin, with a thick carpet and wood-paneled walls and everything from cellophane-sealed shoe rags to television.

Therese sat on her bed in her robe, looking at a road map, spanning it with her hand. A span and a half was about a day's driving, theoretically, though they probably would not do it. "We might get all the way across Ohio today," Therese said.

"Ohio. Noted for rivers, rubber, and certain railroads. On our left the famous Chillicothe drawbridge, where twenty-eight Hurons once massacred a hundred—morons."

Therese laughed.

"And where Lewis and Clark once camped," Carol added. "I think I'll wear my slacks today. Want to see if they're in that suitcase? If not, I'll have to get into the car. Not the light ones, the navy blue gaberdines."

Therese went to Carol's big suitcase at the foot of the bed. It was full of sweaters and underwear and shoes, but no slacks. She saw a nickel-plated tube sticking out of a folded sweater. She lifted the sweater out. It was heavy. She unwrapped it, and started so she almost dropped it. It was a gun with a white handle.

"No?" Carol asked.

"No." Therese wrapped the gun up again and put it back as she had found it.

"Darling, I forgot my towel. I think it's on a chair."

Therese got it and took it to her, and in her nervousness as she put the towel into Carol's outstretched hand her eyes dropped from Carol's face to her bare breasts and down, and she saw the quick surprise in Carol's glance as she turned around. Therese closed her eyes tight and walked slowly toward the bed, seeing before her closed lids the image of Carol's naked body.

Therese took a shower, and when she came out, Carol was standing at the mirror, almost dressed.

"What's the matter?" Carol asked.

"Nothing."

Carol turned to her, combing her hair that was darkened a little by the wet of the shower. Her lips were bright with fresh lipstick, a cigarette between them. "Do you realize how many times a day you make me ask you that?" she said. "Don't you think it's a little inconsiderate?"

During breakfast, Therese said, "Why did you bring that gun along, Carol?"

"Oh. So that's what's bothering you. It's Harge's gun, something else he forgot." Carol's voice was casual. "I thought it'd be better to take it than to leave it."

"Is it loaded?"

"Yes, it's loaded. Harge got a permit, because we had a burglar at the house once."

"Can you use it?"

Carol smiled at her. "I'm no Annie Oakley. I can use it. I think it worries you, doesn't it? I don't expect to use it."

Therese said nothing more about it. But it disturbed her whenever she thought of it. She thought of it the next night, when a bellhop set the suitcase down heavily on the sidewalk. She wondered if a gun could ever go off from a jolt like that.

They had taken some snapshots in Ohio, and because they could get them developed early the next morning, they spent a long evening and the night in a town called Defiance. All evening they walked around the streets, looking in store windows, walking through silent residential streets where lights showed in front parlors, and homes looked as comfortable and safe as birds' nests. Therese had been afraid Carol would be bored by aimless walks, but Carol was the one who suggested going one block further, walking all the way up the hill to see what was on the other side. Carol talked about herself and Harge. Therese tried to sum up in one word what had separated Carol and Harge, but she rejected the words almost at once—boredom, resentment, indifference. Carol told her of one time that Harge had taken Rindy away on a fishing trip and not communicated for days. That was a retaliation for Carol's refusing to spend Harge's vacation with him at his family's summer house in Massachusetts. It was a mutual thing. And the incidents were not the start.

Carol put two of the snapshots in her billfold, one of Rindy in jodhpurs and a derby that had been on the first part of the roll, and one of Therese, with a cigarette in her mouth and her hair blowing back in the wind. There was one unflattering picture of Carol standing huddled in her coat that Carol said she was going to send to Abby because it was so bad.

They got to Chicago late one afternoon, crept into its gray, sprawling disorder behind a great truck of a meat-distributing company. Therese sat up close to the windshield. She couldn't remember anything about the city from the trip with her father. Carol seemed to know Chicago as well as she knew Manhattan. Carol showed her the famous Loop, and they stopped for a while to watch the trains and the homeward rush of five-thirty in the afternoon. It couldn't compare to the madhouse of New York at five-thirty.

At the main post office, Therese found a postcard from Danny, nothing from Phil, and a letter from Richard. Therese glanced at the letter and saw it began and ended affectionately. She had expected just that, Richard's getting the general delivery address from Phil and writing her an affectionate letter. She put the letter in her pocket before she went back to Carol.

"Anything?" Carol said.

"Just a postcard. From Danny. He's finished his exams."

Carol drove to the Drake Hotel. It had a black and white checked floor, a fountain in the lobby, and Therese thought it magnificent. In their room, Carol took off her coat and flung herself down on one of the twin beds.

"I know a few people here," she said sleepily. "Shall we look somebody up?"

But Carol fell asleep before they quite decided.

Therese looked out the window at the light-bordered lake and at the irregular, unfamiliar line of tall buildings against the still grayish sky. It looked fuzzy and monotonous, like a Pissarro painting. A comparison Carol wouldn't appreciate, she thought. She leaned on the sill, staring at the city, watching a distant car's lights chopped into dots and dashes as it passed behind trees. She was happy.

"Why don't you ring for some cocktails?" Carol's voice said behind her.

"What kind would you like?"

"What kind would you?"

"Martinis."

Carol whistled. "Double Gibsons," Carol interrupted her as she was telephoning. "And a plate of canapés. Might as well get four martinis."

Therese read Richard's letter while Carol was in the shower. The whole letter was affectionate. You are not like any of the other girls, he wrote. He had waited and he would keep on waiting, because he was absolutely confident that they could be happy together. He wanted her to write to him every day, send at least a postcard. He told her how he had sat one evening rereading the three letters she had sent him when he had been in Kingston, New York, last summer. There was a sentimentality in the letter that was not like Richard at all, and Therese's first thought was that he was pretending. Perhaps in order to strike at her later. Her second reaction was aversion. She came back to the old decision, that not to write him, not to say anything more, was the shortest way to end it.

The cocktails arrived, and Therese paid for them instead of signing. She could never pay a bill except behind Carol's back.

"Will you wear your black suit?" Therese asked when Carol came in.

Carol gave her a look. "Go all the way to the bottom of that suitcase?" she said, going to the suitcase. "Drag it out, brush it off, steam the wrinkles out of it for half an hour?"

"We'll be a half hour drinking these."

"Your powers of persuasion are irresistible." Carol took the suit into the bathroom and turned the water on in the tub.

It was the suit she had worn the day they had had the first lunch together.

"Do you realize this is the only drink I've had since we left New York?" Carol said. "Of course you don't. Do you know why? I'm happy."

"You're beautiful," Therese said.

And Carol gave her the derogatory smile that Therese loved, and walked to the dressing table. She flung a yellow silk scarf around her neck and tied it loosely, and began to comb her hair. The lamp's light framed her figure like a picture, and Therese had a feeling all this had happened before. She remembered suddenly: the woman in the window brushing up her long hair, remembered the very bricks in the wall, the texture of the misty rain that morning.

"How about some perfume?" Carol asked, moving toward her with the bottle. She touched Therese's forehead with her fingers, at the hairline where she had kissed her that day.

"You remind me of the woman I once saw," Therese said, "somewhere off Lexington. Not you but the light. She was combing her hair up." Therese stopped, but Carol waited for her to go on. Carol always waited, and she could never say exactly what she wanted to say. "Early one morning when I was on the way to work, and I remember it was starting to rain," she floundered on. "I saw her in a window." She really could not go on, about standing there for perhaps three or four minutes, wishing with an intensity that drained her strength that she knew the woman, that she might be welcome if she went to the house and knocked on the door, wishing she could do that instead of going on to her job at the Pelican Press.

"My little orphan," Carol said.

Therese smiled. There was nothing dismal, no sting in the word when Carol said it.

"What does your mother look like?"

"She had black hair," Therese said quickly. "She didn't look anything like me." Therese always found herself talking about her mother in the past tense, though she was alive this minute, somewhere in Connecticut.

"You really don't think she'll ever want to see you again?" Carol was standing at the mirror.

"I don't think so."

"What about your father's family? Didn't you say he had a brother?"

"I never met him. He was a kind of geologist, working for an oil company. I don't know where he is." It was easier talking about the uncle she had never met.

"What's your mother's name now?"

"Esther—Mrs. Nicolas Strully." The name meant as little to her as one she might see in a telephone book. She looked at Carol, suddenly sorry she had said the name. Carol might some day—A shock of loss, of helplessness, came over her. She knew so little about Carol after all.

Carol glanced at her. "I'll never mention it," she said, "never mention it again. If that second drink's going to make you blue, don't drink it. I don't want you to be blue tonight."

The restaurant where they dined overlooked the lake, too. They had a banquet of a dinner with champagne and brandy afterward. It was the first time in her life that Therese had been a little drunk, in fact much drunker than she wanted Carol to see. Her impression of Lakeshore Drive was always to be of a broad avenue studded with mansions all resembling the White House in Washington. In the memory there would be Carol's voice, telling her about a house here and there where she had been before, and the disquieting awareness that for a while this had been Carol's world, as Rapallo, Paris, and other places Therese did not know had for a while been the frame of everything Carol did.

That night, Carol sat on the edge of her bed, smoking a cigarette before they turned the light on. Therese lay in her own bed, sleepily watching her, trying to read the meaning of the restless, puzzled look in Carol's eyes that would stare at something in the room for a moment and then move on. Was it of her she thought, or of Harge, or of Rindy? Carol had asked to be called at seven tomorrow, in order to telephone Rindy before she went to school. Therese remembered their telephone conversation in Defiance. Rindy had had a fight with some other little girl, and Carol had spent fifteen minutes going over it, and trying to persuade Rindy she should take the first step and apologize. Therese still felt the effects of what she had drunk, the tingling of the champagne that drew her painfully close to Carol. If she simply asked, she thought, Carol would let her sleep tonight in the same bed with her. She wanted more than that, to kiss her, to feel their bodies next to each other's. Therese thought of the two girls she had seen in the Palermo bar. They did that, she knew, and more. And would Carol suddenly thrust her away in disgust, if she merely wanted to hold her in her arms? And would whatever affection Carol now had for her vanish in that instant? A vision of Carol's cold rebuff swept her courage clean away. It crept back humbly in the question, couldn't she ask simply to sleep in the same bed with her?

"Carol, would you mind—"

"Tomorrow we'll go to the stockyards," Carol said at the same time, and Therese burst out laughing. "What's so damned funny about that?" Carol asked, putting out her cigarette, but she was smiling, too.

"It just is. It's terribly funny," Therese said, still laughing, laughing away all the longing and the intention of the night.

"You're giggly on champagne," Carol said as she pulled the light out.

• • •

Late the next afternoon they left Chicago and drove in the direction of Rockford. Carol said she might have a letter from Abby there, but probably not, because Abby was a bad correspondent. Therese went to a shoe repair shop to get a moccasin stitched, and when she came back, Carol was reading the letter in the car.

"What road do we take out?" Carol's face looked happier.

"Twenty, going west."

Carol turned on the radio and worked the dial until she found some music. "What's a good town for tonight on the way to Minneapolis?"

"Dubuque," Therese said, looking at the map. "Or Waterloo looks fairly big, but it's about two hundred miles away."

"We might make it."

They took Highway 20 toward Freeport and Galena, which was starred on the map as the home of Ulysses S. Grant.

"What did Abby say?"

"Nothing much. Just a very nice letter."

Carol said little to her in the car, or even in the café where they stopped later for coffee. Carol went over and stood in front of a jukebox, dropping nickels slowly.

"You wish Abby'd come along, don't you?" Therese said.

"No," Carol said.

"You're so different since you got the letter from her."

Carol looked at her across the table. "Darling, it's just a silly letter. You can even read it if you want to." Carol reached for her handbag, but she did not get the letter out.

Sometime that evening, Therese fell asleep in the car and woke up with the lights of a city on her face. Carol was resting both arms tiredly on the top of the wheel. They had stopped for a red light.

"Here's where we stay the night," Carol said.

Therese's sleep still clung to her as she walked across the hotel lobby. She rode up in an elevator and she was acutely conscious of Carol beside her, as if she dreamed a dream in which Carol was the subject and the only figure. In the room, she lifted her suitcase from the floor to a chair, unlatched it and left it, and stood by the writing table, watching Carol. As if her emotions had been in abeyance all the past hours, or days, they flooded her now as she watched Carol opening her suitcase, taking out, as she always did first, the leather kit that contained her toilet articles, dropping it onto the bed. She looked at Carol's hands, at the lock of hair that fell over the scarf tied around her head, at the scratch she had gotten days ago across the toe of her moccasin.

"What're you standing there for?" Carol asked. "Get to bed, sleepy-head."

"Carol, I love you."

Carol straightened up. Therese stared at her with intense, sleepy eyes. Then Carol finished taking her pajamas from the suitcase and pulled the lid down. She came to Therese and put her hands on her shoulders. She squeezed her shoulders hard, as if she were exacting a promise from her, or perhaps searching her to see if what she had said were real. Then she kissed Therese on the lips, as if they had kissed a thousand times before.

"Don't you know I love you?" Carol said.

Carol took her pajamas into the bathroom, and stood for a moment, looking down at the basin.

"I'm going out," Carol said. "But I'll be back right away."

Therese waited by the table while Carol was gone, while time passed indefinitely or maybe not at all, until the door opened and Carol came in again. She set a paper bag on the table, and Therese knew she had only gone to get a container of milk, as Carol or she herself did very often at night.

"Can I sleep with you?" Therese asked.

"Did you see the bed?"

It was a double bed. They sat up in their pajamas, drinking milk and sharing an orange that Carol was too sleepy to finish. Then Therese set the container of milk on the floor and looked at Carol who was sleeping already, on her stomach, with one arm flung up as she always went to sleep. Therese pulled out the light. Then Carol slipped her arm under her neck, and all the length of their bodies touched, fitting as if something had prearranged it. Happiness was like a green vine spreading through her, stretching fine tendrils, bearing flowers through her flesh. She had a vision of a pale white flower, shimmering as if seen in darkness, or through water. Why did people talk of heaven, she wondered.

"Go to sleep," Carol said.

Therese hoped she would not. But when she felt Carol's hand move on her shoulder, she knew she had been asleep. It was dawn now. Carol's fingers tightened in her hair, Carol kissed her on the lips, and pleasure leaped in Therese again as if it were only a continuation of the moment when Carol had slipped her arm under her neck last night. I love you, Therese wanted to say again, and then the words were erased by the tingling and terrifying pleasure that spread in waves from Carol's lips over her neck, her shoulders, that rushed suddenly the length of her body. Her arms were tight around Carol, and she was conscious of Carol and nothing else, of Carol's hand that slid along her ribs, Carol's hair that brushed her bare breasts, and then her body too seemed to vanish in widening circles that leaped further and further, beyond where thought could follow. While a thousand memories and moments, words, the first darling, the second time Carol had met her at the store, a thousand memories of Carol's face, her voice, moments of anger and laughter flashed like the tail of a comet across her brain. And now it was pale blue distance and space, an expanding space in which she took flight suddenly like a long arrow. The arrow seemed to cross an impossibly wide abyss with ease, seemed to arc on and on in space, and not quite to stop. Then she realized that she still clung to Carol, that she trembled violently, and the arrow was herself. She saw Carol's pale hair across her eyes, and now Carol's head was close against hers. And she did not have to ask if this was right, no one had to tell her, because this could not have been more right or perfect. She held Carol tighter against her, and felt Carol's mouth on her own smiling mouth. Therese lay still, looking at her, at Carol's face only inches away from her, the gray eyes calm as she had never seen them, as if they retained some of the space she had just emerged from. And it seemed strange that it was still Carol's face, with the freckles, the bending blonde eyebrow that she knew, the mouth now as calm as her eyes, as Therese had seen it many times before.

"My angel," Carol said. "Flung out of space."

Therese looked up at the corners of the room, that were much brighter now, at the bureau with the bulging front and the shield-shaped drawer pulls, at the frameless mirror with the beveled edge, at the green-patterned curtains that hung straight at the windows, and the two gray tips of buildings that showed just above the sill. She would remember every detail of this room forever.

"What town is this?" she asked.

Carol laughed. "This? This is Waterloo." She reached for a cigarette. "Isn't that awful."

Smiling, Therese raised up on her elbow. Carol put a cigarette between her lips. "There's a couple of Waterloos in every state," Therese said.

# *sixteen*

Therese went out to get some newspapers while Carol was dressing. She stepped into the elevator and turned around in the exact center of it. She felt a little odd, as if everything had shifted and distances were not quite the same, balance was not quite the same. She walked across the lobby to the newspaper stand in the corner.

"The *Courier* and the *Tribune*," she said to the man, taking them, and even to utter words was as strange as the names of the newspapers she bought.

"Eight cents," the man said, and Therese looked down at the change he had given her and saw there was still the same difference between eight cents and a quarter.

She wandered across the lobby, looked through the glass into the barber shop where a couple of men were getting shaves. A black man was shining shoes. A tall man with a cigar and a broad-brimmed hat, with Western boots, walked by her. She would remember this lobby, too, forever, the people, the old-fashioned-looking woodwork at the base of the registration desk, and the man in the dark overcoat who looked at her over the top of his newspaper, and slumped in his chair and went on reading beside the black and cream-colored marble column.

When Therese opened the room door, the sight of Carol went through her like a spear. She stood a moment with her hand on the knob.

Carol looked at her from the bathroom, holding the comb suspended over her head. Carol looked at her from head to foot. "Don't do that in public," Carol said.

Therese threw the newspapers on the bed and came to her. Carol seized her suddenly in her arms. They stood holding each other as if they would never separate. Therese shuddered, and there were tears in her eyes. It was hard to find words, locked in Carol's arms, closer than kissing.

"Why did you wait so long?" Therese asked.

"Because—I thought there wouldn't be a second time, that I wouldn't want it. But that's not true."

Therese thought of Abby, and it was like a slim shaft of bitterness dropping between them. Carol released her.

"And there was something else—to have you around reminding me, knowing you and knowing it would be so easy. I'm sorry. It wasn't fair to you."

Therese set her teeth hard. She watched Carol walk slowly away across the room, watched the space widen, and remembered the first time she had seen her walk so slowly away in the department store, Therese had thought forever. Carol had loved Abby, too, and Carol reproached herself for it. As Carol would one day for loving her, Therese wondered. Therese understood now why the December and January weeks had been made up of anger and indecision, reprimands alternating with indulgences. But she understood now that whatever Carol said in words, there were no barriers and no indecisions now. There was no Abby, either, after this morning, whatever had happened between Carol and Abby before.

"Was it?" Carol asked.

"You've made me so happy ever since I've known you," Therese said.

"I don't think you can judge."

"I can judge this morning."

Carol did not answer. Only the rasp of the door lock answered her. Carol had locked the door and they were alone. Therese came toward her, straight into her arms.

"I love you," Therese said, just to hear the words. "I love you, I love you."

But Carol seemed deliberately to pay almost no attention to her that day. There was more arrogance in the tilt of her cigarette, in the way she backed the car away from a curb, cursing, not quite joking. "Damned if I'll put a dime in a parking meter with a prairie right in sight," Carol said. But when Therese did catch her looking at her, Carol's eyes were laughing. Carol teased her, leaning on her shoulder as they stood in front of a cigarette machine, touching her foot under tables. It made Therese limp and tense at the same time. She thought of people she had seen holding hands in movies, and why shouldn't she and Carol? Yet when she simply took Carol's arm as they stood choosing a box of candy in a shop, Carol murmured, "Don't."

Therese sent a box of candy to Mrs. Robichek from the candy shop in Minneapolis, and a box also to the Kellys. She sent an extravagantly big box to Richard's mother, a double-deck box with wooden compartments that she knew Mrs. Semco would use later for sewing articles.

"Did you ever do that with Abby?" Therese asked abruptly that evening in the car.

Carol's eyes understood suddenly and she blinked. "What questions you ask," she said. "Of course."

Of course. She had known it. "And now—?"

"Therese—"

She asked stiffly, "Was it very much the same as with me?"

Carol smiled. "No, darling."

"Don't you think it's more pleasant than sleeping with men?"

Her smile was amused. "Not necessarily. That depends. Who have you ever known except Richard?"

"No one."

"Well, don't you think you'd better try some others?"

Therese was speechless for a moment, but she tried to be casual, drumming her fingers on the book in her lap.

"I mean sometime, darling. You've got a lot of years ahead."

Therese said nothing. She could not imagine ever leaving Carol either. That was another terrible question that had sprung into her mind at the start, that hammered at her brain now with a painful insistence to be answered. Would Carol ever want to leave her?

"I mean, whom you sleep with depends so much on habit," Carol went on. "And you're too young to make enormous decisions. Or habits."

"Are you just a habit?" she asked, smiling, but she heard the resentment in her voice. "You mean it's nothing but that?"

"Therese—of all times to get so melancholic."

"I'm not melancholic," she protested, but the thin ice was under her feet again, the uncertainties. Or was it that she always wanted a little more than she had, no matter how much she had? She said impulsively, "Abby loves you, too, doesn't she?"

Carol started a little. "Abby has loved me practically all her life—even as you."

Therese stared at her.

"I'll tell you about it one day. Whatever happened is past. Months and months ago," she said, so softly Therese could hardly hear.

"Only months?"

"Yes."

"Tell me now."

"This isn't the time or the place."

"There's never a time," Therese said. "Didn't you say there never was a right time?"

"Did I say that? About what?"

But neither of them said anything for a moment, because a fresh barrage of wind hurled the rain like a million bullets against the hood and windshield, and for a moment they could have heard nothing else. There was no thunder, as if the thunder, somewhere up above, modestly refrained from competing with this other god of rain. They waited in the inadequate shelter of a hill at the side of the road.

"I might tell you the middle," Carol said, "because it's funny—and ironic. It was last winter when we had the furniture shop together. But I can't begin without telling you the first part—and that was when we were children. Our families lived near each other in New Jersey, so we saw each other during vacations. Abby always had a mild crush on me, I thought, even when we were about six and eight. Then she wrote me a couple of letters when she was about fourteen and away at school. And by that time I'd heard of girls who preferred girls. But the books also tell you it goes away after that age." There were pauses between her sentences, as if she left out sentences in between.

"Were you in school with her?" Therese asked.

"I never was. My father sent me to a different school, out of town. Then Abby went to Europe when she was sixteen, and I wasn't at home when she came back. I saw her once at some party around the time I got married. Abby looked quite different then, not like a tomboy anymore. Then Harge and I lived in another town, and I didn't see her again—really for years, till long after Rindy was born. She came once in a while to the riding stable where Harge and I used to ride. A few times we all rode together. Then Abby and I started playing tennis on Saturday afternoons when Harge usually played golf. Abby and I always had fun together. Abby's former crush on me never crossed my mind—we were both so much older and so much had happened. I had an idea about starting a shop, because I wanted to see less of Harge. I thought we were getting bored with each other and it would help. So I asked Abby if she wanted to be partners in it, and we started the furniture shop. After a few weeks, to my surprise, I felt I was attracted to her," Carol said in the same quiet voice. "I couldn't understand it, and I was a little afraid of it—remembering Abby from before, and realizing she might feel the same way, or that both of us could. So I tried not to let Abby see it, and I think I succeeded. But finally—here's the funny part finally—there was the night in Abby's house one night last winter. The roads were snowed in that night, and Abby's mother insisted that we stay together in Abby's room, simply because the room I'd stayed in before hadn't any sheets on the bed then, and it was very late. Abby said she'd fix the sheets, we both protested, but Abby's mother insisted." Carol smiled a little, and glanced at her, but Therese felt Carol didn't even see her. "So I stayed with Abby. Nothing would have happened, if not for that night, I'm sure of it. If not for Abby's mother, that's the ironic thing, because she doesn't know anything about it. But it did happen, and I felt very much as you, I suppose, as happy as you." Carol blurted out the end, though her voice was still level and somehow without emotion of any kind.

Therese stared at her, not knowing if it was jealousy or shock or anger that was suddenly jumbling everything. "And after that?" she asked.

"After that, I knew I was in love with Abby. I don't know, why not call it love, it had all the earmarks. But it lasted only two months, like a disease that came and went." Carol said in a different tone, "Darling, it's got nothing to do with you, and it's finished now. I knew you wanted to know, but I didn't see any reason for telling you before. It's that unimportant."

"But if you felt the same way about her—"

"For two months?" Carol said. "When you have a husband and child, you know, it's a little different."

Different from her, Carol meant, because she hadn't any responsibilities. "Is it? You can just start and stop?"

"When you haven't got a chance," Carol answered.

The rain was abating, but only by so much that she could see it as rain now and not solid silver sheets. "I don't believe it."

"You're hardly in a state to talk."

"Why are you so cynical?"

"Cynical? Am I?"

Therese was not sure enough to answer. What was it to love someone, what was love exactly, and why did it end or not end? Those were the real questions, and who could answer them?

"It's letting up," Carol said. "How about going on and finding a good brandy somewhere? Or is this a dry state?"

They drove on to the next town and found a deserted bar in the biggest hotel. The brandy was delicious, and they ordered two more.

"It's French brandy," Carol said. "Some day we'll go to France."

Therese turned the little bowl of a glass between her fingers. A clock ticked at the end of the bar. A train whistle blew in the distance. And Carol cleared her throat. Ordinary sounds, yet the moment was not an ordinary one. No moment had been an ordinary one since the morning in Waterloo. Therese stared at the bright brown light in the brandy glass, and suddenly she had no doubt that she and Carol would one day go to France. Then out of the shimmering brown sun in the glass, Harge's face emerged, mouth and nose and eyes.

"Harge knows about Abby, doesn't he?" Therese said.

"Yes. He asked me something about her a few months ago—and I told him the whole truth from start to finish."

"You did—" She thought of Richard, imagined how Richard would react. "Is that why you're getting the divorce?"

"No. It's got nothing to do with the divorce. That's another ironic thing—that I told Harge after it was all over. A mistaken effort at honesty, when Harge and I had nothing left to salvage. We'd already talked about a divorce. Please don't remind me of mistakes!" Carol frowned.

"You mean—he certainly must have been jealous."

"Yes. Because however I chose to tell it, I suppose it came out that I'd cared more about Abby at one period than I'd ever cared for him. At one point, even with Rindy I'd have left everything behind to go with her. I don't know how it was that I didn't."

"And taken Rindy with you?"

"I don't know. I know the fact that Rindy existed stopped me from leaving Harge then."

"Do you regret it?"

Carol shook her head slowly. "No. It wouldn't have lasted. It didn't last, and maybe I knew it wouldn't. With my marriage failing, I was too afraid and too weak—" She stopped.

"Are you afraid now?"

Carol was silent.

"Carol—"

"I am not afraid," she said stubbornly, lifting her head.

Therese looked at her face in profile in the dim light. What about Rindy now, she wanted to ask, what will happen? But she knew Carol was on the brink of growing suddenly impatient, giving her a careless answer, or no answer at all. Another time, Therese thought, not this moment. It might destroy everything, even the solidity of Carol's body beside her, and the bend of Carol's body in the black sweater seemed the only solid thing in the world. Therese ran her thumb down Carol's side, from under the arm to the waist.

"I remember Harge was particularly annoyed about a trip I took with Abby to Connecticut. Abby and I went up to buy some things for the shop. It was only a two-day trip, but he said. 'Behind my back. You had to run away.'" Carol said it bitterly. There was more self-reproach in her voice than imitation of Harge.

"Does he still talk about it?"

"No. Is it anything to talk about? Is it anything to be proud of?"

"Is it anything to be ashamed of?"

"Yes. You know that, don't you?" Carol asked in her even, distinct voice. "In the eyes of the world it's an abomination."

The way she said it, Therese could not quite smile. "You don't believe that."

"People like Harge's family."

"They're not the whole world."

"They are enough. And you have to live in the world. You, I mean—and I don't mean anything just now about whom you decide to love." She looked at Therese, and at last Therese saw a smile rising slowly in her eyes, bringing Carol with it. "I mean responsibilities in the world that other people live in and that might not be yours. Just now it isn't, and that's why in New York I was exactly the wrong person for you to know—because I indulge you and keep you from growing up."

"Why don't you stop?"

"I'll try. The trouble is, I like to indulge you."

"You're exactly the right person for me to know," Therese said.

"Am I?"

On the street, Therese said, "I don't suppose Harge would like it if he knew we were away on a trip, either, would he?"

"He's not going to know about it."

"Do you still want to go to Washington?"

"Absolutely, if you've got the time. Can you stay away all of February?"

Therese nodded. "Unless I hear something in Salt Lake City. I told Phil to write there. It's pretty slim chance." Probably Phil wouldn't even write, she thought. But if there was the least chance of a job in New York, she should go back. "Would you go on to Washington without me?"

Carol glanced at her. "As a matter of fact, I wouldn't," she said with a little smile.

• • •

Their hotel room was so overheated when they came back that evening, they had to throw open the windows for a while. Carol leaned on the windowsill, cursing the heat for Therese's amusement, calling her a salamander because she could bear it. Then Carol asked abruptly, "What did Richard have to say yesterday?"

Therese had not even known that Carol knew about the last letter. The one he had promised, in the Chicago letter, to send to Minneapolis and to Seattle. "Nothing much," Therese said. "Just a one-page letter. He still wants me to write to him. And I don't intend to." She had thrown the letter away, but she remembered it:

> I haven't heard from you, and it's beginning to dawn on me what an incredible conglomeration of contradictions you are. You are sensitive and yet so insensitive, imaginative and yet so unimaginative . . . If you get stranded by your whimsical friend, let me know and I'll come after you. This won't last, Terry. I know a little about such things. I saw Danny and he wanted to know what I'd heard from you, what you were doing. How would you like it if I had told him? I didn't say anything, for your sake, because I think one day you'll blush. I still love you, I admit it. I'll come out to you—and show you what America's really like—if you care enough about me to write and say so . . .

It was insulting to Carol, and Therese had torn it up. Therese sat on the bed with her arms around her knees, gripping her wrists inside the sleeves of her robe. Carol had overdone the ventilation, and the room was cold. The Minnesota winds had taken possession of the room, were seizing Carol's cigarette smoke and tearing it to nothing. Therese watched Carol calmly brushing her teeth at the basin.

"Do you mean that about not writing to him? That's your decision?" Carol asked.

"Yes."

Therese watched Carol knock the water out of her toothbrush, and turn from the basin, blotting her face with a towel. Nothing about Richard mattered so much to her as the way Carol blotted her face with a towel.

"Let's say no more," Carol said.

She knew Carol would say no more. She knew Carol had been pushing her toward him, until this moment. Now it seemed it might all have been for this moment as Carol turned and walked toward her and her heart took a giant's step forward.

They went on westward, through Sleepy Eye, Tracy, and Pipestone, sometimes taking an indirect highway on a whim. The West unfolded like a magic carpet, dotted with the neat, tight units of farmhouse, barn, and silo that they could see for half an hour before they came abreast of them. They stopped once at a farmhouse to ask if they could buy enough gas to get to the next station. The house smelled like fresh cold cheese. Their steps sounded hollow and lonely on the solid brown planks of the floor, and Therese thought in a fervid burst of patriotism—*America.* There was a picture of a rooster on the wall, made of colored patches of cloth sewn on a black ground, beautiful enough to hang in a museum. The farmer warned them about ice on the road directly west, so they took another highway going south.

They discovered a one-ring circus that night beside a railroad track in a town called Sioux Falls. The performers were not very expert. Therese and Carol sat on a couple of orange crates in the first row. One of the acrobats invited them into the performers' tent after the show, and insisted on giving Carol a dozen of the circus posters, because she had admired them. Carol sent some of them to Abby and some to Rindy, and sent Rindy as well a green chameleon in a pasteboard box. It was an evening Therese would never forget, and unlike most such evenings, this one registered as unforgettable while it still lived. It was a matter of the bag of popcorn they shared, the circus, and the kiss Carol gave her back of some booth in the performers' tent. It was a matter of that particular enchantment that came from Carol—though Carol took their good times so for granted—and seemed to work on all the world around them, a matter of everything going perfectly, without disappointments or hitches, going just as they wished it to.

Therese walked from the circus with her head down, lost in thought. "I wonder if I'll ever want to create anything again," she said.

"What brought this on?"

"I mean—what was I ever trying to do but this? I'm happy."

Carol took her arm and squeezed it, dug her thumb in so hard that Therese yelled. Carol looked up at a street marker and said, "Fifth and Nebraska. I think we go this way."

"What's going to happen when we get back to New York? It can't be the same, can it?"

"Yes," Carol said. "Till you get tired of me."

Therese laughed. She heard the soft snap of Carol's scarf end in the wind.

"We might not be living together, but it'll be the same."

They couldn't live together with Rindy, Therese knew. It was useless to dream of it. But it was more than enough that Carol promised in words it would be the same.

Near the border of Nebraska and Wyoming, they stopped for dinner at a large restaurant built like a lodge in an evergreen forest. They were almost the only people in the big dining room, and they chose a table near the fireplace. They spread out the road map and decided to head straight for Salt Lake City. They might stay there for a few days, Carol said, because it was an interesting place, and she was tired of driving.

"Lusk," Therese said, looking at the map. "What a sexy-sounding name."

Carol put her head back and laughed. "Where is it?"

"On the road."

Carol picked up her wineglass and said, "Château Neuf-du-Pape in Nebraska. What'll we drink to?"

"Us."

It was something like the morning in Waterloo, Therese thought, a time too absolute and flawless to seem real, though it was real, not merely props in a play—their brandy glasses on the mantel, the row of deers' horns above, Carol's cigarette lighter, the fire itself. But at moments she felt like an actor, remembered only now and then her identity with a sense of surprise, as if she had been playing in these last days the part of someone else, someone fabulously and excessively lucky. She looked up at the fir branches fixed in the rafters, at the man and woman talking inaudibly together at a table against the wall, at the man alone at his table, smoking his cigarette slowly. She thought of the man sitting with the newspaper in the hotel in Waterloo. Didn't he have the same colorless eyes and the long creases on either side of his mouth? Or was it only that this moment of consciousness was so much the same as that other moment?

They spent the night in Lusk, ninety miles away.

## *seventeen*

"Mrs. H. F. Aird?" The desk clerk looked at Carol after she had signed the register. "Are you Mrs. Carol Aird?"

"Yes."

"Message for you." He turned around and got it from a pigeonhole. "A telegram."

"Thank you." Carol glanced at Therese with a little lift of her brows before she opened it. She read it, frowning, then turned to the clerk. "Where's the Belvedere Hotel?"

The clerk directed her.

"I've got to pick up another telegram," Carol said to Therese. "Want to wait here while I get it?"

"Who from?"

"Abby."

"All right. Is it bad news?"

The frown was still in her eyes. "Don't know until I see it. Abby just says there's a telegram for me at the Belvedere."

"Shall I have the bags taken up?"

"Well—just wait. The car is parked."

"Why can't I come with you?"

"Of course, if you want to. Let's walk. It's only a couple of blocks away."

Carol walked quickly. The cold was sharp. Therese glanced around her at the flat, orderly looking town, and remembered Carol's saying that Salt Lake City was the cleanest town in the United States. When the Belvedere was in sight, Carol suddenly looked at her and said, "Abby's probably had a brainstorm and decided to fly out and join us."

In the Belvedere, Therese bought a newspaper while Carol went to the desk. When Therese turned to her, Carol was just lowering the telegram after reading it. There was a stunned expression on her face. She came slowly toward Therese, and it flashed through Therese's mind that Abby was dead, that this second message was from Abby's parents.

"What's the matter?" Therese asked.

"Nothing. I don't know yet." Carol glanced around and slapped the telegram against her fingers. "I've got to make a phone call. It might take a few minutes." She looked at her watch.

It was a quarter to two. The hotel clerk said she could probably get New Jersey in about twenty minutes. Meanwhile, Carol wanted a drink. They found a bar in the hotel.

"What is it? Is Abby sick?"

Carol smiled. "No. I'll tell you later."

"Is it Rindy?"

"No!" Carol finished her brandy.

Therese walked up and down in the lobby while Carol was in the telephone booth. She saw Carol nod slowly several times, saw her fumble to get a cigarette lighted, but by the time Therese got there to light it for her, Carol had it and motioned her away. Carol talked for three or four minutes, then came out and paid her bill.

"What is it, Carol?"

Carol stood looking out the doorway of the hotel for a moment. "Now we go to the Temple Square Hotel," she said.

There they picked up another telegram. Carol opened it and glanced at it, and tore it up as they walked to the door.

"I don't think we'll stay here tonight," Carol said. "Let's go back to the car."

They went back to the hotel where Carol had gotten the first telegram. Therese said nothing to her, but she felt something had happened that meant Carol had to get back east immediately. Carol told the clerk to cancel their room reservation.

"I'd like to leave a forwarding address in case of any other messages," she said. "That's the Brown Palace, Denver."

"Right you are."

"Thank you very much. That's good for the next week at least."

In the car, Carol said, "What's the next town west?"

"West?" Therese looked at the map. "Wendover. This is that stretch. A hundred and twenty-seven miles."

"Christ!" Carol said suddenly. She stopped the car completely and took the map and looked at it.

"What about Denver?" Therese asked.

"I don't want to go to Denver." Carol folded the map and started the car." Well, we'll do it anyway. Light me a cigarette, will you, darling? And watch out for the next place to get something to eat."

They hadn't had lunch yet, and it was after three. They had talked about this stretch last night, the straight road west from Salt Lake City across the Great Salt Lake Desert. They had plenty of gas, Therese noticed, and probably the country wasn't entirely deserted, but Carol was tired. They had been driving since six that morning. Carol drove fast. Now and then she pressed the pedal down to the floor and held it there a long while before letting up. Therese glanced at her apprehensively. She felt they were running away from something.

"Anything behind us?" Carol asked.

"No." On the seat between them, Therese could see a piece of the telegram sticking out of Carol's handbag. "GET THIS. JACOPO." was all she could read. She remembered Jacopo was the name of the little monkey in the back of the car.

They came to a gas station café standing all by itself like a wart on the flat landscape. They might have been the first people who had stopped there in days. Carol looked at her across the white oilcloth table, and sank back in the straight chair. Before she could speak, an old man in an apron came from the kitchen in back, and told them there was nothing but ham and eggs, so they ordered ham and eggs and coffee. Then Carol lighted a cigarette and leaned forward, looking down at the table.

"Do you know what's up?" she said. "Harge has had a detective following us since Chicago."

"A detective? What for?"

"Can't you guess?" Carol said in almost a whisper.

Therese bit her tongue. Yes, she could guess. Harge had found out they were traveling together. "Abby told you?"

"Abby found out." Carol's fingers slid down her cigarette and the fire burned her. When she got the cigarette out of her mouth, her lips began to bleed.

Therese looked around her. The place was empty. "Following us?" she asked. "*With* us?"

"He may be in Salt Lake City now. Checking on all the hotels. It's very dirty business, darling. I'm sorry, sorry, sorry." Carol sat back restlessly in her chair. "Maybe I'd better put you on a train and send you home."

"All right—if you think that's the best idea."

"You don't have to be mixed up in this. Let them follow me to Alaska, if they want to. I don't know what they've got so far. I don't think much."

Therese sat rigidly on the edge of her chair. "What's he doing—making notes about us?"

The old man was coming back, bringing them glasses of water.

Carol nodded. "Then there's the Dictaphone trick," she said as the man went away. "I'm not sure if they'll go that far. I'm not sure if Harge would do that." The corner of her mouth trembled. She stared down at one spot on the worn white oilcloth. "I wonder if they had time for a Dictaphone in Chicago. It's the only place we stayed more than ten hours. I rather hope they did. It's so ironic. Remember Chicago?"

"Of course." She tried to keep her voice steady, but it was pretense, like pretending self-control when something you loved was dead in front of your eyes. They would have to separate here. "What about Waterloo?" She thought suddenly of the man in the lobby.

"We got there late. It wouldn't have been easy."

"Carol, I saw someone—I'm not sure, but I think I saw him twice."

"Where?"

"In the lobby in Waterloo the first time. In the morning. Then I thought I saw the same man in that restaurant with the fireplace." It was only last night, the restaurant with the fireplace.

Carol made her tell completely about both times and describe the man completely. He was hard to describe. But now she racked her brain to extract the last detail she could, even to the color of his shoes. And it was odd and rather terrifying, dragging up what was probably a figment of her imagination and tying it to a situation that was real. She felt she might even be lying to Carol as she watched Carol's eyes grow more and more intense.

"What do you think?" Therese asked.

Carol sighed. "What can anyone think? Just watch out for him the third time."

Therese looked down at her plate. It was impossible to eat. "It's about Rindy, isn't it?"

"Yes." She put down her fork without taking the first bite, and reached for a cigarette. "Harge wants her—in toto. Maybe with this, he thinks he can do it."

"Just because we're traveling together?"

"Yes."

"I should leave you."

"Damn him," Carol said quietly, looking off at a corner of the room.

Therese waited. But what was there to wait for? "I can get a bus somewhere from here, and then get a train."

"Do you want to go?" Carol asked.

"Of course I don't. I just think it's best."

"Are you afraid?"

"Afraid? No." She felt Carol's eyes appraise her as severely as at that moment in Waterloo, when she had told Carol she loved her.

"Then I'm damned if you'll go. I want you with me."

"Do you mean that?"

"Yes. Eat your eggs. Stop being silly." And Carol even smiled a little. "Shall we go to Reno as we'd planned?"

"Any place."

"And let's take our time."

A few moments later, when they were on the road, Therese said again, "I'm still not sure it was the same man the second time, you know."

"I think you're sure," Carol said. Then, suddenly, on the long straight road, she stopped the car. She sat for a moment in silence, looking down the road. Then she glanced at Therese. "I can't go to Reno. That's a little too funny. I know a wonderful place just south of Denver."

"Denver?"

"Denver," Carol said firmly, and backed the car around.

# *eighteen*

In the morning, they lay in each other's arms long after the sun had come into the room. The sun warmed them through the window of the hotel in the tiny town whose name they hadn't noticed. There was snow on the ground outside.

"There'll be snow in Estes Park," Carol said to her.

"What's Estes Park?"

"You'll like it. Not like Yellowstone. It's open all year."

"Carol, you're not worried, are you?"

Carol pulled her close. "Do I act like I'm worried?"

Therese was not worried. That first panic had vanished. She was watching, but not as she had watched yesterday afternoon just after Salt Lake City. Carol wanted her with her, and whatever happened they would meet it without running. How was it possible to be afraid and in love, Therese thought. The two things did not go together. How was it possible to be afraid, when the two of them grew stronger together every day? And every night. Every night was different, and every morning. Together they possessed a miracle.

The road into Estes Park slanted downward. The snowdrifts piled higher and higher on either side, and then the lights began, strung along the fir trees, arching over the road. It was a village of brown logged houses and shops and hotels. There was music, and people walked in the bright street with their heads lifted up, as if they were enchanted.

"I do like it," Therese said.

"It doesn't mean you don't have to watch out for our little man."

They brought the portable phonograph up to their room, and played some records they had just bought and some old ones from New Jersey. Therese played "Easy Living" a couple of times, and Carol sat across the room watching her, sitting on the arm of a chair with her arms folded.

"What a rotten time I give you, don't I?"

"Oh, Carol—" Therese tried to smile. It was only a mood of Carol's, only a moment. But it made Therese feel helpless.

Carol looked around at the window. "And why didn't we go to Europe in the first place? Switzerland. Or fly out here at least."

"I wouldn't have liked that at all." Therese looked at the yellow suede shirt that Carol had bought for her, which hung over the back of a chair. Carol had sent Rindy a green one. She had bought some silver earrings, a couple of books, and a bottle of Triple Sec. Half an hour ago, they had been happy, walking through the streets together. "It's that last rye you got downstairs," Therese said. "Rye depresses you."

"Does it?"

"Worse than brandy."

"I'm going to take you to the nicest place I know this side of Sun Valley," she said.

"What's the matter with Sun Valley?" She knew Carol liked skiing.

"Sun Valley just isn't the place," Carol said mysteriously. "This place is near Colorado Springs."

In Denver, Carol stopped and sold her diamond engagement ring at a jeweler's. Therese felt a little disturbed by it, but Carol said the ring meant nothing to her and she loathed diamonds anyway. And it was quicker than wiring her bank for money. Carol wanted to stop at a hotel a few miles out from Colorado Springs, where she had been before, but she changed her mind almost as soon as they got there. It was too much like a resort, she said, so they went to a hotel that backed on the town and faced the mountains.

• • •

Their room was long from the door to the square floor-length windows that overlooked a garden, and beyond, the red and white mountains. There were touches of white in the garden, odd little pyramids of stone, a white bench or a chair, and the garden looked foolish compared to the magnificent land that surrounded it, the flat sweep that rose up into mountains upon mountains, filling the horizon like half a world. The room had blonde furniture about the color of Carol's hair, and there was a bookcase as smooth as she could want it, with some good books amid the bad ones, and Therese knew she would never read any of them while they were here. A painting of a woman in a large black hat and a red scarf hung above the bookcase, and on the wall near the door was spread a pelt of brown leather, not a real pelt but something someone had cut out of a piece of brown suede. Above it was a tin lantern with a candle. Carol also rented the room next to them, which had a connecting door, though they did not use it even to put their suitcases in. They planned to stay a week, or longer if they liked it.

On the morning of the second day, Therese came back from a tour of inspection of the hotel grounds and found Carol stopped by the bed table. Carol only glanced at her, and went to the dressing table and looked under that, and then to the long built-in closet behind the wall panel.

"That's that," Carol said. "Now let's forget it."

Therese knew what she was looking for. "I hadn't thought of it," she said. "I feel like we've lost him."

"Except that he's probably gotten to Denver by now," Carol said calmly. She smiled, but she twisted her mouth a little. "And he'll probably drop in down here."

It was so, of course. There was even the remotest chance that the detective had seen them when they drove back through Salt Lake City, and followed them. If he didn't find them in Salt Lake City, he might inquire at the hotels. She knew that was why Carol had left the Denver address, in fact, because they hadn't intended to go to Denver. Therese flung herself in the armchair, and looked at Carol. Carol took the trouble to search for a Dictaphone, but her attitude was arrogant. She had even invited trouble by coming here. And the explanation, the resolution of those contradictory facts was nowhere but in Carol herself, unresolved, in her slow, restless step as she walked to the door now and turned, in the nonchalant lift of her head, and in the nervous line of her eyebrows that registered irritation in one second and in the next were serene. Therese looked at the big room, up at the high ceiling, at the large, square, plain bed, the room that for all its modernness had a curiously old-fashioned, ample air about it that she associated with the American West, like the oversized western saddles she had seen in the riding stable downstairs. A kind of cleanness, as well. Yet Carol looked for a dictaphone. Therese watched her, walking back toward her, still in her pajamas and robe. She had an impulse to go to Carol, crush her in her arms, pull her down on the bed, and the fact that she didn't now made her tense and alert, filled her with a repressed but reckless exhilaration.

Carol blew her smoke up into the air. "I don't give a damn. I hope the papers find out about it and rub Harge's nose in his own mess. I hope he wastes fifty thousand dollars. Do you want to take that trip that bankrupts the English language this afternoon? Did you ask Mrs. French yet?'

They had met Mrs. French last night in the game room of the hotel. She hadn't a car, and Carol had asked her if she would like to take a drive with them today.

"I asked her," Therese said. "She said she'd be ready right after lunch."

"Wear your suede shirt." Carol took Therese's face in her hands, pressed her cheeks, and kissed her. "Put it on now."

It was a six- or seven-hour trip to the Cripple Creek gold mine, over Ute Pass and down a mountain. Mrs. French went with them, talking the whole time. She was a woman of about seventy, with a Maryland accent and a hearing aid, ready to get out of the car and climb anywhere, though she had to be helped every foot of the way. Therese felt very anxious about her, though she actually disliked even touching her. She felt if Mrs. French fell, she would break in a million pieces. Carol and Mrs. French talked about the state of Washington, which Mrs. French knew well, since she had lived there for the past few years with one of her sons. Carol asked a few questions, and Mrs. French told her all about her ten years of traveling since her husband's death, and about her two sons, the one in Washington and the one in Hawaii who worked for a pineapple company. And obviously Mrs. French adored Carol, and they were going to see a lot more of Mrs. French. It was nearly eleven when they got back to the hotel. Carol asked Mrs. French to have supper in the bar with them, but Mrs. French said she was too tired for anything but her shredded wheat and hot milk, which she would have in her room.

"I'm glad," Therese said when she had gone. "I'd rather be alone with you."

"Really, Miss Belivet? Whatever do you mean?" Carol asked as she opened the door into the bar. "You'd better sit down and tell me all about that."

But they were not alone in the bar more than five minutes. Two men, one named Dave and the other whose name Therese at least did not know and did not care to, came over and asked to join them. They were the two who had come over last night in the game room and asked Carol and her to play gin rummy. Carol had declined last night. Now she said, "Of course, sit down." Carol and Dave began a conversation that sounded very interesting, but Therese was seated so that she couldn't participate very well. And the man next to Therese wanted to talk about something else, a horseback trip he had just made around Steamboat Springs. After supper, Therese waited for a sign from Carol to leave, but Carol was still deep in conversation. Therese had read about that special pleasure people got from the fact that someone they loved was attractive in the eyes of other people, too. She simply didn't have it. Carol looked at her every now and then and gave her a wink. So Therese sat there for an hour and a half, and managed to be polite, because she knew Carol wanted her to be.

The people who joined them in the bar and sometimes in the dining room did not annoy her so much as Mrs. French, who went with them somewhere almost every day in the car. Then an angry resentment that Therese was actually ashamed of would rise in her because someone was preventing her from being alone with Carol.

"Darling, did you ever think you'll be seventy-one, too, someday?"

"No," Therese said.

But there were other days when they drove out into the mountains alone, taking any road they saw. Once they came upon a little town they liked and spent the night there, without pajamas or toothbrushes, without past or future, and the night became another of those islands in time, suspended somewhere in the heart or in the memory, intact and absolute. Or perhaps it was nothing but happiness, Therese thought, a complete happiness that must be rare enough, so rare that very few people ever knew it. But if it was merely happiness, then it had gone beyond the ordinary bounds and become something else, become a kind of excessive pressure, so that the weight of a coffee cup in her hand, the speed of a cat crossing the garden below, the silent crash of two clouds seemed almost more than she could bear. And just as she had not understood a month ago the phenomenon of sudden happiness, she did not understand her state now, which seemed an aftermath. It was more often painful than pleasant, and consequently she was afraid she had some grave and unique flaw. She was as afraid sometimes as if she were walking about with a broken spine. If she ever had an impulse to tell Carol, the words dissolved before she began, in fear and in her usual mistrust of her own reactions, the anxiety that her reactions were like no one else's, and that therefore not even Carol could understand them.

In the mornings, they generally drove out somewhere in the mountains and left the car so they could climb up a hill. They drove aimlessly over the zigzagging roads that were like white chalk lines connecting mountain point to mountain point. From a distance, one could see clouds lying about the projecting peaks, so it seemed they flew along in space, a little closer to heaven than to earth. Therese's favorite spot was on the highway above Cripple Creek, where the road clung suddenly to the rim of a gigantic depression. Hundreds of feet below lay the tiny disorder of the abandoned mining town. There the eye and the brain played tricks with each other, for it was impossible to keep a steady concept of the proportion below, impossible to compare it on any human scale. Her own hand held up in front of her could look Lilliputian or curiously huge. And the town occupied only a fraction of the great scoop in the earth, like a single experience, a single commonplace event, set in a certain immeasurable territory of the mind. The eye, swimming in space, returned to rest on the spot that looked like a box of matches run over by a car, the man-made confusion of the little town.

Always Therese looked for the man with the creases on either side of his mouth, but Carol never did. Carol had not even mentioned him since their second day at Colorado Springs, and now ten days had passed. Because the restaurant of the hotel was famous, new people came every evening to the big dining room, and Therese always glanced about, not actually expecting to see him, but as a kind of precaution that had become a habit. But Carol paid no attention to anyone except Walter, their waiter, who always came up to ask what kind of cocktail they wanted that evening. Many people looked at Carol, however, because she was generally the most attractive woman in the room. And Therese was so delighted to be with her, so proud of her, she looked at no one else but Carol. Then as she read the menu, Carol would slowly press Therese's foot under the table to make her smile.

"What do you think about Iceland in the summer?" Carol might ask, because they made a point of talking about travel, if there was a silence when they first sat down.

"Must you pick such cold places? When'll I ever work?"

"Don't be dismal. Shall we invite Mrs. French? Think she'd mind our holding hands?"

One morning, there were three letters—from Rindy, Abby, and Danny. It was Carol's second letter from Abby, who had had no further news before, and Therese noticed Carol opened Rindy's letter first. Danny wrote that he was still waiting to hear the outcome of two interviews about jobs. And reported that Phil said Harkevy was going to do the sets for the English play called *The Faint Heart* in March.

"Listen to this," Carol said. "'Have you seen any armadillos in Colorado? Can you send me one, because the chameleon got lost. Daddy and I looked everywhere in the house for him. But if you send me the armadillo it will be big enough not to get lost.' New paragraph. 'I got ninety in spelling but only seventy in arithmetic. I hate it. I hate the teacher. Well I must be closing. Love to you and to Abby. Rindy. XX. P. S. Thank you very much for the leather shirt. Daddy bought me a two-wheel bike regular size that he said I was too small for Christmas. I am not too small. It is a beautiful bike.' Period. What's the use? Harge can always top me." Carol put the letter down and picked up Abby's.

"Why did Rindy say 'Love to you and to Abby'?" Therese asked. "Does she think you're with Abby?"

"No." Carol's wooden letter opener had stopped halfway through Abby's envelope. "I suppose she thinks I write to her," she said, and finished slitting the envelope.

"I mean, Harge wouldn't have told her that, would he?"

"No, darling," Carol said preoccupiedly, reading Abby's letter.

Therese got up and crossed the room, and stood by the window looking out at the mountains. She should write to Harkevy this afternoon, she thought, and ask him if there was a chance of an assistant's job with his group in March. She began composing the letter in her head. The mountains looked back at her like majestic red lions, staring down their noses. Twice she heard Carol laugh, but she did not read any of the letter aloud to her.

"No news?" Therese asked when she was finished.

"No news."

Carol taught her to drive on the roads around the foot of the mountains, where a car almost never passed. Therese learned faster than she had ever learned anything before, and after a couple of days, Carol let her drive in Colorado Springs. In Denver, she took a test and got a license. Carol said she could do half the driving back to New York, if she wanted to.

• • •

He was sitting one evening at the dinner hour at a table by himself to the left of Carol and behind her. Therese choked on nothing, and put her fork down. Her heart began to beat as if it would hammer its way out of her chest. How had she gotten halfway through the meal without seeing him? She lifted her eyes to Carol's face and saw Carol watching her, reading her with the gray eyes that were not quite so calm as a moment ago. Carol had stopped in the middle of saying something.

"Have a cigarette," Carol said, offering her one, lighting it for her. "He doesn't know that you can recognize him, does he?"

"No."

"Well, don't let him find out." Carol smiled at her, lighted her own cigarette, and looked away in the opposite direction from the detective. "Just take it easy," Carol added in the same tone.

It was easy to say, easy to have thought she could look at him when she saw him next, but what was the use of trying when it was like being struck in the face with a cannon ball?

"No baked Alaska tonight?" Carol said, looking at the menu. "That breaks my heart. You know what we're going to have?" She called to the waiter. "Walter!"

Walter came smiling, ardent to serve them, just as he did every evening. "Yes, madame."

"Two Remy Martins, please, Walter," Carol told him.

The brandy helped very little, if at all. The detective did not once look at them. He was reading a book that he had propped up on the metal napkin holder, and even now Therese felt a doubt as strong as in the café outside Salt Lake City, an uncertainty that was somehow more horrible than the positive knowledge would be that he was the detective.

"Do we have to go past him, Carol?" Therese asked. There was a door in back of her, into the bar.

"Yes. That's the way we go out." Carol's eyebrows lifted with her smile, exactly as on any other night. "He can't do anything to us. Do you expect him to pull a gun?"

Therese followed her, passed within twelve inches of the man whose head was lowered toward his book. Ahead of her she saw Carol's figure bend gracefully as she greeted Mrs. French, who was sitting alone at a table.

"Why didn't you come and join us?" Carol said, and Therese remembered that the two women Mrs. French usually sat with had left today.

Carol even stood there a few moments talking with Mrs. French, and Therese marveled at her but she couldn't stand there herself, and went on, to wait for Carol by the elevators.

Upstairs, Carol found the little instrument fastened up in a corner under the bed table. Carol got the scissors and, using both hands, cut through the wire that disappeared under the carpet.

"Did the hotel people let him in here, do you think?" Therese asked, horrified.

"He probably had a key to fit." Carol yanked the thing loose from the table and dropped it on the carpet, a little black box with a trail of wire. "Look at it, like a rat," she said. "A portrait of Harge." Her face had flushed suddenly.

"Where does it go to?"

"To some room where it's recorded. Probably across the hall. *Bless* these fancy wall-to-wall carpets!"

Carol kicked the Dictaphone toward the center of the room.

Therese looked at the little rectangular box, and thought of it drinking up their words last night. "I wonder how long it's been there?"

"How long do you think he could have been here without your seeing him?"

"Yesterday at the worst." But even as she said it, she knew she could be wrong. She couldn't have seen every face in the hotel.

And Carol was shaking her head. "Would it take him nearly two weeks to trace us from Salt Lake City to here? No, he just decided to have dinner with us tonight." Carol turned from the bookshelf with a glass of brandy in her hand. The flush had left her face. Now she even smiled a little at Therese. "Clumsy fellow, isn't he?" She sat down on the bed, swung a pillow behind her and leaned back. "Well, we've been here just about long enough, haven't we?"

"When do you want to go?"

"Maybe tomorrow. We'll get ourselves packed in the morning and take off after lunch. What do you think?"

Later, they went down to the car and took a drive, westward into the darkness. We shall not go farther west, Therese thought. She could not stamp out the panic that danced in the very core of her, that she felt due to something gone before, something that had happened long ago, not now, not this. She was uneasy, but Carol was not. Carol was not merely pretending coolness, she really was not afraid. Carol said, what could he do, after all, but she simply didn't want to be spied upon.

"One other thing," Carol said. "Try and find out what kind of car he's in."

That night, talking over the road map about their route tomorrow, talking as matter of factly as a couple of strangers, Therese thought surely tonight would not be like last night. But when they kissed good night in bed, Therese felt their sudden release, that leap of response in both of them, as if their bodies were of some materials which put together inevitably created desire.

## *nineteen*

Therese could not find out what kind of car he had, because the cars were locked in separate garages, and though she had a view of the garages from the sunroom, she did not see him come out that morning. Neither did they see him at lunchtime.

Mrs. French insisted that they come into her room for a cordial, when she heard they were leaving. "You must have a stirrup cup," Mrs. French said to Carol. "Why, I haven't even got your address yet!"

Therese remembered that they had promised to exchange flower bulbs. She remembered a long conversation in the car one day about bulbs that had cemented their friendship. Carol was incredibly patient to the last. One would never have guessed, seeing Carol sitting on Mrs. French's sofa with the little glass Mrs. French kept filling, that she was in a hurry to get away. Mrs. French kissed them both on the cheek when they said good-bye.

From Denver, they took a highway northward toward Wyoming. They stopped for coffee at the kind of place they always liked, an ordinary restaurant with a counter and a jukebox. They put nickels into the jukebox, but it was not the same as before. Therese knew it would not be the same for the rest of the trip, though Carol talked of going to Washington even yet, and perhaps up into Canada. Therese could feel that Carol's goal was New York.

They spent the first night in a tourist camp that was built like a circle of tepees. While they were undressing, Carol looked up at the ceiling where the tepee poles came to a point, and said boredly, "The trouble some idiots go to," and for some reason it struck Therese as hysterically funny. She laughed until Carol got tired of it and threatened to make her drink a tumbler of brandy, if she didn't stop. And Therese was still smiling, standing by the window with a brandy in her hand, waiting for Carol to come out of the shower, when she saw a car drive up beside the large office tepee and stop. After a moment, the man who had gone into the office came out and looked around in the dark area within the circle of tepees, and it was his prowling step that arrested her attention. She was suddenly sure without seeing his face or even his figure very clearly that he was the detective.

"Carol!" she called.

Carol pushed the shower curtain aside and glanced at her and stopped drying herself. "Is it—"

"I don't know, but I think so," she said, and saw the anger spread slowly over Carol's face and stiffen it, and it shocked Therese to sobriety, as if she had just realized an insult, to herself or to Carol.

"Chr-rist!" Carol said, and flung the towel at the floor. She drew on her robe and tied the belt of it. "Well—what's he doing?"

"I think he's stopping here." Therese stood back at the edge of the window. "His car's still in front of the office, anyway. If we turn out the light, I'll be able to see a lot better."

Carol groaned. "Oh, don't. I couldn't. It bores me," she said with the utmost boredom and disgust.

And Therese smiled, twistedly, and checked another insane impulse to laugh, because Carol would have been furious if she had laughed. Then she saw the car roll under the garage door of a tepee across the circle. "Yes, he's stopping here. It's a black two-door sedan."

Carol sat down on the bed with a sigh. She smiled at Therese, a quick smile of fatigue and boredom, of resignation and helplessness and anger. "Take your shower. And then get dressed again."

"But I don't know if it's him at all."

"That's just the hell of it, darling."

Therese took a shower and lay down in her clothes beside Carol. Carol had turned out the light. She was smoking cigarettes in the dark, and said nothing to her until finally she touched her arm and said, "Let's go." It was three-thirty when they drove out of the tourist camp. They had paid their bill in advance. There was no light anywhere, and unless the detective was watching them with his light out, no one had observed them.

"What do you want to do, sleep again somewhere?" Carol asked her.

"No. Do you?"

"No. Let's see how much distance we can make." She pressed the pedal to the floor. The road was clear and smooth as far as the headlights swept.

As dawn was breaking, a highway patrolman stopped them for speeding, and Carol had to pay a twenty-dollar fine in a town called Central City, Nebraska. They lost thirty miles by having to follow the patrolman back to the little town, but Carol went through with it without a word, unlike herself, unlike the time she had argued and cajoled the patrolman out of an arrest for speeding, and a New Jersey speed cop at that.

"Irritating," Carol said when they got back into the car, and that was all she said, for hours.

Therese offered to drive, but Carol said she wanted to. And the flat Nebraska prairie spread out before them, yellow with wheat stubble, brown-splotched with bare earth and stone, deceptively warm-looking in the white winter sun. Because they went a little slower now, Therese had a panicky sensation of not moving at all, as if the earth drifted under them and they stood still. She watched the road behind them for another patrol car, for the detective's car, and for the nameless, shapeless thing she felt pursuing them from Colorado Springs. She watched the land and the sky for the meaningless events that her mind insisted on attaching significance to, the buzzard that banked slowly in the sky, the direction of a tangle of weeds that bounced over a rutted field before the wind, and whether a chimney had smoke or not. Around eight o'clock, an irresistible sleepiness weighted her eyelids and clouded her head, so she felt scarcely any surprise when she saw a car behind them like the car she watched for, a two-door sedan of dark color.

"There's a car like that behind us," she said. "It's got a yellow license plate."

Carol said nothing for a minute, but she glanced in the mirror and blew her breath out through pursed lips. "I doubt it. If it is, he's a better man than I thought." She was slowing down. "If I let him pass, do you think you can recognize him?"

"Yes." Couldn't she recognize the blurriest glimpse of him by now?

Carol slowed almost to a stop and took the road map and laid it across the wheel and looked at it. The other car approached, and it was him inside, and went by.

"Yes," Therese said. The man hadn't glanced at her.

Carol pressed the gas pedal down. "You're sure, are you?"

"Positive." Therese watched the speedometer go up to sixty-five and over. "What are you going to do?"

"Speak to him."

Carol slacked her speed as they closed the distance. They drew alongside of the detective's car, and he turned to look at them, the wide straight mouth unchanging, the eyes like round gray dots, expressionless as the mouth. Carol waved her hand downward. The man's car slowed.

"Roll your window down," Carol said to Therese.

The detective's car pulled over into the sandy shoulder of the road and stopped.

Carol stopped her car with its rear wheels on the highway, and spoke across Therese. "Do you like our company or what?" she asked.

The man got out of his car and closed his door. Some three yards of ground separated the cars, and the detective crossed half of it and stood. His dead little eyes had darkish rims around their gray irises, like a doll's blank and steady eyes. He was not young. His face looked worn by the weathers he had driven it through, and the shadows of his beard deepened the bent creases on either side of his mouth.

"I'm doing my job, Mrs. Aird," he said.

"That's pretty obvious. It's nasty work, isn't it?"

The detective tapped a cigarette on his thumbnail and lighted it in the gusty wind with a slowness that suggested a stage performance. "At least it's nearly over."

"Then why don't you leave us alone," Carol said, her voice as tense as the arm that supported her on the steering wheel.

"Because I have orders to follow you on this trip. But if you're going back to New York, I won't have to anymore. I advise you to go back, Mrs. Aird. Are you going back now?"

"No, I'm not."

"Because I've got some information—information that I'd say was in your interest to go back and take care of."

"Thanks," Carol said cynically. "Thanks so much for telling me. It's not in my plans to go back just yet. But I can give you my itinerary, so you can leave us alone and catch up on your sleep."

The detective looked at her with a false and meaningless smile, not like a person at all, but like a machine wound up and set on a course. "I think you'll go back to New York. I'm giving you sound advice. Your child is at stake. I suppose you know that, don't you?"

"My child is my property!"

A crease twitched in his cheek. "A human being is not property, Mrs. Aird."

Carol raised her voice. "Are you going to tag along the rest of the way?"

"Are you going back to New York?"

"No."

"I think you will," the detective said, and he turned away slowly toward his car.

Carol stepped on the starter. She reached for Therese's hand and squeezed it for a moment in reassurance, and then the car shot forward. Therese sat up with her elbows on her knees and her hands pressed to her forehead, yielding to a shame and shock she had never known before, that she had repressed before the detective.

"Carol!"

Carol was crying, silently. Therese looked at the downward curve of her lips that was not like Carol at all, but rather like a small girl's twisted grimace of crying. She stared incredulously at the tear that rolled over Carol's cheekbone.

"Get me a cigarette," Carol said.

When Therese handed it to her, lighted, she had wiped the tear away, and it was over. Carol drove for a minute, slowly, smoking the cigarette.

"Crawl in the back and get the gun," Carol said.

Therese did not move for a moment.

Carol glanced at her. "Will you?"

Therese slid agilely in her slacks over the seat back, and dragged the navy blue suitcase onto the seat. She opened the clasps and got out the sweater with the gun.

"Just hand it to me," Carol said calmly. "I want it in the side pocket." She reached her hand over her shoulder, and Therese put the white handle of the gun into it, and crawled back into the front seat.

The detective was still following them, half a mile behind them, back of the horse and farm wagon that had turned into the highway from a dirt road. Carol held Therese's hand and drove with her left hand. Therese looked down at the faintly freckled fingers that dug their strong cool tips into her palm.

"I'm going to talk to him again," Carol said, and pressed the gas pedal down steadily. "If you want to get out, I'll put you off at the next gas station or something and come back for you."

"I don't want to leave you," Therese said. Carol was going to demand the detective's records, and Therese had a vision of Carol hurt, of his pulling a gun with an expert's oily speed and firing it before Carol could even pull the trigger. But those things didn't happen, wouldn't happen, she thought, and she set her teeth. She kneaded Carol's hand in her fingers.

"All right. And don't worry. I just want to talk to him." She swung the car suddenly into a smaller road off the highway to the left. The road went up between sloping fields, and turned and went through woods. Carol drove fast, though the road was bad. "He's coming on, isn't he?"

"Yes."

There was one farmhouse set in the rolling hills, and then nothing but scrubby, rocky land and the road that kept disappearing around the curves before them. Where the road clung to a sloping hill, Carol went round a curve and stopped the car carelessly, half in the road.

She reached for the side pocket and pulled the gun out. She opened something on it, and Therese saw the bullets inside. Then Carol looked through the windshield, and let her hands with the gun fall in her lap. "I'd better not, better not," she said quickly, and dropped the gun back in the side pocket. Then she pulled the car up, and straightened it by the side of the hill. "Stay in the car," she said to Therese, and got out.

Therese heard the detective's car. Carol walked slowly toward the sound, and then the detective's car came around the curve, not fast, but his brakes shrieked, and Carol stepped to the side of the road. Therese opened the door slightly, and leaned on the windowsill.

The man got out of his car. "Now what?" he said, raising his voice in the wind.

"What do you think?" Carol came a little closer to him. "I'd like everything you've got about me—Dictaphone tapes and whatever."

The detective's brows hardly rose over the pale dots of his eyes. He leaned against the front fender of his car, smirking with his wide thin mouth. He glanced at Therese and back at Carol. "Everything's sent away. I haven't a thing but a few notes. About times and places."

"All right, I'd like to have them."

"You mean, you want to buy them?"

"I didn't say that, I said I'd like to have them. Do you prefer to sell them?"

"I'm not one you can buy off," he said.

"What're you doing this for anyway, if not money?" Carol asked impatiently. "Why not make a little more? What'll you take for what you've got?"

He folded his arms. "I told you everything's sent away. You'd be wasting your money."

"I don't think you mailed the Dictaphone records yet from Colorado Springs," Carol said.

"No?" he asked sarcastically.

"No. I'll give you whatever you ask for them."

He looked Carol up and down, glanced at Therese, and again his mouth widened.

"Get them—tapes, records or whatever they are," Carol said, and the man moved.

He walked around his car to the luggage compartment, and Therese heard his keys jingle as he opened it. Therese got out of the car, unable to sit there any longer. She walked to within a few feet of Carol and stopped. The detective was reaching for something in a big suitcase. When he straightened up, the raised lid of the compartment knocked his hat off. He stepped on the brim to hold it from the wind. He had something in one hand now, too small to see.

"There's two," he said. "I guess they're worth five hundred. They'd be worth more if there weren't more of them in New York."

"You're a fine salesman. I don't believe you," Carol said.

"Why? They're in a hurry for them in New York." He picked up his hat, and closed the luggage compartment. "But they've got enough now. I told you you'd better go back to New York, Mrs. Aird." He ground his cigarette out in the dirt, twisting his toe in front of him. "Are you going back to New York now?"

"I don't change my mind," Carol said.

The detective shrugged. "I'm not on any side. The sooner you go back to New York, the sooner we call it quits."

"We can call it quits right now. After you give me those, you can take off and keep going in the same direction."

The detective had slowly extended his hand in a fist, like the fist in a guessing game in which there might be nothing. "Are you willing to give me five hundred for these?" he asked.

Carol looked at his hand, then opened her shoulder-strap bag. She took out her billfold, and then her checkbook.

"I prefer cash," he said.

"I haven't got it."

He shrugged again. "All right, I'll take a check."

Carol wrote it, resting it on the fender of his car.

Now as he bent over, watching Carol, Therese could see the little black object in his hand. Therese came closer. The man was spelling his name. When Carol gave him the check, he dropped the two little boxes in her hand.

"How long have you been collecting them?" Carol asked.

"Play them and see."

"I didn't come out here to joke!" Carol said, and her voice broke.

He smiled, folding the check. "Don't say I didn't warn you. What you've gotten from me isn't all of it. There's plenty in New York."

Carol fastened her bag, and turned toward her car, not even looking at Therese. Then she stopped and faced the detective again. "If they've got all they want, you can knock off now, can't you? Have I got your promise to do that?"

He was standing with his hand on his car door, watching her. "I'm still on the job, Mrs. Aird—still working for my office. Unless you want to catch a plane for home now. Or for some other place. Give me the slip. I'll have to tell my office something—not having the last few days at Colorado Springs—something more exciting than this."

"Oh, let them invent something exciting!"

The detective's smile showed a little of his teeth. He got back into his car. He shoved his gear, put his head out to see behind him, and backed the car in a quick turn. He drove off toward the highway.

The sound of his motor faded fast. Carol walked slowly toward the car, got in and sat staring through the windshield at the dry rise of earth a few yards ahead. Her face was as blank as if she had fainted.

Therese was beside her. She put her arm around Carol's shoulder. She squeezed the cloth shoulder of the coat, and felt as useless as any stranger.

"Oh, I think it's mostly bluff," Carol said suddenly.

But it made Carol's face gray, had taken the energy out of her voice.

Carol opened her hand and looked at the two little round boxes. "Here's as good a place as any." She got out of the car, and Therese followed her. Carol opened a box and took out the coil of tape that looked like celluloid. "Tiny, isn't it. I suppose it burns. Let's burn it."

Therese struck the match in the shelter of the car. The tape burned fast, and Therese dropped it on the ground, and then the wind blew it out. Carol said not to bother, they could throw both of them in a river.

"What time is it?" Carol asked.

"Twenty to twelve." She got back in the car, and Carol started immediately, back down the road toward the highway.

"I'm going to call Abby in Omaha, and then my lawyer."

Therese looked at the road map. Omaha was the next big town, if they made a slight turn south. Carol looked tired, and Therese felt her anger, still unappeased, in the silence she kept. The car jolted over a rut, and Therese heard the bump and clink of the can of beer that rolled somewhere under the front seat, the beer they had not been able to open that first day. She was hungry, had been sickly hungry for hours.

"How about my driving?"

"All right," Carol said tiredly, relaxing as if she surrendered. She slowed the car quickly.

Therese slid across her, under the wheel. "And how about stopping for a breakfast?"

"I couldn't eat."

"Or a drink."

"Let's get it in Omaha."

Therese sent the speedometer up to sixty-five, and held it just under seventy. It was Highway 30. Then 275 into Omaha, and the road was not first-class. "You don't believe him about Dictaphone records in New York, do you?"

"Don't talk about it!—I'm sick of it!"

Therese squeezed the wheel, then deliberately relaxed. She sensed a tremendous sorrow hanging over them, ahead of them, that was just beginning to reveal the edge of itself, that they were driving into. She remembered the detective's face and the barely legible expression that she realized now was malice. It was malice she had seen in his smile, even as he said he was on no side, and she could feel in him a desire that was actually personal to separate them, because he knew they were together. She had seen just now what she had only sensed before, that the whole world was ready to be their enemy, and suddenly what she and Carol had together seemed no longer love or anything happy but a monster between them, with each of them caught in a fist.

"I'm thinking of that check," Carol said.

It fell like another stone inside her. "Do you think they're going over the house?" Therese asked.

"Possibly. Just possibly."

"I don't think they'd find it. It's way under the runner." But there was the letter in the book. A curious pride lifted her spirit for an instant, and vanished. It was a beautiful letter, and she would rather they found it than the check, though as to incrimination they would probably have the same weight, and they would make the one as dirty as the other. The letter she had never given, and the check she had never cashed. It was more likely they would find the letter, certainly. Therese could not bring herself to tell Carol of the letter, whether from plain cowardice or a desire to spare Carol any more now, she didn't know. She saw a bridge ahead. "There's a river," she said. "How about here?"

"Good enough." Carol handed her the little boxes. She had put the half-burned tape back in its box.

Therese got out and flung them over the metal rail, and did not watch. She looked at the young man in overalls walking onto the bridge from the other side, hating the senseless antagonism in herself against him.

Carol telephoned from a hotel in Omaha. Abby was not at home, and Carol left a message that she would call at six o'clock that evening, when Abby was expected. Carol said it was of no use to call her lawyer now, because he would be out to lunch until after two by their time. Carol wanted to wash up, and then have a drink.

They had old-fashioneds in the bar of the hotel, in complete silence. Therese asked for a second when Carol did, but Carol said she should eat something instead. The waiter told Carol that food was not served in the bar.

"She wants something to eat," Carol said firmly.

"The dining room is across the lobby, madame, and there's a coffee shop—"

"Carol, I can wait," Therese said.

"Will you please bring me the menu? She prefers to eat here," Carol said with a glance at the waiter.

The waiter hesitated, then said, "Yes, madame," and went to get the menu.

While Therese ate scrambled eggs and sausage, Carol had her third drink. Finally, Carol said in a tone of hopelessness, "Darling, can I ask you to forgive me?"

The tone hurt Therese more than the question. "I love you, Carol."

"But do you see what it means?"

"Yes." But that moment of defeat in the car, she thought, that had been only a moment, as this time now was only a situation. "I don't see why it should mean this forever. I don't see how this can destroy anything," she said earnestly.

Carol took her hand down from her face and sat back, and now in spite of the tiredness she looked as Therese always thought of her—the eyes that could be tender and hard at once as they tested her, the intelligent red lips strong and soft, though the upper lip trembled the least bit now.

"Do you?" Therese asked, and she realized suddenly it was a question as big as the one Carol had asked her without words in the room in Waterloo. In fact, the same question.

"No. I think you're right," Carol said. "You make me realize it."

Carol went to telephone. It was three o'clock. Therese got the bill, then sat there waiting, wondering when it was going to be over, whether the reassuring word would come from Carol's lawyer or from Abby, or whether it was going to get worse before it got better. Carol was gone about half an hour.

"My lawyer hasn't heard anything," she said. "And I didn't tell him anything. I can't. I'll have to write it."

"I thought you would."

"Oh, you did," Carol said with her first smile that day. "What do you say we get a room here? I don't feel like traveling any more."

Carol had her lunch sent up to their room. They both lay down to take a nap, but when Therese awakened at a quarter to five, Carol was gone. Therese glanced around the room, noticing Carol's black gloves on the dressing table, and her moccasins side by side near the armchair. Therese sighed, tremulously, unrefreshed by her sleep. She opened the window and looked down. It was the seventh or eighth floor, she couldn't remember which. A streetcar crawled past the front of the hotel, and people on the sidewalk moved in every direction, with legs on either side of them, and it crossed her mind to jump. She looked off at the drab little skyline of gray buildings and closed her eyes on it. Then she turned around and Carol was in the room, standing by the door, watching her.

"Where have you been?" Therese asked.

"Writing that damned letter."

Carol crossed the room and caught Therese in her arms. Therese felt Carol's nails through the back of her jacket.

When Carol went to the telephone, Therese left the room and wandered down the hall toward the elevators. She went down to the lobby and sat there reading an article on weevils in the *Corngrower's Gazette*, and wondered if Abby knew all that about corn weevils. She watched the clock, and after twenty-five minutes went upstairs again.

Carol was lying on the bed, smoking a cigarette. Therese waited for her to speak.

"Darling, I've got to go to New York," Carol said.

Therese had been sure of that. She came to the foot of the bed. "What else did Abby say?"

"She saw the fellow named Bob Haversham again." Carol raised herself on her elbow. "But he certainly doesn't know as much as I do at this point. Nobody seems to know anything, except that trouble's brewing. Nothing much can happen until I get there. But I've got to be there."

"Of course." Bob Haversham was the friend of Abby's who worked in Harge's firm in Newark, not a close friend either of Abby's or Harge's, just a link, a slim link between the two of them, the one person who might know something of what Harge was doing, if he could recognize a detective, or overhear part of a telephone call, in Harge's office. It was worth almost nothing, Therese felt.

"Abby's going to get the check," Carol said, sitting up on the bed, reaching for her moccasins.

"Has she got a key?"

"I wish she had. She's got to get it from Florence. But that'll be all right. I told her to tell Florence I wanted a couple of things sent to me."

"Can you tell her to get a letter, too? I left a letter to you in a book in my room. I'm sorry I didn't tell you before. I didn't know you were going to have Abby go there."

Carol gave her a frowning glance. "Anything else?"

"No. I'm sorry I didn't tell you before."

Carol sighed, and stood up. "Oh, let's not worry anymore. I doubt if they'll bother about the house, but I'll tell Abby about the letter anyway. Where is it?"

"In the *Oxford Book of English Verse*. I think I left it on top of the bureau." She watched Carol glance around the room, looking anywhere but at her.

"I don't want to stay here tonight after all," Carol said.

• • •

Half an hour later, they were in the car going eastward. Carol wanted to reach Des Moines that night. After a silence of more than an hour, Carol suddenly stopped the car at the edge of the road, bent her head, and said, "Damn!"

She could see the darkish sinks under Carol's eyes in the glare of passing cars. Carol hadn't slept at all last night. "Let's go back to that last town," Therese said. "It's still about seventy-five miles to Des Moines."

"Do you want to go to Arizona?" Carol asked her, as if all they had to do was turn around.

"Oh, Carol—why talk about it?" A feeling of despair came over her suddenly. Her hands were shaking as she lighted a cigarette. She gave the cigarette to Carol.

"Because I want to talk about it. Can you take another three weeks off?"

"Of course." Of course, of course. What else mattered except being with Carol, anywhere, anyhow? There was the Harkevy show in March. Harkevy might recommend her for a job somewhere else, but the jobs were uncertain and Carol was not.

"I shouldn't have to stay in New York more than a week at most, because the divorce is all set. Fred, my lawyer, said so today. So why don't we have a few more weeks in Arizona? Or New Mexico? I don't want to hang around New York the rest of the winter." Carol drove slowly. Her eyes were different now. They had come alive, like her voice.

"Of course I'd like to. Anywhere."

"All right. Come on. Let's get to Des Moines. How about you driving a while?"

They changed places. It was a little before midnight when they got to Des Moines and found a hotel room.

"Why should you go back to New York at all?" Carol asked her. "You could keep the car and wait for me somewhere like Tucson or Santa Fe, and I could fly back."

"And leave you?" Therese turned from the mirror where she was brushing her hair.

Carol smiled. "What do you mean, leave me?"

It had taken Therese by surprise, and now she saw an expression on Carol's face, even though Carol looked at her intently, that made her feel shut off, as if Carol had thrust her away in a back corner of her mind to make room for something more important. "Just leave you now, I meant," Therese said, turning back to the mirror. "No, it might be a good idea. It's quicker for you."

"I thought you might prefer staying somewhere in the West. Unless you want to do something in New York those few days." Carol's voice was casual.

"I don't." She dreaded the cold days in Manhattan, when Carol would be too busy to see her. And she thought of the detective. If Carol flew, she wouldn't be haunted by his trailing her. She tried to imagine it already, Carol arriving in the East alone, to face something she didn't yet know, something impossible to prepare for. She imagined herself in Santa Fe, waiting for a telephone call, waiting for a letter from Carol. But to be two thousand miles away from Carol, she could not imagine that so easily. "Only a week, Carol?" she asked, drawing the comb along her parting again, flicking the long, fine hair to one side. She had gained weight, but her face was thinner, she noticed suddenly, and it pleased her. She looked older.

In the mirror, she saw Carol come up behind her, and there was no answer but the pleasure of Carol's arms sliding around her, which made it impossible to think, and Therese twisted away more suddenly than she meant to, and stood by the corner of the dressing table looking at Carol, bewildered for a moment by the elusiveness of what they talked about, time and space, and the four feet that separated them now and the two thousand miles. She gave her hair another stroke. "Only about a week?"

"That's what I said," Carol replied with a smile in her eyes, but Therese heard the same hardness in it as in her own question, as if they exchanged challenges. "If you mind keeping the car, I can have it driven east."

"I don't mind keeping it."

"And don't worry about the detective. I'll wire Harge that I'm on my way."

"I won't worry about that." How could Carol be so cold about it, Therese wondered, thinking of everything else but their leaving each other? She put the hairbrush down on the dressing table.

"Therese, do you think I'm going to enjoy it?"

And Therese thought of the detectives, the divorce, the hostility, all Carol had to face. Carol touched her cheek, pressed both palms hard against her cheeks so her mouth opened like a fish's, and Therese had to smile. Therese stood by the dressing table and watched her, watching every move of her hands, of her feet as she peeled off her stockings and stepped into her moccasins again. There were no words, she thought, after this point. What else did they need to explain, or ask, or promise in words? They did not even need to see each other's eyes. Therese watched her pick up the telephone, and then she lay face down on the bed, while Carol made her plane reservation for tomorrow, one ticket, one way, tomorrow at eleven a. M.

"Where do you think you'll go?" Carol asked her.

"I don't know. I might go back to Sioux Falls."

"South Dakota?" Carol smiled at her. "You wouldn't prefer Santa Fe? It's warmer."

"I'll wait and see it with you."

"Not Colorado Springs?"

"No!" Therese laughed, and got up. She took her toothbrush into the bathroom. "I might even take a job somewhere for a week."

"What kind of a job?"

"Any kind. Just to keep me from thinking of you, you know."

"I want you to think of me. Not a job in a department store."

"No." Therese stood by the bathroom door, watching Carol take off her slip and put her robe on.

"You're not worrying about money again, are you?"

Therese slid her hands into her robe pockets and crossed her feet. "If I'm broke, I don't care. I'll start worrying when it's used up."

"I'm going to give you a couple of hundred tomorrow for the car."

Carol pulled Therese's nose as she passed her. "And you're not to use that car to pick up any strangers." Carol went into the bathroom and turned on the shower.

Therese came in after her. "I thought I was using this john."

"I'm using it, but I'll let you come in."

"Oh, thanks." Therese took off her robe as Carol did.

"Well?" Carol said.

"Well?" Therese stepped under the shower.

"Of all the nerve." Carol got under it, too, and twisted Therese's arm behind her, but Therese only giggled.

Therese wanted to embrace her, kiss her, but her free arm reached out convulsively and dragged Carol's head against her, under the stream of water, and there was the horrible sound of a foot slipping.

"Stop it, we'll fall!" Carol shouted. "For Christ's sake, can't two people take a shower in peace?"

## *twenty*

In Sioux Falls, Therese stopped the car in front of the hotel they had stayed in before, the Warrior Hotel. It was nine-thirty in the evening. Carol had got home about an hour ago, Therese thought. She was to call Carol at midnight.

She took a room, had her bags carried up, then went out for a walk through the main street. There was a movie house, and it occurred to her she had never seen a movie with Carol. She went in. But she was in no mood to follow the picture, even though there was a woman in it whose voice was a little like Carol's, not at all like the flat nasal voices she heard all around her. She thought of Carol, over a thousand miles away now, thought of sleeping alone tonight, and she got up and wandered out on the street again. There was the drugstore where Carol had bought paper tissues and toothpaste one morning. And the corner where Carol had looked up and read the street names—Fifth and Nebraska streets. She bought a pack of cigarettes at the same drugstore, walked back to the hotel and sat in the lobby, smoking, savoring the first cigarette since she had left Carol, savoring the forgotten state of being alone. It was only a physical state. She really did not feel at all alone. She read some newspapers for a while, then took the letters from Danny and Phil that had come in the last days at Colorado Springs out of her handbag and glanced over them:

> . . . I saw Richard two nights ago in the Palermo all by himself [Phil's letter said]. I asked about you and he said he wasn't writing to you. I gather there has been a small rupture, but I didn't press for information. He was in no mood for talking. And we are not too chummy lately, as you know . . . Have been talking you up to an angel named Francis Puckett who will put up fifty thousand if a certain play from France comes over in April. Shall keep you posted, as there is not even a producer yet . . . Danny sends his love, I am sure. He is leaving soon for somewhere probably, he has that look, and I'll have to scout for new winter quarters or find a roommate . . . Did you get the clippings I sent you on *Small Rain*?
>
> Best, Phil

Danny's short letter was:

> Dear Therese,
>
> There is a possibility I may go out to the Coast at the end of the month to take a job in California. I must decide between this (a lab job) and an offer in a commercial chemical place in Maryland. But if I could see you in Colorado or anywhere else for a while, I would leave a little early. Shall probably take the California job, as I think it has better prospects. So would you let me know where you'll be? It doesn't matter. There are a lot of ways of getting to California. If your friend wouldn't mind, it would be nice to spend a few days with you somewhere. I'll be in New York until the 28th of February anyway.
>
> Love,
> Danny

She had not yet answered him. She would send him an address tomorrow, as soon as she found a room somewhere in the town. But as to the next destination, she would have to talk to Carol about that. And when would Carol be able to say? She wondered what Carol might already have found tonight in New Jersey, and Therese's courage sank dismally. She reached for a newspaper and looked at the date. February fifteenth. Twenty-nine days since she had left New York with Carol. Could it be so few days?

Upstairs in her room, she put the call through to Carol, and bathed and got into pajamas. Then the telephone rang.

"Hel-*lo*," Carol said, as if she had been waiting a long while. "What's the name of that hotel?"

"The Warrior. But I'm not going to stay here."

"You didn't pick up any strangers on the road, did you?"

Therese laughed. Carol's slow voice went through her as if she touched her. "What's the news?" Therese asked.

"Tonight? Nothing. The house is freezing and Florence can't get here till day after tomorrow. Abby's here. Do you want to say hello to her?"

"Not right there with you."

"No-o. Upstairs in the green room with the door shut."

"I *don't* really want to talk to her now."

Carol wanted to know everything she had done, how the roads were, and whether she had on the yellow pajamas or the blue ones. "I'll have a hard time getting to sleep tonight without you."

"Yes." Immediately, out of nowhere, Therese felt tears pressing behind her eyes.

"Can't you say anything but yes?"

"I love you."

Carol whistled. Then silence. "Abby got the check, darling, but no letter. She missed my wire, but there isn't any letter anyway."

"Did you find the book?"

"We found the book, but there's nothing in it."

Therese wondered if the letter could be in her own apartment after all. But she had a picture of the letter in the book, marking a place. "Do you think anybody's been through the house?"

"No, I can tell by various things. Don't worry about that. Will you?"

A moment later, Therese slid down into bed and pulled her light out. Carol had asked her to call tomorrow night, too. For a while the sound of Carol's voice was in her ears. Then a melancholy began to seep into her. She lay on her back with her arms straight at her sides, with a sense of empty space all around her, as if she were laid out ready for the grave, and then she fell asleep.

• • •

The next morning, Therese found a room she liked in a house on one of the streets that ran uphill, a large front room with a bay window full of plants and white curtains. There was a four-poster bed and an oval hooked rug on the floor. The woman said it was seven dollars a week, but Therese said she was not sure if she would be here a week, so she had better take it by the day.

"That'll be the same thing," the woman said. "Where're you from?"

"New York."

"Are you going to live here?"

"No. I'm just waiting for a friend to join me."

"Man or woman?"

Therese smiled. "A woman," she said. "Is there any space in those garages in back? I've got a car with me."

The woman said there were two garages empty, and that she didn't charge for the garages, if people lived here. She was not old, but she stooped a little and her figure was frail. Her name was Mrs. Elizabeth Cooper. She had been keeping roomers for fifteen years, she said, and two of the three she had started with were still here.

The same day, she made the acquaintance of Dutch Huber and his wife who ran the diner near the public library. He was a skinny man of about fifty with small curious blue eyes. His wife Edna was fat and did the cooking, and talked a great deal less than he. Dutch had worked in New York for a while years ago. He asked her questions about sections of the city she happened not to know at all, while she mentioned places Dutch had never heard of or had forgotten, and somehow the slow, dragging conversation made them both laugh. Dutch asked her if she would like to go with him and his wife to the motorcycle races that were to be held a few miles out of town on Saturday, and Therese said yes.

She bought cardboard and glue and worked on the first of the models she meant to show Harkevy when she got back to New York. She had it nearly done when she went out at eleven-thirty to call Carol from the Warrior.

Carol was not in and no one answered. Therese tried until one o'clock, then went back to Mrs. Cooper's house.

Therese reached her the next morning around ten-thirty. Carol said she had talked over everything with her lawyer the day before, but there was nothing she or her lawyer could do until they knew Harge's next move. Carol was a little short with her, because she had a luncheon appointment in New York and a letter to write first. She seemed anxious for the first time about what Harge was doing. She had tried to call him twice without being able to reach him. But it was her brusqueness that disturbed Therese most of all.

"You haven't changed your mind about anything," Therese said.

"Of course not, darling. I'm giving a party tomorrow night. I'll miss you."

Therese tripped on the hotel threshold as she went out, and she felt the first hollow wave of loneliness break over her. What would she be doing tomorrow night? Reading in the library until it closed at nine? Working on another set? She went over the names of the people Carol had said were coming to the party—Max and Clara Tibbett, the couple who had a greenhouse on some highway near Carol's house and whom Therese had met once, Carol's friend Tessie she had never met, and Stanley McVeigh, the man Carol had been with the evening they went to Chinatown. Carol hadn't mentioned Abby.

And Carol hadn't said to call tomorrow.

She walked on, and the last moment she had seen Carol came back as if it were happening in front of her eyes again. Carol waving from the door of the plane at the Des Moines airport, Carol already small and far away, because Therese had had to stand back of the wire fence across the field. The ramp had been moved away, but Therese had thought, there were still a few seconds of time before they closed the door, and then Carol had appeared again, just long enough to stand still in the doorway for a second, to find her again, and make the gesture of blowing her a kiss. But it meant an absurd lot that she had come back.

• • •

Therese drove out to the motorcycle races on Saturday, and took Dutch and Edna with her, because Carol's car was bigger. Afterward, they invited her to supper at their house, but she did not accept. There hadn't been a letter from Carol that day, and she had expected a note at least. Sunday depressed her, and even the drive she took up the Big Sioux River to Dell Rapids in the afternoon did not change the scene inside her mind.

Monday morning, she sat in the library reading plays. Then around two, when the noonday rush was slacking off in Dutch's diner, she went in and had some tea, and talked with Dutch while she played the songs on the jukebox that she and Carol had used to play. She had told Dutch that the car belonged to the friend for whom she was waiting. And gradually, Dutch's intermittent questions led her to tell him that Carol lived in New Jersey, that she would probably fly out, that Carol wanted to go to New Mexico.

"Carol does?" Dutch said, turning to her as he polished a glass.

Then a strange resentment rose in Therese because he had said her name, and she made a resolution not to speak of Carol again at all, not to anyone in the city.

Tuesday the letter came from Carol, nothing but a short note, but it said Fred was more optimistic about everything, and it looked as if there would be nothing but the divorce to worry about and she could probably leave the twenty-fourth of February. Therese began to smile as she read it. She wanted to go out and celebrate with someone, but there was no one, so there was nothing to do but take a walk, have a lonely drink at the bar of the Warrior, and think of Carol five days away. There was no one she would have wanted to be with, except perhaps Danny. Or Stella Overton. Stella was jolly, and though she couldn't have told Stella anything about Carol—whom could she tell?—it would have been good to see her now. She had meant to write Stella a card days ago, but she hadn't yet.

She wrote to Carol late that night.

> The news is wonderful. I celebrated with a single daiquiri at the Warrior. Not that I am conservative, but did you know that one drink has the kick of three when you are alone? . . . I love this town because it all reminds me of you. I know you don't like it any more

than any other town, but that isn't the point. I mean you are here as much as I can bear you to be, not being here . . .

Carol wrote:

I never liked Florence. I say this as a prelude. It seems Florence found the note you wrote to me and sold it to Harge—at a price. She is also responsible for Harge's knowing where we (or at least I) were going, I've no doubt. I don't know what I left around the house or what she might have overheard, I thought I was pretty silent, but if Harge took the trouble to bribe her, and I'm sure he did, there's no telling. They picked us up in Chicago, anyway. Darling, I had no idea how far this thing had gone. To give you the atmosphere—nobody tells me anything, things are just suddenly discovered. If anyone is in possession of the facts, it is Harge. I spoke with him on the phone, and he refuses to tell me anything, which of course is calculated to terrorize me into giving all my ground before the fight has even begun. They don't know me, any of them, if they think I will. The fight of course is over Rindy, and yes, darling, I'm afraid there will be one, and I can't leave the 24th. That much Harge did tell me when he sprang the letter this morning on the phone. I think the letter may be his strongest weapon (the Dictaphone business only went on in Colorado S. so far as I can possibly imagine) hence his letting me know about it. But I can imagine the kind of letter it is, written even before we took off, and there'll be a limit to what even Harge can read into it. Harge is merely threatening—in the peculiar form of silence—hoping I will back out completely as far as Rindy is concerned. I won't, so there will come some kind of a showdown, I hope not in court. Fred is prepared for anything, however. He is wonderful, the only person who talks straight to me, but unfortunately he knows least of all too.

You ask if I miss you. I think of your voice, your hands, and your eyes when you look straight into mine. I remember your courage that I hadn't suspected, and it gives me courage. Will you call me, darling? I don't want to call you if your phone is in the hall. Call me collect around 7 p.m. preferably, which is 6 your time.

And Therese was about to call her that day when a telegram came:

DON'T TELEPHONE FOR A WHILE. EXPLAIN LATER. ALL MY LOVE, DARLING. CAROL.

Mrs. Cooper watched her reading it in the hall. "That from your friend?" she asked.

"Yes."

"Hope nothing's the matter." Mrs. Cooper had a way of peering at people, and Therese lifted her head deliberately.

"No, she's coming," Therese said. "She's been delayed."

## *twenty-one*

Albert Kennedy, Bert to people he liked, lived in a room at the back of the house, and was one of Mrs. Cooper's original lodgers. He was forty-five, a native of San Francisco, and more like a New Yorker than anyone Therese had met in the town, and this fact alone inclined her to avoid him. Often he asked Therese to go to the movies with him, but she had gone only once. She was restless and she preferred to wander about by herself, mostly just looking and thinking, because the days were too cold and windy for any outdoor sketching. And the scenes she had liked at first had grown too stale to sketch, from too much looking, too much waiting. Therese went to the library almost every evening, sat at one of the long tables looking over half a dozen books, and then took a meandering course homeward.

She came back to the house only to wander out again after a while, stiffening herself against the erratic wind, or letting it turn her down streets she would not otherwise have followed. In the lighted windows she would see a girl seated at a piano, in another a man laughing, in another a woman sewing. Then she remembered she could not even call Carol, admitted to herself she did not even know what Carol was doing at this moment, and she felt emptier than the wind. Carol did not tell her everything in her letters, she felt, did not tell her the worst.

In the library, she looked at books with photographs of Europe in them, marble fountains in Sicily, ruins of Greece in sunlight, and she wondered if she and Carol would really ever go there. There was still so much they had not done. There was the first voyage across the Atlantic. There was simply the mornings, mornings anywhere, when she could lift her head from a pillow and see Carol's face, and know that the day was theirs and that nothing would separate them.

And there was the beautiful thing, transfixing the heart and the eyes at once, in the dark window of an antique shop in a street where she had never been. Therese stared at it, feeling it quench some forgotten and nameless thirst inside her. Most of its porcelain surface was painted with small bright lozenges of colored enamel, royal blue, and deep red and green, outlined with coin gold as shiny as silk embroidery, even under its film of dust. There was a gold ring at the rim for the finger. It was a tiny candlestick holder. Who had made it, she wondered, and for whom?

She came back the next morning and bought it to give to Carol.

A letter from Richard had come that morning, forwarded from Colorado Springs. Therese sat down on one of the stone benches in the street where the library was, and opened it. It was on business stationery: The Semco Bottled Gas Company. Cooks—Heats—Makes Ice. Richard's name was at the top as General Manager of the Port Jefferson Branch.

Dear Therese,

I have Danny to thank for telling me where you are. You may think this letter unnecessary and perhaps it is to you. Perhaps you are still in that fog you were when we talked that evening in the cafeteria. But I feel it is necessary to make one thing clear, and that is that I no longer feel the way I did even two weeks ago, and the letter I wrote you last was nothing but a last spasmodic effort, and I knew it was hopeless when I wrote it, and I knew you wouldn't answer and I didn't want you to. I know I had stopped loving you then, and now the upper-most emotion I feel toward you is one that was present from the first—disgust. It is your hanging on to this woman to the exclusion of everyone else, this relationship which I am sure has become sordid and pathological by now, that disgusts me. I know that it will not last, as I said from the first. It is only regrettable that you will be disgusted later yourself, in proportion to how much of your life you waste now with it. It is rootless and infantile, like living on lotus blossoms or some sickening candy instead of the bread and meat of life. I have often thought of those questions you asked me the day we were flying the kite. I wish I had acted then before it was too late, because I loved you enough then to try to rescue you. Now I don't.

People still ask me about you. What do you expect me to tell them? I intend to tell them the truth. Only that way can I get it out of myself—and I can no longer bear to carry it around with me. I have sent a few things you had at the house back to your apartment. The slightest memory or contact with you depresses me, makes me not want to touch you or anything concerned with you. But I am talking sense and very likely you are not understanding a word of it. Except maybe this: I want nothing to do with you.

Richard

She saw Richard's thin soft lips tensed in a straight line as they must have looked when he wrote the letter, a line that still did not keep the tiny, taut curl in the upper lip from showing—she saw his face clearly for a moment, and then it vanished with a little jolt that seemed as muffled and remote from her as the clamor of Richard's letter. She stood up, put the letter back in the envelope, and walked on. She hoped he succeeded in purging himself of her. But she could only imagine him telling other people about her with that curious attitude of passionate participation she had seen in New York before she left. She imagined Richard telling Phil as they stood some evening at the Palermo bar, imagined him telling the Kellys. She wouldn't care at all, whatever he said.

She wondered what Carol was doing now, at ten o'clock, at eleven in New Jersey. Listening to some stranger's accusations? Thinking of her, or was there time for that?

It was a fine day, cold and almost windless, bright with sun. She could take the car and drive somewhere. She had not used the car for three days. Suddenly she realized she did not want to use it. The day she had taken it out and driven it up to ninety on the straight road to Dell Rapids, exultant after a letter from Carol, seemed very long ago.

Mr. Bowen, another of the roomers, was on the front porch when she came back to Mrs. Cooper's house. He was sitting in the sun with his legs wrapped in a blanket and his cap pulled down over his eyes as if he were asleep, but he called out, "Hi, there! How's my girl?"

She stopped and chatted with him for awhile, asked him about his arthritis, trying to be as courteous as Carol had always been with Mrs. French. They found something to laugh at, and she was still smiling when she went to her room. Then the sight of the geranium ended it.

She watered the geranium and set it at the end of the windowsill, where it would get the sun for the longest time. There was even brown at the tips of the smallest leaves at the top. Carol had bought it for her in Des Moines just before she took the plane. The pot of ivy had died already—the man in the shop had warned them it was delicate, but Carol had wanted it anyway—and Therese doubted that the geranium would live. But Mrs. Cooper's motley collection of plants flourished in the bay window.

"I walk and walk around the town," she wrote to Carol, "but I wish I could keep walking in one direction—east—and finally come to you. When can you come, Carol? Or shall I come to you? I really cannot stand being away from you so long . . ."

She had her answer the next morning. A check fluttered out of Carol's letter onto Mrs. Cooper's hall floor. The check was for two hundred and fifty dollars. Carol's letter—the long loops looser and lighter, the t-bars stretching the length of the word—said that it was impossible for her to come out within the next two weeks, if then. The check was for her to fly back to New York and have the car driven east.

"I'd feel better if you took the plane. Come now and don't wait," was the last paragraph.

Carol had written the letter in haste, had probably snatched a moment to write it, but there was a coldness in it, too, that shocked Therese. She went out and walked dazedly to the corner and dropped the letter she had written the night before into the mailbox anyway, a heavy letter with three airmail stamps on it. She might see Carol within twelve hours. The thought did not bring any reassurance. Should she leave this morning? This afternoon? What had they done to Carol? She wondered if Carol would be furious if she telephoned her, if it would precipitate some crisis into a total defeat if she did?

She was sitting at a table somewhere with coffee and orange juice in front of her, before she looked at the other letter in her hand. In the upper left corner she could just make out the scrawly handwriting. It was from Mrs. R. Robichek.

Dear Therese,

Thank you very much for the delicious sausage that came last month. You are a nice sweet girl and I am glad to have the opportunity to thank you many times. It was nice of you to think of me making such a long trip. I enjoy the pretty postcards, specially the big one from Sioux Falls. How is in South Dakota? Are mountains and cowboys? I have never had chance to travel except Pennsylvania. You are a lucky girl, so young and pretty and kind. Myself I still work. The store is just the same. Everything is the same but it is colder. Please visit me when you come back. I cook a nice dinner for you not from delicatessen. Thank you for the sausage again. I lived from it for many days, really something special and nice. With best regards and yours truly.

Ruby Robichek

Therese slid off the stool, left some money on the counter and ran out. She ran all the way to the Warrior Hotel, put the call in and waited with the receiver against her ear until she heard the telephone ringing in Carol's house. No one answered. It rang twenty times and no one answered. She thought of calling Carol's lawyer, Fred Haymes. She decided she shouldn't. Neither did she want to call Abby.

That day it rained, and Therese lay on her bed in her room, staring up at the ceiling, waiting for three o'clock, when she intended to telephone again. Mrs. Cooper brought her a tray of lunch around midday. Mrs. Cooper thought she was sick. Therese could not eat the food, however, and she did not know what to do with it.

She was still trying to reach Carol at five o'clock. Finally the ringing stopped and there was confusion on the wire, a couple of operators questioning each other about the call, and the first words Therese heard from Carol were "Yes, damn it!" Therese smiled and the ache went out of her arms.

"Hello?" Carol said brusquely.

"Hello?" The connection was bad. "I got the letter—the one with the check. What happened, Carol? . . . What?"

Carol's harassed-sounding voice repeated through the crackling interference, "*This wire I think is tapped, Therese* . . . Are you all right? Are you coming home? I can't talk very long now."

Therese frowned, wordless. "Yes, I suppose I can leave today." Then she blurted, "What is it, Carol? I really can't stand this, not knowing anything!"

"*Therese!*" Carol drew the word all across Therese's words, like a deletion. "Will you come home so I can talk to you?"

Therese thought she heard Carol sigh impatiently. "But I've got to know now. Can you see me at all when I come back?"

"Hang on to yourself, Therese."

Was this the way they talked together? Were these the words they used? "But can you?"

"I don't know," Carol said.

A chill ran up her arm, into the fingers that held the telephone. She felt Carol hated her. Because it was her fault, her stupid blunder about the letter Florence had found. Something had happened and perhaps Carol couldn't and wouldn't even want to see her again. "Has the court thing started yet?"

"It's finished. I wrote you about that. I can't talk any longer. Good-bye, Therese." Carol waited for her to reply. "I've got to say good-bye."

Therese put the receiver slowly back on the hook.

She stood in the hotel lobby, staring at the blurred figures around the front desk. She pulled Carol's letter out of her pocket and read it again, but Carol's voice was closer, saying impatiently, "Will you come home so I can talk to you?" She pulled the check out and looked at it again, upside down, and slowly tore it up. She dropped the pieces into a brass spittoon.

But the tears did not come until she got back to the house and saw her room again, the double bed that sagged in the middle, the stack of letters from Carol on the desk. She couldn't stay here another night.

She would go to a hotel for the night, and if the letter Carol had mentioned wasn't here tomorrow morning, she would leave anyway.

Therese dragged her suitcase down from the closet and opened it on the bed. The folded corner of a white handkerchief stuck out of one of the pockets. Therese took it out and lifted it to her nose, remembering the morning in Des Moines when Carol had put it there, with the dash of perfume on it, and the derisive remark Carol had made about putting it there, which she had laughed at. Therese stood with her hand on the back of a chair and the other hand clenched in a fist that rose and fell aimlessly, and what she felt was as blurred as the desk and the letters that she frowned at in front of her. Then her hand reached out suddenly for the letter propped against the books at the back of the desk. She hadn't seen the letter before, though it was in plain view. Therese tore it open. This was the letter Carol had meant. It was a long letter, and the ink was pale blue on some pages and dark on others, and there were words crossed out. She read the first page, then went back and read it again.

Monday

My darling,

I am not even going into court. This morning I was given a private showing of what Harge intended to bring against me. Yes, they have a few conversations recorded—namely Waterloo, and it would be useless to try to face a court with this. I should be ashamed, not for myself oddly enough, but for my own child, to say nothing of not wanting you to have to appear. Everything was very simple this morning—I simply surrendered. The important thing now is what I intend to do in the future, the lawyers said. On this depends whether I would ever see my child again, because Harge has with ease now complete custody of her. The question was would I stop seeing you (and others like you, they said!). It was not so clearly put. There were a dozen faces that opened their mouths and spoke like the judges of doomsday—reminding me of my duties, my position, and my future. (What future have they fixed up for me? Are they going to look in on it in six months?)—I said I would stop seeing you. I wonder if you will understand, Therese, since you are so young and never even knew a mother who cared desperately for you. For this promise, they present me with their wonderful reward, the privilege of seeing my child a few weeks of the year.

Hours later—

Abby is here. We talk of you—she sends you her love as I send mine. Abby reminds me of the things I know already—that you are very young and you adore me. Abby does not think I should send this to you, but tell you when you come. We have just had quite an argument about it. I tell her she does not know you as well as I, and I think now she does not know me as well as you in some ways, and those ways are the emotions. I am not very happy today, my sweet. I am drinking my ryes and you would tell me they depress me, I know. But I wasn't prepared for these days after those weeks with you. They were happy weeks—you knew it more than I did. Though all we have known is only a beginning. I meant to try to tell you in this letter that you don't even know the rest and perhaps you never will and are not supposed to—meaning destined to. We never fought, never came back knowing there was nothing else we wanted in heaven or hell but to be together. Did you ever care for me that much, I don't know. But that is all part of it and all we have known is only a beginning. And it has been such a short time. For that reason it will have shorter roots in you. You say you love me however I am and when I curse. I say I love you always, the person you are and the person you will become. I would say it in a court if it would mean anything to those people or possibly change anything, because those are not the words I am afraid of. I mean, darling, I shall send you this letter and I think you will understand why I do, why I told the lawyers yesterday I would not see you again and why I had to tell them that, and I would be underestimating you to think you could not and to think you would prefer delay.

She stopped reading and stood up, and walked slowly to her writing table. Yes, she understood why Carol had sent the letter. Because Carol loved her child more than her. And because of that, the lawyers had been able to break her, to force her to do exactly what they wanted her to do. Therese could not imagine Carol forced. Yet here it was in Carol's writing. It was a surrender, Therese knew, no situation in which she was the stake could have wrested from Carol. For an instant there came the fantastic realization that Carol had devoted only a fraction of herself to her, Therese, and suddenly the whole world of the last month, like a tremendous lie, cracked and almost toppled. In the next instant, Therese did not believe that. Yet the fact remained, she had chosen her child. She stared at Richard's envelope on her table, and felt all the words she wanted to say to him, that she had never said to him, rising in a torrent inside her. What right had he to talk about whom she loved or how? What did he know about her? What had he ever known?

> . . . exaggerated and at the same time minimized [she read on another page of Carol's letter]. But between the pleasure of a kiss and of what a man and woman do in bed seems to me only a gradation. A kiss, for instance, is not to be minimized, or its value judged by anyone else. I wonder do these men grade their pleasure in terms of whether their actions produce a child or not, and do they consider them more pleasant if they do. It is a question of pleasure after all, and what's the use debating the pleasure of an ice cream cone versus a football game—or a Beethoven quartet versus the *Mona Lisa*. I'll leave that to the philosophers. But their attitude was that I must be somehow demented or blind (plus a kind of regret, I thought, at the fact a fairly attractive woman is presumably unavailable to men). Someone brought "aesthetics" into the argument, I mean against me of course. I said did they really want to debate that—it brought the only laugh in the whole show. But the most important point I did not mention and was not thought of by anyone—that the rapport between two men or two women can be absolute and perfect, as it can never be between man and woman, and perhaps some people want just this, as others want that more shifting and uncertain thing that happens between men and women. It was said or at least implied yesterday that my present course would bring me to the depths of human vice and degeneration. Yes, I have sunk a good deal since they took you from me. It is true, if I were to go on like this and be spied upon, attacked, never possessing one person long enough so that knowledge of a person is a superficial thing—that is degeneration. Or to live against one's grain, that is degeneration by definition.
>
> Darling, I pour all this out to you [the next lines were crossed out]. You will undoubtedly handle your future better than I. Let me be a bad example to you. If you are hurt now beyond what you think you can bear and if it makes you—either now or one

day—hate me, and this is what I told Abby, then I shan't be sorry. I may have been that one person you were fated to meet, as you say, and the only one, and you can put it all behind you. Yet if you don't, for all this failure and the dismalness now, I know what you said that afternoon is right—it needn't be like this. I do want to talk with you once when you come back, if you're willing, unless you think you can't.

Your plants are still thriving on the back porch. I water them every day . . .

Therese could not read any more. Beyond her door she heard footsteps slowly descending the stairs, walking more confidently across the hall. When the footsteps were gone, she opened her door and stood there a moment, struggling against an impulse to walk straight out of the house and leave everything behind her. Then she went down the hall to Mrs. Cooper's door in the rear.

Mrs. Cooper answered her knock, and Therese said the words she had prepared, about leaving that night. She watched Mrs. Cooper's face that didn't listen to her but only reacted to the sight of her own face, and Mrs. Cooper seemed suddenly her own reflection, which she could not turn away from.

"Well, I'm sorry, Miss Belivet. I'm sorry if your plans have gone wrong," she said, while her face registered only shock and curiosity.

Then Therese went back to her room and began to pack, laying in the bottom of her suitcase the cardboard models she had folded flat, and then her books. After a moment, she heard Mrs. Cooper approaching her door slowly, as if she carried something, and Therese thought, if she was bringing her another tray, she would scream. Mrs. Cooper knocked.

"Where shall I forward your mail to, honey, in case there's any more letters?" Mrs. Cooper asked.

"I don't know yet. I'll have to write and let you know." Therese felt lightheaded and sickish when she straightened up.

"You're not starting back for New York this late at night, are you?" Mrs. Cooper called anything after six "night."

"No," Therese said. "I'll just go a little ways." She was impatient to be alone. She looked at Mrs. Cooper's hand bulging the gray-checked apron under the waistband, at the cracked soft houseshoes worn paper-thin on these floors, which had walked these floors years before she came here and would go on in the same foot-tracks years after she was gone.

"Well, you be sure and let me hear how you make out," Mrs. Cooper said.

"Yes."

She drove to a hotel, a different hotel from the one where she had always called Carol. Then she went out for a walk, restlessly, avoiding all the streets she had been in with Carol. She might have driven to another town, she thought, and stopped, half decided to go back to the car. Then she walked on, not caring, actually, where she was. She walked until she was cold, and the library was the closest place to go and get warm. She passed the diner and glanced in. Dutch saw her, and with the familiar dip of his head, as if he had to look under something to see her through the window, he smiled and waved to her. Automatically, her hand waved back, good-bye, and suddenly she thought of her room in New York, with the dress still on the studio couch, and the corner of the carpet turned back. If she could only reach out now and pull the carpet flat, she thought. She stood staring down the narrowish, solid-looking avenue with its round streetlights. A single figure walked along the sidewalk toward her. Therese went up the library steps.

Miss Graham, the librarian, greeted her as usual, but Therese did not go into the main reading room. There were two or three people there tonight, the bald-headed man with the black-rimmed glasses who was often at the middle table, and how often had she sat in that room with a letter from Carol in her pocket? With Carol beside her. She climbed the stairs, passed the history and art room on the second floor, up to the third floor where she had never been before. There was a single large dusty-looking room with glass-front bookcases around the walls, a few oil paintings and marble busts on pedestals.

Therese sat down at one of the tables, and her body relaxed with an ache. She put her head down on her arms on the table, suddenly limp and sleepy, but in the next second, she slid the chair back and stood up. She felt prickles of terror in the roots of her hair. She had been somehow pretending until this moment that Carol was not gone, that when she went back to New York she would see Carol and everything would be, would have to be, as it had been before. She glanced nervously around the room, as if looking for some contradiction, some redress. For a moment, she felt her body might shatter apart of itself, or might hurl itself through the glass of the long windows across the room. She stared at a pallid bust of Homer, the inquisitively lifted eyebrows delineated faintly by dust. She turned to the door, and for the first time noticed the picture over the lintel.

It was only similar, she thought, not quite the same, not the same, but the recognition had shaken her at the core, was growing as she looked at it, and she knew the picture was exactly the same, only much larger, and she had seen it many times in the hall that led to the music room before they had taken it down when she was still small—the smiling woman in the ornate dress of some court, the hand poised just below the throat, the arrogant head half turned, as if the painter had somehow caught her in motion so that even the pearls that hung from each ear seemed to move. She knew the short, firmly modeled cheeks, the full coral lips that smiled at one corner, the mockingly narrowed lids, the strong, not very high forehead that even in the picture seemed to project a little over the living eyes that knew everything beforehand, and sympathized and laughed at once. It was Carol. Now in the long moment while she could not look away from it, the mouth smiled and the eyes regarded her with nothing but mockery, the last veil lifted and revealing nothing but mockery and gloating, the splendid satisfaction of the betrayal accomplished.

With a shuddering gasp, Therese ran under the picture and down the stairs. In the downstairs hall, Miss Graham said something to her, an anxious question, and Therese heard her own reply like an idiot's babble, because she was still gasping, fighting for breath, and she passed Miss Graham and rushed out of the building.

## *twenty-two*

In the middle of the block, she opened the door of a coffee shop, but they were playing one of the songs she had heard with Carol everywhere, and she let the door close and walked on. The music lived, but the world was dead. And the song would die one day, she thought, but how would the world come back to life? How would its salt come back?

She walked to the hotel. In her room, she wet a face towel with cold water to put over her eyes. The room was chilly, so she took off her dress and shoes and got into bed.

From outside, a shrill voice, muted in empty space, cried: "Hey, *Chicago Sun-Times!*"

Then silence, and she debated trying to fall asleep, while fatigue already began to rock her unpleasantly, like drunkenness. Now there were voices in the hall, talking of a misplaced piece of luggage, and a sense of futility overwhelmed her as she lay there with the wet, medicinally smelling face towel over her swollen eyes. The voices wrangled, and she felt her courage running out, and then her will, and in panic she tried to think of the world outside, of Danny and Mrs. Robichek, of Frances Cotter at the Pelican Press, of Mrs. Osborne, and of her own apartment still in New York, but her mind refused to survey or to renounce, and her mind was the same as her heart now and refused to renounce Carol. The faces swam together like the voices outside. There was also the face of Sister Alicia, and of her mother. There was the last room she had slept in at school. There was the morning she had sneaked out of the dormitory very early and run across the lawn like a young animal crazy with spring, and had seen Sister Alicia running crazily through a field herself, white shoes flashing like ducks through the high grass, and it had been minutes before she realized that Sister Alicia was chasing an escaped chicken. There was the moment, in the house of some friend of her mother's, when she had reached for a piece of cake and had upset the plate on the floor, and her mother had slapped her in the face. She saw the picture in the hall at school, it breathed and moved now like Carol, mocking and cruel and finished with her, as if some evil and long-destined purpose had been accomplished. Therese's body tensed in terror, and the conversation went on and on in the hall obliviously, falling on her ear with the sharp, alarming sound of ice cracking somewhere out on a pond.

"What do you mean you did?"

"No . . ."

"If you did, the suitcase would be downstairs in the checkroom . . ."

"Oh, I told you . . ."

"But you want me to lose a suitcase so you won't lose your job!"

Her mind attached meaning to the phrases one by one, like some slow translator that lagged behind, and at last got lost.

She sat up in bed with the end of a bad dream in her head. The room was nearly dark, its shadows deep and solid in the corners. She reached for the lamp switch and half closed her eyes against the light. She dropped a quarter into the radio on the wall, and turned the volume quite loud at the first sound she got. It was a man's voice, and then music began, a lilting, oriental-sounding piece that had been among the selections in music appreciation class at school. "In a Persian Market," she remembered automatically, and now its undulant rhythm that had always made her think of a camel walking took her back to the rather small room at the Home, with the illustrations from Verdi operas around the walls above the high wainscoting. She had heard the piece occasionally in New York, but she had never heard it with Carol, had not heard it or thought of it since she had known Carol, and now the music was like a bridge soaring across time without touching anything. She picked up Carol's letter opener from the bed table, the wooden knife that had somehow gotten into her suitcase when they packed, and she squeezed the handle and rubbed her thumb along its edge, but its reality seemed to deny Carol instead of affirm her, did not evoke her so much as the music they had never heard together. She thought of Carol with a twist of resentment, Carol like a distant spot of silence and stillness.

Therese went to the basin to wash her face in cold water. She should get a job, tomorrow if she could. That had been her idea in stopping here, to work for two weeks or so, not to weep in hotel rooms. She should send Mrs. Cooper the hotel name as an address, simply for courtesy's sake. It was another of the things she must do, although she did not want to. And was it worthwhile to write to Harkevy again, she wondered, after his polite but inexplicit note in Sioux Falls. ". . . I should be glad to see you again when you come to New York, but it is impossible for me to promise anything this spring. It would be a good idea for you to see Mr. Ned Bernstein, the coproducer, when you get back. He can tell you more of what is happening in designing studios than I can . . ." No, she wouldn't write again about that.

Downstairs, she bought a picture postcard of Lake Michigan, and deliberately wrote a cheerful message on it to Mrs. Robichek. It seemed false as she wrote it, but walking away from the box where she had dropped it, she was conscious suddenly of the energy in her body, the spring in her toes, the youth in her blood that warmed her cheeks as she walked faster, and she knew she was free and blessed compared to Mrs. Robichek, and what she had written was not false, because she could so well afford it. She was not crumpled or half blind, not in pain. She stood by a store window and quickly put on some more lipstick. A gust of wind made her stop to catch her balance. But she could feel in the wind's coldness its core of spring, like a heart warm and young inside it. Tomorrow morning, she would start to look for a job. She should be able to live on the money she had left, and save whatever she earned to get back to New York on. She could wire her bank for the rest of her money, of course, but that was not what she wanted. She wanted two weeks of working among people she didn't know, doing the kind of work a million other people did. She wanted to step into someone else's shoes.

She answered an advertisement for a receptionist-filing clerk that said little typing required and call in person. They seemed to think she would do, and she spent all morning learning the files. Then one of the bosses came in after lunch and said he wanted a girl who knew some shorthand. Therese didn't. The school had taught her typing, but not shorthand, so she was out.

She looked through the Help Wanted columns again that afternoon. Then she remembered the sign on the fence of the lumberyard not far from the hotel. "Girl wanted for general office work and stock. $40 weekly." If they didn't demand shorthand, she might qualify. It was around three when she turned into the windy street where the lumberyard lay. She lifted her head and let the wind blow her hair back from her face. And she remembered Carol saying, I like to see you walking. When I see you from a distance, I feel you're walking on the palm of my hand and you're about five inches high. She could hear Carol's soft voice under the babble of the wind, and she grew tense, with bitterness and fear. She walked faster, ran a few steps, as if she could run out of that morass of love and hate and resentment in which her mind suddenly floundered.

There was a wooden shack of an office at the side of the lumberyard. She went in and spoke with a Mr. Zambrowski, a slow-moving bald-headed man with a gold watch chain that barely stretched across his front. Before Therese asked him about shorthand, he volunteered that he didn't need it. He said he would try her out the rest of the afternoon and tomorrow. Two other girls came in for the job the next morning, and Mr. Zambrowski took their names, but before noon, he said the job was hers.

"If you don't mind getting here at eight in the morning," Mr. Zambrowski said.

"I don't mind." She had come in at nine that morning. But she would have gotten there at four in the morning if he had asked her to.

Her hours were from eight to four-thirty, and her duties consisted simply in checking the mill shipments to the yard against the orders received, and in writing letters of confirmation. She did not see much lumber from her desk in the office, but the smell of it was in the air, fresh as if the saws had just exposed the surface of the white pine boards, and she could hear it bouncing and rattling as the trucks pulled into the center of the yard. She liked the work, liked Mr. Zambrowski, and liked the lumberjacks and truck drivers who came into the office to warm their hands at the fire. One of the lumberjacks named Steve, an attractive young man with a golden stubble of beard, invited her a couple of times to have lunch with him in the cafeteria down the street. He asked her for a date on Saturday night, but Therese did not want to spend a whole evening with him or with anyone yet.

• • •

One night, Abby telephoned her.

"Do you know I had to call South Dakota twice to find you?" Abby said irritably. "What're you doing out there? When're you coming back?"

Abby's voice brought Carol as close as if it were Carol she heard. It brought the hollow tightness in her throat again, and for a moment she couldn't answer anything.

"Therese?"

"Is Carol there with you?"

"She's in Vermont. She's been sick," Abby's hoarse voice said, and there was no smile in it now. "She's taking a rest."

"She's too sick to call me? Why don't you tell me, Abby? Is she getting better or worse?"

"Better. Why didn't you try to call to find out?"

Therese squeezed the telephone. Yes, why hadn't she? Because she had been thinking of a picture instead of Carol. "What's the matter with her? Is she—"

"That's a fine question. Carol wrote you what happened, didn't she?"

"Yes."

"Well, do you expect her to bounce up like a rubber ball? Or chase you all over America? What do you think this is, a game of hide and seek?"

All the conversation of that lunch with Abby crashed down on Therese. As Abby saw it, the whole thing was her fault. The letter Florence had found was only the final blunder.

"When're you coming back?" Abby asked.

"In about ten days. Unless Carol wants the car sooner."

"She doesn't. She won't be home in ten days."

Therese forced herself to say, "About that letter—the one I wrote—do you know if they found it before or after?"

"Before or after what?"

"After the detectives started following us."

"They found it afterward," Abby said, sighing.

Therese set her teeth. But it didn't matter what Abby thought of her, only what Carol thought. "Where is she in Vermont?"

"I wouldn't call her if I were you."

"But you're not me and I want to call her."

"Don't. That much I can tell you. I can give her any message—that's important." And there was a cold silence. "Carol wants to know if you need any money and what about the car."

"I don't need any money. The car's all right." She had to ask one more question. "What does Rindy know about this?"

"She knows what the word *divorce* means. And she wanted to stay with Carol. That doesn't make it easier for Carol, either."

Very well, very well, Therese wanted to say. She wouldn't trouble Carol by telephoning, by writing, by any messages, unless it was a message about the car. She was shaking when she put the telephone down. And she immediately picked it up again. "This is room six eleven," she said. "I don't want to take any more long-distance calls—none at all."

She looked at Carol's letter opener on the bed table, and now it meant Carol, the person of flesh and blood, the Carol with freckles and the corner nicked off one tooth. Did she owe Carol anything, Carol the person? Hadn't Carol been playing with her, as Richard had said? She remembered Carol's words, "When you have a husband and child it's a little different." She frowned at the letter opener, not understanding why it had become only a letter opener suddenly, why it was a matter of indifference to her whether she kept it or threw it away.

Two days later, a letter arrived from Abby enclosing a personal check for a hundred and fifty dollars, which Abby told her to "forget about." Abby said she had spoken with Carol, and that Carol would like to hear from her, and she gave Carol's address. It was a rather cold letter, but the gesture of the check was not cold. It hadn't been prompted by Carol, Therese knew.

"Thank you for the check," Therese wrote back to her. "It's terribly nice of you, but I won't use it and I don't need it. You ask me to write to Carol. I don't think I can or that I should."

• • •

Danny was sitting in the hotel lobby one afternoon when she came home from work. She could not quite believe it was he, the dark-eyed young man who got up from the chair smiling and came slowly toward her. Then the sight of his loose black hair, mussed a little more by the upturned coat collar, the symmetrical broad smile, was as familiar as if she had seen him only the day before.

"Hello, Therese," he said. "Surprised?"

"Well, terrifically! I'd given you up. No word from you in—two weeks." She remembered the twenty-eighth was the day he said he would leave New York, and it was the day she had come to Chicago.

"I'd just about given you up," Danny said, laughing. "I got delayed in New York. I guess it's lucky I did, because I tried to telephone you and your landlady gave me your address." Danny's fingers kept a firm grip on her elbow. They were walking slowly toward the elevators. "You look wonderful, Therese."

"Do I? I'm awfully glad to see you." There was an open elevator in front of them. "Do you want to come up?"

"Let's go have something to eat. Or is it too early? I didn't have any lunch today."

"It's certainly not too early, then."

They went to a place Therese knew about, which specialized in steaks. Danny even ordered cocktails, though he usually never drank.

"You're here by yourself?" he said. "Your landlady in Sioux Falls told me you left by yourself."

"Carol couldn't come out finally."

"Oh. And you decided to stay out longer?"

"Yes."

"Until when?"

"Until just about now. I'm going back next week."

Danny listened with his warm dark eyes fixed on her face, without any surprise. "Why don't you just go west instead of east and spend a little time in California? I've got a job in Oakland. I have to be there day after tomorrow."

"What kind of a job?"

"Researching—just what I asked for. I came out better than I thought I would on my exams."

"Were you first in the class?"

"I don't know. I doubt it. They weren't graded like that. You didn't answer my question."

"I want to get back to New York, Danny."

"Oh." He smiled, looking at her hair, her lips, and it occurred to her Danny had never seen her with this much makeup on. "You look grown up all of a sudden," he said. "You changed your hair, didn't you?"

"A little."

"You don't look frightened anymore. Or even so serious."

"That pleases me." She felt shy with him, yet somehow close, a closeness charged with something she had never felt with Richard. Something suspenseful, that she enjoyed. A little salt, she thought. She looked at Danny's hand on the table, at the strong muscle that bulged below the thumb. She remembered his hands on her shoulders that day in his room. The memory was a pleasant one.

"You did miss me a little, didn't you, Terry?"

"Of course."

"Did you ever think you might care something about me? As much as you did for Richard, for instance?" he asked, with a note of surprise in his own voice, as if it were a fantastic question.

"I don't know," she said quickly.

"But you're not still thinking about Richard, are you?"

"You must know I'm not."

"Who is it then? Carol?"

She felt suddenly naked, sitting there opposite him. "Yes. It was."

"But not now?"

Therese was amazed that he could say the words without any surprise, any attitude at all. "No. It's—I can't talk to anyone about it, Danny," she finished, and her voice sounded deep and quiet in her ears, like the voice of another person.

"Don't you want to forget it, if it's past?"

"I don't know. I don't know just how you mean that."

"I mean, are you sorry?"

"No. Would I do the same thing again? Yes."

"Do you mean with somebody else, or with her?"

"With her," Therese said. The corner of her mouth went up in a smile.

"But the end was a fiasco."

"Yes. I mean I'd go through the end, too."

"And you're still going through it."

Therese didn't say anything.

"Are you going to see her again? Do you mind if I ask you all these questions?"

"I don't mind," she said. "No, I'm not going to see her again. I don't want to."

"But somebody else?"

"Another woman?" Therese shook her head. "No."

Danny looked at her and smiled, slowly. "That's what matters. Or rather, that's what makes it not matter."

"What do you mean?"

"I mean, you're so young, Therese. You'll change. You'll forget."

She did not feel young. "Did Richard talk to you?" she asked.

"No. I think he wanted to one night, but I cut it off before he got started."

She felt the bitter smile on her mouth, and she took a last pull on her short cigarette and put it out. "I hope he finds somebody to listen to him. He needs an audience."

"He feels jilted. His ego's suffering. Don't ever think I'm like Richard. I think people's lives are their own."

Something Carol had said once came suddenly to her mind: every adult has secrets. Said as casually as Carol said everything, stamped as indelibly in her brain as the address she had written on the sales slip in Frankenberg's. She had an impulse to tell Danny the rest, about the picture in the library, the picture in the school. And about the Carol who was not a picture, but a woman with a child and a husband, with freckles on her hands and a habit of cursing, of growing melancholy at unexpected moments, with a bad habit of indulging her will. A woman who had endured much more in New York than she had in South Dakota. She looked at Danny's eyes, at his chin with the faint cleft. She knew that up to now she had been under a spell that prevented her from seeing anyone in the world but Carol.

"Now what are you thinking?" he asked.

"Of what you said once in New York, about using things and throwing them away."

"Did she do that to you?"

Therese smiled. "I shall do it."

"Then find someone you'll never want to throw away."

"Who won't wear out," Therese said.

"Will you write to me?"

"Of course."

"Write me in three months."

"Three months?" But suddenly she knew what he meant. "And not before?"

"No." He was looking at her steadily. "That's a fair time, isn't it?"

"Yes. All right. It's a promise."

"Promise me something else—take tomorrow off so you can be with me. I've got till nine tomorrow night."

"I can't, Danny. There's work to do—and I've got to tell him anyway that I'm leaving in another week." Those weren't quite the reasons, she knew. And perhaps Danny knew, looking at her. She didn't want to spend tomorrow with him; it would be too intense, he would remind her too much of herself, and she still was not ready.

Danny came round to the lumberyard the next day at noon. They had intended to have lunch together, but they walked and talked on Lake Shore Drive for the whole hour instead. That evening at nine, Danny took a plane westward.

Eight days later, she started for New York. She meant to move away from Mrs. Osborne's as soon as possible. She wanted to look up some of the people she had run away from last fall. And there would be other people, new people. She would go to night school this spring. And she wanted to change her wardrobe completely. Everything she had now, the clothes she remembered in her closet in New York, seemed juvenile, like clothes that had belonged to her years ago. In Chicago she had looked around in the stores and hungered for the clothes she couldn't buy yet. All she could afford now was a new haircut.

## *twenty-three*

Therese went into her old room, and the first thing she noticed was that the carpet corner lay flat. And how small and tragic the room looked. And yet hers, the tiny radio on the bookshelf, and the pillows on the studio couch, as personal as a signature she had written long ago and forgotten. Like the two or three set models hanging on the walls that she deliberately avoided looking at.

She went to the bank and took out a hundred of her last two hundred dollars, and bought a black dress and a pair of shoes.

Tomorrow, she thought, she would call Abby and arrange something about Carol's car, but not today.

That same afternoon, she made an appointment with Ned Bernstein, the coproducer of the English show for which Harkevy was to do the sets. She took three of the models she had made in the West and also the *Small Rain* photographs to show him. An apprentice job with Harkevy, if she got it, wouldn't pay enough to live on, but there were other sources, other than department stores, anyway. There was television, for instance.

Mr. Bernstein looked at her work indifferently. Therese said she hadn't spoken to Mr. Harkevy yet, and asked Mr. Bernstein if he knew anything about his taking on helpers. Mr. Bernstein said that was up to Harkevy, but as far as he knew, he didn't need any more assistants. Neither did Mr. Bernstein know of any other set studio that needed anyone at the moment. And Therese thought of the sixty-dollar dress. And of the hundred dollars left in the bank. And she had told Mrs. Osborne she might show the apartment any time she wished, because she was moving. Therese hadn't yet any idea where. She got up to leave, and thanked Mr. Bernstein anyway for looking at her work. She did it with a smile.

"How about television?" Mr. Bernstein asked. "Have you tried to start that way? It's easier to break into."

"I'm going over to see someone at Dumont later this afternoon." Mr. Donohue had given her a couple of names last January. Mr. Bernstein gave her some more names.

Then she telephoned Harkevy's studio. Harkevy said he was just going out, but she could drop her models by his studio today and he could look at them tomorrow morning.

"By the way, there'll be a cocktail party at the St. Regis for Genevieve Cranell tomorrow at about five o'clock. If you care to drop in," Harkevy said, with his staccato accent that made his soft voice as precise as mathematics, "at least we'll be sure to see each other tomorrow. Can you come?"

"Yes. I'd love to come. Where in the St. Regis?"

He read from the invitation. Suite D. Five to seven o'clock. "I shall be there by six."

She left the telephone booth feeling as happy as if Harkevy had just taken her into partnership. She walked the twelve blocks to his studio, and left the models with a young man there, a different young man from the one she had seen in January. Harkevy changed his assistants often. She looked around his workroom reverently before she closed the door. Perhaps he would let her come soon. Perhaps she would know tomorrow.

She went into a drugstore on Broadway and called Abby in New Jersey. Abby's voice was entirely different from the way it had sounded in

Chicago. Carol must be much better, Therese thought. But she did not ask about Carol. She was calling to arrange about the car.

"I can come and get it if you want me to," Abby said. "But why don't you call Carol about it? I know she'd like to hear from you." Abby was actually bending over backward.

"Well—" Therese didn't want to call her. But what was she afraid of? Carol's voice? Carol herself? "All right. I'll take the car to her, unless she doesn't want me to. In that case, I'll call you back."

"When? This afternoon?"

"Yes. In a few minutes."

Therese went to the door of the drugstore and stood there for a few moments, looking out at the Camel advertisement with the giant face puffing smoke rings like gigantic doughnuts, at the low-slung, sullen-looking taxis maneuvering like sharks in the after-matinee rush, at the familiar hodgepodge of restaurant and bar signs, awnings, front steps and windows, that reddish brown confusion of the side street that was like hundreds of streets in New York. She remembered walking in a certain street in the West Eighties once, the brownstone fronts, overlaid and overlaid with humanity, human lives, some beginning and some ending there, and she remembered the sense of oppression it had given her, and how she had hurried through it to get to the avenue. Only two or three months ago. Now the same kind of street filled her with a tense excitement, made her want to plunge headlong into it, down the sidewalk with all the signs and theater marquees and rushing, bumping people. She turned and walked back to the telephone booths.

A moment later, she heard Carol's voice.

"When did you get in, Therese?"

There was a brief, fluttering shock at the first sound of her voice, and then nothing. "Yesterday."

"How are you? Do you still look the same?" Carol sounded repressed, as if someone might be with her, but Therese was sure there was no one else.

"Not exactly. Do you?"

Carol waited. "You sound different."

"I am."

"Am I going to see you? Or don't you want to? Once." It was Carol's voice, but the words were not hers. The words were cautious and uncertain. "What about this afternoon? Have you got the car?"

"I've got to see a couple of people this afternoon. There won't be time." When had she ever refused Carol when Carol wanted to see her? "Would you like me to drive the car out tomorrow?"

"No, I can come in for it. I'm not an invalid. Did the car behave itself?"

"It's in good shape," Therese said. "No scratches anywhere."

"And you?" Carol asked, but Therese didn't answer anything. "Shall I see you tomorrow? Do you have any time in the afternoon?"

They arranged to meet in the bar of the Ritz Tower on Fifty-seventh Street at four-thirty, and then they hung up.

• • •

Carol was a quarter of an hour late. Therese sat waiting for her at a table where she could see the glass doors that led into the bar, and finally she saw Carol push open one of the doors, and the tension broke in her with a small dull ache. Carol wore the same fur coat, the same black suede pumps she had worn the day Therese first saw her, but now a red scarf set off the blonde lifted head. She saw Carol's face, thinner now, alter with surprise, with a little smile, as Carol caught sight of her.

"Hello," Therese said.

"I didn't even know you at first." And Carol stood by the table a moment, looking at her, before she sat down. "It's nice of you to see me."

"Don't say that."

The waiter came, and Carol ordered tea. So did Therese, mechanically.

"Do you hate me, Therese?" Carol asked her.

"No." Therese could smell Carol's perfume faintly, that familiar sweetness that was strangely unfamiliar now, because it did not evoke what it had once evoked. She put down the match cover she had been crushing in her hand. "How can I hate you, Carol?"

"I suppose you could. You did for a while, didn't you?" Carol said, as if she told her a fact.

"Hate you? No." Not quite, she might have said. But she knew that Carol's eyes were reading it in her face.

"And now—you're all grown up—with grown-up hair and grown-up clothes."

Therese looked into her gray eyes that were more serious now, somehow wistful, too, despite the assurance of the proud head, and she looked down again, unable to fathom them. She was still beautiful, Therese thought with a sudden pang of loss. "I've learned a few things," Therese said.

"What?"

"That I—" Therese stopped, her thoughts obstructed suddenly by the memory of the portrait in Sioux Falls.

"You know, you look very fine," Carol said. "You've come out all of a sudden. Is that what comes of getting away from me?"

"No," Therese said quickly. She frowned down at the tea she didn't want. Carol's phrase "come out" had made her think of being born, and it embarrassed her. Yes, she had been born since she left Carol. She had been born the instant she saw the picture in the library, and her stifled cry then was like the first yell of an infant, being dragged into the world against its will. She looked at Carol. "There was a picture in the library at Sioux Falls," she said. Then she told Carol about it, simply and without emotion, like a story that had happened to somebody else.

And Carol listened, never taking her eyes from her. Carol watched her as she might have watched from a distance someone she could not help. "Strange," Carol said quietly. "And horrifying."

"It was." Therese knew Carol understood. She saw the sympathy in Carol's eyes, too, and she smiled, but Carol did not smile back. Carol was still staring at her. "What are you thinking?" Therese asked.

Carol took a cigarette. "What do you think? Of that day in the store."

Therese smiled again. "It was so wonderful when you came over to me. Why did you come to me?"

Carol waited. "For such a dull reason. Because you were the only girl not busy as hell. You didn't have a smock, either, I remember."

Therese burst out laughing. Carol only smiled, but she looked suddenly like herself, as she had been in Colorado Springs, before anything had happened. All at once, Therese remembered the candlestick in her handbag. "I bought you this," she said, handing it to her. "I found it in Sioux Falls."

Therese had only twisted some white tissue around it. Carol opened it on the table.

"I think it's charming," Carol said. "It looks just like you."

"Thank you. I thought it looked like you." Therese looked at Carol's hand, the thumb and the tip of the middle finger resting on the thin rim of the candlestick, as she had seen Carol's fingers on the saucers of coffee cups in Colorado, in Chicago, and places forgotten. Therese closed her eyes.

"I love you," Carol said.

Therese opened her eyes, but she did not look up.

"I know you don't feel the same about me. Do you?"

Therese had an impulse to deny it, but could she? She didn't feel the same. "I don't know, Carol."

"That's the same thing." Carol's voice was soft, expectant, expecting affirmation or denial.

Therese stared at the triangles of toast on the plate between them. She thought of Rindy. She had put off asking about her. "Have you seen Rindy?"

Carol sighed. Therese saw her hand draw back from the candlestick. "Yes, last Sunday for an hour or so. I suppose she can come and visit me a couple of afternoons a year. Once in a blue moon. I've lost completely."

"I thought you said a few weeks of the year."

"Well, a little more happened—privately between Harge and me. I refused to make a lot of promises he asked me to make. And the family came into it, too. I refused to live by a list of silly promises they'd made up like a list of misdemeanors—even if it did mean that they'd lock Rindy away from me as if I were an ogre. And it did mean that. Harge told the lawyers everything—whatever they didn't know already."

"God," Therese whispered. She could imagine what it meant, Rindy visiting one afternoon, accompanied by a staring governess who had been forewarned against Carol, told not to let the child out of her sight, probably, and Rindy would soon understand all that. What would be the pleasure in a visit at all? Harge—Therese did not want to say his name. "Even the court was kinder," she said.

"As a matter of fact, I didn't promise very much in court, I refused there, too."

Therese smiled a little in spite of herself, because she was glad Carol had refused, that Carol had still been that proud.

"But it wasn't a court, you know, just a roundtable discussion. Do you know how they made that recording in Waterloo? They drove a spike into the wall, probably just about as soon as we got there."

"A *spike*?"

"I remember hearing somebody hammering something. I think it was when we'd just finished in the shower. Do you remember?"

"No."

Carol smiled. "A spike that picks up sound like a Dictaphone. He had the room next to us."

Therese didn't remember the hammering, but the violence of all of it came back, shattering, destroying—

"It's all over," Carol said. "You know, I'd almost prefer not to see Rindy at all anymore. I'm never going to demand to see her, if she stops wanting to see me. I'll just leave that up to her."

"I can't imagine her ever not wanting to see you."

Carol's eyebrows lifted. "Is there any way of predicting what Harge can do to her?"

Therese was silent. She looked away from Carol, and saw a clock. It was five thirty-five. She should be at the cocktail party before six, she thought, if she went at all. She had dressed for it, in the new black dress with a white scarf, in her new shoes, with her new black gloves. And how unimportant the clothes seemed now. She thought suddenly of the green woolen gloves that Sister Alicia had given her. Were they still in the ancient tissue at the bottom of her trunk? She wanted to throw them away.

"One gets over things," Carol said.

"Yes."

"Harge and I are selling the house, and I've taken an apartment up on Madison Avenue. And a job, believe it or not. I'm going to work for a furniture house on Fourth Avenue as a buyer. Some of my ancestors must have been carpenters." She looked at Therese. "Anyway, it's a living and I'll like it. The apartment's a nice big one—big enough for two. I was hoping you might like to come and live with me, but I guess you won't."

Therese's heart took a jump, exactly as it had when Carol had telephoned her that day in the store. Something responded in her against her will, made her feel happy all at once, and proud. She was proud that Carol had the courage to do such things, to say such things, that Carol always would have the courage. She remembered Carol's courage, facing the detective on the country road. Therese swallowed, trying to swallow the beating of her heart. Carol had not even looked at her. Carol was rubbing her cigarette-end back and forth in the ashtray. To live with Carol? Once that had been impossible, and had been what she wanted most in the world. To live with her and share everything with her, summer and winter, to walk and read together, to travel together. And she remembered the days of resenting Carol, when she had imagined Carol asking her this, and herself answering no.

"Would you?" Carol looked at her.

Therese felt she balanced on a thin edge. The resentment was gone now. Nothing but the decision remained now, a thin line suspended in the air, with nothing on either side to push her or pull her. But on the one side, Carol, and on the other an empty question mark. On the one side, Carol, and it would be different now, because they were both different. It would be a world as unknown as the world just past had been when she first entered it. Only now, there were no obstacles. Therese thought of Carol's perfume that today meant nothing. A blank to be filled in, Carol would say.

"Well," Carol said smiling, impatient.

"No," Therese said. "No, I don't think so." Because you would betray me again. That was what she had thought in Sioux Falls, what she had intended to write or say. But Carol had not betrayed her. Carol loved her more than she loved her child. That was part of the reason why she had not promised. She was gambling now as she had gambled on getting everything from the detective that day on the road, and she lost then, too. And now she saw Carol's face changing, saw the little signs of astonishment and shock so subtle that perhaps only she in the world could have noticed them, and Therese could not think for a moment.

"That's your decision," Carol said.

"Yes."

Carol stared at her cigarette lighter on the table. "That's that."

Therese looked at her, wanting still to put out her hands, to touch

Carol's hair and to hold it tight in all her fingers. Hadn't Carol heard the indecision in her voice? Therese wanted suddenly to run away, to rush quickly out the door and down the sidewalk. It was a quarter to six. "I've got to go to a cocktail party this afternoon. It's important because of a possible job. Harkevy's going to be there." Harkevy would give her some kind of a job, she was sure. She had called him at noon today about the models she had left at his studio. Harkevy had liked them all. "I got a television assignment yesterday, too."

Carol lifted her head, smiling. "My little big shot. Now you look like you might do something good. Do you know, even your voice is different?"

"Is it?" Therese hesitated, finding it harder and harder to sit there. "Carol, you could come to the party if you want to. It's a big party in a couple of rooms at a hotel—welcoming the woman who's going to do the lead in Harkevy's play. I know they wouldn't mind if I brought someone." And she didn't know quite why she was asking her, why Carol would possibly want to go to a cocktail party now any more than she did.

Carol shook her head. "No, thanks, darling. You'd better run along by yourself. I've got a date at the Elysée in a minute as a matter of fact."

Therese gathered her gloves and her handbag in her lap. She looked at Carol's hands, the pale freckles sprinkled on their backs—the wedding ring was gone now—and at Carol's eyes. She felt she would never see Carol again. In two minutes, less, they would part on the sidewalk. "The car's outside. Out in front to the left. And here's the keys."

"I know, I saw it."

"Are you going to stay on?" Therese asked her. "I'll take care of the check."

"I'll take care of the check," Carol said. "Go on, if you have to."

Therese stood up. She couldn't leave Carol sitting here at the table where their two teacups were, with the ashes of their cigarettes in front of her. "Don't stay. Come out with me."

Carol glanced up with a kind of questioning surprise in her face. "All right," she said. "There are a couple of things of yours out at the house. Shall I—"

"It doesn't matter," Therese interrupted her.

"And your flowers. Your plants." Carol was paying the check the waiter had brought over. "What happened to the flowers I gave you?"

"The flowers you gave me—they died."

Carol's eyes met hers for a second, and Therese looked away.

They parted on the sidewalk, at the corner of Park Avenue and Fifty-seventh Street. Therese ran across the avenue, just making it ahead of the green lights that released a pack of cars behind her, that blurred her view of Carol when she turned on the other sidewalk. Carol was walking slowly away, past the Ritz Tower doorway, and on. And that was the way it should be, Therese thought, not with a lingering handclasp, not with backward glances. Then as she saw Carol touch the handle of the car door, she remembered the beer can still under the front seat, remembered its clink as she had driven up the ramp from the Lincoln Tunnel coming into New York. She had thought then, she must get it out before she gave the car back to Carol, but she had forgotten. Therese hurried on to the hotel.

• • •

People were already spilling out of the two doorways into the hall, and a waiter was having difficulty pushing his rolling table of ice buckets into the room. The rooms were noisy, and Therese did not see Bernstein or Harkevy anywhere. She didn't know anyone, not a soul. Except one face, a man she had talked to months ago, somewhere, about a job that didn't materialize. Therese turned around. A man poked a tall glass into her hand.

"Mademoiselle," he said with a flourish. "Are you looking for one of these?"

"Thank you." She didn't stay with him. She thought she saw Mr. Bernstein over in the corner. There were several women with big hats in the way.

"Are you an actress?" the same man asked her, thrusting with her through the crowd.

"No. A set designer."

It was Mr. Bernstein, and Therese sidled between a couple of groups of people and reached him. Mr. Bernstein held out a plump, cordial hand to her, and got up from his radiator seat.

"Miss Belivet!" he shouted. "Mrs. Crawford, the makeup consultant—"

"Let's not talk business!" Mrs. Crawford shrieked.

"Mr. Stevens, Mr. Fenelon," Mr. Bernstein went on, and on and on, until she was nodding to a dozen people and saying "How do you do?" to about half of them. "And Ivor—Ivor!" Mr. Bernstein called.

There was Harkevy, a slim figure with a slim face and a small mustache, smiling at her, reaching a hand over for her to shake. "Hello," he said. "I'm glad to see you again. Yes, I liked your work. I see your anxiety." He laughed a little.

"Enough to let me squeeze in?" she asked.

"You want to know," he said, smiling. "Yes, you can squeeze in. Come up to my studio tomorrow at about eleven. Can you make that?"

"Yes."

"Come and join me later. I must say good-bye to these people who are leaving." And he went away.

Therese set her drink down on the edge of a table, and reached for a cigarette in her handbag. It was done. She glanced at the door. A woman with upswept blonde hair, with bright, intense blue eyes had just come into the room and was causing a small furor of excitement around her. She had quick, positive movements as she turned to greet people, to shake hands, and suddenly Therese realized she was Genevieve Cranell, the English actress who was to play the lead. She looked different from the few stills Therese had seen of her. She had the kind of face that must be seen in action to be attractive.

"Hello, hello!" she called to everyone finally as she glanced around the room, and Therese saw the glance linger on her for an instant, while in Therese there took place a shock a little like that she had known when she had seen Carol for the first time, and there was the same flash of interest in the woman's blue eyes that had been in her own, she knew, when she saw Carol. And now it was Therese who continued to look, and the other woman who glanced away, and turned around.

Therese looked down at the glass in her hand, and felt a sudden heat in her face and her fingertips, the rush inside her that was neither quite her blood nor her thoughts alone. She knew before they were introduced that this woman was like Carol. And she was beautiful. And she did not look like the picture in the library. Therese smiled as she sipped her drink. She took a long pull at the drink to steady herself.

"A flower, madame?" A waiter was extending a tray full of white orchids.

"Thank you very much." Therese took one. She had trouble with the pin, and someone—Mr. Fenelon or Mr. Stevens it was—came up and helped. "Thanks," she said.

Genevieve Cranell was coming toward her, with Mr. Bernstein behind her. The actress greeted the man with Therese as if she knew him very well.

"Did you meet Miss Cranell?" Mr. Bernstein asked Therese.

Therese looked at the woman. "My name is Therese Belivet." She took the hand the woman extended.

"How do you do? So you're the set department?"

"No. Only part of it." She could still feel the handclasp when the woman released her hand. She felt excited, wildly and stupidly excited.

"Isn't anybody going to bring me a drink?" Miss Cranell asked anybody.

Mr. Bernstein obliged. Mr. Bernstein finished introducing Miss Cranell to the people around him who hadn't met her. Therese heard her tell someone that she had just gotten off a plane and that her luggage was piled in the lobby, and while she spoke, Therese saw her glance at her a couple of times past the men's shoulders. Therese felt an exciting attraction in the neat back of her head, in the funny, careless lift of her nose at the end, the only careless feature of her narrow, classic face. Her lips were rather thin. She looked extremely alert, and imperturbably poised. Yet Therese sensed that Genevieve Cranell might not talk to her again at the party for the simple reason that she probably wanted to.

Therese made her way to a wall mirror, and glanced to see if her hair and her lipstick were still all right.

"Therese," said a voice near her. "Do you like champagne?"

Therese turned and saw Genevieve Cranell. "Of course."

"Of course. Well, toddle up to six-nineteen in a few minutes. That's my suite. We're having an inner circle party later."

"I feel very honored," Therese said.

"So don't waste your thirst on highballs. Where did you get that lovely dress?"

"Bonwit's—it's a wild extravagance."

Genevieve Cranell laughed. She wore a blue woolen suit that actually looked like a wild extravagance. "You look so young, I don't suppose you'll mind if I ask how old you are."

"I'm twenty-one."

She rolled her eyes. "Incredible. Can anyone still be only twenty-one?"

People were watching the actress. Therese was flattered, terribly flattered, and the flattery got in the way of what she felt, or might feel, about Genevieve Cranell.

Miss Cranell offered her cigarette case. "For a while, I thought you might be a minor."

"Is that a crime?"

The actress only looked at her, her blue eyes smiling, over the flame of her lighter. Then as the woman turned her head to light her own cigarette, Therese knew suddenly that Genevieve Cranell would never mean anything to her, nothing apart from this half hour at the cocktail party, that the excitement she felt now would not continue, and not be evoked again at any other time or place. What was it that told her? Therese stared at the taut line of her blonde eyebrow as the first smoke rose from the cigarette, but the answer was not there. And suddenly a feeling of tragedy, almost of regret, filled Therese.

"Are you a New Yorker?" Miss Cranell asked her.

"*Vivy!*"

The new people who had just come in the door surrounded Genevieve Cranell and bore her away. Therese smiled again, and finished her drink, felt the first soothing warmth of the Scotch spreading through her. She talked with a man she had met briefly in Mr. Bernstein's office yesterday, and with another man she didn't know at all, and she looked at the doorway across the room, the doorway that was an empty rectangle at that moment, and she thought of Carol. It would be like Carol to come after all, to ask her once more. Or rather, like the old Carol, but not like this one. Carol would be keeping her appointment now at the Elysée bar. With Abby? With Stanley McVeigh? Therese looked away from the door, as if she were afraid Carol might appear, and she would have to say again, "No." Therese accepted another highball, and felt the emptiness inside her slowly filling with the realization she might see Genevieve Cranell very often, if she chose, and though she would never become entangled, might be loved herself.

One of the men beside her asked, "Who did the sets for *The Lost Messiah*, Therese? Do you remember?"

"Blanchard?" she answered out of nowhere, because she was still thinking of Genevieve Cranell, with a feeling of revulsion, of shame, for what had just occurred to her, and she knew it would never be. She listened to the conversation about Blanchard and someone else, even joined in, but her consciousness had stopped in a tangle where a dozen threads crossed and knotted. One was Danny. One was Carol. One was Genevieve Cranell. One went on and on out of it, but her mind was caught at the intersection. She bent to take a light for her cigarette, and felt herself fall a little deeper into the network, and she clutched at Danny. But the strong black thread did not lead anywhere. She knew as if some prognostic voice were speaking now that she would not go further with Danny. And loneliness swept over her again like a rushing wind, mysterious as the thin tears that covered her eyes suddenly, too thin to be noticed, she knew, as she lifted her head and glanced at the doorway again.

"Don't forget." Genevieve Cranell was beside her, patting her arm, saying quickly, "Six-nineteen. We're adjourning." She started to turn away and came back. "You are coming up? Harkevy's coming up, too."

Therese shook her head. "Thanks, I—I thought I could, but I remember I've got to be somewhere else."

The woman looked at her quizzically. "What's the matter, Therese? Did anything go wrong?"

"No." She smiled, moving toward the door. "Thanks for asking me. No doubt I'll see you again."

"No doubt," the actress said.

Therese went into the room beside the big one and got her coat from the pile on the bed. She hurried down the corridor toward the stairs, past the people who were waiting for the elevator, among them Genevieve Cranell, and Therese didn't care if she saw her or not as she plunged down the wide stairs as if she were running away from something. Therese smiled to herself. The air was cool and sweet on her forehead, made a feathery sound like wings past her ears, and she felt she flew across the streets and up the curbs. Toward Carol. And perhaps Carol knew at this moment, because Carol had known such things before. She crossed another street, and there was the Elysée awning.

The headwaiter said something to her in the foyer, and she told him, "I'm looking for somebody," and went on to the doorway.

She stood in the doorway, looking over the people at the tables in the room where a piano played. The lights were not bright, and she did not see her at first, half hidden in the shadow against the far wall, facing her. Nor did Carol see her. A man sat opposite her, Therese did not know who. Carol raised her hand slowly and brushed her hair back, once on either side, and Therese smiled because the gesture was Carol, and it was Carol she loved and would always love. Oh, in a different way now, because she was a different person, and it was like meeting Carol all over again, but it was still Carol and no one else. It would be Carol, in a thousand cities, a thousand houses, in foreign lands where they would go together, in heaven and in hell. Therese waited. Then as she was about to go to her, Carol saw her, seemed to stare at her incredulously a moment while Therese watched the slow smile growing, before her arm lifted suddenly, her hand waved a quick, eager greeting that Therese had never seen before. Therese walked toward her.

# AFTERWORD

My inspiration for this book came in late 1948, when I was living in New York. I had just finished *Strangers on a Train*, but it wasn't to be published until 1949. Christmas was approaching, I was vaguely depressed and also short of money, and to earn some I took a job as salesgirl in a big department store in Manhattan during the period known as the Christmas rush, which lasts about a month. I think I lasted two and a half weeks.

The store assigned me to the toy section, in my case the doll counter. There were many types of doll, expensive and not so expensive, real hair or artificial, and size and clothing were of utmost importance. Children, some whose noses barely reached the glass showcase top, pressed forward with their mother or father or both, dazzled by the display of brand-new dolls that cried, opened and closed their eyes, stood on their two feet sometimes, and, of course, loved changes of clothing. A rush it was, and I and the four or five young women I worked with behind the long counter could not sit down from eight-thirty in the morning until the lunch break. And even then? The afternoon was the same.

One morning, into this chaos of noise and commerce, there walked a blondish woman in a fur coat. She drifted toward the doll counter with a look of uncertainty—should she buy a doll or something else?—and I think she was slapping a pair of gloves absently into one hand. Perhaps I noticed her because she was alone, or because a mink coat was a rarity, and because she was blondish and seemed to give off light. With the same thoughtful air, she purchased a doll, one of two or three I had shown her, and I wrote her name and address on the receipt, because the doll was to be delivered to an adjacent state. It was a routine transaction, the woman paid and departed. But I felt odd and swimmy in the head, near to fainting, yet at the same time uplifted, as if I had seen a vision.

As usual, I went home after work to my apartment, where I lived alone. That evening I wrote out an idea, a plot, a story about the blondish and elegant woman in the fur coat. I wrote some eight pages in longhand in my then current notebook or cahier. This was the entire story of *The Price of Salt.* It flowed from my pen as if from nowhere—beginning, middle, and end. It took me about two hours, perhaps less.

The following morning I felt even odder, and was aware that I had a fever. It must have been a Sunday, because I remember taking the subway (underground) in the morning, and in those days people had to work Saturday mornings, and all of Saturday in the Christmas rush. I recall nearly fainting while hanging on to a strap in the train. The friend I had an appointment with had some medical knowledge, and I said that I felt sickish, and had noticed a little blister on the skin of my abdomen, when I had taken a shower that morning. My friend took one look at the blister and said, "Chickenpox." Unfortunately, I had never had this childhood ailment, though I'd had just about everything else. The disease is not pleasant for adults, as the fever goes up to 104° Fahrenheit for a couple of days, and, worse, the face, torso, upper arms, even ears and nostrils are covered or lined with pustules that itch and burst. One must not scratch them in one's sleep, otherwise scars and pits result. For a month one goes about with bleeding spots, visible to the public on the face, looking as if one has been hit by a volley of air-gun pellets.

I had to give notice to the department store on Monday that I could not return to work. One of the small runny nosed children there must have passed on the germ, but in a way the germ of a book too: fever is stimulating to the imagination. I did not immediately start writing the book. I prefer to let ideas simmer for weeks. And, too, when *Strangers on a Train* was published and shortly afterward sold to Alfred Hitchcock, who wished to make a film of it, my publishers and also my agent were saying, "Write another book of the same type, so you'll strengthen your reputation as . . ." As what? *Strangers on a Train* had been published as "A Harper Novel of Suspense" by Harper & Bros., as the house was then called, so overnight I had become a "suspense" writer, though *Strangers* in my mind was not categorized, and was simply a novel with an interesting story. If I were to write a novel about a lesbian relationship, would I then be labeled a lesbian-book writer? That was a possibility, even though I might never be inspired to write another such book in my life. So I decided to offer the book under another name. By 1951, I had written it. I could not push it into the background for ten months and write something else, simply because for commercial reasons it might have been wise to write another "suspense" book.

Harper & Bros. rejected *The Price of Salt*, so I was obliged to find another American publisher—to my regret, as I much dislike changing publishers. *The Price of Salt* had some serious and respectable reviews when it appeared in hardcover in 1952. But the real success came a year later with the paperback edition, which sold nearly a million copies and was certainly read by more. The fan letters came in addressed to Claire Morgan, care of the paperback house. I remember receiving envelopes of ten and fifteen letters a couple of times a week and for months on end. A lot of them I answered, but I could not answer them all without a form letter, which I never arranged.

My young protagonist Therese may appear a shrinking violet in my book, but those were the days when gay bars were a dark door somewhere in Manhattan, where people wanting to go to a certain bar got off the subway a station before or after the convenient one, lest they be suspected of being homosexual. The appeal of *The Price of Salt* was that it had a happy ending for its two main characters, or at least they were going to try to have a future together. Prior to this book, homosexuals male and female in American novels had had to pay for their deviation by cutting their wrists, drowning themselves in a swimming pool, or by switching to heterosexuality (so it was stated), or by collapsing—alone and miserable and shunned—into a depression equal to hell. Many of the letters that came to me carried such messages as "Yours is the first book like this with a happy ending! We don't all commit suicide and lots of us are doing fine." Others said, "Thank you for writing such a story. It is a little like my own story . . ." And, "I am eighteen and I live in a small town. I feel lonely because I can't talk to anyone . . ." Sometimes I wrote a letter suggesting that the writer go to a larger town where there would be a chance to meet more people. As I remember, there were as many letters from men as from women, which I considered a good omen for my book. This turned out to be true. The letters trickled in for years, and even now a letter comes once or twice a year from a reader. I never wrote another book like this. My next book was *The Blunderer*. I like to avoid labels. It is American publishers who love them.

May 24, 1989

# LATER STORIES

# OONA, THE JOLLY CAVE WOMAN

She was a bit hairy, one front tooth missing, but her sex appeal was apparent at a distance of two hundred yards or more, like an odor, which perhaps it was. She was round, round-bellied, round-shouldered, round-hipped, and always smiling, always jolly. That was why men liked her. She had always something cooking in a pot on a fire. She was simpleminded and never lost her temper. She had been clubbed over the head so many times, her brain was addled. It was not necessary to club Oona to have her, but that was the custom, and Oona barely troubled to dodge to protect herself.

Oona was constantly pregnant and had never experienced the onset of puberty, her father having had at her since she was five, and after him, her brothers. Her first child was born when she was seven. Even in late pregnancy she was interfered with, and men waited impatiently the half hour or so it took her to give birth before they fell on her again.

Oddly, she kept the birthrate of the tribe more or less steady, and if anything tended to decrease the population, since men neglected their own wives because of thinking of her, or occasionally were killed in fighting over her.

Oona was at last killed by a jealous woman whose husband had not touched her in many months. This man was the first to fall in love. His name was Vipo. His men-friends had laughed at him for not taking some other woman, or his own wife, in the times when Oona was not available. Vipo had lost an eye in fighting his rivals. He was only a middle-sized man. He had always brought Oona the choicest things he had killed. He worked long and hard to make an ornament out of flint, so he became the first artist of his tribe. All the others used flint only for arrowheads or knives. He had given the ornament to Oona to hang around her neck by a string of leather.

When Vipo's wife slew Oona out of jealousy, Vipo slew his wife in hatred and wrath. Then he sang a loud and tragic song. He continued to sing like a madman, as tears ran down his hairy cheeks. The tribe considered killing him, because he was mad and different from everyone else, and they were afraid. Vipo drew images of Oona in the wet sand by the sea, then pictures of her on the flat stones on the mountains near by, pictures that could be seen from a distance. He made a statue of Oona out of wood, then one of stone. Sometimes he slept with these. Out of the clumsy syllables of his language, he made a sentence which evoked Oona whenever he uttered it. He was not the only one who learned and uttered this sentence, or who had known Oona.

Vipo was slain by a jealous woman whose man had not touched her for months. Her man had purchased one of Vipo's statues of Oona for a great price—a vast piece of leather made of several bison hides. Vipo made a beautiful watertight house of it, and had enough left over for clothing for himself. He created more sentences about Oona. Some men had admired him, others had hated him, and all the women had hated him because he had looked at them as if he did not see them. Many men were sad when Vipo was dead.

But in general people were relieved when Vipo was gone. He had been a strange one, disturbing some people's sleep at night.

## TWO DISAGREEABLE PIGEONS

They lived in Trafalgar Square, two pigeons which for convenience shall be called Maud and Claud, though they didn't give each other names. They were simply mates, for two or three years now, loyal in a way, though at the bottom of their little pigeon hearts they detested each other. Their days were spent pecking grain and peanuts strewn by endless tourists and Londoners who bought the stuff from peddlers. *Peck-peck*, all day amid hundreds of other pigeons who like Maud and Claud had nearly lost the ability to fly, because it was hardly necessary any longer. Often Maud was separated from Claud in a bobbing field of pigeons, but by nightfall they somehow found each other and made their way to a cranny in the back of a stone parapet near the National Gallery. *Uff!* and they'd heave their bulging breasts up the two or three feet to their domicile.

Maud would make disagreeable noises in her throat, signifying both pique and scorn. She was the same age as Claud, which wasn't young. Her first mate had been hit in the prime of life by a bus while trying to capture part of a sandwich.

Maud's standoffish sounds could have been interpreted as "At it again today, eh?" or various other taunts at Claud's virility and his groundless self-esteem. Perhaps Claud hadn't been at it again today, but his was a roving eye. Often Maud had the satisfaction of seeing Claud bested by a younger male who swooped down at the wrong moment for Claud and his newly found female. Claud would put up a blustering show, pretend he was willing to fight, but the younger male would go for his eyes and Claud would retreat.

"Shut up," Claud would reply finally, and settle himself for sleep.

Once in a while, for a change of scene, Claud and Maud took the tube to Hampstead Heath. Rather, once they had taken the tube and found themselves at Hampstead Heath, much to their delight. Space! Plenty of things to peck at! No people! Or almost no people. Sometimes they took the tube for amusement, not caring where they might be when they got off. They could always find their way back to Trafalgar Square, even if they had to make a bit of an effort and fly a few yards here and there. Buses were safer as to direction, though there wasn't much to hang on to on the top of a bus. They certainly remembered the direction of Hampstead Heath, and by hopping a bus starting in that direction there was a fair chance they'd get there, and if the bus veered, they simply flew to another bus that looked more promising. They'd made it twice by bus.

However, tubes were more fun, because Maud and Claud enjoyed making people step out of their way. People laughed and pointed when Maud and Claud rode the escalators up and down. Sometimes people whipped out cameras, as in the Square, and they'd be photographed by flash.

"Look out! Don't step on the pigeons! Ha-ha!" That was a familiar cry by now.

Maud was haunted by a vague memory of a daughter who had been clubbed before her eyes on a pavement near the Square. That had been an offspring by her first mate. Or had she imagined it? Maud was shy to this day of people carrying sticks, even umbrellas, of which she saw plenty. Maud would flinch and sidle away a few inches. Maud fancied that she could acquire another mate if she wished, but something—she couldn't say what—kept her with boring Claud.

With mutual consent, they decided to head for Hampstead Heath one Saturday morning. Something awful was going on in Trafalgar Square. There were hordes of people, and bleachers and loudspeakers were being set up. Not a day for peanuts and popcorn. Maud and Claud descended to the underground in Whitehall.

"Ooh, lookie, Mummy!" cried a little girl. "Pigeons!"

Maud and Claud ignored it and kept hopping down. They went under the turnstile, unnoticed but kicked by someone, then took the escalator down. Claud led, though he didn't know where he was going. He hopped onto the first train.

"Look at that! Pigeons!" someone said.

A couple of people laughed.

Maud and Claud were among the few passengers not jostled. They had a clear circle around them. Again it was Claud who led when they got off, his head bobbing authoritatively. He didn't know where he was, but liked giving the impression that he did.

"They're getting on the lift! Ha-haa-aa!"

A way was cleared for them as if they were VIPs.

In the rush of people up the stairs to pavement level, Maud and Claud had to take to their wings. This left them exhausted when they stood finally in the sunlight near a news vendor. Maud started out, leading. The pavement sloped upward, and this direction she took. The pavements near Hampstead Heath usually sloped upward, she remembered. Claud followed.

"Ah, romance," a male voice said.

The voice was wrong. Often Claud led, when he wanted to appear superior to Maud, knowing Maud would follow no matter what. Sometimes it was just the reverse, and it had nothing to do with the mating urge. After three streets, hopping down and up curbs, Maud was becoming tired. Claud had made a wrong decision, detraining when he did, and Maud got beside him and indicated this with a glance and a derogatory rattle. She didn't know where she was, either, though she knew that Trafalgar Square was somewhere behind and to her right. No problem getting home, at least. But this wasn't the Heath.

Then Maud sensed or spotted a patch of green ahead on the left, and with a toss of her head, which made her breast glisten blue and green in the sunlight, she steered Claud to the left. They paused to let a taxi turn, then continued. Up the curb. Now Maud could see the greenery, and she put on some speed, fluttering her wings as her feet moved in double time on the pavement. She mustered the energy to fly over the three-foot-high rail of a little park.

There were benches on which people sat peacefully, and a fair-sized expanse of green grass, untrammeled. A pond in the center. Maud began to peck.

Claud noticed three other pigeons, a female and two males, not far away on the grass. They wouldn't take kindly to him and Maud. But the males were otherwise absorbed at the moment. Maud said something to the effect that Claud might try his luck there, and Claud replied promptly that she might try hers. Maud walked off, turning her back on the lot of them, including Claud. Claud was pecking at a worm, and thinking that he preferred dried corn, when one of the males swooped on him.

The attacking bird was in better physical shape. Claud only rose a few inches in the air, and slammed himself down, not to much effect. Claud beat a retreat, walking, flapping his wings and making noises to indicate that he was annoyed but by no means vanquished and that he simply wasn't going to bother to fight.

Maud affected amusement and indifference.

It began to rain, quite suddenly. Claud and Maud walked toward the nearest tree. The rain had the look of lasting. Should they take the tube for home? It was only midafternoon. Rain would bring the worms out, maybe a snail or two. Suddenly Maud flew at Claud and attacked him in the neck.

Claud was already in a bad mood, and he stalked off toward a path. When he reached the pavement, he turned smartly left. This was the way back to the tube, he thought, and it was even the direction of home.

Maud followed, hating herself for following, but consoled by the fact that she had Claud under her eye and that it was the general direction of Trafalgar Square. Claud's day would come, Maud thought. If she made sufficient effort, a younger male might actually invade their home and rout Claud from his own premises. That would pay him back for—

*Clomp!*

What was that?

A blackness had descended. Claud was in it with her, squawking and flapping.

Maud heard children's laughter. A box! Maud had had it once before, and she'd escaped, she reminded herself. The cardboard box scraped along the pavement, catching one of her legs painfully. She and Claud were tumbled suddenly upside down, they saw a brief patch of sky, then a nasty coat or something was thrown over the box. They were jiggled and jostled as the children ran. They went down steps. Maud and Claud were tossed onto the floor of a brightly lighted room. They were inside a house.

A woman shouted something.

The children, two boys, laughed.

Maud flew onto a table. It was a kitchen in one of those edifices she and Claud had often looked into through a semi-basement window.

"What're you going to do with them?—A-aak!"

Claud had taken off, up to the sink rim. A boy came for him, and Claud hopped down into a corner by a door that was open only a crack.

One boy strewed bread on the floor, which Claud ignored. Claud was interested in the door, Maud saw, but the rest of the house might not be open anywhere, so what good was the door? Maud defecated.

This produced a yelp from the woman. Good! Maud knew that a dropping could go a long way: it meant contempt, for one thing. Maud had been kicked a few times—deliberately—when she'd done it on her own land, Trafalgar Square, not even meaning it as an insult. But then people weren't normal, they were insane, most of them. You could never tell what people were going to do. Peanuts one minute and a club the next.

The woman was still jabbering, and there was a whoop from the boys, and they lunged at Claud with open arms, trying to grab him. Claud flew up and loosed a dropping, hitting one boy in the face. Laughter. Claud teetered on a clothes dryer near the ceiling, oscillating.

A big man with a loud voice came in. Maud detested him on sight. He made a long, bellowing speech, then bent close to Maud and spoke more softly. Maud took two steps backward, knocking a china lid off something, keeping an eye on the man, ready to join Claud if he came any closer. The man left the kitchen.

The woman was making popcorn at the stove. Maud and Claud recognized the smell. Meanwhile the children tittered stupidly by the sink. The man came back with a tall tripod affair. Bright lights came on. Then Maud and Claud understood. They'd seen the same thing in Trafalgar Square on a larger scale—tripods, moving platforms, awful lights everywhere that turned night into day. Now the light was right in Maud's eyes, and she turned in a circle. The camera buzzed. Maud would have defecated again, but at the moment was not able.

"Popcorn!" the man cried.

"Coming!" The woman swung around with the pan just in time to collide with Claud, who had been going to try the window. He had hoped that the top part might be open, but before he had time to see, he was on his side on the floor. He got to his feet. The woman spilled some popcorn on the floor near him, and Claud backed away as if it were poison.

"Ha-ha!" the man laughed. "Scare 'em up again, Simon!"

The smaller of the odious two flailed his arms at Maud, while the other boy stomped toward Claud.

Maud and Claud rose, wings flapping wildly. Claud dropped like a fat eagle onto the forehead and hair of the bigger boy, all claws out.

"Ow!" the boy cried.

Maud contented herself with two hard pecks at the smaller boy's cheeks and as much clawing as she could get in, before she pushed herself off just in time to avoid a swat of the man's fist. It was going to be a fight for life, Maud realized, and she and Claud were trapped.

The woman took a broom to Claud, missing at every swing. "Open the window! Get them *out*!"

"I'll wring their necks! They're insane!" yelled the red-faced man, striding toward the window.

Maud could see that the man was *angry*, but who had brought them here but his own nauseating children? Maud attacked the man just as he was pulling the window down from the top. He fended Maud off with an elbow and ducked.

Claud flew out the window.

"Use the broom!" said the woman, handing it to the man.

Maud evaded the broom, flew to the dish rack over the sink, seized a saucer to brace herself, and as she took off toward the window, the saucer fell in the sink and shattered.

Another cry from the woman, a roar from the man, both of which faded as Maud flew, flew several yards with the energy of her wrath, and then she sank to the civilized pavement, where she could walk normally again and recover her breath. What a relief to get out of that madhouse! Good Lord! Such people should be reported! Maud held her head high and thrust her beak forward with every step. There were groups—*people*, in fact—who fought for pigeons. She'd seen people in Trafalgar Square stopping boys from using guns or even from throwing things at pigeons. If they ever got hold of this family, there'd be hell to pay.

Where was Claud?

Maud stopped and turned. Not that she cared much where Claud was. If she went straight home, as she intended to do, Claud would turn up this evening, she had no doubt. What help had he been to her just now? None.

She heard his voice. Then he appeared behind her, rushing toward her on legs and wings, looking exhausted. Maud shook her feathers and walked on. Claud walked beside her, grumbling a little, as did Maud, but gradually their sounds became calmer. They were, after all, free again, and they were walking in the direction of home. Suddenly Maud made for a bus. Claud followed, getting himself with some difficulty up to the roof. They crouched for better grip. Some buses lurched horribly. They had to switch to another bus, hoping for the best, but their instinct was right and they soon found themselves jolting down the Haymarket. Home! And it wasn't yet dark. The sky was a smoky blue where the sun was setting.

Still time to find a few pickings in the Square before retiring, Maud thought. Claud was thinking the same thing, so they left the bus in Whitehall, and glided down to the familiar ground.

There were not many pigeons still about. Lights were coming on in shop windows. The pickings were poor and trampled. And Maud felt tired and out of sorts.

Claud thrust his head in her way and seized a peanut fragment that Maud had been about to peck.

Maud flew at him, flapping her wings. Why did she put up with him? Selfish, greedy—she couldn't count on him for anything, not even to guard the nest when there was an egg!

Claud retaliated with an ill-meant peck at Maud's eye, which missed her and got her in the head.

Then suddenly—it was impossible to tell whether Maud or Claud moved first—they attacked a passing perambulator. They went for the baby, pecking its cheeks, its eyes. The young woman pushing the pram let out a scream and hit at the pigeons, knocking the breath out of Maud, but she rejoined Claud in the pram in a matter of seconds. A couple of people ran toward the pram, and the pigeons took off. They flew over the heads of their would-be attackers and settled in a group of twenty-odd pigeons who were pecking around a litter basket.

When the two people, plus the woman with the pram, came close to the pigeons, Maud and Claud were not in the least afraid, though some of the other pigeons looked up, startled by the angry voices.

One of the people, a man, rushed among the pigeons, kicking, waving his arms and yelling. Most of the pigeons took lazy flight. Maud headed for home, the nook behind the low stone wall, and when she got there, Claud had already arrived. They settled themselves for sleep, too tired even to grumble to each other. But Maud was not too tired to recall the half peanut that Claud had snatched. Why did she live with him? Why did she, or they, live *here*, running the risk daily of being captured, as they'd been today, or kicked by people who objected even to their droppings? Why? Maud fell asleep, exhausted by her discontent.

The incident of the pecked baby, blinded in one eye, in Trafalgar Square, inspired a couple of letters to the *Times*. But nothing was done about it.

# NOT ONE OF US

It wasn't merely that Edmund Quasthoff had stopped smoking and almost stopped drinking that made him different, slightly goody-goody and therefore vaguely unlikable. It was something else. What?

That was the subject of conversation at Lucienne Gauss's apartment in the East 80s one evening at the drinks hour, seven. Julian Markus, a lawyer, was there with his wife Frieda, also Peter Tomlin, a journalist aged twenty-eight and the youngest of the circle. The circle numbered seven or eight, the ones who knew Edmund well, meaning for most of them about eight years. The others present were Tom Strathmore, a sociologist, and Charles Forbes and his wife, Charles being an editor in a publishing house, and Anita Ketchum, librarian at a New York art museum. They gathered more often at Lucienne's apartment than at anyone else's, because Lucienne liked entertaining and, as a painter working on her own, her hours were flexible.

Lucienne was thirty-three, unmarried, and quite pretty with fluffy reddish hair, a smooth pale skin, and a delicate, intelligent mouth. She liked expensive clothes, she went to a good beauty parlor, and she had style. The rest of the group called her, behind her back, a lady, shy even among themselves at using the word (Tom the sociologist had), because it was an old-fashioned or snob word, perhaps.

Edmund Quasthoff, a tax accountant in a law firm, had been divorced a year ago, because his wife had run off with another man and had therefore asked for a divorce. Edmund was forty, quite tall, with brown hair, a quiet manner, and was neither handsome nor unattractive, but lacking in that spark which can make even a rather ugly person attractive. Lucienne and her group had said after the divorce, "No wonder. Edmund *is* sort of a bore."

On this evening at Lucienne's, someone said out of the blue, "Edmund didn't used to be such a bore—did he?"

"I'm afraid so. *Yes!*" Lucienne yelled from the kitchen, because at that moment she had turned on the water at the sink in order to push ice cubes out of a metal tray. She heard someone laugh. Lucienne went back to the living room with the ice bucket. They were expecting Edmund at any moment. Lucienne had suddenly realized that she wanted Edmund out of their circle, that she actively disliked him.

"Yes, what *is* it about Edmund?" asked Charles Forbes with a sly smile at Lucienne. Charles was pudgy, his shirt front strained at the buttons, a patch of leg often showed between sock and trousers cuff when he sat, but he was well loved by the group, because he was good-natured and bright, and could drink like a fish and never show it. "Maybe we're all jealous because he stopped smoking," Charles said, putting out his cigarette and reaching for another.

"I admit *I'm* jealous," said Peter Tomlin with a broad grin. "I know I should stop and I damned well can't. Tried to twice—in the last year."

Peter's details about his efforts were not interesting. Edmund was due with his new wife, and the others were talking while they could.

"Maybe it's his wife!" Anita Ketchum whispered excitedly, knowing this would get a laugh and encourage further comments. It did.

"Worse than the first by far!" Charles avowed.

"Yes, Lillian wasn't bad at all! I agree," said Lucienne, still on her feet and handing Peter the Vat 69 bottle, so he could top up his glass the way he liked it. "It's true Magda's no asset. That—" Lucienne had been about to say something quite unkind about the scared yet aloof expression which often showed on Magda's face.

"Ah, marriage on the rebound," Tom Strathmore said musingly.

"Certainly was, yes," said Frieda Markus. "Maybe we have to forgive that. You know they say men suffer more than women if their spouses walk out on them? Their egos suffer, they say—worse."

"Mine would suffer with *Magda,* matter of fact," Tom said.

Anita gave a laugh. "And what a name, Magda! Makes me think of a lightbulb or something."

The doorbell rang.

"Must be Edmund." Lucienne went to press the release button. She had asked Edmund and Magda to stay for dinner, but they were going to a play tonight. Only three were staying for dinner, the Markuses and Peter Tomlin.

"But he's changed his job, don't forget," Peter was saying as Lucienne came back into the room. "You can't say he has to be clammed up—secretive, I mean. It's not *that.*" Like the others, Peter sought for a word, a phrase to describe the unlikability of Edmund Quasthoff.

"He's stuffy," said Anita Ketchum with a curl of distaste at her lips.

A few seconds of silence followed. The apartment doorbell was supposed to ring.

"Do you suppose he's happy?" Charles asked in a whisper.

This was enough to raise a clap of collective laughter. The thought of Edmund radiating happiness, even with a two-month-old marriage, was risible.

"But then he's probably never been happy," said Lucienne, just as the bell rang, and she turned to go to the door.

"Not late, I hope, Lucienne dear," said Edmund coming in, bending to kiss Lucienne's cheek, and by inches not touching it.

"No-o. I've got the time but you haven't. How are *you,* Magda?" Lucienne asked with deliberate enthusiasm, as if she really cared how Magda was.

"Very well, thank you, and you?" Magda was in brown again, a light and dark brown cotton dress with a brown satin scarf at her neck.

Both of them looked brown and dull, Lucienne thought as she led them into the living room. Greetings sounded friendly and warm.

"No, just tonic, please . . . Oh well, a smidgen of gin," Edmund said to Charles, who was doing the honors. "Lemon slice, yes, thanks." Edmund as usual gave an impression of sitting on the edge of his armchair seat.

Anita was dutifully making conversation with Magda on the sofa.

"And how're you liking your new job, Edmund?" Lucienne asked. Edmund had been with the accounting department of the United Nations for several years, but his present job was better paid and far less cloistered, Lucienne gathered, with business lunches nearly every day.

"O-oh," Edmund began, "different crowd, I'll say that." He tried to smile. Smiles from Edmund looked like efforts. "These boozy lunches . . ." Edmund shook his head. "I think they even resent the fact I don't smoke. They want you to be like them, you know?"

"Who's them?" asked Charles Forbes.

"Clients of the agency and a lot of the time *their* accountants," Edmund replied. "They all prefer to talk business at the lunch table instead of face to face in my office. 'S funny." Edmund rubbed a forefinger along the side of his arched nose. "I have to have one or two drinks with them—my usual restaurant knows now to make them weak—otherwise our clients might think I'm the Infernal Revenue Department itself putting—honesty before expediency or some such." Edmund's face again cracked in a smile that did not last long.

*Pity,* Lucienne thought, and she almost said it. A strange word to think of, because pity she had not for Edmund. Lucienne exchanged a glance with Charles, then with Tom Strathmore, who was smirking.

"They call me up at all hours of the night too. California doesn't seem to realize the time dif—"

"Take your phone off the hook at night," Charles' wife Ellen put in.

"Oh, can't afford to," Edmund replied. "Sacred cows, these worried clients. Sometimes they ask me questions a pocket calculator could answer. But Babcock and Holt have to be polite, so I go on losing sleep . . . No, thanks, Peter," he said as Peter tried to pour more drink for him. Edmund also pushed gently aside a nearly full ashtray whose smell perhaps annoyed him.

Lucienne would ordinarily have emptied the ashtray, but now she didn't. And Magda? Magda was glancing at her watch as Lucienne looked at her, though she chatted now with Charles on her left. Twenty-eight she was, enviably young to be sure, but what a drip! A bad skin. Small wonder she hadn't been married before. She still kept her job, Edmund had said, something to do with computers. She knitted well, her parents were Mormons, though Magda wasn't. Really wasn't, Lucienne wondered?

A moment later, having declined even orange or tomato juice, Magda said gently to her husband, "Darling . . ." and tapped her wristwatch face.

Edmund put down his glass at once, and his old-fashioned brown shoes with wing tips rose from the floor a little before he hauled himself up. Edmund looked tired already, though it was hardly eight. "Ah, yes, the theater—Thank you, Lucienne. It's been a pleasure as usual."

"But such a short one!" said Lucienne.

When Edmund and Magda had left, there was a general "Whew!" and a few chuckles, which sounded not so much indulgent as bitterly amused.

"I really wouldn't like to be married to that," said Peter Tomlin, who was unmarried. "Frankly," he added. Peter had known Edmund since he, Peter, was twenty-two, having been introduced via Charles Forbes, at whose publishing house Peter had applied for a job without success. The older Charles had liked Peter, and had introduced him to a few of his friends, among them Lucienne and Edmund. Peter remembered his first good impression of Edmund Quasthoff—that of a serious and trustworthy man—but whatever virtue Peter had seen in Edmund was somehow gone now, as if that first impression had been a mistake on Peter's part. Edmund had not lived up to life, somehow. There was something cramped about him, and the crampedness seemed personified in Magda. Or was it that Edmund didn't really like *them*?

"Maybe he deserves Magda," Anita said, and the others laughed.

"Maybe he doesn't like us either," said Peter.

"Oh, but he does," Lucienne said. "Remember, Charles, how pleased he was when—we sort of accepted him—at that first dinner party I asked Edmund and Lillian to here at my place. One of my birthday dinners, I remember. Edmund and Lillian were beaming because they'd been admitted to our charmed circle." Lucienne's laugh was disparaging of their circle and also of Edmund.

"Yes, Edmund did try," said Charles.

"His clothes are so boring even," Anita said.

"True. Can't some of you men give him a hint? You, Julian." Lucienne glanced at Julian's crisp cotton suit. "You're always so dapper."

"Me?" Julian settled his jacket on his shoulders. "I frankly think men pay more attention to what women say. Why should I say anything to him?"

"Magda told me Edmund wants to buy a car," said Ellen.

"Does he drive?" Peter asked.

"May I, Lucienne?" Tom Strathmore reached for the scotch bottle which stood on a tray. "Maybe what Edmund needs is to get thoroughly soused one night. Then Magda might even leave him."

"Hey, we've just invited the Quasthoffs for dinner at our place Friday night," Charles announced. "Maybe Edmund *can* get soused. Who else wants to come?—Lucienne?"

Anticipating boredom, Lucienne hesitated. But it might not be boring. "Why not? Thank you, Charles—and Ellen."

Peter Tomlin couldn't make it because of a Friday night deadline. Anita said she would love to come. Tom Strathmore was free, but not the Markuses, because it was Julian's mother's birthday.

It was a memorable party in the Forbeses' big kitchen which served as dining room. Magda had not been to the penthouse apartment before. She politely looked at the Forbeses' rather good collection of framed drawings by contemporary artists, but seemed afraid to make a comment. Magda was on her best behavior, while the others as if by unspoken agreement were unusually informal and jolly. Part of this, Lucienne realized, was meant to shut Magda out of their happy old circle, and to mock her stiff decorum, though in fact everyone went out of his or her way to try and get Edmund and Magda to join in the fun. One form that this took, Lucienne observed, was Charles's pouring gin into Edmund's tonic glass with a rather free hand. At the table, Ellen did the same with the wine. It was especially good wine, a vintage Margaux that went superbly with the hot-oil-cooked steak morsels which they all dipped into a pot in the center of the round table. There was hot, buttery garlic bread, and paper napkins on which to wipe greasy fingers.

"Come on, you're not working tomorrow," Tom said genially, replenishing Edmund's wine glass.

"I—yam working tomorrow," Edmund replied, smiling. "Always do. Have to on Saturdays."

Magda was giving Edmund a fixed stare, which he missed, because his eyes were not straying her way.

After dinner, they adjourned to the long sun parlor which had a terrace beyond it. With the coffee those who wanted it had a choice of Drambuie, Bénédictine or brandy. Edmund had a sweet tooth, Lucienne knew, and she noticed that Charles had no difficulty in persuading Edmund to accept a snifter of Drambuie. Then they played darts.

"Darts're as far as I'll go toward exercising," said Charles, winding up. His first shot was a bull's-eye.

The others took their turns, and Ellen kept score.

Edmund wound up awkwardly, trying to look amusing, they all knew, though still making an effort to aim right. Edmund was anything but limber and coordinated. His first shot hit the wall three feet away from the board, and since it hit sideways, it pierced nothing and fell to the floor. So did Edmund, having twisted somehow on his left foot and lost his balance.

Cries of "Bravo!" and merry laughter.

Peter extended a hand and hauled Edmund up. "Hurt yourself?"

Edmund looked shocked and was not laughing when he stood up. He straightened his jacket. "I don't think—I have the definite feeling—" His eyes glanced about, but rather swimmily, while the others waited, listening. "I have the feeling I'm not exactly well liked here—so I—"

"Oh-h, Edmund!" said Lucienne.

"What're you talking about, Edmund?" asked Ellen.

A Drambuie was pressed into Edmund's hand, despite the fact that Magda tried gently to restrain the hand that offered it. Edmund was soothed, but not much. The darts game continued. Edmund was sober enough to realize that he shouldn't make an ass of himself by walking out at once in a huff, yet he was drunk enough to reveal his gut feeling, fuzzy as it might be to him just then, that the people around him were not his true friends anymore, that they really didn't like him. Magda persuaded him to drink more coffee.

The Quasthoffs took their leave some fifteen minutes later.

There was an immediate sense of relief among all.

"She is the end, let's face it," said Anita, and flung a dart.

"Well, we got him soused," said Tom Strathmore. "So it's possible."

Somehow they had all tasted blood on seeing Edmund comically sprawled on the floor.

Lucienne that night, having had more to drink than usual, mainly in the form of two good brandies after dinner, telephoned Edmund at four in the morning with an idea of asking him how he was. She knew she was calling him also in order to disturb his sleep. After five rings, when Edmund answered in a sleepy voice, Lucienne found she could not say anything.

"Hello?—Hello? Qu-Quasthoff here . . ."

When she awakened in the morning, the world looked somehow different—sharper edged and more exciting. It was not the slight nervousness that might have been caused by a hangover. In fact Lucienne felt very well after her usual breakfast of orange juice, English tea and toast, and she painted well for two hours. She realized that she was busy detesting Edmund Quasthoff. Ludicrous, but there it was. And how many of her friends were feeling the same way about Edmund today?

The telephone rang just after noon, and it was Anita Ketchum. "I hope I'm not interrupting you in the middle of a masterstroke."

"No, no! What's up?"

"Well—Ellen called me this morning to tell me Edmund's birthday party is off."

"I didn't know any was on."

Anita explained. Magda last evening had invited Charles and Ellen to a birthday dinner party for Edmund at her and Edmund's apartment nine days from now, and had told Ellen she would invite "everybody" plus some friends of hers whom everybody might not have met yet, because it would be a stand-up buffet affair. Then this morning, without any explanation such as that Edmund or she were ill with a lingering ailment, Magda had said she had "decided against" a party, she was sorry.

"Maybe afraid of Edmund's getting pissed again," Lucienne said, but she knew that wasn't the whole answer.

"I'm sure she thinks we don't like her—or Edmund much—which unfortunately is true."

"What *can* we do?" asked Lucienne, feigning chagrin.

"Social outcasts, aren't we? Hah-hah. Got to sign off now, Lucienne, because someone's waiting."

The little contretemps of the canceled party seemed both hostile and silly to Lucienne, and the whole group got wind of it within a day or so, even though they all might not as yet have been invited.

"We can also invite and disinvite," chuckled Julian Markus on the telephone to Lucienne. "What a childish trick—with no excuse such as a business trip."

"No excuse, no. Well, I'll think of something funny, Julian dear."

"What do you mean?"

"A little smack back at them. Don't you think they deserve it?"

"Yes, my dear."

Lucienne's first idea was simple. She and Tom Strathmore would invite Edmund out for lunch on his birthday, and get him so drunk he would be in no condition to return to his office that afternoon. Tom was agreeable. And Edmund sounded grateful when Lucienne rang him up and extended the invitation, without mentioning Magda's name.

Lucienne booked a table at a rather expensive French restaurant in the East 60s. She and Tom and three dry martinis were waiting when Edmund arrived, smiling tentatively, but plainly glad to see his old friends again at a small table. They chatted amiably. Lucienne managed to pay some compliments in regard to Magda.

"She has a certain dignity," said Lucienne.

"I wish she weren't so *shy,*" Edmund responded at once. "I try to pull her out of it."

Another round. Lucienne delayed the ordering by having to make a telephone call at a moment when Tom was able to order a third round to fill the time until Lucienne got back. Then they ordered their meal, with white wine to be followed by a red. On the first glass of white, Tom and Lucienne sang a soft chorus of "Happy Birthday to You" to Edmund as they lifted their glasses. Lucienne had rung Anita, who worked only three blocks away, and Anita joined them when the lunch ended just after three with a Drambuie for Edmund, though Lucienne and Tom abstained. Edmund kept murmuring something about a three o'clock appointment, which maybe would be all right for him to miss, because it really wasn't a top-level appointment. Anita and the others told him it would surely be excusable on his birthday.

"I've just got half an hour," Anita said as they went out of the restaurant together, Anita having partaken of nothing, "but I did want to see you on this special day, Edmund old thing. I insist on inviting you for a drink or a beer."

The others kissed Edmund's cheek and left, then Anita steered Edmund across the street into a corner bar with a fancy decor that tried to be an old Irish pub. Edmund fairly fell into his chair, having nearly slipped a moment before on sawdust. It was a wonder he was served, Anita thought, but hers was a sober presence, and they were served. From this bar, Anita rang Peter Tomlin and explained the situation, which Peter found funny, and Peter agreed to come and take over for a few minutes. Peter arrived. Edmund had a second beer, and insisted upon a coffee, which was ordered, but the combination seemed to make him sick. Anita had left minutes before. Peter waited patiently, prattling nonsense to Edmund, wondering if Edmund was going to throw up or slip under the table.

"Mag's got people coming at six," Edmund mumbled. "Gotta be home—little before—or else." He tried in vain to read his watch.

"Mag you call her? . . . Finish your beer, chum." Peter lifted his first glass of beer, which was nearly drained. "Bottoms up and many happy returns!"

They emptied their glasses.

Peter delivered Edmund to his apartment door at 6:25 and ran. A cocktail party was in swing *chez* Magda and Edmund, Peter could tell from the hum of voices behind the closed door. Edmund had been talking about his "boss" being present, and a couple of important clients. Peter smiled to himself as he rode down in the elevator. He went home, put in a good report to Lucienne, made himself some instant coffee, and got back to his typewriter. Comical, yes! Poor old Edmund! But it was Magda who amused Peter the more. Magda was the stuffy one, their real target, Peter thought.

Peter Tomlin was to change his opinion about that in less than a fortnight. He watched with some surprise and gathering alarm as the attack, led by Lucienne and to a lesser extent Anita, focused on Edmund. Ten days after the sousing of Edmund, Peter looked in one evening at the Markuses' apartment—just to return a couple of books he had borrowed—and found both smirking over Edmund's latest mishap. Edmund had lost his job at Babcock and Holt and was now in the Payne-Whitney for drying out.

"What?" Peter said. "I hadn't heard a word!"

"We just found out today," said Frieda. "Lucienne called me up. She said she tried to call Edmund at his office this morning, and they said he was absent on leave, but she insisted on finding out where he was—said it concerned an emergency in his family, you know how good she is at things like that. So they told her he was in the Payne-Whitney, and she phoned there and talked with Edmund personally. He also had an accident with his car, he said, but luckily he didn't hurt himself or anyone else."

"Holy cow," said Peter.

"He always had a fondness for the bottle, you know," Julian said, "and a thimble-belly to go with it. He really had to go on the wagon five or six years ago, wasn't it, Frieda? Maybe you didn't know Edmund then, Peter. Well, he did, but it didn't last long. Then it got worse when Lillian walked out. But now *this* job—"

Frieda Markus giggled. "This job!—Lucienne didn't help and you know it. She invited Edmund to her place a couple of times and plied him. Made him talk about his troubles with Mag."

Troubles. Peter felt a twinge of dislike for Edmund for talking about his "troubles" after only three months or so of marriage. Didn't everyone have troubles? Did people have to bore their friends with them? "Maybe he deserved it," Peter murmured.

"In a way, *yes,*" Julian said forcefully, and reached for a cigarette. Julian's aggressive attitude implied that the anti-Edmund campaign wasn't over. "He's weak," Julian added.

Peter thanked Julian for the loan of the two books, and took his leave. Again he had work to do in the evening, so he couldn't linger for a drink. At home, Peter hesitated between calling Lucienne or Anita, decided on Lucienne, but she didn't answer, so he tried Anita. Anita was home and Lucienne was there. Both spoke with Peter, and both sounded merry. Peter asked Lucienne about Edmund.

"Oh, he'll be sprung in another week or so, he said. But he won't be quite the same man, I think, when he comes out."

"How do you mean that?"

"Well, he's lost his job and this story isn't going to make it easier for him to get another one. He's probably lost Magda too, because Edmund told me she'd leave him if they didn't move out of New York."

"So . . . maybe they will move," said Peter. "He told you he'd definitely lost his job?"

"Oh yes. They call it a leave of absence at his office, but Edmund admitted they're not taking him back." Lucienne gave a short, shrill laugh. "Just as well they do move out of New York. Magda hates *us,* you know. And frankly Edmund never was one of us—so in a way it's understandable."

Was it understandable, Peter wondered as he got down to his own work. There was something vicious about the whole thing, and he'd been vicious plying Edmund with beers that day. The curious thing was that Peter felt no compassion for Edmund.

One might have thought that the group would leave Edmund alone, at least, even make some effort to cheer him up (without drinks) when he got out of the Payne-Whitney, but it was just the opposite, Peter observed. Anita Ketchum invited Edmund for a quiet dinner at her apartment, and asked Peter to come too. She did not ply him with drink, though Edmund had at least three on his own. Edmund was morose, and Anita did not make his mood any better by talking against Magda. She fairly said that Edmund could and should do better than Magda, and that he ought to try as soon as possible. Peter had to concur here.

"She doesn't seem to make you very happy, Ed," Peter remarked in a man-to-man way, "and now I hear she wants you to move out of New York."

"That's true," Edmund said, "and I dunno where else I'd get a decent job."

They talked until late, getting nowhere, really. Peter left before Edmund did. Peter found that the memory of Edmund depressed him: a tall, hunched figure in limp clothes, looking at the floor as he strolled around Anita's living room with a glass in his hand.

Lucienne was home in bed reading when the telephone rang at one in the morning. It was Edmund, and he said he was going to get a divorce from Mag.

"She just walked out—just now," Edmund said in a happy but a bit drunk-sounding voice. "Said she was going to stay in a hotel tonight. I don't even know where."

Lucienne realized that he wanted a word of praise from her, or a congratulation. "Well, dear Edmund, it may be for the best. I hope it can all be settled smoothly. After all, you haven't been married long."

"No. I think I'm doing—I mean she's doing—the right thing," said Edmund heavily.

Lucienne assured him that she thought so too.

Now Edmund was going to look for another job. He didn't think Mag would make any difficulties, financial or otherwise, about the divorce. "She's a young woman w-who likes her privacy quite a bit. She's surprisingly . . . *independent,* y'know?" Edmund hiccuped.

Lucienne smiled, thinking any woman would want independence from Edmund. "We'll all be wishing you luck, Edmund. And let us know if you think we can pull strings anywhere."

Charles Forbes and Julian Markus went to Edmund's apartment one evening, to discuss business, Charles later said to Lucienne, as Charles had an idea of Edmund's becoming a freelance accountant, and in fact Charles' publishing house needed such a man now. They drank hardly anything, according to Charles, but they did stay up quite late. Edmund had been down in the dumps, and around midnight had lowered the scotch bottle by several inches.

That was on a Thursday night, and by Tuesday morning, Edmund was dead. The cleaning woman had come in with her key and found him asleep in bed, she thought, at nine in the morning. She hadn't realized until nearly noon, and then she had called the police. The police hadn't been able to find Magda, and notifying anybody had been much delayed, so it was Wednesday evening before any of the group knew: Peter Tomlin saw an item in his own newspaper, and telephoned Lucienne.

"A mixture of sleeping pills and alcohol, but they don't suspect suicide," Peter said.

Neither did Lucienne suspect suicide. "What an end," she said with a sigh. "Now what?" She was not at all shocked, but vaguely thinking about the others in their circle hearing the news, or reading it now.

"Well—funeral service tomorrow in a Long Island—um—funeral home, it says."

Peter and Lucienne agreed they should go.

The group of friends, Lucienne Gauss, Peter Tomlin, the Markuses, the Forbeses, Tom Strathmore, Anita Ketchum, were all there and formed at least a half of the small gathering. Maybe a few of Edmund's relatives had come, but the group wasn't sure: Edmund's family lived in the Chicago area, and no one had ever met any of them. Magda was there, dressed in gray with a thin black veil. She stood apart, and barely nodded to Lucienne and the others. It was a nondenominational service to which Lucienne paid no attention, and she doubted if her friends did—except to recognize the words as empty rote and close their ears to it. Afterwards, Lucienne and Charles said they didn't wish to follow the casket to the grave, and neither did the others.

Anita's mouth looked stony, though it was fixed in a pensive, very faint smile. Taxis waited, and they straggled towards them. Tom Strathmore walked with his head down. Charles Forbes looked up at the late summer sky. Charles walked between his wife, Ellen, and Lucienne, and suddenly he said to Lucienne:

"You know, I rang Edmund up a couple of times in the night—just to annoy him. I have to confess that. Ellen knows."

"Did you," said Lucienne calmly.

Tom, just behind them, had heard this. "I did worse," he said with a twitch of a smile. "I told Edmund he might lose his job if he started taking Magda out with him on his business lunches."

Ellen laughed. "Oh, that's not serious, Tom. That's—" But she didn't finish.

*We killed him,* Lucienne thought. Everybody was thinking that, and no one had the guts to say it. Anyone of them might have said, "We killed him, you know?" but no one did. "We'll miss him," Lucienne said finally, as if she meant it.

"Ye-es," someone replied with equal gravity.

They climbed into three taxis, promising to see each other soon.

# WOODROW WILSON'S NECKTIE

The façade of Madame Thibault's Waxwork Horrors glittered and throbbed with red and yellow lights, even in the daytime. Golden balls like knobs—the yellow lights—pulsated amid the red lights, attracting the eye, holding it.

Clive Wilkes loved the place, the inside and outside equally. Since he was a delivery boy for a grocery store, it was easy for him to say a certain delivery had taken him longer than might be expected—he'd had to wait for Mrs. So-and-so to get home, because the doorman had told him she was due any minute, or he'd had to go five blocks to find some change, because Mrs. Zilch had had only a fifty-dollar bill. At these spare moments, and Clive found one or two a week, he visited Madame Thibault's Waxwork Horrors.

Inside the establishment, you went through a dark passage to get in the mood, and then you were confronted by a bloody murder scene: a girl with long blonde hair was sticking a knife into the neck of an old man who sat at a kitchen table eating his dinner. His dinner was a couple of wax frankfurters and wax sauerkraut. Then came the Lindbergh kidnapping, with Hauptmann climbing down a ladder outside a nursery window. You could see the top of the ladder outside the window, and the top half of Hauptmann's figure, clutching the little boy. Also there was Marat in his bath with Charlotte nearby. And Christie with his stocking throttlings of women. Clive loved every tableau, and they never became stale. But he didn't look at them with the solemn, vaguely startled expression of the other people who looked at them. Clive was inclined to smile, even to laugh. They were amusing. Why not laugh? Farther on in the museum were the torture chambers—one old, one modern, purporting to show twentieth-century torture methods in Nazi Germany and in French Algeria. Madame Thibault—who Clive strongly suspected did not exist—kept up to date. There were the Kennedy assassinations, of course, the Tate massacre, and as like as not a murder that had happened just a month ago somewhere.

Clive's first definite ambition in regard to Madame Thibault's Waxwork Horrors was to spend a night there. This he did one night, providently taking along a cheese sandwich in his pocket. It was fairly easy to accomplish. Clive knew that three people worked in the museum proper, down in the bowels as he thought of it, though the museum was on street level, while another man, a plumpish middle-aged fellow in a nautical cap, sold tickets out in front at a booth. There were two men and a woman who worked in the bowels. The woman, also plump with curly brown hair and glasses and about forty, took the tickets at the end of the dark corridor, where the museum began. One of the men lectured constantly, though not more than half the people ever bothered to listen. "Here we see the fanatical expression of the true murderer, captured by the wax artistry of Madame Thibault . . . blah-blah-blah . . ." The other man had black hair and black-rimmed glasses, and he just drifted around, shooing away kids who wanted to climb into the tableaux, maybe watching for pickpockets, or maybe protecting women from unpleasant assaults in the semi-darkness of the place, Clive didn't know.

He only knew it was quite easy to slip into one of the dark corners or into a nook next to one of the Iron Molls—maybe even into one of the Iron Molls, but slender as he was, the spikes might poke him, Clive thought, so he ruled out this idea. He had observed that people were gently urged out around 9:15 p.m. as the museum closed at 9:30 p.m. And lingering as late as possible one evening, Clive had learned that there was a sort of cloak room for the staff behind a door in one back corner, from which he had also heard the sound of a toilet flushing.

So one night in November, Clive concealed himself in the shadows, which were abundant, and listened to the three people as they got ready to leave. The woman—whose name seemed to be Mildred—was lingering to take the money box from Fred, the ticket-seller, and to count it and deposit it somewhere in the cloak room. Clive was not interested in the money, at least not very interested. He was interested in spending a night in the place, to be able to say that he had.

"Night, Mildred! See you tomorrow!" called one of the men.

"Anything else to do? I'm leaving now," said Mildred. "Boy, am I tired! But I'm still going to watch Dragon Man tonight."

"Dragon Man," the other man repeated, uninterested.

Evidently the ticket-seller Fred left from the front of the building after handing in the money box, and in fact Clive recalled seeing him close up the front once, cutting the lights from inside the entrance door, locking it.

Clive stood in a nook by an Iron M[illegible]l. When he heard the back door shut, and the key turn in the lock, he waited for a moment in delicious silence, aloneness, and suspense, then ventured out. He went first on tiptoe to the room where they kept their coats, because he had never seen it. He had brought matches (also cigarettes, though smoking was not allowed, according to several signs), and with the aid of a match, he found the light switch. The room contained an old desk, four or five metal lockers, a tin wastebasket, an umbrella stand, and some books in a bookcase against a rather grimy wall that had once been white. Clive slid open a drawer or two, and found the well-worn wooden box which he had once seen the ticket-seller carrying in through the front door. The box was locked. He could walk out with the box, he thought, but in fact he didn't care to, and he considered this rather decent of himself. He gave the box a wipe with the side of his hand, not forgetting the bottom where his fingertips had touched. That was funny, he thought, wiping something he hadn't stolen.

Clive set about enjoying the night. He found the lights, and put them on, so that the booths with the gory tableaux were all illuminated. He was hungry, and took one bite of his sandwich and put it back in the paper napkin in his pocket. He sauntered slowly past the John F. Kennedy assassination—Robert, Jackie, doctors bending anxiously over the white table on which JFK lay, leaking an ocean of blood which covered the floor. This time Hauptmann's descent of the ladder made Clive giggle. Charles Lindbergh Jr.'s face looked so untroubled, one might have thought he was sitting on the floor of his nursery playing with blocks. Clive swung a leg over a metal bar and climbed into the Judd-Snyder fracas. It gave him a thrill to be standing right *with* them, inches from the throttling-from-behind which the lover was administering to the husband. Clive put a hand out and touched the red-paint blood that was beginning to come from the man's throat where the wire pressed. Clive also touched the cool cheekbones of the victim. The popping eyes were of glass, vaguely disgusting, and Clive did not touch those.

Two hours later, he was singing a church hymn, "Nearer My God to Thee" and "Jesus Wants Me for a Sunbeam." Clive didn't know all the words. He smoked.

By 2 a.m. he was bored, and tried to get out by both front door and back, but couldn't. No spare keys anywhere that he could find. He'd thought of having a hamburger at an all-night place between here and home. His incarceration didn't bother him, however, so he finished the now dry cheese sandwich, made use of the toilet, and slept for a bit on three straight chairs which he arranged in a row. It was so uncomfortable, he knew he would wake up in a while, which he did at 5 a.m. He washed his face, and went for another look at the wax exhibits. This time he took a souvenir—Woodrow Wilson's necktie.

As the hour of nine approached—Madame Thibault's Waxwork Horrors opened at 9:30 a.m.—Clive hid himself in an excellent spot, behind one of the tableaux whose backdrop was a black and gold Chinese screen. In front of the screen was a bed and in the bed lay a wax man with a handlebar mustache, who was supposed to be dead from poisoning by his wife.

The public began trickling in shortly after 9:30 a.m., and the taller, solemn man began mumbling his boring lecture. Clive had to wait till a few minutes past ten before he felt safe enough to mingle with the crowd and make his exit, with Woodrow Wilson's necktie rolled up in his pocket. He was a bit tired, but happy. Though on second thought, who would he tell about it? Joey Vrasky, that blond idiot who worked behind the counter at Simmons's Grocery? Hah! Why bother? Joey didn't deserve a good story. Clive was half an hour late for work.

"I'm sorry, Mr. Simmons, I overslept," Clive said hastily, but he thought quite politely, as he came into the store. There was a delivery job awaiting him. Clive took his bicycle and put the box in front of the handlebars on a platform which had a curb, so a box would not fall off.

Clive lived with his mother, a thin, highly strung woman who was a saleswoman in a shop that sold stockings, girdles, and underwear. Her husband had left her when Clive was five. She had no other children but Clive. Clive had quit high school a year before graduating, to his mother's regret, and for a year he had done nothing but lie around the house or stand on street corners with his chums. But Clive had never been very chummy with any of his friends, for which his mother was thankful, as she considered them a worthless lot. Clive had had the delivery job at Simmons's for nearly a year now, and his mother felt that he was settling down.

When Clive came home that evening at 6:30 p.m., he had a story ready for his mother. Last night he had run into his old friend Richie, who was in the army and home on leave, and they had sat up at Richie's talking so late, that Richie's parents had invited him to stay, and Clive had slept on the couch. His mother accepted this explanation. She made a supper of beans, bacon and eggs.

There was really no one to whom Clive felt like telling his exploit of the night. He couldn't have borne someone looking at him and saying, "Yeah? Well, so what?" because what he had done had taken a bit of planning, even a little daring. He put Woodrow Wilson's tie among his others that hung over a string on the inside of his closet door. It was a gray silk tie, conservative and expensive. Several times that day, Clive imagined the two men in the place, or maybe the woman named Mildred, glancing at Woodrow Wilson and exclaiming:

"Hey! What happened to Woodrow Wilson's tie, I wonder?"

Each time Clive thought of this, he had to duck his head to hide his smile.

After twenty-four hours, however, the exploit had begun to lose its charm and excitement. Clive's excitement arose only again—and it could arise every day and two or three times a day—when he cycled past the twinkling façade of Madame Thibault's Waxwork Horrors. His heart would give a leap, his blood would run a little faster, and he would think of all the motionless murders going on in there, and all the stupid faces of Mr. and Mrs. Johnny Q. Public gaping at them. But Clive didn't even buy another ticket—price sixty-five cents—to go in and look at Woodrow Wilson and see that his tie was missing and his collar button showing—his work.

Clive did get another idea one afternoon, a hilarious idea that would make the public sit up and take notice. Clive's ribs trembled with suppressed laughter as he pedaled towards Simmons's, having just delivered a carton of groceries.

When should he do it? Tonight? No, best to take a day or so to plan it. It would take brains. And silence. And sure movements—all the things Clive admired. He spent two days thinking about it. He went to his local snack bar and drank Coca-Cola and beer, and played the pinball machines with his pals. The pinball machines had pulsating lights, too—MORE THAN ONE CAN PLAY and IT'S MORE FUN TO COMPETE—but Clive thought only of Madame Thibault's as he stared at the rolling, bouncing balls that mounted a score he cared nothing about. It was the same when he looked at the rainbow-colored jukebox whose blues, reds and yellows undulated, and when he went over to drop a few coins in it. He was thinking of what he was going to do in Madame Thibault's Waxwork Horrors.

On the second night, after a supper with his mother, Clive went to Madame Thibault's and bought a ticket. The old guy who sold tickets barely looked at people, he was so busy making change and tearing off tickets, which was just as well. Clive went in at 9 p.m.

He looked at the tableaux, though they were not so fascinating to him tonight as usual. Woodrow Wilson's tie was still missing, as if no one had noticed it, and Clive had a good chuckle over this, which he concealed behind his hand. Clive remembered that the solemn-faced pickpocket-watcher—the drifting snoop—had been the last to leave the night Clive had stayed, so Clive assumed he had the keys, and therefore he ought to be the last to be killed.

The woman was the first. Clive hid himself beside one of the Iron Molls again, while the crowd oozed out, and as Mildred walked past him, in her hat and coat, to leave via the back door, Clive stepped out and wrapped an arm around her throat from behind.

She made only a small "Ur-rk" sound.

Clive squeezed her throat with his hands, stopping her voice. At last she slumped, and Clive dragged her into a dark, recessed corner to the left of the cloakroom as one faced that room, and he knocked an empty cardboard box of some kind over, but it didn't make enough noise to attract the attention of the other two men.

"Mildred's gone?" one of the men said.

"She might be still in the office."

"No, she's not." This voice had already gone into the corridor where Clive crouched over Mildred, and had looked into the empty cloakroom where the light was still on. "She's left. Well, I'm calling it a day, too."

Clive stepped out then, and encircled this man's neck in the same manner. The job was more difficult, because the man struggled, but Clive's arm was thin and strong, he acted with swiftness, and he knocked the man's head against the nearest wall.

"What's going on?" The thump had brought the second man.

This time, Clive tried a punch to the man's jaw, but missed and hit his neck. However, this so stunned the man—the solemn fellow, the snoop—that a second blow was easy, and then Clive was able to take him by the shirtfront and bash his head against the wall which was harder than the wooden floor. Then Clive made sure all three were dead. The two men's heads were bleeding. The woman was bleeding slightly from the mouth. Clive reached for the keys in the second man's pockets. They were in his left trousers pocket and with them was a penknife. Clive took the knife also.

Then the taller man moved slightly. Alarmed, Clive opened the pearl-handled penknife and went to work with it. He plunged it into the man's throat three or four times.

*Close call!* Clive thought, and he checked again to make sure they were all dead now. They most certainly were, and that was most certainly real blood coming out, not the red paint of Madame Thibault's Waxwork Horrors. Clive switched on the lights for the tableaux, and went into the exhibition hall for the interesting task of choosing the right places for the corpses.

The woman belonged in Marat's bath, not much doubt about that, and Clive debated removing her clothing, but decided against it, simply because she would look much funnier sitting in a bath with a fur-trimmed coat and hat on than naked. The figure of Marat sent him off in laughter. He'd expected sticks for legs, and nothing between the legs, because you couldn't see any more of Marat than from the middle of his torso up, but Marat had no legs at all, and his wax body ended just below the waist in a fat stump which was planted on a wooden platform so it would not topple. This crazy item Clive carried into the cloakroom and set squarely in the middle of the desk, like a Buddha. He then carried Mildred—who weighed a good bit—onto the Marat scene and stuck her in the bath. Her hat fell off and he pushed it on again, a bit over one eye. Her bleeding mouth hung open.

God, it *was* funny!

Now for the men. Obviously, the one whose throat he had cut would look good in the place of the old man who was eating franks and sauerkraut, because the girl behind him was supposed to be stabbing him in the throat. This work took Clive some fifteen minutes. Since the wax figure of the old man was in a seated position, Clive stuck him on the toilet off the cloakroom. It was amusing to see the old man on the toilet, throat bleeding, a knife in one hand and a fork in the other, apparently waiting for something to eat. Clive lurched against the doorjamb laughing loudly, not even caring if someone heard him, because it was so ludicrous, it was worth getting caught for.

Next, the little snoop. Clive looked around him, and his eye fell on the Woodrow Wilson scene, which depicted the signing of the armistice in 1918. A wax figure—Woodrow Wilson—sat at a huge desk signing a paper, and that was the logical place for a man whose head was split open and bleeding. With some difficulty Clive got the pen out of Woodrow Wilson's fingers, laid it to one side on the desk, and carried the figure—they did not weigh very much—into the cloakroom where Clive seated him at the desk, rigid arms in attitude of writing, and Clive stuck a ballpoint pen into his right hand. Now for the last heave. Clive saw that his jacket was now quite spotted with blood, and he would have to get rid of it, but so far no blood was on his trousers.

Clive dragged the second man to the Woodrow Wilson tableau, heaved him up onto the platform, and rolled him towards the desk. His head was still leaking blood. Clive got him up onto the chair, but the head toppled forward onto the green-blottered desk, onto the phony blank pages, and the pen barely stood upright in the limp hand.

But it was done. Clive stood back and smiled. Then he listened. Clive sat down on a straight chair somewhere and rested for a few minutes, because his heart was beating fast, and he suddenly realized that every muscle in his body was tired. Ah, well, now he had the keys. He could get out, go home, have a good night's rest, because he wanted to be ready to enjoy tomorrow. Clive took a sweater from one of the male figures in a log cabin tableau. He had to pull the sweater down over the feet to get it off, because the arms would not bend, and it stretched the neck of the sweater but that couldn't be helped. Now the wax figure had a bib of a shirtfront, and naked arms and chest.

Clive wadded up his jacket and went everywhere with it, erasing fingerprints wherever he thought he had touched. He turned the lights off, and made his way carefully to the back door, which was not locked. Clive locked it behind him, and would have left the keys in a mailbox, if there had been one, but there was none, so he dropped the keys on the doorstep. In a wire rubbish basket, he found some newspapers, and he wrapped his jacket in them, and walked on with it until he found another wire rubbish basket, where he forced the bundle down among candy wrappers and beer cans.

"A new sweater?" his mother asked that night.

"Richie gave it to me—for luck."

Clive slept like the dead, too tired even to laugh again at the memory of the old man sitting on the toilet.

The next morning, Clive was standing across the street when the ticket-seller arrived just before 9:30 a.m. By 9:35 a.m., only three people had gone in (evidently Fred had a key to the front door, in case his colleagues were late), but Clive could not wait any longer, so he crossed the street and bought a ticket. Now the ticket-seller was doubling as ticket-taker, or telling people, "Just go on in. Everybody's late this morning." The ticket man stepped inside the door to put on some lights, then walked all the way into the place to put on the display lights, which worked from switches in the hall that led to the cloakroom. And the funny thing to Clive, who was walking behind him, was that the ticket man didn't notice anything odd, didn't notice Mildred in hat and coat sitting in Marat's bathtub.

The customers so far were a man and woman, a boy of fourteen or so in sneakers, and a single man. They looked expressionlessly at Mildred in the tub, as if they thought it quite "normal," which could have sent Clive into paroxysms of mirth, except that his heart was thumping madly, and he was hardly breathing for suspense. Also, the man with his face in franks and sauerkraut brought no surprise either. Clive was a bit disappointed.

Two more people came in, a man and a woman.

Then at last by the Woodrow Wilson tableau, there was a reaction. One of the women clinging to a man's arm, asked:

"Was there someone shot when the armistice was signed?"

"I don't know. I don't *think* so," the man replied vaguely. "Yes-s—Let me think."

Clive's laughter pressed like an explosion in his chest, he spun on his heel to control himself, and he had the feeling he knew all about history, and that no one else did. By now, of course, the real blood had turned dark red. The green blotter was now dark red, and blood had run down the side of the desk.

A woman on the other side of the hall, where Mildred was, let out a scream.

A man laughed, but only briefly.

Suddenly everything happened. A woman shrieked, and at the same time, a man yelled, "My God, it's *real*!"

Clive saw a man climbing up to investigate the corpse with its face in the frankfurters.

"The blood's *real*! It's a dead man!"

Another man—one of the public—slumped to the floor. He had fainted!

The ticket-seller came bustling in. "What's the trouble?"

"Coupla corpses here! Real ones!"

Now the ticket-seller looked at Marat's bathtub and fairly jumped into the air with surprise. "Holy Christmas! Holy *cripes*!—*Mildred*!"

"And this one!"

"And the one here!"

"My God, got to—got to call the police!" said the ticket-seller Fred. "Could you all, please—just leave?"

One man and woman went out hurriedly. But the rest lingered, shocked, fascinated.

Fred had trotted into the cloakroom, where the telephone was, and Clive heard him yell something. He'd seen the man at the desk, of course, Woodrow Wilson, and Marat on the desk.

Clive thought it was time to drift out, so he did, sidling his way through four or five people who were peering in the door, coming in maybe because there was no ticket-seller.

That was good, Clive thought. That was all right. Not bad.

He had not intended to go to work that day, but suddenly he thought it wiser to check in and ask for the day off. Mr. Simmons was of course as sour as ever when Clive said he was not feeling well, but as Clive held his stomach and appeared weak, there was little old Simmons could do. Clive left the store. He had brought with him all his ready cash, about twenty-three dollars.

Clive wanted to take a long bus ride somewhere. He realized that suspicion was likely to fall on him, if the ticket-seller remembered his coming to Madame Thibault's very often, or especially if he remembered his being there last night, but this had little to do with his desire to take a bus ride. His longing for a bus ride was simply, somehow, irresistible and purposeless. He bought a ticket westward for something over seven dollars, one way. This brought him, by about 7 p.m., to a good-sized town in Indiana, whose name Clive paid no attention to.

The bus spilled a few passengers, Clive included, at a terminal where there was a cafeteria and a bar. Clive by now was curious about the newspapers, and went at once to the newsstand near the street door of the cafeteria. And there it was:

TRIPLE MURDER IN WAXWORKS

MASS MURDER IN WAXWORKS MUSEUM

MYSTERY KILLER: THREE DEAD IN WAXWORKS MUSEUM

Clive liked the last headline best. He bought the three newspapers, and stood at the bar with a beer.

> This morning at 9:30 a.m., ticket man Fred J. Keating and several of the public who had come to see Madame Thibault's Waxworks Horrors, a noted attraction of this city, were confronted by three genuine corpses among the displays. They were the bodies of Mrs. Mildred Veery, 41; George P. Hartley, 43; and Richard K. MacFadden, 37, all employed at the waxworks museum. The two men were killed by concussions to the head, and in the case of one also by stabbing, and the woman by strangulation. Police are searching for clues on the premises. The murders are believed to have

> taken place shortly before 10 p.m. last evening, when the three employees were about to leave the museum. The murderer or murderers may have been among the last patrons of the museum before closing time at 9:30 p.m. It is thought that he or they may have concealed themselves somewhere in the museum until the rest of the patrons had left . . .

Clive was pleased. He smiled as he sipped his beer. He hunched over the papers, as if he did not wish the rest of the world to share his pleasure, but this was not true. After a few minutes, Clive looked to right and left to see if anyone else among the men and a few women at the bar were reading the story also. Two men were reading newspapers, but Clive could not tell if they were reading about him necessarily, because their newspapers were folded. Clive lit a cigarette and went through all three newspapers to see if there was any clue about him. He found none at all. One paper said specifically that Fred J. Keating had not noticed any person or persons entering the museum last evening who looked suspicious.

> . . . Because of the bizarre arrangement of the victims and of the displaced wax figures in the exhibitions, in whose places the victims were put, police are looking for a psychopathic killer. Residents of the area have been warned by radio and television to take special precautions on the street and to keep their homes locked . . .

Clive chuckled over that one. Psychopathic killer. He was sorry about the lack of detail, the lack of humor in the three write-ups. They might have said something about the old guy sitting on the toilet. Or the fellow signing the armistice with the back of his head bashed in. Those were strokes of genius. Why didn't they appreciate them?

When he had finished his beer, Clive walked out onto the sidewalk. It was now dark and the streetlights were on. He enjoyed looking around in the new town, looking into shop windows. But he was aiming for a hamburger place, and he went into the first one he came to. It was a diner made up to look like a crack train made of chromium. Clive ordered two hamburgers and a cup of coffee. Next to him were two Western-looking men in cowboy boots and rather soiled broad-brimmed hats. Was one a sheriff, Clive wondered? But they were talking, in a drawl, about acreage somewhere. Land. Money. They were hunched over hamburgers and coffee, one so close his elbow kept brushing Clive's. Clive was reading his newspapers all over again, and he had propped one against the napkin container in front of him.

One of the men asked for a napkin and disturbed Clive, but Clive smiled, and said in a friendly way:

"Did you read about the murders in the waxworks?"

The man looked blank, then said, "Saw the headlines."

"Someone killed the three people who worked in the place. Look." There was a photograph in one of the papers, but Clive didn't much like it, because it showed the corpses lined up on the floor. He would have preferred Mildred in the bathtub.

"Yeah," said the Westerner, edging away from Clive as if he didn't like him.

"The bodies were put into a few of the exhibitions. Like the wax figures. They say that, but they don't show a picture of it," said Clive.

"Yeah," said the Westerner, and went on with his hamburger.

Clive felt let down and somehow insulted. His face grew a little warm as he stared back at his newspapers. In fact, anger was growing very quickly inside him, making his heart go faster, as it did when he passed Madame Thibault's Waxwork Horrors, though now the sensation was not at all pleasant. Clive put on a smile, however, and turned again to the man on his left. "I mention it, because I did it. That's my work there." He pointed at the picture of the corpses.

"Listen, boy," said the Westerner, chewing, "you just keep to yourself tonight. Okay? We ain't botherin' you, and don't you go botherin' us." He laughed a little, and glanced at his companion.

His friend was staring at Clive, but looked away at once when Clive looked at him.

This was a double rebuff, and quite enough for Clive. Clive got his money out and paid for his unfinished food with a dollar bill and a fifty-cent piece. He left the change and walked to the sliding door exit.

"But y'know, maybe that kid ain't kiddin'," Clive heard one of the men say.

Clive turned and said, "*I* ain't kiddin'!" Then he went out into the night.

Clive slept at a YMCA. The next day, he half expected he would be picked up by any passing cop on the beat, but he wasn't, and he passed a few. He got a lift to another town, nearer his home town. The day's newspapers brought no mention of his name, and no clues. In another café that evening almost the identical conversation took place between Clive and a couple of fellows around his own age. They didn't believe him. It was stupid of them, Clive thought, and he wondered if they were pretending? Or lying?

Clive hitched his way to his hometown, and headed for the police station. He was curious to see what *they* would say. He imagined what his mother would say after he confessed. Probably the same thing she had said to her friends sometimes, or that she'd said to a policeman when he was sixteen and had stolen a car:

"Clive hasn't been the same boy since his father went away. I know he needs a man around the house, a man to look up to, imitate, y'know. That's what people tell me. Since fourteen, Clive's been asking me questions like, 'Who am I, anyway?' and 'Am I a person, mom?' " Clive could see and hear her already in the police station.

"I have an important confession to make," Clive said to a guard, or somebody, sitting at a desk at the front of the station.

The guard's attitude was rude and suspicious, Clive thought, but he was told to walk to an office, where he spoke with a police officer who had gray hair and a fat face. Clive told his story.

"Where do you go to school, Clive?"

"I don't. I'm eighteen." Clive told him about his job at Simmons's Grocery.

"Clive, you've got troubles, but they're not the ones you're talking about," said the officer.

Clive had to wait in a room, and nearly an hour later a psychiatrist was brought in. Then his mother. Clive became more and more impatient. They didn't believe him. They were saying he was a typical case of false confessing in order to attract attention to himself. His mother's repeated statements about his asking questions like "Am I a person?" only seemed to corroborate the psychiatrist and the police in their opinion.

Clive was to report somewhere twice a week for psychiatric therapy.

He fumed. He refused to go back to Simmons's Grocery, but found another delivery job, because he liked having a little money in his pocket, and he was fast on his bicycle and honest with the change.

"You haven't *found* the murderer, have you?" Clive said to the psychiatrist, associating him, Clive realized, with the police. "You're all the biggest bunch of jackasses I've ever seen in my life!"

The psychiatrist lost his temper, which was at least human.

"You'll never get anywhere talking to people like that, boy."

Clive said, "Some perfectly ordinary strangers in Indiana said, 'Maybe that kid ain't kiddin'.' They seem to have had more sense than *you*!"

The psychiatrist laughed.

Clive smoldered. One thing might have helped to prove his story, Woodrow Wilson's necktie, which still hung in his closet. But these bastards damned well didn't deserve to see that tie. Even as he ate his suppers with his mother, went to movies with her, and delivered groceries, he was planning. He'd do something more important next time: start a fire in the depths of a big building, plant a bomb somewhere, take a machine gun up to some penthouse and let 'em have it down on the street. Kill a hundred people at least. They'd have to come up in the building to get him. They'd know then. They'd treat him like somebody who existed.

# THE TERRORS OF BASKET-WEAVING

Diane's terror began in an innocent and fortuitous way. She and her husband, Reg, lived in Manhattan, but had a cottage on the Massachusetts coast near Truro where they spent most weekends. Diane was a press relations officer in an agency called Retting. Reg was a lawyer. They were both thirty-eight, childless by choice, and both earned good salaries.

They enjoyed walks along the beach, and usually they took walks alone, not with each other. Diane liked to look for pretty stones, interesting shells, bottles of various sizes and colors, bits of wood rubbed smooth by sand and wind. These items she took back to the unpainted gray cottage they called "the shack," lived with them for a few weeks or months, then Diane threw nearly all of them out, because she didn't want the shack to become a magpie's nest. One Sunday morning she found a wicker basket bleached nearly white and with its bottom stoved in, but its frame and sides quite sturdy. This looked like an old-fashioned crib basket for a baby, because one end of it rose higher than the other, the foot part tapered, and it was just the size for a newborn or for a baby up to a few months. It was the kind called a Moses basket, Diane thought.

Was the basket even American? It was amusing to think that it might have fallen overboard or been thrown away, old and broken, from a passing Italian tanker, or some foreign boat that might have had a woman and child on board. Anyway, Diane decided to take it home, and she put it for the nonce on a bench on the side porch of the shack, where colored stones and pebbles and sea glass already lay. She might try to repair it, for fun, because in its present condition it was useless. Reg was then shifting sand with a snow shovel from one side of the wooden front steps, and was going to plant more beach grass from the dunes, like a second line of troops, between them and the sea to keep the sand in place. His industry, which Diane knew would go on another hour or so until lunchtime—and cold lobster and potato salad was already in the fridge—inspired her to try her hand at the basket now.

She had realized a few minutes before that the kind of slender twigs she needed stood already in a brass cylinder beside their small fireplace. Withes or withies—the words sounded nice in her head—might be more appropriate, but on the other hand the twigs would give more strength to the bottom of a basket which she might use to hold small potted plants, for instance. One would be able to move several pots into the sun all at once in a basket—if she could mend the basket.

Diane took the pruning shears, and cut five lengths of reddish-brown twigs—results of a neighbor's apple-tree pruning, she recalled—and then snipped nine shorter lengths for the crosspieces. She estimated she would need nine. A ball of twine sat handy on a shelf, and Diane at once got to work. She plucked out what was left of the broken pieces in the basket, and picked up one of her long twigs. The slightly pointed ends, an angle made by the shears, slipped easily between the sturdy withes that formed the bottom rim. She took up a second and a third. Diane then, before she attempted to tie the long pieces, wove the shorter lengths under and over the longer, at right angles. The twigs were just flexible enough to be manageable, and stiff enough to be strong. No piece projected too far. She had cut them just the right length, measuring only with her eye or thumb before snipping. Then the twine.

Over and under, around the twig ends at the rim and through the withes already decoratively twisted there, then a good solid knot. She was able to continue with the cord to the next twig in a couple of places, so she did not have to tie a knot at each crosspiece. Suddenly to her amazement the basket was repaired, and it looked splendid.

In her first glow of pride, Diane looked at her watch. Hardly fifteen minutes had passed since she had come into the house! How had she done it? She held the top end of the basket up, and pressed the palm of her right hand against the floor of the basket. It gave out firm-sounding squeaks. It had spring in it. And strength. She stared at the neatly twisted cord, at the correct over-and-under lengths, all about the diameter of pencils, and she wondered again how she had done it.

That was when the terror began to creep up on her, at first like a faint suspicion or surmise or question. Had she some relative or ancestor not so far in the past, who had been an excellent basket-weaver? Not that she knew of, and the idea made her smile with amusement. Grandmothers and great-grandmothers who could quilt and crochet didn't count. This was more primitive.

Yes, people had been weaving baskets thousands of years before Christ, and maybe even a million years ago, hadn't they? Baskets might have come before clay pots.

The answer to her question, how had she done it, might be that the ancient craft of basket-weaving had been carried on for so long by the human race that it had surfaced in her this Sunday morning in the late twentieth century. Diane found this thought rather frightening.

As she set the table for lunch, she upset a wine glass, but the glass was empty and it didn't break. Reg was still shoveling, but slowing up, nearly finished. It was still early for lunch, but Diane had wanted the table set, the salad dressing made in the wooden bowl, before she took a swat at the work she had brought with her. Finally she sat with a yellow pad and pencil, and opened the plastic-covered folder marked RETTING, plus her own name, DIANE CLARKE, in smaller letters at the bottom. She had to write three hundred words about a kitchen gadget that extracted air from plastic bags of apples, oranges, potatoes or whatever. After the air was extracted, the bags could be stored in the bottom of the fridge as usual, but the product kept much longer and took up less space because of the absence of air in the bag. She had seen the gadget work in the office, and she had a photograph of it now. It was a sixteen-inch-long tube which one fastened to the cold water tap in the kitchen. The water from the tap drained away, but its force moved a turbine in the tube, which created a vacuum after a hollow needle was stuck into the sealed bag. Diane understood the principle quite well, but she began to feel odd and disoriented.

It was odd to be sitting in a cottage built in a simple style more than a hundred years ago, to have just repaired a basket in the manner that people would have made or repaired a basket thousands of years ago, and to be trying to compose a sentence about a gadget whose existence depended upon modern plumbing, sealed packaging, transport by machinery of fruit and vegetables grown hundreds of miles (possibly thousands) from the places where they would be consumed. If this weren't so, people could simply carry fruit and vegetables home in a sack from the fields, or in baskets such as the one she had just mended.

Diane put down the pencil, picked up a ballpoint pen, lit a cigarette, and wrote the first words. "Need more space in your fridge? Tired of having to buy more lemons at the supermarket than you can use in the next month? Here is an inexpensive gadget that might interest you." It wasn't particularly inexpensive, but no matter. Lots of people were going to pay thousands of dollars for this gadget. She would be paid a sizable amount also, meaning a certain fraction of her salary for writing about it. As she worked on, she kept seeing a vision of her crib-shaped basket and thinking that the basket—per se, as a thing to be used—was far more important than the kitchen gadget. However, it was perfectly normal to consider a basket more important or useful, she supposed, for the simple reason that a basket was.

"Nice walk this morning?" Reg asked, relaxing with a pre-lunch glass of cold white wine. He was standing in the low-ceilinged living room, in shorts, an unbuttoned shirt, sandals. His face had browned further, and the skin was pinkish over his cheekbones.

"Yes. Found a basket. Rather nice. Want to see it?"

"Sure."

She led the way to the side porch, and indicated the basket on the wooden table. "The bottom was all broken—so I fixed it."

"*You* fixed it?" Reg was leaning over it with admiration. "Yeah, I can see. Nice job, Di."

She felt a tremor, a little like shame. Or was it fear? She felt uncomfortable as Reg picked up the basket and looked at its underside. "Might be nice to hold kindling—or magazines, maybe," she said. "We can always throw it away when we get bored with it."

"Throw it away, no! It's sort of amusing—shaped like a baby's cradle or something."

"That's what I thought—that it must have been made for a baby." She drifted back into the living room, wishing now that Reg would stop examining the basket.

"Didn't know you had such talents, Di. Girl Scout lore?"

Diane gave a laugh. Reg knew she'd never joined the Girl Scouts. "Don't forget the Gartners are coming at seven-thirty."

"Um-m. Yes, thanks. I didn't forget.—What's for dinner? We've got everything we need?"

Diane said they had. The Gartners were bringing raspberries from their garden plus cream. Reg had meant he was willing to drive to town in case they had to buy anything else.

The Gartners arrived just before eight, and Reg made dacquiris. There was scotch for any who preferred it, and Olivia Gartner did. She was a serious drinker and held it well. An investment counselor, she was, and her husband Pete was a professor in the math department at Columbia.

Diane, after a swim around four o'clock, had collected some dry reeds from the dunes and among these had put a few long-stemmed blossoming weeds and wild flowers, blue and pink and orangy-yellow. She had laid all these in the crib-shaped basket which she had set on the floor near the fireplace.

"Isn't this pretty!" said Olivia during her second scotch, as if the drink had opened her eyes. She meant the floral arrangement, but Reg at once said:

"And look at the basket, Olivia! Diane found it on the beach today and *repaired* it." Reg lifted the basket as high as his head, so Olivia and Pete could admire its underside.

Olivia chuckled. "That's fantastic, Diane! Beautiful! How long did it take you?—It's a sweet basket."

"That's the funny thing," Diane began, eager to express herself. "It took me about twelve minutes!"

"Look how proud she is of it!" said Reg, smiling.

Pete was running his thumb over the apple twigs at the bottom, nodding his approval.

"Yes, it was almost terrifying," Diane went on.

"Terrifying?" Pete lifted his eyebrows.

"I'm not explaining myself very well." Diane had a polite smile on her face, though she was serious. "I felt as if I'd struck some hidden talent or knowledge—just suddenly. Everything I did, I felt sure of. I was amazed."

"Looks strong too," Pete said, and set the basket back where it had been.

Then they talked about something else. The cost of heating, if they used their cottages at all in the coming winter. Diane had hoped the basket conversation would continue a little longer. Another round of drinks, while Diane put their cold supper on the table. Bowls of jellied consommé with a slice of lemon to start with. They sat down. Diane felt unsatisfied. Or was it a sense of disturbance? Disturbance because of what? Just because they hadn't pursued the subject of the basket? Why should they have? It was merely a basket to them, mended the way anyone could have mended it. Or could just anyone have mended it that well? Diane happened to be sitting at the end of the table, so the basket was hardly four feet from her, behind her and to her right. She felt bothered somehow even by the basket's nearness. That was very odd. She must get to the bottom of it—that was funny, in view of the basket repair—but now wasn't the time, with three other people talking, and half her mind on seeing that her guests had a good meal.

While they were drinking coffee, Diane lit three candles and the oil lamp, and they listened to a record of Mozart *divertimenti*. They didn't listen, but it served as background music for their conversation. Diane listened to the music. It sounded skillful, even modern, and extremely civilized. Diane enjoyed her brandy. The brandy too seemed the epitome of human skill, care, knowledge. Not like a basket any child could put together. Perhaps a child in years couldn't, but a child as to progress in the evolution of the human race could weave a basket.

Was she possibly feeling her drinks? Diane pulled her long cotton skirt farther down over her knees. The subject was lobbies now, the impotence of any president, even Congress against them.

Monday morning early Diane and Reg flew back to New York by helicopter. Neither had to be at work before eleven. Diane had supposed that New York and work would put the disquieting thoughts re the basket out of her head, but that was not so. New York seemed to emphasize what she had felt up at the shack, even though the origin of her feelings had stayed at the shack. What were her feelings, anyway? Diane disliked vagueness, and was used to labeling her emotions jealousy, resentment, suspicion or whatever, even if the emotion was not always to her credit. But this?

What she felt was most certainly not guilt, though it was similarly troubling and unpleasant. Not envy either, not in the sense of desiring to master basketry so she could make a truly great basket, whatever that was. She'd always thought basket-weaving an occupation for the simple-minded, and it had become in fact a symbol of what psychiatrists advised disturbed people to take up. That was not it at all.

Diane felt that she had lost herself. Since repairing that basket, she wasn't any longer Diane Clarke, not completely, anyway. Neither was she anybody else, of course. It wasn't that she felt she had assumed the identity, even partially, of some remote ancestor. How remote, anyway? No. She felt rather that she was living with a great many people from the past, that they were in her brain or mind (Diane did not believe in a soul, and found the idea of a collective unconscious too vague to be of importance), and that people from human antecedents were bound up with her, influencing her, controlling her every bit as much as, up to now, she had been controlling herself. This thought was by no means comforting, but it was at least a partial explanation, maybe, for the disquietude that she was experiencing. It was not even an explanation, she realized, but rather a description of her feelings.

She wanted to say something to Reg about it and didn't, thinking that anything she tried to say along these lines would sound either silly or fuzzy. By now five days had passed since she had repaired the basket up at Truro, and they were going up to the shack again this weekend. The five working days at the office had passed as had a lot of other weeks for Diane. She had had a set-to with Jan Heyningen, the art director, on Wednesday, and had come near telling him what she thought of his stubbornness and bad taste, but she hadn't. She had merely smoldered. It had happened before. She and Reg had gone out to dinner at the apartment of some friends on Thursday. All as usual, outwardly.

The unusual was the schizoid atmosphere in her head. Was that it? Two personalities? Diane toyed with this possibility all Friday afternoon at the office while she read through new promotion-ready material. Was she simply imagining that several hundred prehistoric ancestors were somehow dwelling within her? No, frankly, she wasn't. That idea was even less credible than Jung's collective unconscious. And suddenly she rejected the simple schizo idea or explanation also. Schizophrenia was a catch-all, she had heard, for a lot of derangements that couldn't otherwise be diagnosed. She didn't feel schizoid, anyway, didn't feel like two people, or three, or more. She felt simply scared, mysteriously terrified. But only one thing in the least awkward happened that week: she had let one side of the lettuce-swinger slip out of her hand on the terrace, and lettuce flew everywhere, hung from the potted bamboo trees, was caught on rose thorns, lay fresh and clean on the red tile paving, and on the seat of the glider. Diane had laughed, even though there was no more lettuce in the house. She was tense, perhaps, therefore clumsy. A little accident like that could happen any time.

During the flight to the Cape, Diane had a happy thought: she'd use the basket not just for floral arrangements but for collecting more *objets trouvés* from the beach, or better yet for potatoes and onions in the kitchen. She'd treat it like any old basket. That would take the mystique out of it, the terror. To have felt terror was absurd.

So Saturday morning while Reg worked on the nonelectric typewriter which they kept at the shack, Diane went for a walk on the beach with the basket. She had put a piece of newspaper in the basket, and she collected a greater number than usual of colored pebbles, a few larger smooth rocks—one orange in color, making it almost a *trompe l'oeil* for a mango—plus an interesting piece of sea-worn wood that looked like a boomerang. Wouldn't that be odd, she thought, if it really were an ancient boomerang worn shorter, thinner, until only the curve remained unchanged? As she walked back to the shack, the basket emitted faint squeaks in unison with her tread. The basket was so heavy, she had to carry it in two hands, letting its side rest against her hip, but she was not at all afraid that the twigs of the bottom would give. *Her work.*

*Stop it*, she told herself.

When she began to empty the basket on the porch's wooden table, she realized she had gathered too many stones, so she dropped more than half of them, quickly choosing the less interesting, over the porch rail onto the sand. Finally she shook the newspaper of its sand, and started to put it back in the basket. Sunlight fell on the glossy reddish-brown apple twigs. Over and under, not every one secured by twine, because for some twigs it hadn't been necessary. New work, and yet—Diane felt the irrational fear creeping over her again, and she pressed the newspaper quickly into the basket, pressed it at the crib-shaped edges, so that all her work was hidden. Then she tossed it carelessly on the floor, could have transferred some potatoes from a brown paper bag into it but she wanted to get away from the basket now.

An hour or so later, when she and Reg were finishing lunch, Reg laughing and about to light a cigarette, Diane felt an inner jolt as if—What? She deliberately relaxed, and gave her attention, more of it, to what Reg was saying. But it was as if the sound had been switched off a TV set. She saw him, but she wasn't listening or hearing. She blinked and forced herself to listen. Reg was talking about renting a tractor to clear some of their sand away, about terracing, and maintaining their property with growing things. They'd drawn a simple plan weeks ago, Diane remembered. But again she was feeling not like herself, as if she had lost herself in millions of people as an individual might get lost in a huge crowd. No, that was too simple, she felt. She was still trying to find solace in words. Or was she even dodging something? If so, what?

"What?" Reg asked, leaning back in his chair now, relaxed.

"Nothing. Why?"

"You were lost in thought."

Diane might have replied that she had just had a better idea for a current project at Retting, might have replied several things, but she said suddenly, "I'm thinking of asking for a leave of absence. Maybe just a month. I think Retting would do it, and it'd do me good."

Reg looked puzzled. "You're feeling tired, you mean? Just lately?"

"No. I feel somehow upset. Turned around, I don't know. I thought maybe a month of just being away from the office . . ." But work was supposed to be good in such a situation as hers. Work kept people from dwelling on their problems. But she hadn't a problem, rather a state of mind.

"Oh . . . well," Reg said. "Heyningen getting on your nerves maybe."

Diane shifted. It would have been easy to say yes, that was it. She took a cigarette, and Reg lit it. "Thanks. You're going to laugh, Reg. But that basket bothers me." She looked at him, feeling ashamed, and curiously defensive.

"The one you found last weekend? You're worried a child might've drowned in it, lost at sea?" Reg smiled as if at a mild joke he'd just made.

"No, not at all. Nothing like that. I told you last weekend. It simply bothers me that I repaired it so easily. There. That's it. And you can say I'm cracked—I don't care."

"I do not—quite—understand what you mean."

"It made me feel somehow—prehistoric. And funny. Still does."

Reg shook his head. "I can sort of understand. Honestly. But—another way of looking at it, Di, is to realize that it's a very simple activity after all, mending or even making a basket. Not that I don't admire the neat job you did, but it's not like—sitting down and playing Beethoven's Emperor Concerto, for instance, if you've never had a piano lesson in your life."

"No." She'd never had a basket-making lesson in her life, she might have said. She was silent, wondering if she should put in her leave of absence request on Monday, as a gesture, a kind of appeasement to the uneasiness she felt? Emotions demanded gestures, she had read somewhere, in order to be exorcised. Did she really believe that?

"Really, Di, the leave of absence is one thing, but that basket—It's an interesting basket, sure, because it's not machine-made and you don't see that shape anymore. I've seen you get excited about stones you find. I understand. They're beautiful. But to let yourself get upset about—"

"Stones are different," she interrupted. "I can admire them. I'm not upset about them. I told you I feel I'm not exactly myself—me—any longer. I feel lost in a strange way—*Identity*, I mean," she broke in again, when Reg started to speak.

"Oh, Di!" He got up. "What do you mean you told me that? You didn't."

"Well, I have now. I feel—as if a lot of other people were inside me besides myself. And I feel lost because of that. Do you understand?"

Reg hesitated. "I understand the words. But the feeling—no."

Even that was something. Diane felt grateful, and relieved that she had said this much to him.

"Go ahead with the leave of absence idea, darling. I didn't mean to be so abrupt."

Diane put her cigarette out. "I'll think about it." She got up to make coffee.

That afternoon, after tidying the kitchen, Diane put another newspaper in the basket, and unloaded the sack of potatoes into it, plus three or four onions—familiar and contemporary objects. Perishable too. She made herself not think about the basket or even about the leave of absence for the rest of the day. Around 7:30, she and Reg drove off to Truro, where there was a street party organized by an ecology group. Wine and beer and soft drinks, hot dogs and jukebox music. They encountered the Gartners and a few other neighbors. The wine was undrinkable, the atmosphere marvelous. Diane danced with a couple of merry strangers and was for a few hours happy.

A month's leave of absence, she thought as she stood under the shower that night, was absurd and unnecessary. Temporary aberration to have considered it. If the basket—a really simple object as Reg had said—annoyed her so much, the thing to do was to get rid of it, burn it.

Sunday morning Reg took the car and went to deliver his Black & Decker or some appliance of it to the Gartners, who lived eight miles away. As soon as he had left, Diane went to the side porch, replaced the potatoes and onions in the brown paper bag which she had saved as she saved most bags that arrived at the shack, and taking the basket with its newspaper and a book of matches, she walked out onto the sand in the direction of the ocean. She struck a match and lit the newspaper, and laid the basket over it. After a moment's hesitation, as if from shock, the basket gave a crack and began to burn. The drier sides burned more quickly than the newer apple twigs, of course. With a stick, Diane poked every last pale withe into the flames, until nothing remained except black ash and some yellow-glowing embers, and finally these went out in the bright sunshine and began to darken. Diane pushed sand with her feet over the ashes, until nothing was visible. She breathed deeply as she walked back to the shack, and realized that she had been holding her breath, or almost, the entire time of the burning.

She was not going to say anything to Reg about getting rid of the basket, and he was not apt to notice its absence, Diane knew.

Diane did mention, on Tuesday in New York, that she had changed her mind about asking for a leave of absence. The implication was that she felt better, but she didn't say that.

The basket was gone, she would never see it again, unless she deliberately tried to conjure it up in memory, and that she didn't want to do. She felt better with the thing out of the shack, destroyed. She knew that the burning had been an action on her part to get rid of a feeling within her, a primitive action, if she thought about it, because though the basket had been tangible, her thoughts were not tangible. And they proved damned hard to destroy.

Three weeks after the burning of the basket, her crazy idea of being a "walking human race" or some such lingered. She would continue to listen to Mozart and Bartók, they'd go to the shack most weekends, and she would continue to pretend that her life counted for something, that she was part of the stream or evolution of the human race, though she felt now that she had spurned that position or small function by burning the basket. For a week, she realized, she had grasped something, and then she had deliberately thrown it away. In fact, she was no happier now than during that week when the well-mended basket had been in her possession. But she was determined not to say anything more about it to Reg. He had been on the verge of impatience that Saturday before the Sunday when she had burned it. And in fact could she even put any more into words? No. So she had to stop thinking about it. Yes.

# THE TROUBLE WITH MRS. BLYNN, THE TROUBLE WITH THE WORLD

Mrs. Palmer was dying, there was no doubt of that to her or to anyone else in the household. The household had grown from two, Mrs. Palmer and Elsie the housemaid, to four in the past ten days. Elsie's daughter Liza, age fourteen, had come to help her mother, and had brought their shaggy sheepdog Princy—who to Mrs. Palmer made a fourth presence in the house. Liza spent most of her time doing things in the kitchen, and slept in the little low-ceilinged room with double-deck bunks down the steps from Mrs. Palmer's room. The cottage was small—a sitting room and dining alcove and kitchen downstairs, and upstairs Mrs. Palmer's bedroom, the room with the two bunks, and a tiny back room where Elsie slept. All the ceilings were low and the doorways and the ceiling above the stairway even lower, so that one had to duck one's head constantly.

Mrs. Palmer reflected that she would have to duck her head very few times more, as she rose only a couple of times a day, making her way, her lavender dressing gown clutched about her against the chill, to the bathroom. She had leukemia. She was not in any pain, but she was terribly weak. She was sixty-one. Her son Gregory, an officer in the R.A.F., was stationed in the Middle East, and perhaps would come in time and perhaps wouldn't. Mrs. Palmer had purposely not made her telegram urgent, not wanting to upset or inconvenience him, and his telegraphed reply had simply said that he would do his best to get leave to fly to her, and would let her know when. A cowardly telegram hers had been, Mrs. Palmer thought. Why hadn't she had the courage to say outright, "Am going to die in about a week. Can you come to see me?"

"Missus Palmer?" Elsie stuck her head in the door, one floury hand resting against the doorjamb. "Did Missus Blynn say four-thirty or five-thirty today?"

Mrs. Palmer did not know, and it did not seem in the least important. "I think five-thirty."

Elsie gave a preoccupied nod, her mind on what she would serve for five-thirty tea as opposed to four-thirty tea. The five-thirty tea could be less substantial, as Mrs. Blynn would already have had tea somewhere. "Anything I can get you, Missus Palmer?" she asked in a sweet voice, with a genuine concern.

"No, thank you, Elsie, I'm quite comfortable." Mrs. Palmer sighed as Elsie closed the door again. Elsie was willing, but unintelligent. Mrs. Palmer could not talk to her, not that she would have wanted to talk intimately to her, but it would have been nice to have the feeling that she could talk to someone in the house if she wished to.

Mrs. Palmer had no close friends in the town, because she had been here only a month. She had been en route to Scotland when the weakness came on her again and she had collapsed on a train platform in Ipswich. A long journey to Scotland by train or even airplane had been out of the question, so on a strange doctor's recommendation, Mrs. Palmer had hired a taxi and driven to a town on the east coast called Eamington, where the doctor knew there was a visiting nurse, and where the air was splendid and bracing. The doctor had evidently thought she needed only a few weeks' rest and she would be on her feet again, but Mrs. Palmer had had a premonition that this wasn't true. She had felt better the first few days in the quiet little town, she had found the cottage called Sea Maiden and rented it at once, but the spurt of energy had been brief. In Sea Maiden she had collapsed again, and Mrs. Palmer had the feeling that Elsie and even a few other acquaintances she had made, like Mr. Frowley the real estate agent, resented her faiblesse. She was not only a stranger come to trouble them, to make demands on them, but her relapse belied the salubrious powers of Eamington air—just now mostly gale-force winds which swept from the northeast day and night, tearing the buttons from one's coat, plastering a sticky, opaque film of salt and spray on the windows of all the houses on the seafront. Mrs. Palmer was sorry to be a burden herself, but at least she could pay for it, she thought. She had rented a rather shabby cottage that would otherwise have stayed empty all winter, since it was early February now, she was employing Elsie at slightly better than average Eamington wages, she paid Mrs. Blynn a guinea per half-hour visit (and most of that half hour was taken up with her tea), and she soon would bring business to the undertaker, the sexton, and perhaps the shopkeeper who sold flowers. She had also paid her rent through March.

Hearing a quick tread on the pavement, in a lull in the wind's roar, Mrs. Palmer sat up a little in bed. Mrs. Blynn was arriving. An anxious frown touched Mrs. Palmer's thin-skinned forehead, but she smiled faintly, too, with beforehand politeness. She reached for the long-handled mirror that lay on her bedtable. Her gray face had ceased to shock her or to make her feel shame. Age was age, death was death, and not pretty, but she still had the impulse to do what she could to look nicer for the world. She tucked some hair back into place, moistened her lips, tried a little smile, pulled a shoulder of her nightdress even with the other and her pink cardigan closer about her. Her pallor made the blue of her eyes much bluer. That was a pleasant thought.

Elsie knocked and opened the door at the same time. "Missus Blynn, ma'am."

"Good afternoon, Mrs. Palmer," said Mrs. Blynn, coming down the two steps from the threshold into Mrs. Palmer's room. She was a full-bodied, dark blond woman of middle height, about forty-five, and she wore her usual bulky, two-piece black suit with a rose-colored floral pin on her left breast. She also wore a pale pink lipstick and rather high heels. Like many women in Eamington, she was a sea widow, and had taken up nursing after she was forty. She was highly thought of in the town as an energetic woman who did useful work. "And how are you this afternoon?"

"Good afternoon. Well as can be expected, I think you'd say," said Mrs. Palmer with an effort at cheerfulness. Already she was loosening the covers, preparatory to pushing them back entirely for her daily injection.

But Mrs. Blynn was standing with an absent smile in the center of the room, hands folded backward on her hips, surveying the walls, gazing out the window. Mrs. Blynn had once lived in this house with her husband, for six months when they were first married, and every day Mrs. Blynn said something about it. Mrs. Blynn's husband had been the captain of a merchant ship, and had gone down with it ten years ago in a collision with a Swedish ship only fifty nautical miles from Eamington. Mrs. Blynn had never married again. Elsie said her house was filled with photographs of the captain in uniform and of his ship.

"Yes-s, it's a wonderful little house," said Mrs. Blynn, "even if the wind does come in a bit." She looked at Mrs. Palmer with brighter eyes, as if she were about to say, "Well, now, a few more of these injections and you'll be as fit as can be, won't you?"

But in the next seconds, Mrs. Blynn's expression changed. She groped in her black bag for the needle and the bottle of clear fluid that would do no good. Her mouth lost its smile and drooped, and deeper lines came at its corners. By the time she plunged the needle into Mrs. Palmer's fleshless body, her bulging green-gray eyes were glassy, as if she saw nothing and did not need to see anything: this was her business, and she knew how to do it. Mrs. Palmer was an object, which paid a guinea a visit. The object was going to die. Mrs. Blynn became apathetic, as if even the cutting off of the guinea in three days or eight days mattered nothing to her, either.

Guineas as such mattered nothing to Mrs. Palmer, but in view of the fact she was soon quitting this world, she wished that Mrs. Blynn could show something so human as a desire to prolong the guineas. Mrs. Blynn's eyes remained glassy, even when she glanced at the door to see if Elsie was coming in with her tea. Occasionally the floorboards in the hall cracked from the heat or the lack of it, and so they did when someone walked just outside the door.

The injection hurt today, but Mrs. Palmer did not flinch. It was really such a small thing, she smiled at the slightness of it. "A little sunshine today, wasn't there?" Mrs. Palmer said.

"Was there?" Mrs. Blynn jerked the needle out.

"Around eleven this morning. I noticed it." Weakly she gestured toward the window behind her.

"We can certainly use it," Mrs. Blynn said, putting her equipment back in her bag. "Goodness, we can use that fire, too." She had fastened her bag, and now she chafed her palms, huddling toward the grate.

Princy was stretched full length before the fire, looking like a rolled-up shag rug.

Mrs. Palmer tried to think of something pleasant to say about Mrs. Blynn's husband, their time in this house, the town, anything. She could only think of how lonely Mrs. Blynn's life must be since her husband died. They had had no children. According to Elsie, Mrs. Blynn had worshiped her husband, and took a pride in never having remarried. "Have you many patients this time of year?" Mrs. Palmer asked.

"Oh, yes. Like always," Mrs. Blynn said, still facing the fire and rubbing her hands.

*Who?* Mrs. Palmer wondered. *Tell me about them.* She waited, breathing softly.

Elsie knocked once, by bumping a corner of the tray against the door.

"Come in, Elsie," they both said, Mrs. Blynn a bit louder.

"Here we are," said Elsie, setting the tray down on a hassock made by two massive olive-green pillows, one atop the other. Butter slid down the side of a scone, spread onto the plate, and began to congeal while Elsie poured the tea.

Elsie handed Mrs. Palmer a cup of tea with three lumps of sugar, but no scone, because Mrs. Blynn said they were too indigestible for her. Mrs. Palmer did not mind. She appreciated the sight of well-buttered scones, anyway, and of healthy people like Mrs. Blynn eating them. She was offered a ginger biscuit and declined it. Mrs. Blynn talked briefly to Elsie about her water pipes, about the reduced price of something at the butcher's this week, while Elsie stood with folded arms, leaning against the edge of the door, letting in a frigid draft on Mrs. Palmer. Elsie was taking in all Mrs. Blynn's information about prices. Now it was catsup at the health store. On sale this week.

"Call me if you'd like something," Elsie said as usual, ducking out the door.

Mrs. Blynn was sunk in her scones, leaning over so the dripping butter would fall on the stone floor and not her skirt.

Mrs. Palmer shivered, and drew the covers up.

"Is your son coming?" Mrs. Blynn asked in a loud, clear voice, looking straight at Mrs. Palmer.

Mrs. Palmer did not know what Elsie had told Mrs. Blynn. She had told Elsie that he might come, that was all. "I haven't heard yet. He's probably waiting to tell me the exact time he'll come—or to find out if he can or not. You know how it is in the Air Force."

m-m," said Mrs. Blynn through a scone, as if of course she knew, ng had a husband who had been in service. "He's your only son and , I take it."

"My only one," said Mrs. Palmer.

"Married?"

"Yes." Then, anticipating the next question, "He has one child, a aughter, but she's still very small."

Mrs. Blynn's eyes kept drifting to Mrs. Palmer's bedtable, and suddenly Mrs. Palmer realized what she was looking at—her amethyst pin. Mrs. Palmer had worn it for a few days on her cardigan sweater, until she had felt so bad, the pin ceased to lift her spirits and became almost tawdry, and she had removed it.

"That's a beautiful pin," said Mrs. Blynn.

"Yes. My husband gave it to me years ago."

Mrs. Blynn came over to look at it, but she did not touch it. The rectangular amethyst was set in small diamonds. She stood up, looking down at it with alert, bulging eyes. "I suppose you'll pass it on to your son—or his wife."

Mrs. Palmer flushed with embarrassment, or anger. She hadn't thought to whom she would pass it on, particularly. "I suppose my son will get everything, as my heir."

"I hope his wife appreciates it," Mrs. Blynn said, turning on her heel with a smile, setting her cup down in its saucer.

Then Mrs. Palmer realized that for the last few days it was the pin Mrs. Blynn had been looking at when her eyes drifted over to the bedtable. When Mrs. Blynn had gone, Mrs. Palmer picked up the pin and held it in her palm protectively. Her jewel box was across the room. Elsie came in, and Mrs. Palmer said, "Elsie, would you mind handing me that blue box over there?"

"Certainly, ma'am," Elsie said, swerving from the tea tray to the box on the top of the bookshelf. "This the one?"

"Yes, thank you." Mrs. Palmer took it, opened the lid, and dropped the pin on her pearls. She had not much jewelry, perhaps ten or eleven pieces, but each piece meant a special occasion in her life, or a special period, and she loved them all. She looked at Elsie's blunt, homely profile as she bent over the tray, arranging everything so that it could be carried out at once.

"That Missus Blynn," said Elsie, shaking her head, not lookig at Mrs. Palmer. "Asked me if I thought your son was coming. How s I to know? I said yes, *I* thought so." Now she stood with the tray, lo g at Mrs. Palmer, and she smiled awkwardly, as if she had said perhap much. "The trouble with Missus Blynn is she's always nosing—if y pardon me saying so. Asking questions, you know?"

Mrs. Palmer nodded, feeling too low just at that moment to mal comment. She had no comment anyway. Elsie, she thought, had pas back and forth by the amethyst pin for days and never mentioned never touched it, maybe never even noticed it. Mrs. Palmer sudden realized how much more she liked Elsie than she liked Mrs. Blynn.

"The trouble with Missus Blynn—she means well, but . . ." Els floundered and jiggled the tray in her effort to shrug. "It's too bad Everyone's always saying it about her," she finished, as if this summed it up, and started out the door. But she turned with the door open. "At tea, for instance. It's always get this and get that for her, as if she were a grand lady or something. A day ahead she tells me. I don't see why she don't bring what she wants from the bakery now and then herself. If you know what I mean."

Mrs. Palmer nodded. She supposed she knew. She knew. Mrs. Blynn was like a nursemaid she had for a time for Gregory. Like a divorcée she and her husband had known in London. She was like a lot of people.

Mrs. Palmer died two days later. It was a day when Mrs. Blynn came in and out, perhaps six times, perhaps eight. A telegram had arrived that morning from Gregory, saying he had at last wangled leave and would take off in a matter of hours, landing at a military field near Eamington. Mrs. Palmer did not know if she would see him again or not, she could not judge her strength that far. Mrs. Blynn took her temperature and felt her pulse frequently, then pivoted on one foot in the room, looking about as if she were alone and thinking her own thoughts. Her expression was blankly pleasant, her peaches-and-cream cheeks aglow with health.

"Your son's due today," Mrs. Blynn half said, half asked, on one of her visits.

"Yes," said Mrs. Palmer.

It was then dusk, though it was only four in the afternoon.

That was the last clear exchange she had with anyone, for she sank into a kind of dream. She saw Mrs. Blynn staring at the blue box on the top of the bookshelf, staring at it even as she shook the thermometer down. Mrs. Palmer called for Elsie and had her bring the box to her. Mrs. Blynn was not in the room then.

"This is to go to my son when he comes," Mrs. Palmer said. "All of it. Everything. You understand? It's all written . . ." But even though it was all itemized, a single piece like the amethyst pin might be missing and Gregory would never do anything about it, maybe not even notice, maybe think she'd lost it somewhere in the last weeks and not reported it. Gregory was like that. Then Mrs. Palmer smiled at herself, and also reproached herself. *You can't take it with you.* That was very true, and people who tried to were despicable and rather absurd. "Elsie, this is yours," Mrs. Palmer said, and handed Elsie the amethyst pin.

"Oh, Missus Palmer! Oh, no, I couldn't take *that*!" Elsie said, not taking it, and in fact retreating a step.

"You've been very good to me," Mrs. Palmer said. She was very tired, and her arm dropped to the bed. "Very well," she murmured, seeing it was really of no use.

Her son came at six that evening, sat with her on the edge of her bed, held her hand and kissed her forehead. But when she died, Mrs. Blynn was closest, bending over her with her great round, peaches-and-cream face and her green-gray eyes as expressionless as some fantastic reptile's. Mrs. Blynn to the last continued to say crisp, efficient things to her like, "Breathe easily. That's it," and "Not chilly, are you? Good." Somebody had mentioned a priest earlier, but this had been overruled by both Gregory and Mrs. Palmer. So it was Mrs. Blynn's eyes she looked into as her life left her. Mrs. Blynn so authoritative, strong, efficient, one might have taken her for God Himself. Especially since when Mrs. Palmer looked toward her son, she couldn't really see him, only a vague pale blue figure in the corner, tall and erect, with a dark spot at the top that was his hair. He was looking at her, but now she was too weak to call him. Anyway, Mrs. Blynn had shooed them all back. Elsie was also standing against the closed door, ready to run out for something, ready to take any order. Near her was the smaller figure of Liza, who occasionally whispered something and was shushed by her mother. In an instant,

Mrs. Palmer saw her entire life—her carefree childhood and youth, her happy marriage, the blight of the death of her other son at the age of ten, the shock of her husband's death eight years ago—but all in all a happy life, she supposed, though she could wish her own character had been better, *purer*, that she had never shown temper or selfishness, for instance. All that was past now, but what remained was a feeling that she had been imperfect, wrong, like Mrs. Blynn's presence now, like Mrs. Blynn's faint smile, wrong, wrong for the time and the occasion. Mrs. Blynn did not understand her. Mrs. Blynn did not know her. Mrs. Blynn, somehow, could not comprehend goodwill. Therein lay the flaw, and the flaw of life itself. Life is a long failure of understanding, Mrs. Palmer thought, a long, mistaken shutting of the heart.

Mrs. Palmer had the amethyst pin in her closed left hand. Hours ago, sometime in the afternoon, she had taken it with an idea of safekeeping, but now she realized the absurdity of that. She had also wanted to give it to Gregory directly, and had forgotten. Her closed hand lifted an inch or so, her lips moved, but no sound came. She wanted to give it to Mrs. Blynn: one positive and generous gesture she could still make to this essence of nonunderstanding, she thought, but now she had not the strength to make her want known—and that was like life, too, everything a little too late. Mrs. Palmer's lids shut on the vision of Mrs. Blynn's glassy, attentive eyes.

# COPYRIGHT NOTICES

*Strangers on a Train*
Copyright 1950 by Patricia Highsmith
Copyright © 1993 by Diogenes Verlag AG, Zurich
Originally published by Harper & Brothers, New York, and Cresset Press, London, in 1950

"A Mighty Nice Man," "The Still Point of the Turning World," "Where the Door Is Always Open and the Welcome Mat Is Out," "Quiet Night," "In the Plaza," The Great Cardhouse," "Two Disagreeable Pigeons," and "The Trouble with Mrs. Blynn, the Trouble with the World" from *Nothing That Meets the Eye*
Copyright © 2002 by Diogenes Verlag AG, Zurich
Copyright © 1993 by Diogenes Verlag AG, Zurich
This collection first published in the United States of America by W. W. Norton & Company, Inc. in 2002
"A Mighty Nice Man" First published in *Barnard Quarterly*, vol. XV, no. 3, Spring 1940, pp. 34–40.
"The Still Point of the Turning World" First published as "The Envious One" in *Today's Woman*, March 1949.
"Quiet Night" Two versions; the first version first published in *Barnard Quarterly*, Fall 1939, pp. 5–10; revised and lengthened story published as "The Cries of Love" in *Woman's Home Journal*, January 1968, and in book form in *Eleven*, London: Heinemann 1970 (U.S. edition titled *The Snail-Watcher and Other Stories*, published by Doubleday, 1970).
"The Great Cardhouse" First published in *Story*, vol. 36, issue 3, no. 140, May–June 1963, pp. 32–48.
"Two Disagreeable Pigeons" First published in *Harper's Magazine*, vol. 305, no. 1829, October 2002, pp. 29–32.
"The Trouble with Mrs. Blynn, the Trouble with the World" First published in *The New Yorker*, vol. LXXVIII, no. 13 (May 27, 2002), pp. 106–11.

"The Baby Spoon" and "Woodrow Wilson's Necktie" from *Slowly, Slowly in the Wind*
Copyright © 1972, 1973, 1974, 1976, 1977, and 1979 by Patricia Highsmith

This selection of short stories first published in volume form in Great Britain by William Heinemann Ltd in 1979

First published in the United States of America by Penzler Books in 1985 (Warner Books, Inc.)

*The Price of Salt*



First published in the United States of America by Coward McCann, Inc., New York, in 1952

Revised edition with an afterword by the author, 1984

Published in Great Britain under the title *Carol*

"Oona, the Jolly Cave Woman" from *Little Tales of Misogyny*

First published in German as *Kleine Geschichten für Weiberfeinde* in a translation by W. E. Richartz. Copyright © 1975 by Diogenes Verlag AG, Zurich. Original English text first published in Great Britain in 1977. Copyright © 1977 by Diogenes Verlag AG, Zurich



First published in Great Britain by Heinemann in 1977

First published in the United States of America by Penzler Books in 1986

"Not One of Us" and "The Terrors of Basket-Weaving" from *The Black House*



This collection first published in Great Britain by William Heinemann Ltd in 1981

First published in the United States of America by Penzler Books in 1988 (Warner Books, Inc.)

# ABOUT THE EDITOR

Joan Schenkar is the author of the landmark biography *The Talented Miss Highsmith: The Secret Life and Serious Art of Patricia Highsmith*. Her other works include the widely praised *Truly Wilde: The Unsettling Story of Dolly Wilde, Oscar's Unusual Niece*, as well as a collection of award-winning plays, *Signs of Life: Six Comedies of Menace*. She lives and writes in Paris and Greenwich Village.

# ABOUT THE AUTHOR

Born in Fort Worth, Texas, in 1921, Patricia Highsmith spent much of her adult life in Switzerland and France. She was educated at Barnard College, where she studied English, Latin, and Greek. Her first novel, *Strangers on a Train*, published initially in 1950, proved to be a major commercial success, and was filmed by Alfred Hitchcock. Despite this early recognition, Highsmith was unappreciated in the United States for the entire length of her career.

Writing under the pseudonym of Claire Morgan, she then published *The Price of Salt* in 1952, which had been turned down by her previous American publisher because of its frank exploration of homosexual themes. Her most popular literary creation was Tom Ripley, the dapper sociopath who first debuted in her 1955 novel, *The Talented Mr. Ripley*. She followed with four other Ripley novels. Posthumously made into a major motion picture, *The Talented Mr. Ripley* has helped bring about a renewed appreciation of Highsmith's work in the United States, as have the posthumous publications of *The Selected Stories* and *Nothing That Meets the Eye: The Uncollected Stories*, both of which received widespread acclaim when they were published by W. W. Norton & Company.

The author of more than twenty books, Highsmith won the O. Henry Memorial Award, the Edgar Allan Poe Award, Le Grand Prix de Littérature Policière, and the Award of the Crime Writers' Association of Great Britain. She died in Switzerland on February 4, 1995, and her literary archives are maintained in Berne.